THE ESSENTIAL READER'S COMPANION

THE ESSENTIAL READER'S COMPANION

PABLO HIDALGO

Illustrations by
JEFF CARLISLE, JOE CORRONEY, BRIAN ROOD,
CHRIS SCALF, DARREN TAN,
and CHRIS TREVAS

BALLANTINE BOOKS • NEW YORK

*To Sue Rostoni, for her encouragement,
guidance, and friendship*

ILLUSTRATION CREDITS

JEFF CARLISLE · Pages ii, 10, 19, 25, 31, 41, 57, 86, 105, 116, 125, 148, 153, 170, 181, 189, 219, 236, 244, 261, 285, 301, 317, 320, 332, 338, 348, and 355

JEFF CARLISLE/CHRIS SCALF · Pages 15, 197, 274, and 307

JOE CORRONEY · Pages 422 and 436

JOE CORRONEY (pencils)/CHRIS SCALF(colors) · Page 359

BRIAN ROOD · Character portrait galleries on pages 2, 28, 74, 122, 178, 246, 368, and 416

CHRIS SCALF · Pages 35, 36, 53, 67, 72, 77, 90, 102, 110, 134, 140, 142, 145, 150, 159, 163, 174, 185, 193, 213, 265, 315, 326, 330, 345, 381, 385, 414, 419, 427, 439, 446, 451, 454, and 465

DARREN TAN · Pages 4, 129, 132, 208, 268, 279, 297, 304, 323, 371, 402, and 409

CHRIS TREVAS · Pages 13, 22, 45, 47, 62, 71, 80, 84, 96, 99, 108, 114, 120-121, 137, 168, 231, 240, 249, 253, 294, 341, 351, and 394

A Del Rey Trade Paperback Original

Copyright © 2012 Lucasfilm Ltd. & ® or ™ where indicated. All Rights Reserved. Used Under Authorization.

Published in the United States by Del Rey, an imprint of The Random House Publishing Group, a division of Random House, Inc., New York.

DEL REY is a registered trademark and the Del Rey colophon is a trademark of Random House, Inc.

ISBN 978-0-345-51119-5

Printed in the United States of America

www.starwars.com
www.star-wars.suvudu.com

9 8 7 6 5 4 3 2 1

Book design by Simon Sullivan

CONTENTS

Introduction vii

CHAPTER 1. TALES OF ANCIENT JEDI AND SITH 3

CHAPTER 2. HEIGHT OF THE REPUBLIC 29

CHAPTER 3. THE CLONE WARS 75

CHAPTER 4. THE DARK TIMES 123

CHAPTER 5. THE GALACTIC CIVIL WAR 179

CHAPTER 6. THE NEW REPUBLIC 247

CHAPTER 7. THE NEW JEDI ORDER 369

CHAPTER 8. LEGACY 417

APPENDIX A. *Works in Publication Order* 471

APPENDIX B. *Works by Author* 477

INTRODUCTION

Before *Star Wars* graced the silver screens of packed movie houses, its story was presented to an eager public via the printed word. A tie-in novel based on the screenplay of *Star Wars* arrived in bookstores over five months prior to the film's debut on May 25, 1977, helping to spread awareness of the movie to come in a pre-digital, word-of-mouth age. As such, the very first *Star Wars* fans were readers.

It was soon evident that *Star Wars* would surpass the bounds of summer entertainment to become much more than just a movie. The faraway galaxy became a setting for legends. As production promptly began on a sequel to the first film, creator George Lucas opened up his universe to exploration by other storytellers. Comic book tales came first and proved to be a medium that would be integral to the genesis of the *Star Wars* universe. Within a year of the film's release, Alan Dean Foster's follow-up novel, *Splinter of the Mind's Eye*, became a bestseller.

Since that time, over 145 full-length novels have expanded the *Star Wars* story. More than one hundred juvenile novels helped open the door for young readers into a lifetime of reading. Over 170 short stories added to the saga. It can be a very daunting task to navigate among these works. *The Essential Reader's Companion* hopes to guide you through these rich stories.

The Essential Reader's Companion is a summary of *Star Wars* fiction for *Star Wars* readers of any level. The novice reader, unsure of where to start, may find guidance by browsing through the curated summaries. It is also meant for the intermediate *Star Wars* reader who has sampled some works, but never realized how immense the library is. And, for the experts, it's a fresh look at what they may already know, hopefully with some new surprises thrown in—not to mention all-new illustrations of characters and scenes previously only imagined.

What's Not in This Book

The Essential Reader's Companion focuses on prose fiction. Graphic novels, every bit as essential to the Expanded Universe, are beyond the scope of this book, though where relevant mentions of certain stories are given in the text. The younger end of children's literature—the illustrated storybooks, chapter books, and beginner books—is also excluded, though works for young adults (ages twelve and up) are included. Stories with variable plots—Solitaire Adventures, Choose Your Own Adventure, Decide Your Destiny, and similar works—are also not included.

Stories of videogames, which often form important chapters in the lives of *Star Wars* characters, are not covered unless they've been adapted into a book. Sometimes game books—such as roleplaying game supplements and videogame strategy guides—include fictional sidebars or a fictional story that frames the rules and game information. These, too, are not in the *Companion*.

indicia of the publication, though the dates books were actually available for purchase may vary by weeks.

Where the story fits into the *Star Wars* time line follows, with a year annotated as BBY (for events before the Battle of Yavin, as seen in the movie *Star Wars*: Episode IV *A New Hope*) and ABY (for events after the Battle of Yavin). For those interested in galactic cartography, a roster of the planets visited in the story is given, complete with grid coordinates for use with the maps found in *Star Wars: The Essential Atlas*. The *Companion* next identifies the main characters in a story, summarizes its events, and in some cases offers "behind-the-scenes" information about a story's creation or impact.

What's in This Book

Most of this book consists of summaries of novels, whether for adults or young adults. In some cases, multibook stories that flow into one another are collected in a single entry. Short stories published in official *Star Wars* periodicals or online are afforded their own entries or are described in sidebars when they directly connect to a larger story.

Each entry includes the cover art—in some cases, multiple examples if more than one version of the cover exists. It is important to note that in the case of multiple entries from the same source, the *Companion* will show the cover only for the first entry from that source. An entry credits the author(s) and cover artist(s), then lists the work's publication history—format and release date. A note about release dates: For consistency's sake, the *Companion* uses the date as recorded in the

Reading Order

The *Companion* presents *Star Wars* fiction in a recommended reading order that follows a chronological flow within the Expanded Universe. However, the order presented prioritizes reading experience over rigid adherence to chronology. For example, the Jedi Academy Trilogy and the novel *I, Jedi* occur at the same time, often covering the same events. A rigid adherence to chronology would recommend reading alternate parts of each work. Instead, the *Companion* recommends reading the Jedi Academy Trilogy first; it was the first work published, and *I, Jedi* was written with the expectation that it likely would be the second work read. If a book covers large spans of time, it's often where the story ends that determines its chronological placement, not where it begins.

Canon and Continuity

Common questions are: How "real" are these stories? Do they count? Did they really happen?

The most definitive canon of the *Star Wars* universe is encompassed by the feature films and television productions in which George Lucas is directly involved. The movies and the *Clone Wars* television series are what he and his handpicked writers reference when adding cinematic adventures to the *Star Wars* oeuvre.

But Lucas allows for an Expanded Universe that exists parallel to the one he directly oversees. In many cases, the stewards of the Expanded Universe—editors within the licensing division of Lucasfilm Ltd. who work with authors and publishers—will ask for his input or blessing on projects. Though these stories may get his stamp of approval, they don't enter his canon unless they are depicted cinematically in one of his projects.

That said, unless something occurs in a canon project to directly contradict a published source, it can reliably be said to have occurred. Extensive records track the growth of the Expanded Universe, cataloging planets, characters, technology, and events, to allow for a sprawling, believable continuity connecting the published works of the *Star Wars* universe. It's not perfect—when errors occur, the *Companion* does sometimes call them out. This is not to diminish these tales in any way, but rather to illustrate that the *Star Wars* Expanded Universe is a living document that grows and evolves over time.

The *Reader's Companion* is not meant as a replacement for the experience of reading these works firsthand. Those truly interested in the stories are strongly encouraged to read them whole. No matter how detailed, a summary is no substitute for experiencing a story as the author intended.

THE ESSENTIAL READER'S COMPANION

Yaru Korsin

Orielle "Ori" Kitai

Zeerid "Z-man" Korr

Aryn Leneer

Darth Scabrous

Darth Zannah

CHAPTER I

TALES OF ANCIENT JEDI AND SITH

Civilization in the *Star Wars* galaxy stretches back more than twenty-five thousand years, to an ancient past where history and mythology are inextricably braided. There are legends of enormously powerful alien cultures that were architects of some of the galaxy's greatest wonders—the unlikely conglomeration of black holes called the Maw, the peculiar alignment of the five worlds in the Corellian system, and the remarkable spread of humanity across the stars in "prehistoric" times.

Star Wars storytelling has presented these fantastic origins as historical backstory, with most tales beginning no earlier than five thousand years before the Battle of Yavin. An exception, the *Dawn of the Jedi* comics series from Dark Horse Comics published in 2012, set 25,000 years in the past, indicates that this frontier is open for narrative exploration.

Before the late 1990s, when George Lucas and his crew began work on *Star Wars:* Episode I *The Phantom Menace*, Jedi lore was a precious rarity in the Expanded Universe. Lucasfilm kept a tight guard on Jedi mythology, to give the stories Lucas wished to explore in Episodes I, II, and III as wide a berth as possible. Enterprising authors found a way to tell Jedi stories by going far back in time, millennia before the fall of the Republic. Thus, they afforded themselves considerable creative freedom since differences of interpretation could be smoothed out by the passage of centuries.

LOST TRIBE OF THE SITH: THE COLLECTED STORIES

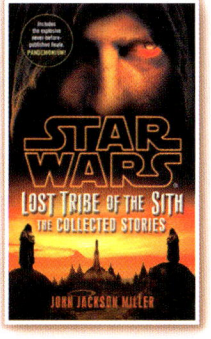

AUTHOR · John Jackson Miller

COVER ARTIST · David Stevenson and Scott Biel

PUBLICATION HISTORY · Novel, Del Rey Books
· Trade paperback, July 2012
Originally serialized as eight eBook novellas:
· *Precipice* (May 2009), *Skyborn* (July 2009), *Paragon* (February 2010), *Savior* (April 2010), *Purgatory* (October 2010), *Sentinel* (February 2011), *Pantheon* (July 2011), and *Secrets* (March 2012)

TIME LINE PLACEMENT · 5000 BBY (*Precipice, Skyborn*), 4985 BBY (*Paragon*), 4975 BBY (*Savior*), 3960 BBY (*Purgatory, Sentinel*), 3000 BBY (*Pantheon, Secrets*), 2975 BBY (*Pandemonium*)

WORLD VISITED · Kesh [U-10]

MAIN CHARACTERS · Yaru Korsin, Grand Lord of the Skyborn (human male); Adari Vaal, resistance leader (Keshiri female); Seelah, Sith crèche tender (human female); Jariad Korsin, Sith High Lord (human male); Nida Korsin, Skyborn Ranger (human female); Orielle "Ori" Kitai, Sith Saber (human female); Jelph Marrian, Jedi Covenant agent (human male); Varner Hilts, caretaker (human male); Quarra Thayn, wardmaster (Keshiri female); Edell Vrai, Sith High Lord (human male); Jogan Halder, watchman (Keshiri male)

SUMMARY · During the Great Hyperspace War, the Sith mining vessel *Omen* crashes into Kesh, a world unknown to either Republic or Sith. The ship's commander, an enslaved human named Yaru Korsin, tries to keep his tempestuous crew in line. Kesh is a relatively primitive world with a superstitious population contained on the continent of Keshtar. At the very apex of Keshiri mythology are the Skyborn, gods from above. The Sith newcomers are venerated as the gods incarnate by the Keshiri. Within fifteen years, the new arrivals rule unchallenged over their Keshiri subjects. Yaru Korsin becomes Grand Lord of the Skyborn.

Years later, an underground movement of Keshiri rebels conspires to rid their world of these offworld intruders. The wicked machinations of Seelah, Yaru Korsin's wife, wipe out the pureblood Sith from among the *Omen* survivors, allowing the humans alone to survive. Seelah's son, Jariad, mortally wounds the Grand Lord in a coup. Although Yaru dies, he is survived by his daughter, Nida, who punishes Seelah for her treachery.

More than a thousand years later, the *Omen* crash site becomes sacred ground to the Keshiri, concealed by a temple in the mountains. The Sith dynasty continues, no longer propagated by bloodline, but rather as a meritocracy shaped by bold examples of power and skillful political maneuvering.

A botched assassination attempt targets the reigning Grand Lord, a doddering crone named Lillia Venn. Culpability for the assault is pegged on High Lord Candra Kitain. She and her daughter, Orielle Kitain, are stripped of status and enslaved. Ori flees to the countryside, finding some peace with a lowly gardener named Jelph. Jelph, in truth, is a secret Jedi agent who has recently and accidentally arrived on Kesh. Ori uncovers Jelph's secrets, finding his Republic starfighter hidden in his shed. Venn and a retinue of Sith Lords arrive at Jelph's, also discovering the spacecraft. When Venn boards

Adari Vaal, atop her flying uvak, spots the half brothers Yaru and Devore Korsin fighting near the crash site of the Sith vessel *Omen*.

TALES OF ANCIENT JEDI AND SITH

5

the starfighter, she unwittingly trips an antitheft device rigged by Jelph that destroys the ship and Venn in an explosion. This leaves Jelph and Ori together as exiles, in the wilderness, where they begin a new life together.

After another millennium of stagnation, the Sith dynasty has splintered into squabbling factions that only begrudgingly unite to honor the traditions of Yaru Korsin. Varner Hilts, a caretaker of Sith customs, plays a traditional holographic recording made by Korsin at the end of his reign and intended for his daughter, Nida. Before the assembled Sith factions, Hilts allows the recording to play past its conclusion, revealing fragments of an earlier transmission never meant for public display—an image of Naga Sadow identifying the crew of the *Omen* as slaves. This sends the Sith factions into disarray as their view of their ancestors as godly conquerors is turned upside down. As the disillusioned Sith factions begin to self-destruct, Hilts realizes there is more to Korsin's recording. He has hidden a message to Nida, with the cryptic words that "the true power lies behind the throne."

Hilts finds Korsin's old command chair that he used as a throne in a secret chamber within the *Omen* temple. Korsin has hidden a map of the entire world of Kesh, revealing an unexplored continent on the far side of the planet, a landmass recorded by *Omen*'s sensors during the crash but left unrevealed to Korsin's crew. Hilts realizes the key to unifying the disintegrating Sith factions is to give them a target of conquest.

After twenty-five years of planning and advancements, the Sith have constructed a fleet of airships to travel across the ocean and invade the new world. A gifted engineer, Edell Vrai, leads a scouting fleet to Alanciar, the new land. The Keshiri of Alanciar are prepared, though, for they have remained vigilant since being warned centuries earlier by Adari Vaal, a Keshiri who first greeted the Sith and fled their rule

SPOTLIGHT   *Tales of the Jedi* Comics

Dark Horse Comics first blazed into the uncharted history of the ancient Sith and Jedi in their seminal series *Tales of the Jedi* (1993–94). Written by Tom Veitch, who would be joined by Kevin J. Anderson in sequels, the various *Tales of the Jedi* titles introduced a new cast of Jedi and Sith legends, such as Ulic Qel-Droma, Freedon Nadd, Nomi Sunrider, Exar Kun, and Naga Sadow. These characters and their actions would impact stories told in novels for years to come.

As groundwork for the comics, Veitch prepared a questionnaire about Jedi and Sith lore that George Lucas answered. With this information, the *Tales of the Jedi* comics were the first to identify the Sith as an order of ambitious dark siders built around a master-and-apprentice relationship.

The *Tales of the Jedi* comics chronicle two major events in the Republic's history: the Great Hyperspace War (5000 BBY) that brought the expanding Sith Empire and the Republic into violent collision, and the Great Sith War (4000 BBY) that saw the resurgence of the Sith with the corruption of the mighty Jedi Exar Kun.

during the reign of Yaru Korsin. Enormous ballistae shoot down the Sith airships, and Edell crashes onto the coast. He takes a pair of Keshiri watchers, Quarra Thayn and Jogan Halder, prisoner. While Edell has his Sith lieutenants take Halder back to the Keshtar homeland via boat, he forces Quarra to bring him into the Alanciar civilization.

Edell admires the advanced architecture and engineering exhibited by these Keshiri, advancements made necessary by their long-held fear of Sith invasion from afar. Edell is shocked to see a Sith invasion force, impulsively launched from Keshtar before his scouting expedition could return, attempting conquest of Alanciar. Its leader, the Sith Lord Bentado, seeks to betray his tribe and destroy any remaining airships so he can rule the new land unchallenged. Quarra and Edell work together and defeat Bentado.

Caretaker Hilts, now Grand Lord of the Lost Tribe, arrives as a benevolent contrast to Bentado's force. He brings with him Jogan, who sings the praises of the distant Sith, alleviating the concerns of the Alanciar. Hilts, a far more pragmatic and even-minded ruler than the Grand Lords past, sees the unification of Kesh as the key to the continued survival of the Lost Tribe. He make sure Jogan sees only the best of Keshtar. Hilts even welcomes Keshiri blood into their ranks to ensure their future. A new era of Kesh begins.

THE LOST TRIBE SERIES is a tie-in to Del Rey's Fate of the Jedi novels, which were published from 2009 through 2012 and set more than forty years after *A New Hope*. The Fate books featured a new, previously undiscovered faction of Sith that had escaped notice for thousands of years, since being marooned on a primitive world. Each Lost Tribe story told an important tale of their history and debuted as a free eBook concurrent with the release of books two through nine of the Fate series. *Pandemonium* was an original story written for the trade paperback collection.

The Lost Tribe series begins in the thick of the Great Hyperspace War, a conflict between the ancient Republic and the Sith that was the subject of two series from Dark Horse Comics, *Tales of the Jedi: The Golden Age of the Sith* (1996–97) and *Tales of the Jedi: The Fall of the Sith Empire* (1997). The Lost Tribe story continued in *Lost Tribe of the Sith: Spiral*, a comic book mini-series published by Dark Horse Comics in the Fall of 2012.

The novel *Crosscurrent* (2010) also begins in 5000 BBY. The opening chapters feature a cameo by the ship *Omen* and occur just before the events of *Precipice*. However, because *Crosscurrent* occurs in multiple eras, the *Companion* includes it much later in the time line, at 40 ABY.

THE OLD REPUBLIC: REVAN

AUTHOR · Drew Karpyshyn
COVER ARTIST · LucasArts
PUBLICATION HISTORY ·
Novel, Del Rey Books
 · Hardcover, November 2011
 · Paperback, September 2012

TIME LINE PLACEMENT ·
3954–3950 BBY; c. 3900 BBY (epilogue)

WORLDS VISITED · Bosthirda [R-5]; Coruscant [L-9]; Dromund Kaas [R-5]; Hallion [R-5]; Nathema [S-4]; Rekkiad [S-4]

MAIN CHARACTERS · Revan, Jedi Knight (human male); Lord Scourge, Sith Lord (Sith male); Meetra Surik, Jedi Knight (human female); Canderous Ordo, Mandalorian mercenary (human male); T3-M4, astromech droid; Darth Nyris, Dark Councilor (Sith female); Darth Xedrix, Dark Councilor (human male); Bastila Shan, Jedi Knight (human female); Emperor Vitiate, Sith Emperor (human male)

SUMMARY · Years after having returned from the dark side to save the galaxy from the Star Forge crisis, Revan is a rehabilitated Jedi Knight who has married Bastila Shan. He is plagued by his fragmented memories of the events that led him to the dark side, as well as nightmares of a storm-shrouded world. Revan enlists the aid of his friend and teammate Canderous Ordo and the astromech droid T3-M4 to retrace his steps before his fall, to see if he can stir some recollection.

Meanwhile, in the Sith Empire, the Dark Councilor Darth Nyris summons Lord Scourge to find who is responsible for the attempts on her life. Scourge's investigations find proof that Lord Xedrix, also a Dark Councilor, is conspiring against the Emperor with separatists on Bosthirda. Scourge kills Xedrix, but not before the Councilor plants the seeds of doubt in his mind concerning Nyris's motives.

Ordo, Revan, and T3 voyage to the icy planet Rekkiad aboard the freighter *Ebon Hawk*. The icy planet is the current home of the nomadic Mandalorian clans. Visions of the past help Revan find items he hid there years ago—Mandalore's Mask and a datacron belonging to a Sith Lord exile, Dramath. Revan recalls that Mandalore the Ultimate revealed to him that he had been corrupted and betrayed by a Sith Lord, who promised a successful campaign of conquest against the Republic. Revan returns the mask to the Mandalorians, allowing Canderous to adopt the mantle of Mandalore the Protector and lead his people. Revan follows his trail of memories to Nathema, the planet that Dramath fled.

Scourge confronts Nyris about her plans, and she reveals the truth to him. She did indeed manipulate him to kill Xedrix, a co-conspirator and one of several Dark Councilors plotting to stop the Emperor before the tyrant launches an ill-advised attack against the Republic. Xedrix was sacrificed to protect the Dark Council. To impress upon Scourge the importance of the Council's motives, Nyris brings him to Nathema, former homeworld of the Emperor.

The Emperor is one thousand years old. In a dark side ritual, he drained the life of his home planet, Nathema, to achieve immortality. The world is now a lifeless husk, devoid of the Force. Scourge comes to understand that such power is madness, and the Emperor has lost all reason. While on Nathema, Scourge and Nyris cross paths with Revan, who arrives aboard the *Ebon Hawk*. Nyris blasts Revan's ship out of the sky, and the Sith take Revan prisoner.

Years pass. T3-M4 returns to Bastila Shan on Coruscant, helped by a Jedi exile, Meetra Surik. Meetra and Bastila learn from T3 that the Sith, long thought extinct, are somehow involved in Revan's disappearance. Meetra and T3 return to Nathema, where she finds the location of Dromund Kaas, the Sith homeworld. There she meets with Scourge, the Sith Lord whose image T3-M4 managed to record holographically at the time of Revan's capture.

In the years since Revan's imprisonment, Scourge has been meeting with the Jedi Knight and has learned secrets of the Force from Revan. Scourge is still wary of the Emperor and has become convinced that Revan holds the key to stopping the ruler's plans. Scourge needs to rescue Revan from Nyris's prison and allies with Meetra to that end.

TALES OF ANCIENT JEDI AND SITH

Scourge reveals to the Emperor Nyris's plot against him, presenting him with evidence of her treachery. The Emperor orders the Imperial Guard to strike against Nyris. Using the chaos of this reprisal as cover, Scourge and Meetra free Revan but are nearly stopped by Nyris. Revan's raw power in the Force bends Nyris's Sith lightning back at her, utterly destroying the Sith Lord. The trio of Scourge, Meetra, and Revan escape into secret caves, where T3 projects an image for Revan of Bastila and his now three-year-old son, Vaner. The Emperor, meanwhile, destroys *all* twelve Dark Councilors to send a message against any who would plot against him.

Revan is determined to keep the galaxy safe for his child. Scourge, Meetra, and Revan enter the Emperor's citadel and challenge the supreme ruler. The Emperor's power is too much for Revan. Recognizing that the Emperor is undefeatable, Scourge kills Meetra and betrays Revan. Scourge tells the Emperor that he had plotted to expose these assassins once he realized he alone would not be powerful enough to stop them. The Emperor believes Scourge and rewards him with the title of Emperor's Wrath.

In truth, Scourge still thinks the Emperor must be stopped. His betrayal of the Jedi was a bid to buy himself more time. Revan languishes in a Sith prison, mentally exhibiting subtle pressure against the Emperor's mind to keep the dark ruler from attacking the Republic. As it is, the Emperor is preoccupied with securing the Sith Empire, rebuilding the Dark Council, and rooting out traitors.

In this way, peace lasts for another fifty years. Bastila and Revan's child, Vaner, grows into an influential man of politics with children of his own.

SPOTLIGHT   Knights of the Old Republic

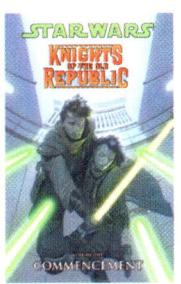

In 2003, LucasArts and BioWare released the critically acclaimed videogame **Knights of the Old Republic** (also known as **KotOR**). As a roleplaying game, it focuses heavily on storytelling driven by character choices, meaning its central story can take a wide variety of shapes depending on the player's actions. A true canonical order of specific events has not been established, but the "light side" ending (as opposed to the ending achievable if the player concentrates on dark side actions) is accepted to be the historically accurate account.

The game takes place during the Jedi Civil War, when two renegade Jedi—Malak and Revan—take an offensive role in repulsing Mandalorian invaders. The Jedi succumb to the dark side to emerge as Sith Lords, and the Republic must then stop Malak from uncovering an ancient relic created by the Rakatan species that could turn the tide in the conflict.

KotOR would spawn a sequel, **Knights of the Old Republic II: The Sith Lords** (2004), and a *KotOR* comic series that began in 2006 and is set before the events of the games. These titles became an essential part of the backstory to the *Star Wars:* **The Old Republic** massively multiplayer online game and its tie-in books and comics.

In the videogame **Knights of the Old Republic** (2003), the character Revan is by necessity a blank slate, a Jedi hero whose gender, appearance, and name could be customized by the player. As more stories and source material referenced Revan, the character underwent further refinement. This novel canonically defines his appearance, history, and personality. It does the same for the similarly unnamed Jedi Exile hero from **Knights of the Old Republic II: The Sith Lords** (2004), who is identified as Meetra Surik in this novel.

Revan looks upon a hologram of his wife, Bastila, and their child, Vaner.

"THE OLD REPUBLIC: SMUGGLER'S VANGUARD"

AUTHOR · Rob Chestney

PUBLICATION HISTORY · Short story, StarWars.com, March 2010

TIME LINE PLACEMENT · c. 3660 BBY

WORLD VISITED · Corellia [M-11]

MAIN CHARACTERS · Hylo Visz, smuggler (Mirialan female)

TALES OF ANCIENT JEDI AND SITH

SHORT STORY | *Knights of the Old Republic* Prose

Completists attempting to read all *Star Wars* prose fiction will want to include a pair of online short stories written by John Jackson Miller for StarWars.com that tie into the *Knights of the Old Republic* series from Dark Horse Comics. Both published in 2008, these stories connect to Miller's ongoing narrative of the comic and should be read as part of that series. "Labor Pains" occurs after issue #12 of the comic, after the *Flashpoint* trade paperback, and features con man Gryph trying to sell scrap as fine works of art. "Interference" takes place after issue #21 of the comic, or midway through the *Daze of Hate, Knights of Suffering* trade paperback. This story has an unusual format in that it is told as a series of intercepted propaganda transmissions during the Mandalorian invasion of Taris. Both stories are set in 3963 BBY. Readers can find these stories at star-wars.suvudu.com.

SUMMARY · A superstitious smuggler, Hylo pilots her ship, the *Crimson Fleece*, to Corellia, delivering prototype engines to the Rendili Vehicle Corporation on behalf of crime lord Barrga the Hutt. After the transaction is completed, her instincts save her when her ship erupts in an explosion, and she is stranded at the corporate offices. Knocking out an absentminded Jedi Knight, she escapes Corellia by stealing a prototype *Vanguard*-class light corvette.

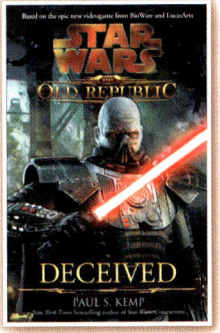

THE OLD REPUBLIC: DECEIVED

AUTHOR · Paul S. Kemp
COVER ARTIST · LucasArts
PUBLICATION HISTORY · Novel, Del Rey Books
 · Hardcover, March 2011
 · Paperback, May 2012

TIME LINE PLACEMENT ·
c. 3653 BBY

WORLDS VISITED · Alderaan [M-10]; Coruscant [L-9]; Ord Mantell [L-7]; Vulta [N-7]

MAIN CHARACTERS · Zeerid "Z-Man" Korr, smuggler (human male); Aryn Leneer, Jedi Knight (human female); Darth Malgus, Sith Lord (human male); Eleena, servant (Twi'lek female); Darth Angral, Sith Lord (human male); Darth Adraas, Sith Lord (human male); Vrath Xizor, mercenary (human male)

SUMMARY · As representatives of the Sith Empire and the Galactic Republic convene on Alderaan to finalize a peace treaty ending their long-standing conflict, the Sith launch a lightning attack on Coruscant. Darth Malgus leads the devastating sacking of the Republic capital. Much to his consternation, it is not an act of conquest; Coruscant is held hostage to exact key concessions from the Republic at the ne-

TALES OF ANCIENT JEDI AND SITH

gotiating table. Malgus feels diplomacy is beneath the Sith and loathes such displays of weakness.

Malgus slays Jedi Master Ven Zallow before bringing down the entire Temple in an explosive collapse. Zallow's death reverberates through the Force and is keenly felt by the empathic Aryn Leneer, his former Padawan. She is at the Alderaan peace conference when word of the Coruscant attack reaches her. Aryn impetuously departs to seek vengeance on her mentor's killer.

Meanwhile, Zeerid Korr, smuggler captain of the freighter *Fatman*, is desperate to eke out a living to support his disabled daughter. A delivery to Ord Mantell botched by pirates puts him further in debt to the criminal organization The Exchange. With deep misgivings, he takes a job to deliver narcotics past the blockade on Coruscant. He returns home to Vulta to see his daughter prior to his dangerous journey. While he's there, a mercenary hired by rival Hutt gangsters targets Zeerid and his cargo. With the help of Aryn Leneer—who voyaged to Vulta to recruit Zeerid's help in returning to Coruscant—he escapes the gangsters.

Malgus's blockading flagship, *Valor*, blasts the approaching *Fatman* out of the sky over Coruscant, but Zeerid and Aryn survive and land on the besieged capital's surface. Probing the ruins of the Temple, Aryn finds evidence that it was Malgus who killed her Master. She also unravels the nature of the relationship between Malgus and Eleena, his Twi'lek servant. Despite his cruel nature, the Dark Lord has come to love Eleena. Determined to make the Dark Lord suffer for his crimes, Aryn kidnaps Eleena. Before doing her harm, however, Aryn comes to her senses and spares Eleena's life. Malgus and Aryn duel, and though he could kill Aryn, he likewise returns the favor and lets the Jedi live. Malgus instead turns his blade on Eleena, realizing how vulnerable his emotions toward her have made him.

Having finally escaped his underworld pursuers, Zeerid and his daughter retire to a quiet life on a farm on Dantooine.

SHORT STORY: "The Third Lesson"

"The Third Lesson" is a short story by Paul S. Kemp published in *Star Wars Insider* #124 (March 2011) by Titan Publishing. Set prior to the events of the novel *Deceived*, the tale involves Darth Malgus surviving a Jedi ambush during the Sith attack on Alderaan. Malgus flashes back to lessons imparted to him by his father, an Imperial biologist, using natural examples from the family's menagerie.

This book expands upon a cinematic trailer for the videogame *Star Wars: The Old Republic* that was released on the Internet in 2009. The fallout from the Coruscant blitz is also the focus of the comic story *The Old Republic: Threat of Peace* (2009).

Author James Luceno was originally slated to write a tie-in novel to *The Old Republic*, developing an outline that would explore the history of Darth Malgus. His early concepts, which had Malgus as a former slave hardened in gladiatorial combat, ultimately did not fit with the direction that BioWare and LucasArts mapped out for Malgus. Luceno reworked some of these into Darth Maul's history in the novel *Darth Plagueis* (2012), and as he concentrated on that project, Paul S. Kemp began his writing duties on *Deceived*. As Kemp's story developed,

Jedi Knight Aryn Leneer and pilot Zeerid "Z-Man" Korr leap from the doomed vessel *Fatman* as the freighter crashes through the atmosphere of Coruscant.

some of the darker details of Malgus and the Sith were trimmed—a scene depicting the triumphant Sith playing a game of ball with severed Jedi heads, for example, was left out of the final text.

RED HARVEST

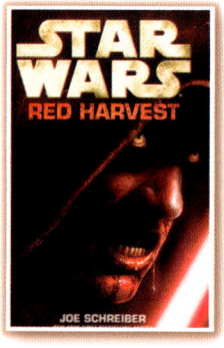 

AUTHOR · Joe Schreiber

COVER ARTIST · Indika (hardcover and paperback)

PUBLICATION HISTORY · Novel, Del Rey Books
- Hardcover, December 2010
- Paperback, February 2012

TIME LINE PLACEMENT · 3645 BBY

WORLDS VISITED · Geonosis [R-16]; Marfa [M-10]; Odacer-Faustin [Q-5]

MAIN CHARACTERS · Hestizo "Zo" Trace, Jedi AgriCorps worker (human female); Tulkh, bounty hunter (Whiphid male); Darth Scabrous, Sith Lord (human male); Dail'Liss, librarian (Neti male); Rojo Trace, Jedi Knight (human male); Hartwig, Sith student (human male); Kindra, Sith student (human female); Pergus Frode, mechanic (human male)

SUMMARY · Seeking the secrets of immortality, Darth Scabrous uncovers a Sith Holocron housed in an ancient temple hidden beneath a Sith Academy on the snow-covered world of Odacer-Faustin. With the writings of Darth Drear guiding him, Scabrous subjects unwilling Academy students to foul experiments. The Dark Lord lacks an essential ingredient: a unique, Force-sensitive plant called the Murakami orchid. One of his dispatched agents, a fierce Whiphid bounty hunter named Tulkh, captures the sentient flower along with its tender, Jedi Agricultural Corps member Hestizo "Zo" Trace, who uses her Force abilities to communicate with and nurture the orchid.

When Scabrous infuses the orchid into test subjects, he creates a blood-borne infection. The Sickness transforms those exposed into ravenous undead. The plague spreads quickly through the Academy, turning students and faculty into zombies. The infection leaps from host to host, regardless of species. Ordinarily cutthroat Sith students band together for survival, but they cannot outrun the pathogen or the clawing, bloodied corpses that pursue them. Even the corralled tauntauns turn into crazed, shambling undead.

Despite the spread of the Sickness, Zo can still feel the presence of the orchid and can influence it. She entreats the plant with the command *Grow*, which causes vine-like masses to sprout from the bodies of the zombies, stopping them in their shuffling tracks. This greatly taxes the orchid, though it saves Zo's life several times.

Though Scabrous is himself infected, he remains collected enough to carry out Drear's rituals. By sacrificing a Jedi with a Sith sword at the height of the infestation, Scabrous intends to bring forth everlasting life. Zo becomes his prisoner, though she is spared death by the sudden appearance of her brother, Rojo Trace, who saves his sister but dies on Scabrous's blade.

Hunter Tulkh stares at the horrific sight of infected undead Sith students at the academy on Odacer-Faustin riding within similarly afflicted tauntaun zombies.

Zo flees the hellish Academy with Tulkh and a mechanic named Pergus Frode aboard the Whiphid's starship. Leaving Odacer-Faustin behind, the survivors still cannot escape infection: Tulkh carries the Sickness in him. He stoically orders Zo to eject him into space. With regret, Zo jettisons the proud Whiphid warrior out the air lock.

Zo and Pergus return to the Jedi greenhouses of Marfa. Exposed to the dangers of the galaxy, and perhaps given a window into her own mortality, Zo decides to end her sequestered lifestyle in a greenhouse and voyages to Coruscant instead.

Originally called *Black Orchid*, a reference to the Murakami orchid at the bloody heart of the Sickness, this horror novel was rechristened *Red Harvest*, a title that not only fits the plot but is also a nod to a piece of *Star Wars* history. *Return of the Jedi* (1983) was code-named *Blue Harvest: Horror Beyond Imagination* during its stateside filming as a smokescreen to draw attention away from it being a *Star Wars* film.

Red Harvest is a prequel to *Death Troopers* (2009), a zombie horror novel set before the events of *A New Hope* (1977). Since a gulf of thousands of years separates the novels, they share no recurring characters, though the Sickness is occasionally personified and can be thought of as a character in both books.

At story's end, Zo intends to visit the Jedi Temple on Coruscant. However, at this point in the time line—eight years after the events of The Old Republic: *Deceived* (2011)—the Temple should be in ruins.

THE OLD REPUBLIC: FATAL ALLIANCE

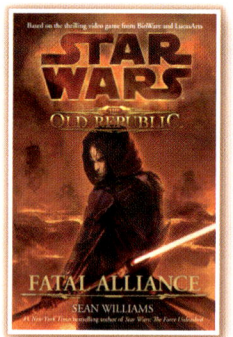

AUTHOR · Sean Williams

COVER ARTIST · LucasArts

PUBLICATION HISTORY ·
Novel, Del Rey Books
· Hardcover, July 2010
· Paperback, May 2011

TIME LINE PLACEMENT ·
c. 3643 BBY

WORLDS VISITED · Coruscant [L-9]; Dromund Kaas [R-5]; Nal Hutta [S-12]; Sebaddon [Q-11]; Tatooine [R-16]

MAIN CHARACTERS · Shigar Konshi, Padawan learner (Kiffar male); Eldon Ax, Sith apprentice (human female); Larin Moxla, former Republic trooper (Kiffar female); Ula Vii, Republic envoy and Imperial agent (Epicanthix male); Jet Nebula, smuggler (human male); Satele Shan, Jedi Grand Master (human female); Darth Chratis, Sith Lord (human male); Dao Stryver, Mandalorian warrior (Gektl female)

SUMMARY · The discovery of the starship *Cinzia* has grave ramifications for the galaxy. Privateer Jet Nebula brings back two crucial remains of the vessel to his Hutt masters—a navicomp pointing to the ship's origins and a mysterious cylinder made of exotic metals. The Hutts rightly surmise that there will be many parties interested in these enigmatic trophies. Factions from across the galaxy gather their envoys to take up the invitation to the Hutt homeworld of Nal Hutta.

Gathering intelligence for the Jedi Order is young Shigar Konshi, a Padawan learner. He brings with him a former Republic trooper, Larin Moxla. Serving the Republic is the stuffy Epicanthix envoy Ula Vii, who is secretly an Imperial double agent. For the Sith, the decrepit Darth Chratis dispatches his fiery-tempered apprentice, Eldon Ax. Most mysterious is the armored Mandalorian warrior Dao Stryver.

The cylinder is a miniaturized droid factory of incredibly advanced engineering. The device saps raw materials and power from its surroundings and deploys combat droids nicknamed hexes. The mastermind who devised this powerful technology must be found. This brings all parties to Sebaddon, a mineral-rich world far from the galactic plane, orbiting a black hole at a safe yet terrifying distance.

The droids are the creation of Lema Xandret, a genius engineer who fled the Sith Empire. Her daughter, Eldon Ax, was stolen from her by the Sith Lords for training, and Lema longed for vengeance. She created the instruments of her revenge—the hex droids—to be self-generating, inadvertently releasing a scourge of geometrically replicating warrior droids. If left unchecked, the droids could overrun the galaxy within a generation.

The Republic and Imperial forces unite to destroy the hexes. Eldon Ax penetrates deep into a laboratory concealed on Sebaddon's surface. She finds a clone of herself and discovers the twisted truth of her mother's plot. Lema had found a way to infuse adaptability into the droids through an organic fluid that served as their lifeblood. Lema's spirit seemingly inhabited this fluid to some degree and was primarily tasked with protecting the developing clone of her long-lost daughter. The hexes took that order of protection to the extreme, killing *any* life-form that threatened the clone. In their cold logic, this even included killing Lema.

Eldon destroys the cylinder containing the clone and then genetically imprints herself on the hexes. She orders them to call off their attack and self-destruct, but not before using them to destroy her Master, Darth Chratis. The Republic and Imperial forces retreat, and Sebaddon's unbalanced orbit decays, eventually dooming it to a destructive embrace with the black hole.

THE OLD REPUBLIC: ANNIHILATION

AUTHOR · Drew Karpyshyn

COVER ARTIST · LucasArts

PUBLICATION HISTORY · Novel, Del Rey Books · Hardcover, November 2012

TIME LINE PLACEMENT · 3640 BBY

WORLDS VISITED (partial list) · Alderaan (flashbacks) [M-10]; Coruscant [L-9]; Dromund Kaas [R-5]; Nar Shaddaa, moon of Nal Hutta [S-12]; Ziost [R-4]

MAIN CHARACTERS · Theron Shan, covert agent (human male); Gnost-Dural, Jedi Master (Kel Dor male); Jace Malcom, Supreme Commander of Republic forces (human male); Darth Karrid, Sith Lord (Umbaran female)

SUMMARY · The Sith Empire is in disarray, but it still holds military might in the massive warship, *Ascendant Spear*. The huge vessel is under the control of Darth Karrid, a Sith Lord who espouses a polarizing belief that the Sith Empire should adopt a pan-species unity, a viewpoint held by her former Master, Darth Malgus.

SHORT STORY: "The Last Battle of Colonel Jace Malcom"

Published in *Star Wars Insider* #137 (October 2012, from Titan Publishing), this short story by Alexander Freed tells of Colonel Malcom's last battlefield assignment. On a desolate, alien world, Jace Malcom leads teams of Republic troopers into a Sith Imperial spaceport. They plant target beacons for an incoming Republic starfighter squadron. Malcom spots a docked Sith command ship and decides to capture it before it departs. Infiltrating the vessel, Malcom fails to stop its commanding Sith Lord from activating a self-destruct countdown. The Colonel leaps from the ship, accepting death as his fate — but his life is spared when he is caught by a Republic starfighter. A Jedi takes Malcom from the battlefield — he's been recalled by the Supreme Chancellor and will be assigned a new mission away from the frontlines. The grizzled Colonel doesn't have time to reflect on the casualties suffered on this battlefield. It's time to move onto the next battle.

The Republic is plotting to destroy the *Spear*. To that end, Republic Strategic Information Services assembles a team made up of Theron Shan and Master Gnost-Dural, commanded from Coruscant by the hardened Jace Malcom, Supreme Commander of all Republic military forces. To succeed in their mission, Theron and Gnost-Dural must capture Imperial code-breaking technology that will allow them to tap into Sith transmissions and strike when the *Ascendant Spear* is most vulnerable. The impulsive and rule-bending Theron uses his underworld contacts to his advantage when carrying out this most important assignment.

As a senior writer for BioWare, author Drew Karpyshyn helped establish the complex storylines of the **Knights of the Old Republic** and *Star Wars: The Old Republic* videogames, putting him in the ideal position to expand upon those epic narratives through novels. This book draws from the vast history built for the **Old Republic** franchise. The *Ascendant Spear* and Theron Shan were first introduced in *The Old Republic: The Lost Suns* comics series, which began publication in June 2011 from Dark Horse Comics. It also includes flashbacks to a battle on Alderaan, when Jace Malcom was a soldier serving alongside Satele Shan. This scenario was vividly realized as a computer-generated cinematic trailer for the **Old Republic** videogame, released in June 2010.

KNIGHT ERRANT

AUTHOR ·
John Jackson Miller

COVER ARTIST ·
John VanFleet

PUBLICATION HISTORY ·
Novel, Del Rey Books
· Paperback, January 2011

TIME LINE PLACEMENT ·
1032 BBY

Kerra Holt discovers the Celagian telepaths who have helped the Sith subjugate the world of Byllura.

TALES OF ANCIENT JEDI AND SITH

WORLDS VISITED · Byllura [N-17]; Darkknell [M-17]; Gazzari [M-17]; Syned [N-17]

MAIN CHARACTERS · Kerra Holt, Jedi Knight (human female); Narsk Ka'hane, spy (Bothan male); Jarrow Rusher, brigadier mercenary (human male); Lord Daiman, Sith Lord (human male); Lord Odion, Sith Lord (human male); Quillan and Dromika, Sith influencers (human male and female twins); Arkadia Calimondra, Sith Lord (human female); Vilia Calimondra, Sith Lord (human female)

SUMMARY · During the New Sith Wars, advancing Sith conquests chased the Republic from its territories, plunging vast swaths of the galaxy into a terrifying dark age. The many Sith Lords of this era are perpetually locked in violent rivalries for power. In the Grumani sector, Kerra Holt is a lone Jedi operating behind enemy lines, trying to scuttle Sith operations and free as many of the enslaved civilians as possible.

The Daimanate is an expanse of worlds dominated by the monomaniacal Lord Daiman, a deranged solipsist who believes he is the creator of the universe. Kerra, operating undercover within the cracks of his empire, learns of an impending confrontation with Daiman's brother, Lord Odion. With a prototype stealth suit stolen from a Bothan spy, Kerra slips into the front line of this combat on the planet Gazzari. Discovering that Daiman has brought more than a thousand young students to the battlefield to bait his brother to attack, Kerra seizes the initiative and rallies these refugees away from the battle, bringing them aboard a mercenary artillery vessel, *Diligence*.

The battlefield erupts into bewildering chaos as Daiman and Odion, sworn enemies, briefly ally to conquer a third Sith Lord, Bactra. Escaping in this confusion, the *Diligence* soars to nearby Byllura, while Kerra becomes acquainted with the vessel's commander, Brigadier Jarrow Rusher. A pragmatic

gun-for-hire, Rusher works for the Sith but claims no real loyalty to anyone other than his crew. He complains loudly about Kerra bringing the refugee children aboard and is eager to drop them off on the nearest suitable world.

That planet is deceptively tranquil Byllura. Though its principal city of Hestobyll seems peaceful enough, set against a beautiful ocean view, it is the heart of the Dyarchy, another Sith stronghold. Here Quillan and Dromika—twin teenage Sith Lords—hold the population in check through the Force, spreading their mental influence through a network of telepathic Celagians. Kerra scuttles this operation by liberating the Celagians from their brainwashing, shattering the mental grip of the twins over the planet's population. Immediately swooping in to claim the power vacuum on Byllura is a neighboring Sith Lord, Lady Arkadia Calimondra.

SPOTLIGHT   *Knight Errant* in Comics

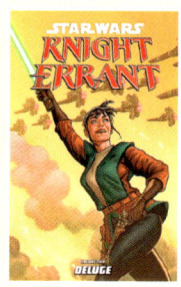
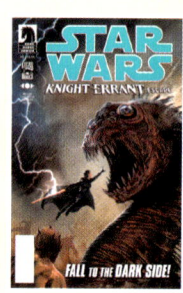

Knight Errant is a close collaboration of *Star Wars* storytelling between comic book publisher Dark Horse Comics and novel publisher Del Rey. Author John Jackson Miller wrote not only the *Knight Errant* novel, but also a comic book series of the same name featuring the same characters and setting. The comic began publication in October 2010. A full-color preview of the comic was included as an insert in the novel, and a chapter excerpt from the novel appeared in one of the issues of the comic.

In the five-issue *Aflame* story line, Kerra Holt is the sole Jedi survivor left behind enemy lines after a disastrous mission to Chelloa. She is caught in the middle of Lord Odion and Lord Daiman's destructive struggle for control of the baradium deposits on the planet. With difficulty, Kerra puts aside her desire to defeat the Sith and concentrates instead on evacuating the planet's beleaguered slave population.

The follow-up series, *Deluge*, takes place after the *Knight Errant* novel. On her home planet, Aquilaris, Kerra finds a daring Republic captain, Jeen Devaad, continuing the fight against the Sith. But she also discovers the truth behind Devaad's mission—it's a rogue intel op meant to slow the Sith by addicting their slaves to a drug called Deluge. Despite her misgivings, Kerra joins Devaad in the fight against a Hutt interloper, Zodoh, who is attempting to impress the Sith with a new weapon based on the moisture vaporator.

In the third series, *Escape*, Kerra Holt infiltrates Lord Daiman's death cult, which is focused on uncovering a great Sith relic, the Helm of Ieldis. Kerra discovers shocking information about the survivors of the assault upon her homeworld of Aquilaris.

Arkadia brings Kerra, the *Diligence*, and one of the twins, Quillan, to her icebound palace on Syned. Arkadia rules through a program of careful social engineering that keeps Syned's citizens forever changing occupations, always living to serve yet never to excel. Arkadia reveals to Kerra the true nature of the Sith conflict in the Grumani sector: Power rests in her grandmother, Vilia Calimondra, who keeps her grandchildren in intense conflict for her favor. Arkadia tries to convince Kerra to kill her grandmother, but Kerra refuses.

Arkadia imprisons Kerra and turns to the Bothan spy, Narsk Ka'hane, to carry out the deed, unaware that Ka'hane is working for Vilia. Ka'hane frees Kerra and, together with Rusher, engineers an explosive escape from Syned. The enigmatic Bothan supplies Kerra and Rusher with hyperspace coordinates that will return them to Republic space. Rusher is happy to leave the endless Sith conflict, and the refugees will find safe harbor in the Republic, though Kerra intends to return to Grumani to continue her fight against the Sith.

KNIGHT ERRANT is filled with meticulous world-building and history. Author John Jackson Miller specifically carved out the Grumani sector as the setting for his Kerra Holt stories. Prior to the publication of the comics and novel, Miller penned the short story "Influx" (2010), which served as a lead-in to the comic series and was published on StarWars.com. Also posted to the website was *The Essential Atlas* Extra: *Knight Errant* Gazetteer, an introductory guide to the worlds of the Grumani sector written by Miller and *Star Wars: The Essential Atlas* authors Daniel Wallace and Jason Fry.

THE DARTH BANE SAGA

DARTH BANE: PATH OF DESTRUCTION • DARTH BANE: RULE OF TWO • DARTH BANE: DYNASTY OF EVIL

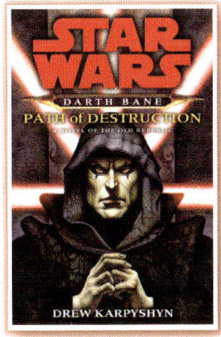 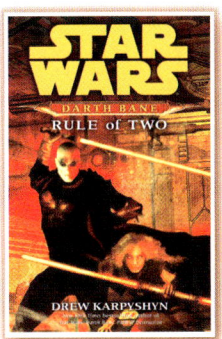 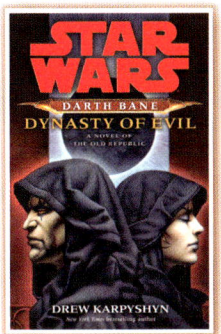

AUTHOR · Drew Karpyshyn
COVER ARTISTS · John Jude Palencar (*Path of Destruction* and *Dynasty of Evil*) and John VanFleet (*Rule of Two*)

TALES OF ANCIENT JEDI AND SITH

PUBLICATION HISTORY · Novels, Del Rey Books

DARTH BANE: *Path of Destruction*
- Hardcover, September 2006
- Paperback, June 2007

DARTH BANE: *Rule of Two*
- Hardcover, December 2007
- Paperback, October 2008

DARTH BANE: *Dynasty of Evil*
- Hardcover, December 2009
- Paperback, September 2010

TIME LINE PLACEMENT · 1003–980 BBY

WORLDS VISITED · Ambria [O-10]; Apatros [Q-16]; Ciutric IV [N-5]; Coruscant [L-9]; Doan [M-6]; Korriban [R-5]; Lehon (aka Unknown World, Rakata Prime) [G-11]; Nal Hutta [S-12]; Onderon (and its moon Dxun) [O-9]; Phaseera [P-8]; Prakith [K-10]; Ruusan [P-11]; Serenno [P-5]; Tython [L-10]

MAIN CHARACTERS · Darth Bane, Sith Lord (human male); Darth Zannah, Sith apprentice (human female); Githany, Sith Lord and former Jedi (human female); Lord Kaan, Dark Lord (human male); Johun Othone, Jedi Knight (human male); Serra, princess of Doan (human female); Set Harth, Dark Jedi (human male); Darovit, healer (human male); the Huntress, assassin (Iktotchi female)

SUMMARY · Using his instinctive Force abilities, an indentured miner named Dessel flees the bleak planet Apatros and joins the ranks of the Sith army. He proves to be a formidable soldier, coaxing hard-won victories against the Jedi and the Republic. Dessel draws the attention of the ruling Sith Lords, who enroll him at the Sith Academy on Korriban, where he adopts the name Bane.

In studying the philosophies of ancient Dark Lords, Bane grows increasingly disillusioned with modern Sith doctrine, particularly the Brotherhood

of Darkness led by Lord Kaan. In defiance, Bane resurrects the lost title of Darth and leaves Korriban. On Lehon, he finds a Holocron constructed by Darth Revan. Studying its contents, Bane realizes that the modern Sith are doomed to extinction due to the unyielding ambitions of competing warlords. Bane envisions another structure with only two Sith Lords active at a time: the Master, to embody the power, and the apprentice, to crave it.

Bane plots to reinfiltrate the Brotherhood and destroy it from within. He offers Lord Kaan a peculiar gift discovered among Revan's teachings: instructions for the creation of a powerful Sith weapon, the thought bomb. Kaan, wary of Bane's power and loyalty, dispatches the wily seductress Githany to retrieve him at a rendezvous point on Ambria. Githany poisons Bane with deadly synox. Reeling from the toxin, Bane threatens a local healer's daughter, forcing the healer to rid Bane's body of the contamination.

Bane voyages to Ruusan. The planet has been ravaged by an intense war between the Brotherhood of Darkness and the Jedi Army of Light led by Lord Hoth. It is here that the Jedi and the Sith Orders prepare for a final battle. Darth Bane arrives at Kaan's command tent and offers him assistance. The increasingly desperate Lord Kaan resorts to using the thought bomb.

The Sith retreat into caves, drawing the Jedi into the dark warrens. There, with all forces concentrated, Kaan ignites the arcane weapon. The blast destroys the Force-users—the assembled Brotherhood and Jedi who ventured into the caverns—and sucks their spirits into a single egg-like orb, where the disembodied souls swirl about in eternal madness.

Because he avoided the thought bomb, Darth Bane is alive in secret. As he departs the devastated world, he comes across a young girl named Zannah, whom he selects as his apprentice.

Seeking out ancient Sith lore, Bane crashes his ship in the jungles of Dxun, a moon of Onderon. In an ancient sepulchre, he uncovers a Sith Holocron. As Bane claims the repository of dark lore, he is overcome by orbalisks, hard-shelled parasites that cover his body.

Ten years pass. Bane has relocated to a camp on Ambria, where he has spent years studying how to assemble his own Holocron. Bane's grotesque orbalisk infestation has forced him to remain in the shadows, while Darth Zannah serves as his remote executor, helping the Sith build a shadowy network of benefactors and informants. Zannah's strongest dark side talent is to conjure horrors from a victim's mind, destroying sanity with illusory threats.

By insinuating herself into a separatist movement on Serenno, Zannah uncovers hyperspace charts in the trove of a Sith artifact collector. These routes wind through the dangerous Deep Core to the ancient world of Tython, said to hold the secrets of Holocron construction. While Bane embarks for Tython, he tasks Zannah with infiltrating the Jedi Temple and seeking out lore regarding the safe removal of the debilitating orbalisk parasites.

Undercover amid the Jedi, Zannah crosses paths with her cousin Darovit, a Ruusan veteran. He recognizes Zannah despite her disguise. Unwilling to break her cover or kill Darovit, she takes him prisoner and returns to her Master with the orbalisk cure. Rushing to depart, Zannah inadvertently leaves a trail to Tython that the Jedi can follow. There the Sith destroy the Jedi pursuers, but Bane is badly wounded. Desperate to heal her Master, Zannah and Darovit bring the fallen Sith Lord to Caleb, the healer who once saved his life on Ambria.

After Bane is healed of both his injuries and the orbalisks, Zannah kills Caleb and uses her Force abilities to drive Darovit mad. She carefully ar-

Dessel—the future Darth Bane—leads his elite Sith squad known as the Gloom Walkers.

SHORT STORY — "Bane of the Sith"

In 2001, Wizards of the Coast published the short story "Bane of the Sith" by Kevin J. Anderson in *Star Wars Gamer* #3. The tale describes Bane's uncovering of Freedon Nadd's Holocron, and his infestation by orbalisk parasites. These events would be retold in *Darth Bane: Rule of Two* (2007). The magazine story has a number of incongruities compared with the later Bane novels. Bane is not presented as the scheming mastermind behind the use of the devastating thought bomb, for instance. Bane's apprentice, Zannah, is also not mentioned in the short story.

ranges clues to lead the Jedi to misidentify Darovit as the rumored Sith Lord. In killing the raving Darovit, the Jedi mistakenly assume they have destroyed the last Sith survivor.

Ten years later, Bane and Zannah have adopted the aliases of a wealthy brother and sister living on an estate on Ciutric IV. Bane's research has uncovered the teachings of Darth Andeddu, an ancient Sith Lord said to have revealed the secret of eternal life through the arcane ritual of essence transfer. Doubting Zannah's abilities and fearing for his health, Bane is determined to ensure the continuation of the Sith. Bane voyages to Prakith to claim Andeddu's Holocron and memorize its contents.

The ambitious Zannah seeks out a possible apprentice to allow her to supplant Bane. She considers a former Jedi named Set Harth as a candidate. He is insouciant and obsessed with material possessions, but nonetheless a formidable warrior, strong in the Force.

Princess Serra of Doan has a secret connection with Darth Bane. Before marrying into the royal family, she had lived with her father Caleb. Upon hearing the descriptions of the Sith Lord killed there, she comes to realize that the Jedi were mistaken and that Darth Bane may still live. Serra hires a Force-sensitive assassin known as the Huntress to track him down.

Mercenaries led by the Huntress attack Bane as he returns to Ciutric IV. The intruders defeat and drug Bane, taking him to Doan. The Huntress, impressed by Bane's power, pockets Andeddu's Holocron and brings it with her. Bane is shackled and kept in a chemical stupor within the Stone Prison, far below the metropolitan surface of Doan.

When Zannah learns of Bane's quest for immortality, she is incensed, deciding it to be an affront to his Rule of Two. She tracks her Master to the Stone Prison and confronts him there. Serra detonates fail-safe demolitions within the prison, tearing the facility apart. A cave-in separates Bane from Zannah. In his escape from Doan, Bane encounters the Huntress, who bows before him, promising to be his apprentice. Bane, intrigued by her abilities, accepts the Huntress as his student.

Fleeing to Ambria, Zannah and Bane resume their duel. Zannah uses her skill in Sith sorcery to overwhelm Bane's psyche. Bane, sensing defeat, initiates the essence transfer, attempting to force his consciousness into Zannah's body. Bane's physical form disintegrates in a burst of Force energy, leaving only Zannah standing triumphant. Zannah adopts as her apprentice the Huntress, who takes the title Darth Cognus.

Darth Bane and Darth Zannah enter a final lightsaber duel from which only one of them will walk away.

> ### CHRONOLOGICAL NOTE | Jedi vs. Sith
>
>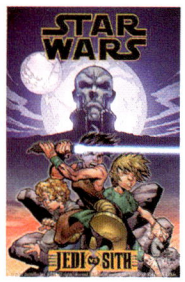
>
> Published in 2001 by Dark Horse Comics, the *Jedi vs. Sith* series was the first dramatized depiction of the Battle of Ruusan, an event introduced in the backstory to the videogame **Dark Forces II: Jedi Knight** (1997). *Darth Bane: Path of Destruction* (2006) encompasses this tale in its final chapters, but it focuses on Bane as the protagonist, whereas the comic concentrates on three Force-sensitive children, Zannah, Darovit, and Hardin (aka Rain, Tomcat, and Bug), who are scarcely mentioned in the novel. The two sources also differ from each other in a number of mostly superficial ways, particularly in dialogue and the order of certain events. Githany's death differs notably. In the novel, she is immediately swept up in the thought bomb blast. In the comic, she lives long enough after the detonation to encounter Bane one last time and beg to be his apprentice before her body falls apart from the bomb's effects.

Elsewhere in the galaxy, Set Harth survives, having appropriated Darth Andeddu's Holocron from Doan before escaping, and studies its secrets intently.

The saga of Darth Bane is an excellent example of the collaborative, iterative, and cumulative nature of Expanded Universe storytelling. The evolution of the Sith Order was told through many sources to become a single narrative with no one author.

The motion picture *Star Wars* (1977) makes no mention of Darth Vader's title, but the term *Dark Lord of the Sith* is indeed in the script and in tie-in publications, like the film's novelization. In the development of *Heir to the Empire* (1991), author Timothy Zahn attempted to establish the Sith as a species of assassins completely subservient to Darth Vader. Lucasfilm rejected this idea, and Zahn's imagined Sith instead became the Noghri. With insights from George Lucas, author Tom Veitch began revealing more about the Sith in the *Tales of the Jedi* comic series (1993). They were dark side practitioners, the antithesis of the Jedi Order. This backstory reveals that only one Sith may wear the mantle of Dark Lord, while another Sith serves as an apprentice, though there was no restriction on the number of Sith present at any time. *Tales of the Jedi: The Freedon Nadd Uprising* (1994) used the term Sith civilization, revealing the Sith to be an entire species. The Sith would be visibly depicted as red-skinned humanoids in *Tales of the Jedi: The Golden Age of the Sith* (1996–97).

The LucasArts videogame **Dark Forces II: Jedi Knight** (1997) and accompanying *Dark Forces* novellas from Dark Horse Comics describe an epic struggle for the ancient world of Ruusan. The planet is home to the fabled Valley of the Jedi, site of an ancient battle between a Jedi Army of Light and the Brotherhood of Darkness. The dark practitioners are not explicitly called Sith in the source, and the battle is said to occur "hundreds and hundreds of years ago." Though not intended at the time, this story would become an essential piece of Sith history.

In 1999, *The Phantom Menace* finally shed light on George Lucas's vision of the Sith, which at first glance would not seem to align with what had appeared previously in the Expanded Universe. This canonical history describes a strict limitation to two Sith at one time—a Master and an apprentice—and establishes that the Sith have been extinct for a millennium. Working with author Terry Brooks, Lucas revealed more specific details in the Episode I novelization. Two thousand years in the past, a Jedi had left the Order to found the Sith. A thousand years after that, the Sith Order disintegrated due to infighting, and a sole survivor—Darth Bane—restructured the order to number only two.

It is here that the history of the Sith begins to coalesce. The extinction of the *old* Sith Order was merged with the tales of Ruusan, and Darth Bane became the sole survivor from that encounter, living on to found the new Sith Order. This point was explicitly made in *The Essential Chronology* (2000) and *Secrets of the Sith* (2000), a young reader sourcebook, before being dramatized in the *Jedi vs. Sith* comic series (2001) and, later still, the Darth Bane books.

"DARKNESS SHARED"

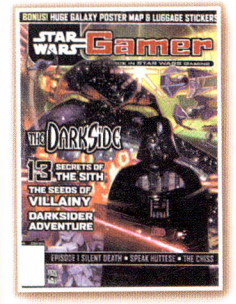

AUTHOR · Bill Slavicsek

PUBLICATION HISTORY · Short story, Wizards of the Coast
· *Star Wars Gamer* #5, August 2001

TIME LINE PLACEMENT · 1000 BBY

WORLD VISITED · Balowa [Q-12]

MAIN CHARACTERS · Kaox Krul, Sith marauder (human male); Dree Vandap, Padawan learner (Rodian female); Crian Maru, Jedi Knight (human female)

SUMMARY · A Sith marauder, Krul, hunts a Jedi Knight and her Padawan in the underbrush of an untamed world. After Krul kills the Padawan, the Jedi is enraged and engages him in an intense duel. Both Sith and Jedi fall in battle, and their intense emotions leave behind a concentration of the dark side on the world.

Xanatos

Tahl

Bruck Chun

Siri Tachi

Jenna Zan Arbor

Granta Omega

CHAPTER 2

HEIGHT OF THE REPUBLIC

Star Wars: Episode II Attack of the Clones (2002) had two lines of dialogue with major implications for galactic history: "I will not let this Republic that has stood for a thousand years be split in two," says Chancellor Palpatine to the Jedi in the face of the Separatist crisis. As the galaxy teeters toward war, Sio Bibble laments, "There hasn't been a full-scale war since the foundation of the Republic." At first, these seem hard to reconcile with the vast history of war and galactic strife in the Old Republic era.

When Darth Bane engineered the detonation of the thought bomb on Ruusan, the New Sith Wars came to a sudden end. Every known Sith Lord was instantly wiped out, and the Jedi ranks were decimated. The galaxy restructured in such a profound way that, in recognition of this new dawn, the Republic reset their calendars, and a millennium of peace began.

Thus, the Expanded Universe material that occurred prior to approximately a thousand years BBY is of an older epoch. Characters in the *Clone Wars* animated series refer to it as the Old Republic, differentiating it from the modern Galactic Republic. And since the Republic does not experience any major conflicts after this time, the books set in this period tell of minor struggles and focus more on the growth of characters such as Obi-Wan Kenobi and Anakin Skywalker before they became major players on the galactic scene.

The era is not devoid of menace; evil remains in the shadows. After Bane's purge of the old Sith, the new Sith Lords continue in hiding, biding their time. As the prologue to the very first *Star Wars* novel (1976) describes, "So it was with the Republic at its height. Like the greatest of trees . . . the Republic rotted from within though the danger was not visible from the outside."

JEDI APPRENTICE #1: THE RISING FORCE

AUTHOR · Dave Wolverton

COVER ARTIST · Cliff Nielsen

PUBLICATION HISTORY · Juvenile novel, Scholastic Inc. · Paperback, June 1999

TIME LINE PLACEMENT · 44 BBY

WORLDS VISITED · Bandomeer [O-6]; Coruscant [L-9]; unnamed planet [O-7]

MAIN CHARACTERS · Obi-Wan Kenobi, youngling (human male); Qui-Gon Jinn, Jedi Master (human male); Jemba, Offworld Mining boss (Hutt); Si Treemba, miner (Arcona male); Clat'Ha, mining leader (human female); Yoda, Jedi Master (male)

SUMMARY · Twelve-year-old Obi-Wan Kenobi fails to be selected as a Padawan learner by a Jedi Master and is instead assigned to the Agricultural Corps. En route to Bandomeer aboard a decrepit mining vessel, he is caught in a violent rivalry between competing mining collectives, as well as a sudden attack by Togorian pirates. He teams up with Qui-Gon Jinn to defend the miners once the ship crash-lands on an untamed world.

The JEDI APPRENTICE series of young reader novels would ultimately comprise twenty installments covering approximately five years of Obi-Wan and Qui-Gon's relationship. There is still plenty of unexplored time in Obi-Wan's apprenticeship to allow for further adventures in this era to be told. The *Clone Wars* animated series (2010) revealed that Obi-Wan and Qui-Gon once spent a year on Mandalore, a lengthy event not chronicled in these books.

JEDI APPRENTICE #2: THE DARK RIVAL

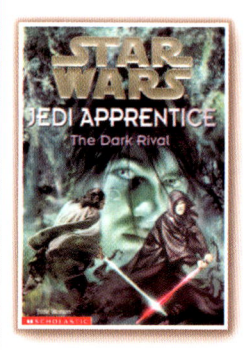

AUTHOR · Jude Watson

COVER ARTIST · Cliff Nielsen

PUBLICATION HISTORY · Juvenile novel, Scholastic Inc. · Paperback, June 1999

TIME LINE PLACEMENT · 44 BBY

WORLD VISITED · Bandomeer [O-6]

MAIN CHARACTERS · Obi-Wan Kenobi, youngling (human male); Qui-Gon Jinn, Jedi Master (human male); SonTag, governor (Meerian female); Xanatos, fallen Jedi (human male); Clat'Ha, mining leader (human female); Guerra Derida, miner/thief (Phindian male); Si Treemba, miner (Arcona male)

SUMMARY · On separate assignments, Obi-Wan and Qui-Gon investigate sabotage on the mining world of Bandomeer. Qui-Gon is unsettled to discover that the representative of the unscrupulous Offworld Mining Corporation is his former Padawan, the fallen Jedi Xanatos. He and Obi-Wan foil Xanatos's plot to devastate Bandomeer, and Qui-Gon finally accepts Obi-Wan as his apprentice.

Qui-Gon Jinn and Obi-Wan Kenobi, marooned on an unknown world, defend themselves from draigons.

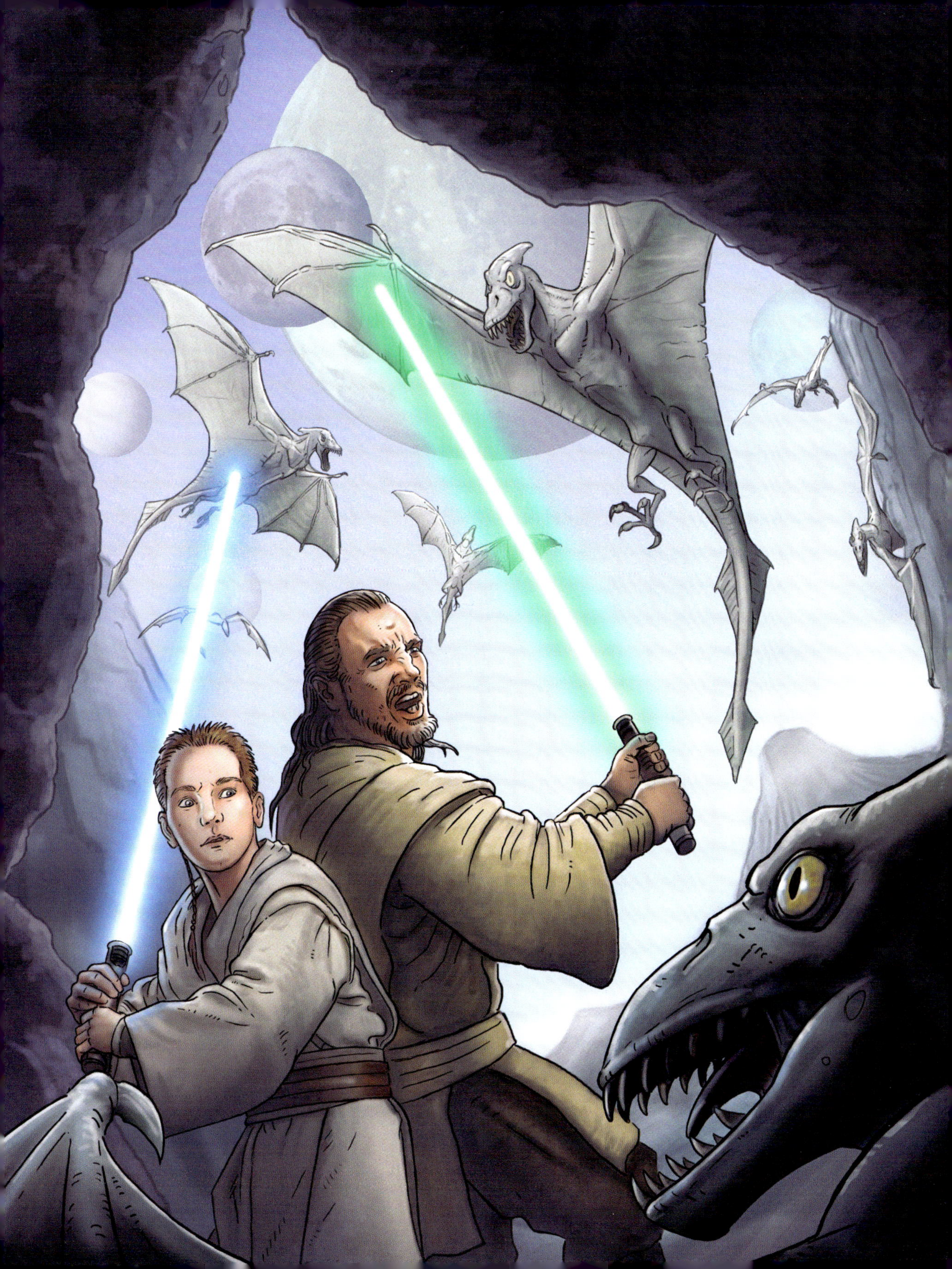

Presented as backstory and flashbacks in *The Dark Rival*, Qui-Gon's history with Xanatos and the planet Telos became the focus of a 2011 comic series, *Star Wars: Jedi—The Dark Side*, from Dark Horse Comics.

JEDI APPRENTICE #3: THE HIDDEN PAST

AUTHOR · Jude Watson
COVER ARTIST · Cliff Nielsen
PUBLICATION HISTORY · Juvenile novel, Scholastic Inc. · Paperback, August 1999
TIME LINE PLACEMENT · 44 BBY
WORLDS VISITED · Bandomeer [O-7]; Gala [Q-7]; Phindar [P-6]
MAIN CHARACTERS · Obi-Wan Kenobi, Padawan learner (human male); Qui-Gon Jinn, Jedi Master (human male); Guerra Derida, thief (Phindian male); Paxxi Derida, thief and pilot (Phindian male); Baftu, Syndicat leader (Phindian male); Prince Beju, conspirator (Galacian male)
SUMMARY · Phindian thieves Paxxi and Guerra Derida redirect Obi-Wan and Qui-Gon to Phindar and request their help against the ruling Syndicat. The criminal organization has created shortages of vital supplies to keep the populace cowed, and uses a mind-wiping "renewal" technique to neutralize the most dangerous rebels. Obi-Wan is captured by the Syndicat and undergoes the renewal, but he draws upon the Force to withstand its effects. He is able to expose the Syndicat's wicked ways to Phindar's populace.

Undergoing the renewal, Obi-Wan holds on to memories of his brother, Owen. This stems from the earlier, now-apocryphal idea introduced in the screenplay of *Return of the Jedi* (1983) that Owen Lars and Obi-Wan were brothers.

JEDI APPRENTICE #4: THE MARK OF THE CROWN

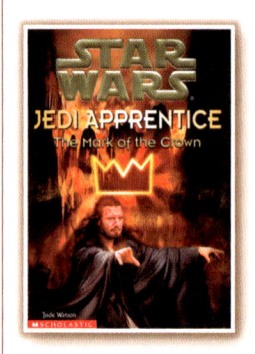

AUTHOR · Jude Watson
COVER ARTIST · Cliff Nielsen
PUBLICATION HISTORY · Juvenile novel, Scholastic Inc. · Paperback, October 1999
TIME LINE PLACEMENT · 44 BBY
WORLD VISITED · Gala [Q-7]
MAIN CHARACTERS · Obi-Wan Kenobi, Padawan learner (human male); Qui-Gon Jinn, Jedi Master (human male); Prince Beju, heir apparent (Galacian male); Queen Veda, monarch (Galacian female); Jono Dunn, royal retainer (Galacian male); Lonnag Giba, councilor (Galacian male); Elan, hill people leader (Galacian female)

SUMMARY · Queen Veda, the ailing monarch of Gala, is introducing democracy to her world, much to the chagrin of her son, Prince Beju, presumed heir to the throne. When Qui-Gon and Obi-Wan arrive to monitor and ensure peaceful elections, they become ensnared in palace intrigue. As Qui-Gon journeys to the outcast hill people to find a lost heir, Elan, Obi-Wan thwarts a plot to poison the queen.

JEDI APPRENTICE #5: THE DEFENDERS OF THE DEAD

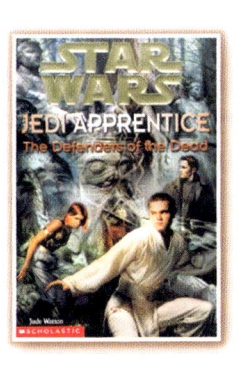

AUTHOR · Jude Watson
COVER ARTIST · Cliff Nielsen
PUBLICATION HISTORY · Juvenile novel, Scholastic Inc.
 · Paperback, December 1999
TIME LINE PLACEMENT · 44 BBY
WORLD VISITED · Melida/Daan [P-17]
MAIN CHARACTERS · Obi-Wan Kenobi, Padawan learner (human male); Qui-Gon Jinn, Jedi Master (human male); Wehutti, Melida/Daan leader (human male); Cerasi, Young revolutionary (human female); Nield, Young leader (human male); Tahl, Jedi Knight (humanoid female)
SUMMARY · Civil war has consumed Melida/Daan for so long simple concensus on the planet's name is impossible. After generations of fighting the youths of the planet have banded together to form a revolutionary movement called the Young. With their help, Qui-Gon and Obi-Wan seek out a missing Jedi, Tahl, who has been held hostage by one of the factions. Though the Jedi succeed in rescuing Tahl, Obi-Wan is so moved by the plight of the Young that he abandons the Jedi Order to join their ranks.

In *The Empire Strikes Back* (1980), a disembodied Obi-Wan admits he was reckless in his youth, a trait exemplified by his departure from the Order here. This book also shows Obi-Wan to be an exuberant pilot, a far cry from the reluctance he demonstrates in *Star Wars:* Episode II *Attack of the Clones* (2002).

JEDI APPRENTICE #6: THE UNCERTAIN PATH

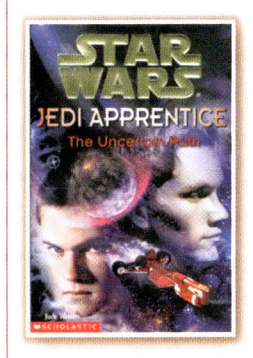

AUTHOR · Jude Watson
COVER ARTIST · Cliff Nielsen
PUBLICATION HISTORY · Juvenile novel, Scholastic Inc.
 · Paperback, February 2000
TIME LINE PLACEMENT · 44 BBY
WORLDS VISITED · Coruscant [L-9]; Melida/Daan [P-17]
MAIN CHARACTERS · Obi-Wan Kenobi, former Padawan (human male); Qui-Gon Jinn, Jedi Master (human male); Nield, Young leader (human male); Cerasi, Young councilor (human female); Tahl, Jedi Knight (humanoid female);

HEIGHT OF THE REPUBLIC

Bruck Chun, youngling (human male); Bant Eerin, youngling (Mon Calamari female)

SUMMARY · The victorious Young face the challenge of transitioning from a revolutionary movement to a functioning government. Despite his role in the Young's victory, Obi-Wan is cast aside as an outsider by the fractious leadership. Meanwhile, on Coruscant, an escalating series of thefts puts the Jedi Temple on alert and draws the attention of the Jedi Council. Qui-Gon leaves for Melida/Daan at his former Padawan's request. There he helps Obi-Wan unravel a plot by a faction of the Young to perpetuate the war.

JEDI APPRENTICE #7: THE CAPTIVE TEMPLE

AUTHOR · Jude Watson
COVER ARTIST · Cliff Nielsen
PUBLICATION HISTORY · Juvenile novel, Scholastic Inc. · Paperback, April 2000
TIME LINE PLACEMENT · 44 BBY
WORLD VISITED · Coruscant [L-9]

MAIN CHARACTERS · Obi-Wan Kenobi, former Padawan (human male); Qui-Gon Jinn, Jedi Master (human male); Mace Windu, Jedi Master (human male); Yoda, Jedi Master (male); Bant Eerin, youngling (Mon Calamari female); Siri Tachi, youngling (human female); Bruck Chun, youngling (human male)

SUMMARY · The Jedi Temple is under siege by unseen saboteurs who wreak havoc in a bid to steal a cache of valuable crystals. Qui-Gon and Obi-Wan discover that Xanatos, Jinn's former apprentice, is the mastermind. Xanatos has corrupted youngling Bruck Chun as his accomplice. While Qui-Gon chases Xanatos away from the Temple, Obi-Wan duels with Bruck, who dies in a fall. Ultimately, Xanatos's plot is foiled, and the Jedi Temple is saved.

THIS BOOK DEPICTS Ki-Adi-Mundi as a member of the Jedi Council. However, according to the comics, Ki-Adi-Mundi does not join that body until after the death of Councilor Micah Giiett, which occurs in 33 BBY, in the comic series *Jedi Council: Acts of War* (2000). The Jedi Apprentice book *The Evil Experiment* (2001) corrects this inconsistency by explaining that Ki-Adi-Mundi would occasionally sit on the Council in Micah's absence.

JEDI APPRENTICE #8: THE DAY OF RECKONING

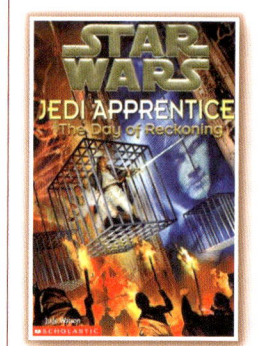

AUTHOR · Jude Watson
COVER ARTIST · Cliff Nielsen
PUBLICATION HISTORY · Juvenile novel, Scholastic Inc. · Paperback, June 2000
TIME LINE PLACEMENT · 44 BBY
WORLD VISITED · Telos [Q-4]

Young Obi-Wan Kenobi squares off against his rival Bruck Chun in the Room of a Thousand Fountains, a lush greenhouse within the Jedi Temple.

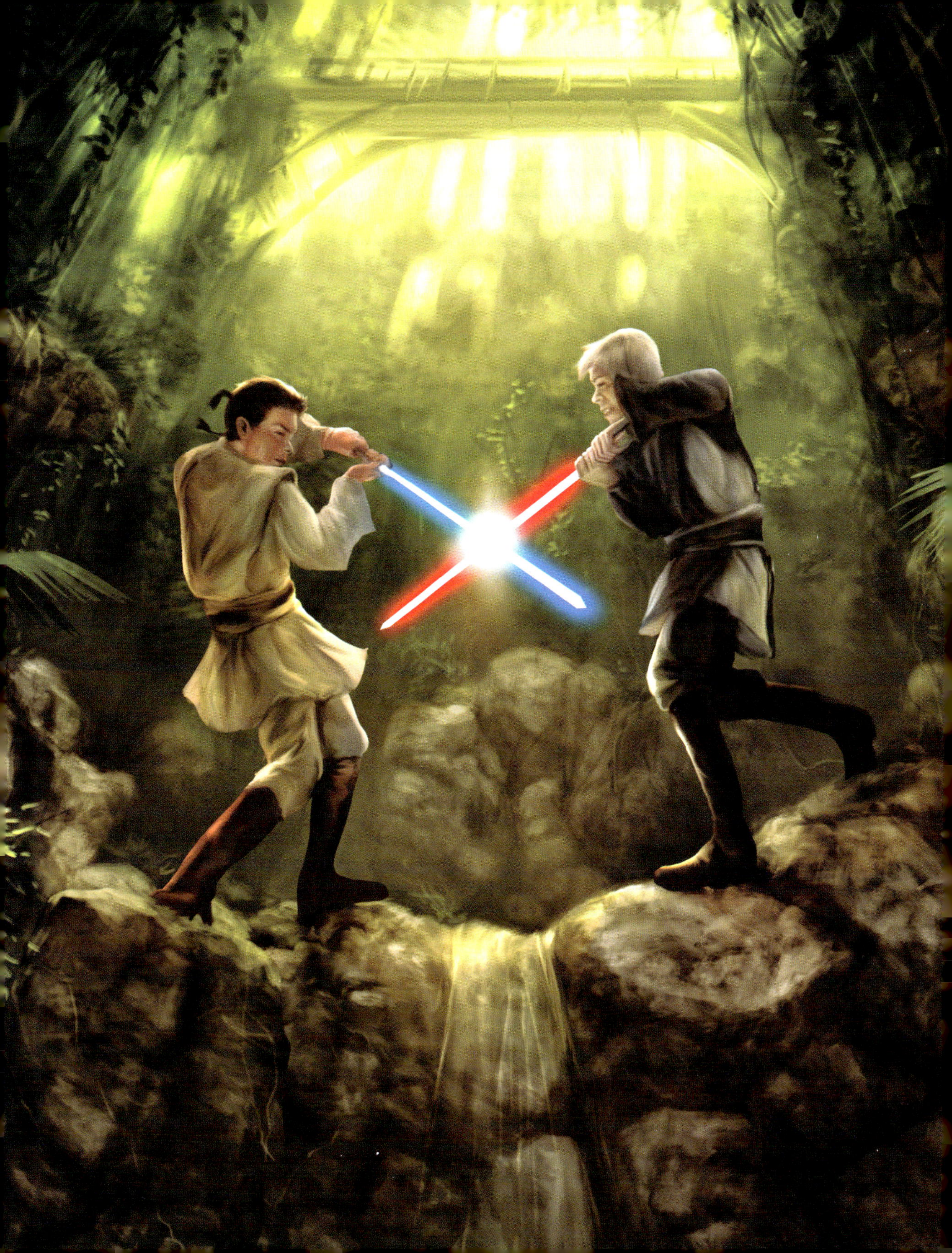

MAIN CHARACTERS · Obi-Wan Kenobi, former Padawan (human male); Qui-Gon Jinn, Jedi Master (human male); Andra, POWER leader (human female); Denetrus, tech worker (human male); Vox Chun, treasurer (human male); Xanatos, former Jedi (human male)

SUMMARY · Qui-Gon and Obi-Wan voyage to Xanatos's homeworld of Telos, host to Katharsis, an immensely popular gladiatorial sporting and lottery event that appeals to the populace's greed and bloodlust. It is an event secretly engineered as a distraction by the Offworld Mining Corporation, which seeks to exploit Telos's resources. Despite Xanatos's efforts to kill the Jedi, Obi-Wan and Qui-Gon work together to defeat and destroy him, in the process reforging their bond as Padawan and Master.

The first eight books of the Jedi Apprentice series tell a continuous tale, with the events of one book flowing directly into those of the next, spanning about four months. A break of several months occurs between this story and the next, during which Obi-Wan and Qui-Gon are said to have visited other worlds.

Padawan Obi-Wan Kenobi and his mentor, Qui-Gon Jinn, watch helplessly as their enemy, Xanatos, takes his own life by leaping into a corrosive pool.

JEDI APPRENTICE #9: THE FIGHT FOR TRUTH

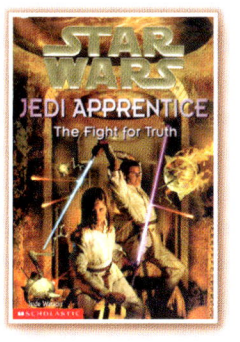

AUTHOR · Jude Watson
COVER ARTIST · Cliff Nielsen
PUBLICATION HISTORY · Juvenile novel, Scholastic Inc. · Paperback, August 2000
TIME LINE PLACEMENT · 44 BBY
WORLDS VISITED · Coruscant [L-9]; Kegan [T-9]
MAIN CHARACTERS · Obi-Wan Kenobi, Padawan learner (human male); Qui-Gon Jinn, Jedi Master (human male); Adi Gallia, Jedi Master (Tholothian female); Siri Tachi, Padawan learner (human female); O-Bin, teacher (human female); V-Haad, Hospitality Guide (human male); Davi, student (human male)

SUMMARY · The birth of a Force-sensitive girl on isolationist Kegan prompts the Jedi Council to dispatch Masters Jinn and Gallia to see if she is suitable for inclusion in the Order. The cloistered leaders of the planet spin a web of deception over the visiting Jedi to prevent them from examining the girl. Meanwhile, the Padawans Obi-Wan and Siri are accidentally mistaken for truant children and are imprisoned in a harsh school where students are indoctrinated with the dogmatic and untrue views of the Keganites. The Jedi expose the worst of the freedom-stripping measures to the public, who demand a return to democracy.

The KEGANITE LEADERS have visions of the future: Jedi Knights engulfed by darkness, masked soldiers, and a device that could destroy entire worlds. These mercurial images appear to predict the rise of the Galactic Empire. Qui-Gon Jinn likewise has a vision in this story, of Obi-Wan as an old man living alone on a desolate planet.

JEDI APPRENTICE #10: THE SHATTERED PEACE

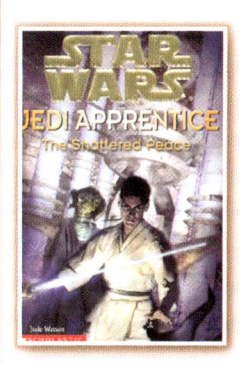

AUTHOR · Jude Watson
COVER ARTIST · Cliff Nielsen
PUBLICATION HISTORY · Juvenile novel, Scholastic Inc. · Paperback, October 2000
TIME LINE PLACEMENT · 44 BBY
WORLDS VISITED · Rutan [L-20]; Senali [L-20].
MAIN CHARACTERS · Obi-Wan Kenobi, Padawan learner (human male); Qui-Gon Jinn, Jedi Master (human male); Leed, prince of Rutan (Rutanian male); Taroon, royalty of Rutan (Rutanian male); Drenna, Leed's adopted sister (Senali female); Frane, king of Rutan (Rutanian male)

SUMMARY · The adversarial worlds of Rutan and Senali ensure a tentative peace by having their rulers exchange firstborns to be raised on the opposite planet. Rutanian prince Leed refuses to return from Senali when it is time. Qui-Gon and Obi-Wan attempt to stem the tide of war by bringing Leed back

HEIGHT OF THE REPUBLIC 37

to confront his enraged father, King Frane of Rutan. Leed accepts his responsibility, and the Jedi defuse a plot by Leed's brother to spark a war.

ANOTHER BREAK IN TIME occurs between this and the previous book, advancing the time line by months and aging Obi-Wan Kenobi to fourteen. This marks the first appearance of Didi Oddo, who will in the future sell his café to Dexter Jettster.

JEDI APPRENTICE #11: THE DEADLY HUNTER

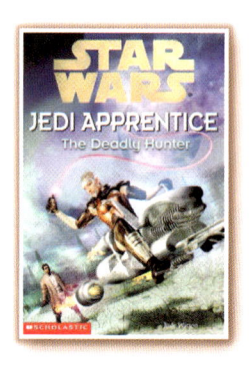

AUTHOR · Jude Watson
COVER ARTIST · Cliff Nielsen
PUBLICATION HISTORY · Juvenile novel, Scholastic Inc. · Paperback, December 2000
TIME LINE PLACEMENT: 43 BBY
WORLDS VISITED · Coruscant [L-9]; Duneeden [K-9]
MAIN CHARACTERS · Obi-Wan Kenobi, Padawan learner (human male); Qui-Gon Jinn, Jedi Master (human male); Ona Nobis, bounty hunter (Sorrusian female); Didi Oddo, café owner (human male); Astri Oddo, café worker (human female); Uta S'orn, Senator from Belasco (human female); Jenna Zan Arbor, scientist (human female)
SUMMARY · Didi Oddo, an information broker and longtime friend of Qui-Gon Jinn, runs a café in Coruscant's Senate District. He finds himself the target of a mysterious bounty hunter. Qui-Gon and Obi-Wan are on the case. Together they uncover a murder mystery that implicates renowned scientist Jenna Zan Arbor. As the Jedi close in on the answer, Qui-Gon is captured by the hunter.

JEDI APPRENTICE #12: THE EVIL EXPERIMENT

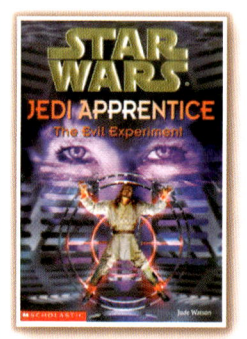

AUTHOR · Jude Watson
COVER ARTIST · Cliff Nielsen
PUBLICATION HISTORY · Juvenile novel, Scholastic Inc. · Paperback, February 2001
TIME LINE PLACEMENT · 43 BBY
WORLDS VISITED · Coruscant [L-9]; Simpla-12 [O-5]; Sorrus [O-5]
MAIN CHARACTERS · Obi-Wan Kenobi, Padawan learner (human male); Qui-Gon Jinn, Jedi Master (human male); Ona Nobis, bounty hunter (Sorrusian female); Astri Oddo, café worker (human female); Jenna Zan Arbor, scientist (human female); Cholly, Weez, and Tup, scoundrels (humanoid males)
SUMMARY · Obi-Wan and Astri voyage to Sorrus to track down the mysterious bounty hunter who has kidnapped Qui-Gon. Meanwhile, Qui-Gon weakens as Jenna Zan Arbor subjects him to experiments in her secret laboratory in an endeavor to understand the biological underpinnings of the Force.

HEIGHT OF THE REPUBLIC

JEDI APPRENTICE #13: THE DANGEROUS RESCUE

AUTHOR · Jude Watson
COVER ARTIST · Cliff Nielsen
PUBLICATION HISTORY · Juvenile novel, Scholastic Inc. · Paperback, April 2001
TIME LINE PLACEMENT · 43 BBY
WORLDS VISITED · Belasco [O-11]; Coruscant [L-9]; Simpla-12 [O-5]; Sorrus [O-5]
MAIN CHARACTERS · Obi-Wan Kenobi, Padawan learner (human male); Qui-Gon Jinn, Jedi Master (human male); Ona Nobis, bounty hunter (Sorrusian female); Astri Oddo, café worker (human female); Jenna Zan Arbor, scientist (human female); Cholly, Weez, and Tup, scoundrels (humanoid males); Uta S'orn, Senator from Belasco (human female)
SUMMARY · Together with Adi Gallia and Siri Tachi, Obi-Wan rescues Qui-Gon from Jenna Zan Arbor's lab, but the scientist escapes. Obi-Wan and Siri return to Sorrus, where they tangle with vengeful bounty hunter Ona Nobis. Their search leads them to Belasco, where a bacterial outbreak in the water supply threatens the oldest and youngest of the planet's population. The Jedi capture Jenna Zan Arbor, who was behind the outbreak, engineered with the complicity of Senator Uta S'orn.

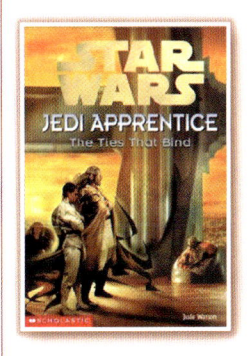

JEDI APPRENTICE #14: THE TIES THAT BIND

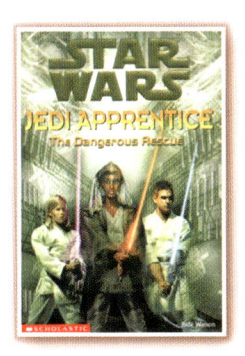

AUTHOR · Jude Watson
COVER ARTIST · Cliff Nielsen
PUBLICATION HISTORY · Juvenile novel, Scholastic Inc. · Paperback, August 2001
TIME LINE PLACEMENT · 41 BBY
WORLDS VISITED · Coruscant [L-9]; New Apsolon [P-10]; Ragoon VI [K-9]
MAIN CHARACTERS · Obi-Wan Kenobi, Padawan learner (human male); Qui-Gon Jinn, Jedi Master (human male); Tahl, Jedi Knight (humanoid female); Balog, Chief Security Controller (human male); Eritha and Alani, twins (human females); Roan, planetary leader (human male)
SUMMARY · A vision of fellow Jedi Tahl imperiled sends Qui-Gon racing to New Apsolon with Obi-Wan in tow. On the politically unstable world, Qui-Gon admits his love for Tahl, which she returns in kind. But she is kidnapped by a treacherous security chief, Balog. Together with the twins Eritha and Alani they seek to upend the current government.

Qui-Gon and Tahl's pledge of love for each other runs counter to the Jedi stricture on emotional attachments, a rule first revealed in *Star Wars: Episode II Attack of the Clones* (2002). This transgression further bolsters Qui-Gon's reputation as a maverick.

HEIGHT OF THE REPUBLIC

JEDI APPRENTICE #15: THE DEATH OF HOPE

AUTHOR · Jude Watson
COVER ARTIST · Cliff Nielsen
PUBLICATION HISTORY · Juvenile novel, Scholastic Inc. · Paperback, October 2001
TIME LINE PLACEMENT · 41 BBY
WORLDS VISITED · Coruscant (flashback) [L-9]; New Apsolon [P-10]; Zekulae (flashback) [N-8]
MAIN CHARACTERS · Obi-Wan Kenobi, Padawan learner (human male); Qui-Gon Jinn, Jedi Master (human male); Eritha and Alani, twins (human females); Yanci, rock worker (human female); Tahl, Jedi Knight (humanoid female); Balog, Chief Security Controller (human male)

SUMMARY · Obsessed with saving Tahl, Qui-Gon leads a trek across the desert to confront her kidnappers, the fanatical Absolute movement. The treacherous Balog kills Tahl, sparking a vow of vengeance from Qui-Gon.

This book includes several flashbacks to Qui-Gon Jinn's youth, but deftly avoids any scenes with his Master, who would not be identified as Dooku until Episode II (2002).

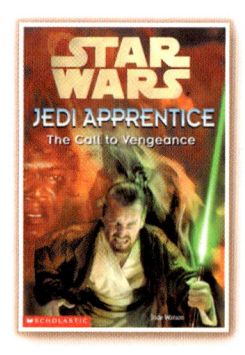

JEDI APPRENTICE #16: THE CALL TO VENGEANCE

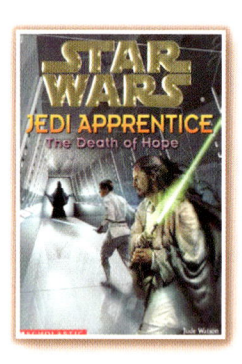

AUTHOR · Jude Watson
COVER ARTIST · Cliff Nielsen
PUBLICATION HISTORY · Juvenile novel, Scholastic Inc. · Paperback, December 2001
TIME LINE PLACEMENT · 41 BBY
WORLD VISITED · New Apsolon [P-10]
MAIN CHARACTERS · Obi-Wan Kenobi, Padawan learner (human male); Qui-Gon Jinn, Jedi Master (human male); Mace Windu, Jedi Master (human male); Eritha and Alani, Absolutist twins (human females); Yanci, rock worker (human female); Balog, Chief Security Controller (human male)

SUMMARY · Word of Tahl's shocking death and the instability on New Apsolon brings Mace Windu to the planet. Qui-Gon grapples with the dark side as his desire for revenge against Balog dominates his thoughts. When he finally catches his quarry, he resists temptation. The Jedi successfully thwart the coup engineered by the radical Absolute movement, allowing New Apsolon to continue on a more honest path in redefining its government.

A grief-stricken Qui-Gon Jinn sits at the side of his beloved Tahl as she succumbs to her injuries and dies.

JEDI APPRENTICE #17: THE ONLY WITNESS

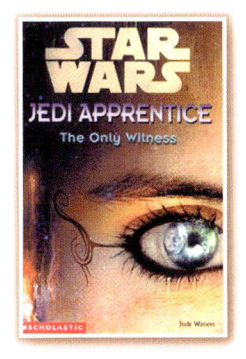

AUTHOR · Jude Watson

COVER ARTIST · Cliff Nielsen

PUBLICATION HISTORY · Juvenile novel, Scholastic Inc. · Paperback, February 2002

TIME LINE PLACEMENT · 40 BBY

WORLDS VISITED · Coruscant (flashback) [L-9]; Frego [L-13]

MAIN CHARACTERS · Obi-Wan Kenobi, Padawan learner (human male); Qui-Gon Jinn, Jedi Master (human male); Jocasta Nu, Jedi librarian (human female); Lena Cobral, informant (human female); Mica, Lena's cousin (human female); Cobral, familial matriarch (human female)

SUMMARY · Lena Cobral has agreed to testify against the rulers of the planet Frego, the Cobral criminal family. Obi-Wan and Qui-Gon protect her as she gathers evidence and returns to Coruscant.

———

As an indication of Episode II's impending release, this 2002 book features an early appearance by that movie's Jedi librarian, Jocasta Nu. A scene set in the Galactic Senate mentions Chancellor Valorum, but term limitations would prevent this from being the same chancellory seen in Episode I—Valorum would not become chancellor until 39 BBY, according to *Cloak of Deception* (2001).

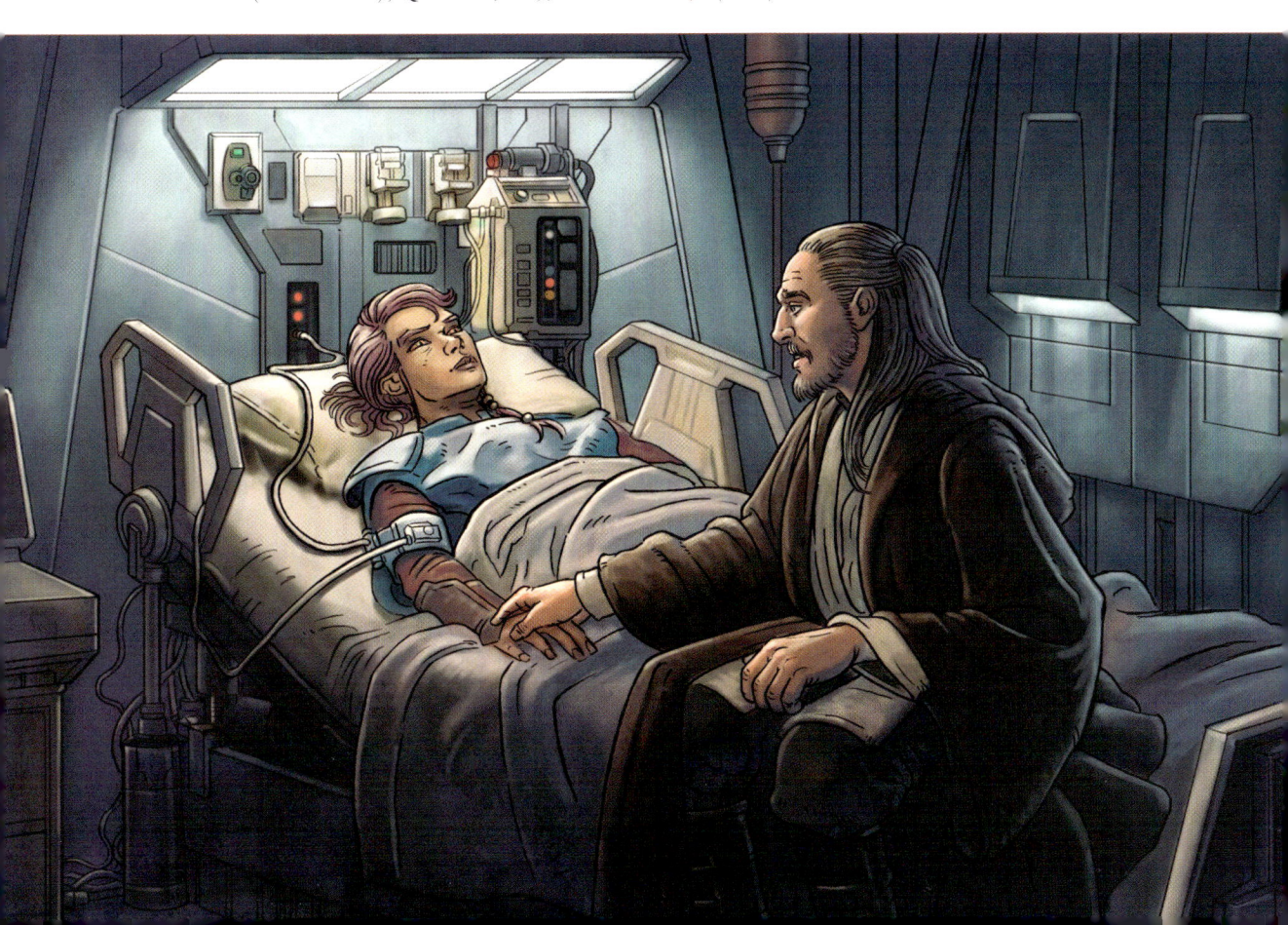

JEDI APPRENTICE #18: THE THREAT WITHIN

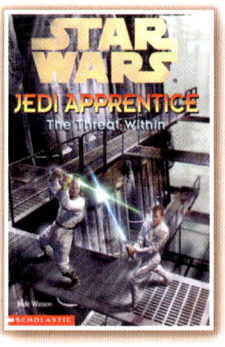

AUTHOR · Jude Watson
COVER ARTIST · Cliff Nielsen
PUBLICATION HISTORY ·
Juvenile novel, Scholastic Inc.
· Paperback, March 2002
TIME LINE PLACEMENT ·
40 BBY
WORLDS VISITED · Coruscant [L-9]; Vorzyd IV [R-6]
MAIN CHARACTERS · Obi-Wan Kenobi, Padawan learner (human male); Qui-Gon Jinn, Jedi Master (human male); Chairman Port, Vorzyd IV official (Vorzydiak male); Grath, Freelie (Vorzydiak male); Tray, Freelie (Vorzydiak female)

SUMMARY · A rash of sabotage threatening the productivity of Vorzyd IV casts suspicion on its frivolous neighbor, Vorzyd V. Obi-Wan discovers that a group of rebellious teens called the Freelies are the real culprits. Qui-Gon and Obi-Wan prevent the Freelie pranks from turning deadly and get the generational representatives speaking to one another peacefully.

V ORZYD V WAS ONE of the earliest planets explored in the Expanded Universe, as it was the backdrop for the first story arc of the *Star Wars* daily newspaper strip published in 1979. This series was reprinted as *Classic Star Wars: The Early Adventures* by Dark Horse Comics from 1994 to 1995.

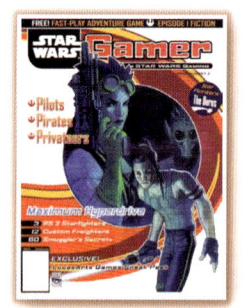

"THE MONSTER"

AUTHOR · Daniel Wallace
PUBLICATION HISTORY ·
Short story, Wizards of the Coast
· *Star Wars Gamer* #2, November 2000
TIME LINE PLACEMENT ·
36 BBY
WORLD VISITED · Naboo [O-17]
MAIN CHARACTERS · Lieutenant Panaka, security officer (human male); Captain Magneta, security officer (human female); Sate Pestage, Senatorial aide (human male); Veermok, criminal (human male)

SUMMARY · An enormous sando aqua monster beaches itself on the shores of a Naboo lake, exposing a series of secret tunnels. Security officer Lieutenant Panaka explores the tunnels and encounters a criminal code-named Veermok who claims the lair holds evidence that can implicate highly placed Naboo officials. To protect the dark secrets Sate Pestage, aide to Senator Palpatine, kills Veermok and a proton torpedo strike is ordered by Captain Magneta, Panaka's superior, which blasts the subterranean secrets into dust.

S ATE PESTAGE has grown considerably in the Expanded Universe from his humble origins as a character cut from *The Empire Strikes Back* (1980). In an earlier draft of the movie script, Darth Vader was to initiate holographic contact with the Emperor during the pursuit of the *Millennium*

HEIGHT OF THE REPUBLIC

Falcon, only to be stalled by the Imperial Grand Vizier Sate Pestage. Pestage's role was cut from the film, but his name appeared in print in the *Empire Strikes Back: Collector's Edition* souvenir magazine (1980), the Darth Vader's Star Destroyer playset from Kenner, and the *Dark Empire Sourcebook* (1993).

DARTH MAUL: SABOTEUR

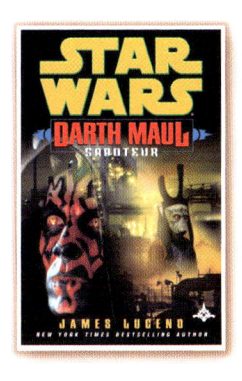

AUTHOR · James Luceno
COVER ARTIST · David Stevenson
PUBLICATION HISTORY · Short story, Del Rey Books · EBook novella, February 2001
Included with *Darth Maul: Shadow Hunter* paperback, December 2001 and reissue December 2011

TIME LINE PLACEMENT · 33 BBY

WORLDS VISITED · Coruscant [L-9]; Dorvalla [M-18]; Eriadu [M-18]; Neimoidia [M-10]; Riome [M-18]

MAIN CHARACTERS · Darth Maul, Sith apprentice (Dathomirian Zabrak male); Patch Bruit, chief of field operations (human male); Jurnel Arrant, executive officer (human male); Hath Monchar, Trade Federation official (Neimoidian male); Darth Sidious, Sith Lord (human male)

SUMMARY · Darth Sidious's complex schemes target the mining and transport of lommite, a valuable mineral found on the jungle world of Dorvalla. The Sith Lord secretly dispatches his apprentice, Darth Maul, to exploit the heated rivalry between the mining companies of Lommite Limited and InterGalactic Ore. Maul stealthily maneuvers both firms to sabotage their own efforts, effectively crippling them. Maul's killing of the survivors, which leaves no evidence of Sith involvement, paves the way for Nute Gunray's faction within the Trade Federation to take control of the planet.

Darth Maul: Saboteur was the first *Star Wars* eBook. It features a brief appearance by Hath Monchar, a Neimoidian who would figure prominently in *Darth Maul: Shadow Hunter* (2001). Also appearing is Lieutenant Governor Tarkin of Eriadu, an early chronological appearance of the Imperial officer who would later command the Death Star. The tale ends with Sidious advising Maul to study up on Black Sun, a reference to Maul's assignment in Dark Horse Comics' *Darth Maul* mini series (2000).

"THE STARFIGHTER TRAP"

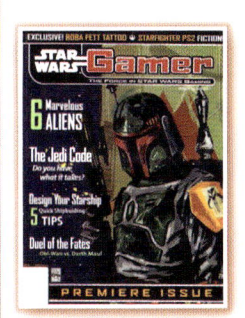

AUTHOR · Steve Miller
PUBLICATION HISTORY · Short story, Wizards of the Coast · *Star Wars Gamer* #1, September 2000

TIME LINE PLACEMENT · 33 BBY

WORLD VISITED · Naboo [O-17]

MAIN CHARACTERS · Essara Till, flight leader (human female); Dren Melne, starfighter pilot (human male)

HEIGHT OF THE REPUBLIC

SUMMARY · An attack on a space station in the outskirts of the Naboo system draws Royal Starfighter Corps Bravo and Delta squadrons to its defense. Flight leader Essara Till is heartbroken to discover that her lover and wingmate Dren Melne has engineered a trap to capture Naboo fighters for Agamarian mercenaries. Essara and her pilots thwart the theft, and she is forced to shoot Dren down.

This short story is a tie-in to the LucasArts videogame *Star Wars: Starfighter* (2000).

CLOAK OF DECEPTION

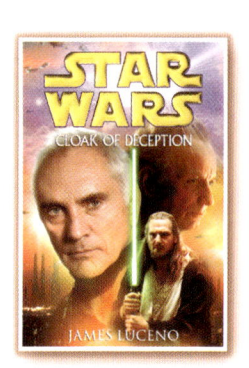

AUTHOR · James Luceno
COVER ARTIST · Steven D. Anderson
PUBLICATION HISTORY ·
Novel, Del Rey Books
· Hardcover, June 2001
· Paperback, July 2002
TIME LINE PLACEMENT · 32 BBY
WORLDS VISITED · Asmeru [L-17]; Coruscant [L-9]; Dorvalla [M-18]; Eriadu [M-18]; Karfeddion [L-18]; Neimoidia [M-10]
MAIN CHARACTERS · Qui-Gon Jinn, Jedi Master (human male); Obi-Wan Kenobi, Padawan learner (human male); Palpatine, Naboo Senator (human male); Finis Valorum, Supreme Chancellor (human male); Arwen Cohl, mercenary (Mirialan male); Eru "Havac" Matalis, Nebula Front leader (human male); Rella, outlaw raider (human female); Nute Gunray, Trade Federation official (Neimoidian male); Darth Sidious, Sith Lord (human male)

SUMMARY · Mercenary Arwen Cohl has been hired by a radical terrorist arm of the Nebula Front to mount a campaign of audacious attacks on Trade Federation freighters. Cohl's actions have drawn the attention of the Jedi Order, with Qui-Gon Jinn and Obi-Wan Kenobi leading the hunt for the raiders' secret base.

Such rampant violence prompts the Trade Federation representatives in the Senate to petition the government to relax restrictions on their droid security forces. In a controversial bid to balance such increased power to the Trade Federation, Supreme Chancellor Valorum—with the support of Senator Palpatine of Naboo—counters with a move to tax outlying trade routes. This causes great tumult in the Senate.

The Nebula Front leader, known only as Havac, hires Cohl and his team to assassinate the Chancellor at a trade summit on Eriadu. Cohl and his band are unaware of Havac's true intent: Havac works for Darth Sidious, and the shadowy Sith Lord has engineered an attack on the summit to wipe out the Trade Federation Directorate, allowing for the ascension of Nute Gunray to command of the shipping conglomerate. Havac tries to kill Cohl for a perceived failure, but Cohl survives long enough to kill Havac before dying himself, thus eliminating a direct chain of contacts that could have pointed back to the Sith.

Originally titled *Vergence*, *Cloak of Deception* was the earliest adult novel in the time line upon its publication. Because his novel preceded the events of Episode I, author James Luceno likened its relationship with the rest of the

HEIGHT OF THE REPUBLIC

Supreme Chancellor Valorum confers with Jedi Masters Yoda and Mace Windu on the deteriorating state of the Galactic Republic.

saga to *The Hobbit*'s relationship with the *Lord of the Rings* trilogy. Luceno made a conscious effort to fully introduce and explain concepts that are usually taken for granted in *Star Wars* literature—the Jedi Order, lightsabers, the Republic, the Senate, and more.

Luceno's rogue character Arwen Cohl was originally named Margrave M'Buele in the outline, a nod to Katya M'Buele, a minor character from the *Star Wars* Marvel Comics run.

The book has numerous notable cameo appearances. The Jedi Anoon Bondara and Darsha Assant and the Neimoidian Hath Monchar figure prominently in *Darth Maul: Shadow Hunter* (2001); many of the commerce entities that help fund the Separatist Alliance in Episode II make an early appearance here, as does the Jedi Master Luminara Unduli.

Jorus C'baoth appears in one scene—he is a Jedi Master integral to the plot of *Heir to the Empire* (1991) and *Outbound Flight* (2006).

One sly inclusion is Senator Grebleips from Brodo Asogi—a reference to the aliens who resemble E.T. the Extra Terrestrial in the Senate scene of Episode I (1999). Grebleips is Spielberg spelled backward, and Brodo Asogi is a name given to E.T.'s home planet in *E.T.: The Book of the Green Planet*, a spin-off novel to the movie *E.T. The Extra Terrestrial*.

HEIGHT OF THE REPUBLIC 45

DARTH MAUL: SHADOW HUNTER

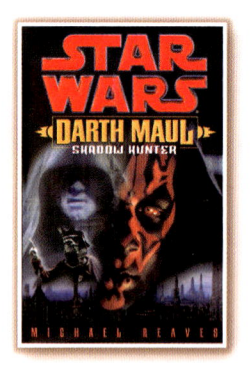

AUTHOR · Michael Reaves

COVER ARTIST · David Stevenson

PUBLICATION HISTORY · Novel, Del Rey Books
- Hardcover, February 2001
- Paperback, November 2001
- Paperback reissue, December 2011

TIME LINE PLACEMENT · 32 BBY

WORLD VISITED · Coruscant [L-9]

MAIN CHARACTERS · Darth Maul, Sith apprentice (Dathomirian Zabrak male); Lorn Pavan, information broker (human male); Darsha Assant, Padawan learner (human female); I-5YQ "I-Five," modified protocol droid; Hath Monchar, Trade Federation official (Neimoidian male); Darth Sidious, Sith Lord (human male); Obi-Wan Kenobi, Padawan learner (human male)

SUMMARY · As Darth Sidious plots his invasion of Naboo, Hath Monchar, one of his Neimoidian conspirators, absconds with crucial information in a misbegotten bid to personally profit from the endeavor. Rather than risk exposing his carefully formulated plans, Sidious sends his deadly apprentice, Darth Maul, in pursuit of the missing Trade Federation official.

This chase leads into the disreputable underbelly of Coruscant. Down-on-his-luck information broker Lorn Pavan stumbles into this intrigue when the holocron containing the Sith plans falls into his

SHORT STORY | "Restraint"

In conjunction with the 3-D theatrical release of *Star Wars: Episode I The Phantom Menace* and Darth Maul's return in the animated *Star Wars: The Clone Wars* series in 2012, Del Rey Books reissued *Shadow Hunter* in paperback with a new short story, "Restraint," by James Luceno. It features a teenaged Darth Maul undergoing combat training at a brutal mercenary academy on Orsis. At his Master's command, Maul cannot divulge that he has Force abilities, and instead must rely on his physical prowess to survive. Meltch Krakko, a Mandalorian rival who knows Maul to be a Nightbrother from Dathomir, voyages to the world of witches and lures Mother Talzin and her Nightsisters to Orsis to "rescue" Maul from his current life. Krakko is hardly benevolent; he's sold out the Nightsisters and Maul to a Rattataki warlord, Osika Kirske, who arrives at Orsis to conquer and capture the Dathomirians. After Maul and the Nightsisters fight their way past the Rattataki warriors, Darth Sidious orders his apprentice to hunt down and destroy all the students on Orsis.

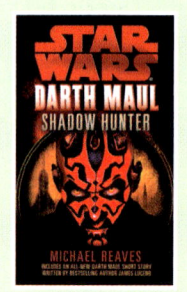

HEIGHT OF THE REPUBLIC

Padawan Darsha Assant defends herself against the fierce deadliness of Darth Maul in the industrial depths of Coruscant.

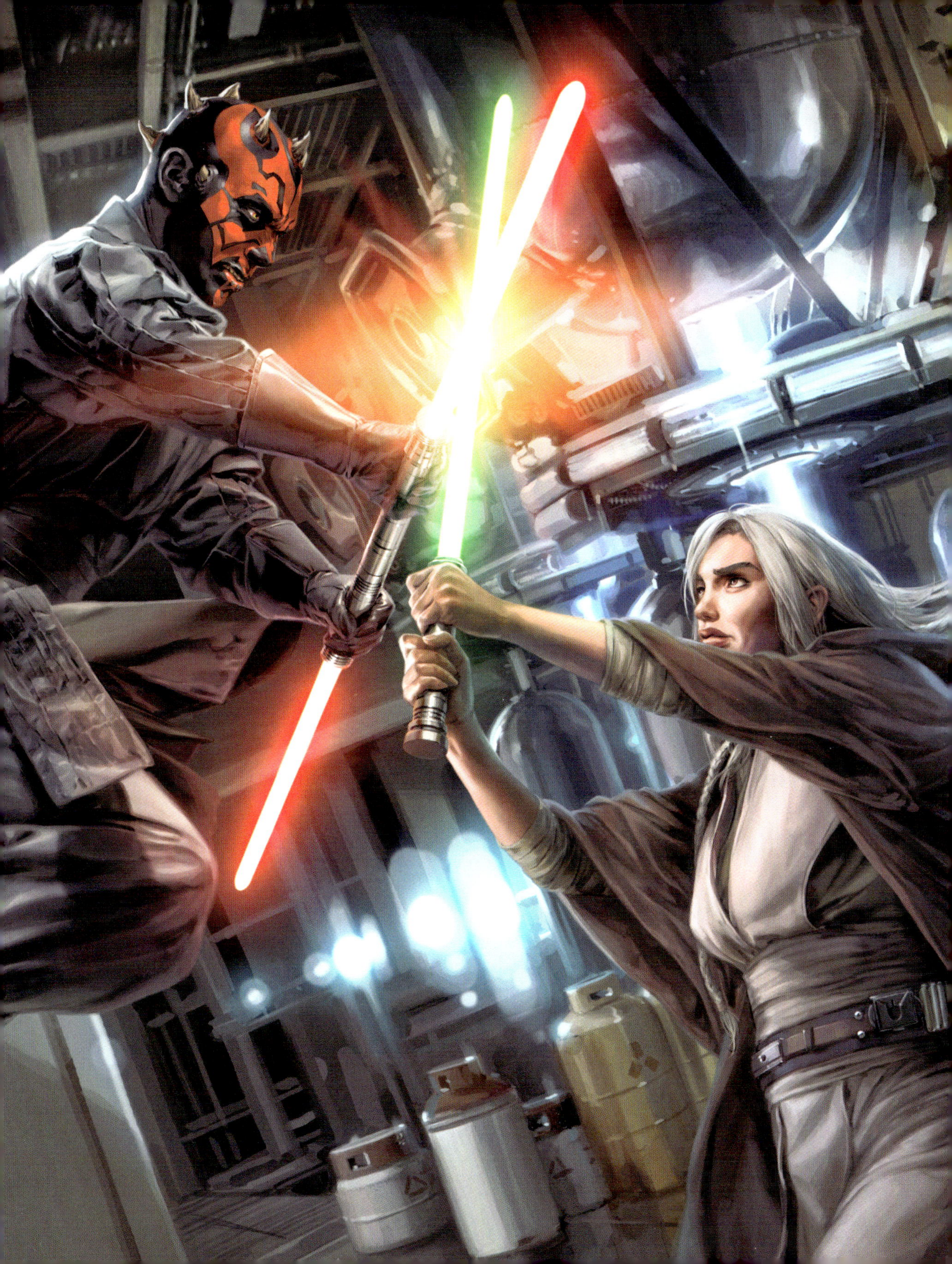

possession. Maul, having killed Monchar, next targets Pavan, who for a time survives the dangers of the Coruscant urban wilderness with the help of his uncanny droid I-5YQ and a Padawan learner, Darsha Assant. In the end, the Sith plot remains a secret, as Assant and Pavan are both killed.

The movies Episodes I and II include deliberate hints connecting Palpatine and Darth Sidious, but any explicit statement that they were the same person was carefully avoided by all *Star Wars* media until the 2005 release of Episode III. This novel has one of the more overt connections, with Lorn Pavan delivering the coveted invasion plans to Senator Palpatine, yet the Sith conspiracy continues unabated.

Lorn Pavan is survived by his droid I-5YQ, who would resurface during the Clone Wars in the *MedStar* novels, and by his son, Jax Pavan, who was taken into the Jedi Order as an infant. Jax would feature in the Coruscant Nights novels.

STAR WARS: EPISODE I THE PHANTOM MENACE

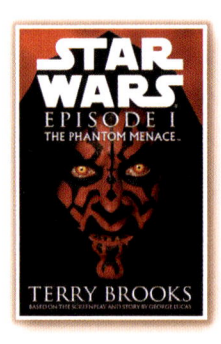

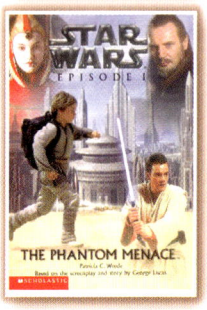

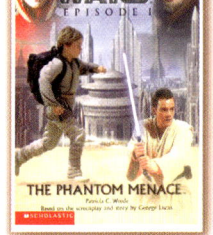

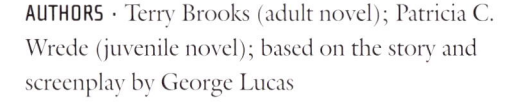

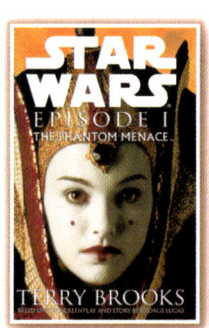

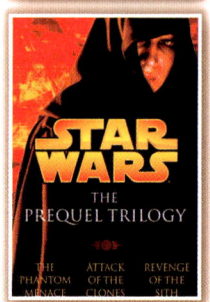

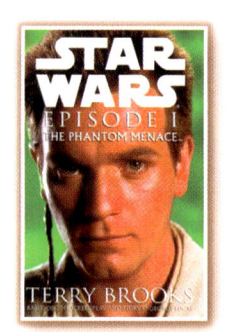

AUTHORS · Terry Brooks (adult novel); Patricia C. Wrede (juvenile novel); based on the story and screenplay by George Lucas

COVER ARTISTS · Lucasfilm Ltd. (Del Rey novelizations and omnibus); Paul Colin (Scholastic Junior novelization)

HEIGHT OF THE REPUBLIC

PUBLICATION HISTORY · Adult novel, Del Rey Books
- Hardcover, April 1999
- Paperback, March 2000
- Paperback reissue, January 2012

Compiled as part of *The Prequel Trilogy* omnibus, Del Rey Books. Paperback, May 2007

Young reader novel, Scholastic Inc.
- Paperback, April 1999

TIME LINE PLACEMENT · 32 BBY

WORLDS VISITED · Coruscant [L-9]; Naboo [O-17]; Tatooine [R-16]

MAIN CHARACTERS · Qui-Gon Jinn, Jedi Master (human male); Anakin Skywalker, slave (human male); Queen Amidala/Padmé Naberrie, leader of the Naboo (human female); Obi-Wan Kenobi, Padawan learner (human male); Jar Jar Binks, outcast (Gungan male); Darth Maul, Sith apprentice (Dathomirian Zabrak male); R2-D2, astromech droid; Nute Gunray, Trade Federation Viceroy (Neimoidian male)

SUMMARY · To protest Republic taxation, the Trade Federation brazenly invades the peaceful planet of Naboo. Its leader, young Queen Amidala, escapes capture with the help of Jedi ambassadors Qui-Gon Jinn and Obi-Wan Kenobi. Setting down on nearby Tatooine to repair their vessel, the fugitives cross paths with a nine-year-old slave boy, Anakin Skywalker, who is a Force prodigy.

Proceeding to the capital, Amidala is dismayed to find the Republic ineffective in helping her people. She spearheads a campaign to unite her planet's human populace with the native Gungans to repel the invaders. The Naboo crisis earns Senator Palpatine a sympathy nomination, which leads him to be elected Supreme Chancellor of the Republic.

In truth, the evil Sith were the masterminds behind the invasion. The appearance of a Sith, Darth Maul, in the course of these events reveals to the Jedi that their long-gone enemies have returned. Maul slays Qui-Gon, but is killed in turn by Obi-Wan Kenobi. Obi-Wan honors Qui-Gon Jinn's dying request and takes Anakin Skywalker as his apprentice.

SHORT STORY — "End Game"

Del Rey Books reissued the Episode I novelization as a paperback to accompany the theatrical release of *The Phantom Menace* in 3-D in 2012. The novel included a new Darth Maul short story, "End Game," by James Luceno. Set during the events of Episode I, the story follows Maul's mission to Naboo to oversee the Neimoidian conquest of the planet. Disgusted by the Neimoidians' incompetence, Maul ventures into the swamps of the planet to find the hidden Gungan cities, lest the armed indigents prove a threat. During his search, he comes across Captain Magneta, King Veruna's former head of security, living in self-imposed exile in a simple shed in the forests. Magneta tells Maul that she believes Veruna was killed by a Muun financier, Hego Damask, a political ally of Senator Palpatine. From this Maul infers that Damask was Darth Sidious's Sith Master. The story ends with Obi-Wan defeating Maul by using his lightsaber to slice him in two.

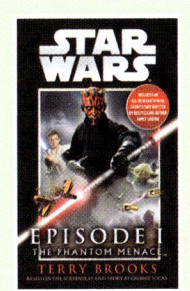

HEIGHT OF THE REPUBLIC

The identity of the second Sith, Darth Sidious, remains a mystery.

T HE THEATRICAL RELEASE of *Star Wars: Episode I The Phantom Menace* in 1999 brought with it adaptations of the screenplay across multiple forms of media, from the adult and juvenile novels featured here to comics, storybooks, videogames, picture books, and others.

Like all novelizations, these adaptations have a number of superficial differences from the finished film, the result of being based on the screenplay and not the final edit. Lines of dialogue, sequences of action, and visual descriptions differ from the movie.

Author Terry Brooks built upon the screenplay by George Lucas for his novel, benefiting from direct input from Lucas to confidently expand the story. Episode I was the first *Star Wars* movie novelization to add newly created scenes unique to the book. Unlike the film, it begins on Tatooine and introduces Anakin Skywalker first. Other chapters unique to the novel depict Anakin's humanitarian side when he saves the life of an injured Tusken Raider. These story threads would be picked up by other adaptations, such as children's books.

One continuity curiosity is the mention of the Jedi Master under whom Qui-Gon trained. This unnamed mentor described Qui-Gon as the best he had taught in more than four hundred years of the Jedi Order. Though it is possible this is a needlessly veiled reference to Yoda, it certainly does not fit Dooku, who is revealed to be Qui-Gon's mentor in Episode II.

EPISODE I JOURNALS

EPISODE I JOURNAL: ANAKIN SKYWALKER · EPISODE I JOURNAL: QUEEN AMIDALA · EPISODE I JOURNAL: DARTH MAUL

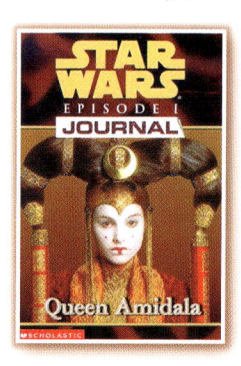

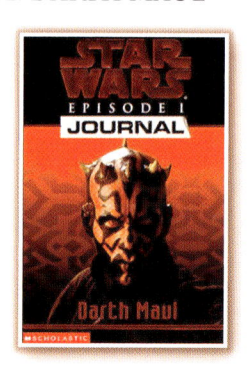

AUTHORS · Todd Strasser (*Skywalker*); Jude Watson (*Amidala* and *Maul*)
COVER ARTIST · Lucasfilm Ltd.

PUBLICATION HISTORY · Juvenile novel, Scholastic Inc.
· Paperback, June 1999 (*Skywalker* and *Amidala*); March 2000 (*Maul*)

TIME LINE PLACEMENT · 32 BBY

WORLDS VISITED · Coruscant [L-9]; Naboo [O-17]; Tatooine [R-16]

MAIN CHARACTERS · Anakin Skywalker, slave (human male); Queen Amidala/Padmé Naberrie, leader of the Naboo (human female); Darth Maul, Sith apprentice (Dathomirian Zabrak male)

SUMMARY · The journals provide firsthand accounts of the events surrounding the Battle of Naboo, by those who witnessed it.

Anakin's journal is written after the Battle of Naboo, as he wishes to have a record of the momentous events that spirited him away from Tatooine. Amidala's journal is kept during these events, recorded on a datapad hidden in her robes. Darth Maul keeps his diary in the hope of it becoming a record in the Sith archives when they have conquered the galaxy.

The *Darth Maul* journal has the most embellished plot compared with the other two journals, as Maul's minimal screen time allows for more opportunities for new storytelling. New scenes include Maul's combat with Togorian pirates in space and Tusken Raiders on Tatooine.

DARTH PLAGUEIS

AUTHOR · James Luceno

COVER ARTIST · Torstein Nordstrand

PUBLICATION HISTORY · Novel, Del Rey Books
· Hardcover, January 2012
· Paperback, October 2012

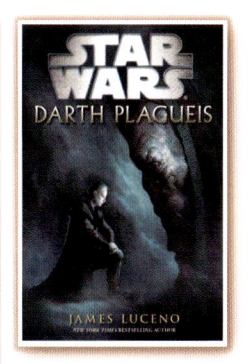

TIME LINE PLACEMENT · 67–65 BBY (Part 1); 54–52 BBY (Part 2); 34–32 BBY (Part 3)

WORLDS VISITED · Bal'demnic [R-7]; Bedlam [O-7]; Buoyant [J-14]; Chandrila [L-9]; Dathomir [O-6]; Hypori [S-16]; Kamino [S-15]; Kursid [Q-5]; Lianna [S-6]; Malastare [N-16]; Muunilinst [K-4]; Mygeeto [K-5]; Naboo [O-17]; Saleucami [S-8]; Serenno [P-5]; Sojourn moon [J-4]

MAIN CHARACTERS · Darth Plagueis/Hego Damask, Sith Lord/Magistrate (Muun male); Darth Sidious/Palpatine, Sith apprentice (human male); Cosinga Palpatine, Naboo noble (human male); Darth Tenebrous, Sith Lord (Bith male); Vidar Kim, Senator (human male); Sate Pestage, operative (human male); Ars Veruna, Naboo king (human male); 11-4D, multipurpose droid

SUMMARY · The Sith Lord Darth Tenebrous and his apprentice Darth Plagueis continue the millennium-long conspiracy of the Sith Order, plotting the downfall of the Jedi Knights and the Republic. A sudden explosion and cave-in at a cortosis mine on Bal'demnic threatens Tenebrous's life. Rather than save his injured mentor, Plagueis snaps Tenebrous's neck, watching closely as the Sith Lord dies. Plagueis is fascinated by the biological underpinnings of life and the Force, hypothesizing that the midi-chlorians found in the bloodstream of all living things can unlock the most powerful secrets of the Force.

Even in his public guise as Hego Damask, a powerful CEO of a Muun corporation, Plagueis is entrenched in clandestine plotting as part of the Order of the Canted Circle secret society. On the moon of Sojourn, Damask hosts brokers of industrial and commercial power, arranging alliances and

HEIGHT OF THE REPUBLIC 51

deals to ensure the continued prosperity of the galaxy's wealthiest businessbeings. His affluent lifestyle affords him the ability to continue biological experiments on Force-sensitive life-forms and their midi-chlorians within a hidden laboratory on Sojourn. When Plagueis is confronted by Darth Venamis, a secret apprentice to Tenebrous, he defeats and imprisons the failed usurper, subjecting him to tests and procedures in his laboratory that cause Venamis to hover at the brink of death.

Plagueis's business attentions are drawn to the rich plasma lodes beneath Naboo's surface. Damask arranges support for the campaign of a Naboo king who wishes to open the otherwise insular world to offworld exploitation. Damask's efforts are staunchly opposed by Cosinga Palpatine, an influential noble who rejects foreign interest in Naboo. Cosinga's iconoclast seventeen-year-old son, a youth known only as Palpatine, finds such isolationism backward, and helps Damask's efforts by supplying inside information on the political opposition. Damask is intrigued by Palpatine's sharp mind and his natural strength in the Force, and encourages the lad to follow his darkest desires. In a dark fit of rebellion, Palpatine uses the Force to kill his family, who attempted to cut him off from his newfound Muun friend and mentor.

Over the following decade, Plagueis trains Palpatine as his apprentice, granting him the title Darth Sidious and unlocking his potential as a Force-user and politician. Plagueis plots an ascent for Palpatine that will see him one day named Supreme Chancellor, with Hego Damask serving as his co-chancellor. By arranging for the death of Vidar Kim—Senator of Naboo and one of Palpatine's oldest friends—the Sith Lords pave the way for Palpatine to claim that title.

The ambitious Sidious begins hatching his own agenda. When he is presented with a Force-strong Zabrak infant during a visit to Dathomir, Sidious decides to raise the child, Maul, in secret to become a Sith apprentice. To Plagueis, Sidious explains Maul is to be but an enforcer, a brute warrior to unleash when circumstances demand it.

Plagueis's dealings as Damask endanger his life. Pax Teem, a political rival marginalized by Damask's affairs, launches a deadly attack by Maladin assassins that slaughters many of the Canted Circle members and grievously wounds Plagueis. Sidious kills Teem in return. Damask must wear a transpirator mask due to his injuries, and he recedes from public view, becoming all the more obsessed with immortality through the power of the Force. He even experiments with coaxing midi-chlorians to spontaneously create life, though his results are frustratingly inconclusive. In his continued biological experimentations, Plagueis enlists the aid of the cloners of Kamino to examine the Force-resistance exhibited by the reptilian Yinchorri species, and even considers creating a cloned army of Yinchorri.

On Naboo, King Veruna wants his world to throw off financial dependency on the Trade Federation and reap more profits from its own resources. To that end, he begins a program to arm the planet with state-of-the-art starfighters. He willfully defies Plagueis, launching a nuclear strike against Damask's headquarters on Sojourn. Tipped off by his ally Jabba the Hutt, Damask leaves the moon before the devastating assault and survives to kill Veruna, leaving a vacant throne to be filled by young Queen Amidala.

Plagueis and Palpatine together maneuver the ineffective Chancellor Valorum and the rapacious leadership of the Trade Federation into position to spark the Battle of Naboo. As Palpatine nears his goal of becoming Supreme Chancellor, Plagueis resumes a more public profile as Damask, hoping to ascend alongside the Naboo Senator so that he can control the Republic from behind his more politically astute apprentice. Palpatine, however, betrays

Darth Plagueis fights for his life as the secret gathering of the Order of the Canted Circle is ambushed by assassins.

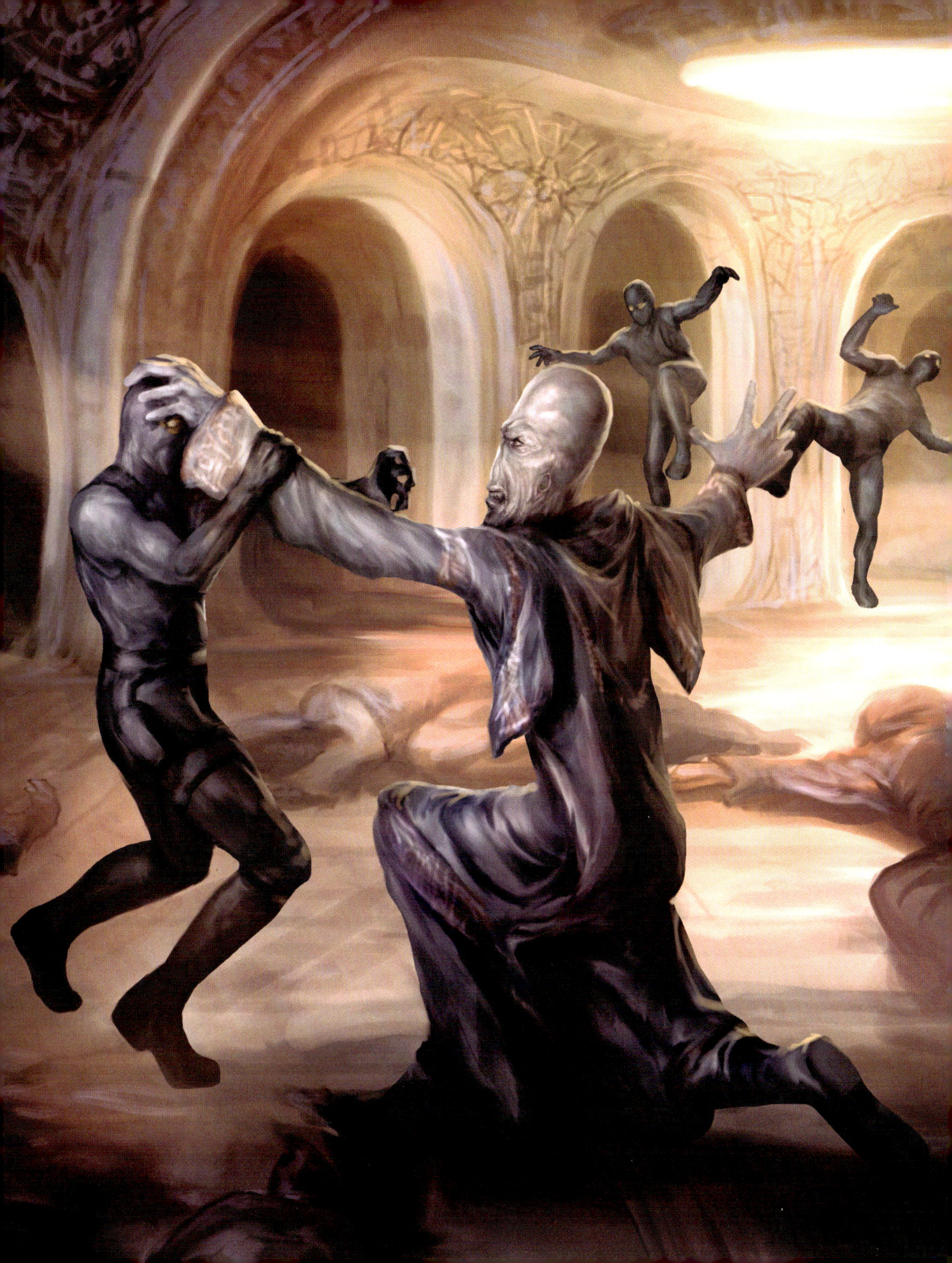

SHORT STORY — "The Tenebrous Way"

Published alongside the novel's release was the short story "The Tenebrous Way" by Matthew Stover. Appearing in *Star Wars Insider* #130 (2011, Titan Publishing), the story deals with Tenebrous's efforts to cheat death. Tenebrous has bioengineered a variant of midi-chlorian capable of passing on his consciousness, and in this way, he infects the body of Darth Plagueis, stowing away silently in his apprentice's veins. When Tenebrous experiences a jarring vision of Plagueis's doomed future, he vacates the body immediately. It would seem, however, that perceptions of time and space are very skewed to the disembodied Tenebrous—for he is now in a strange loop, reliving his moment of death and transference for centuries within the buried depths of Bal'demnic.

---

and kills Plagueis, hatefully revealing that he was never truly loyal to his master and had in fact conspired to betray him from the start.

Elected Supreme Chancellor, Palpatine achieves a crucial victory, rising to the top of Republic political power. He must weather the apparent death of Darth Maul as well as other events with great repercussions that will shape the future: a Jedi named Sifo-Dyas has been goaded into engaging the Kaminoans to create a clone army, a disenchanted Jedi Master named Dooku has left the Order, and a young boy named Anakin Skywalker—seemingly conjured to life by the midi-chlorians—has begun study at the Jedi Temple.

The *Reader's Companion* assumes that newcomers to *Star Wars* fiction have already been exposed to the story of the six films of the saga. For this reason, *Darth Plagueis* is placed here in the time line, earlier than Palpatine's exposure as a Sith Lord during the events of Episode III (2005). Episode III was the first source to identify Darth Plagueis as Sidious's Master.

Author James Luceno initially pitched *Darth Plagueis* as a first-person narrative—a retelling of Plagueis's life story as recorded in a holocron discovered by Sidious immediately after his murder. As inspiration, Luceno pointed to works such as Anne Rice's Vampire Chronicles novels. This direction evolved as the story grew to tell of Palpatine's beginnings as much as the origin of Plagueis.

Mirroring Plagueis's deepest aspirations, the novel that bears his name was able to stave off a premature death. LucasBooks nearly canceled the book in its earliest development due to sensitivities regarding shining too direct a spotlight on these shadowy Sith characters. The novel survived, though, as the story underwent careful refinement with direct input from Howard Roffman, president of Lucas Licensing.

Luceno gathers story elements from across the Expanded Universe as part of this narrative. The novel builds upon fragments of Palpatine's history revealed in *Wild Space* (2008)—that he was a speed demon as a young man—and the short story "The Monster" (2000), which features Palpatine's co-

conspirator Sate Pestage during King Veruna's reign. Also referenced is the Episode I lead-in story *Cloak of Deception* (2001) and Maul's early assignments from *Darth Maul: Shadow Hunter* (2001) and *Darth Maul: Saboteur* (2001).

From Dark Horse Comics stories, the Yinchorri Uprising was originally depicted in *Jedi Council: Acts of War* (2000) mini series, while Vidar Kim—Palpatine's Senatorial predecessor—first appeared in *Star Wars: Republic* #64 (2004). Darth Maul's mission to behead Black Sun is from the *Darth Maul* comics series (2000).

The novel also features Romeo Treblanc, a Coruscant mover and shaker who dabbles in the criminal world, and the planet Bal'demnic—elements created by fans and officially sanctioned as *Star Wars* lore by the *Star Wars* Fan Club in 2008.

The book also weaves elements from concurrently developed projects, like Luceno's short stories "Restraint" and "End Game," both created in anticipation of the 2012 3-D release of *Star Wars: Episode I The Phantom Menace*. *Plagueis* also includes elements from Ryder Windham's *The Wrath of Darth Maul* (2012) novel, and the developing story of the fourth and fifth seasons of *Star Wars: The Clone Wars* animated series (2011–2013).

WORLD VISITED · Naboo [O-17]

MAIN CHARACTERS · Spleed Nukkels, bongo pilot (Gungan female); Neb Neb Goodrow, bongo pilot (Gungan male); Squidfella Quiglee, outlaw racer (Gungan male); Lob Dizz, engineer (Gungan female); Boss Rugor Nass, leader (Gungan male)

SUMMARY · Boss Nass is having his old heyblibber submarine restored to a racing model and wants input from the infamous pilots Spleed Nukkels and Neb Neb Goodrow. The two crash-prone Gungans end up capturing would-be bongo thief Squidfella Quiglee.

M**ANY OF THE CHARACTERS** in this short story were first introduced in the Episode I Adventures game books by Ryder Windham, published by Scholastic Inc.

JEDI APPRENTICE SPECIAL EDITION: DECEPTIONS
"DEEP SPOILERS"

AUTHOR · Ryder Windham

PUBLICATION HISTORY · Short story, Wizards of the Coast · *Star Wars Gamer* #4, June 2001

TIME LINE PLACEMENT · 33 BBY

AUTHOR · Jude Watson

COVER ARTIST · Cliff Nielsen

PUBLICATION HISTORY · Juvenile novel, Scholastic Inc. · Paperback, July 2001

TIME LINE PLACEMENT · 44 BBY (Part 1); 29 BBY (Part 2)

HEIGHT OF THE REPUBLIC

WORLDS VISITED · Coruscant [L-9]; Hilo [O-13]; Tentrix [N-15]

MAIN CHARACTERS · Obi-Wan Kenobi, Padawan learner/Jedi Knight (human male); Qui-Gon Jinn, Jedi Master (human male); Anakin Skywalker, Padawan learner (human male); Uni/Kad Chun, *BioCruiser* leader (human male); Vox Chun, Telosian leader (human male); Sano Sauro, prosecutor (human male); Garen Muln, Jedi Knight (human male); Den, thief (human male)

SUMMARY · THE PAST: The grieving Chun family attempts in vain to hold Obi-Wan and the Jedi Order responsible for the death of Bruck Chun. Meanwhile, Qui-Gon and Tahl study incidents of sabotage in a fledgling Jedi starfighter program. Though their search stalls, they find clues that someone in the Senate may be behind it.

THE PRESENT: Obi-Wan Kenobi and twelve-year-old Anakin Skywalker are sent to assess the *BioCruiser*, an enormous shipbound community of disenfranchised citizens fleeing the Republic. Aboard, Obi-Wan discovers that Kad Chun, his sworn enemy, is the leader of the ship. Despite their animosity, they eventually work together to thwart a plot engineered by Vox Chun, Kad's father, to steal the wealth of the *BioCruiser*'s passengers.

ROGUE PLANET

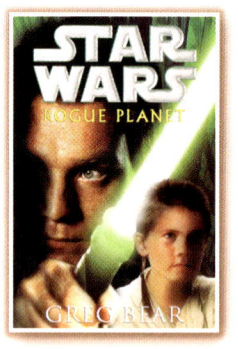

AUTHOR · Greg Bear

COVER ARTIST · David Stevenson

PUBLICATION HISTORY · Novel, Del Rey Books
· Hardcover, May 2000
· Paperback, May 2001

TIME LINE PLACEMENT · 29 BBY

WORLDS VISITED · Coruscant [L-9]; Seline [M-3]; Zonama Sekot [M-3]

MAIN CHARACTERS · Anakin Skywalker, Padawan learner (human male); Obi-Wan Kenobi, Jedi Knight (human male); Raith Sienar, industrialist (human male); Wilhuff Tarkin, Republic Outland Regions Security Force commander (human male); Ke Daiv, assassin (Blood Carver male); Jabitha, guide (Ferroan female); Charza Kwinn, pilot (Priapulin male)

SUMMARY · The Jedi Council dispatches Obi-Wan and Anakin to seek out Jedi Knight Vergere, who has been missing for a year. They venture to the mysterious world of Zonama Sekot, a remote, verdant planet teeming with life. It is said to be the source of the fastest ships in the galaxy, and indeed Anakin is fascinated to discover the bizarre, organic process through which these ships are created.

The two pose as customers interested in purchasing one of these custom-made vessels. The complex procedure begins with prospective buyers being paired with eager seed-partners that will grow into the vessel. Anakin's strong attunement to the Force creates an unprecedented number of seed-partners, resulting in a superlative ship.

An anguished twelve-year-old Anakin Skywalker stands over Ke Daiv, a Blood Carver who he has killed through an uncontrolled burst of Force power in order to save the life of young Jabitha.

HEIGHT OF THE REPUBLIC

Ultimately, the Jedi investigation reveals Zonama Sekot to be a unique living planet of unknown origins. Its biosphere is conscious and able to cloud the minds of even Jedi through illusions. Obi-Wan and Anakin learn that Vergere has vanished, taken by an aggressive alien culture known only as the Far Outsiders, who show an affinity for organic technology.

Others are interested in Zonama Sekot. The ambitious Outland Regions commander Wilhuff Tarkin sees the galaxy at a turning point and is determined to cement himself into a position of power when the change comes. He views Zonama Sekot's technology as an unparalleled asset and allies himself with industrialist Raith Sienar. Sienar leads an expedition to seek out this planet and steal a Sekotan ship. Accompanying Sienar is Ke Daiv, an assassin-for-hire ready to do Sienar's dirty work.

Unable to secure the ship through other means, Sienar and Tarkin's task force endeavors to take Zonama Sekot by force. During the battle, Daiv tries to steal Anakin's vessel. Anakin gives in to his growing rage and unleashes a torrent of Force energy that kills Daiv. Anakin is deeply regretful that he has taken a life through the Force.

Tarkin and Sienar ultimately fail to conquer Zonama Sekot. The planet harbors enormous hyperdrive cores and launches itself into hyperspace, fleeing the battle into parts unknown. Obi-Wan and Anakin are left behind by the planet, as is the ship that Anakin constructed, which withers and dies when cut off from its home.

In 2000, Del Rey Books had already begun publishing the epic multibook series The New Jedi Order, which is set twenty-five years after the events of *A New Hope*. *Rogue Planet* can be seen as essentially a chapter in that story line, which describes the galaxy threatened by brutal invaders who wield organic technology. Those aliens, the Yuuzhan Vong, are not detailed by name in *Rogue Planet*, but their presence is implied in the sketchy descriptions of the Far Outsiders. Furthermore, the planet Zonama Sekot returns to play a crucial role in The New Jedi Order by the end of the series.

Tarkin makes an appearance here wearing a different hat than lieutenant governor, as seen in *Cloak of Deception* (2001). Despite the lack of a centralized galactic military—as established in Episode II (2002)—there is a Republic Outland Regions Security Force, where Tarkin holds the rank of commander. *The Essential Guide to Warfare* (2012) reveals that Ranulph Tarkin built the ORSF out of local defense forces and made use of confiscated Trade Federation warships—moves that alarmed the Republic.

Set more than two years after the end of Episode I, this book reveals some of the repercussions to the Trade Federation from their botched invasion of Naboo. They have been ordered by the Senate to demilitarize, but given the sizable droid armies seen in Episode II, this decree was evidently poorly enforced.

Raith Sienar is an extension of Expanded Universe lore that began in *The Star Wars Sourcebook* (1987), which identified the manufacturer of the TIE fighter as Sienar Fleet Systems. In *Rogue Planet*, Sienar describes to Tarkin a radical dream project: an immense space station, the size of a moon. This marks the first chronological appearance of the germ of an idea that will develop into the Death Star.

The book introduces a Jedi named Thracia Cho Leem who remarks with disdain that Mace Windu has never married, whereas she has been married and has children. This is in direct opposition to the rules of the Jedi Code established later in Episode II.

JEDI APPRENTICE SPECIAL EDITION: THE FOLLOWERS

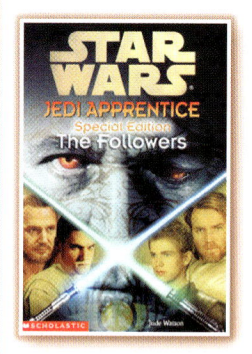

AUTHOR · Jude Watson
COVER ARTIST · Cliff Nielsen
PUBLICATION HISTORY · Juvenile novel, Scholastic Inc. · Paperback, April 2002
TIME LINE PLACEMENT · 39 BBY (Part 1); 29 BBY (Part 2)
WORLDS VISITED · Coruscant [L-9]; Kodai [R-6]; Ploo II [N-7]
MAIN CHARACTERS · Obi-Wan Kenobi, Padawan learner/Jedi Knight (human male); Qui-Gon Jinn, Jedi Master (human male); Anakin Skywalker, Padawan learner (human male); Dr. Murk Lundi, professor (Quermian male); Norval, Sith follower (human male)

SUMMARY · THE PAST: The rise of Sith-worshipping cults alarms the Jedi Council. Obi-Wan Kenobi (age eighteen) and Qui-Gon Jinn scrutinize Dr. Murk Lundi, a popular history professor on Coruscant who is obsessed with uncovering a long-lost Sith Holocron. This investigation leads to the tide-swept world of Kodai where, once every ten years, the oceans part to reveal the sunken landscape. Lundi believes a Holocron is hidden under the surface. Driven mad by the Holocron's influence, Lundi fails to recover the artifact and is incarcerated by the Jedi.

THE PRESENT: A decade later, the Kodai oceans once again part. The return of the Sith leads the Jedi to try to locate the Holocron to prevent it from falling into Sith hands. Obi-Wan and Anakin

Skywalker bring the addled Lundi back to Kodai, to the site where the Holocron lies. But the Jedi find themselves a step behind Lundi's student, Norval, who has already seized the Holocron and plans to deliver it to an unknown but powerful benefactor. Obi-Wan and Anakin chase Norval to the Ploo sector, where they recapture the Holocron and take it to the Jedi Temple for safe storage in the Jedi Archives.

Norval's benefactors are never identified beyond their sending a "sleek gray ship" to rendezvous with Norval for delivery of the Holocron. Source material subsequently published would track this Holocron's passage from the vaults of the Jedi Archives to the hands of Lumiya, much later in the time line.

This book features an early appearance by Kit Fisto, the tentacle-headed Jedi Master memorably introduced in Episode II. He is revealed to be Bant Eerin's Jedi Master.

JEDI QUEST: PATH TO TRUTH

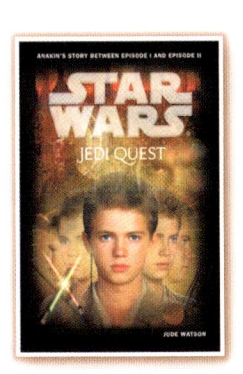

AUTHOR · Jude Watson

COVER ARTISTS · Alicia Buelow and David Mattingly

PUBLICATION HISTORY · Juvenile novel, Scholastic Inc. · Hardcover, September 2001

TIME LINE PLACEMENT · 28 BBY

WORLDS VISITED · Coruscant [L-9]; Ilum [G-7]; Nar Shaddaa (moon of Nal Hutta) [M-9]; Tatooine (flashback) [R-16]

MAIN CHARACTERS · Anakin Skywalker, Padawan learner (human male); Obi-Wan Kenobi, Jedi Knight (human male); Anf Dec, starship captain (Colicoid male); Krayn, slave raider (T'surr male); Siri Tachi, Jedi Knight (human female)

SUMMARY · At age thirteen, Anakin Skywalker climbs the icy cliffs of Ilum to seek out the crystal necessary to construct his own lightsaber. Anakin stares down visions of his worst fears, including images of his mother imperiled and the evil Sith Lord, Darth Maul. Returning with a lightsaber of his own, Anakin is soon given a new assignment with his Master, Obi-Wan Kenobi: protecting a starship from the pirate Krayn. Anakin has long known of Krayn, for the dreadful raider terrorized the Mos Espa Slave Quarters in Anakin's youth.

Infiltrating Krayn's spice-processing operation on Nar Shaddaa, Anakin makes it his personal mission to confront and destroy Krayn. He finds out that Krayn's lieutenant, Zora, is actually Jedi Knight Siri Tachi operating deep undercover. Obi-Wan likewise surreptitiously enters Krayn's compound, posing as a bounty hunter. The Jedi work together to liberate the enslaved workers, and Anakin kills Krayn with his lightsaber.

This hardcover release launched a new young reader book series focused on Anakin Skywalker's early teen years apprenticed to Obi-Wan Kenobi. In 2000, the publishing and product development teams at Lucas Licensing first planned the Jedi Quest banner to encompass books, comics, toys, and roleplaying games.

An internal Lucasfilm memo dated March 13, 2000, describes six possible action figures from

Hasbro: a "full body tattoo Darth Maul," Obi-Wan in Jedi pilot training outfit, Anakin Skywalker in cold-weather gear, the pirate Krayn, a Wookiee pirate, and "a possible prototype battle droid." The memo also listed two Action Fleet vehicles for the Micro Machines line (though it does not elaborate on their type), a roleplaying book from Wizards of the Coast for October 2001, a six-part Dark Horse Comics series, and tentative plans for an online interactive comic (possibly included as a CD-ROM with the action figures), as well as an audio drama.

The Jedi Quest multimedia project ultimately did not come to full fruition, though the Scholastic young reader series proved popular enough to carry on without any ancillary product support. Dark Horse only adapted the first book, *Path to Truth*, as a four-part *Jedi Quest* series by writer Ryder Windham and artist Pop Mhan in 2001. That year, Hasbro did release several Expanded Universe *Star Wars* action figures—the shirtless Darth Maul; training gear Qui-Gon Jinn, Obi-Wan Kenobi, and Darth Maul; and a cold-weather gear Obi-Wan—but none bore any mention of the Jedi Quest series. Hasbro did use the Jedi Quest name for a Kids Club, an online promotion for kids age four through twelve that included a short-lived magazine spotlighting Hasbro *Star Wars* toys. The roleplaying, interactive, and audio tie-ins never materialized.

The Jedi Quest series was also meant to offer glimpses of Episode II, but only *Path to Truth* arrived in advance of the 2002 Episode II tie-in titles. The insectoid Colicoid aliens featured in the book were at one point planned to be the first appearance of Geonosian aliens prior to *Attack of the Clones*.

JEDI QUEST #1: THE WAY OF THE APPRENTICE

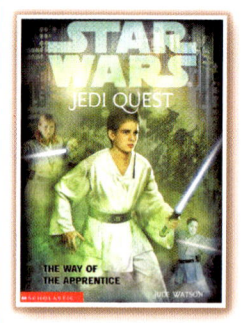

AUTHOR · Jude Watson

COVER ARTISTS · Alicia Buelow and David Mattingly

PUBLICATION HISTORY · Juvenile novel, Scholastic Inc. · Paperback, May 2002

TIME LINE PLACEMENT · 27 BBY

WORLDS VISITED · Coruscant [L-9]; Radnor [Q-16]

MAIN CHARACTERS · Anakin Skywalker, Padawan learner (human male); Obi-Wan Kenobi, Jedi Knight (human male); Tru Veld, Padawan learner (Teevan male); Darra Thel-Tanis, Padawan learner (human female); Ferus Olin, Padawan learner (human male); Siri Tachi, Jedi Knight (human female)

SUMMARY · The Jedi help the evacuation and relief efforts following a toxic disaster on Radnor, but quarantine requirements cause the Padawans to become separated from their Masters. Anakin Skywalker has difficulty working with fellow apprentice Ferus Olin, a naturally gifted leader. Nonetheless, the students together discover that the disaster was orchestrated by the neighboring Avoni as a prelude to their invasion of the planet. The Jedi are able to stop the plot and reveal the Radnoran conspirators who allowed it to happen.

OUTBOUND FLIGHT

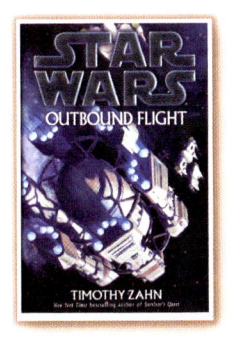

AUTHOR · Timothy Zahn
COVER ARTIST · Dave Seeley
PUBLICATION HISTORY ·
Novel, Del Rey Books
 · Hardcover, January 2006
 · Paperback, January 2007
TIME LINE PLACEMENT · 27 BBY
WORLDS VISITED · Barlok [L-8]; Coruscant [L-9]; Crustai [H-8]; Geroon [I-8]; Lonnaw [K-6]; Roxuli [I-8]; Yaga Minor [K-5]

MAIN CHARACTERS · Mitth'raw'nuruodo, commander (Chiss male); Jorj Car'das, navigator (human male); Dubrak "Rak" Qennto, smuggler captain (human male); Maris Ferasi, smuggler first mate (human female); Jorus C'baoth, Jedi Master (human male); Lorana Jinzler, Padawan learner/Jedi Knight (human female); Kinman Doriana, adviser/conspirator (human male); Mitth'ras'safis, syndic (Chiss male); Obi-Wan Kenobi, Jedi Knight (human male); Anakin Skywalker, Padawan learner (human male)

SUMMARY · Desperate to escape pursuit by a vengeful Hutt enemy, the smuggling vessel *Bargain Hunter* leaps into Unknown Space. Its crew is discovered by the starship *Springhawk*, commanded by a cool, calculating blue-skinned Chiss alien named Mitth'raw'nuruodo. The alien—called Thrawn— takes great interest in the visitors from the Republic and brings them aboard his vessel. He is quite intrigued by navigator Jorj Car'das, and the two enjoy a rapport and exchange of information about their respective cultures.

Thrawn plots to engage the dangerous Vagaari species before they prove a threat, but preemptive strikes are anathema to the Chiss. Thrawn's brother, Mitth'ras'safis, attempts to have him stripped of command—for his own good—by bringing a Chiss admiral to monitor Thrawn's actions.

Meanwhile, in the Republic, Jedi Master Jorus C'baoth transforms political capital gained from a successful treaty negotiation into the launch of his dream project: Outbound Flight. The ambitious program is a mobile complex of six linked Dreadnought heavy cruisers crewed for a lengthy exploration mission beyond the borders of the galaxy. C'baoth sees it as an essential step in preserving the Jedi Order and the ideals of the Republic in increasingly troubled times.

C'baoth has hard-line views of the Jedi's role in society and tries to force a command structure aboard the vessel with the Jedi as absolute authorities. Many crewmembers aboard *Outbound Flight* balk at this overreach, causing deep resentment and tension early in the ship's maiden voyage. The Jedi Council sends Obi-Wan Kenobi and Anakin Skywalker aboard briefly to monitor the expedition as it begins its journey, but they are called away on other duties before *Outbound Flight* departs Republic space.

Darth Sidious wants *Outbound Flight* destroyed. Sidious has learned of a mysterious alien menace beyond the frontier of the galaxy and fears that *Outbound Flight* may provoke an invasion from these Far Outsiders. As a precaution, the Sith Lord sends his aide, Kinman Doriana, and a Trade Federation task force to intercept and destroy *Outbound Flight*. The task force instead comes across Thrawn's smaller fleet, and the force's foolish Neimoidian commander attempts to destroy the Chiss starships. Thrawn outmaneuvers them with cunning tactics, destroying the task force save for its command ship. Doriana speaks with Thrawn and

HEIGHT OF THE REPUBLIC 61

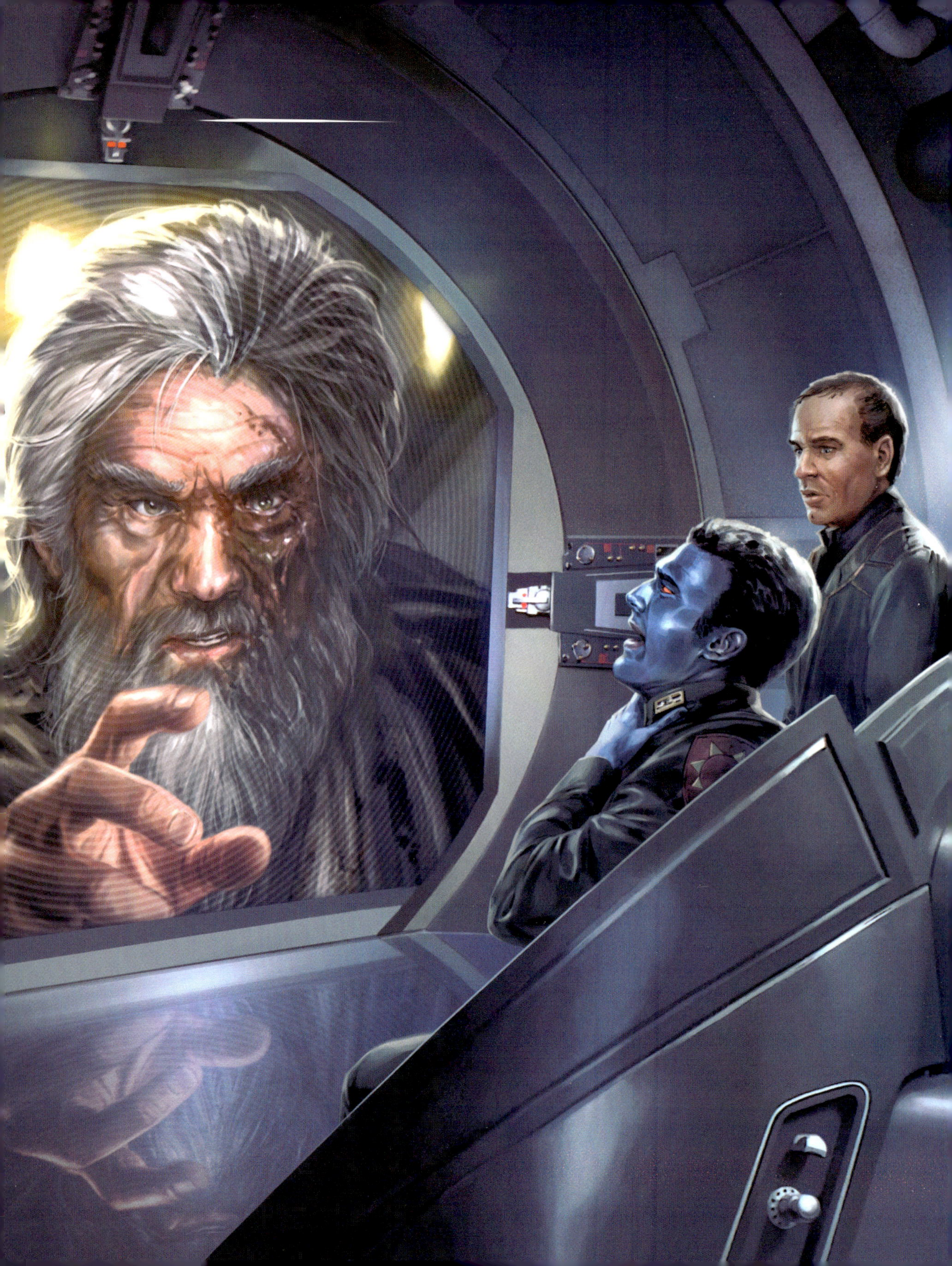

impresses upon him the magnitude of the extragalactic threat. Thrawn, aware that the Chiss have had contact with these aliens, agrees to destroy *Outbound Flight*.

Car'das, meanwhile, escapes the company of his Chiss hosts in a seemingly foolhardy plan. He voyages to the Vagaari, stoking their conquering instincts to provoke an attack on the Chiss base. The Vagaari imprison Car'das and launch their attack. En route to the base, they are caught in an artificial gravitational field erected by Thrawn to capture *Outbound Flight*.

Thrawn's meticulous plan unfurls precisely: His reprogrammed droid starfighters, appropriated from Doriana's task force, ravage the Vagaari fleet and likewise destroy much of *Outbound Flight*. An enraged C'baoth turns to the dark side in an attempt to telekinetically strangle Thrawn from across the void between their ships. The detonation of deadly radiation bombs throughout *Outbound Flight* kills most of those aboard the Dreadnoughts, leaving only a skeleton crew—including Jedi Lorana Jinzler and the colonist children who exhibited Force potential—alive in the complex's storage core.

A Chiss potentate, attracted by reports of Thrawn's provocative actions, arrives and tries to take control of *Outbound Flight*. Thrawn recognizes that the alien technology of *Outbound Flight* would be too unsettling to the tenuous balance maintained in Chiss society, but he has no choice except to follow orders. Not beholden to Chiss military command, Thrawn's brother Thrass and Car'das take control of *Outbound Flight* and escape with it into hyperspace. Aboard the ruined vessel, they come across the wounded Jinzler. Thrass plots a journey to a hidden clutch of stars patrolled by the Chiss while Car'das returns to Thrawn aboard a shuttle. Despite their best efforts, Thrass and Lorana cannot keep *Outbound Flight* running, and it slams into an unnamed planet.

Thrawn has avoided political reprisal and retains his command. He finally returns the *Bargain Hunter* to her crew and says farewell to Car'das. Doriana, intrigued by Car'das's initiative and insight, offers the navigator an influential position erecting an information network within the Republic.

AN IMPORTANT CHAPTER in *Star Wars* history, *Outbound Flight* marks the first novel in the time line by author Timothy Zahn, the writer most often credited with starting the modern *Star Wars* Expanded Universe with *Heir to the Empire* (1991). That first book introduced the characters of Thrawn and C'baoth and made fleeting mention of the *Outbound Flight* expedition, though the full details of the failed mission and C'baoth's final days would not be explored until the *Outbound Flight* novel. Car'das first appeared in an earlier Zahn work, *Specter of the Past* (1997), though this is his first time line appearance.

C'baoth uses the power of a Jedi meld to increase the effectiveness of Jedi gunners aboard *Outbound Flight*. This talent is presented as an intense and potentially dangerous use of Jedi ability, and seasoned Jedi such as Obi-Wan Kenobi speak of it with caution and awe. Later, in the New Jedi Order series and beyond, Jedi battle-melds are increasingly commonplace, suggesting either an increase in power and control in "modern" Jedi Knights, or a less potent incarnation of the meld itself.

The fate of *Outbound Flight*—as well as Lorana Jinzler—after the crash would be revealed in the novel *Survivor's Quest* (2004). Thrawn would next appear in the short story "Mist Encounter" (1995).

An infuriated Jorus C'baoth reaches out through the Force to throttle Thrawn, the alien tactical genius who has thwarted his plans for *Outbound Flight*.

JEDI QUEST #2: THE TRAIL OF THE JEDI

AUTHOR · Jude Watson
COVER ARTISTS · Alicia Buelow and David Mattingly
PUBLICATION HISTORY · Juvenile novel, Scholastic Inc. · Paperback, May 2002
TIME LINE PLACEMENT · 27 BBY
WORLDS VISITED · Coruscant [L-9]; Ragoon VI [K-9]
MAIN CHARACTERS · Anakin Skywalker, Padawan learner (human male); Obi-Wan Kenobi, Jedi Knight (human male); Floria, bounty hunter (human female); Dane, bounty hunter (human male); Wren Honoran, Jedi Knight (human male); Granta Omega, master of disguise (human male)

SUMMARY · A training mission meant to strengthen the bond between Master and Padawan instead becomes a dangerous game as Obi-Wan Kenobi and Anakin Skywalker are pursued by tenacious bounty hunters on the beautiful world of Ragoon VI. Two of the hunters, the brother-and-sister team of Dane and Floria, end up assisting the Jedi, and reveal that they were hired by a mysterious wealthy benefactor named Granta Omega. The Jedi survive the hunt and return to Coruscant, where they can find no information about Omega.

In this story, Obi-Wan warns Anakin about using absolute statements—a lesson he will memorably repeat during their fateful duel in *Star Wars:* Episode III *Revenge of the Sith* (2005). This book reveals that Didi Oddo has sold his café to Dexter Jettster, who now runs it as a greasy spoon diner.

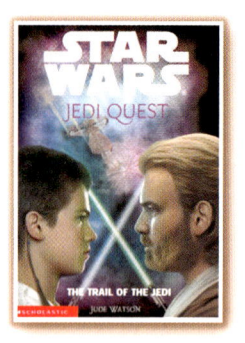

JEDI QUEST #3: THE DANGEROUS GAMES

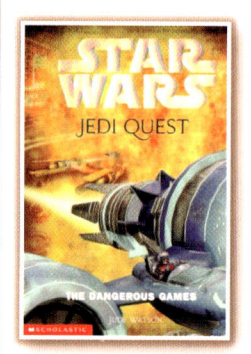

AUTHOR · Jude Watson
COVER ARTISTS · Alicia Buelow and David Mattingly
PUBLICATION HISTORY · Juvenile novel, Scholastic Inc. · Paperback, August 2002
TIME LINE PLACEMENT · 27 BBY
WORLD VISITED · Euceron [Q-7]
MAIN CHARACTERS · Anakin Skywalker, Padawan learner (human male); Obi-Wan Kenobi, Jedi Knight (human male); Hekula, outlaw Podracer (Dug male); Doby and Deland Tyerell, Podracing mechanic and pilot (Aleena brothers); Didi Oddo, gambler (human male); Astri Oddo, Games attendee (human female); Bog Divinian, Games Councilor (human male); Maxo Vista, athlete (Euceron male)

SUMMARY · A Jedi security team is on Euceron during the Galactic Games and discovers a plot engineered by the Commerce Guild to discredit certain Senators by implicating them in illegal gambling. Meanwhile, reports of an outlawed Podracing competition in the caves of Euceron draw Anakin Skywalker's curiosity, and he finds that Hekula, son of Sebulba, is piloting his old Podracer. Anakin volunteers to enter the race on behalf of the Tyerell brothers to free their enslaved sister.

The book states that Anakin has not raced since he was eight years old, when in fact he was nine years old during the Boonta Eve Podrace that saw his liberation.

JEDI QUEST #4: THE MASTER OF DISGUISE

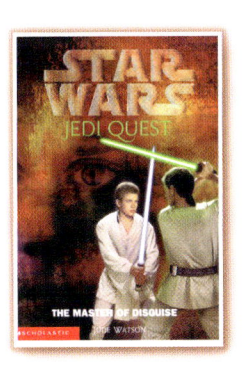

AUTHOR · Jude Watson

COVER ARTISTS · Alicia Buelow and David Mattingly

PUBLICATION HISTORY · Juvenile novel, Scholastic Inc. · Paperback, November 2002

TIME LINE PLACEMENT · 25 BBY

WORLDS VISITED · Coruscant [L-9]; Eeropha (and its moon, Nierport 7)[L-8]; Haariden [O-9]

MAIN CHARACTERS · Anakin Skywalker, Padawan learner (human male); Obi-Wan Kenobi, Jedi Knight (human male); Soara Antana, Jedi Knight (human female); Darra Thel-Tanis, Padawan learner (human female); Jocasta Nu, Jedi librarian (human female); Granta Omega, master of disguise (human male)

SUMMARY · Anakin Skywalker and Obi-Wan Kenobi once again run afoul of Granta Omega. Their enigmatic enemy hires soldiers on Haariden to attack a team of Jedi tasked with protecting a scientific expedition on the seismically active world. Though the Jedi survive, Anakin's impulsiveness results in fellow Padawan Darra Thel-Tanis being inadvertently injured in the attack. Back on Coruscant, Omega poses as a scientist and lures Anakin into a trap, but Obi-Wan rescues his apprentice. The two learn that Omega, though not Force-sensitive, is a cultist who wishes to attract the attention of the unseen Sith Lord by moving against the Jedi. Omega attempts to exploit a volcanic eruption on Haariden to reap its mineral wealth in a bid to corner the bacta market. The Jedi chase Omega to Haariden, but he once again escapes.

A jump in time advances Anakin to sixteen years of age, as revealed in book five of this series.

JEDI QUEST #5: THE SCHOOL OF FEAR

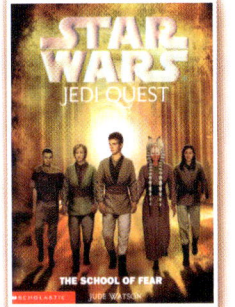

AUTHOR · Jude Watson

COVER ARTISTS · Alicia Buelow and David Mattingly

PUBLICATION HISTORY · Juvenile novel, Scholastic Inc. · Paperback, February 2003

TIME LINE PLACEMENT · 25 BBY

WORLDS VISITED · Andara [L-13]; Coruscant [L-9]

HEIGHT OF THE REPUBLIC

65

MAIN CHARACTERS · Anakin Skywalker, Padawan learner (human male); Ferus Olin, Padawan learner (human male); Obi-Wan Kenobi, Jedi Knight (human male); Sano Sauro, Senator (human male); Tyro Caladian, Senatorial aide (Svivreni male); Reymet Autem, student (human male); Marit Dice, student (human female); Gillam Tarturi, student (human male)

SUMMARY · The Leadership School on Andara trains the next generation of the galaxy's privileged and elite beings to excel, but the sudden disappearance of one of its pupils—Gillam Tarturi, son of an influential Senator—is cause for a Jedi probe. Rivals Anakin Skywalker and Ferus Olin go undercover, and Anakin discovers a secret mercenary group at the heart of this conspiracy. Gillam engineered his own disappearance as a vengeful strike against his father. Though the Jedi are able to scuttle this plot, Obi-Wan Kenobi is deeply disappointed in Anakin's decision to support the mercenaries and his poor focus on the Jedi Code throughout this mission.

The supporting character of Reymet Autem first appeared in the *Star Wars: Republic* comic book story "Honor and Duty" (published in issues #46–48, 2002), which occurs later in the time line. The Autem family story would be more fully explored in comic books.

JEDI QUEST #6: THE SHADOW TRAP

AUTHOR · Jude Watson
COVER ARTISTS · Alicia Buelow and David Mattingly

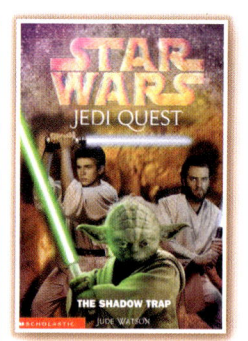

PUBLICATION HISTORY · Juvenile novel, Scholastic Inc. · Paperback, May 2003
TIME LINE PLACEMENT · 25 BBY
WORLD VISITED · Mawan [M-11]
MAIN CHARACTERS · Anakin Skywalker, Padawan learner (human male); Obi-Wan Kenobi, Jedi Knight (human male); Yaddle, Jedi Master (female); Granta Omega, master of disguise (human male)

SUMMARY · Unsettling visions of the future trouble Anakin Skywalker as he accompanies Obi-Wan Kenobi and Jedi Master Yaddle to Mawan, a lawless world ruled by competing crime groups that have forced the innocent population underground. The Jedi are led into a trap by their old foe, Granta Omega, who is secretly running one of the crime groups. To prevent Granta from launching a biological attack on the populace, Yaddle sacrifices herself by blocking the path of a weapon with her body. Anakin blames himself for Yaddle's death, for in her sacrifice, she rescued him from Omega's clutches. Though Omega escapes, Obi-Wan learns the truth behind their persistent enemy: he is the son of Xanatos, Qui-Gon Jinn's late fallen apprentice.

A change in the roster of the Jedi Council from Episode I (1999) to Episode II (2002) allowed the intervening stories of the Expanded Universe to eliminate prominent Jedi Masters in a dramatic fashion. The comic book *Star Wars: Zam Wesell* (2002) had Yarael Poof sacrifice himself to save Coruscant from a Force talisman weapon, while Yaddle sacrifices herself in this book. Their vacant spots on the Council would be filled by newcomers Coleman Trebor and Shaak Ti.

On the rooftops of Mawan, Padawan Anakin Skywalker witnesses Jedi Master Yaddle sacrifice herself to contain a deadly bio-weapon explosion.

HEIGHT OF THE REPUBLIC

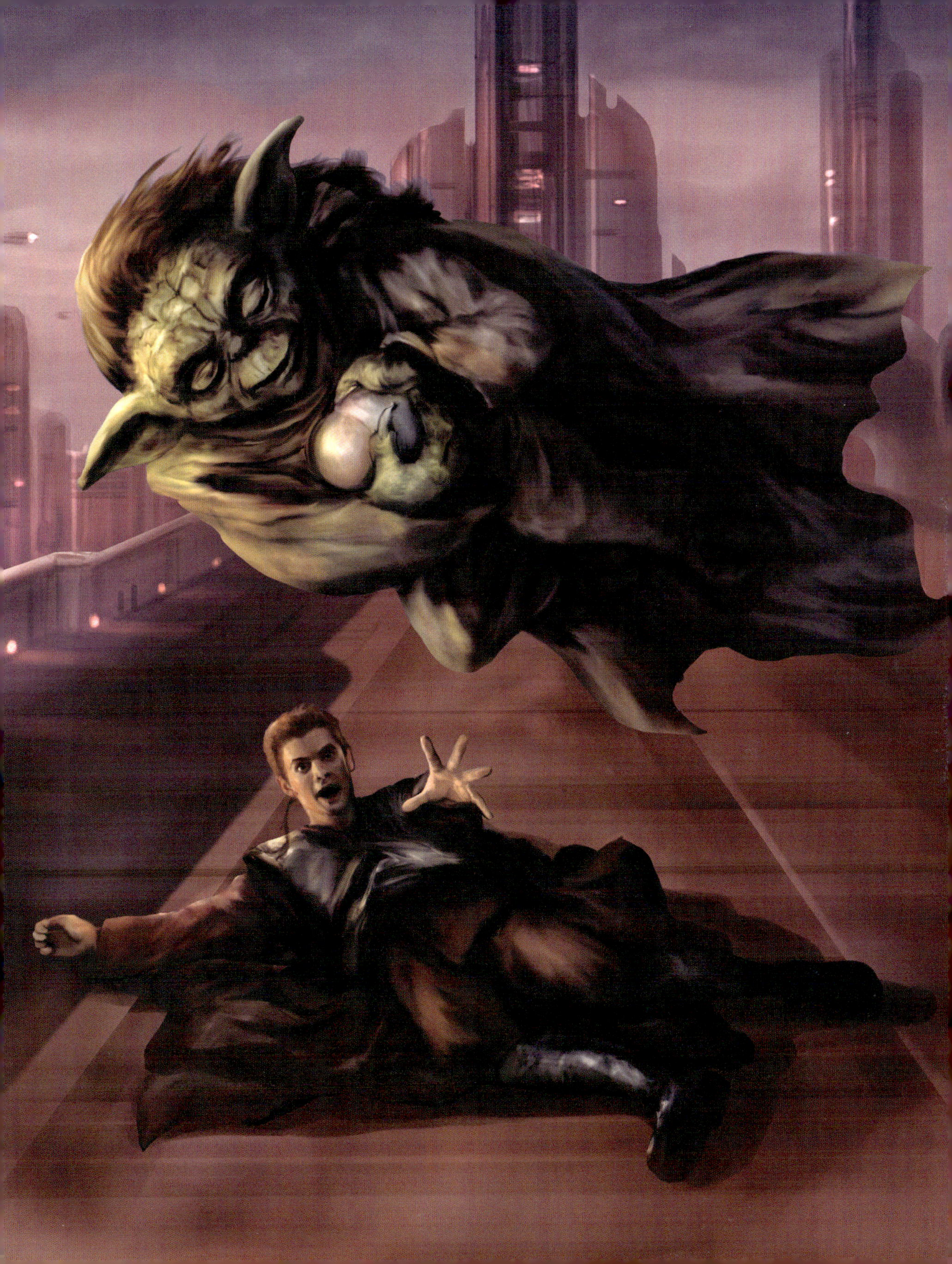

JEDI QUEST #7: THE MOMENT OF TRUTH

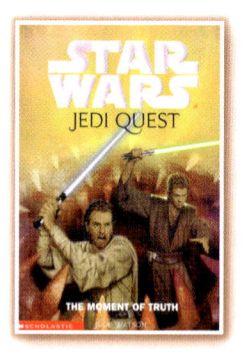

AUTHOR · Jude Watson
COVER ARTISTS · Alicia Buelow and David Mattingly
PUBLICATION HISTORY · Juvenile novel, Scholastic Inc. · Paperback, August 2003
TIME LINE PLACEMENT · 25 BBY
WORLDS VISITED · Typha-Dor [R-5]; Vanqor [R-5]
MAIN CHARACTERS · Anakin Skywalker, Padawan learner (human male); Obi-Wan Kenobi, Jedi Knight (human male); Jenna Zan Arbor, scientist (human female)

SUMMARY · Anakin Skywalker and Obi-Wan Kenobi are on Typha-Dor to rescue a team of scientists who have crucial information about an impending invasion from the neighboring world of Vanqor. A traitor in their ranks causes their escape vessel to crash on Vanqor, and Anakin is taken prisoner by none other than Obi-Wan's old nemesis, Jenna Zan Arbor. The unscrupulous scientist subjects Anakin to a drug called the Zone of Self-Containment, a stupefying agent that causes the Padawan moments of profound self-reflection. Obi-Wan rescues Anakin from prison, and the apprentice quickly repays the favor by saving his Master from a nest of enraged gundarks. The Jedi are able to prevent the Vanqor invasion. Anakin voices to Obi-Wan his long-held fears about being the prophesied Chosen One, a moment of trust that strengthens their connection.

The gundark nest in this book was inspired by a casual aside by Obi-Wan to Anakin in *Star Wars: Episode II Attack of the Clones* (2002). The two would once again face gundarks on Vanqor in a first-season episode of the *Star Wars: The Clone Wars* television series (2009).

JEDI QUEST #8: THE CHANGING OF THE GUARD

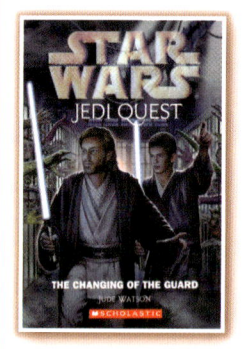

AUTHOR · Jude Watson
COVER ARTISTS · Alicia Buelow and David Mattingly
PUBLICATION HISTORY · Juvenile novel, Scholastic Inc. · Paperback, March 2004
TIME LINE PLACEMENT · 24 BBY
WORLDS VISITED · Coruscant [L-9]; Romin [Q-8]; Tentator [L-9]
MAIN CHARACTERS · Anakin Skywalker, Padawan learner (human male); Obi-Wan Kenobi, Jedi Knight (human male); Siri Tachi, Jedi Knight (human female); Ferus Olin, Padawan learner (human male); Roy Teda, planetary leader (Romin male); Jenna Zan Arbor, scientist (human female)

SUMMARY · The Jedi track Zan Arbor to lawless Romin, a haven for criminal fugitives. Obi-Wan, Siri, Anakin, and Ferus go undercover as gang members, seeking out the scientist in an effort to extradite her from the world. Anakin and Ferus become caught up with the Romin underground, whose members aid them in their mission to corner Zan Arbor. Obi-Wan discovers that the scientist is collaborating with Granta Omega. Though Zan Arbor escapes in the chaos that accompanies a bloody revolt on Romin, the Jedi track her in the hope that she will lead them to Omega.

JEDI QUEST #9: THE FALSE PEACE

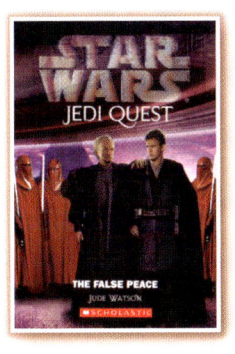

AUTHOR · Jude Watson

COVER ARTISTS · Alicia Buelow and David Mattingly

PUBLICATION HISTORY · Juvenile novel, Scholastic Inc. · Paperback, July 2004

TIME LINE PLACEMENT · 24 BBY

WORLDS VISITED · Coruscant [L-9]; Falleen [P-15]

MAIN CHARACTERS · Anakin Skywalker, Padawan learner (human male); Obi-Wan Kenobi, Jedi Knight (human male); Palpatine, Supreme Chancellor (human male); Siri Tachi, Jedi Knight (human female); Jenna Zan Arbor, scientist (human female); Ferus Olin, Padawan learner (human male); Bog Divinian, Senator (human male); Dexter Jettster, diner owner (Besalisk male); Granta Omega, master of disguise (human male); Tyro Caladian, Senatorial aide (Svivreni male)

SUMMARY · The hunt for Jenna Zan Arbor and Granta Omega is cut short when the Jedi are recalled to Coruscant by Chancellor Palpatine. A rising tide of anti-Jedi sentiment risks Senatorial support for the Order. Leading this political movement is the ambitious Bog Divinian, shortsighted lackey of Senator Sano Sauro. The two conspire to replace Palpatine in a coup with the secret assistance of Zan Arbor and Omega. Divinian's wife, Astri Oddo, gives Obi-Wan Kenobi the information he needs to uncover the impending attack on the Senate. Obi-Wan, Anakin Skywalker, Siri Tachi, and Ferus Olin are central to deflecting the assault of deadly seeker droids, though once again Zan Arbor and Omega escape. Palpatine neutralizes Sauro's ambitions by promoting him to deputy chancellor, thus keeping his enemy close. Anakin learns much from watching Palpatine's decisiveness in action, and he admires the man's convictions. The Jedi help relocate Astri and her son, Lune, away from Bog.

Though set between Episodes I and II, this book was written as Episode III was in development. Palpatine and Anakin's relationship is portrayed in a manner that better reflects their camaraderie in *Revenge of the Sith* (2005). Obi-Wan's Senatorial informant, Tyro Caladian, is killed in the course of the story for uncovering a shocking truth about the Senate. Though it isn't explicitly stated in the story, Tyro is presumably silenced for learning about the Sith presence on Coruscant.

"REPUTATION"

AUTHOR · Ari Marmell

PUBLICATION HISTORY · Short story, Titan Publishing · *Star Wars Insider* #136, October 2012

TIME LINE PLACEMENT · c. 24 BBY

WORLDS VISITED · Coruscant [L-9]

MAIN CHARACTERS · Cad Bane, bounty hunter (Duros male); Akris Ur'etu, gangster (Bothan male)

SUMMARY · Bothan criminal Akris Ur'etu, head of the Skar'kla Consortium, has hired an up-and-coming bounty hunter named Cad Bane for protection. But Bane is nowhere to be found when a Jedi assassin smashes through the Bothan's defenses to kill the gangster. Bane has been watching the assassin's progress, and realizes that he is no Jedi—he is a Hutt-hired killer disguised as a Jedi to cover the true culprit behind the hit. Bane outmaneuvers the faux Jedi and holds him at gunpoint. Rather than kill him, though, Bane offers the "Jedi" a chance to live if he shares the secrets of the miniaturized technology that he carries—the rocket boots, as well as the various gadgets secreted about his person. Bane realizes that with such gear, he would be well-equipped to become the preeminent bounty hunter in a galaxy that teeters on the brink of war.

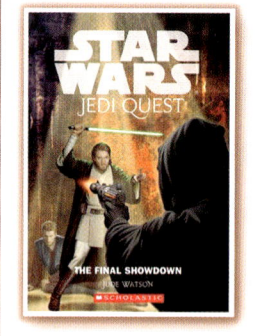

JEDI QUEST #10: THE FINAL SHOWDOWN

AUTHOR · Jude Watson

COVER ARTISTS · Alicia Buelow and David Mattingly

PUBLICATION HISTORY · Juvenile novel, Scholastic Inc. · Paperback, November 2004

TIME LINE PLACEMENT · 23 BBY

WORLDS VISITED · Coruscant [L-9]; Korriban [R-5]

MAIN CHARACTERS · Anakin Skywalker, Padawan learner (human male); Obi-Wan Kenobi, Jedi Knight (human male); Ferus Olin, Padawan learner (human male); Tru Veld, Padawan learner (Teevan male); Darra Thel-Tanis, Padawan learner (human female); Siri Tachi, Jedi Knight (human female); Jenna Zan Arbor, scientist (human female); Granta Omega, master of disguise (human male); Ry-Gaul, Jedi Knight (human male); Soara Antana, Jedi Knight (human female)

SUMMARY · Granta Omega, still desperate to curry favor with the secret Sith Lord, arranges a meeting on Korriban, ancient tombworld of the long-vanished Sith Empire. A team of Jedi Knights and their Padawans arrives in time to stop this union. The Sith Lord, unseen by the Jedi, vanishes without a trace, as does Jenna Zan Arbor, abandoning Omega and his impassioned vendetta. Obi-Wan Kenobi is forced to slay Omega in the ruins of a Sith temple when the crazed son of Xanatos will not relent.

While on the mission to the dark side–enshrouded world, Anakin Skywalker struggles with his feelings

Obi-Wan Kenobi, Anakin Skywalker, and Siri Tachi battle deadly seeker droids that swarm the Galactic Senate chambers.

HEIGHT OF THE REPUBLIC

of rivalry toward Ferus Olin. With deep-seated jealousy he observes the growing friendship between Ferus and Tru Veld, his best friend among the Padawans. Anakin's desire to see Ferus trip up causes him to keep quiet about a potentially disastrous repair Ferus has made on Tru's lightsaber. The weapon fails in combat with Commerce Guild droids, leading to the death of Padawan Darra Thel-Tanis. Ferus resigns from the Jedi Order as penance, while Anakin forever loses his friendship with Tru Veld.

The Sith Lord's presence is spoken of in the book, but he is not specified as Darth Tyranus until *The Desperate Mission* (2005), the first book of the Last of the Jedi series. At one point in this story, the events in *The Dangerous Games* (2002) are described as occurring six years earlier, but the time line fits in such events as being four years earlier.

THE APPROACHING STORM

AUTHOR · Alan Dean Foster
COVER ARTIST · Steven D. Anderson
PUBLICATION HISTORY · Novel, Del Rey Books
· Hardcover, January 2002
· Paperback, January 2003

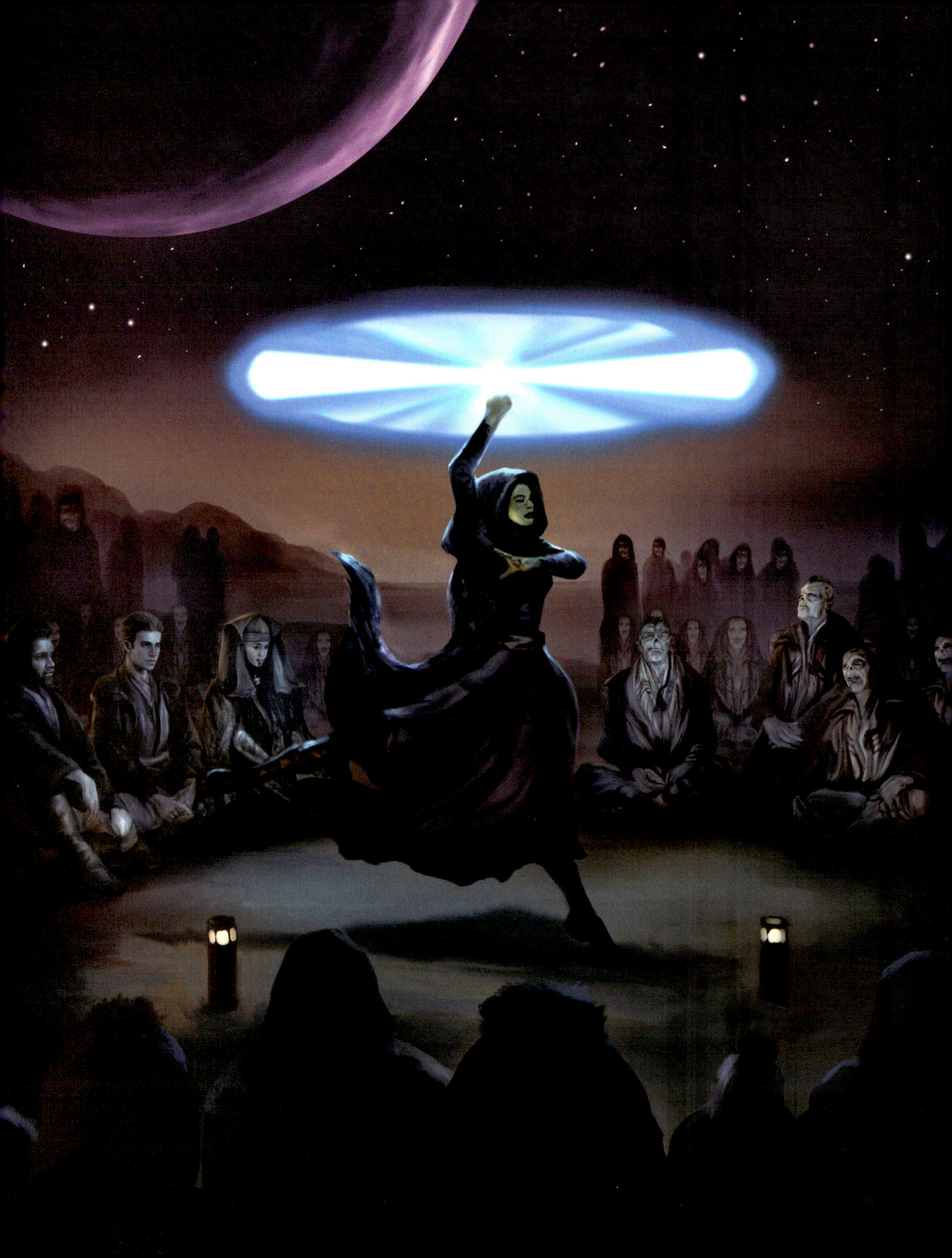

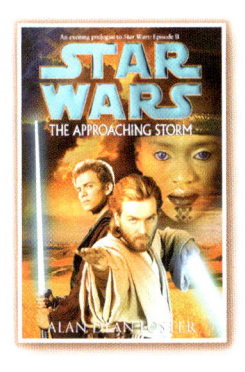

TIME LINE PLACEMENT ·
22 BBY

WORLDS VISITED · Ansion [I-6]; Coruscant [L-9]

MAIN CHARACTERS · Anakin Skywalker, Padawan learner (human male); Obi-Wan Kenobi, Jedi Knight (human male); Luminara Unduli, Jedi Knight (Mirialan female); Barriss Offee, Padawan learner (Mirialan female); Soergg Vosadii Bezhin, bossban (Hutt); Ogomoor, major-domo (Ansionian male); Bulgan, guide (Ansionian male); Kyakhta, guide (Ansionian male); Shu Mai, president of the Commerce Guild (Gossam female); Tooqui, tagalong (Gwurran male)

SUMMARY · The otherwise unremarkable world of Ansion finds itself at the center of a multitude of treaties and alliances. Should it secede from the Republic, it would bring dozens of influential worlds with it into the growing Separatist movement. This is precisely the outcome being cleverly engineered by Shu Mai, president of the Commerce Guild, on behalf of former Jedi Count Dooku. In response, the Jedi Council dispatches a team of four Jedi to win the loyalty of Ansion by settling a long-standing border dispute. Joining Luminara Unduli and Barriss Offee on this assignment are Obi-Wan Kenobi and Anakin Skywalker.

On Ansion, Soergg the Hutt has been secretly contracted by the Separatists to disrupt the Jedi mission. He tasks two deranged Ansionian underlings—Kyakhta and Bulgan—with kidnapping the Padawans. Their addled nature makes their motives and actions difficult for the Jedi to detect, and the twisted duo succeed in capturing Barriss. She uses the Force to heal their fractured minds, however, and gains their loyalty. The Jedi and their newfound Ansionian allies set off into the prairies on a mission to convince the nomadic Alwari people to cede half of their land to the city dwellers of Cuipernam to allow for the expansion of developed territory.

After tangling with a variety of wildlife and several Alwari tribes, the Jedi make contact with the Borokii overclan and convince them to make peace with the civilized Unity. During their journey back the Jedi narrowly avoid assassins hired by Soergg. The four Jedi present the treaty resolving the border dispute to the ruling council of Ansion. The planet votes to remain in the Republic, and the Separatists decide to bide their time just a little longer.

The springboard of this novel's story is a single line of dialogue spoken by Mace Windu in *Attack of the Clones* (2002) describing Obi-Wan and Anakin as returning from a border dispute on Ansion. Curiously, Luminara Unduli is beside Windu at the time he says this, even though she, too, was on this mission.

The visiting Jedi delegation of Obi-Wan Kenobi, Anakin Skywalker, Luminara Unduli, and Barriss Offee performs feats of physical perfection to impress the Alwari nomads.

Nejaa Halcyon

Nuru Kungurama

Vokara Che

Kal Skirata

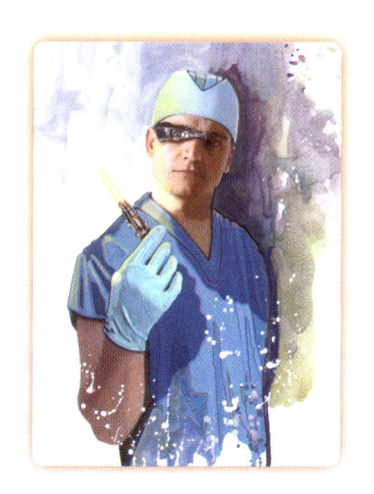

Jos Vondar

Tallisibeth "Scout" Enwandung-Esterhazy

CHAPTER 3

THE CLONE WARS

With the first volleys of the explosive Clone Wars fired in *Attack of the Clones*, LucasBooks and its publishers embarked on an ambitious program set in this long-roped-off area of continuity. Starting in 2003, interconnected books, comics, magazine articles, and videogames chronicled the war with a level of detail that would, in time, prove to be a double-edged sword.

The authors of the first Clone Wars books exercised creative license in filling out the conflict. Unbeknownst to them, there was a plan percolating to dramatize the conflict on television. In some notable cases, these early stories did not align with the version of events that would later be established by George Lucas and his team at Lucasfilm Animation. Some differences have proven more irreconcilable than others, and are noted where appropriate. It is not the intent of this *Companion* to discard any Clone Wars tales, though it is evident that some published events must have at least transpired *differently*, or in a different order, than first presented.

One of the biggest surprises offered by *The Clone Wars* animated series was the introduction of Ahsoka Tano, Anakin's Padawan learner. Since the books published before her introduction lead all the way in to the events of *Revenge of the Sith*, the complete lack of any reference to so major a character is obvious. However, most of the Clone Wars novels avoided using Anakin and Obi-Wan as central characters, thus blunting the conspicuous nature of Ahsoka's absence.

The Clone Wars stories from 2002 through 2005 provided a detailed time line that comprised a month-by-month account of the estimated three-year war. The animated series does not adhere to this time line, thus requiring that all published dates be taken with a grain of salt. Anakin Skywalker's ascension from Padawan to Jedi Knight, for example, is pegged by the novel *Jedi Trial* (2004) as happening around thirty months after the start of the war. Yet the animated series advances Anakin to this rank at the very beginning of the conflict. This leaves few options: either the date provided in *Jedi Trial* is incorrect, or all television stories are compressed to the last six months of the war. As always, a story line direct from George Lucas trumps publishing continuity, and it's the *Jedi Trial* date that gets discarded. However, it's important to note that it's not the novel's *story* that is disavowed as a result.

By beginning production after the release of Episode III, the TV show greatly benefits from a level of hindsight unavailable to the earlier book publishers. For example, none of the creators of the original Clone Wars literature knew that General Grievous would be a key player in the conflict until 2004, by which time the early months of the Clone Wars had already been extensively detailed. Thus a key figure makes a relatively late appearance in the war, according to the Expanded Universe. *The Clone Wars* animated series, however, having full knowledge of Grievous's prominence, depicts him as active from the very start.

STAR WARS: EPISODE II ATTACK OF THE CLONES

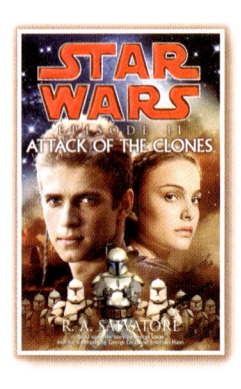

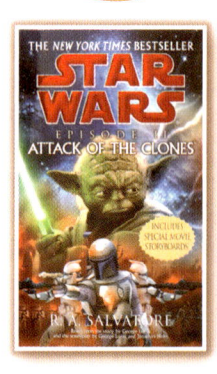

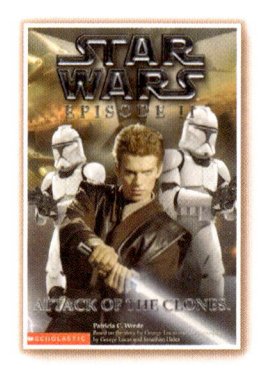

AUTHORS · R. A. Salvatore (adult novel); Patricia C. Wrede (juvenile novel); based on the story by George Lucas and the screenplay by George Lucas and Jonathan Hales

COVER ARTISTS · Steven D. Anderson (hardcover); David Stevenson (paperback); Louise Bova and Lucasfilm (juvenile novel)

PUBLICATION HISTORY · Adult novel, Del Rey Books
- Hardcover, April 2002
- Paperback, April 2003

Compiled as part of the Prequel Trilogy omnibus, Del Rey Books
- Paperback, May 2007

Juvenile novel, Scholastic Inc.
- Paperback, April 2002

TIME LINE PLACEMENT · 22 BBY

WORLDS VISITED · Coruscant [L-9]; Geonosis [R-16]; Kamino [S-15]; Naboo [O-17]; Tatooine [R-16]

MAIN CHARACTERS · Anakin Skywalker, Padawan learner (human male); Padmé Amidala, Galactic Senator (human female); Obi-Wan Kenobi, Jedi Knight (human male); Palpatine, Supreme Chancellor (human male); Jango Fett, bounty hunter (human male); Yoda, Jedi Master (alien male); Mace Windu, Jedi Master (human male); Count Dooku, Separatist leader (human male)

SUMMARY · A Separatist movement led by former Jedi Count Dooku is creating turmoil in the galaxy. Rushing back to Coruscant to vote against the creation of an army to deal with the increasing threats,

Young Boba Fett attempts to help his father, Jango Fett, as the bounty hunter tangles with Jedi Knight Obi-Wan Kenobi on Kamino.

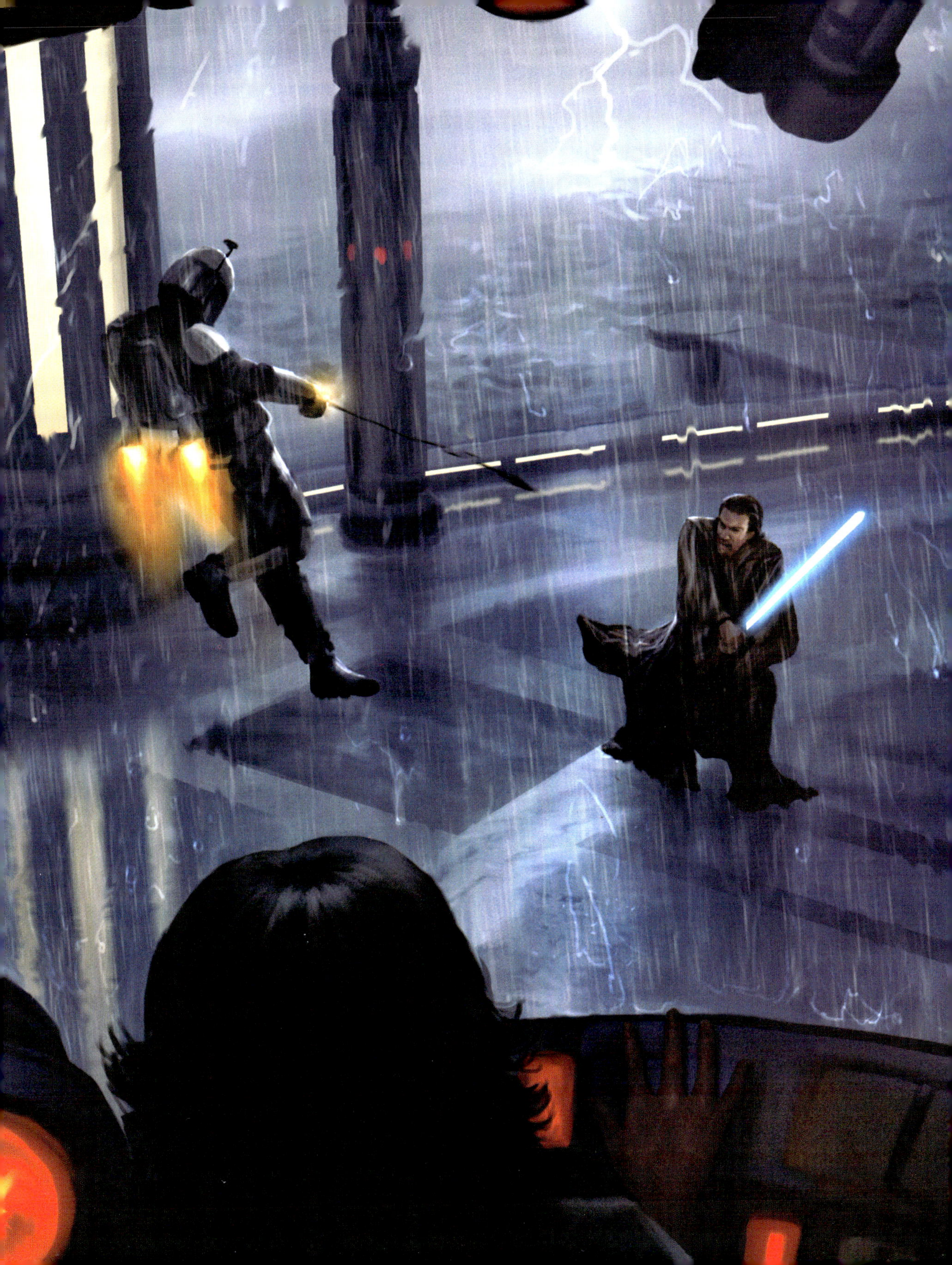

Senator Padmé Amidala is targeted for assassination by unknown agents. The Jedi Council assigns Anakin Skywalker to protect her, while Obi-Wan Kenobi investigates the incident. Anakin and Padmé begin to fall in love, though the Padawan is haunted by visions of his mother imperiled. These visions compel Anakin to rush to Tatooine, where he discovers that his mother, Shmi Skywalker, has been abducted and tortured by Tusken Raiders. Shmi dies of her injuries, and Anakin massacres the entire village's populace in revenge.

Meanwhile, Obi-Wan's search uncovers a secret army created for the Republic within the clone hatcheries on the planet Kamino. The army is activated in response to the Separatists amassing an immense droid army within the foundries of Geonosis, and the first battle of the Clone Wars erupts on that arid, distant world. To better handle this threat, Supreme Chancellor Palpatine assumes emergency powers over the Galactic Senate.

The Jedi attempt to apprehend Count Dooku, but the skilled swordsman cuts through them, injuring Obi-Wan and severing Anakin's arm. Not even Yoda can stop the renegade Jedi from fleeing Geonosis. Unknown to the Republic, Dooku is the Sith Lord Darth Tyranus, and he engineered the war at the behest of his Sith Master, Darth Sidious.

GEORGE LUCAS REVEALED new information about his universe in Episode II that ran counter to earlier stories of the Expanded Universe. Among the surprises: the Jedi Order is monastic, with love and marriage forbidden to its members. This would necessitate reforms to the Jedi Code over time to separate the ancient era when Nomi Sunrider was married to a Jedi, seen in the *Tales of the Jedi* (1993–94) comics, as well as the post-Empire era when Luke Skywalker married Mara Jade in the comic series *Union* (1999–2000). LucasBooks also needed to create plausible exceptions for Ki-Adi-Mundi, a Jedi Master who had multiple wives in the *Prelude to Rebellion* comics (1999).

Another revelation: the Republic had been without a military or a sizable conflict in over a thousand years. This means that incidents such as the Stark Hyperspace War (dramatized in a comic series of the same name in 2001) and organizations such as the Katana Fleet (from the Thrawn Trilogy, 1991–93) are exceptions, rather than the rule.

Perhaps the biggest surprise to longtime readers was the true history of Boba Fett. The future bounty hunter began life as the perfect clone of Jango Fett, the genetic template of the Republic clone army. Prior to this revelation, Fett already had several EU backstories charted out in comics. *Star Wars* #68: "The Search Begins" (Marvel Comics, 1983) describes Fett as one of three survivors out of 212 Mandalorian Supercommandos from the Clone Wars. *Dark Empire II* #2 (Dark Horse Comics, 1995) reveals that Fett was a former Imperial stormtrooper who murdered his superior officer. *The Essential Guide to Characters* (Del Rey Books, 1995) gives the most detailed account of Fett's background: he was a former Journeyman Protector from Concord Dawn named Jaster Mereel exiled for murdering a fellow lawman. Fett's true roots have revealed these narratives to be historically inaccurate, as the legends of notorious characters often are.

"PRECIPICE"

AUTHOR · Chris Cassidy
PUBLICATION HISTORY · Short story, StarWars.com, August 2008
TIME LINE PLACEMENT · 22 BBY

WORLDS VISITED · Geonosis [R-16]

MAIN CHARACTERS · Obi-Wan Kenobi, Jedi Knight (human male); Count Dooku, Separatist leader (human male)

SUMMARY · As Count Dooku holds Obi-Wan Kenobi captive on Geonosis and tries to lure him to the side of the Separatists, Kenobi steels his resolve by thinking back to other difficult moments when on the brink.

BOBA FETT #1: THE FIGHT TO SURVIVE

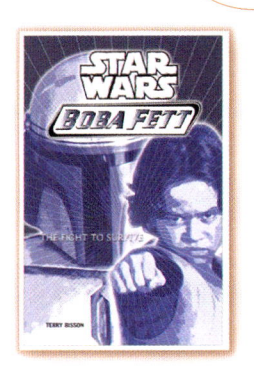

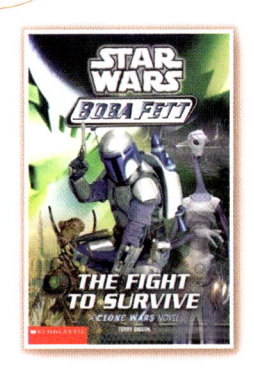

AUTHOR · Terry Bisson

COVER ARTISTS · Louisa Bova (hardcover); Peter Bollinger (paperback)

PUBLICATION HISTORY · Juvenile novel, Scholastic Inc.
 · Hardcover, May 2002
 · Paperback, April 2003

TIME LINE PLACEMENT · 22 BBY

WORLDS VISITED · Bogden [M-8]; Coruscant [L-9]; Geonosis [R-16]; Kamino [S-15]; Raxus Prime [S-5]

MAIN CHARACTERS · Boba Fett, fugitive (human male); Jango Fett, bounty hunter (human male); Aurra Sing, bounty hunter (humanoid female)

SUMMARY · After witnessing his father's death at the blade of a Jedi, young Boba Fett is alone in the galaxy. He buries Jango Fett's body, stashes his father's armor in a cave, and returns to his home on Kamino. Boba recovers a book left for him by his father with advice and information essential to his survival. Boba's first task is to find Darth Tyranus, the man who hired Jango to be the clone template. Tyranus holds the key to Jango's wealth, which Boba will need to survive on his own. Boba's search takes him to the moons of Bogden and to Coruscant. On the capital world, he is nabbed by Aurra Sing, who delivers him to Count Dooku on Raxus Prime.

The FIRST HALF of this novel is a retelling of the events before and during *Attack of the Clones* (2002) from Boba's point of view, including scenes written specifically for the movie's novelization. This is the first source to pair up Aurra Sing and young Boba, something that would also occur in the second season of *The Clone Wars* animated series (2010).

"DEATH IN THE CATACOMBS"

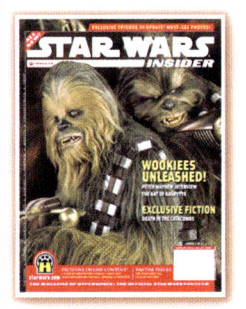

AUTHOR · Mike W. Barr

PUBLICATION HISTORY · Short story, Paizo Publishing
 · *Star Wars Insider* #79, December 2004

TIME LINE PLACEMENT · 22 BBY

WORLD VISITED · Geonosis [R-16]

MAIN CHARACTERS · Jyl Sontay, Jedi Knight (human female); Naj Pandoor, smuggler (human male); Dr. Frayne, scientist (human female)

SUMMARY · Jedi Jyl Sontay leads a Republic team that has remained on Geonosis, tasked with disarming the natives and cataloging their technology. A devious scientist, Dr. Frayne, who intends to sell the research to the black market, knocks Sontay unconscious. Sontay soon awakens and teams up with a rakish smuggler, Naj Pandoor. Together they fight past Geonosians only to discover that Dr. Frayne has been killed by a nexu.

Though Sontay has been recently promoted to Jedi Knight, the clone troopers in this story refer to her as a "commander," a rank held by a Padawan.

"ELUSION ILLUSION: A TALE OF THE CLONE WARS"

AUTHOR · Michael A. Stackpole
PUBLICATION HISTORY · Short story, Paizo Publishing
· *Star Wars Insider* #66, March 2003
TIME LINE PLACEMENT · 22 BBY
WORLDS VISITED · Corellia [M-11]; Coruscant [L-9]
MAIN CHARACTERS · Aayla Secura, Jedi Knight (Twi'lek female); Ylenic It'kla, Jedi

---

After the outbreak of the Clone Wars, young Boba Fett encounters Count Dooku on Raxus Prime and learns a secret about the Separatist leader's true identity.

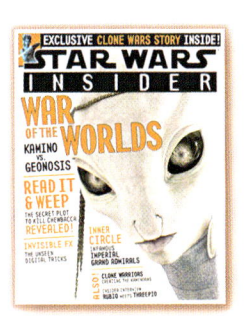

Knight (Caamasi male); Mace Windu, Jedi Master (human male); Nejaa Halcyon, Jedi Knight (human male)

SUMMARY · On Corellia, a neutral world in the Clone Wars, Jedi Knights Aayla Secura and Ylenic It'kla pose as traders while tracking down Ratri Tane, a former Techno Union technician who has fled his employers with valuable technology. The operation is an elaborate ruse abetted by Nejaa Halcyon and the Corellian Security Force (CorSec) to smuggle Tane offplanet, while falsely convincing bounty hunters that Tane was killed.

This story takes place within a week of the Battle of Geonosis. Nejaa Halcyon was created as part of Corran Horn's backstory in X-Wing: *Rogue Squadron* (1996), though this short story was the first time he appeared in a narrative tale. He would later figure prominently in *Jedi Trial* (2004).

BOBA FETT #2: CROSSFIRE

AUTHOR · Terry Bisson

COVER ARTISTS · Lucasfilm (hardcover); Peter Bollinger (paperback)

PUBLICATION HISTORY · Juvenile novel, Scholastic Inc.
· Hardcover, November 2002
· Paperback, April 2003

TIME LINE PLACEMENT · 22 BBY

WORLDS VISITED · Bespin [K-18]; Raxus Prime [S-5]

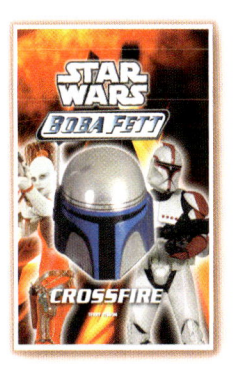

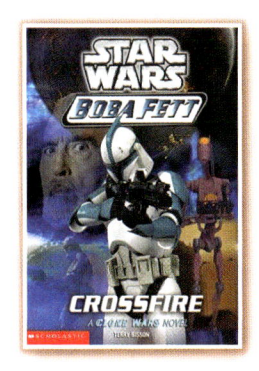

MAIN CHARACTERS · Boba Fett, fugitive (human male); Count Dooku, aka Darth Tyranus, Sith Lord (human male); Garr, war orphan (young Excargan); Aurra Sing, bounty hunter (humanoid female)

SUMMARY · Boba Fett's encounter with Count Dooku is cut short when Republic forces attack Raxus Prime, causing the Separatists gathered there to scatter. Clone troopers misidentify Fett as a war orphan and take him to Bespin as a refugee. There Fett is reunited with Aurra Sing, who wants to use him to recover the riches secreted away by his father, Jango Fett. Chased by Jedi, the two use his father's ship, *Slave I*, to escape the pursuit by threading their way through a dangerous Bespin storm and then leaving the gas giant.

A Separatist archaeological mission to uncover an ancient Sith weapon called the Dark Reaper is alluded to in this book. That threat is from the 2002 **Clone Wars** videogame from LucasArts.

THE CLONE WARS

BOBA FETT #3: MAZE OF DECEPTION

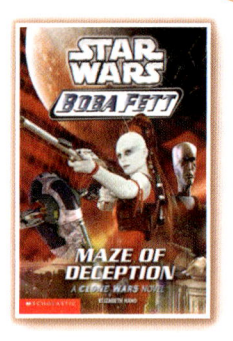

AUTHOR · Elizabeth Hand
COVER ARTIST · Peter Bollinger
PUBLICATION HISTORY · Juvenile novel, Scholastic Inc. · Paperback, April 2003
TIME LINE PLACEMENT · 22 BBY
WORLD VISITED · Aargau [L-10]
MAIN CHARACTERS · Boba Fett, fugitive (human male); Aurra Sing, bounty hunter (humanoid female); Nuri, con artist (Clawdite male)
SUMMARY · Boba Fett and Aurra Sing realize they need each other to retrieve part of Jango Fett's fortune. Aurra knows where it is, but only Boba can access it. Soon after they arrive on the banking planet Aargau, young Boba is able to get his hands on Aurra's data card containing the location of the fortune. He makes his break from her by fleeing into the massive maze-like pyramid city. Boba eventually secures his father's money—though he loses a substantial portion of it to a Clawdite con artist named Nuri—and returns to *Slave I* to continue his journey in accord with his late father's instructions.

Aargau first appeared in the Marvel Comics series in 1980. In this book, Boba recounts tales his father told of navigating the labyrinth on Balmorra, which are taken from the *Star Wars* Adventures game book *Warlords of Balmorra* (2003). *Maze of Deception* makes the claim that Boba Fett is eleven at this time, though most time lines would peg his age at ten.

"SCHOLASTIC PRESENTS: STORM FLEET WARNINGS"

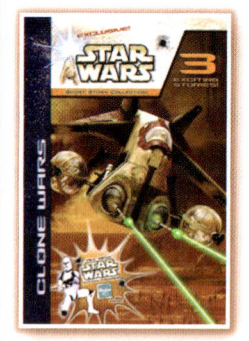

AUTHOR · Jude Watson
PUBLICATION HISTORY · Short story, Paizo Publishing · *Hasbro Short Story Collection*, July 2003
TIME LINE PLACEMENT · 22 BBY
WORLD VISITED · Llon Nebula [K-15]
MAIN CHARACTERS · Anakin Skywalker, Padawan learner (human male); Obi-Wan Kenobi, Jedi Knight (human male)
SUMMARY · Aboard their starfighters, Anakin Skywalker and Obi-Wan Kenobi intercept the Separatist Storm Fleet. Anakin lures the Separatist fleet into a treacherous stretch of the Llon Nebula, delaying the ships from an engagement in the Cyphar system.

Since Anakin is presented as a Padawan in this tale, the *Companion* moves this story to earlier in the time line than its original dating of four months into the Clone Wars.

LEGACY OF THE JEDI

AUTHOR · Jude Watson
COVER ARTISTS · David Mattingly; Lucasfilm

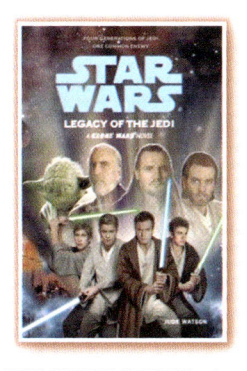

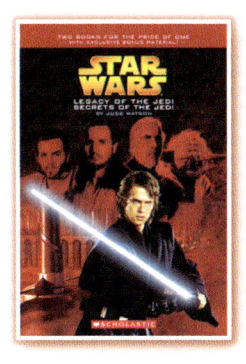

PUBLICATION HISTORY · Juvenile novel, Scholastic Inc. · Hardcover, August 2003 Collected with *Secrets of the Jedi* into single omnibus · Paperback, May 2006

TIME LINE PLACEMENT · 89 BBY (part 1); 76 BBY (part 2); 44 BBY (part 3); 22 BBY (part 4)

WORLDS VISITED · Coruscant [L-9]; Delaluna (Junction moon) [J-7]; Null [N-7]; Pirin [O-8]; Von-Alai [O-8]

MAIN CHARACTERS · Count Dooku, former Jedi (human male); Lorian Nod, former Jedi (human male); Qui-Gon Jinn, Jedi Master (human male); Obi-Wan Kenobi, Jedi Knight (human male); Anakin Skywalker, Padawan learner (human male); Floria, bounty hunter (human female); Dane, bounty hunter (human male)

SUMMARY · THE PAST: As a thirteen-year-old Padawan learner, Count Dooku sees his friendship with fellow student Lorian Nod come to an end when the troublemaker Nod is expelled from the Jedi Order for lying and impulsively stealing a Sith Holocron from the Jedi Archives.

Thirteen years later, Dooku and his apprentice Qui-Gon Jinn discover that Nod has become a space pirate who targets wealthy Senators for ransom. An enraged Dooku captures Nod, who is imprisoned by the Republic.

Three decades later, Qui-Gon and Obi-Wan Kenobi are Master and apprentice. The two Jedi discover that Lorian Nod is responsible for deceiving the populace of Delaluna. He has led them to believe that they are living under threat of a superweapon—one that doesn't actually exist. The Jedi liberate the Delalunans by proving Nod to be a fraud, and he is once again imprisoned.

THE PRESENT: A redeemed Lorian Nod becomes the legitimately elected leader of Junction and is now genuinely interested in helping his people. During the Clone Wars, the Separatists—led by Count Dooku—entreat Junction and its allies to join their cause. Nod remains loyal to the Republic, requesting aid from the Jedi. Anakin Skywalker and Obi-Wan secretly travel to Null, site of the diplomatic conference. The evil Dooku tries to kill the rulers who would not pledge their loyalty, but the Jedi intervene. As Dooku hurriedly departs, Nod tries to stop him, but Dooku slays his onetime friend and escapes.

SPANNING NEARLY SEVEN DECADES, this novel is divided into four segments, each focusing on a Jedi apprentice: Dooku, Qui-Gon, Obi-Wan, and Anakin. An early concept for this book would have gone back to Yoda's youthful days. Episode II revealed that Count Dooku was a former student of Yoda, but this book clarifies—at the behest of George Lucas—that he learned under Yoda as all younglings did, and his official Padawan apprenticeship was actually to another Jedi Master.

Since Anakin is presented as a Padawan in this tale, this story has been moved up to earlier in the time line than its original dating of six months into the Clone Wars.

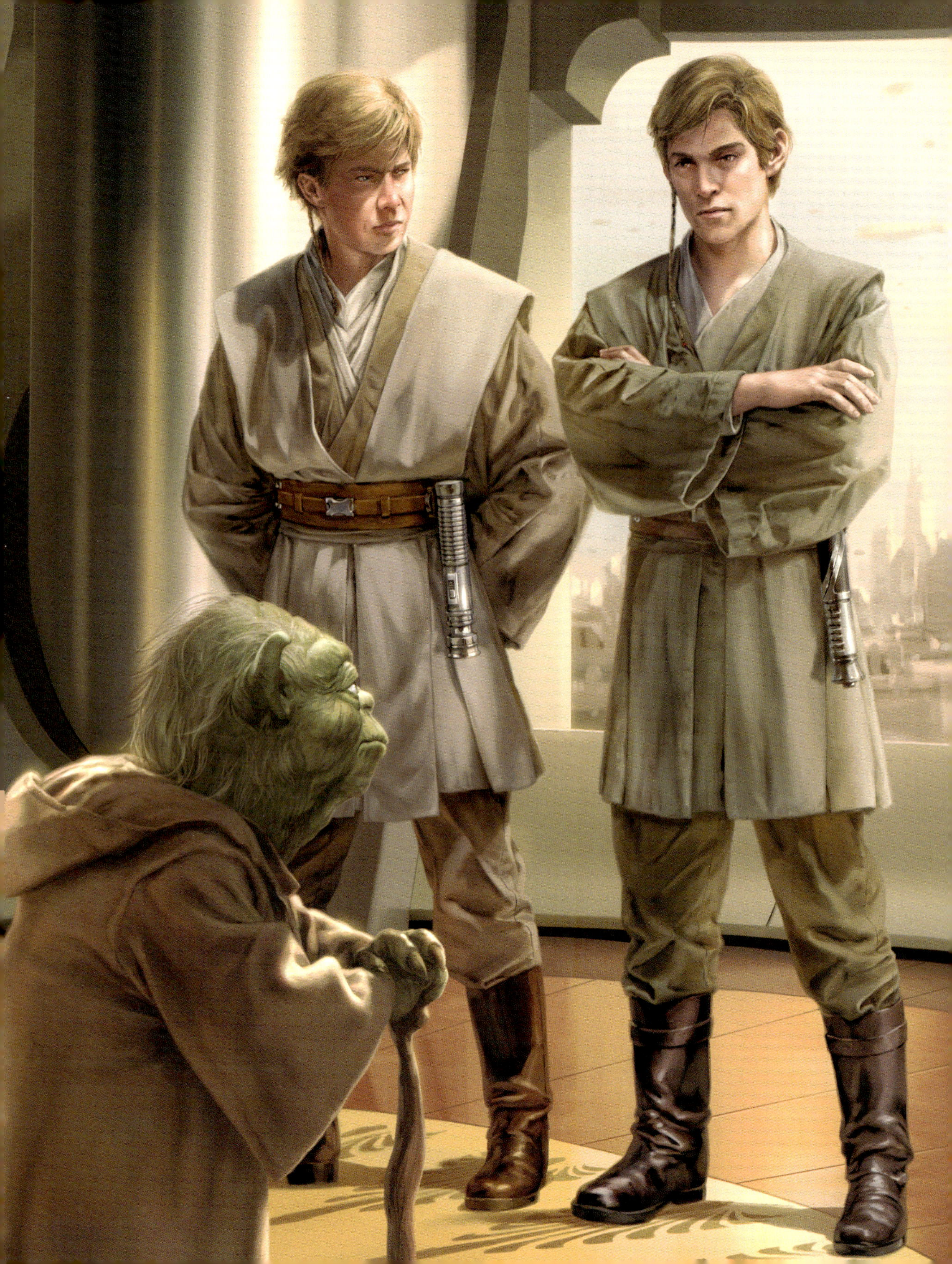

THE CESTUS DECEPTION

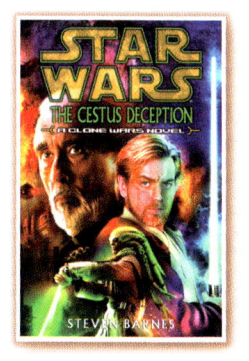

AUTHOR · Steven Barnes

COVER ARTIST · Steven D. Anderson

PUBLICATION HISTORY ·
Novel, Del Rey Books
· Hardcover, June 2004
· Paperback, March 2005

TIME LINE PLACEMENT ·
c. 22 BBY

WORLDS VISITED · Coruscant [L-9]; Ord Cestus [O-6]; Vandor-3 [L-9]

MAIN CHARACTERS · Obi-Wan Kenobi, Jedi Knight (human male); Kit Fisto, Jedi Knight (Nautolan male); G'Mai Duris, regent (X'Ting female); Nate/Jangotat, ARC trooper (human male); Sheeka Tull, pilot (human female); Doolb Snoil, barrister (Vippit male); Asajj Ventress, Separatist commander (Dathomirian female)

SUMMARY · Reports reach Coruscant that the Cestus Corporation has agreed to supply the Separatists with combat droids. Though JK-series droids—as in "Jedi Killer"—had been successfully exported as security units, weaponizing them for use in the Clone Wars would prove a grave threat to the Jedi. JK droids possess a degree of Force sensitivity due to a unique living component—a Dashta eel.

Obi-Wan Kenobi and barrister Doolb Snoil seek a diplomatic solution to secure Ord Cestus's alliance through the world's regent, G'Mai Duris. Though she is the nominal leader the planet's insectoid species the X'Ting, her power is checked by the Five Families, rulers of Cestus Corporation. Meanwhile, Kit Fisto and a team of clone commandos rally the tattered remains of a resistance group called Desert Wind. Fisto and the Desert Wind raiders ambush a train carrying the Five Families leadership as part of a ruse to force those leaders to reconsider their neutrality. Obi-Wan thwarts the faked attack, but his efforts are undone when Asajj Ventress supplies proof of the deception to the Five Families. Ventress then launches a droid attack on the Desert Wind camps in the Dashta Mountains, killing many rebels and Doolb Snoil.

ARC trooper Nate is wounded in the droid attack, but recovers in the secret Zantay Caves with the tender help of a local pilot, Sheeka Tull. Through the course of the Cestus operation, Nate and Sheeka fall in love. She is a former lover of Jango Fett, and seeing Nate rekindles confusing emotions in her. In Sheeka's presence, Nate aspires to be more than his defined role as an ARC trooper. He adopts a more personalized name, Jangotat, which literally means "brother of Jango." As Jangotat recovers in the presence of the Dashta eels, he learns their truth. The creatures are sentient and benevolent. They have donated nonsentient offspring to the Cestians for the development of nonlethal security droids—it is against their nature to inflict mortal injuries, and thus their use in war droids would be an impossibility.

The situation on Cestus grows dire. With no alliance secured, a Republic task force is en route to bombard the planet as a contingency. The ultimate goal of the Separatists was to force the Republic into such destructive action. A desperate Obi-Wan and Kit Fisto return to the city to salvage the situation, but must engage Ventress in a duel. Jangotat, meanwhile, disobeys an order and infiltrates the Five Families' bunker, calling in a precise orbital strike at his location. Jangotat's sacrifice supersedes the planned wide-scale planetary bombardment, destroys the Five Families, and returns rule of the planet to the X'Ting. Sheeka Tull is left to mourn Jangotat, and carries his child.

Two headstrong Padawan learners, Lorian Nod and young Dooku, stand before the wise Jedi Master Yoda.

THE CLONE WARS

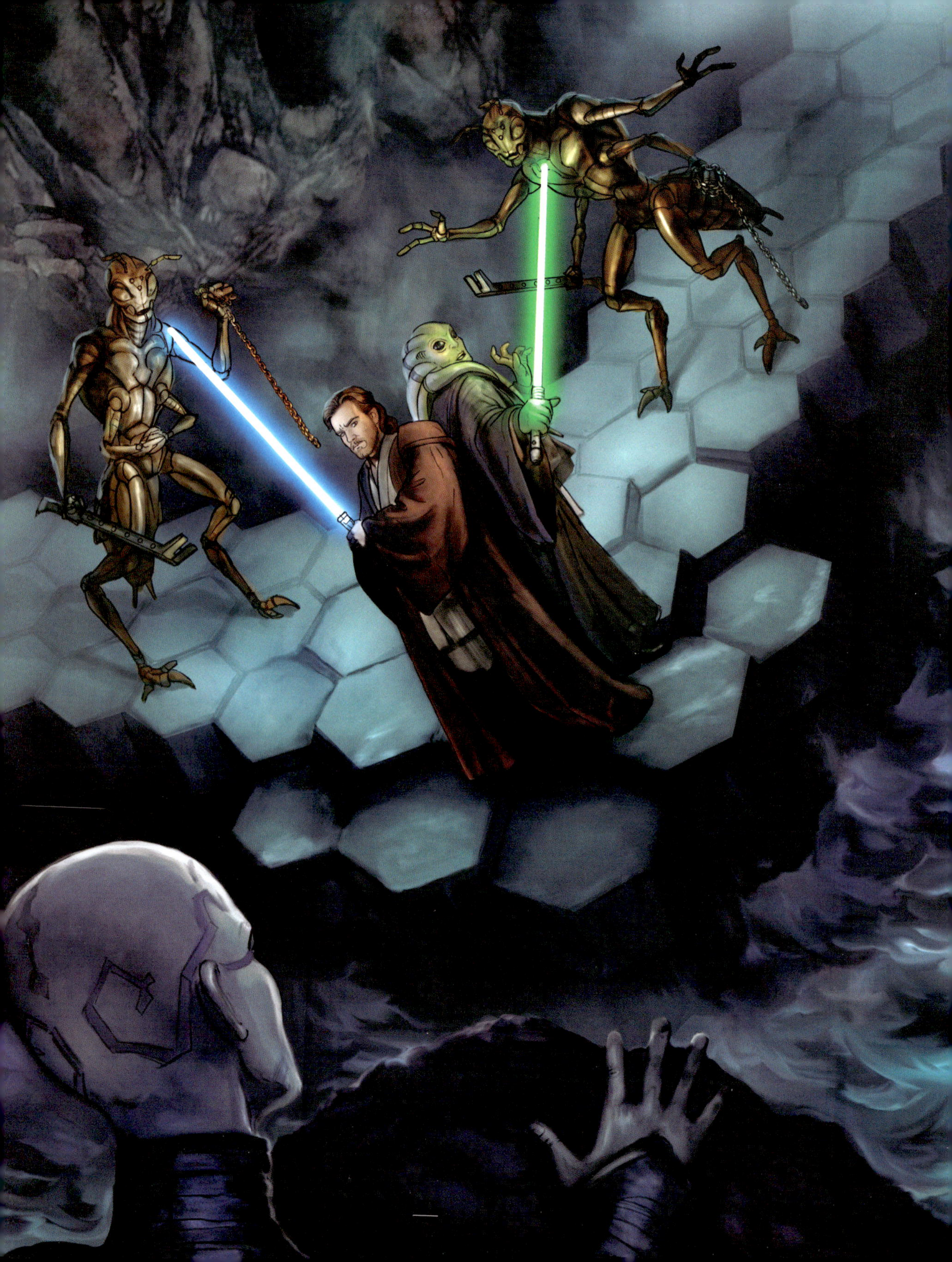

SHORT STORY — *The Hive*

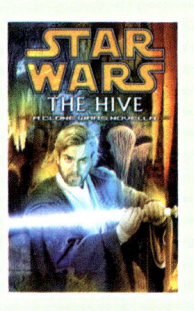

Published in conjunction with *The Cestus Deception*, the eBook novella *The Hive*, also by author Steven Barnes with cover art by Steven D. Anderson, takes place during the events of the novel. In it, Obi-Wan Kenobi and an X'Ting guide, Jesson Di Blinth, spelunk into the depths of an abandoned X'Ting hive, past ancient booby traps, to uncover royal eggs that could return authority to the insectoid X'Ting species. "The Hive" was included in the paperback edition of *The Cestus Deception*.

Readers attempting to be as inclusive as possible with the details of the text will experience some time line problems with *The Cestus Deception*. First, Anakin Skywalker's brief appearance at the start of the novel describes him as a Padawan, which means this book must occur within four weeks of the Battle of Geonosis, and not twelve months after, as originally presented.

In the novel, Obi-Wan notes that a clone has never before disobeyed orders. This is contradicted in the *Clone Wars* episode "The Hidden Enemy," which includes a clone traitor.

The name of memorable character Doolb Snoil is *Lion's Blood* spelled backward, the title of a non–*Star Wars* novel by author Steven Barnes.

"CHANGING SEASONS"

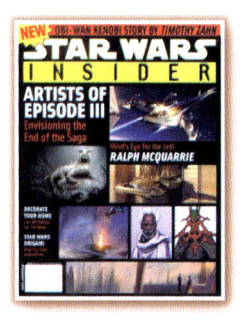

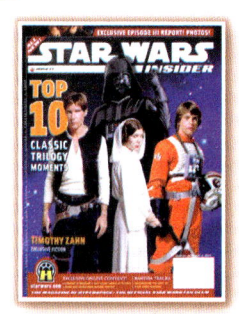

AUTHOR · Timothy Zahn

PUBLICATION HISTORY · Serialized short story, Paizo Publishing/IDG Entertainment · *Star Wars Insider* #76–77, June–September 2004

TIME LINE PLACEMENT · c. 22 BBY

WORLD VISITED · Dagro [P-7]

MAIN CHARACTERS · Obi-Wan Kenobi, Jedi Knight (human male); Anakin Skywalker, Padawan learner (human male); Kirlan Swens, farmer (human male); Fivvic, Republic task force commander (Barabel male)

SUMMARY · Obi-Wan Kenobi and Anakin Skywalker uncover a Separatist droid factory on Dagro that specializes in experimental anti-city terror droid deployers called crawl carriers. After scuttling the facility, the Jedi destroy the last of the carriers with the help of local farmers.

Though the story was originally set two years after the Battle of Geonosis, Anakin's portrayal as a Padawan requires it to occur within the first four weeks of the Clone Wars.

The wicked Asajj Ventress sends a pair of X'Ting thugs to do battle with Obi-Wan Kenobi and Kit Fisto.

THE CLONE WARS

SECRETS OF THE JEDI

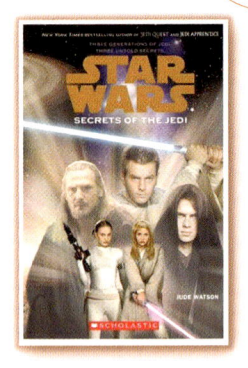

AUTHOR · Jude Watson
COVER ARTISTS · David Mattingly
PUBLICATION HISTORY · Juvenile novel, Scholastic Inc. · Hardcover, March 2005 Collected with *Legacy of the Jedi* into single omnibus · Paperback, May 2006
TIME LINE PLACEMENT · 39 BBY (part 1); c. 22 BBY (part 2)
WORLDS VISITED · Azure [P-8]; Cirrus [J-6]; Coruscant [L-9]; Genian [P-10]; Haven (spaceport moon) [J-6]; Quadrant Seven [J-6]; Rondai 2 [J-8]
MAIN CHARACTERS · Obi-Wan Kenobi, Jedi Knight (human male); Qui-Gon Jinn, Jedi Master (human male); Anakin Skywalker, Padawan learner (human male); Adi Gallia, Jedi Master (Tholothan female); Talesan Fry, industrialist (human male); Siri Tachi, Jedi Knight (human female); Padmé Amidala, Galactic Senator (human female); Magus, bounty hunter (human male)
SUMMARY · THE PAST: Talesan Fry, a young technology whiz, has intercepted a message revealing that twenty planetary leaders are being targeted for assassination by bounty hunters hired by the Corporate Alliance. The Jedi Council sends the team of Masters Qui-Gon Jinn and Adi Gallia, and their respective Padawans Obi-Wan Kenobi and Siri Tachi, to protect young Fry. Although the Jedi are able to thwart the assault, they are unable to stop the vengeful bounty hunter Magus from killing Fry's parents in retribution.

During the course of the assignment, Obi-Wan and Siri discover their deep love for each other, but they refuse to break the Jedi Code, and are forced to turn their backs on their feelings.

THE PRESENT: Years later, during the Clone Wars, Talesan Fry emerges as a leading technological innovator and the mastermind behind Fry Industries. He develops a powerful code breaker that he offers to sell to the Republic in exchange for a lucrative military contract. Obi-Wan Kenobi, his Padawan Anakin Skywalker, Siri Tachi, and Senator Padmé Amidala venture to Genian to broker the deal.

After ferreting out a Separatist spy from within the company, the Jedi bring Fry to a secret Republic outpost on Azure to activate his code-breaking device. The device has been secretly rigged with a tracker that alerts the Separatist fleet to their whereabouts. Among the Separatists is Magus, who once again guns for Fry. In a wildly dangerous attack, Siri Tachi leaps from her starfighter onto Magus's vessel during an aerial pursuit and downs the hunter's vessel. The Jedi capture Magus, but Siri tragically dies from blaster wounds suffered at his hands. The Republic has no choice but to destroy the code breaker, lest it fall into Separatist hands.

When the Prequel Trilogy was in production, the editors at Lucasfilm restricted authors from including Padmé Amidala in the spin-off fiction, particularly in the period between Episodes II and III, as her pregnancy was not yet known to many beyond George Lucas. As such, her appearance here in *Secrets of the Jedi* is a rare exception. Padmé would be more routinely featured in Clone Wars material published after the launch of the animated series in 2008.

Among the bounty hunters in Magus's posse is Gorm the Dissolver, a cyborg first created as a background character in Dark Horse Comics' *Dark Empire* series (1991–92).

The story was originally dated as occurring at twenty-nine months—over two years—after the start of the Clone Wars, but since Anakin is presented as a Padawan, it must occur within the first four weeks of the war. Early published time lines list this book as *Jedi Quest Special Edition*, which was a placeholder title.

The book features the appearance of a non-Jedi Republic general named Solomahal, who was an original *A New Hope* (1977) cantina alien once known only as "The Colonel." The 1996 customizable card game from Decipher, Inc., gave the character his name and revealed that he was a Clone Wars veteran. *Secrets of the Jedi* shrinks the scope of character connections by revealing that Obi-Wan Kenobi had previously worked with Solomahal, meaning he was in the cantina with a fellow veteran during the events of the original *Star Wars*.

JEDI TRIAL

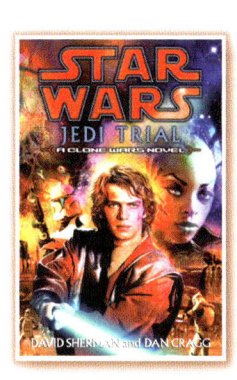

AUTHORS · David Sherman and Dan Cragg

COVER ARTIST · Steven D. Anderson

PUBLICATION HISTORY · Novel, Del Rey Books
- Hardcover, October 2004
- Paperback, May 2005

TIME LINE PLACEMENT · c. 22 BBY

WORLDS VISITED · Coruscant [L-9]; Praesitlyn [M-19]

MAIN CHARACTERS · Anakin Skywalker, Padawan learner (human male); Nejaa Halcyon, Jedi Master (human male); Zozridor Slayke, Freedom's Sons and Daughters commander (human male); Odie Subu, scout (human female); Erk H'Arman, pilot (human male); Pors Tonith, Separatist admiral (Muun male); Grudo, mercenary (Rodian male); Reija Momen, communications center administrator (human female)

SUMMARY · A massive droid army led by the evil Admiral Tonith invades Praesitlyn, site of a vital Republic communications center. The Separatist forces decimate the local defenses, turning scout Odie Subu and pilot Erk H'Arman into survivors who must band together to withstand the harsh deserts of the planet. On their grueling trek back to a command outpost, they forge a bond of trust and love.

Tonith captures the communications center, taking the staff hostage. The strained Republic military responds with a task force commanded by General Nejaa Halcyon and Anakin Skywalker, bolstered by the private military force known as Freedom's Sons and Daughters, led by Zozridor Slayke. Slayke and Halcyon have a tangled history together, as Halcyon failed to bring in the privateer captain during Slayke's unauthorized attacks against the Separatists prior to the start of the Clone Wars. Despite this rivalry, they maintain a mutual respect. Anakin also bonds with Halcyon, for the Padawan and the unorthodox Corellian Jedi have a shared secret: each has a wife despite the Jedi Order forbidding marriage.

The campaign to retake the communications center succeeds, with the hostages rescued and Tonith defeated, but it is not easy. Anakin once again skirts the dark side of the Force while engaged in the intense ground battle. In the final attack against an orbiting Separatist battleship, Skywalker survives a near-suicidal run by jumping his modified

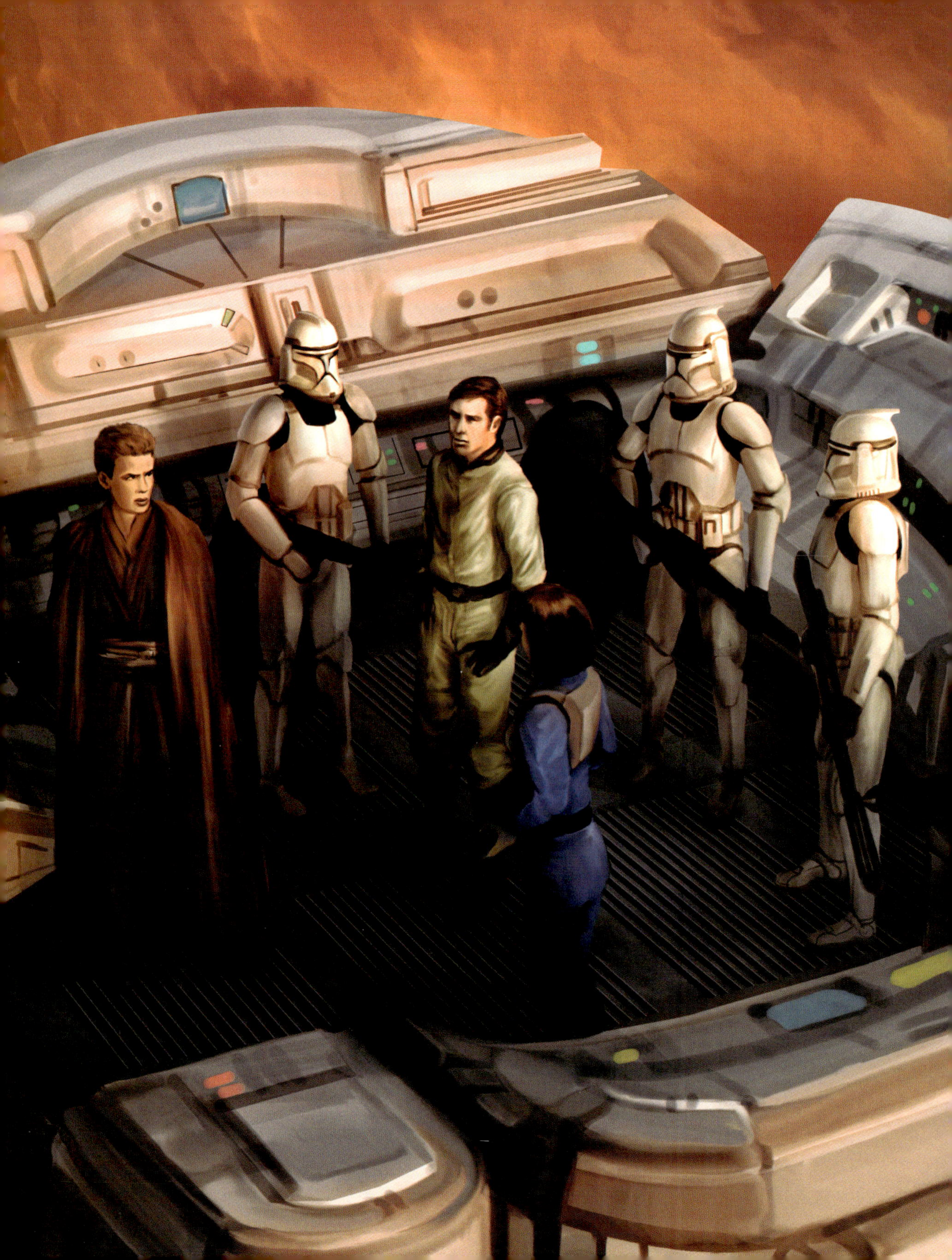

fighter into hyperspace before the Separatist ship explodes.

For his valor, Anakin is promoted to the rank of full Jedi Knight by the Jedi Council, and thus general in the Republic army. One of his first acts with this elevated authority is to preside over the marriage of Odie and Erk.

Jedi Trial was originally set thirty months after the Battle of Geonosis, a mere six months before the end of the Clone Wars. The new time line established by *The Clone Wars* animated series makes it clear that Anakin was Knighted near the start of the war. This tale therefore must occur within the first four weeks of the conflict. This change fits with Nejaa Halcyon's relationship with Slayke—Halcyon's prewar pursuit of Slayke is more of a fresh memory for the Jedi rather than an event nearly three years past.

Much of the setting for *Jedi Trial* is pieced together from earlier Expanded Universe material. Praesitlyn and its communications center were first mentioned in *Heir to the Empire* (1991), while Nejaa Halcyon was first introduced as part of Corran Horn's backstory from X-Wing: *Rogue Squadron* (1996). Freedom's Sons and Daughters is a very old reference to a glancing mention of Freedom's Sons in *Han Solo at Stars' End* (1979).

THE CLONE WARS

AUTHORS · Karen Traviss (adult novel); Tracey West (juvenile novel); based on the movie *Star Wars: The Clone Wars*

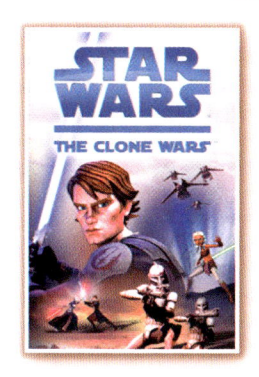

COVER ARTISTS · John VanFleet (adult novel); Lucasfilm (juvenile novel)

PUBLICATION HISTORY · Adult novel, Del Rey Books
· Hardcover, July 2008
Juvenile novel, Grosset & Dunlap
· Paperback, July 2008

TIME LINE PLACEMENT · 22 BBY

WORLDS VISITED · Christophsis [Q-16]; Coruscant [L-9]; Kem Stor Ai* [Q-7]; Tatooine [R-16]; Teth [U-12]

MAIN CHARACTERS · Anakin Skywalker, Jedi Knight (human male); Ahsoka Tano, Padawan learner (Togruta female); Obi-Wan Kenobi, Jedi Knight (human male); Rex, clone trooper captain (human male); Asajj Ventress, assassin (Dathomirian female); Rotta, child (Hutt); Jabba, crime lord (Hutt); Ziro, criminal (Hutt); Padmé Amidala, Galactic Senator (human female); Palpatine, Supreme Chancellor (human male)

SUMMARY · After triumphing at the Battle of Christophsis, General Anakin Skywalker is surprised to be assigned a Padawan learner, the spirited Togruta girl Ahsoka Tano. In order for the Republic to curry favor with the Hutts and gain access to their hyperspace routes throughout the Outer Rim, Anakin and Ahsoka are tasked with rescuing Jabba the Hutt's

*Adult novel only.

In a Republic command center on Praesitlyn, Anakin Skywalker commands Erk H'Arman and Odie Subu, for whom he will perform marriage services in a rare moment of calm in the Clone Wars.

THE CLONE WARS 91

infant son, Rotta. The squirming Huttlet has been kidnapped and left in an abandoned monastery on Teth. The kidnapping was engineered by Count Dooku and Asajj Ventress to discredit the Republic in the eyes of the Hutts, but Anakin and Ahsoka persevere and safely deliver the child to Jabba on Tatooine. Meanwhile, Padmé Amidala discovers that Jabba's uncle Ziro conspired with the Separatists in the kidnapping plot in a bid for power.

THE ANIMATED MOVIE *The Clone Wars* served as a big-screen introduction to the television series. In addition to the adult and junior novels, there were also young reader storybooks and activity books based on the movie's plot.

The novels are listed as "based on the movie," yet unlike other movie novelizations, they do not list screenwriting credits. *The Clone Wars* movie was actually built out of four episodes—"The New Padawan," "Castle of Deception," "Castle of Salva-

SPOTLIGHT | The Clone Wars Adaptations

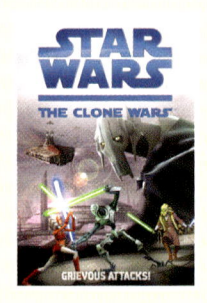

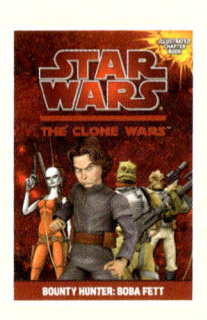

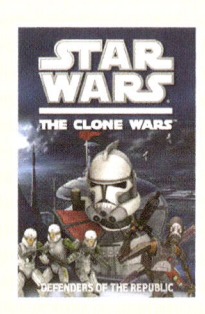

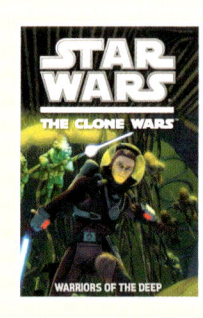

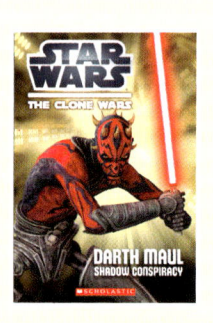

With so many new young fans introduced to *Star Wars* via the weekly animated adventures of *The Clone Wars* series, Grosset & Dunlap (part of The Penguin Group) began adapting episodes into young reader novelizations. The brief running time of each episode (about twenty-two minutes) meant that these adaptations appeared in anthologies, and like the series itself occupy a span of the overall time line.

The Clone Wars: Grievous Attacks! (2009). By Veronica Wasserman, Tracey West, and Rob Valois. Adapting the episodes "Rookies," "Downfall of a Droid," and "Lair of Grievous."

The Clone Wars: Bounty Hunter: Boba Fett (2010). By Jason Fry. Adapting the episodes "Death Trap," "R2 Come Home," and "Lethal Trackdown."

The Clone Wars: Defenders of the Republic (2010). By Rob Valois. Adapting the episodes "Clone Cadets," "Rookies," and "ARC Troopers."

The Clone Wars: Warriors of the Deep (2011). By Rob Valois. Adapting the episodes "Water War," "Gungan Attack," and "Prisoners."

The Clone Wars: Darth Maul: Shadow Conspiracy (2013). By Jason Fry. Adapting the episodes "Revival," "Eminence," "Shades of Reason," and "The Lawless" (from Scholastic Inc.).

tion," and "Castle of Doom"—which have never aired in their original formats. Writing credits go to Henry Gilroy, Scott Murphy, and Steven Melching.

As a note of caution for chronological readers, Karen Traviss's novel depicts Darth Sidious's double identity in the open, under the assumption that this secret was exposed in *Star Wars*: Episode III *Revenge of the Sith* (2005). The adult novelization includes many more Expanded Universe connections than the junior novelization or the movie itself. Traviss's text makes repeated mention of Asajj Ventress's original EU backstory as told in the *Star Wars: Republic* comics, as well as an incident in Dooku's past on Galidraan from the *Jango Fett: Open Seasons* (2002) comics.

A brief mention of the conflict on Jabiim in the adult novel refers to *Star Wars: Republic* comics #55–58 (2003). The Battle of Jabiim was originally listed as occurring fifteen months after the start of the Clone Wars, and chronicled a pivotal experience of Anakin as a Padawan. The animated series, however, begins with Anakin already Knighted, thus compressing all of his apprentice adventures into the first four weeks of the Clone Wars. The Battle of Jabiim may have still occurred in Expanded Universe continuity, but it must have occurred months earlier than originally presented in the time line.

The young reader book suggests that the usual age to become a Padawan is sixteen, and that Ahsoka, at fourteen, is remarkably young for apprenticeship. This runs counter to the Jedi Apprentice series, which states that a youngling needs to become an apprentice before age thirteen.

"STAR WARS: THE CLONE WARS: OUT FOXED"

AUTHOR · Rob Valois

PUBLICATION HISTORY · Short story, Grosset & Dunlap · Published online at Target.com, July 2008

TIME LINE PLACEMENT · 22 BBY

WORLDS VISITED · Coruscant [L-9]

MAIN CHARACTERS · Clone Commander Fox, clone trooper (human male); T'doshok, bounty hunter (Trandoshan male)

SUMMARY · Clone Commander Fox of the Coruscant Guard, protector of the Galactic Republic's most important officials, stops a Trandoshan bounty hunter before he kidnaps a Senator.

THE CLONE WARS: SECRET MISSIONS

SECRET MISSIONS #1: BREAKOUT SQUAD · SECRET MISSIONS #2: CURSE OF THE BLACK HOLE PIRATES · SECRET MISSIONS #3: DUEL AT SHATTERED ROCK · SECRET MISSIONS #4: GUARDIANS OF THE CHISS KEY

AUTHOR · Ryder Windham

COVER ARTISTS · Wayne Lo, with Tara Rueping (colors, cover #4)

PUBLICATION HISTORY · Juvenile novels, Grosset & Dunlap · Paperback, September 2009 (book 1), July 2010 (book 2), March 2011 (book 3), March 2012 (book 4)

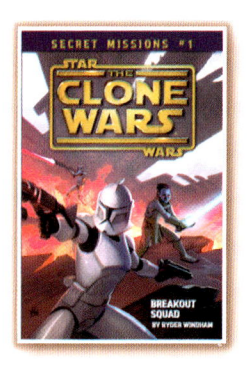

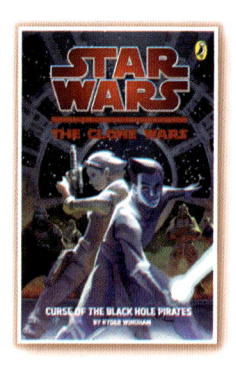

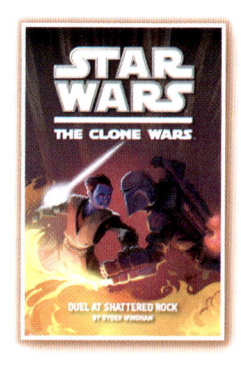

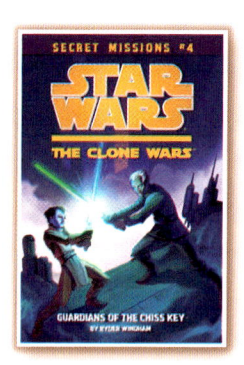

TIME LINE PLACEMENT · 22 BBY (with a flashback to 33 BBY)

WORLDS VISITED · Antar (moon) [N-12]; Bilbringi [J-8]; Bogden (moons) [M-8]; Coruscant [L-9]; Kynachi [J-5]; Plunder Moon [G-8]; Vaced [J-7]

MAIN CHARACTERS · Nuru Kungurama, Padawan learner (Chiss male); Ring-Sol Ambase, Jedi Master (Kynachi male); Breaker, Chatterbox, Knuckles, Sharp: Breakout Squad clone troopers (human males); Cleaver, reprogrammed commando droid; Gizman, aka "Big Gizz," swoop pilot (Moggonite half-breed male); Cad Bane, bounty hunter (Duros male); Lalo Gunn, smuggler (human female); Count Dooku, Separatist leader (human male); Aristocra "Veeren" Sev'eere'nuruodo, diplomatic envoy (Chiss female)

SUMMARY · The discovery of Kynachi technology amid the wreckage of a Separatist warship leads Chancellor Palpatine to send Jedi Master Ring-Sol Ambase and his team of clones to the distant and unallied planet Kynachi. Though Master Ambase instructs his Padawan Nuru Kungurama to stay behind, the impetuous boy is driven by visions of his Master in danger and sneaks aboard the departing vessel. The Trade Federation and the Techno Union have established a blockade around Kynachi and their picket vessels blast Ambase's vessel from orbit. Nuru and the clones, also known as Breakout Squad, escape in life-pods, but are separated from Master Ambase. Unbeknownst to Nuru, the wily bounty hunter Cad Bane captures Ambase and delivers him to Count Dooku on Bogden. Nuru and the clones leave Kynachi with the help of smuggler Lalo Gunn and her ship, *Hasty Harpy*.

Palpatine assigns Nuru and Breakout Squad to meet with a Chiss diplomatic envoy. Desperate to escape a sudden Separatist attack, the clones bring the Chiss envoy, Aristocra Veeren, with them as they flee into hyperspace. The *Harpy* emerges near a black hole and is met by pirates who are likewise stranded in this area of space. Together, they uncover an ancient alien transdimensional device that enables them to return to Republic space.

The Chancellor then assigns Breakout Squad to protect a Kynachi diplomat who intends to ally his world with the Republic. Nuru and the squad—aided by a burly swoop rider called Big Gizz—narrowly save the diplomat's life from an assassination attempt by a Mandalorian sniper.

The Sith Lords Count Dooku and Darth Sidious are masterminding a plot to make Master Ambase doubt the intentions and allegiance of his apprentice. Dooku, once a close friend to Ambase, was with him eleven years earlier when they found the alien life-pod that carried the infant Nuru.

THE CLONE WARS

Now, Dooku tells Ambase that a vital discovery has been made in the pod by Jedi researchers. Following separate threads planted by the Sith, Ambase and Nuru rush to Coruscant to secure the pod. The Sith Lords, working through agents and intermediaries, have caused Ambase and Nuru to distrust one another's motives. Ambase arrives at the research laboratory first and steals the pod to keep Nuru from reaching it. In trying to stop Ambase, Nuru cripples his Master's ship, causing the vessel to crash and destroy the pod.

Ambase, confused by Dooku's deception, engages Nuru in a lightsaber duel, but the young Chiss is able to see that his Master has been tricked. The depths of the ruse become clear when one of the clones of Breakout Squad proves to be a Clawdite imposter and saboteur. Ambase eventually sees the light, but decides to leave the Jedi Order, acknowledging that his convictions are too easily swayed in the fog of war. Nuru, though without a Master, continues to serve as a special operative during the Clone Wars, leading Breakout Squad on secret missions.

THE FIRST BOOK BEGINS right after the three-part *Malevolence* story arc from the start of *The Clone Wars* animated series (2008), while a mention by Count Dooku of Weequay pirates in the fourth book suggests it occurs shortly after the first season episode "Dooku Captured." Written by Ryder Windham, a longtime contributor to Expanded Universe fiction, Secret Missions include references to many longstanding EU elements. Examples include the Kwa Star Temples from the Dark Horse Comics series *Star Wars: Infinity's End* (2000–2001), the Black Hole Pirates from the original Marvel run of the *Star Wars* comics, and the swoop brute Big Gizz, who was developed for *Shadows of the Empire* (1996).

In addition to these four books, Nuru also appeared in the Dark Horse Comics story *The Clone Wars: "Strange Allies"* (2011), written by Windham with pencils by Ben Dewey.

THE CLONE WARS: WILD SPACE

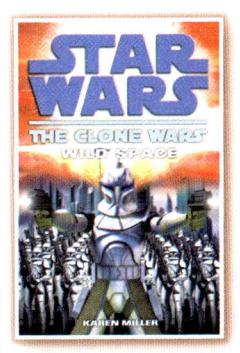

AUTHOR · Karen Miller
COVER ARTIST · Lucasfilm
PUBLICATION HISTORY ·
Novel, Del Rey Books
· Trade paperback, December 2008
TIME LINE PLACEMENT · 22 BBY
WORLDS VISITED · Atzerri (system) [M-13]; Coruscant [L-9]; Geonosis (flashback) [R-16]; Munto Codru (system) [T-6]; Zigoola [U-6]
MAIN CHARACTERS · Obi-Wan Kenobi, Jedi Knight (human male); Bail Organa, Galactic Senator (human male); Yoda, Jedi Master (alien male); Anakin Skywalker, Jedi Knight (human male); Ahsoka Tano, Padawan learner (Togruta female); Padmé Amidala, Galactic Senator (human female); Palpatine, Supreme Chancellor (human male); Vokara Che, Jedi healer (Twi'lek female)
SUMMARY · The Republic stands on edge after an explosive terrorist strike at the heart of Coruscant. Jedi Knight Obi-Wan Kenobi is gravely injured in the blast, but not before securing a fragment of key intelligence from his informant, Dexter Jettster: General

Grievous is about to target the Bothan spy network. Convalescing, Obi-Wan cannot act on this information, so the Jedi Council assigns Anakin Skywalker and his Padawan Ahsoka Tano to lead a task force to Bothawui.

As Obi-Wan recuperates, Darth Sidious sees the Jedi Knight as a growing threat to his plans. Using a densely layered array of anonymous contacts, Sidious sends a message to Senator Bail Organa, a cryptic warning that the Sith intend to strike. This leads Bail and a recovered Obi-Wan on a quest to find out more about the Sith. Their lengthy journey takes them deep into uncharted Wild Space, to a barren planet, Zigoola, site of an ancient Sith Temple.

There Obi-Wan is overwhelmed by terrifying visions broadcast telepathically into his mind by a Sith

Senator Bail Organa carries an ailing Obi-Wan Kenobi across the blighted surface of Zigoola.

Holocron. Believing Obi-Wan would surely lose his sanity, Sidious underestimates Bail and Obi-Wan's ability to look past their differences and forge a true friendship. It is this bond that allows them to persevere, and Bail helps Obi-Wan keep his strength and destroy the Sith artifact. When Bail and Obi-Wan return to Coruscant, Sidious is dismayed that they have survived.

THE STORY OF *Wild Space* begins right after the events of Episode II (2002), and describes several noteworthy moments of character history: Anakin discovering that his arm has been amputated

THE CLONE WARS

and Obi-Wan suspecting and confronting Padmé about her relationship with Anakin. Following these early chapters, the novel jumps ahead seven weeks, after the events of *The Clone Wars* feature film (2008). It is this specific gap of time that necessitates the compression of time for all of Anakin's Padawan Clone Wars stories from before the animated series.

Anakin's mission to stop General Grievous at Bothawui is from *The Clone Wars* episodes "Downfall of a Droid" and "Duel of the Droids," meaning the *Wild Space* story is what Obi-Wan Kenobi was doing offscreen at the time. Based on the production order of Season One episodes, *Wild Space* assumes that the Bothawui mission happens soon after the events of the movie—the missions on Christophsis and Teth. But in the series time line, the "hunt for *Malevolence*" story arc takes place *before* Bothawui.

This gets tricky since Anakin is specifically given command of the *Resolute* in *Wild Space*, a vessel he commands in the *Malevolence* episodes. Further complicating matters is the *Resolute*'s involvement at Christophsis prior to the feature, under Anakin's command.

Another continuity hiccup: the explosion on Coruscant is at odds with the Season Three episode "Heroes on Both Sides," which makes it clear that the capital world has not been attacked in a thousand years.

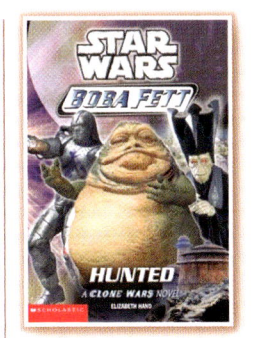

TIME LINE PLACEMENT · 22 BBY

WORLD VISITED · Tatooine [R-16]

MAIN CHARACTERS · Boba Fett, fugitive (human male); Durge, bounty hunter (Gen'Dai male); Gilramos Libkath, exile (Neimoidian male); Jabba, crime lord (Hutt); Ygabba, urchin (human female); Gab'borah Hise, dessert chef (human male)

SUMMARY · Eager to prove himself as a bounty hunter, Boba Fett hires out his services to Jabba the Hutt on Tatooine. The amused gangster tasks him with bringing in Neimoidian exile Gilramos Libkath. Fett competes against the ancient hunter Durge for this quarry, but succeeds in eliminating Libkath, thus freeing a group of street urchins held in thrall by the Neimoidian.

This book is the sole prose appearance of Durge, a character created for the Clone Wars comic stories published by Dark Horse in 2003. Durge would also appear in the *Clone Wars* animated micro-series in 2003.

BOBA FETT #4: HUNTED

AUTHOR · Elizabeth Hand
COVER ARTIST · Peter Bollinger
PUBLICATION HISTORY · Juvenile novel, Scholastic Inc.
· Paperback, October 2003

"THE PENGALAN TRADE-OFF"

AUTHOR · Aaron Allston
PUBLICATION HISTORY ·
Short story, Paizo Publishing
· *Star Wars Insider* #65, February 2003

TIME LINE PLACEMENT · 22 BBY

WORLD VISITED · Pengalan IV [O-8]

MAIN CHARACTERS · Joram Kithe, Republic bureaucrat/inspector (human male); Tooth, Mapper, Digger, Spots: clone troopers (human males)

SUMMARY · Their gunship shot down during an escape from a Separatist trap on Pengalan IV, Joram Kith and his squad of clone troopers crash-land in the wilderness. Joram, a self-admitted coward, takes the initiative to lead his clones to a nearby city, where they discover a secret weapons plant that they must destroy.

"THE LEAGUE OF SPIES"

AUTHOR · Aaron Allston

PUBLICATION HISTORY · Short story, Paizo Publishing · *Star Wars Insider* #73, February 2004

TIME LINE PLACEMENT · 22 BBY

WORLD VISITED · Tarhassan [O-11]

MAIN CHARACTERS · Joram Kithe, intelligence (human male); Mapper Gann, clone intelligence (human male)

SUMMARY · The sole Republic intelligence agent on the now-Separatist-allied world of Tarhassan has disappeared. Joram Kithe leads a bumbling group of bureaucrats-turned-spies to track him down and rescue him from a planetary security prison.

REPUBLIC COMMANDO: HARD CONTACT

AUTHOR · Karen Traviss

COVER ARTIST · Greg Knight

PUBLICATION HISTORY · Novel, Del Rey Books · Paperback, November 2004

TIME LINE PLACEMENT · 22 BBY

WORLDS VISITED · Geonosis (flashback) [R-16]; Ord Mantell [L-7]; Qiilura [L-7]

MAIN CHARACTERS · Darman, Niner, Atin, Fi: clone commandos (human males); Etain Tur-Mukan, Padawan learner (human female); Ovolot Qail Uthan, scientist (human female); Ghez Hokan, warlord (human male); Lik Ankkit, overseer (Neimoidian male)

SUMMARY · The Republic dispatches a newly assembled squad of clone commandos—Omega Squad—to the neutral world of Qiilura. Their objective is to destroy a Separatist laboratory developing a clone-killing nanovirus and capture the biotech expert who developed it, Ovolot Qail Uthan. During insertion, the squad's covert transport crashes, and clone commando Darman is separated from the others.

Darman makes contact with Padawan Etain Tur-Mukan. The Padawan and her master, Kast Fulier, were on assignment on Qiilura when Kast was killed by the local militia, she has been in hiding since his death. Etain is surprised to learn that the Republic now has a clone army and the Jedi are effectively tasked with serving as military leaders for this new force. Lacking confidence in her abilities, she learns many crucial survival skills by working with Darman, forging a strong bond with him.

Padawan Etain Tur-Mukan is wary upon first meeting clone commando Darman in the wilderness of Qiilura as he hands her her dropped lightsaber.

THE CLONE WARS

Darman reunites with his squad, and the team receives help from two shapeshifting Gurlanin natives named Jinart and Valaquil. Together, this small group of special operatives takes on an enemy target with much larger numbers: a Separatist laboratory protected by battle droids and hired guns commanded by the Mandalorian mercenary Ghez Hokan. The clones succeed, though Atin is wounded during extraction. Etain refuses to leave her troops behind despite orders from arriving Jedi Master Arligan Zey. Etain recognizes that she is developing a strong emotional attachment to the commandos, particularly to Darman. After successful extraction from Qiilura, Etain opts to stay on the planet to help keep the world free of Separatist control, though she finds parting from Darman to be a true test of her Jedi oaths.

H*ard Contact* is the first of four Republic Commando novels inspired by the videogame of the same name released by LucasArts in 2005. The game focuses on Delta Squad—a team of specialized commandos that operate as a quartet behind enemy lines. Though the novel instead spotlights Omega Squad, the feel of the missions, the squad tactics involved, and the equipment used are all directly tied to the game.

The **Republic Commando** videogame and tie-in novels built much upon a strong cultural connection among the clone commandos and Mandalorian warriors, something that would be downplayed in the animated series with the establishment of Mandalorian pacifists who have turned their back on their martial heritage. The *Clone Wars* TV series also brings into question whether Jango Fett was ever truly a Mandalorian.

However, there is still room for Mandalorian heritage among clones since the second-season episode "Clone Cadets" makes it clear that bounty hunters are involved in the training of clones. This is consistent with what is presented in the Republic Commando books: mercenaries with Mandalorian roots were involved in the training of the commandos specifically. The books, which focus on these commandos, are therefore steeped in Mandalorian lore, but these traditions weren't necessarily applicable across the entirety of the clone ranks.

"OMEGA SQUAD: TARGETS"

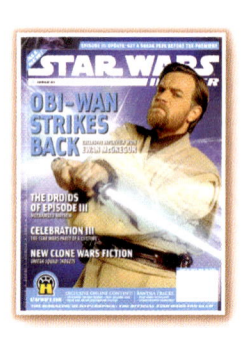

AUTHOR · Karen Traviss
PUBLICATION HISTORY · Short story, IDG Entertainment · *Star Wars Insider* #81, March 2005
Reprinted in Republic Commando: *Triple Zero* novel, Del Rey Books · Paperback, February 2006
TIME LINE PLACEMENT · 22 BBY
WORLDS VISITED · Coruscant [L-9]; Kamino (flashbacks) [S-15]
MAIN CHARACTERS · Fi, Darman, Atin, Niner, clone commandos (human males); Kal Skirata, mercenary (human male); Ordo, ARC trooper (human male); Meena Tills, Galactic Senator (Mon Calamari)

SUMMARY · The clone commandos of Omega Squad, advised by their former instructor Kal Skirata, are called upon to help settle a tense hostage crisis on Coruscant. Aided by Ordo, an ARC trooper also trained by Skirata, Omega Squad storms the building in which the terrorists are holding the hostages. In the course of the action and the chaos of the attack, Commando Atin is shaken at how readily he might have mistakenly killed Skirata based on his deeply embedded obedience to orders first and foremost.

Atin's shock is meant to foreshadow the clones' eventual carrying out of Order 66, regardless of their relationship with their commanding officers. In this story, Senator Meena Tills is male, though the fourth season of *The Clone Wars* would canonically establish her as female.

"STAR WARS INSIDER PRESENTS: DUEL"

AUTHOR · Timothy Zahn
PUBLICATION HISTORY · Short story, Paizo Publishing · *Hasbro Short Story Collection*, July 2003
TIME LINE PLACEMENT · 22 BBY
WORLD VISITED · Axion [P-10]
MAIN CHARACTERS · Yoda, Jedi Master (alien male); Brolis, clone commander (human male)
SUMMARY · Yoda engages in battle with a Hailfire droid, defeating the missile-firing automaton in order to rescue a stranded clone commander.

SHATTERPOINT

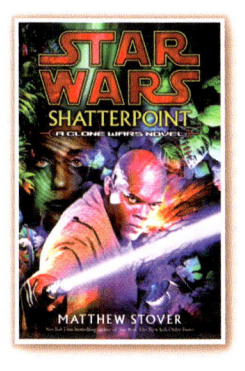

AUTHOR · Matthew Stover
COVER ARTIST · Steven D. Anderson
PUBLICATION HISTORY · Novel, Del Rey Books
· Hardcover, June 2003
· Paperback, May 2004
TIME LINE PLACEMENT · 22 BBY
WORLDS VISITED · Coruscant [L-9]; Haruun Kal [M-17]

MAIN CHARACTERS · Mace Windu, Jedi Master (human male); Nick Rostu, Korun guide (human male); Depa Billaba, Jedi Master (human female); Lorz Geptun, Balawai colonel (human male); Kar Vastor, *lor pelek* (human male)

SUMMARY · Mace Windu's homeworld of Haruun Kal is the site of a terribly violent seasonal civil war between native jungle dwellers—the Korunnai—and the Balawai colonists who seek to harvest valuable resources found there. The conflict is indiscriminate, often targeting innocents and turning children into victims or merciless soldiers. Early in the Clone Wars, Jedi Master Depa Billaba went to Haruun Kal to rally the natives to repulse the Separatist-leaning government, but there has been no communication with Depa for months. A disturbing holographic message of a Balawai slaughter suggests that Depa has lost her way and fallen to the dark side. Because Depa was his former Padawan, the mission to return to his home and find her is extremely personal for Mace, a Jedi who normally keeps a tight rein on his emotions.

Upon his arrival, Mace is almost instantly exposed to violence. One of Depa's followers, Nick Rostu, alongside Korun allies, leads Mace into the jungle on a lengthy and deadly trek to meet with Depa. Along the journey, Mace realizes that the raw savagery, merciless lethality, and insidious contagion of the jungle is the dark side of the Force given form. Its destructive impulses bleed into the psyche of those around it. The Korun, descended from ancient Jedi, have long tried to tame the wilderness, to push back its encroaching death, because that is what the Jedi do: they stand opposed to darkness.

During his journey, Mace keeps a journal of his innermost thoughts. He is troubled by Kar Vastor, a fierce shaman lieutenant loyal to Depa Billaba. Vastor is a cruel and deadly warrior, who makes no secret of his hatred for Mace. Vastor stills his instinct to kill Mace out of deference to Depa. When Mace arrives at the Korunnai camp, he is saddened to see how frayed Depa's sanity has become from her time on Haruun Kal. Mace places her under arrest for the atrocities carried out under her command.

Mace's flagship, *Halleck*, moves in to Haruun Kal to extract Mace and Depa, prompting a harried defense from Separatist droid fighters. The air battle spills over the cityscape of Pelek Baw, leading to much destruction. Hoping to end the conflict, Mace willingly surrenders to Colonel Lorz Geptun, leader of the local militia. This allows Mace to penetrate the control center in Pelek Baw, in a bid to destroy the computer controlling the starfighters. Geptun, tired of the carnage, ultimately helps Mace in this effort, but Vastor and Depa try to stop him. Influenced by the chaos of the dark side, they want the destruction to continue.

With Nick's help, Mace ultimately incapacitates Vastor. Depa, defeated and with her will broken, attempts suicide, but Mace stops her at great physical and mental cost. By destroying the droid control systems on Haruun Kal, Mace has eliminated any obstacles the Republic would face in controlling the world. Mace has brought an end to the civil war on Haruun Kal.

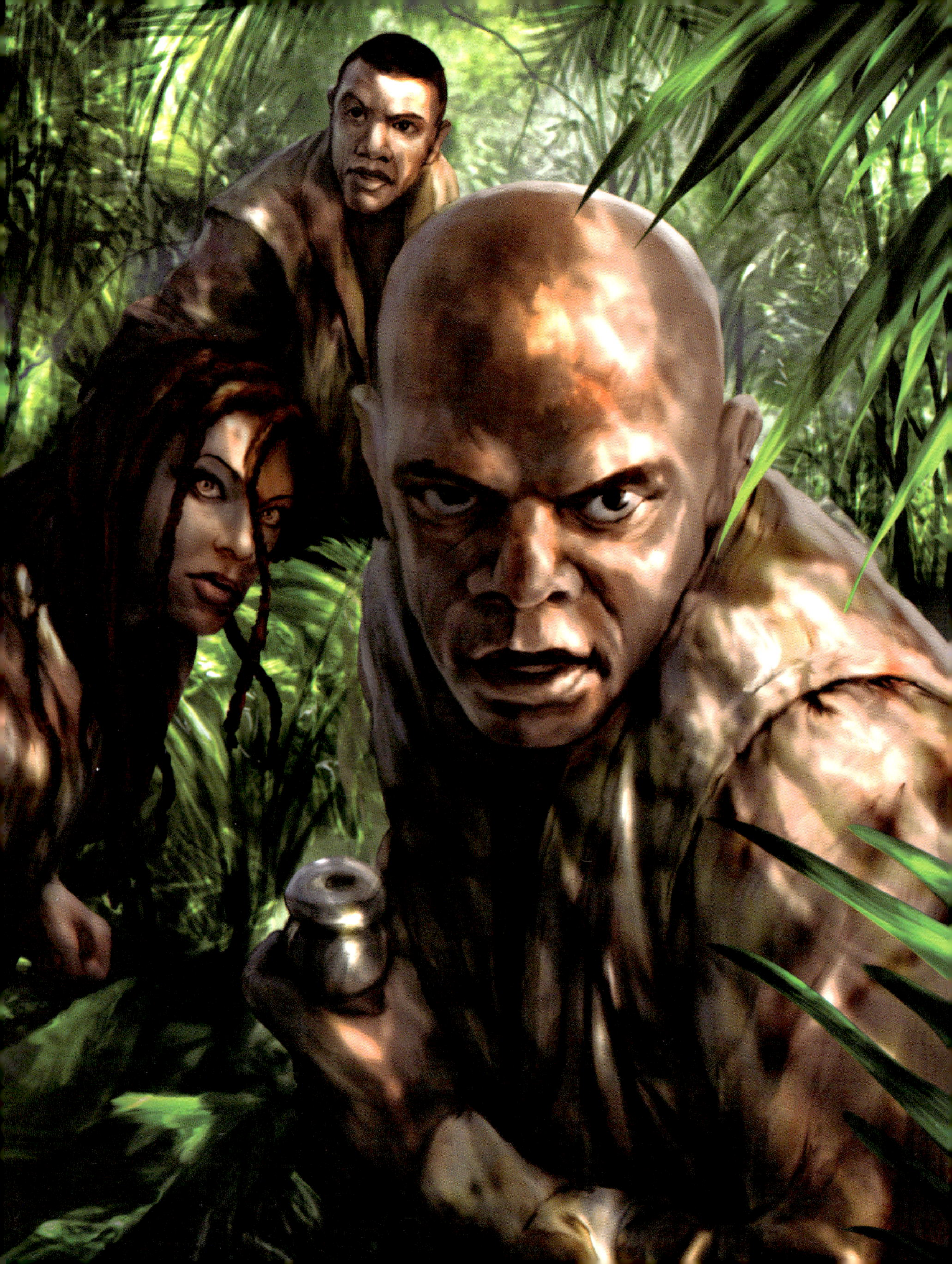

SHORT STORY — "Del Rey Presents: Equipment"

Originally printed by Paizo Publishing in the *Hasbro Short Story Collection* (2003), this story by Matthew Stover takes place during the events of his novel *Shatterpoint*. It tells the personal account of clone trooper CT-6/774, who thanks to the careful upkeep of his equipment survives a harrowing space battle trapped in the severed turret of his gunship. The short story was reprinted in the paperback edition of *Shatterpoint* in 2004.

For his valor, Nick Rostu is awarded an officer rank in the Grand Army of the Republic. Geptun also joins the Republic military, with Mace recommending him for intelligence service. Republic forces imprison Kar Vastor, holding him for trial to answer for his atrocities. Depa Billaba, rendered catatonic after her defeat by her Master, is left recuperating in the Jedi Temple.

Though he is successful in his mission, Mace is shaken by his encounters on Haruun Kal, and worries about how involvement in the war may affect the Jedi Knights.

A stark and unblinking look at the inhumane horrors of war, *Shatterpoint* was Matthew Stover's ode to Joseph Conrad's novella *Heart of Darkness* (1902) and the film that it inspired, *Apocalypse Now* (1979). The deadly jungles of Haruun Kal stand in for the untamed darkness of the Congo or Southeast Asia in the earlier works.

The book is notable for introducing Mace's history and home planet. Prior to this, the only connection to Mace's past was a reference to akk dogs in the *Star Wars: Republic* comics story arc *Emissaries to Malastare*, published by Dark Horse in 1999–2000. That story, depicting Mace and Depa corralling akk dogs used by the Circus Horrificus on Nar Shaddaa, is mentioned in the novel.

Shatterpoint removes Depa Billaba, a Jedi Master seen in Episode I, from the story line of the Clone Wars, explaining her absence from the Jedi Council in Episode III. She would not be seen again in the Expanded Universe save for a brief appearance in her catatonic state in the comic book *Star Wars: Republic* #65 (2004). Putting her into a coma was a hedge against her possibly appearing in Episode III. Nick Rostu would next appear in *Coruscant Nights I: Jedi Twilight* (2008), set after the events of Episode III.

THE CLONE WARS: NO PRISONERS

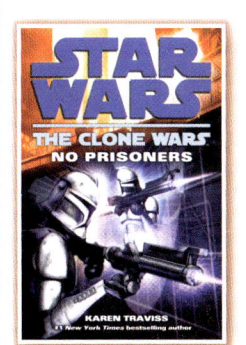

AUTHOR · Karen Traviss

COVER ARTIST · Craig Howell

PUBLICATION HISTORY ·
Novel, Del Rey Books
· Trade paperback, May 2009

TIME LINE PLACEMENT · 22 BBY

WORLDS VISITED · Coruscant [L-9]; JanFathal [K-6]; Yarille [K-6]

In the thick of the Haruun Kal jungles, Mace Windu treks through the dense underbrush with local warriors Liane "Chalk" Trevval and Nick Rostu.

MAIN CHARACTERS · Gilad Pellaeon, Republic fleet captain (human male); Hallena Devis, Republic Intelligence agent (human female); Rex, clone captain (human male); Ahsoka Tano, Padawan learner (Togruta female); Anakin Skywalker, Jedi Knight (human male); Djinn Altis, Jedi Master (human male); Callista Masana, Jedi Knight (human female); Geith Eris, Jedi Knight (human male)

SUMMARY · During a shakedown cruise of the new Republic cruiser *Leveler*, Captain Gilad Pellaeon intercepts a distress signal from a Republic Intelligence agent captured in the Separatist-backed revolution on the planet JanFathal. Pellaeon pauses to assess his own personal involvement in risking his ship in a rescue mission, since he is romantically involved with the captive agent, Hallena Devis.

Aboard his vessel are Clone Captain Rex and Jedi Padawan Ahsoka Tano, along with a group of Jedi from a nontraditionalist sect led by Djinn Altis. The so-called Altisian Jedi do not follow the Jedi Code and are not actively involved as military leaders in the Clone Wars. These Jedi allow for a Master to train multiple simultaneous apprentices and permit romantic relationships among their ranks, even marriages. When Anakin Skywalker meets the Altisian Jedi, he longs for the independence granted them, because of the struggle to keep his marriage to Padmé Amidala a secret.

The Jedi rescue Hallena, though at the cost of a clone trooper's life. Hallena is shaken by the sacrifice. She begins to question her loyalty to the Republic, since her government backed a dictatorship on JanFathal. She decides to leave Republic Intelligence, end her relationship with Pellaeon, and aid civilians in this time of war. The Altisian Jedi likewise continue their philanthropic work, and as Djinn departs, he leaves an open invitation for Anakin to join his order. Anakin declines, committing to the Jedi and his role as general in the Clone Wars.

Featured in this story is Gilad Pellaeon, a fleet officer first introduced as the Imperial captain of the Star Destroyer *Chimaera* in *Heir to the Empire* (1991). He would be a major player in the New Jedi Order and Legacy of the Force novels further along in the time line. Similarly, Djinn Altis, Callista Masana, and Geith Eris are all characters first introduced in *Children of the Jedi* (1995), a novel by Barbara Hambly. At the time of their first appearance, the various strictures of the Jedi Order present in the prequel era were not known to Expanded Universe authors. Thus, the notions of multiple apprentices and Jedi relationships were not presented as anything out of the ordinary. In *No Prisoners*, their first chronological appearance is carefully presented as out of step from the mainline Jedi, a remarkable exception to the Jedi Code that serves to rankle Anakin Skywalker.

REPUBLIC COMMANDO: TRIPLE ZERO

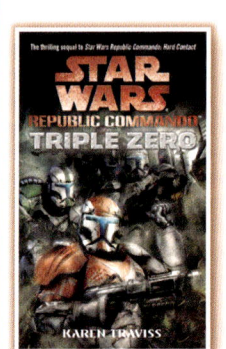

AUTHOR · Karen Traviss
COVER ARTIST · Greg Knight
PUBLICATION HISTORY ·
Novel, Del Rey Books
· Paperback, February 2006
TIME LINE PLACEMENT · 22 BBY
WORLDS VISITED · Coruscant [L-9]; Fest [L-5]; Kamino (flashback) [S-15]
MAIN CHARACTERS · Darman, Niner, Atin, Fi: Omega Squad clone commandos (human males); Boss,

In the rubble-strewn streets of JanFathal stand Callista Masana, Clone Captain Rex, and Ahsoka Tano ready for action.

THE CLONE WARS

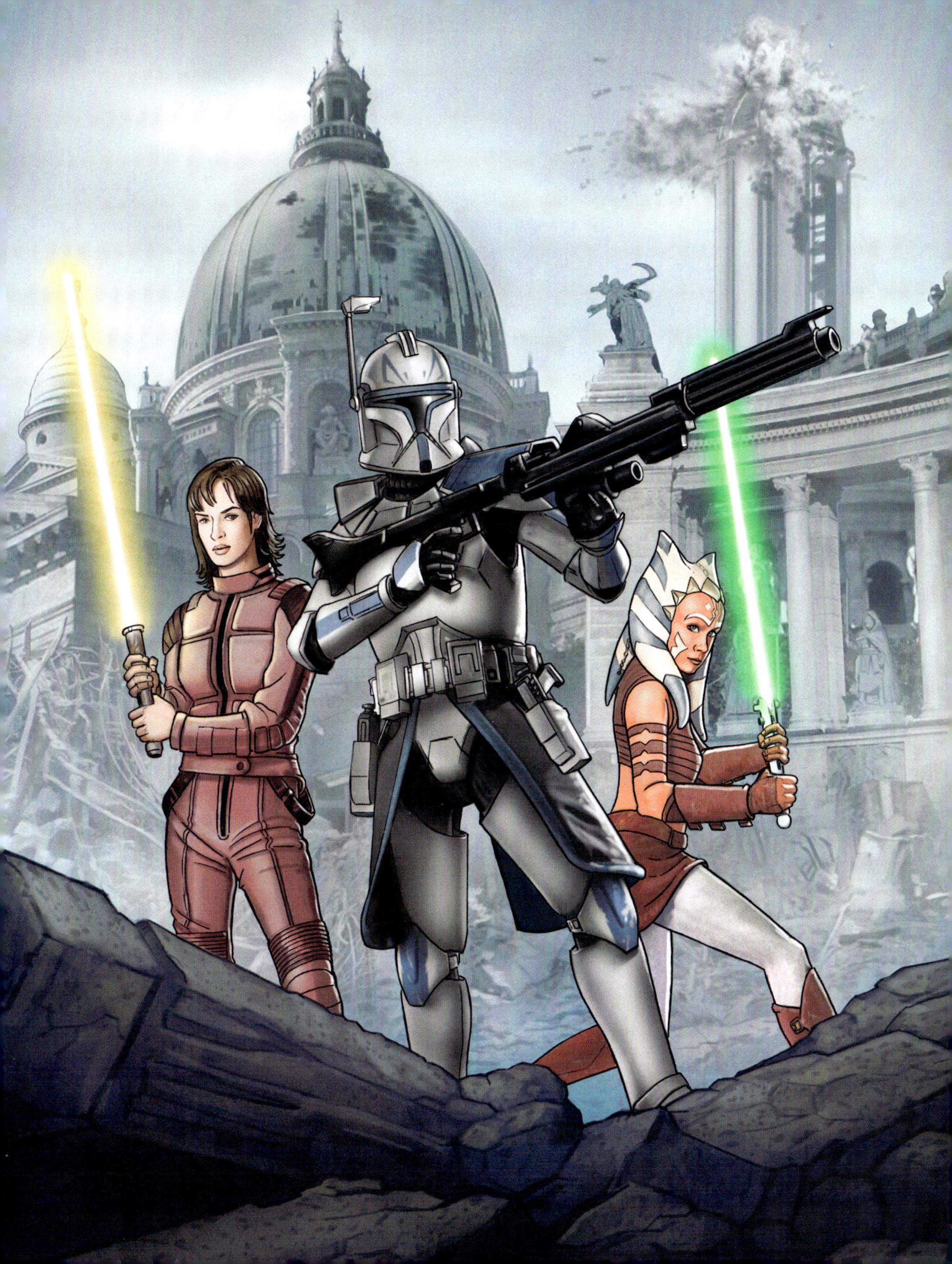

Scorch, Fixer, Sev: Delta Squad clone commandos (human males); Kal Skirata, mercenary (human male); Etain Tur-Mukan, Padawan learner (human female); Walon Vau, mercenary (human male); Ordo, Mereel, ARC troopers (human males); Bardan Jusik, Jedi Knight (human male); Corr, clone trooper (human male)

SUMMARY · Separatist terrorist cells are operating on Coruscant. The Republic turns to Kal Skirata, a seasoned mercenary and a member of the Cuy'val Dar, a group of Mandalorians handpicked by Jango Fett to train many of the Republic's most effective clone commandos. Skirata leads a mixed team of commandos, ARC troopers, and Jedi Knights in an undercover surveillance operation in the heart of the Republic capital. Etain Tur-Mukan reunites with the commandos of Omega Squad, rekindling her friendship with Darman, which soon blossoms into a secret love affair. Etain becomes pregnant with his child and chooses to not tell him for fear it will be a distraction to him in battle.

Omega Squad member Atin is forced to work with his former instructor, Walon Vau, who also becomes part of Skirata's op. Atin loathes Vau for his brutal training techniques and lashes out at his former instructor, nearly killing him before Jedi Knight Bardan Jusik intervenes.

Skirata's mission uncovers a mole within command headquarters. The Republic team is aided by two shapeshifting Gurlanin, who continue to press the Republic to fulfill their overdue promise of ridding their world, Qiilura, of settlers. The team uncovers and destroys the cell of Jabiimi terrorists.

THE BOOK'S TITLE is a reference to the astrogational coordinates of Coruscant: 0-0-0. The novel includes the clones of Delta Squad, the featured commandos in the **Republic Commando** videogame. At the back of the novel is not only a reprint of the short story "Omega Squad: Targets" (2005), but also a glossary of Mando'a terms, the language Mandalorian-trained clone commandos use to liberally pepper their speech in author Karen Traviss's stories.

CLONE WARS GAMBIT

CLONE WARS GAMBIT: STEALTH
CLONE WARS GAMBIT: SIEGE

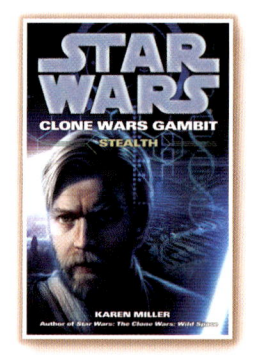

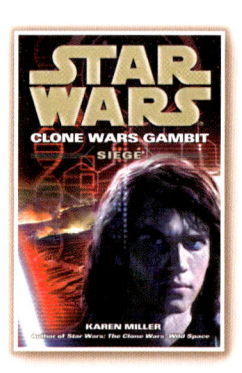

AUTHOR · Karen Miller

COVER ARTIST · Craig Howell (series)

PUBLICATION HISTORY · Novels, Del Rey Books
· Trade paperback, February 2010 (book 1), July 2010 (book 2)

TIME LINE PLACEMENT · 21 BBY

WORLDS VISITED · Corellia [M-11]; Coruscant [L-9]; Kaliida Shoals [O-17]; Kothlis [R-14]; Lanteeb [I-17]

MAIN CHARACTERS · Anakin Skywalker, Jedi Knight (human male); Obi-Wan Kenobi, Jedi Knight (human male); Ahsoka Tano, Padawan learner (Togruta female); Bant'ena Fhernan, scientist (human female); Lok Durd, Separatist general (Neimoidian male); Taria Damsin, Jedi Knight (human female); Bail Organa, Galactic Senator (human male); Padmé Amidala, Galactic Senator (human female); Wullf Yularen, admiral (human male); Palpatine, Supreme Chancellor (human male)

SUMMARY · Bail Organa's intelligence contacts report an inexplicable Separatist interest in the distant and obscure world of Lanteeb. Research uncovers that the planet is home to a potentially toxic mineral, damotite, which could be weaponized. Obi-Wan Kenobi and Anakin Skywalker go undercover to Lanteeb, posing as natives, to investigate.

In charge of the bioweapon is the evil Neimoidian general Lok Durd. By threatening the loved ones of captive scientist Bant'ena Fhernan, Durd forces her to create a damotite-based gaseous chemical that liquefies living matter on contact. Obi-Wan and Anakin infiltrate her laboratory and Anakin, feeling sympathy for anyone so enslaved, promises to free her and her targeted family, though Obi-Wan thinks he is overstepping their mandate. With hope that her family and friends may be spared, Fhernan agrees to help the Jedi by stalling her progress. She also provides them with the names of offworld colleagues capable of developing an antidote to her project.

Durd discovers that the Jedi have helped Fhernan, and he orders one of her loved ones killed. He shows Fhernan holographic evidence of the murder, breaking her spirit. She gives up the Jedi and lures them into a trap. When Obi-Wan and Anakin return to the laboratory, they barely escape being blasted by Separatist droids.

Anakin and Obi-Wan flee into the countryside to the damotite-mining town of Torbel. Still posing as locals, they work in the mines and save the town during an intense radiation storm. Anakin's use of the Force in doing so alerts the locals that they are Jedi. Though the townspeople are by their nature wary, the selflessness displayed by the Jedi earns their loyalty.

Meanwhile, Ahsoka Tano and Jedi Knight Taria Damsin journey to Corellia to ensure the safety of Fhernan's mother. Similar missions are carried out across the galaxy, and the Jedi secure the rest of Fhernan's loved ones. Durd, however, continues to pressure her, using holographic illusions to make her think they are still in jeopardy. Desperate to prove the damotite weapon's effectiveness, Durd impetuously launches an attack on Chandrila with it, killing thousands.

The Republic launches a limited task force of three vessels to Lanteeb. Senators Padmé Amidala and Bail Organa, on their own initiative, bolster this fleet with volunteer civilian ships. Taria Damsin soars past the Separatist blockade of Lanteeb to land on the surface. She contacts Fhernan, revealing the safety of her loved ones. Fhernan destroys the samples of the bioweapon, sacrificing herself in the process as penance for the Chandrilan massacre.

Durd orders his battle droids to lay siege to Torbel. Anakin jury-rigs the town's storm shield to deflect the enemy droids. Taria reunites with Obi-Wan, and Anakin discovers that Obi-Wan has feelings for this Jedi, a close colleague he has known for most of his life. Noting this strong personal bond between them, Anakin can't help but see hypocrisy in the Jedi strictures against romantic commitment.

The Republic overpowers the Separatist blockade, but Durd escapes with the fleeing Confederacy vessels. With the help of the villagers, the Republic is able to synthesize an antidote to the bioweapon, nullifying its threat.

THE OUTER RIM SIEGES are mentioned in the novels. During the production of Episode III, this campaign—mentioned in the script—was at

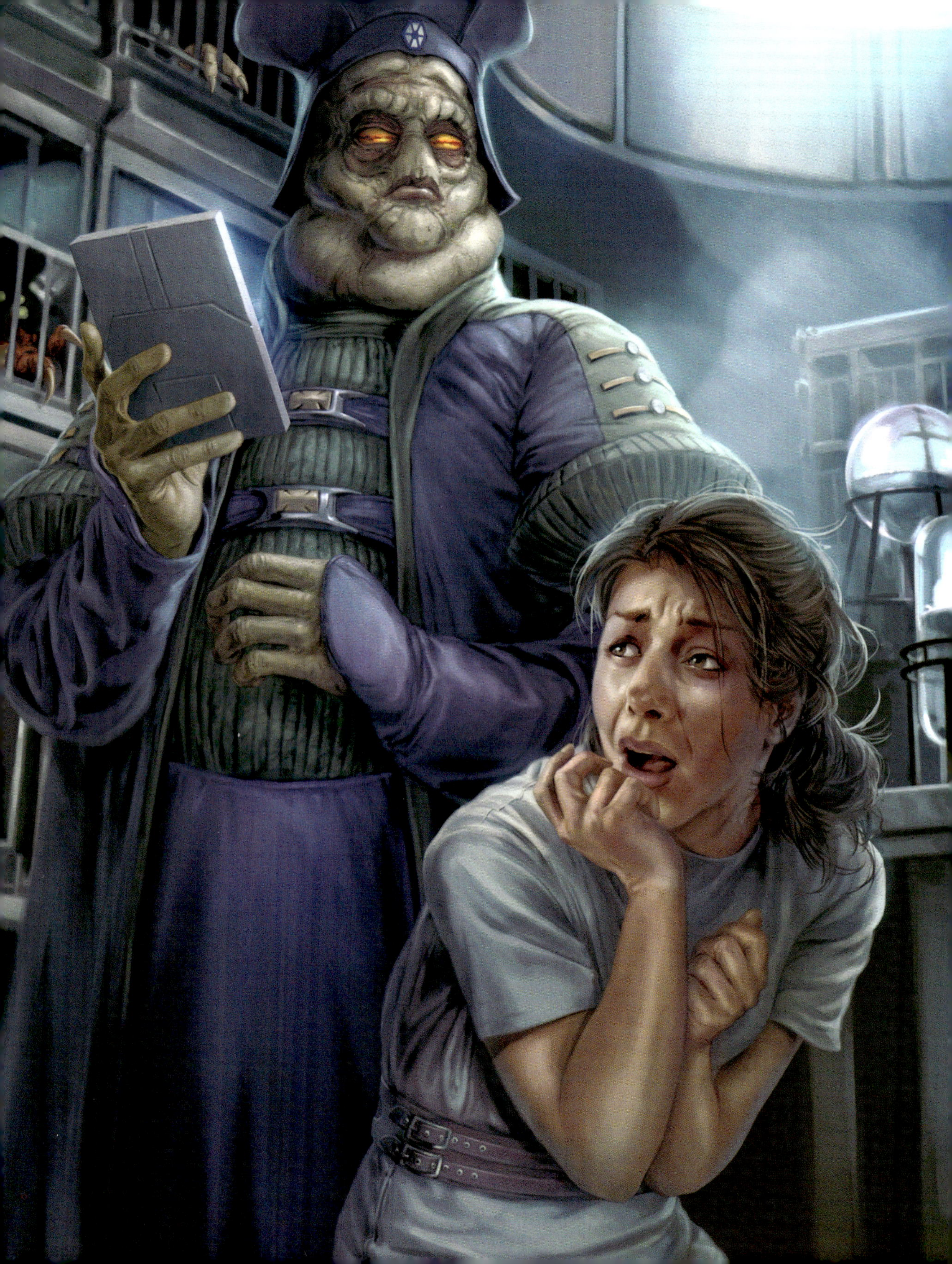

one point described as starting within six months of war's end (20–19 BBY). The books seem to take place earlier than that, in 21 BBY, given that Ahsoka is described as only serving under Anakin for months, and she is hesitant about repairing technology—a skill she possesses in the third season of the animated series. Furthermore, Obi-Wan is depicted as not being on the Jedi Council, though he is seen with a Council seat in the second-season episode "Senate Spy." Lok Durd is a villain from the first season episode "Defenders of Peace."

Though Taria Damsin is presented as being a dear old friend of Obi-Wan's, this is her first appearance. The intimation of romantic feelings between her and Obi-Wan now means that he has had such feelings for at least three women, despite the Jedi Code forbidding it: Taria Damsin, Siri Tachi, and Duchess Satine Kryze.

"ODDS"

AUTHOR · Karen Traviss
PUBLICATION HISTORY · Short story, IDG Entertainment · *Star Wars Insider* #87, April 2006
Included in Republic Commando: *True Colors* novel, Del Rey Books · Paperback, October 2007
TIME LINE PLACEMENT · 21 BBY
WORLDS VISITED · Cato Neimoidia (space) [N-11]; Drall (space) [M-11]; Kamino [S-15]; Olanet [R-17].
MAIN CHARACTERS · Atin, clone commando (human male); Prudii, Mereel, ARC troopers (human males); Kal Skirata, mercenary (human male); General Arligan Zey, Jedi Master (human male)

SUMMARY · Commandos Atin and Prudii discover, while on an assignment that saw them sabotage a droid factory on Olanet, the true number of droids the Separatist factories are creating for the war effort. Meanwhile, on Kamino, Commando Mereel, seeking information about the missing Kaminoan scientist Ko Sai, has infiltrated the clone facility in Tipoca City to extract highly classified information from the clone factory databases. Later, under the supervision of Kal Skirata, the clones compare notes, finding that the numbers of enemy droids quoted by Republic Intelligence are highly erratic, and that the Chancellor's true agenda in the war may not be what it seems.

REPUBLIC COMMANDO: TRUE COLORS

AUTHOR · Karen Traviss
COVER ARTIST · Greg Knight
PUBLICATION HISTORY · Novel, Del Rey Books · Paperback, October 2007
TIME LINE PLACEMENT · 21 BBY
WORLDS VISITED · Agamar [M-5]; Bogden [M-8]; Coruscant [L-9]; Dorumaa (moon of Almas) [P-14]; Gaftikar [P-5]; Mygeeto [K-5]; Napda (moon of Da Soocha) [S-11]; Qiilura [L-7]
MAIN CHARACTERS · Niner, Darman, Fi, Atin: Omega Squad clone commandos (human males); Kal Skirata, mercenary (human male); Besany Wennen, Treasury agent (human female); Etain Tur-Mukan,

The evil Neimoidian general Lok Durd looms over his cowering captive, scientist Bant'ena Fhernan.

Jedi Knight (human female); Ko Sai, fugitive scientist (Kaminoan female); Walon Vau, mercenary (human male); Boss, Scorch, Fixer, Sev: Delta Squad clone commandos (human males)

Jedi Knight Bardan Jusik, who has adopted the Mandalorian culture as his own, uses the Force to stabilize the condition of Fi, a wounded clone commando.

SUMMARY · When Ko Sai, the chief scientist responsible for the development of the Republic's clone army, flees into the unknown, she becomes a wanted Kaminoan by more than just the warring Separatist and Republic forces. Realizing that Ko Sai may hold the secret to undoing the age acceleration that dooms the clones to a less-than-full life, Kal Skirata wants to capture her. Ko Sai's cruel history of destroying young clones that failed to measure up to her standards adds a streak of vengeance to Skirata's quest. To find the fugitive Kaminoan, Skirata buys a submersible starship to plumb the depths of ocean planets, working with Null ARC troopers Ordo and Mereel, as well as fellow Mandalorian Walon Vau.

On Gaftikar, Omega Squad assists the local rebels in overthrowing a Separatist-backed government. While on undercover assignment, commandos Darman and Atin are shocked to spot a clone trooper deserter, Sull. The AWOL trooper is being hunted by Republic Intelligence agents who have targeted him for death, an alarming revelation that raises many disturbing questions about the ultimate fate of freethinking clones. During the Battle of Gaftikar, Omega Squad commando Fi is critically wounded, suffering brain damage and plunging into a coma.

THE CLONE WARS

He and the rest of Omega Squad are extracted by the cruiser *Leveler* and returned to Coruscant.

On the capital, Skirata's ally in the Treasury Department, Besany Wennen, pores through tax data searching for clues about the creation of the clone army. Her search leads to many dead ends, but she uncovers evidence of a cloning operation slated for development far from Kamino, on Coruscant's moon Centax. Evidence mounts that there is no long-term future for the Kaminoan-created clones.

When Fi is taken to a civilian medcenter on Coruscant and declared brain-dead, Besany rescues his body and smuggles him out of the facility. Jedi Bardan Jusik, also an ally of Skirata, uses Force healing to stabilize Fi's condition.

Meanwhile on Qiilura, Jedi Knight Etain Tur-Mukan oversees the forced relocation of human colonists from that planet, in compliance with the demands of the native Gurlanin. When violence erupts, she suffers hemorrhaging that endangers her secret pregnancy. One of the clones, Ordo, rushes to her aid and takes her to Kal Skirata.

Skirata's search uncovers Ko Sai hiding in her secret laboratory underneath the waves of Dorumaa, a resort moon. Ko Sai proves resistant to interrogation, and Skirata and the clones loyal to him bring the Kaminoan to Mandalore. Etain, noting how intrigued Ko Sai is with Jedi physiology, offers to allow Ko Sai to study her tissue after her child is born. Though at first Ko Sai seems willing to cooperate, the scientist commits suicide while in custody, leaving Skirata without a cure for clone age acceleration, though he does keep her research notes.

On Mandalore, Etain gives birth to a boy, Venku. The father, Darman, has no idea of the child's parentage. Besany Wennen agrees to help take care of the child.

REPUBLIC COMMANDO: *True Colors* raises questions about where the clone army will get its future funding, presenting it as a mystery to those characters with a vested interest in the survival of the clones. This runs counter to what is established in *The Clone Wars* animated series, where the continued payment for clones is an issue of public debate, and the Kaminoans are afforded influential Senate representation for their role in the war.

Similarly, Skirata and Besany continue to find no evidence of any long-term health plan for the clones, though the animated series depicts the health of the clones to be important enough to build massive facilities like the Kaliida Shoals medical center, which can house sixty thousand convalescing troopers.

The Republic warship *Leveler*, under the command of Captain Pellaeon, is mentioned in this book, its first time in print. Published after *True Colors*, *No Prisoners* (2008) takes place prior to this story and describes the *Leveler*'s shakedown cruise.

THE WRATH OF DARTH MAUL

AUTHOR · Ryder Windham

COVER ARTIST · Mike Butkus

PUBLICATION HISTORY · Young reader novel, Scholastic Inc. · Hardcover, January 2012

TIME LINE PLACEMENT · c. 21 BBY, with flashbacks to 51 BBY, 48 BBY, 44 BBY, 41 BBY, 39 BBY, and 32 BBY

WORLDS VISITED · Hypori [S-16]; Lotho Minor [I-17]; Mustafar [L-19]; Orsis [Q-15]; Tosste [L-19]

MAIN CHARACTERS · Darth Maul, Sith Lord (Dathomirian Zabrak male); Darth Sidious, Sith Lord (human male); TD-D9, training droid;

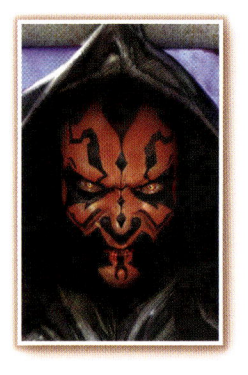

Trezza, Academy headmaster (Falleen male); Savage Opress, warrior (Dathomirian Zabrak male)

SUMMARY · In the wretched depths of the junk world Lotho Minor, Darth Maul is a shattered madman held together only by his longing for vengeance. His mind reels back to his childhood, recalling the grueling tests undertaken as young as three, as he was raised by droids on Mustafar and served his dark mentor, Darth Sidious. Maul recalls his teen years spent at the brutal Orsis Academy, a combat school where he was prohibited from using the Force while learning martial and survival skills. He recalls his ascension to Sith Lord after passing cruel trials on Hypori, and his defeat by Obi-Wan Kenobi during the Battle of Naboo. Maul snaps out of his reflection with the arrival of his brother, Savage Opress, who has been sent on a quest to find him.

THE FRAME STORY of Maul living in the depths of Lotho Minor is from the episode "Brothers," written by Katie Lucas, from the fourth season of *Star Wars: The Clone Wars* (2012). Part of the biography series of novels written by Ryder Windham, *The Wrath of Darth Maul* includes scenes also depicted in the stories "Restraint" (2012), "End Game" (2012), and *Star Wars* Episode I Journal: *Darth Maul* (2000).

STAR WARS: MEDSTAR

MEDSTAR I: BATTLE SURGEONS
MEDSTAR II: JEDI HEALER

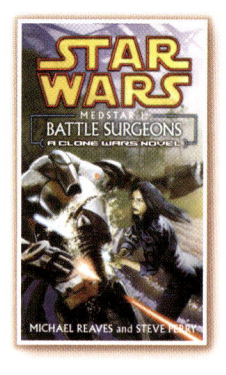

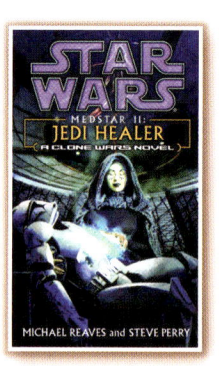

AUTHORS · Michael Reaves and Steve Perry

COVER ARTIST · Dave Seeley (series)

PUBLICATION HISTORY · Novels, Del Rey Books · Paperback, July 2004 (book I), September 2004 (book II)

TIME LINE PLACEMENT · 20 BBY

WORLD VISITED · Drongar [T-5]

MAIN CHARACTERS · Jos Vondar, surgeon (human male); Tolk le Trene, nurse (human female); Barriss Offee, Padawan learner (Mirialan female); Kornell "Uli" Divini, surgeon (human male); I-5YQ, protocol droid; Den Dhur, reporter (Sullustan male); Phow Ji, mercenary (human male); Zan Yant, surgeon (Zabrak male); Kaird, Black Sun agent (Nadiji male); Klo Merit, minder (Equanii male); Tarnese Bleyd, Republic admiral (Sakiyan male); Erel Kersos, Republic admiral (human male)

SUMMARY · On the tropical planet Drongar, Republic and Separatist forces wage war for control of bota, a powerful adaptogenic plant that can be refined into

112 THE CLONE WARS

a wonder drug with a wide range of effects. The rapidly mutating nature of the planet's biosphere ensures that Drongar is the only source for bota, and the plant needs to be refined or frozen in carbonite quickly lest it become useless.

To patch together the clone troopers wounded in this ongoing battlefront, the Republic maintains an orbital MedStar frigate, as well as a scattering of Republic Mobile Surgical Units on the surface. These RMSUs (or "Rimsoos") are temporary hospitals that can be packed up and transported to new locations on short notice.

Padawan Barriss Offee joins the doctors of Rimsoo 7, using her Jedi healing abilities to assist in their near-constant treatment of wounded clone forces. Among the Rimsoo staff are Jos Vondar, a weary surgeon who struggles with his feelings for Tolk le Trene, a Lorrdian nurse. Vondar's conservative Corellian upbringing prohibits him from coupling with a non-Corellian. When it becomes evident that life in a battlefield may end with little notice, he forgoes social taboos and openly shows his love for Tolk.

Vondar's best friend is Zan Yant, a gifted Zabrak surgeon who is also a sensitive musician. Yant is secretly stealing small samples of bota to cure ailing clones who are beyond traditional treatment. The strictly regulated nature of the bota makes it, ironically, illegal to use on the warriors who are defending it. Yant is killed in a Separatist attack. His position is filled by a young doctor from Tatooine, Kornell "Uli" Divini.

A friend to the surgeons is Den Dhur, a quick-witted but cynical HoloNet News reporter sniffing out stories, often while planted in the cantina. Dhur strikes up an unusual friendship with I-5YQ, a modified protocol droid of mysterious origin and unusual wisdom. Intrigued by the droid's vivid personality, Dhur helps I-Five find a means of achieving the electronic equivalent of inebriation. As a side effect of its digital drunkenness, I-Five's memory blockage disappears, and he recalls being the property of Lorn Pavan, an information broker who once operated in the Coruscant underworld. I-Five's new purpose is to return to the capital and watch over Jax Pavan, Lorn's young son who has been taken into the Jedi Order.

Amid the endless cycles of combat and surgery, intrigue also permeates the Rimsoo. A shadowy being named Kaird is secretly a Black Sun agent, tasked with ensuring that bota shipments make their way to the criminal organization. Also lurking on the scene is a *triple* agent, Klo Merit. In plain view, he is a sympathetic minder—a psychotherapist assigned to help the overworked surgeons. For the Separatists, he is a saboteur named Column, seeking vengeance against the suffering his people endured in the Clone Wars. For Black Sun, he is a spy known as Lens. Merit secretly carries out explo-

---

SHORT STORY — "MedStar: Intermezzo"

Published in *Star Wars Insider* #83 (September 2005, IDG Entertainment), this short story is by duology authors Michael Reaves and Steve Perry. As its title implies, it is a composition meant to sit between the two other works—that is, a short piece of fiction that occurs in the week of time between MedStar I and II. In it, a grieving Jos Vondar must operate on a Zabrak mercenary responsible for the attack that killed his best friend, Zan Yant.

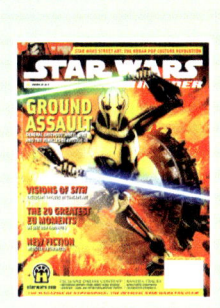

THE CLONE WARS

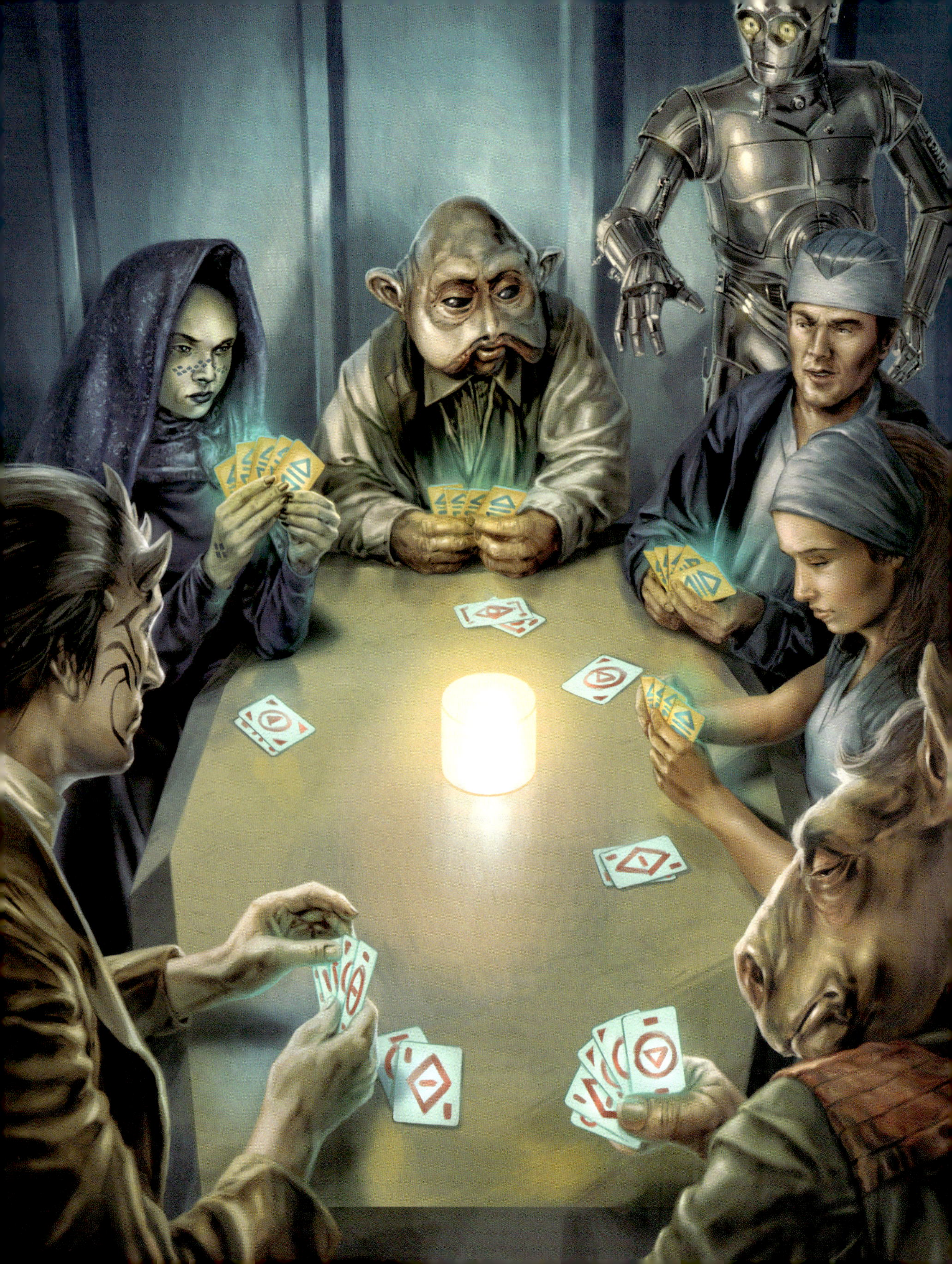

sive sabotage on the orbiting MedStar to benefit the Confederacy, resulting in the loss of thousands of Republic souls.

While treating a mortally wounded clone trooper with illicit bota, Barriss Offee accidentally injects herself with the refined plant extract. It results in a temporary surge in the Force, granting her unprecedented access to the universal energy field. Such a huge increase in power is very tempting to Barriss, but she refuses to give in to its allure. Still, it gives her enough insight to realize that there is a traitor at Rimsoo 7. Vondar confronts Merit and is forced to shoot the minder dead when Merit tries to kill his accuser.

Bota's constant mutation leads to its inevitable obsolescence. Within a generation, it will modify itself until it is useless. Kaird's attempt to steal a final viable batch of bota fails when his grifter accomplices betray him, replacing the bota in his carbonite carrying case with an explosive.

With bota no longer a potent miracle drug, the Separatists and Republic both abandon Drongar. Dhur and I-5YQ depart for Coruscant, as does Barriss Offee, who is returning to the Jedi Temple. For her resistance to power for power's sake, she is considered to have passed the Jedi trials and is elevated to the rank of Jedi Knight.

THE MEDSTAR BOOKS were envisioned as the *Star Wars* answer to the *M*A*S*H* movie and television series, replacing the mobile army surgical hospital of the Korean War with an RMSU on Drongar. Inspiration so firmly rooted in the real world resulted in several nods to our terrestrial culture hidden in the text. For example, in *Jedi Healer*, the RMSU is visited by an entertainment troupe that includes Epoh Trebor, Annloc Yerj, and Eyar Marath—references to USO entertainers Bob Hope, Jerry Colonna, and Martha Raye.

Other sly references include such cantina beverages as Janx spirit and an interrupted order of Pan Galactic Gargle Blaster, both drinks famously featured in the *Hitchhikers' Guide to the Galaxy* novels by Douglas Adams.

I-5YQ, Dhur, Kaird, and the bota return in the Coruscant Nights series of novels by Michael Reaves, while Uli Divini appears in *Death Star* (2007) by Reaves and Steve Perry.

"HERO OF CARTAO"

EPISODE I "HERO'S CALL"
EPISODE II "HERO'S RISE"
EPISODE III "HERO'S END"

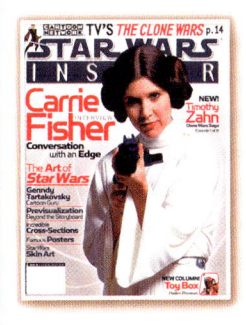

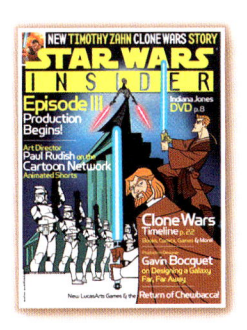

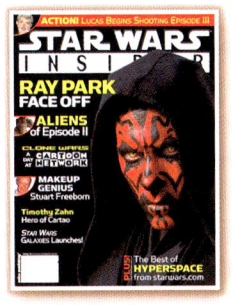

AUTHOR · Timothy Zahn

PUBLICATION HISTORY ·
Serialized short story, Paizo Publishing
· *Star Wars Insider* #68–70, June, August, and September 2003

TIME LINE PLACEMENT ·
20 BBY

WORLDS VISITED · Cartao [O-8]

At an RMSU on Drongar, a game of sabacc plays out with medical staff, support personnel, and other curious onlookers.

THE CLONE WARS

115

MAIN CHARACTERS · Kinman Doriana, Republic aide (human male); Lord Binali, nobleman (human male); Corf Binali, boy (human male); Jafer Torles, Jedi Knight (human male); Darth Sidious, Sith Lord (human male)

SUMMARY · Republic and Separatist forces battle over Spaarti Creations, a unique factory operated by Cranscoc aliens and administered by the Binali noble family on Cartao. Secretly, Doriana is a double agent working for Darth Sidious. Sidious's plot culminates in a Republic assault transport crashing into and destroying the factory, with all appearances suggesting that the Jedi are solely culpable for crippling the planet's manufacturing economy. The factory's last output, containing a wealth of advanced Spaarti cloning cylinders, is then secretly transported to a storage facility on the planet Wayland.

Though a dateline in the first part of the story identifies it as occurring a year into the Clone Wars, a passage within the story sets it at over two years after the Battle of Geonosis. One indicator of it being late in the war is mention of strained relations between the Supreme Chancellor and the Jedi Order. Further muddling the chronology, *The Cestus Deception* (2004), which takes place earlier in the war, mentions Cortao, which might be a garbled reference to this story.

Spaarti cloning cylinders date back to *Heir to the Empire* (1991), where they were presented as the most effective cloning technology in the galaxy. Since they were introduced long before the history of the Clone Wars came to be known, Spaarti cylinders remained the de facto cloning technology in the Expanded Universe until the Kaminoans were revealed in Episode II (2002).

YODA: DARK RENDEZVOUS

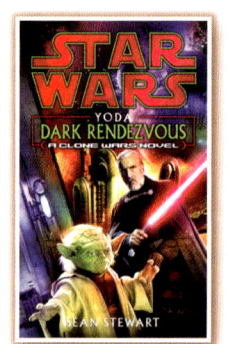

AUTHOR · Sean Stewart
COVER ARTIST · Steven D. Anderson
PUBLICATION HISTORY · Novel, Del Rey Books · Paperback, December 2004
TIME LINE PLACEMENT · 19 BBY
WORLDS VISITED · Arkania [M-8]; Coruscant [L-9]; Ithor (system) [M-6]; Jovan Station [P-6]; Phindar [P-6]; Vjun [Q-6]

MAIN CHARACTERS · Yoda, Jedi Master (alien male); Count Dooku, aka Darth Tyranus, Sith Lord (human male); Tallisibeth "Scout" Enwandung-Esterhazy, Padawan learner (human female); Whie Malreaux, Padawan learner (human male); Asajj Ventress, assassin (Dathomirian female); Jai Maruk, Jedi Knight (human male); Maks Leem, Jedi Master (Gran female); Solis and Fidelis, protector droids

SUMMARY · Jedi Master Jai Maruk escapes capture by Asajj Ventress and delivers a surprising message from Count Dooku to Jedi Master Yoda. The leader of the Separatists and former Jedi is suing for peace. Though Yoda suspects the overture to be a trap, with so many lives hanging in the balance of the Clone Wars, he cannot resist the offer to parlay. Yoda reflects on the past, when Dooku was a powerful Padawan whose pride distanced him from the rest of the Order. It was then that Yoda offered to always welcome Dooku back into the fold. The wizened Jedi Master intends to honor this promise.

Padawan Whie Malreaux is in shock as Asajj Ventress holds another Padawan, Scout, in a Force grip.

THE CLONE WARS

To keep Yoda's voyage to the gloomy world of Vjun a secret, an actor poses as the Jedi Master for a very public departure for the Ithorian system. The decoy gambit works too well for the actor—his vessel is attacked by Asajj Ventress upon arrival.

Yoda, meanwhile, travels to Vjun disguised within the hollowed-out shell of an astromech droid, with undercover Jedi accompanying him: Jai Maruk and his newly appointed Padawan, a spirited young girl nicknamed Scout, and Master Maks Leem and her Padawan, the soulful and sensitive young Whie Malreaux. Malreaux hails from Vjun, a world forever tainted by tragedy when a contagious insanity destroyed the ruling noble family. Malreaux is heir to the family; he worries about becoming lost to the dark side and fears visions of his future in which he is killed by a Jedi Knight.

During their multi-leg journey to Vjun, the Jedi encounter a peculiar pair of antique droids, Solis and Fidelis. Both come from Vjun, and it turns out Fidelis is the property of the Malreaux family. The droid has been watching over Whie from a distance on behalf of Malreaux's addled mother. Asajj Ventress soon picks up Yoda's trail and attacks the group. The droids are able to protect Malraeaux, but the Jedi Maruk and Leem both die in the assault. As a result the Jedi Council dispatches Obi-Wan Kenobi and Anakin Skywalker to Vjun to assist Master Yoda.

On the dreary world, Yoda engages Dooku not with a lightsaber or the Force, but with conversation. The two debate their incompatible ideals, and Dooku is surprised to find Yoda still willing to forgive his fallen pupil. The moment is broken by the arrival of Anakin and Obi-Wan, and an angered Dooku now battles Yoda with more than words. As he did in a previous confrontation with Master Yoda, Count Dooku uses a threat against the lives of others to distract Yoda and allow for his escape.

The Jedi return to Coruscant, and the war continues throughout the galaxy.

The hardcover *Clone Wars* novels published between 2003 and 2005 focused on major Jedi characters—Mace Windu, Anakin Skywalker, Obi-Wan Kenobi—while the paperbacks were intended to give supporting characters like Barriss Offee and clone commandos a spotlight. It seems surprising, then, that Yoda's sole starring role in a *Star Wars* novel should be in a paperback original. *Yoda: Dark Rendezvous* arrived as a replacement novel for *Escape from Dagu*, a canceled paperback that was to have focused on Shaak Ti. Author Sean Stewart made his participation in *Star Wars* novels contingent on being able to write a Yoda story, a rare exception to Lucasfilm's policy of keeping this character reserved. This novel is unique in its exploration of the psychology and motivations of characters such as Yoda and Dooku.

Supporting character Whie Malreaux is actually a background Padawan from the *Star Wars*: Episode III *Revenge of the Sith* movie (2005). Malreaux's prophetic and confusing visions of being killed by a Jedi come true when Anakin Skywalker, fallen to the dark side, kills him during the assault on the Jedi Temple.

BOBA FETT #5: A NEW THREAT

AUTHOR · Elizabeth Hand
COVER ARTIST · Peter Bollinger
PUBLICATION HISTORY · Juvenile novel, Scholastic Inc. · Paperback, April 2004
TIME LINE PLACEMENT · 19 BBY
WORLDS VISITED · Tatooine [R-16]; Xagobah [M-18]

MAIN CHARACTERS · Boba Fett, bounty hunter (human male); Jabba, crime lord (Hutt); Anakin Skywalker, Jedi Knight (human male); General Grievous, droid general (Kaleesh cyborg male); Wat Tambor, Techno Union foreman (Skakoan male)

SUMMARY · Boba Fett is assigned by Jabba to hunt down Wat Tambor on the fungus-covered world Xagobah, where the evil Techno Union foreman hides within the Mazariyan Citadel. Boba must maneuver past an intense battlefield of Republic and Separatist forces. He works his way into the heart of the Citadel, but is battered by General Grievous. Boba plays dead with the help of the stasis-inducing xabar fungus.

Though always intended to take place after *Jedi Trial* (2004), this book makes reference to Anakin being a Padawan, rather than a Jedi Knight.

BOBA FETT #6: PURSUIT

AUTHOR · Elizabeth Hand
COVER ARTIST · Peter Bollinger
PUBLICATION HISTORY · Juvenile novel, Scholastic Inc. · Paperback, December 2004
TIME LINE PLACEMENT · 19 BBY
WORLDS VISITED · Xagobah [M-18]; Coruscant [L-9]
MAIN CHARACTERS · Boba Fett, bounty hunter (human male); Mace Windu, Jedi Master (human male); Asajj Ventress, assassin (Dathomirian female); Anakin Skywalker, Jedi Knight (human male); Wilhuff Tarkin, governor (human male)

SUMMARY · Boba Fett awakens from his temporary stasis to escape the Citadel. In his ship *Slave I*, Boba pursues the fleeing Wat Tambor but is attacked by Asajj Ventress, aboard her starfighter. Boba must set down for repairs on a Xagobah moon. He encounters Anakin Skywalker, who offers to help repair *Slave I*, but also attempts to take him into custody. Boba instead bargains for escort to Coruscant, claiming he has crucial information about the war that can only be shared with Supreme Chancellor Palpatine.

Prior to returning to the capital, Boba modifies his inherited Mandalorian armor, adopting a different paint scheme than that of his father. Boba procures weapons from the Coruscant underworld. He intends to avenge his father's death by killing Mace Windu. Boba confronts Mace in the executive building, but the battle is interrupted by the Chancellor. Palpatine listens to Boba's secret: Darth Tyranus, developer of the clone army, and Count Dooku, enemy of the Republic, are one and the same. Palpatine does not seem surprised by this, and buys Boba's silence in exchange for a fortune. With his newfound riches, Boba disappears, determined to become the galaxy's best bounty hunter.

In *The Clone Wars* animated series, produced well after this book, Anakin has an encounter with Boba that should have colored his perceptions of the young bounty hunter here. Boba's destruction of a Jedi cruiser and attempted assassination of Mace Windu would have prevented his unfettered access to the Jedi Temple as seen in *Pursuit*. The book erroneously claims that Boba had never been to Coruscant, even though the first book in the series, *The Fight to Survive* (2002), has him visiting the capital. Furthermore, the animated series has Boba incarcerated on Coruscant for an unknown period of time.

LABYRINTH OF EVIL

AUTHOR · James Luceno
COVER ARTISTS · Steven D. Anderson; Lucasfilm (omnibus)
PUBLICATION HISTORY · Novel, Del Rey Books · Hardcover, January 2005 · Paperback, September 2005
Collected as part of *The Dark Lord Trilogy* · Trade paperback, August 2008
TIME LINE PLACEMENT · 19 BBY

THE CLONE WARS

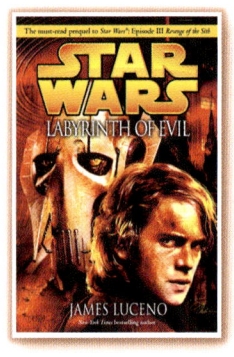

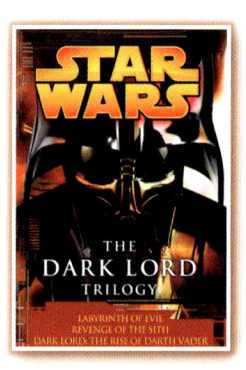

WORLDS VISITED · Belderone [R-6]; Cato Neimoidia [N-11]; Charros IV [R-9]; Coruscant [L-9]; Escarte [T-6]; Kaon [S-6]; Naos III [S-18]; Tythe [Q-16]; Utapau [N-19]

MAIN CHARACTERS · Obi-Wan Kenobi, Jedi Master (human male); Anakin Skywalker, Jedi Knight (human male); General Grievous, droid general (Kaleesh cyborg male); Count Dooku, Separatist leader (human male); Palpatine, Supreme Chancellor (human male); Mace Windu, Jedi Master (human male); Yoda, Jedi Master (alien male); Nute Gunray, Trade Federation viceroy (Neimoidian male); Padmé Amidala, Galactic Senator (human female); Bail Organa, Galactic Senator (human male); Captain Dyne, Republic Intelligence officer (human male)

SUMMARY · A concerted Republic strike against the Separatist stronghold of Cato Neimoidia sends Trade Federation viceroy Nute Gunray and his underlings scattering. Leading the charge are Jedi Obi-Wan Kenobi and Anakin Skywalker. Among the spoils of war is a peculiar mechno-chair that conceals a holographic communicator built into it for contact with the Sith Lord Darth Sidious. For the Jedi, this is the first solid lead they've uncovered that may reveal the identity of their mysterious Sith enemy.

Obi-Wan and Anakin begin a planet-hopping quest, following tenuous clues. Engravings on the chair point to a Xi Charrian artisan on Charros IV, who directs the Jedi to Escarte to find the Bith who developed the hyperwave transceiver and holoprojector built into the chair.

Meanwhile, Republic Intelligence agents crack the chair's encrypted interface, allowing them to intercept a transmission from General Grievous describing an impending attack on Belderone. With advance notice of the assault, the Republic scrambles to evacuate the world. Grievous realizes that the most secret of Separatist communication networks has been compromised. The Sith masterminds behind the Confederacy, Darth Sidious and Count Dooku, discuss this alarming turn of events in their secret lair on Coruscant. Sidious advances his plans to conquer the Republic and to corrupt Anakin to the dark side.

Anakin and Obi-Wan's search next takes them to Naos III, where they find the pilot who had originally delivered a prototype Sith infiltrator vessel to Darth Maul. She points the Jedi in the direction of the Works, a derelict area of decrepit factories and warehouses on Coruscant. Mace Windu, Shaak Ti, and a team of Padawans and Republic Intelligence agents scour the burned-out district, finding an active landing platform connected to the Senate District of Coruscant via a network of tunnels.

Just then, the Separatists' fleet of warships attacks the Republic capital. Destruction rains down over the gleaming cityscape, and droid infiltrators attack the Senate District. General Grievous kidnaps Supreme Chancellor Palpatine, escaping from the Jedi to return to his well-armed flagship, *Invisible Hand*. Obi-Wan and Anakin, who have been occupied with pursuing Count Dooku on Tythe, rush back to Coruscant to help repel the surprise attack from the Separatists.

During his attack on Coruscant, General Grievous confronts Jedi Masters Stass Allie and Shaak Ti, who defend Supreme Chancellor Palpatine.

When author Matthew Stover visited Skywalker Ranch to interview George Lucas to lay the groundwork for his novelization of Episode III, he took with him questions prepared by James Luceno to help with what was then known simply as the Episode III prequel novel. In its earliest outlines, the book was to build upon the opening text crawl from the movie *Revenge of the Sith*, setting up the kidnapping of Chancellor Palpatine. Asajj Ventress, not included in the final story, was at one point slated to die in the novel as a means of tying up her fate, though that story would ultimately be told elsewhere.

The storyline for *Labyrinth of Evil* was finalized before the original animated *Clone Wars* microseries sought to also lead into the events of Episode III. The Cartoon Network team, led by Genndy Tartakovsky, built their animated climax around the novel plot, but departed from the details in the interest of telling a more explosive animated story. This included a more drawn-out sequence of Coruscant under attack by droid starfighters, additional Jedi defending Chancellor Palpatine (Roron Corobb and Foul Moudama, who were then inserted into the novel text), and an entirely separate story of Anakin and Obi-Wan on the planet Nelvaan, which is fleetingly mentioned in the final chapters of the book.

Jax Pavan

Den Dhur

Bria Tharen

Rahm Kota

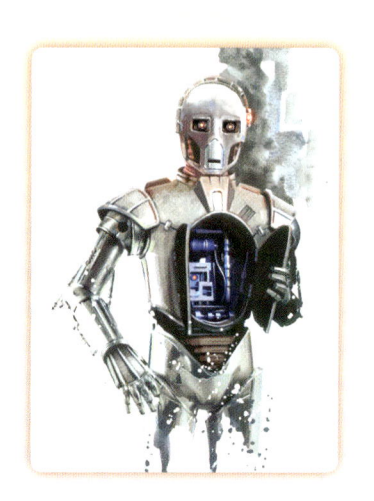

Bollux

Gallandro

CHAPTER 4

THE DARK TIMES

The generational gap between the adventures of Anakin Skywalker and the start of Luke Skywalker's heroics spans about two decades. During this time, the few Jedi survivors from the Clone Wars remain in hiding, desperate to champion causes of freedom, but assiduously avoiding drawing the attention of the Galactic Empire. In this time, the mythos of Anakin Skywalker as the fearless hero of the Republic will be forgotten. Instead, the galaxy's most potent symbol will be Darth Vader, Dark Lord of the Sith.

The Emperor shrinks from the galactic spotlight, content to build his power from behind a veil of darkness. From the shadows, he spins conspiracies even greater than the one that unseated the Republic. Embers of resistance spark across the galaxy, many of which are promptly snuffed out by the rapid strikes of Imperial stormtroopers. A few, however, continue to smolder, fed by idealists in the Senate like Bail Organa and Mon Mothma.

Relatively few Expanded Universe stories dot this span of time, which has long been roped off from active exploration. For decades, uncertainty regarding the details of Episode III kept storytellers from venturing too deeply into this era. Even now, other potential projects in development mean that Expanded Universe storytellers need to tread lightly on an area filled with possibility.

Despite such boundaries, this era contains some of the first Expanded Universe tales ever published. These early romps, featuring scoundrels Han Solo and Lando Calrissian, occupy this space not because of their proximity to the bygone era of the Republic. Rather, these stories were dated just prior to the events of Episode IV.

STAR WARS: EPISODE III REVENGE OF THE SITH

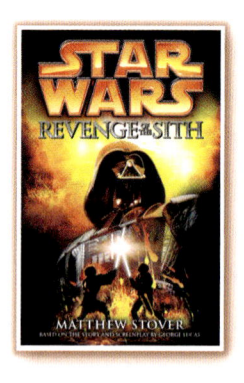

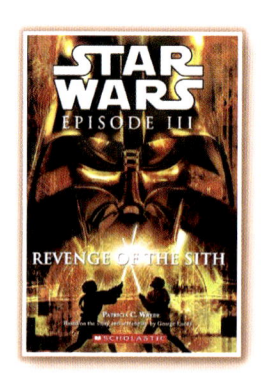

AUTHORS · Matthew Stover (adult novel); Patricia C. Wrede (juvenile novel); based on the story and screenplay by George Lucas

COVER ARTISTS · Steve Anderson (Del Rey novel); Louise Bova and Lucasfilm Ltd. (Scholastic novel)

PUBLICATION HISTORY · Novel, Del Rey Books
· Hardcover, April 2005
· Paperback, October 2005
Compiled as part of the Prequel Trilogy omnibus, Del Rey Books
· Paperback, May 2007
Compiled as part of the Dark Lord Trilogy omnibus, Del Rey Books
· Paperback, August 2008
Young reader novel, Scholastic Inc.
· Paperback, April 2005

TIME LINE PLACEMENT · 19 BBY

WORLDS VISITED · Coruscant [L-9]; Dagobah [M-19]; Kashyyyk [P-9]*; Mustafar [L-19]; Naboo [O-17]; Polis Massa [K-20]; Tatooine [R-16]; Utapau [N-19]

MAIN CHARACTERS · Anakin Skywalker, Jedi Knight (human male); Obi-Wan Kenobi, Jedi Master (human male); Palpatine, Supreme Chancellor (human male); Padmé Amidala, Galactic Senator (human female); Yoda, Jedi Master (male); Mace Windu, Jedi Master (human male); General Grievous, droid general (Kaleesh cyborg male); Count Dooku, Separatist leader (human male); Bail Organa, Galactic Senator (human male)

SUMMARY · The Separatists launch a major strike on Coruscant resulting in the kidnapping of Chancellor Palpatine. Anakin Skywalker and Obi-Wan Kenobi infiltrate General Grievous's fleeing starship to extricate the Chancellor. Though Anakin kills Count Dooku in the rescue, the war continues after Grievous escapes.
  Anakin's wife, Senator Padmé Amidala, is pregnant, and he is plagued by terrifying nightmares of

*Appears in junior novelization, but not in adult novelization.

After centuries of peace, the long-dormant battle between Sith and Jedi erupts anew as Darth Sidious duels with Yoda in the Galactic Senate Chamber.

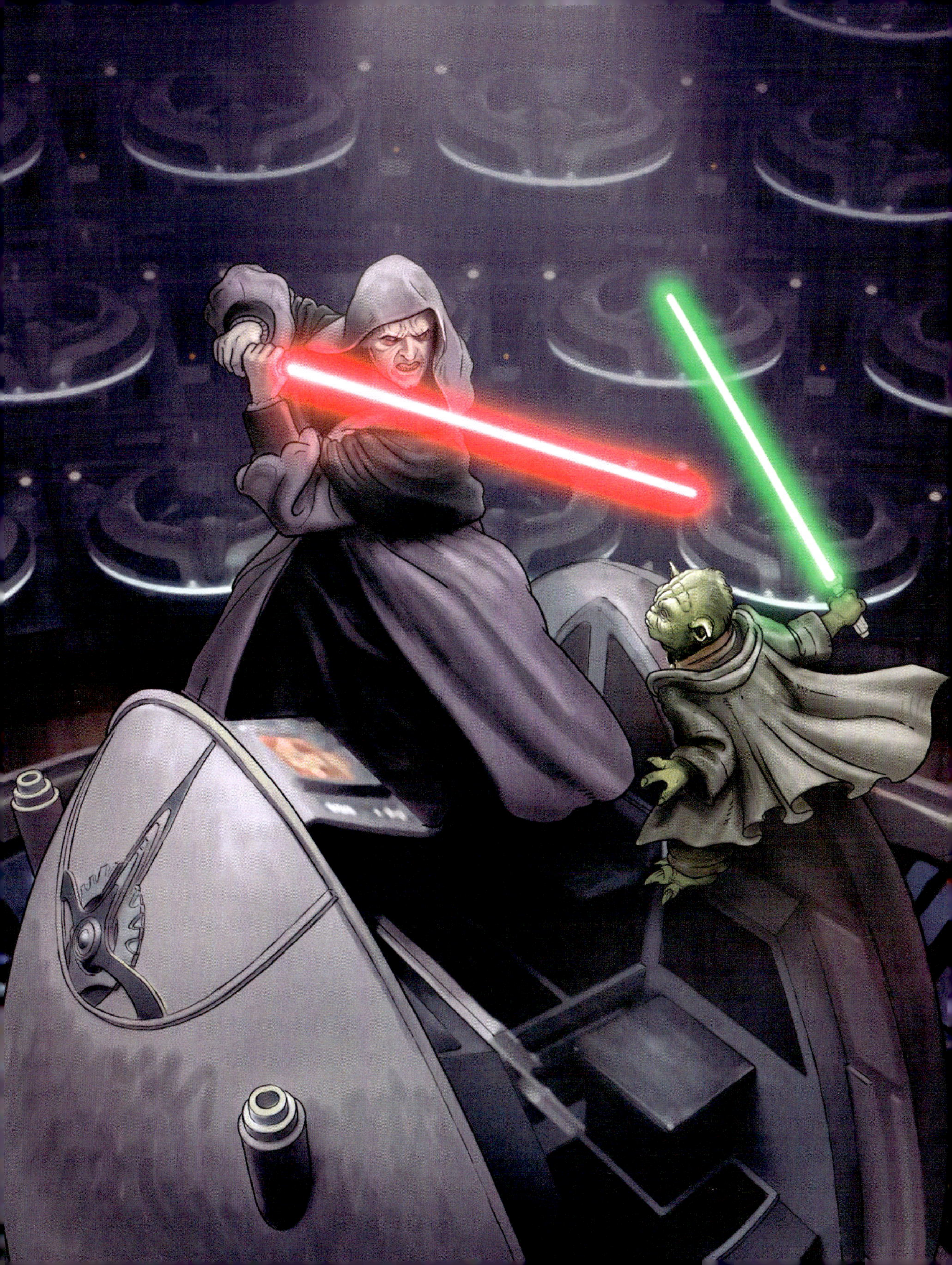

her dying during childbirth. Seeking to prevent this tragedy, Anakin looks for power beyond the Jedi: power offered to him by Palpatine, who reveals himself to be the Sith Lord, Darth Sidious. Anakin knows that the Sith are the sworn enemies of the Republic and the Jedi, but he cannot pass up the chance to save Padmé.

Though wavering in his loyalty and disappointed with the Jedi, Anakin nonetheless reports Sidious's revelation to Jedi Master Mace Windu. When Windu attempts to arrest the Chancellor, Anakin implores him to spare Palpatine's life, but Windu deems Palpatine too dangerous to be taken alive. Before Windu can kill the Dark Lord, Anakin cuts off Windu's sword hand. Palpatine then uses his dark power to destroy Windu.

Anakin embraces the dark side, kneeling before Darth Sidious to become his Sith apprentice. Sidious orders Anakin to march against the Jedi Temple with a legion of clone troopers and destroy all those within. Sidious then broadcasts a message to all clone commanders scattered across the galaxy: execute Order 66. The decree marks the Jedi as traitors and enemies of the state. Clones everywhere open fire on their generals.

On Utapau, Obi-Wan defeats General Grievous just prior to the issuing of Order 66. He escapes and leaves Utapau to reunite with Senator Bail Organa of Alderaan, who has intercepted Yoda fleeing from a battlefront on Kashyyyk.

Worried that other Jedi survivors may fall into Sidious's trap Yoda and Obi-Wan infiltrate the Jedi Temple to disable a beacon recalling the Jedi. There they discover disturbing evidence of Anakin's betrayal. Meanwhile, Chancellor Palpatine declares to the Senate that the war is over, and the Jedi insurrection has been quashed. To ensure peace and security, he announces that the Republic will transform into the Galactic Empire, with himself as sovereign.

Palpatine sends Anakin to the hellish planet of Mustafar to eliminate the Separatist leaders. Padmé follows Anakin to the lava world and confronts him about his radical actions. He offers Padmé a chance to join him in his conquest, but she is horrified at her husband's dark transformation. When Anakin sees Obi-Wan emerge from Padmé's vessel, he is consumed by jealousy. He reaches out with the Force and telekinetically chokes Padmé. Obi-Wan engages Anakin in a fierce lightsaber duel, defeating his former apprentice by amputating his legs and remaining arm. Anakin's ruined body bursts into flames amid the fires of Mustafar. Obi-Wan leaves the planet with an ailing Padmé.

On Coruscant, Yoda confronts Darth Sidious in a lightsaber duel that causes great destruction in the vacant Senate chamber. Sidious defeats Yoda, forcing the Jedi Master to flee the capital with Bail. Sidious departs for Mustafar, to collect his new Sith apprentice.

On remote Polis Massa, Padmé dies while giving birth to the twins Luke and Leia. Yoda decides the existence of the children should be kept secret: Bail takes the girl to live as his adoptive daughter on Alderaan, while Obi-Wan takes the boy to Tatooine to live with the Lars family. Yoda goes into exile on remote and uncharted Dagobah.

Within a surgical laboratory on Coruscant, Anakin Skywalker is rebuilt with cybernetic machinery to become the mechanized embodiment of Sidious's new empire: Darth Vader.

Though the Episode III adult novelization by Matthew Stover follows the Episodes I and II precedent of adding new scenes, its greatest additions to the screenplay are extensive internal viewpoints exploring the psychological underpinnings to character actions. To do this, the text often switches tenses and time frames to present the story as both an event of the past, and one "currently" unfolding. In this way, it skips cutaways to side stories, meaning the Order 66 montage that spans many worlds in the movie is instead distilled to action directly faced by Obi-Wan on Utapau. Even Yoda's mission to Kashyyyk to protect the Wookiee homeworld is only referred to as happening "off-screen" in the adult novel.

REPUBLIC COMMANDO: ORDER 66

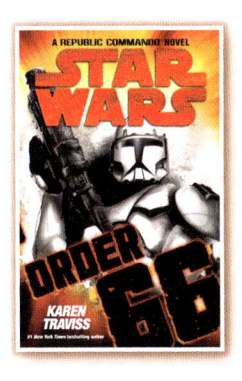

AUTHOR · Karen Traviss
COVER ARTIST · Greg Knight
PUBLICATION HISTORY · Novel, Del Rey Books
· Hardcover, September 2008
· Paperback, May 2009
TIME LINE PLACEMENT · 19 BBY

WORLDS VISITED · Anaxes [L-9]; Coruscant [L-9]; Haurgab [L-16]; Kashyyyk [P-9]; Mandalore [O-7]; Mes Cavoli (flashback) [O-7]; Nerrif [O-16]; Thyferra [L-14]

MAIN CHARACTERS · Darman, Niner, Corr, Atin: Omega Squad (human males); Mereel, Jaing, Ordo, A'den: Null ARCs (human males); Kal Skirata, mercenary (human male); Etain Tur-Makan, Jedi Knight (human female); Walon Vau, mercenary (human male); Bardan Jusik, former Jedi Knight (human male); Boss, Scorch, Fixer, Sev: Delta Squad (human males); Arligan Zey, Jedi Master (human male); Maze, Sull, Spar: ARC troopers (human males); Besany Wennen, Treasury investigator (human female)

SUMMARY · Kal Skirata continues his plot to liberate his personally trained clone commandos from service to the Republic. He is building a hidden refuge in the city Kyrimorut on Mandalore. Kal also persists in his search for a cure to the genetically encoded age-acceleration that robs the clones of a full life span. Toward that end, he searches for Dr. Ovolot Qail Uthan, a Separatist bioscientist captured by the Republic at the start of the war.

The clones living in Kal's enclave continue to aspire to a life beyond military service. The Null ARC Ordo proposes to Besany Wennen, and trooper Fixer proposes to Parja, a Mandalorian woman who has been helping him rehabilitate from his head injury. The Omega Squad commando Atin likewise ends up proposing to Laseema, a Twi'lek ally of Kal's operation.

The face of the war is changing. Omega Squad reports the battlefield appearance of new clone troopers with differing temperaments. These troops must hail from secret secondary cloning facilities hidden on Centax, part of Palpatine's machinations uncovered by Besany Wennen's data-mining.

The Delta and Omega commandos are recalled to Coruscant from the grueling front on Haurgab. Jedi general Arligan Zey needs their help in investigating strange activity within the data centers of the Republic Treasury.

Etain Tur-Makan has been joyfully snatching secret visits with her son, but is plagued by guilt because Darman isn't aware of his fatherhood. With Darman back in the capital, Etain tells him of his child. He is shaken to his core by this revelation. He lashes out against Kal for his role in keeping this information from him and beats him severely. Kal holds no ill will toward Darman, he also feels guilty for keeping the child a secret.

Kal suddenly finds himself targeted by Palpatine. Word of his investigations into genetic research has exposed his whole operation. Kal gathers his clones and allies, and they escape Coruscant using a contingency plan involving his submersible freighter. In the midst of this exodus, the Separatists attack Coruscant. Thousands of Republic ships emerge to defend the planet—the fruits of Palpatine's secret military development program. In the chaos that follows, Kal and his team free Dr. Uthan.

General Zey assigns Etain and Delta Squad to Kashyyyk, site of an intense battle between the natives and the Separatists. Delta Squad loses commando Sev in the wilderness and must leave him behind. In the thick of ground combat on Coruscant, Darman transmits a marriage proposal to Etain. She returns to Coruscant with Delta Squad to accept.

Order 66 is enacted, and Jedi Masters across the galaxy are murdered by clone troopers. The Coruscant Security Force joins with the Republic military in rounding up Jedi fugitives. While trying to escape a checkpoint, Etain is killed by a skittish Padawan's undisciplined lightsaber strike. Darman is devastated by Etain's death. Kal's group departs Coruscant, forced to leave Darman and Niner behind.

Kal takes Etain's body to Mandalore, to burn it on a pyre in a funeral befitting a Jedi Knight. Kal posthumously adopts Etain as his daughter. While at the refuge on Kyrimorut, he catches up with his biological daughter, Ruusaan, recently freed from a Republic prison. Other clones from beyond Kal's influence also join his enclave.

The attack on Coruscant here spans several days, while in *Labyrinth of Evil* it occurs in the course of a single day. The Delta Squad mission to Kashyyyk—and specifically the abandonment of Sev during extraction—is taken directly from the last mission of the 2004 videogame **Republic Commando**. To date, Sev's fate has yet to be resolved.

DARK LORD: THE RISE OF DARTH VADER

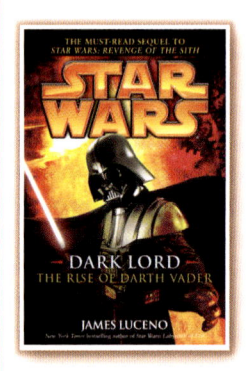

AUTHOR · James Luceno

COVER ARTISTS · David Stevenson; Lucasfilm

PUBLICATION HISTORY · Novel, Del Rey Books
· Hardcover, November 2005
· Paperback, June 2006
Compiled as part of the Dark Lord Trilogy omnibus, Del Rey Books
· Paperback, August 2008

TIME LINE PLACEMENT · 19 BBY

WORLDS VISITED · Alderaan [M-10]; Coruscant [L-9]; Jaguada [R-5]; Kashyyyk [P-9]; Murkhana [S-6]; Tatooine [R-16]

MAIN CHARACTERS · Darth Vader, Dark Lord of the Sith (human cyborg male); Roan Shryne, Jedi Knight (human male); Olee Starstone, Padawan learner (human female); Bol Chatak, Jedi Knight (Zabrak female); Palpatine, Emperor (human male); Bail Organa, Galactic Senator (human male)

SUMMARY · At the end of the Clone Wars, while the Republic attempts to conquer the Corporate Alliance

On the planet Kashyyyk, Darth Vader and the loyal troopers of the 501st Legion battle against Jedi survivors.

THE DARK TIMES

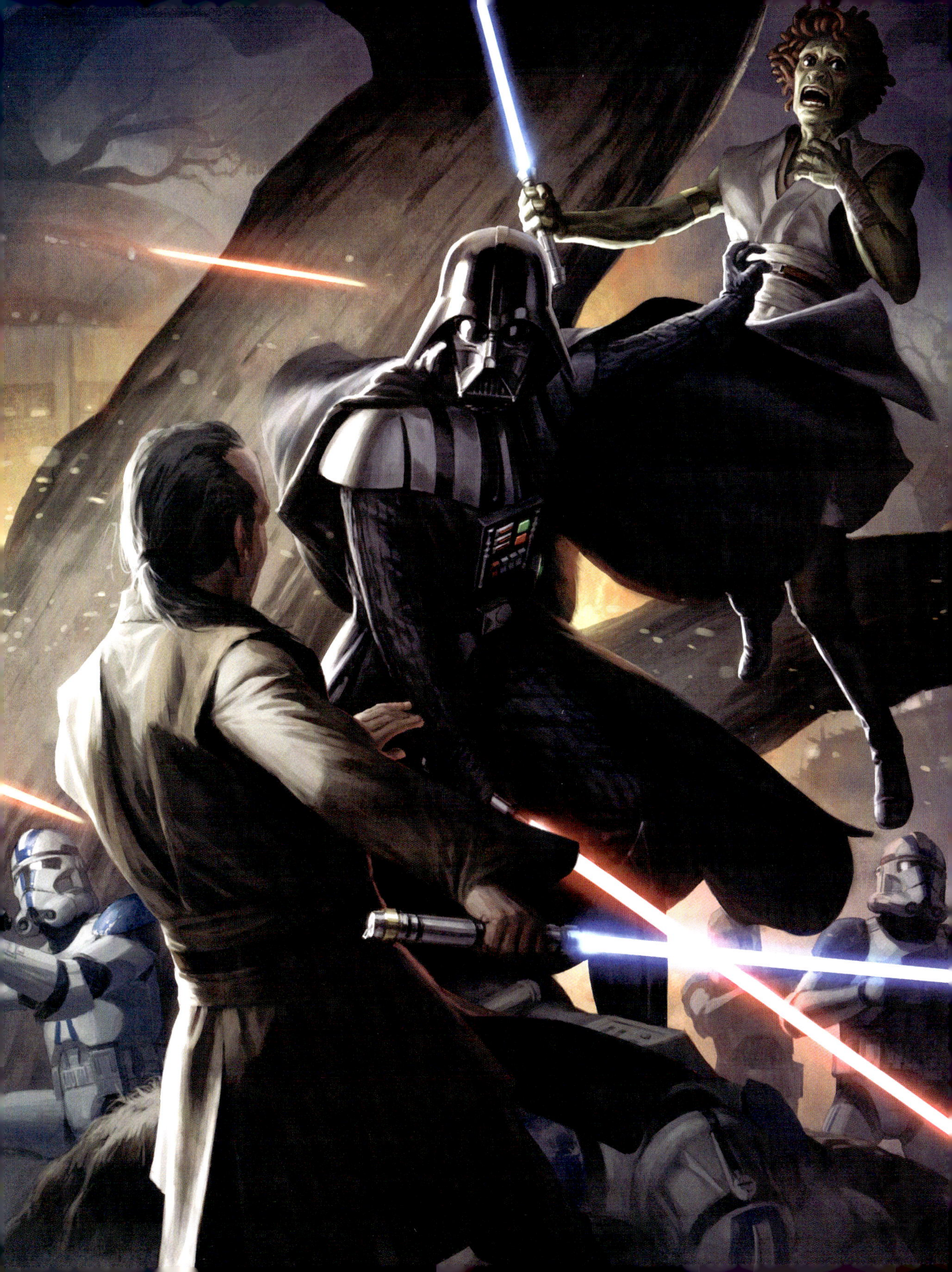

stronghold of Murkhana, Chancellor Palpatine enacts Order 66. Jedi Knights Roan Shryne, Olee Starstone, and Bol Chatak narrowly avoid the execution order when their clone troopers hesitate. The Jedi fugitives disguise themselves as Separatist mercenary prisoners.

Darth Vader, still becoming accustomed to the shortcomings of his new mechanical body, is dispatched by the Emperor to investigate clone disloyalty on Murkhana. He briefly tangles with the fugitive Jedi and kills Bol during her attempted escape. Roan and Olee flee aboard the freighter *Drunk Dancer*, a transit arranged by an underworld contact, Cash Garrulan. Roan is astounded to learn that *Dancer*'s captain, Jula, is his mother, whom he has not seen since his adoption into the Jedi Order decades before.

Olee is determined to stop Vader and learn more about the state of the Jedi in the galaxy, though Roan is more pragmatic and wants to stay beneath Imperial notice. The *Drunk Dancer* arrives at a Separatist communications center on the moon of Jaguada and taps into the data banks of the distant Jedi Temple. This breach alerts the Empire to the Jedi presence, prompting a hasty exit, but not before Olee secures a list of a hundred Jedi Masters and their whereabouts during the issuance of Order 66. She wishes to seek them out, while Shryne wants to stay in hiding. Unable to reconcile their differences, they agree to part ways.

Jula has a new assignment: to ferry a wanted Senator, Fang Zar, from his haven on Alderaan. Roan feels obligated to carry it out as a posthumous favor to Garrulan, who has been killed by the Empire. On Alderaan, Darth Vader is also trying to collect the Senator. The Dark Lord meets with Bail Organa, who secretly comes to realize that Vader is Anakin Skywalker—all the more reason to keep the true identity of his adopted daughter, Leia, a secret. Roan fails to free Zar before Vader strikes. The Dark Lord, in an effort to stop the extraction, throws his lightsaber at Zar, cutting down the Senator and injuring Jula.

Olee voyages to Kashyyyk, hoping to find any trace of Master Yoda and the other Jedi stationed there during the war. The world is in the midst of Imperial subjugation. The mighty Wookiees have been enslaved for the Imperial war effort. Roan, not wanting to see Olee fall into an Imperial trap, intercepts Lord Vader during his onslaught on the jungle world. Roan dies by Vader's power, buying Olee time to escape.

Meanwhile, on Tatooine, Obi-Wan Kenobi lives in exile as a desert hermit named Ben. While in a cantina, he hears reports of Darth Vader and sees the image of the dark armored warrior. This gives him his first inkling that Anakin Skywalker still lives.

The novel begins during the final moments of *Revenge of the Sith*, with the bulk of the story line starting four weeks later. Springing off the events of the movie, the book features cameo appearances by C-3PO and R2-D2 on Alderaan and Chewbacca on Kashyyyk. By coincidence, the Roan Shryne of this book shares a given name with Roan Land, a character featured in the Last of the Jedi books, also set in this era.

IMPERIAL COMMANDO: 501ST

AUTHOR · Karen Traviss
COVER ARTIST · Greg Knight

THE DARK TIMES

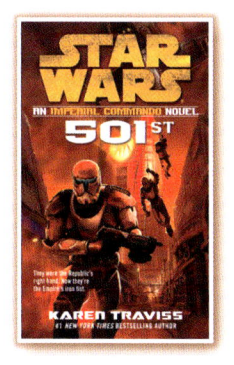

PUBLICATION HISTORY · Novel, Del Rey Books · Paperback, October 2009

TIME LINE PLACEMENT · 19 BBY

WORLDS VISITED · Celen [R-9]; Coruscant (Imperial Center) [L-9]; Coth Fuuras space station [J-8]; Fradian [Q-8]; Gibad [S-15]; Meserian [O-4]; Mezeg [N-7]; Ralltiir system [L-9]

MAIN CHARACTERS · Darman, Niner, Bry, Ennen: Imperial commandos (human males); Kal Skirata, mercenary (human male); Walon Vau, mercenary (human male); Tallisibeth "Scout" Enwandung-Esterhazy, Padawan fugitive (human female); Kina Ha, Jedi fugitive (Kaminoan female); Ny Vollen, transport pilot (human female); Ovolot Qail Uthan, scientist (human female); Djinn Altis, maverick Jedi (human male); Mij Gilamar, doctor and warrior (human male)

SUMMARY · Darman and Niner, left behind on Coruscant weeks earlier during the fighting following Order 66, are now Imperial commandos in the 501st Legion. Under direct orders from Darth Vader himself, the legion is to seek out Jedi and clone fugitives and capture Padawans for potential indoctrination into the Emperor's service. Darman is still deeply affected by the death of Etain. He has subsumed his compassionate personality, replacing it with cold Imperial implacability.

On Mandalore, Kal Skirata receives two unlikely fugitives into his Kyrimorut refuge: the Padawan Tallisibeth "Scout" Enwandung-Esterhazy, and a millennium-old Kaminoan Jedi, Kina Ha, who has been genetically engineered for exceedingly long life. Kal wants to exploit Kina's genetic structure to search for a cure for the clone age-acceleration, but his anti-Jedi sentiment begins to falter as he comes to genuinely like Scout and Kina. Kal's plan also risks the security of the Kyrimorut haven, for the Jedi's Force attunement allows them to pinpoint their location on Mandalore. They may compromise the location should they ever be interrogated. Adding to Kal's dilemma is the arrival of ARC trooper Maze, who brings with him Jedi Master Arligan Zey.

The coldly pragmatic Walon Vau suggests simply killing the Jedi, but Kal comes up with an alternate plan. He reaches out to Djinn Altis, the unorthodox leader of a splinter Jedi group, and offers the Jedi trio to him, in exchange for having their memories wiped of Kyrimorut's location.

Kal's principal agent in reversing the clone aging is Dr. Ovolot Qail Uthan, but he loses her focus when the Empire destroys her home planet of Gibad. Adding to Uthan's pain, the Empire did so by unleashing a toxin of her own creation. Uthan devotes her efforts to developing a virus to use against the Empire, distracting her from the age-acceleration research.

Eager to see his original squads return, Kal dispatches his troops to Coruscant to rescue Darman and Niner from the Empire. Darman decides to stay with the 501st, reasoning that he can monitor the legion's activities from within and thus better ensure the safety of his son, Kad, who would likely be a target of the Empire. Niner remains with Darman but vows to stay in touch with Kal Skirata through specialized comlinks.

Darman comes to view the Jedi as a threat, for he wants to see his son raised as a free Mandalorian rather than a Jedi to be hunted by the Empire. Darman vows to begin hunting what Jedi he can.

THE BOOK DRAWS ITS TITLE from the 501st Legion of costumers, a fan group founded in 1997. Members of the worldwide group build their own intricate Imperial armor, which sometimes surpasses screen-used costumes in detail. They arrange impressive group appearances for fun and charity. The 501st Legion was first included as part of the *Star Wars* story line in *Survivor's Quest* (2004) by Timothy Zahn.

"MIST ENCOUNTER"

AUTHOR · Timothy Zahn
COVER ARTIST · Gábor Szikszal and Zoltán Boros
PUBLICATION HISTORY · Short story, West End Games · *Star Wars Adventure Journal* #7, August 1995 Reprinted in paperback release of *Outbound Flight* by Del Rey Books, January 2007

TIME LINE PLACEMENT ·
19 BBY
WORLD VISITED · Unnamed world [I-5]
MAIN CHARACTERS ·
Colonel Mosh Barris, Imperial officer (human male); Voss Parck, Imperial captain (human male); Major Wyan, Imperial officer (human male); Mitth'raw'nuruodo, exile (Chiss male); Booster Terrik, smuggler (human male); Llollulion, smuggler (Borlovian male)

SUMMARY · The *Victory*-class Star Destroyer *Strikefast* pursues smugglers who take to ground on an uncharted, mist-shrouded world. Mosh Barris leads a team of Imperials searching the forests, but they continue to run afoul of traps and tricks laid by an alien exiled on the planet. Captain Parck, impressed by the alien's keen strategies and cunning tactics, offers him a position in the new Imperial fleet. The alien, Mitth'raw'nuruodo, accepts.

Published in 1995, for years "Mist Encounter" served as the earliest origin story for Grand Admiral Thrawn, though it still did not reveal who his people were and what specific circumstances led to his exile—some of that would wait until *Outbound Flight* (2006). Timothy Zahn wrote "Mist Encounter" well before any details of Episodes I, II, and III were shared with Expanded Universe authors, and though it aligns fairly well with modern continuity, there is a conspicuous absence of any mention of the recently completed Clone Wars. The original short story included a mention of "President Palpatine," which was changed to "Chancellor Palpatine" when it was reprinted in the *Outbound Flight* paperback in 2007. By virtue of its chronology, this story inadvertently marks the debut of the TIE fighter. It also marks the first chronological appearance of Booster Terrik, who will figure prominently in the X-Wing novels and beyond.

"THE LAST ONE STANDING"

AUTHOR · Jude Watson

PUBLICATION HISTORY · Short story, Scholastic Inc. Compiled as part of the Legacy of the Jedi / Secrets of the Jedi omnibus
· Paperback, May 2006

TIME LINE PLACEMENT · 19 BBY

WORLD VISITED · Tatooine [R-16]

MAIN CHARACTERS · Obi-Wan Kenobi, Jedi exile (human male); Owen and Beru Lars, moisture farmers (human male and female)

SUMMARY · The Lars homestead, where Luke Skywalker is being raised by his step-aunt and step-uncle, is plagued by repeated attacks by the Sand People. Though Owen asks Obi-Wan not to get involved, the Jedi confronts the Tuskens. When they become violent, rather than strike them down, Obi-Wan forces them to flee by exposing their faces—a deep-rooted cultural taboo among the desert nomads. Unlike Anakin years earlier, Obi-Wan finds a solution to the problem that does not require bloodshed.

This short story shares a title with a Boba Fett story published in the anthology *Tales of the Bounty Hunters* (1996).

CORUSCANT NIGHTS I: JEDI TWILIGHT

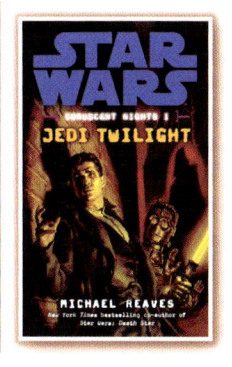

AUTHOR · Michael Reaves

COVER ARTIST · Glen Orbik

PUBLICATION HISTORY ·
Novel, Del Rey Books
· Paperback, June 2008

TIME LINE PLACEMENT · 19 BBY

WORLD VISITED · Coruscant (Imperial Center) [L-9]

Imperial officers Colonel Mosh Barris and Captain Voss Parck scrutinize Mitth'raw'nuruodo, an exiled Chiss.

THE DARK TIMES

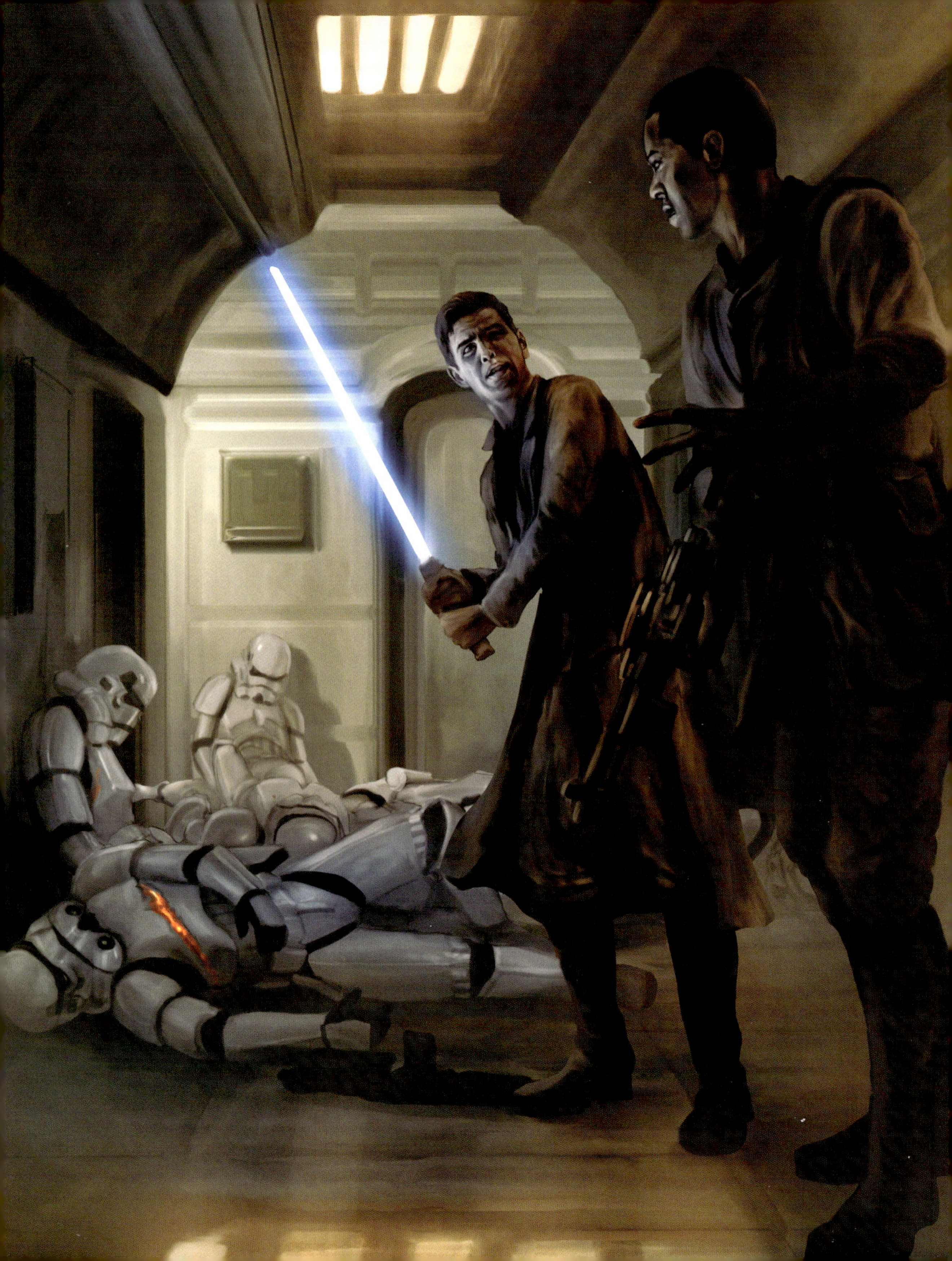

MAIN CHARACTERS · Jax Pavan, Jedi fugitive (human male); I-5YQ, self-aware droid; Den Dhur, journalist (Sullustan male); Nick Rostu, freedom fighter (human male); Kaird, underworld assassin (Nediji male); Laranth Tarak, Gray Paladin (Twi'lek female); Prince Xizor, Black Sun operative (Falleen male); Darth Vader, Dark Lord of the Sith (human cyborg male)

SUMMARY · Jax Pavan is a surviving Jedi Knight living undercover on the mean streets of Coruscant. The dying words of his Jedi Master, Even Piell, cause him to seek out a droid carrying information vital to the Whiplash, an underground group devoted to smuggling political dissidents out of Imperial Center. During his quest, Jax crosses paths with Laranth Tarak, an unorthodox Force-user aligned with the Whiplash, as well as the odd pair of Den Dhur, Sullustan cynic, and his best friend, the self-aware protocol droid I-5YQ.

In finding Jax, I-Five is continuing a mission begun more than a decade earlier by Lorn Pavan, Jax's father. I-Five looks out for Jax, but Jax is at first uncertain what to make of the droid's unusually vivid personality. Jax's intermittent connection to the Force—caused by him deliberately living a life counter to the ideals of the Jedi—exacerbates his sour spirit.

Darth Vader seeks out Jax. The Dark Lord's interest extends beyond the hunt for any surviving Jedi. Anakin Skywalker once had a fleeting friendship with Jax, and Vader wants to bury this remnant from his past. One of Jax's key contacts, Whiplash agent Nick Rostu, is coerced by Darth Vader to give up Jax.

Meanwhile, court intrigue abounds in the upper echelons of the Black Sun criminal organization. The Falleen noble Prince Xizor and the Nediji assassin Kaird vie for a position of power. Part of Xizor's plot involves capturing the very droid that Pavan seeks, which causes Jax and his crew to encounter the Falleen prince within a secret laboratory in the abandoned factory districts of Coruscant. The district is overrun by horrifying feral droids bent on the mindless destruction of all intruders.

The object of Jax's quest—the missing Whiplash droid—is in reality a lure concocted by Vader to capture Jax. Sensing Vader's approach, Jax triggers a thermonuclear explosion in the vacant factories by sacrificing his lightsaber to overload a generator. Though Jax fails to destroy Vader, the Dark Lord does mistakenly believe his quarry is dead.

With renewed spirit and purpose—and a more confident connection to the Force—Jax and his newfound associates agree to help the Whiplash cause and do their bit in challenging the rule of the Empire.

SET ABOUT TWO MONTHS AFTER the events of Episode III, the Coruscant Nights series picks up story threads begun in Darth Maul: *Shadow Hunter* (2000), also by Michael Reaves, and the MedStar duology (2004).

The inclusion of Even Piell at the start of this story line does not align with canon as presented in the subsequent *Clone Wars* animated series. A 2011 episode ("Counterattack") kills Piell off at the height of the war, while this 2008 book presents him as a survivor of Order 66. Though Jax Pavan being Piell's Padawan is still accepted as part of continuity, exactly who begins the hunt for the Whiplash droid has yet to be redefined.

In the corridors of a dingy underworld apartment on Coruscant, Jax Pavan and Nick Rostu meet after dispatching their common foe: a patrol of Imperial stormtroopers.

THE DARK TIMES

"IN HIS IMAGE"

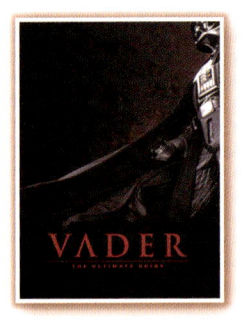

AUTHOR · Karen Traviss
COVER ARTIST · Lucasfilm
PUBLICATION HISTORY · Short story, IDG Entertainment · *Vader: The Ultimate Guide*, July 2005
TIME LINE PLACEMENT · 19 BBY
WORLDS VISITED · Coruscant (Imperial Center) [L-9]; Vohai [O-18]
MAIN CHARACTERS · Darth Vader, Dark Lord of the Sith (human cyborg male); Palpatine, Galactic Emperor (human male); Sa Cuis, Emperor's Hand (human male); Erv Lekauf, aide-de-camp (human male)

SUMMARY · As Darth Vader searches for a possible new clone template to bolster the Imperial stormtrooper ranks, the Emperor sends assassins to test his apprentice. Sa Cuis, an Emperor's Hand and Dark Jedi, attacks Vader, but the Sith Lord defeats him. Vader, impressed by Cuis's devotion, physical power, and Force ability, orders that a genetic sample be taken from him prior to execution, so that Cuis can become a clone template.

LAST OF THE JEDI #1: THE DESPERATE MISSION

AUTHOR · Jude Watson
COVER ARTIST · John VanFleet 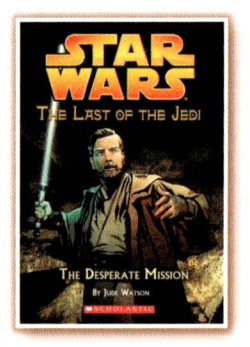
PUBLICATION HISTORY · Juvenile novel, Scholastic Inc. · Paperback, May 2005
TIME LINE PLACEMENT · c. 18 BBY
WORLDS VISITED · Bellassa [M-11]; Red Twins [I-7]; Tatooine [R-16]
MAIN CHARACTERS · Obi-Wan Kenobi, Jedi exile (human male); Ferus Olin, revolutionary (human male); Trever Flume, thief (human male); Boba Fett, bounty hunter (human male); D'harhan, bounty hunter (human cyborg male); Malorum, Imperial Inquisitor (human male)

SUMMARY · Intriguing rumors of the escape of former Padawan Ferus Olin from Imperial imprisonment on Bellassa bring Obi-Wan Kenobi out of his Tatooine exile. While trying to avoid Imperial stormtrooper patrols, Obi-Wan encounters a young thief and colleague of Ferus's, Trever Flume. Trever leads Obi-Wan to make contact with the Eleven, Bellassa's rebel underground.

As the Empire begins rounding up innocent Bellassan citizens in its search for Ferus, Obi-Wan finds him. Ferus feigns surrender to spare the Bellassans, but ultimately escapes Imperial custody with Obi-Wan and Trever's help. The fugitives leave the planet for the Red Twins spaceport, pursued by bounty hunters Boba Fett and D'harhan.

Early in development, the *Last of the Jedi* series was envisioned as the continuing adventures of Obi-Wan Kenobi, but Lucasfilm ultimately vetoed this concept, reasoning that Kenobi would never venture far from Luke Skywalker unless exceptional circumstances demanded it. Almost a year has passed between the events of Episode III and

Obi-Wan Kenobi and Ferus Olin attempt to outrun a determined Boba Fett through the abandoned mining tunnels beneath the surface of Bellassa.

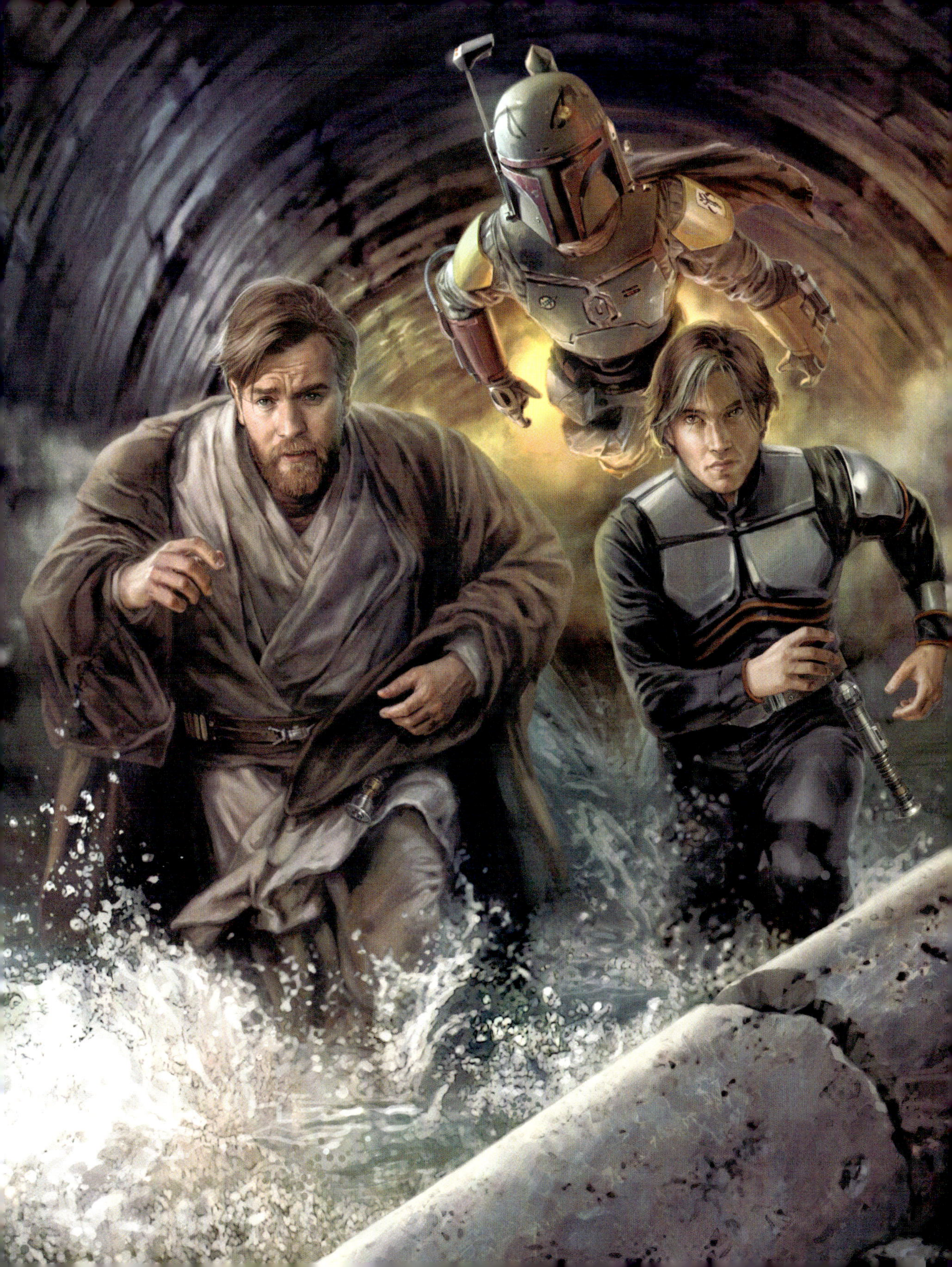

the start of this series. The heavily armored bounty hunter D'harhan was first introduced in *The Mandalorian Armor* (1998), book 1 of the Bounty Hunter Wars trilogy by K. W. Jeter, set after the events of *Return of the Jedi*.

LAST OF THE JEDI #2: DARK WARNING

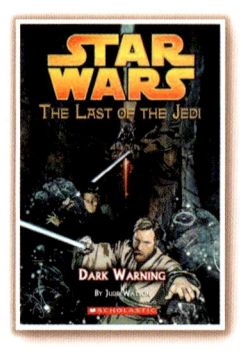

AUTHOR · Jude Watson
COVER ARTIST · John VanFleet
PUBLICATION HISTORY · Juvenile novel, Scholastic Inc. · Paperback, September 2005
TIME LINE PLACEMENT · c. 18 BBY

WORLDS VISITED · Acherin [I-7]; Coruscant (Imperial Center) [L-9]; Ilum [G-7]; Polis Massa [K-20]; Tatooine [R-16]; unnamed asteroid [I-7]

MAIN CHARACTERS · Obi-Wan Kenobi, Jedi exile (human male); Ferus Olin, revolutionary (human male); Trever Flume, thief (human male); Boba Fett, bounty hunter (human male); Garen Muln, Jedi exile (human male); Toma, revolutionary leader (human male)

SUMMARY · Obi-Wan, Ferus, and Trever ditch their violent bounty hunter pursuers in the occluded depths of a nebula, but the limited range of their escape vessel forces them to set down on Acherin, in the Red Twins system. A former front in the Clone Wars, the planet is now home to open rebellion against Imperial rule. It is here that Obi-Wan and Ferus learn that Jedi Knight Garen Muln is still alive and hiding on Ilum. From Acherin, Ferus also finds a rogue asteroid, perfectly concealed in turbulent gas clouds, which he chooses as a secret base of operations for fugitives from the Empire.

After a side trip to Polis Massa to ensure that any trails leading to Padmé's children are erased, Obi-Wan decides to part ways with Ferus and return to Tatooine. He asks Ferus to take care of Garen and to ensure that the Imperial Inquisitors do not pursue any leads to or from Polis Massa.

CHRONOLOGICAL NOTE | Imperial Inquisitors

Imperial Inquisitors—dark-side-imbued agents of the Empire tasked with seeking out any Force-users—began as a storytelling concept in *Star Wars* role-playing games. A "Grand Inquisitor Torbin" is given the briefest of passing mentions in *The Star Wars Sourcebook* (1987). Later guidebooks such as *Galaxy Guide 9: Fragments from the Rim* (1993) and *The Dark Empire Sourcebook* (1993) give more detailed accounts of the Inquisitors, primarily as a means of providing Force-wielding opponents for players of the game. The Inquisitors rarely appeared in fiction because, until relatively recently, so few tales were told in their most pertinent era.

"GHOSTS OF THE SITH"

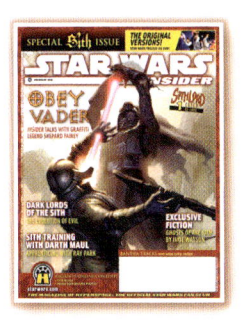

AUTHOR · Jude Watson
PUBLICATION HISTORY · Short story, IDG Entertainment
 · *Star Wars Insider* #88, June 2006
TIME LINE PLACEMENT · c. 18 BBY
WORLD VISITED · Korriban [R-5]

MAIN CHARACTERS · Ferus Olin, fugitive (human male); Trever Flume, thief (human male); Jenna Zan Arbor, scientist (human female)

SUMMARY · Ferus Olin sets down on Korriban to refuel. He is surprised to see Jenna Zan Arbor there, eager to venture into the Valley of the Dark Lords. Though Ferus is compelled to learn what she is up to, he must attend to other matters.

LAST OF THE JEDI #3: UNDERWORLD

AUTHOR · Jude Watson
COVER ARTIST · John VanFleet
PUBLICATION HISTORY · Juvenile novel, Scholastic Inc.
 · Paperback, December 2005
TIME LINE PLACEMENT · c. 18 BBY
WORLD VISITED · Coruscant (Imperial Center) [L-9]

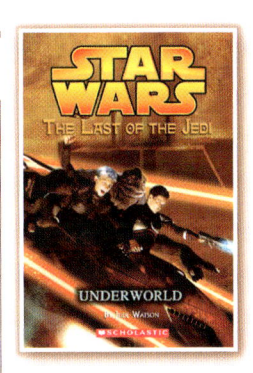

MAIN CHARACTERS · Ferus Olin, fugitive (human male); Trever Flume, thief (human male); Solace, aka Fy-Tor Ana, Jedi Knight (human female); Malorum, Imperial Inquisitor (human male); Darth Vader, Dark Lord of the Sith (human cyborg male); Dexter Jettster, underworld contact (Besalisk male)

SUMMARY · Ferus and Trever explore the burned-out Jedi Temple, which persistent rumors describe as having been converted into a prison for surviving Jedi. In the heart of the Temple, they realize that the rumors were a trap set by Imperial Inquisitors to lure any Jedi survivors. Ferus narrowly avoids Malorum and Vader, venturing into the "orange district" deep in Coruscant, where he meets Dexter Jettster, who has been helping Imperial fugitives. In the underworld, Ferus and Trever find an enclave of survivors led by a Jedi, Fy-Tor Ana, who now operates under the name Solace. A spy in her ranks alerts Imperial stormtroopers to their secret base deep beneath the crust of Coruscant. Ferus is again captured by the Empire.

LAST OF THE JEDI #4: DEATH ON NABOO

AUTHOR · Jude Watson
COVER ARTIST · John VanFleet

THE DARK TIMES

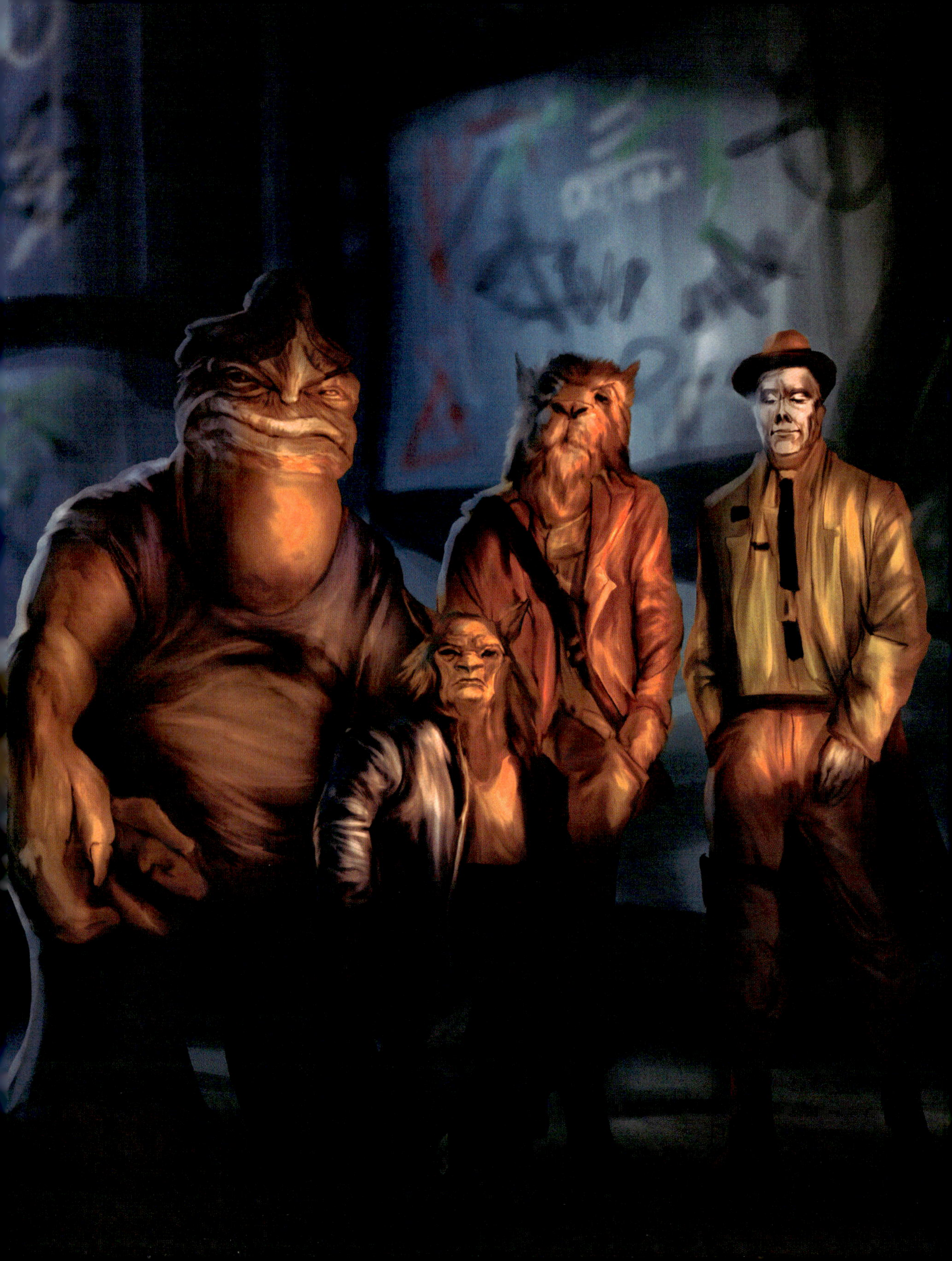

PUBLICATION HISTORY · Juvenile novel, Scholastic Inc. · Paperback, April 2006

TIME LINE PLACEMENT · c. 18 BBY

WORLDS VISITED · Alba-16 [O-6]; Coruscant (Imperial Center) [L-9]; Dontamo [J-6]; Naboo [O-17]; Polis Massa [K-20]

MAIN CHARACTERS · Ferus Olin, fugitive (human male); Trever Flume, thief (human male); Solace, aka Fy-Tor Ana, Jedi Knight (human female); Malorum, Imperial Inquisitor (human male); Clive Flax, infiltrator (human male); Ryoo Thule, Padmé's grandmother (human female); Gregar Typho, Naboo captain (human male)

SUMMARY · Ferus is sentenced to an Imperial prison camp on Dontamo, where he is reunited with Clive Flax, a former spy and colleague. The two escape captivity and are rescued by Trever and Solace.

Meanwhile, Inquisitor Malorum, following a tenuous lead regarding the mystery of Padmé Amidala's death, voyages to Polis Massa and Naboo to investigate the details surrounding the Senator's funeral. Ferus hears of this and—remembering his promise to Obi-Wan—speeds to Naboo to intercept the Inquisitor. In his search, Malorum kills Padmé's grandmother Ryoo and discovers that Padmé's child survived. Before Malorum can do anything with this information, however, he dies in a duel with Ferus.

CORUSCANT NIGHTS II: STREET OF SHADOWS

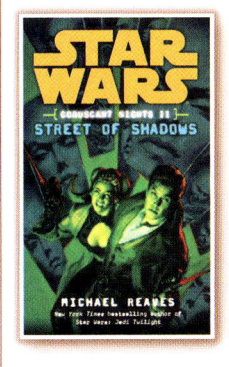

AUTHOR · Michael Reaves

COVER ARTIST · Glen Orbik

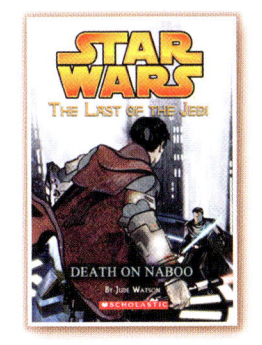

PUBLICATION HISTORY · Novel, Del Rey Books · Paperback, August 2008

TIME LINE PLACEMENT · c. 18 BBY

WORLDS VISITED · Coruscant (Imperial Center) [L-9]; Oovo-4 [S-8]

MAIN CHARACTERS · Jax Pavan, private investigator (human male); I-5YQ, self-aware droid; Den Dhur, journalist (Sullustan male); Laranth Tarak, Gray Paladin (Twi'lek female); Dejah Duare, artist's assistant (Zeltron female); Aurra Sing, bounty hunter (humanoid female); Darth Vader, Dark Lord of the Sith (human cyborg male); Gregar Typho, Naboo captain (human male); Baron Vlaçan and Baroness Kirma Umber, nobles (male and female Vindalians); Ves Volette, light sculptor (Caamasi male)

SUMMARY · Jax Pavan, working as a private detective, must solve the murder of outspoken Caamasi artist Ves Volette. Jax's renewed attunement to the Force is vital both in the investigation as well as in warding off the pheromonic allure of Volette's Zeltron art assistant, the sultry Dejah Duare. Jax's persistent digging uncovers a likely culprit in either Baron or Baroness Umber, wealthy art patrons who supported Ves. Though there were several possible motives—increasing the value of the late artist's works, for example—the two are innocent. The real

---

The Erased of the Coruscant underworld: Dexter Jettster, Curran Caladian, Oryon, and Keets Freely.

THE DARK TIMES

killer was their protocol droid, who witnessed how much the Baron's attraction toward Dejah upset the Baroness.

I-Five continues his friendship with Jax, becoming a vital partner in their efforts on behalf of the Whiplash underground group. I-Five reveals to Jax that his father, Lorn, was killed by the Sith Lord Darth Maul. I-Five also secretly carries within him a preserved sample of bota, a Force-enhancing medicine, which he entrusts to Jax.

Meanwhile, Darth Vader frees bounty hunter Aurra Sing from a lengthy prison sentence to resume the hunt for Jax on his behalf. Aurra's Force attunement allows her to track down her quarry. She attacks Jax, though he escapes by causing her to fall into heavy machinery at a construction site.

Amid this drama, Captain Typho of Naboo carries out a mission of vengeance rooted in love. He is

In the mirrored chamber of an amusement park, Laranth Tarak is goaded by the many reflections of bounty hunter Aurra Sing.

seeking answers regarding Padmé Amidala's mysterious death. His own investigation into the Coruscant underworld and the various information fonts there uncovers the presence of a Sith Lord on Mustafar at the time of Padmé's demise. To avenge her, he confronts Vader in an attempt to kill him. Vader kills Typho instead, though he is deeply affected by Typho's invoking Padmé's name.

TRUE TO THE PULP NOIR ROOTS celebrated in the Coruscant Nights series, *Street of Shadows* has several essential ingredients of a murder mystery: There is an alluring femme fatale and an exposi-

142   THE DARK TIMES

tory "parlor scene" where the investigator calls out the true killer. And sure enough, the butler (droid) did it.

Street of Shadows is, thus far, the only story that includes the destruction of Caamas as a contemporaneous event in its plot, though the event was introduced as part of galactic history in Timothy Zahn's *Specter of the Past* (1997).

Typho's first name, Gregar, is not mentioned in this book, though he was given it in *Death on Naboo* (2006). Given the chronological placement of both works, it's possible that Malorum's investigation into Padmé's demise in *Death on Naboo* renewed or further fueled Typho's quest in *Street of Shadows*. The novel erroneously suggests, through Typho's recollections, that Padmé's death had occurred before Palpatine declared himself Emperor, though the movie *Revenge of the Sith* has Typho seated next to a very-much-alive Padmé at that exact moment.

MAIN CHARACTERS · Ferus Olin, double agent (human male); Trever Flume, thief (human male); Solace, aka Fy-Tor Ana, Jedi Knight (human female); Sano Sauro, Galactic Senator (human male); Bog Divinian, Imperial dignitary (human male); Palpatine, Galactic Emperor (human male)

SUMMARY · The Emperor surprises Ferus Olin with an offer of amnesty in exchange for helping solve the mystery behind the computer sabotage that has crippled the high-tech world of Samaria. Ferus discovers that the saboteur was Astri Oddo, the estranged wife of Bog Divinian, the ranking Imperial official on Samaria. Her computer work has helped cover up the erasure of records of Imperial political targets on the planet.

Trever returns to Bellassa with Solace, discovering that the Empire has moved the prosecution of political prisoners offworld, away from prying eyes, to a roaming starship called *True Justice*. They pose as Imperials and commandeer the ship, an embarrassing development that discredits Senator Sauro, the developer of the *True Justice* initiative.

LAST OF THE JEDI #5: A TANGLED WEB

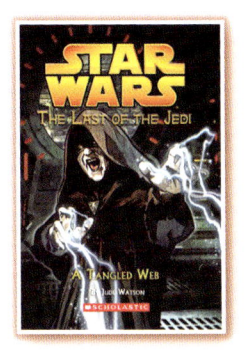

AUTHOR · Jude Watson
COVER ARTIST · John VanFleet
PUBLICATION HISTORY · Juvenile novel, Scholastic Inc.
· Paperback, August 2006
TIME LINE PLACEMENT · c. 18 BBY
WORLDS VISITED · Bellassa [M-11]; Coruscant (Imperial Center) [L-9]; Samaria [M-11]

LAST OF THE JEDI #6: RETURN OF THE DARK SIDE

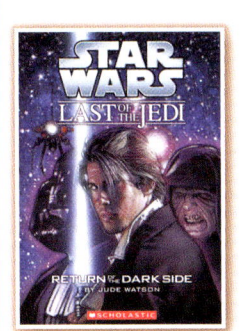

AUTHOR · Jude Watson
COVER ARTIST · Drew Struzan
PUBLICATION HISTORY · Juvenile novel, Scholastic Inc.
· Paperback, December 2006

TIME LINE PLACEMENT · c. 18 BBY

WORLDS VISITED · Bellassa [M-11]; Coruscant (Imperial Center) [L-9]; Samaria [M-11]; unnamed asteroid [I-7]

MAIN CHARACTERS · Ferus Olin, double agent (human male); Trever Flume, thief (human male); Darth Vader, Dark Lord of the Sith (human cyborg male); Bog Divinian, Imperial dignitary (human male); Palpatine, Galactic Emperor (human male); Flame, resistance leader (human female)

SUMMARY · Bog Divinian blames the Samarian sabotage on the neighboring world of Rosha, a finger-pointing political exercise he uses to elevate his influence on Samaria. The Emperor takes a personal interest in the intrigue, asking Ferus to make contact with the Samarian rebels. Palpatine commands that Ferus report directly to him, a show of favoritism that rankles Lord Vader. Independently, Trever Flume also makes contact with the resistance, led by an agent named Flame. Her freedom fighters spirit visiting Roshan officials back to their homeworld, unaware that the Empire is ready to invade the planet. Ferus comes to realize that the Empire wanted to keep Samarians and Roshans apart, for together they could combine their achievements in droid technology in a way that would threaten the Empire.

LAST OF THE JEDI #7: SECRET WEAPON

AUTHOR · Jude Watson
COVER ARTIST · Drew Struzan

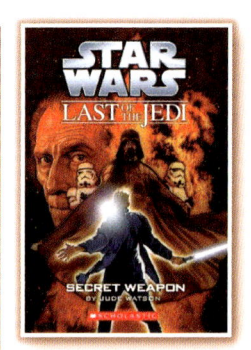

PUBLICATION HISTORY · Juvenile novel, Scholastic Inc. · Paperback, April 2007

TIME LINE PLACEMENT · c. 18 BBY

WORLDS VISITED · Bellassa [M-11]; Coruscant (Imperial Center) [L-9]; Omman [S-6]; unnamed asteroid [I-7]

MAIN CHARACTERS · Ferus Olin, double agent (human male); Trever Flume, thief (human male); Flame, resistance leader (human female); Roan Land, resistance fighter (human male); Amie Antin, doctor (human female); Astri Oddo, resistance fighter (human female); Lune Oddo, Force-sensitive child (human male); Darth Vader, Dark Lord of the Sith (human cyborg male); Palpatine, Galactic Emperor (human male); Solace, Jedi Knight (human female); Clive Flax, infiltrator (human male); Dona Telemark, fugitive (human female)

SUMMARY · To ward off stir-craziness on the asteroid refuge, Ferus's crew splits up to undertake two separate missions. Solace, Clive, Astri, and her son, Lune, voyage to the Coruscant underworld, while Flame, Roan, Dona, and Trever return to Bellassa.

Bellassa is undergoing transformation. The Empire is resuscitating the world's depressed economy. Bellassa's industrial factories are being refitted for weapons and technology production for a top-secret Imperial project overseen by Moff Tarkin. In trying to uncover more information about it, Trever, Roan, and Amie break into a factory to steal data, their infiltration facilitated by Ferus. Darth Vader catches the thieves. Though Trever escapes with the data, Vader captures Ferus and Amie, and kills Roan right before Ferus's disbelieving eyes.

On Coruscant, Solace finds Jedi Knight Ry-Gaul

In a starfighter training simulator, young cadets Lune Oddo and Trever Flume train for Imperial service.

surviving in the underworld. An Imperial patrol witnesses Lune Oddo exhibiting Force abilities. Astri is devastated when she learns that her son has been kidnapped and enrolled in the Imperial Naval Academy, no doubt due to the machinations of her ex-husband, Bog Divinian.

LAST OF THE JEDI #8: AGAINST THE EMPIRE

AUTHOR · Jude Watson

COVER ARTIST · Drew Struzan

PUBLICATION HISTORY · Juvenile novel, Scholastic Inc. · Paperback, October 2007

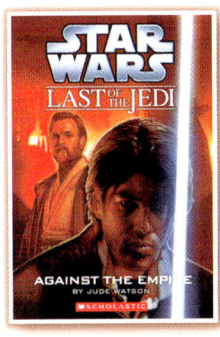

TIME LINE PLACEMENT · c. 18 BBY

WORLDS VISITED · Acherin [I-7]; Bellassa [M-11]; Coruscant (Imperial Center) [L-9]

MAIN CHARACTERS · Ferus Olin, double agent (human male); Trever Flume, thief (human male); Flame, resistance leader (human female); Amie Antin, doctor (human female); Lune Oddo, Force-sensitive child (human male); Darth Vader, Dark Lord of the Sith (human cyborg male); Clive Flax, infiltrator (human male); Jenna Zan Arbor, scientist (human female)

SUMMARY · To rescue young Lune Oddo from the Imperial Naval Academy, Trever enrolls under a false identity. Lune's ambitious father, Bog, volunteers his son as a test subject for an experiment being undertaken by Dr. Jenna Zan Arbor on behalf of Darth Vader. She is developing a drug that can target and erase specific memories. Trever, with help from Ferus, frees Lune just in time.

The Bellassan resistance, bolstered by Solace and Flame, stages a daring rescue of Amie during a prisoner transfer. Despite Flame's involvement, Clive has his doubts about her. He voyages to Acherin to find out more about her. Astri agrees to help Clive in his investigation.

Ferus, still shaken by Roan's death, is given a new assignment by the Emperor. He is made one of the Imperial Inquisitors, tasked with hunting down Force-sensitives. As a double agent, Ferus sees much opportunity in this: he'll have access to records of potential Jedi. But his exposure to the dark side threatens to corrupt him. Wanting to avenge Roan's death, Ferus seeks Vader's origins, which leads him to the Imperial surgical suite where the Dark Lord was rebuilt. There he uncovers a Sith Holocron that he plots to use against Vader.

LAST OF THE JEDI #9: MASTER OF DECEPTION

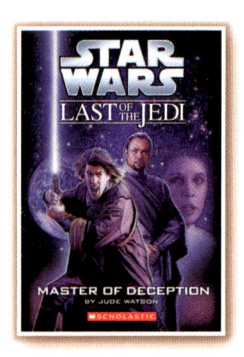

AUTHOR · Jude Watson
COVER ARTIST · Drew Struzan
PUBLICATION HISTORY · Juvenile novel, Scholastic Inc. · Paperback, February 2008
TIME LINE PLACEMENT · c. 18 BBY

WORLDS VISITED · Alderaan [M-10]; Coruscant (Imperial Center) [L-9]; Niro 11 [O-12]; Revery [N-6]

MAIN CHARACTERS · Ferus Olin, double agent (human male); Trever Flume, thief (human male); Bail Organa, Galactic Senator (human male); Clive Flax, infiltrator (human male); Astri Oddo, resistance fighter (human female); Darth Vader, Dark Lord of the Sith (human cyborg male); Jenna Zan Arbor, scientist (human female); Flame, resistance leader (human female); Hydra, Imperial Inquisitor (human female)

SUMMARY · Bail Organa is worried about his adoptive daughter, Leia. A reported display of Force ability by her has brought Imperial Inquisitors Ferus Olin and Hydra to Alderaan. Little does Bail know that Ferus is coming at the behest of Obi-Wan. While Ferus works hard to discredit the report—and thus draw suspicion away from Leia—he uncovers an Imperial spy on Alderaan. Vader was trying to disseminate weapons on the world as "proof" of sedition to warrant an Imperial crackdown, but Ferus thwarts that plan.

On Coruscant, Trever breaks into Jenna Zan Arbor's apartment to find out more about the memory agent she is developing. Together with Ry-Gaul's help, he liberates Zan Arbor's assistant, Linna Naltree, who injects the scientist with the drug as she escapes. The powerful drug effectively destroys Zan Arbor's evil genius.

Although Leia is less than a year old, she is described as walking and talking in this story—remarkably advanced development for a child that age . . . at least, by our terrestrial standards.

LAST OF THE JEDI #10: RECKONING

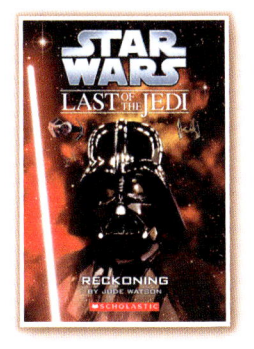

AUTHOR · Jude Watson

COVER ARTIST · Drew Struzan

PUBLICATION HISTORY · Juvenile novel, Scholastic Inc. · Paperback, June 2008

TIME LINE PLACEMENT · c. 18 BBY

WORLDS VISITED · Alderaan [M-10]; Coruscant (Imperial Center) [L-9]; Dexus-12 [L-9]; Hallitron-7 [J-7]; Kayuk [P-13]; Revery [N-6]; Telepan [M-11]; unnamed asteroid [I-7]; XT987 [J-8]

MAIN CHARACTERS · Ferus Olin, double agent (human male); Trever Flume, thief (human male); Clive Flax, infiltrator (human male); Astri Oddo, resistance fighter (human female); Darth Vader, Dark Lord of the Sith (human cyborg male); Solace, Jedi Knight (human female); Ry-Gaul, Jedi Knight (human male); Flame, resistance leader (human female)

SUMMARY · Ferus has pieced together the mystery of Darth Vader: he is Anakin Skywalker. Ferus confirms this through communication with Obi-Wan Kenobi, who worries that Ferus is so focused on vengeance that he may be falling under the sway of the dark side and the Emperor.

Moonstrike, the growing coalition of resistance leaders organized by Flame, needs a locale to gather. Ferus offers up his asteroid base. Together with Ry-Gaul and Solace, Ferus will ferry the resistance leaders to the secret location. Flame arranges the purchase of new starships for the transit. When Ferus discovers a tracking device aboard one of them, he comes to realize what Clive has suspected: Flame is a double agent gathering together resistance leaders so the Emperor can crush them in one strike. Influenced by the Sith Holocron, Ferus orders Flame's execution, but calmer heads prevail. The Jedi opt instead to strand Flame on a moon with enough supplies to survive while they continue, untracked, to the refuge asteroid.

Ferus returns to Coruscant to confront Vader within the ruins of the Jedi Temple. Ferus tries to unsettle the Sith Lord by invoking Padmé's name and reminding him of his past as Anakin. Despite such distraction, Vader injures and defeats Ferus, though Ferus survives the encounter. Ferus reaffirms his commitment to the Jedi Code and destroys the Sith Holocron by tossing it into a power conduit.

On the asteroid moon, Toma, a resistance leader from Acherin, proves to be a mole. The Empire has offered him a chance to rule Acherin if he gives up the location of the asteroid base. He activates a homing beacon that summons an Imperial Star Destroyer. The massive warship is fitted with a prototype weapon from the top-secret Death Star project. It fires and completely annihilates the asteroid, instantly killing the resistance leaders, as well as Solace, Ry-Gaul, and Garen Muln. The Jedi save the life of young Lune Oddo by placing him aboard an escape pod.

Ferus is devastated by this turn of events. Lune is reunited with his mother, Astri, who is now partners with Clive. They will raise him on Bellazura, along with Trever, who has been given the mind-wiping drug to erase his specific memories of Ferus's resistance movement for his own safety. Ferus, upon advice from Obi-Wan, retires to Alderaan to keep watch over young Leia Organa from a distance.

THE DARK TIMES
147

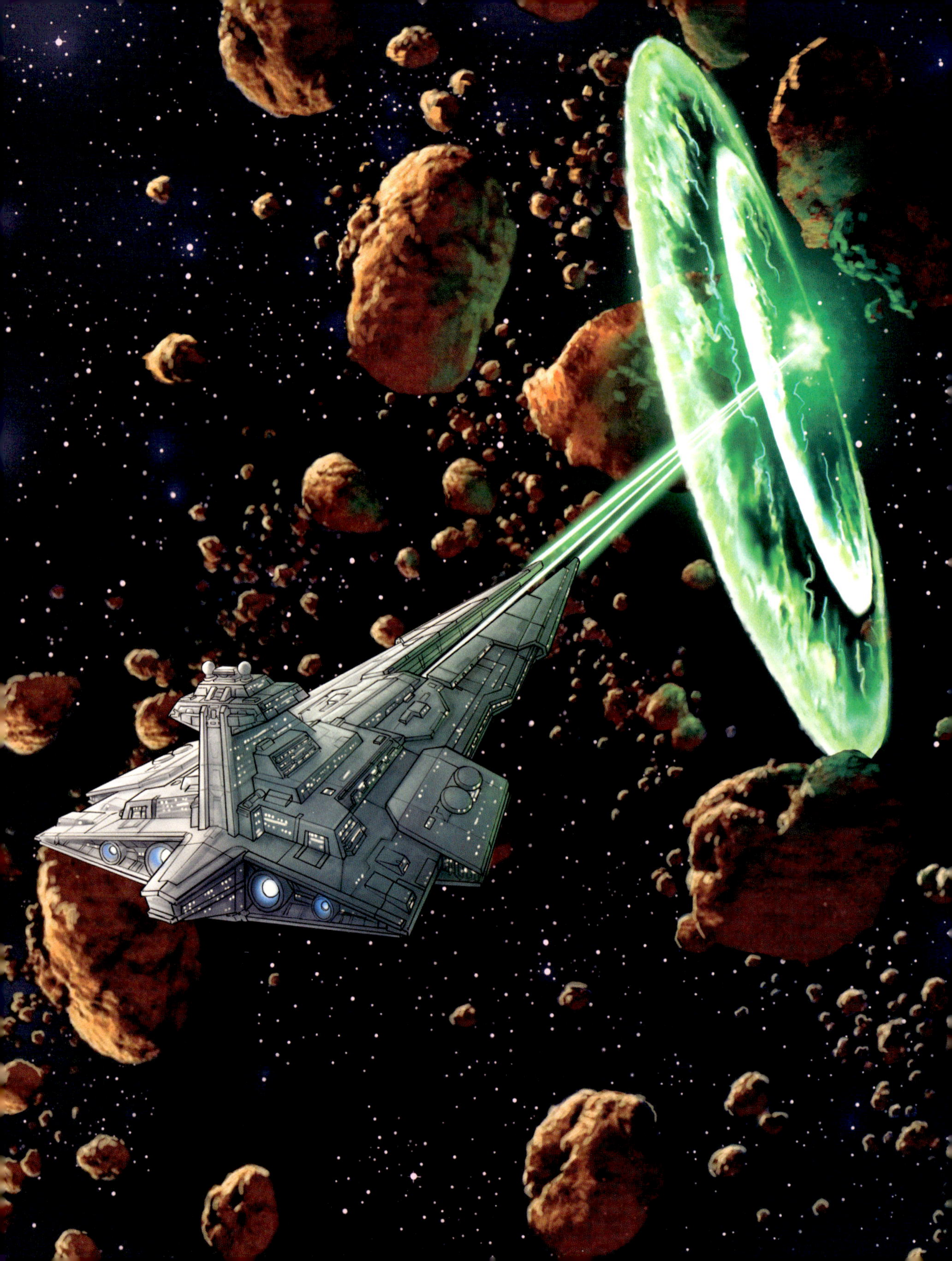

CORUSCANT NIGHTS III: PATTERNS OF FORCE

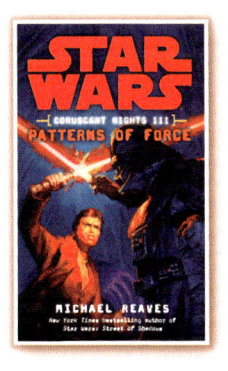

AUTHOR · Michael Reaves
COVER ARTIST · Glen Orbik
PUBLICATION HISTORY ·
Novel, Del Rey Books
· Paperback, January 2009
TIME LINE PLACEMENT ·
c. 18 BBY
WORLD VISITED · Coruscant (Imperial Center) [L-9]

MAIN CHARACTERS · Jax Pavan, former Jedi Knight (human male); I-5YQ, self-aware droid; Den Dhur, journalist (Sullustan male); Kajin Savaros, Force prodigy (human male); Laranth Tarak, Gray Paladin (Twi'lek female); Dejah Duare, artist's assistant (Zeltron female); Haninum Tyk Rhinann, former aide-de-camp to Darth Vader (Elomin male); Probus Tesla, Inquisitor (human male); Tuden Sal, Whiplash associate (Sakiyan male)

SUMMARY · In the shadowy Coruscant underworld, Kajin Savaros, a young man with unusually intense raw Force talent, draws the attention of both Imperial Inquisitors and Jax Pavan. In escaping pursuing Imperials, Kaj is welcomed by Jax and Laranth. While they recognize his potential as a Jedi, they also know that his undisciplined outbursts of Force energy risk their activities on behalf of the Whiplash. Jax begins training Kaj to control his abilities, and also discovers a peculiar attribute of Ves Volette's light sculptures: they can disrupt the broadcast of Force signatures.

Lorn Pavan's former associate Tuden Sal, who betrayed him and left I-Five to be mindwiped years ago, apologetically approaches the self-aware protocol droid. Tuden wants to make amends for his past betrayal and to use I-Five in a bid to assassinate Emperor Palpatine. Tuden figures I-Five to be the perfect assassin—invisible in the Force, and unexpected. I-Five considers the assignment, but Jax has reservations about using the droid in such a way. When he sees a recording of his father, made just prior to Lorn Pavan committing to kill the Sith warrior Darth Maul, Jax has a change of heart, recognizing that such extreme actions must be taken because no one else will dare do so. An added complication to this assignment emerges when I-Five's intentions begin registering in the Force—truly remarkable for a droid.

One of Jax's agents, Rhinann, obsesses over his inability to touch the Force. When he learns that I-Five smuggled a sample of the Force-amplifying bota plant from Drongar, he attempts to finagle his way into using the miracle extract.

When Imperial agents capture Kaj and Laranth—facilitated by an act of betrayal by Dejah Duare—I-Five and Jax agree to undertake a rescue mission in addition to their assassination attempt. Since the Emperor never arrives at the proposed rendezvous site, this part of the mission is scrubbed. Vader tortures Laranth in front of Jax, demanding that he hand over the bota sample along with other trophies. As Vader samples it, he is overcome by a tempestuous outburst of Force energy. An enraged Rhinann, seeing his chance at using the bota evaporate, charges the distracted Vader, knocking both out a shattered window.

Vader's Force storm kills Dejah and damages I-Five, but Jax and Laranth survive. They rescue Kaj, and the Whiplash smuggles the Force prodigy offworld to be rehabilitated on Shili. A rebuilt and modified I-Five joins Jax, Laranth, and Den in re-

---

A modified Imperial Star Destroyer fires its experimental super-laser weapon to devastate Ferus Olin's secret asteroid refuge.

THE DARK TIMES
149

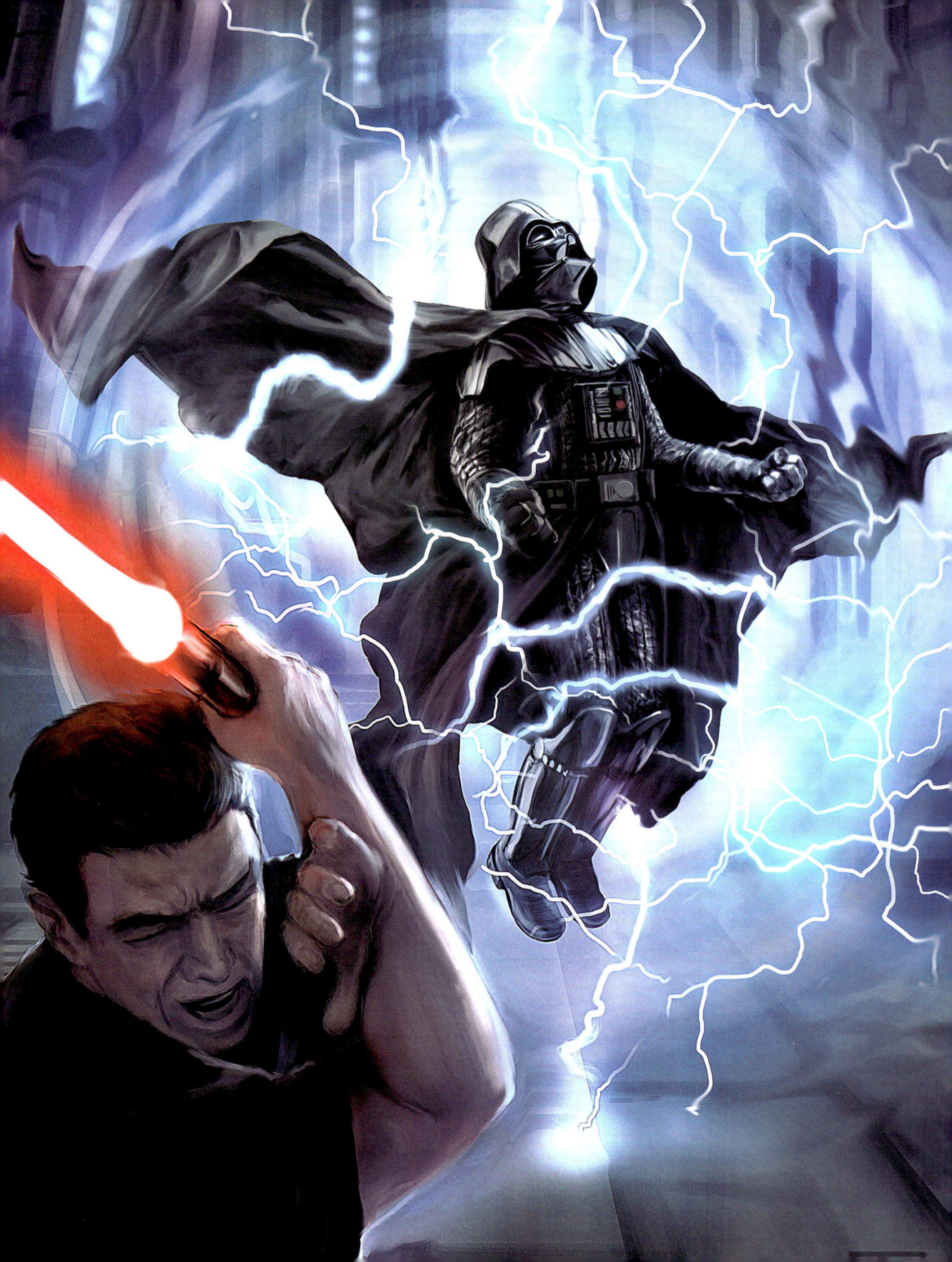

newed rescue activities on behalf of the Whiplash, while Jax begins to suspect—through impressions gleaned via the Force—that Vader was once Anakin Skywalker.

"TWO-EDGED SWORD"

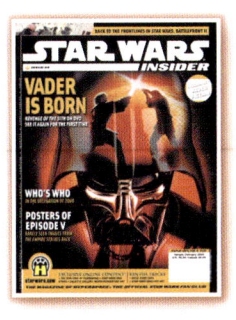

AUTHOR · Karen Traviss

PUBLICATION HISTORY · Short story, IDG Entertainment · *Star Wars Insider* #85, January 2006

TIME LINE PLACEMENT · 18 BBY

WORLDS VISITED · Coruscant (Imperial Center) [L-9]; Yinchorr [L-8]

MAIN CHARACTERS · Darth Vader, Dark Lord of the Sith (human cyborg male); Erv Lekauf, Imperial officer (human male); Palpatine, Galactic Emperor (human male); Sheyvan, Emperor's Hand (human male)

SUMMARY · Vader tests newly created Sa Cuis and Err Lekauf clones in combat drills at a training facility on Yinchorr, with Erv Lekauf and Emperor Palpatine in attendance. Satisfied with the results, they board a shuttle to return to Coruscant. En route, a disgruntled Emperor's Hand, Sheyvan, leads a revolt of the Cuis clones against the Emperor. Vader and the Lekauf clones put down the insurrection, though Lekauf is badly burned in the attack. Impressed with the officer's sacrifice, Vader orders a battalion of Lekauf clones.

"THE GUNS OF KELRODO-AI"

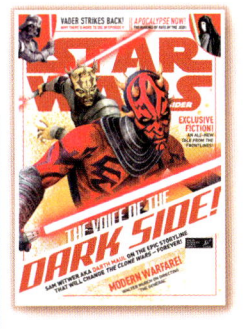

AUTHOR · Jason Fry

PUBLICATION HISTORY · Short story, Titan Publishing · *Star Wars Insider* #132, April 2012

TIME LINE PLACEMENT · 17 BBY

WORLD VISITED · Kelrodo-Ai [L-18]

MAIN CHARACTER · Shea Hublin, starfighter pilot (human male)

SUMMARY · Imperial hero Shea Hublin leads his V-wing starfighter squadron on a mission to pacify a seditionist pocket on the volcanic world of Kelrodo-Ai. The assignment requires twisting the nimble fighters through tunnels to blow a facility's hypermatter reactor, but the squadron must fly at agonizingly slow speeds through one stretch to avoid triggering an attack by a native tentacled lifeform.

SHEA HUBLIN FIRST APPEARED briefly in the 1979 newspaper strip "Princess Leia: Imperial Servant," by Russ Manning. In it, he is an older, distinguished gentleman decorated with military campaign ribbons and known as "The Rebel Destroyer."

Consumed by the Force-power unleashed by an extract of bota, Darth Vader crackles with energy that overwhelms Jax Pavan.

THE DARK TIMES

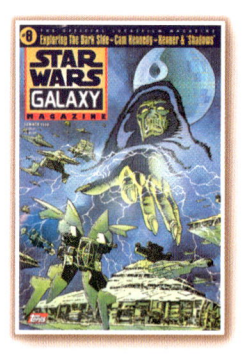

"DARK VENDETTA"

AUTHOR · Eric S. Trautmann

PUBLICATION HISTORY · Short story, The Topps Company · *Star Wars Galaxy* #8, Summer 1996

TIME LINE PLACEMENT · 10 BBY

WORLD VISITED · Coruscant (Imperial Center) [L-9]

MAIN CHARACTERS · Tremayne, Imperial High Inquisitor (human male); Corwin Shelvay, Jedi apprentice (human male); Darth Vader, Dark Lord of the Sith (human cyborg male); Darrin Arkanian, Jedi Knight (Sullustan male)

SUMMARY · Jedi Darrin Arkanian braves the Imperial capital to rescue his captured apprentice, Corwin Shelvay. The Imperial High Inquisitor tracks the fugitive Jedi and kills Darrin in a lightsaber duel. Enraged, Corwin maims and disfigures Tremayne, leaving the High Inquisitor for dead. Corwin escapes, and Lord Vader's surgical droids rebuild Tremayne with cybernetic prosthetics.

High Inquisitor Tremayne was introduced in 1993 by West End Games as a potential villain for players of *Star Wars* roleplaying games. Tremayne's flashbacks in "Dark Vendetta" don't mesh easily with the continuity established years later with the release of Episode III. For example, the tale states that he was recruited by Palpatine to aid Vader in the culling of corrupt Jedi Knights prior to the Emperor cementing his rule.

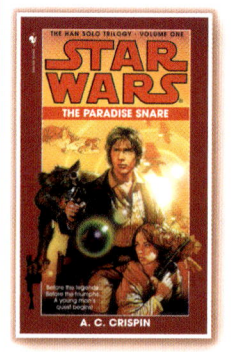

THE HAN SOLO TRILOGY: THE PARADISE SNARE

AUTHOR · A. C. Crispin

COVER ARTIST · Drew Struzan

PUBLICATION HISTORY · Novel, Bantam Spectra Books · Paperback, July 1997

TIME LINE PLACEMENT · c. 10 BBY

WORLDS VISITED · Alderaan [M-10]; Corellia [M-11]; Coruscant (Imperial Center) [L-9]; Togoria [P-9]; Ylesia [T-12]

MAIN CHARACTERS · Han Solo, pilot (human male); Bria Tharen, pilgrim (human female); Garris Shrike, pirate (human male); Teroenza, high priest (t'landa Til male); Muuurgh, enforcer (Togorian male)

SUMMARY · The brutal pirate Garris Shrike runs a tight ship aboard the *Trader's Luck*. Among his petty rackets, Shrike conscripts street urchins to beg and steal on his behalf. That's how he first brought Han Solo aboard his vessel. Han would come to exhibit other talents, most notably as a foolhardy yet skilled swoop pilot. Tired of living under Shrike's thumb, Han stows away aboard an automated freighter, fleeing Shrike with barely enough oxygen to arrive intact on the tropical world of Ylesia.

Ylesia is a religious sanctuary administered by t'landa Til priests. Pilgrims come from across the galaxy to experience "the Exultation," a euphoric state evoked by the subsonic harmonies sung by the t'landa Til. In truth, the harmonies act like a narcotic, and the religion is a cult of addicted subjects

---

152 THE DARK TIMES

Han Solo witnesses an Exultation ceremony, where slave workers prostrate themselves before the t'landa Til priests of Ylesia.

forced to toil away in spice-processing facilities that profit the Besadii Hutt clan.

Han's piloting skills impress the t'landa Til high priest, Teroenza. Han, unwilling to reveal his true name, poses as "Vyyk Drago" and finds employment as a spice freighter pilot. In his trips across the Ylesian colonies, Han is smitten by Pilgrim 921, who was once a Corellian woman named Bria Tharen before coming under the influence of the Exultation. Han tries to prove to her that the Exultation is just a scam, and though Bria comes to believe his words, she cannot break her addiction. Han uses his influence in Teroenza's organization to relocate her from more unsavory jobs to serve as archivist for the t'landa Til's extensive art and antiquities collection.

Han realizes he is in love with Bria and that he wants to escape Ylesia with her. He ransacks Teroenza's treasures and sets the spice operation ablaze as a distraction so they can escape aboard Teroenza's stolen starship, *Talisman*.

With money gained from selling Teroenza's relics, Han and Bria hope to start a new life together. Han goes to Coruscant to enroll in the Imperial Academy. He then discovers a heartbreaking note from Bria, who leaves him because she cannot shake her addiction to the Exultation. His ill fortunes continue when he is ambushed by an old enemy: a vengeful Garris Shrike. Shrike savagely attacks Han, nearly defeating him, but the old pirate chief is killed by a bounty hunter who is also after Han. Han kills that

THE DARK TIMES

hunter in turn, and uses the hunter's anonymous, unidentifiable corpse to dispose of his ersatz identity Vyyk Drago. He then starts anew as Han Solo, Imperial cadet.

Han Solo estimates that he is nineteen years old at the start of this story, which would make him twenty-nine at the start of *A New Hope*, though his age is heavily caveated with uncertainty—he's not sure when he was born. During a visit to Alderaan, Han sees a pre-recorded transmission from Senator Bail Organa with a dark-haired girl on his lap. This would be the first time Han sets eyes on his future wife, Leia, who would be ten years old at the time.

Among the host of false identities that Han employs is Jenos Idanian, an anagram of Indiana Jones—another character made famous by actor Harrison Ford. This identity is particularly appropriate when Han is trying to fence stolen antiquities.

"TURNING POINT"

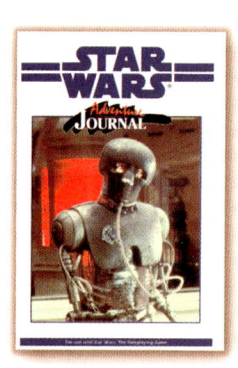

AUTHOR · Charlene Newcomb

COVER ARTIST · Lucasfilm

PUBLICATION HISTORY · Short story, West End Games · *Star Wars Adventure Journal* #5, February 1995

TIME LINE PLACEMENT · 6 BBY

WORLD VISITED · Garos IV

[P-7]

MAIN CHARACTERS · Dair Haslip, Academy recruit (human male); Keriin Haslip, retired mine owner (human female); Tork Winger, government minister (human male)

SUMMARY · With an interest in the mines of Garos IV, the Galactic Empire steps up its presence on the planet, imposing its brand of order and quelling an ongoing civil war among the inhabitants. Young Dair Haslip is eager to join the Imperial Academy, but the glow of his acceptance is dimmed by the knowledge that his best friend, Jos Mayda, will not attend after his father is arrested on suspicion of Rebel activity. The two enjoy one last summer evening together exploring the Garosian caves as they did in their youth, but are stopped by Imperial scout troopers who suspect they are spies. The troopers callously shoot and kill Jos, and Dair fires back, killing the scouts in self-defense. After confessing this to his grandmother, Dair is surprised to find that she is part of the local underground. Having witnessed the true nature of the Empire, Dair agrees to help the underground from within the Imperial ranks by going through with his Academy training.

Though this was the fifth of Charlene Newcomb's short stories to focus on Garos IV, it is the first one in the time line. Thus it is an "introduction" to many of the supporting characters in the tales starring Alex Winger set after the events of *Return of the Jedi*. Winger makes an appearance in this story as a little girl, just adopted into her new family. She made her publication debut in "A Glimmer of Hope" (1994).

"THE FINAL EXIT"

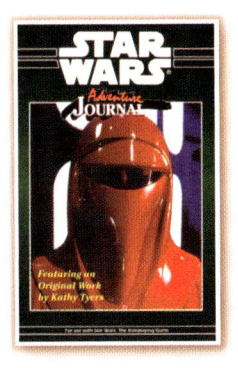

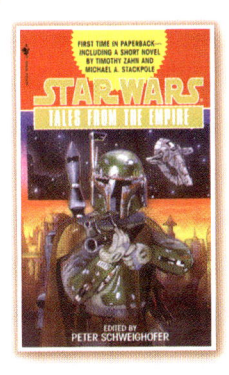

AUTHOR · Patricia Jackson

COVER ARTIST · Lucasfilm (*Star Wars Adventure Journal*); Matt Busch (*Tales from the Empire*)

PUBLICATION HISTORY · Short story, West End Games · *Star Wars Adventure Journal* #4, November 1994 Compiled as part of the *Tales from the Empire* anthology, Bantam Spectra Books · Paperback, November 1997

TIME LINE PLACEMENT · 5 BBY

WORLDS VISITED · Najiba [R-17]; Trulalis [R-17]

MAIN CHARACTERS · Adalric Brandl, fallen Jedi (human male); Thaddeus Ross, smuggler (human male); Otias, dramatist (human male); Kierra, droid intelligence (female personality)

SUMMARY · A moody fallen Jedi named Adalric Brandl hires a smuggling vessel to take him to the planet Trulalis. The dark sider pays for the ship's captain, Thaddeus Ross, to accompany him to Kovit Settlement. There, Adalric visits the theater stage where he once performed as an actor, seeking forgiveness from his old mentor, Master Otias. But there is no salvation to be found in the past for Adalric—not in his former career onstage, nor in the presence of his young son, Jaalib.

Leaving Trulalis aboard Thaddeus's vessel, Adalric is tracked down by the Imperial Star Destroyer *Interrogator*, flagship of High Inquisitor Tremayne. The Imperials capture Adalric, and Thaddeus is surprised to receive a hefty portion of a bounty for returning a fugitive of the Emperor. Adalric, however, does not surrender himself quietly. Stealing one of Thaddeus's thermal detonators, he creates havoc aboard the Star Destroyer.

Though the story leaves Adalric's fate vague—he might have perished in the explosion—he proves to be alive in the follow-up tale, "Uhl Eharl Khoehng," set in 0 ABY.

THE HAN SOLO TRILOGY: THE HUTT GAMBIT

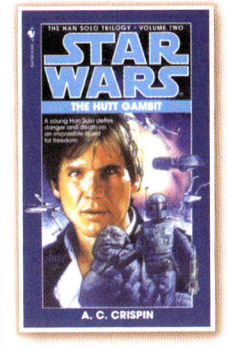

AUTHOR · A. C. Crispin

COVER ARTIST · Drew Struzan

PUBLICATION HISTORY · Novel, Bantam Spectra Books · Paperback, September 1997

TIME LINE PLACEMENT · c. 5–4 BBY

WORLDS VISITED · Coruscant (Imperial Center) [L-9]; Devaron [M-13]; Kessel [T-10]; Nal Hutta and Nar Shaddaa [S-12]; Smuggler's Run asteroid field [S-18]; Tatooine [R-16]; Teth [U-12]; Ylesia [T-12]

THE DARK TIMES

MAIN CHARACTERS · Han Solo, smuggler (human male); Chewbacca, mechanic (Wookiee male); Jabba, crime lord (Hutt); Jiliac, crime lord (Hutt); Sarn Shild, Imperial Moff (human male); Aruk, crime lord (Hutt); Durga, crime lord (Hutt); Lando Calrissian, gambler (human male)

SUMMARY · Han Solo is drummed out of the Imperial Academy and finds himself with a new lifelong friend—a Wookiee named Chewbacca who has sworn a life debt to him. With the help of his old Academy classmate Mako Spince, Han makes a name for himself as a peerless pilot in the smuggling underworld. Soon clocking impressive times on the Kessel Run, Han draws the attention of Jabba the Hutt.

Han still has a hefty bounty on his head from his Ylesian getaway, and he is targeted by bounty hunter Boba Fett. Fett lands a toxic dart on Han, temporarily paralyzing him, but the smuggler is saved by a brave young gambler, Lando Calrissian. Lando turns the tables on Fett and uses the same toxin on the bounty hunter. Though Fett is vulnerable, Han and Lando are not heartless killers, so they spare Fett's life.

Lando needs to hire the best pilot around. He also wants to become a pilot himself, so in exchange for giving Han a new vessel, he receives flying lessons. Han names his new ship *Bria*.

The lawlessness of Hutt space is increasingly becoming a blemish on Imperial security and order. For years, Moff Sarn Shild has taken bribes from the Hutts to turn a blind eye to the most egregious law-bending. Asked by the Emperor to put his house in order, he betrays those who lined his coffers and plans to crack down on Nar Shaddaa, the notorious Smuggler's Moon. The Hutts, eager to stave off any Imperial action that might affect their business, send a human envoy to meet with Shild on Coruscant: Han Solo.

Han is stunned to find his old flame Bria Tharen, now seemingly Moff Shild's mistress. Distracted by this development, he fails to dissuade Shild, but does discover who the task force commander will be for the impending assault. The Hutts are able to bribe the commander into revealing his attack strategy, and thus are able to plan an adequate defense with smugglers running interference. The Imperial attack is parried, and Moff Shild takes his own life rather than report failure to the Emperor.

THIS BOOK PIECES TOGETHER many fragments from Han's past that surfaced in previously published works. Mentors, colleagues, rivals, and acquaintances from past books make their first chronological appearance in Han's history: Roa from *Han Solo's Revenge* (1979); Rik Duel from the Marvel Comics series (1983); Shug Ninx, Salla Zend, and Mako Spince from the *Dark Empire* comics series (1992); Zeen Afit, Kid DXo'ln, Sinewy Ana Blue, and Xaverri from *The New Rebellion* (1996); and Soontir Fel from the *X-Wing: Rogue Squadron* comics series (1997). For all its elaboration of Han's history, the book does notably skip past the meeting of Han Solo and Chewbacca, which occurs between *The Paradise Snare* and *The Hutt Gambit*. This stemmed from a request from Lucasfilm to not dramatize this important event in the lives of these two characters.

"PASSAGES"

AUTHOR · Charlene Newcomb

PUBLICATION HISTORY · Short story, West End Games · *Star Wars Adventure Journal* #7, August 1995

TIME LINE PLACEMENT · 3 BBY

WORLDS VISITED · Kabaira [P-17]; Tatooine [R-16]

MAIN CHARACTERS · Matt Turhaya, free trader (human male); Tere Metallo, free trader (Riileb female)

SUMMARY · Tere Metallo, captain of the freighter *Star Quest*, takes on a down-on-his-luck mechanic, Matt Turhaya, as part of her crew. During an Imperial crackdown on Rebel activity on Kabaira, an Imperial officer identifies Matt as a deserter and arrests him. Tere frees Matt, as well as several other captive Rebels, with the help of the local underground.

Charlene Newcomb's story connects to her larger Alex Winger series, though this tale is set many years before it. Matt mourns the loss of his wife and young daughter, the girl who would grow up to be Alex Winger after being adopted into a prominent family on Garos IV.

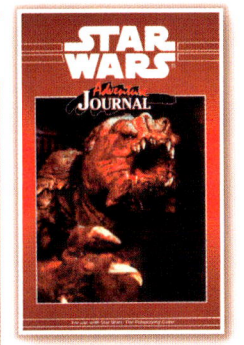

"OUT OF THE CRADLE"

AUTHOR · Patricia A. Jackson

COVER ARTIST · Lucasfilm

PUBLICATION HISTORY · Short story, West End Games · *Star Wars Adventure Journal* #2, May 1994

TIME LINE PLACEMENT · 3 BBY

WORLDS VISITED · Socorro [Q-17]; Tro'Har [M-19]

MAIN CHARACTERS · Drake Paulsen, smuggler (human male); Elias Halbert, smuggler (human male); Abdi-Badawzi, crime lord (Twi'lek male); Kaine Paulsen, smuggler (human male)

SUMMARY · Against the wishes of his father, fifteen-year-old Drake Paulsen is forced to serve as a navigator aboard a smuggling vessel at the behest of a Twi'lek gangster on Socorro. Drake is aboard the *Seldom Different*, a ship that will serve as a decoy to his father's vessel. An Imperial cruiser inspects the *Seldom Different*, and an impulsive stormtrooper shoots and injures Drake for back talk. The ship is let go, and Drake recovers. The run is considered his coming of age.

THE FORCE UNLEASHED I AND II

AUTHOR · Sean Williams, based on a story by Haden Blackman

COVER ARTISTS · Petrol Advertising; LucasArts

PUBLICATION HISTORY · Novels, Del Rey Books · Hardcover, August 2008 · Paperback, August 2009 (book I)

THE DARK TIMES 157

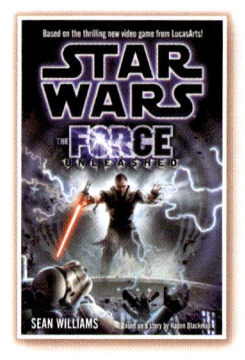

- Hardcover, October 2010
- Paperback, August 2011 (book II)

TIME LINE PLACEMENT · 3–1 BBY

WORLDS VISITED · Bespin [K-18]; Cato Neimoidia [N-11]; Corellia [M-11]; Coruscant (Imperial Center) [L-9]; Dac (aka Mon Cala) [U-6]; Dagobah [M-19]; Despayre [L-5]; Felucia [R-6]; Itani Nebula [N-14]; Kamino [S-15]; Kashyyyk [P-9]; Malastare [N-16]; Nordra [N-14]; Raxus Prime [S-5]; Rhommamool [N-13]; Scarl system [L-13]

MAIN CHARACTERS · Starkiller, secret apprentice (human male); Darth Vader, Dark Lord of the Sith (human cyborg male); Rahm Kota, former Jedi general (human male); Juno Eclipse, pilot (human female); PROXY, training droid; Palpatine, Galactic Emperor (human male); Bail Organa, Rebel leader (human male); Maris Brood, fallen apprentice (Zabrak female); Boba Fett, bounty hunter (human male); Ackbar, Rebel leader (Mon Calamari male); Mon Mothma, Rebel leader (human female); Garm Bel Iblis, Rebel leader (human male)

SUMMARY · In the hidden confines of Darth Vader's incomplete Star Destroyer *Executor*, Lord Vader has been training Starkiller, his secret apprentice. The shadowy agent has already disposed of some of Vader's enemies, but now the Dark Lord deems him ready to take on a more powerful opponent—a Jedi survivor. Starkiller, ferried by his pilot Juno Eclipse and accompanied by his training droid PROXY, infiltrates a TIE fighter production facility on Nar Shaddaa, just as it is attacked by Rebel forces led by Jedi general Rahm Kota. Starkiller and Kota duel, and the secret assassin defeats the old Jedi, leaving him for dead. Kota's prophetic words haunt the apprentice, however. Kota predicts Starkiller will not always be Vader's apprentice.

More missions follow. On the junk world of Raxus Prime, Starkiller hunts down the addled Jedi Master Kazdan Paratus. On Felucia, he stalks Shaak Ti and her Padawan, Maris Brood. As Shaak Ti dies by Starkiller's blade, she warns that the Sith way is always poisoned by betrayal. Upon returning to the *Executor*, Starkiller finds this to be true. Emperor Palpatine has learned of the apprentice's existence and orders Vader to kill his pupil. The Dark Lord has no choice and runs his lightsaber through Starkiller.

Starkiller later awakens in a medical lab aboard Vader's science ship, *Empirical*. He has been healed, the attempt against his life carefully orchestrated to fool the Emperor. Vader conspires with Starkiller, whose existence is now known only to the Dark Lord, to create a distraction for the Emperor—to foment rebellion across the galaxy—while Vader plots against his master.

Along with PROXY and Juno, Starkiller tracks down General Kota on Bespin. The former war hero has become a broken, ragged drunk since his defeat by Starkiller. Cleaning himself up, Kota takes Starkiller to Kashyyyk, where the apprentice has a Force vision of his father, a Jedi Knight, defeated by Darth Vader. Starkiller realizes that he was stolen by Vader as a child, and that this was not the fate intended for him.

While on Kashyyyk, Starkiller comes to the rescue of Princess Leia Organa, an Imperial Senator captured by the overzealous Imperial captain Ozzik

In the wilds of Felucia, Starkiller blasts Maris Brood and a tamed rancor with the power of the Force.

THE DARK TIMES

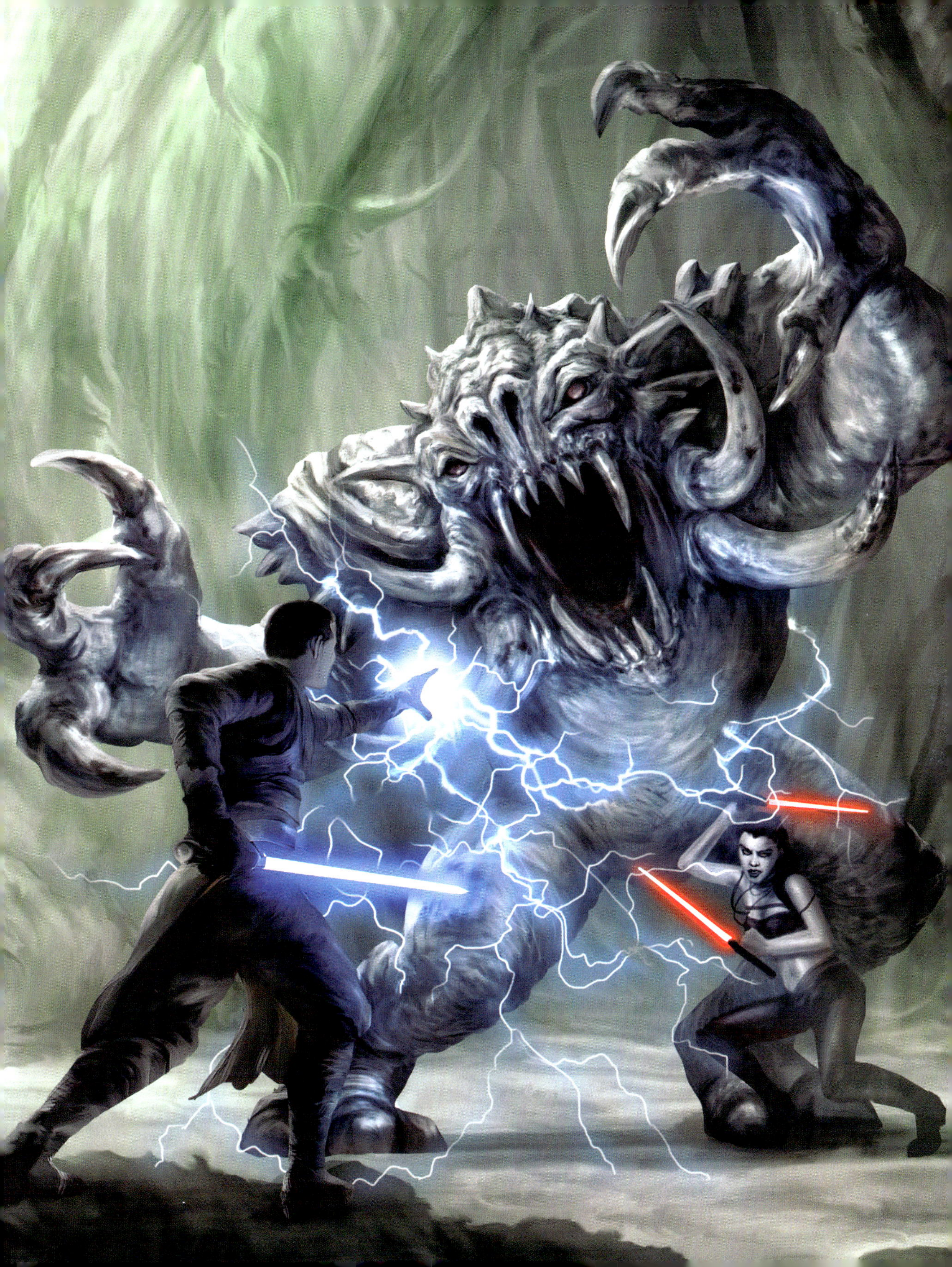

SPOTLIGHT — "Pax Empirica—The Wookiee Annihilation"

In November 2001, LucasArts and Ensemble Studios released the real-time strategy game **Star Wars: Galactic Battlegrounds**, in which players could amass the fighting forces of various factions in the *Star Wars* galaxy, manage resources and combat units, and wage large-scale battles across various points in the time line. That month also saw the release of *Star Wars: Galactic Battlegrounds: Prima's Official Strategy Guide* from Prima Games. Written by Steven L. Kent, the 204-page paperback book devoted its first chapter to a short story, "Pax Empirica—The Wookiee Annihilation," a tale that has as yet never been reprinted anywhere else.

In it, Corporal Wayson Dower is an Imperial stormtrooper who is briefed along with his unit on the impending invasion of Kashyyyk. The planet's dense foliage make a mechanized invasion impractical—the troopers must land without vehicle and fighter support. The troopers underestimate the native Wookiees, believing them to be unintelligent brutes. It is a grueling assault that proves to be merely a diversion—the main invasion force lands elsewhere on the planet.

The story is a rare example of a pre–Episode II publication explicitly stating that stormtroopers ranks include clones—according to the text, at least 40 percent of all stormtroopers come from a single genetic template, one shared by Dower's friend Milo Strander. These cloned troopers are called GeNodes and are genetically programmed to not self-identify as clones.

There are no specific indications in the story to suggest when it takes place beyond a mention of Grand Moff Tarkin, which would mean it occurs some time before Episode IV.

Sturn. On Felucia, Starkiller rescues Senator Bail Organa from a demented Maris Brood, and at Raxus Prime he demolishes the Imperial Star Destroyer construction yard high in orbit.

Starkiller's efforts to create a rebellion have become a cause he believes in. Leaders Mon Mothma, Garm Bel Iblis, and Bail Organa gather on Corellia to forge a true Alliance to Restore the Republic. However, they are ambushed by Imperial forces. Vader and the Emperor have exploited Starkiller into gathering this resistance so that it can be crushed in a single blow. The Imperials take the Rebel leaders and General Kota captive aboard their nearly completed Death Star battle station. Starkiller enters the station and confronts Vader and the Emperor. He sacrifices himself so that the Rebels and Kota can escape. Starkiller dies a martyr for the Rebel cause. His family crest becomes the very symbol of the Rebel Alliance.

Juno Eclipse, mourning Starkiller's death, becomes a member of the Rebel Alliance. She is assigned command of the Rebel frigate *Salvation* and often works alongside General Kota. Juno grows dismayed by the often conflicted and overly cautious leadership of the Rebellion. Disobeying orders, she seeks to recruit the brilliant strategist Ackbar and the Mon Calamari people into the Rebel fold.

Some time later, Starkiller awakens, somehow alive and in the Imperial cloning facilities on Kamino. He is once again the loyal pupil of Darth Vader. He is plagued by fragmented visions of his past life. Vader tells him he is a clone, inexplicably experiencing memories of his former life. Unstable and haunted by his love for Juno Eclipse, Starkiller breaks his shackles and escapes Kamino, leaving destruction in his wake.

Eager to get his secret apprentice back under his control, Vader tasks Boba Fett with tracking down his most dangerous quarry. Starkiller seeks out Kota, who is imprisoned on opulent Cato Neimoidia and forced to fight gladiator battles for the amusement of pampered Imperial Baron Merillion Tarko. Starkiller joins the fight, and together Kota and Starkiller destroy Tarko's savage arena beasts. They escape aboard the *Rogue Shadow*, piloted by PROXY. Kota once again gives Starkiller pause with prophetic words. The old Jedi does not believe that Starkiller is a clone.

Seeking answers about his identity, Starkiller is compelled to visit Dagobah. The world is strong with the Force, and he is greeted by Jedi Master Yoda, who invites him to enter a cave steeped in the dark side. There Starkiller experiences intense visions of conflict, of battling himself. More specifically, he receives a vision of Juno in danger. After he reports this to Kota, the two hurry to the Rebel fleet, aboard the flagship *Salvation*. Starkiller's visions prove true. Juno has been captured by Boba Fett.

Starkiller shares the coordinates to the Imperial facilities on Kamino with the Rebellion, prompting a major assault by the Rebels on the planet. Starkiller joins the strike, returning to the clone hatchery. He discovers that Darth Vader has created an army of Starkiller clones. Starkiller also finds Vader, who has used Juno to lure Starkiller into a final confrontation. In the fierce, destructive duel that follows, Starkiller defeats the Dark Lord, ordering him to surrender. Vader is taken captive by Rebel forces, and Starkiller is reunited with Juno, his love.

The Force Unleashed was an ambitious video-game series launched by LucasArts in 2008, its first foray into next-generation console gaming, featuring unique technology for unparalleled visuals, game physics, and character intelligence. The story line by Haden Blackman, set between Episodes III and IV, had sweeping implications for the larger Expanded Universe, by giving Vader an apprentice, imbuing him with unfathomable Force abilities, and positing that the very origin of the Rebel Alliance was a plot by the Emperor. The surprising tale and concept for the game received personal approval from George Lucas, but it does not occupy a higher standard of canon than any other Expanded Universe lore. That is, it still exists outside the movies and television series produced by Lucas and would be subordinate to mythology revealed in those media. For example, Lucas's alternate explanations for the roots of the Rebel Alliance appear in season five of *Star Wars: The Clone Wars,* which take precedence over Starkiller's involvement.

The Force Unleashed benefited from a multi-pronged licensing release, not unlike the movies, with the novelization from Del Rey Books, a graphic novel from Dark Horse Comics, and toys from Hasbro and LEGO. The Force Unleashed II ends as a cliffhanger; its story line has yet to be resolved.

THE LANDO CALRISSIAN ADVENTURES

LANDO CALRISSIAN AND THE MINDHARP OF SHARU · LANDO CALRISSIAN AND THE FLAMEWIND OF OSEON · LANDO CALRISSIAN AND THE STARCAVE OF THONBOKA

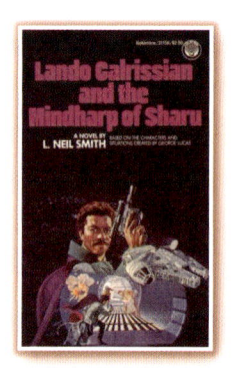

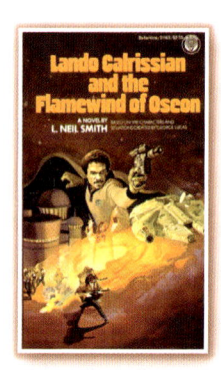

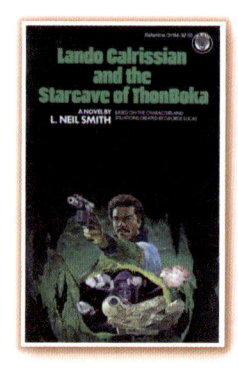

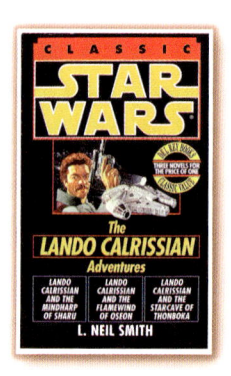

AUTHOR · L. Neil Smith

COVER ARTIST · William Schmidt (series)

PUBLICATION HISTORY · Novels, Del Rey Books
· Paperback, July 1983 (book 1)
· Paperback, September 1983 (book 2)
· Paperback, November 1983 (book 3)
Compiled as *The Lando Calrissian Adventures*
· Paperback, June 1994

TIME LINE PLACEMENT · 3–2 BBY

WORLDS VISITED · Dilonexa XXIII [U-8]; Oseon system [T-8]; Rafa system [T-8]; ThonBoka Nebula [U-8]

MAIN CHARACTERS · Lando Calrissian, gambler (human male); Vuffi Raa, droid scout; Rokur Gepta, Sorcerer of Tund (Croke male); Osuno Whett, professor (human male); Waywa Fybot, narcotics agent (Quor'sav male); Klyn Shanga, fleet admiral (human male); Lehesu, adventurous spacefarer (Oswaft male)

SUMMARY · Lando Calrissian, card player, scoundrel, and captain of the *Millennium Falcon*, is in the Oseon asteroid belt, a systemwide trove of valuable minerals and also home to the galaxy's superwealthy in an area of space called the Centrality. He is attempting to win a fortune in a game of sabacc, but ends up with a meager haul of credits and a droid of unknown origins that he must pick up from Rafa IV. The droid is unlike any Lando has ever seen: with the unusual moniker of Vuffi Raa, the chrome-plated starfish-shaped automaton has a vivid and keen personality.

On Rafa IV, Lando is arrested by local authorities on trumped-up charges. Rafa's governor, Duttes Mer, and his enigmatic ally Rokur Gepta force Lando to procure a mystical artifact of unspeakable

Lando Calrissian stares, enthralled by the beauty of the Mindharp of Sharu.

THE DARK TIMES

power: the Mindharp of Sharu. With few options, Lando and Vuffi embark on this treasure hunt, starting within Rafa V's enormous pyramids. A bizarre, mind-twisting journey later, they inexplicably emerge from a pyramid back on Rafa IV, with the eye-defying Mindharp. Governor Mer confiscates the Mindharp, which Gepta plans to use for his own nefarious ends. The instrument, when plucked and tuned accordingly, can control every sentient mind in the system.

The artifact is more than it seems. The pyramids that cover the worlds of the Rafa system are actually the hidden cities of the Sharu, a long-vanished species that disappeared in fear of a coming invasion from a powerful alien force. The Sharu disguised themselves as witless subservient beings, the Toka, by transferring their higher intelligence into the crystalline orchards of the system. By activating the Mindharp, Governor Mer inadvertently returns intelligence to the Toka, though he is destroyed by an outburst of energy from the artifact. Rokur Gepta barely survives this reversal and swears vengeance upon Lando.

Lando next tries his hand as a freelance freighter captain, but finds he doesn't have the knack for that business. He returns to playing cards in the Oseon system. The asteroid field is about to experience its Flamewind spectacle, a seasonal flaring of the star Oseon that is a galactic tourist draw. Lando once again finds himself forced into government dirty work when local law enforcement extorts him to serve as transport captain in a drug raid. The Flamewind makes travel in the Oseon treacherous, but Lando has no option except to comply.

He smuggles a shipment of the drug lesai along with an Imperial narcotics agent to the home of Bohhuah Mutdah, one of the wealthiest beings in the galaxy. The operation is a trap—Mutdah is Rokur Gepta in disguise. Gepta has arranged Lando's capture and subjects him to insidious memory torture—

forcing him to relive his most horrible moments. Gepta's vengeance is cut short when his asteroid base is attacked by starfighters of the Renatasian Confederation, who are also bent on revenge. Led by Klyn Shanga, the fighter group is seeking out Vuffi Raa, calling the droid the "Butcher of Renatasia." Lando and Vuffi escape in the confusion. Gepta allies with the Renatasian Confederation, as they are both targeting the crew of the *Millennium Falcon.*

When Lando learns that the Centrality fleet is blockading the peculiar sack-shaped nebulosity called the ThonBoka and effectively starving the enormous space-dwelling creatures within, he and Vuffi are compelled to intervene. The Oswaft are sentient, large, gelatinous, winged-looking gas feeders capable of deep-space travel. To the Centrality, these aliens represent a new threat—a living starfleet of undefined power. Lando, looking to save the Oswaft, uses his charms as an independent salesman, offering a variety of wares to move through the fleet.

Meeting with the Oswaft, Lando advises them how to defeat the blockade using their natural abilities. The Oswaft are capable of "shouting" through intense radiation—bursts of destructive microwaves. They can also cast off replicated shells of their bodies, creating instant decoys as they make short leaps into hyperspace. In this manner, the Oswaft destroy the Centrality fleet.

Rokur Gepta challenges Lando to a one-on-one fight, and Lando defeats the sorcerer, revealing him to be a sluglike Croke concealed beneath Gepta's robes.

Shanga, upon finally understanding that Vuffi Raa is a droid, ends his misguided vendetta—it was Vuffi Raa's former master, Osuno Whett, who ordered the devastation of Renatasia. Vuffi Raa's originators—a race of enormous saucer-like sentient machines—arrive at the ThonBoka to collect their observer scout. Lando says farewell to Vuffi and ends his adventures with a vessel full of precious gems, enough money to buy a city.

Like *The Han Solo Adventures* published earlier (1979–80), *The Lando Calrissian Adventures* trilogy of novels sets its focus on a scoundrel in an isolated sector of space prior to the events of his cinematic exploits. The unique locale, in this case the Centrality, allowed the author to world-build without fear of continuity conflicts with the larger Galactic Empire. The Lando novels are most notable for describing sabacc, the preeminent Galactic card game. West End Games expanded on the details of these novels to make a playable version of sabacc in 1989. All depictions of sabacc that have appeared in the Expanded Universe are built on the foundations of the Lando books.

The enormous mechanical beings that collect Vuffi Raa are introduced but not explored in detail in these novels. They were given the name Silentium in *The New Essential Guide to Droids* (2006).

Although art commissioned to depict this series often shows Lando as he looks in *The Empire Strikes Back*, Lando does not grow a mustache until the second book.

"WHEN THE DOMINO FALLS"

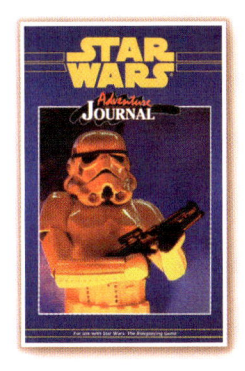

AUTHOR · Patricia A. Jackson

COVER ARTIST · Lucasfilm

PUBLICATION HISTORY · Short story, West End Games. · *Star Wars Adventure Journal* #3, August 1994

TIME LINE PLACEMENT · 2 BBY

WORLDS VISITED · Omman [S-6]; Socorro [Q-17]

MAIN CHARACTERS · Drake Paulsen, smuggler (human male); Karl Ancher, smuggler (human male); Nikaede Celso, smuggler (Wookiee female); Tait Ransom, smuggler (human male)

SUMMARY · Drake Paulsen and his smuggling colleagues break out of an Imperial prison cell on Omman. Returning to Socorro, Drake hears the news that his father, Kaine, died while on a smuggling run to Thrugii. Determined to carry on his father's occupation and assignment, Drake and his newfound Wookiee companion, Nikaede Celso, begin their smuggling career aboard the *Steadfast*.

"REBEL BASS"

AUTHOR · Kathy Tyers

PUBLICATION HISTORY · Short story, Wizards of the Coast · *Star Wars Gamer* #6, October 2001

TIME LINE PLACEMENT · 2 BBY

WORLDS VISITED · Beltrix [M-14]; Tuttin IV [M-14]

MAIN CHARACTERS · Ryley Ancum, bass vye player (human male); Hannis D'Lund, touchboard player (human male); Erik Lauderslag, percussionist (human male); Shran Etison, Imperial governor (human male); Onjo Fegel, Imperial Intelligence agent (human male); Keth Beamis, Alliance Intelligence agent (human male)

SUMMARY · Ryley Ancum is a bass player in a local garage band, Far Cry. He's also a secret supporter of the Rebellion, transmitting coded signals in his bass lines. Ry's main contact, a talent scout named Keth Beamis, has been nabbed by the Imperials and commits suicide under interrogation before implicating Ry. A well-meaning Imperial governor assigns Ry to ferret out any Rebel activity at Beamis's talent agency on Beltrix, but Ry is able to surreptitiously send out a message of warning.

THE DARK TIMES

THE HAN SOLO ADVENTURES

HAN SOLO AT STARS' END · HAN SOLO'S REVENGE · HAN SOLO AND THE LOST LEGACY

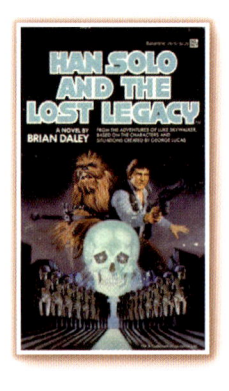

AUTHOR · Brian Daley

COVER ARTISTS · Wayne Douglas Barlow (*Han Solo at Stars' End*); Dean Ellis (*Han Solo's Revenge*); William Schmidt (*Han Solo and the Lost Legacy* and *The Han Solo Adventures* omnibus)

PUBLICATION HISTORY · Novels, Del Rey Books
· Paperback, April 1979 (book 1)
· Paperback, October 1979 (book 2)
· Paperback, August 1980 (book 3)
Compiled as *The Han Solo Adventures*
· Paperback, April 1992

TIME LINE PLACEMENT · 2–1 BBY

WORLDS VISITED · Ammuud [S-4]; Bonadan [S-3]; Brigia [T-6]; Dellalt [T-6]; Duroon [S-4]; Etti IV [S-4]; Kamar [S-4]; Lur [N-10]; Mytus VIII [S-3]; Orron III [S-4]; Roonadan [S-3]; Rudrig [S-6]; Saheelindeel [S-6]; Sarlucif [S-4]; Urdur [S-4]

MAIN CHARACTERS · Han Solo, smuggler (human male); Chewbacca, copilot and mechanic (Wookiee male); Bollux, labor droid; Blue Max, computer probe; Gallandro, gunfighter (human male); Doc, outlaw tech (human male); Jessa, outlaw tech (human female); Ewwen Glayyd, Mor Glayyd (human male); Hart-and-Parn Gorra Fiolla of Lorrd, auditor (human female); Odumin aka Spray, territorial manager (Tynnan male); Rekkon, scholar (human male); Roa, retired smuggler (human male); Badure, treasure seeker (human male); Atuarre, ranger (Trianii female); Pakka, cub (Trianii male); Mirkovig Hirken, Corporate Sector Authority Viceprex (human male); Ploovo Two-for-One, loan shark (human male)

SUMMARY · Working in the Corporate Sector, taking odd and often dangerous jobs from the unsavory likes of loan sharks and gangsters, Han Solo and Chewbacca need to upgrade their beloved *Millennium Falcon*. Han strikes a deal with a group of outlaw techs run by Doc and Jessa: parts and labor in exchange for running a mission to a Corporate Sector Authority data center on Orron III. The mission is decidedly political—a scholar named Rekkon is investigating the disappearance of dissidents in the Corporate Sector. To help him slice

THE DARK TIMES
166

into the Authority network, he is equipped with a unique droid duo: the antiquated labor droid, Bollux, conceals within him a chipper young computer probe, Blue Max.

Though the pragmatic and cash-focused Han tries to ignore altruistic endeavors, he cannot help getting involved when the Orron III mission fails, Chewbacca is taken captive by the Authority, and Rekkon is killed by a traitor. Desperate to find Chewie, Han continues Rekkon's work, finding the Authority prison installation known as Stars' End. In the bleak facility, prisoners are kept in stasis booths for ease of control. Han infiltrates the prison, audaciously posing as an entertainment act, and in true Han Solo fashion blows up its power generator, launching the prison tower into orbit. He frees the prisoners—including Chewbacca—before Stars' End comes to a crashing demise.

Bad investments put Han and Chewie in the red. They take a no-questions-asked assignment on Lur, in the Corporate Sector, where they're forced—at gunpoint—to pick up a cargo of slaves. Han turns the tables on the slavers, freeing the captives. The slavers die in the breakout, and Han wants to collect the money owed him. He recovers clues from the dead slavers pointing him toward Bonadan. There he stumbles upon Fiolla of Lorrd's Corporate Sector Authority investigation into a slavery ring that may implicate highly placed Authority figures.

They team up to chase down the slavers, a search that brings them to Ammuud. A young noble there, Mor Ewwen Glayyd, is honoring a code of silence to protect his late father's dealings with slavers. When Han steps in for the Mor to prevent him from entering a shooting duel with Gallandro, the best gunfighter in the galaxy, Glayyd is indebted. He reveals documents regarding his father's dealings. The gunfight—and much of the investigation—was craftily engineered by Odumin, a Corporate Sector territorial administrator.

After a stint as a mechanic on Saheelindeel, and delivering educational materials to Rudrig, Han comes across his old friend Badure, who has fallen on hard times. Badure offers Han a stake in the fabled lost treasure of Xim the Despot on Dellalt, if they can find it. The quest involves braving rival treasure seekers, rough terrain, a bloodthirsty cult of Xim-worshipping Survivors, and a reawakened pre-Republic-era droid army. As the battle among the treasure hunters escalates, the gunslinger Gallandro arrives to settle his score with Han. Though Gallandro would have beaten Han at the draw, he accidentally sets off ancient booby traps in the treasure vaults and gets blasted to pieces.

Han and his companions uncover the treasure, though it proves to be of little value since most of the rare materials it contains have been rendered obsolete by centuries of technological progress.

Author Brian Daley set *The Han Solo Adventures* prior to the events of *A New Hope*, within an isolated patch of space, the Corporate Sector. Standing in for the Empire, stormtroopers, and TIE fighters are, respectively, the Authority, Espos (security police), and IRD fighters. As one of the earliest works in the Expanded Universe, Daley's trilogy was extremely influential in developing elements that would continue well beyond the scope of these three books. Vehicles such as *Victory*-class Star Destroyers, Z-95 headhunters, and swoop bikes; technology and innovations like vibroblades, transparisteel, and repulsorlifts; and cultural concepts including outlaw techs, Wookiee life debts, Corellian Bloodstripes, and the legends of Xim the Despot all owe their origin to Brian Daley.

Han Solo at Stars' End was adapted by Archie Goodwin and Alfredo Alcala into a newspaper comic strip format in 1980. That version of the story differs from the novel—events have been truncated

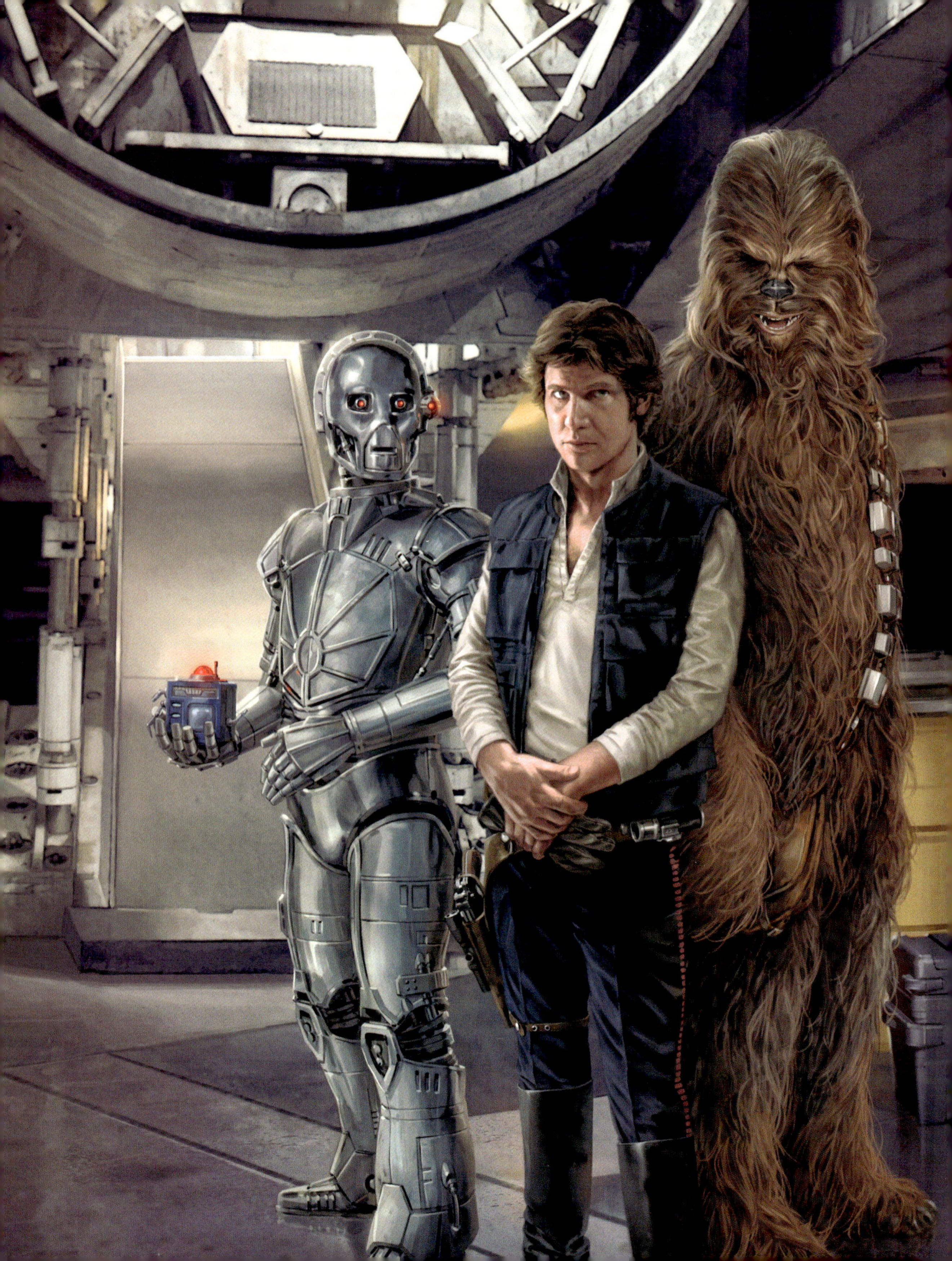

and action sequences restaged to better fit daily comic installments. It was reprinted by Dark Horse Comics in 1997.

The 1979 *Stars' End* novel has a notable moment of prescience in its characterization of Han. In chapter 6, Han says to Rekkon the scholar: "I happen to *like* to shoot first, Rekkon. As opposed to shooting second"—an ironic statement given fan sentiment expressed about the 1997 Special Edition edit that had Han shoot second when confronted by Greedo.

"TINIAN ON TRIAL"

AUTHOR · Kathy Tyers

PUBLICATION HISTORY · Short story, West End Games · *Star Wars Adventure Journal* #4, November 1994 Compiled as part of the *Tales of the Empire* anthology, Bantam Spectra Books
· Paperback, November 1997

TIME LINE PLACEMENT · 1 BBY

WORLD VISITED · Druckenwell [P-15]

MAIN CHARACTERS · Tinian I'att, armaments heir (human female); Daye Azur-Jamin, armaments executive (human male); Eisen Kerioth, Imperial Moff (human male)

SUMMARY · I'att Armaments demonstrates its revolutionary portable shielding technology, which could render stormtroopers invulnerable to blasterfire. The unscrupulous Moff Kerioth seizes the weapons factory by force, killing the company leaders. Tinian I'att, young heir to the company, flees with the sole sample of the shield, running into the streets of Druckenwell while her fiancé, Daye Azur-Jamin, stays behind to detonate the reactor at the factory.

DARK FORCES: SOLDIER FOR THE EMPIRE

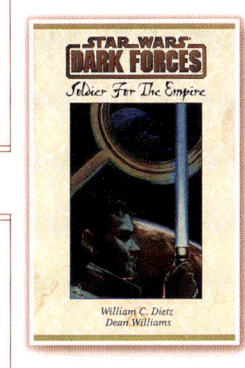

AUTHOR · William C. Dietz

ILLUSTRATOR · Dean Williams

COVER ARTIST · Dean Williams

PUBLICATION HISTORY · Illustrated novella, Dark Horse Comics & Boulevard Putnam Books
· Hardcover, February 1997
· Trade paperback, August 1998

TIME LINE PLACEMENT · 1 BBY

WORLDS VISITED · AX-456 asteroid [M-9]; Carida [M-9]; Danuta [S-9]; Sulon (moon of Sullust) [M-17]

MAIN CHARACTERS · Kyle Katarn, Imperial cadet (human male); Jan Ors, Rebel agent (human female); Morgan Katarn, resistance leader (human male); Jerec, Dark Jedi (human male); Mon Mothma, Rebel leader (human female)

SUMMARY · The enigmatic and blind Dark Jedi Jerec launches an Imperial assault on Sulon, the moon of Sullust, with his forces disguised as Rebels. Local farmer Morgan Katarn is captured and brutally killed by Jerec. Unbeknownst to his son, Kyle, Morgan was a leader in the local Rebel forces.

The intrepid crew of the *Millennium Falcon*: computer probe Blue Max, labor droid Bollux, ship captain Han Solo, first mate Chewbacca.

THE DARK TIMES

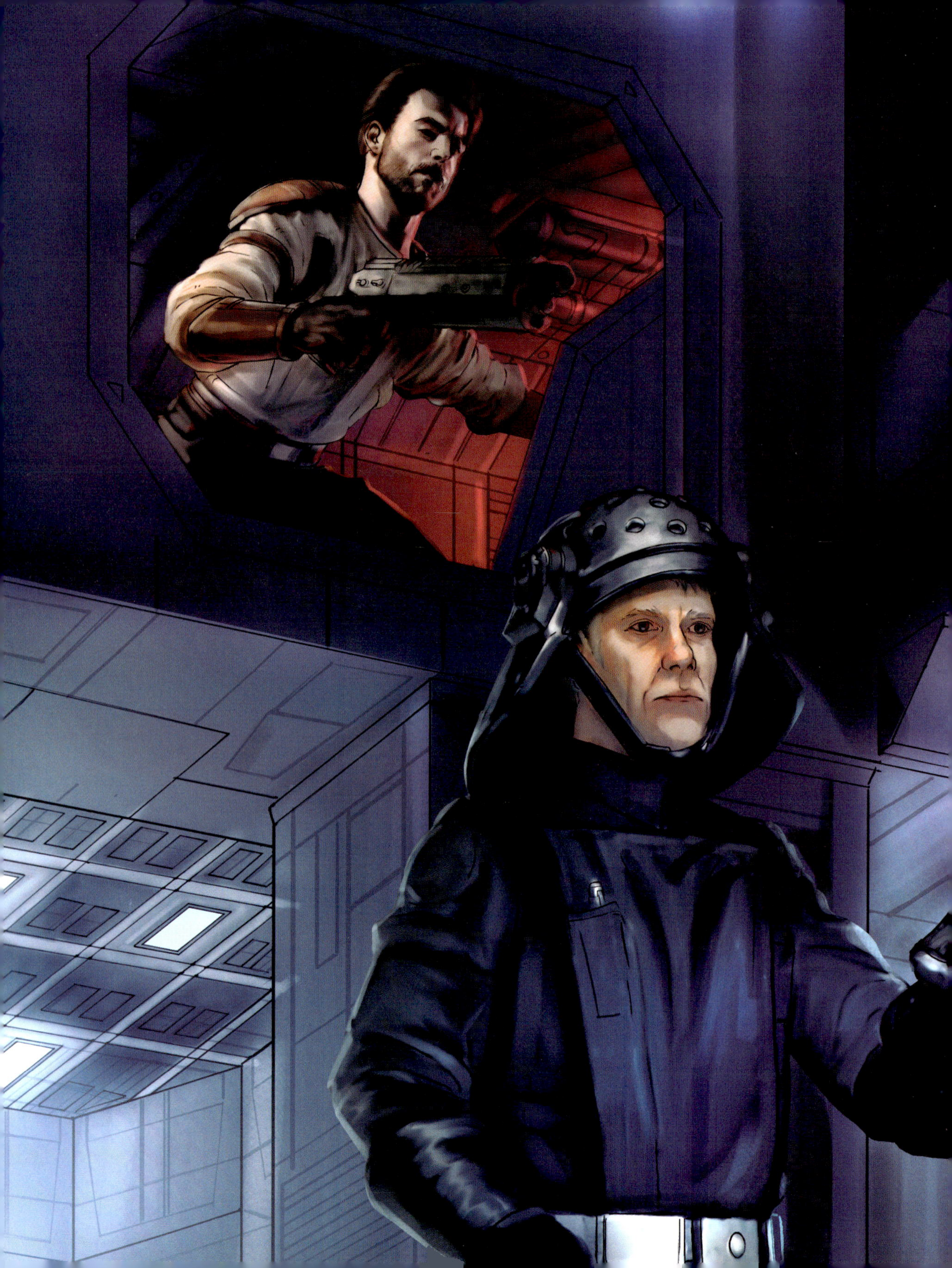

Kyle graduates as a decorated Imperial cadet. During his last training mission—a real assault on a Rebel asteroid base—Kyle opts not to kill surrendered Rebels, letting them leave alive. This makes a deep impression on one of the Rebels, Jan Ors.

After his graduation, Kyle travels aboard the starliner *Star of Empire* and once again encounters Jan. When Jan learns his name, she shows Kyle holographic evidence that his father was killed by the Empire. Kyle's allegiance is shaken, and he agrees to join the Rebel Alliance.

Mon Mothma recruits Kyle to steal the Death Star plans from an Imperial research facility on Danuta. Wary of Kyle's loyalties, Mothma also sends Jan to terminate Kyle should he attempt to betray the Rebellion. Kyle proves both loyal and successful in procuring the Imperial schematics.

THE FIRST IN A TRILOGY of graphic novellas—prose stories embellished throughout with full-page illustrations—the Dark Forces series is based on the story of the **Dark Forces** (1995) and **Jedi Knight: Dark Forces II** (1997) videogames, written by Justin Chin. The LucasArts titles introduced the character of Kyle Katarn, the avatar in both first-person-shooter games. By serving as the player's extension into the *Star Wars* universe, Kyle proved to be an extremely popular character among *Star Wars* gamers.

DEATH TROOPERS

AUTHOR · Joe Schreiber
COVER ARTIST · Indika

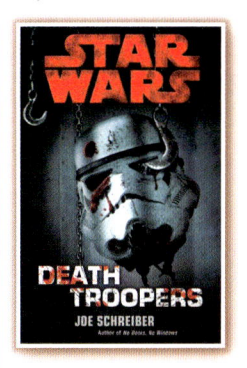

Kyle Katarn infiltrates a top-secret Imperial facility on Danuta to capture the Death Star plans.

PUBLICATION HISTORY ·
Novel, Del Rey Books
- Hardcover, October 2009
- Paperback, October 2010

TIME LINE PLACEMENT · 1 BBY

WORLDS VISITED · Chandrila [L-9]; Galantos [K-10]

MAIN CHARACTERS · Zahara Cody, medical officer (human female); Jareth Sartoris, Imperial captain (human male); Kale and Trig Longo, prisoners (human males, brothers); Han Solo, smuggler (human male); Chewbacca, mechanic (Wookiee male); Waste, 2-1B surgical droid

SUMMARY · The Imperial prison ship *Purge* suffers an engine malfunction en route to a detention moon. The ship drifts across the path of a strangely derelict Imperial Star Destroyer, *Vector*, that registers only ten life-forms aboard. Seeking parts, an Imperial crew led by Captain Jareth Sartoris investigates the eerily empty ship. The search party returns with a strange bronchial infection. The *Purge*'s doctor, Zahara Cody, proves immune and tries desperately to contain the contagion. Though she concocts a vaccine, death sweeps through the prison ship, killing most of the five hundred or so prisoners aboard.

The survivors—Zahara, Sartoris, and freed prisoners Kale and Trig Longo, Chewbacca, and Han Solo—flee the reanimated corpses of the *Purge*'s passengers. The *Purge* is overrun by zombies, and the survivors cross over to the *Vector*, only to find thousands more undead—the crew of the massive warship, stormtroopers, pilots, technicians, and more—transformed into mindless, ravenous animated corpses.

Finding her way to a laboratory aboard the *Vector*, Zahara discovers proof that the virus was the

THE DARK TIMES

result of an Imperial bioweapons research program—the Blackwing virus—gone terribly awry. She also finds the key flaw in the virus: The infected cannot travel far from the source of the contamination. The zombies would not spread from their starships.

Kale is infected by the virus and attempts to bite Trig. Realizing that nothing remains of his brother, Trig shoves Kale into a vent shaft to tumble into an engine turbine. The cruel and implacable prison officer Sartoris sacrifices himself to allow the other survivors to escape. Commandeering a shuttle and deactivating the *Vector*'s constraining tractor beams, Zahara, Trig, Han, and Chewbacca are the only survivors of this horrific incident.

THE FIRST FULLY FOCUSED adult horror novel in the *Star Wars* series, *Death Troopers* enjoyed considerable notoriety when its gruesome cover art—a bloody stormtrooper helmet hanging from a chained hook—was revealed on StarWars.com. The surprise and anticipation registered by readers prompted Del Rey to elevate the book from a mass market paperback release to a hardcover, complete with a printed cover in addition to the removable jacket.

Death Troopers saw a great deal of online promotion and social media interaction. Author Joe Schreiber penned an online series of letters from the crew of the *Purge* that appeared across various official and unofficial *Star Wars* websites. A Twitter account belonging to TK 329, a stormtrooper stationed aboard the *Vector*, sent out cryptic messages. Del Rey also reached out to the fan community to produce horror-movie-style video trailers for *Death Troopers*'s release.

The massively multiplayer online roleplaying game *Star Wars: Galaxies* joined the zombie excitement in the lead-up to the book's release by including game content directly tied to the novel. Gentle Giant also produced a Death Trooper mini bust released in 2010.

"INTERLUDE AT DARKKNELL"

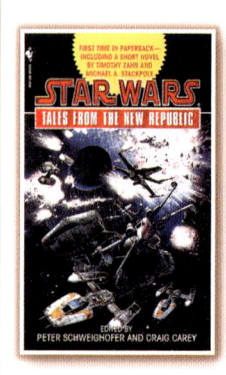

AUTHORS · Timothy Zahn and Michael A. Stackpole

COVER ARTIST · Paul Youll

PUBLICATION HISTORY ·
Short story, featured in *Tales from the New Republic*. Bantam Spectra Books
· Paperback, December 1999

TIME LINE PLACEMENT · 0 BBY

WORLDS VISITED · Anchoron [M-18]; Coruscant (Imperial Center) [L-9]; Darkknell [M-17]

MAIN CHARACTERS · Hal Horn, CorSec inspector (human male); Moranda Savich, thief and con artist (human female); Garm Bel Iblis, Galactic Senator (human male); Ysanne Isard, Imperial Intelligence (human female); Trabler, Imperial Intelligence (human male); Colonel Nyroska, Darkknell security (human male)

SUMMARY · Senator Garm Bel Iblis is targeted by assassins just prior to giving an anti-Imperial speech on Anchoron. The explosive strike kills his family. Shaken but galvanized by the tragedy, Garm undertakes a mission to Darkknell to pick up stolen technical data vital to the Rebellion.

The thief who is selling the plans finds himself pickpocketed by *another* thief—Moranda Savich.

THE DARK TIMES

She in turn is on the run from CorSec inspector Hal Horn. Hal arrives on Darkknell to find Moranda, only to get caught up in Imperial Intelligence's search for her. Moranda, feeling attachment to her nemesis, actually helps Hal escape Isard's wrath, all the while smuggling the data to Garm Bel Iblis.

Though Ysanne Isard ends the caper empty-handed, she avoids disgrace by pinning the whole incident on her father, Armand Isard, director of Imperial Intelligence.

A TWISTING TALE full of reversals and surprises, "Interlude at Darkknell" was originally written for *Star Wars Adventure Journal*, which ceased publication before it could be printed. The story comprises four parts and an epilogue; Zahn wrote parts 1 and 4, while Stackpole wrote parts 2, 3, and the epilogue.

The story line of *The Force Unleashed* makes this tale very difficult to place in the overall chronology. The Rebel Alliance exists, meaning the Corellian treaty among Alderaan, Corellia, and Chandrila has been signed—an event depicted in *The Force Unleashed*. However, Garm does not know much about the Death Star, and the game story has Garm immediately captured and taken aboard the battle station.

Furthermore, *The Force Unleashed* takes place a few years before the Battle of Yavin. "Darkknell" gives no date, but Hal describes his son Corran as being eighteen. This pins the short story as occurring in the same year as the Battle of Yavin.

SHADOW GAMES

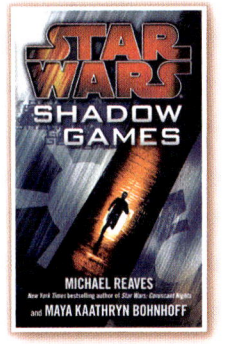

AUTHORS · Michael Reaves and Maya Kaathryn Bohnhoff

COVER ARTIST · Scott Biel

PUBLICATION HISTORY · Novel, Del Rey Books · Paperback, November 2011

TIME LINE PLACEMENT · 0 BBY

WORLDS VISITED · Alderaan [M-10]; Bannistar Station [O-15]; Christophsis [Q-16]; Circarpous system [O-12]; Commenor [N-10]; Falleen [P-15]; Kessel (surrounding space) [T-10]; Rodia [R-16]; Tatooine [R-16]

MAIN CHARACTERS · Dash Rendar, smuggler (human male); Javul Charn, holostar (human female); Eaden Vrill, smuggler (Nautolan male); Leebo, repair droid; Han Solo, smuggler (human male); Hityamun "Hitch" Kris, Black Sun Vigo (human male); Kendara "Spike" Farlion, road manager (human female); Yanus Melikan, cargo master (human male); Edge, assassin (Anomid male)

SUMMARY · With his ship, the *Outrider*, needing repairs, Dash Rendar and his copilot, Eaden Vrill, take on work as bodyguards for pop star Javul Charn, who reports being stalked by an overzealous fan. Dash, Eaden, and their smart-mouthed repair droid Leebo join Javul and her crew aboard her state-of-the-art yacht, the *Nova's Heart*. A series of escalating malfunctions aboard the ship lead Dash to believe the threat is far more than some crazed fan; the nature of the sabotage would require someone with connections.

THE DARK TIMES

Dash Rendar, Eaden Vrill, Han Solo, and Javul Charn try to avoid the deadly Anomid killer known as Edge.

Dash confronts Javul, demanding to know if she has earned any enemies. She denies it, but after a spectacular malfunction during a concert rehearsal on Rodia nearly claims her life, she finally tells Dash that she has been mistaken for the girlfriend of a Black Sun Vigo named Hityamun "Hitch" Kris, a brutal criminal of Mandalorian roots. Javul claims that she's being targeted by Kris's enemies in a deadly case of mistaken identity.

Though Dash warns Javul to be cautious, she indulges in dangerous behavior such as disappearing into the city after concerts in disguise and alone. The sabotage continues—an explosion in the cargo hold on the *Nova's Heart* forces the ship to put down on Tatooine. Dash can't repair his ship in time to make Javul's concert date, so the entourage must travel aboard Han Solo's *Millennium Falcon*, much to Dash's dismay. When his rival flirts with Javul, Dash is forced to confront his feelings for the pop idol.

Dash presses Javul on her past, and she reluctantly confesses it's more than a case of mistaken identity. Javul *was* romantically involved with Hitch and broke off the relationship when she realized the gangster was using her ship and her tour dates as a means of smuggling illegal cargo and disposing of dead bodies. Not only did Javul dump Hitch, she also informed the legal authorities of Black Sun operations, earning the enmity of none other than Prince Xizor. Dash realizes this assignment is far more dangerous than he originally believed.

> ### SHORT STORY — "And Leebo Makes Three"
>
> This short story, written by Michael Reaves and Maya Kaathryn Bohnhoff, was published in *Star Wars Insider* #128 (August 2011) from Titan Publishing and precedes *Shadow Games*. In it, Dash and Eaden acquire Leebo from a Rodian desperate to sell the droid and discover that the wisecracking mechanic carries a memory stick with all sorts of incriminating evidence on Black Sun. The *Outrider* must outrun a number of interested—and extremely dangerous—parties.

At a gig on Falleen, Javul is targeted by a deadly assassin named Edge. Their lives endangered one too many times, Dash once more presses Javul to level with him. She finally admits she is an operative of the Rebel Alliance, using her touring as cover to move Rebel leaders, political prisoners, and vital information. Even now, she is transporting a vital shipment of data from Bannistar Station to Bail Organa, a key Rebel leader on Alderaan. After another strike by Edge—one that kills Dash's partner, Eaden—Dash and Han team up to drop the shipment off on Alderaan while avoiding pursuit from Hitch, Xizor, and the Empire.

On Alderaan, as the *Falcon* rests in a landing bay, Han and Dash are once more attacked by Edge, who has stowed away within one of the ship's secret smuggling compartments. Leebo blasts Edge, killing the assassin—a remarkable achievement for a droid who cannot, by its programming, harm a sentient. Leebo cagily attributes the blasting of Edge as a misfire—the droid had been aiming to shoot the compartment hatch and shot the killer instead.

Han and Dash part ways when Solo drops him off on Tatooine. Dash eventually gets word from Javul that the delivery to the Organas was successful, and in gratitude, she has paid for the repairs required on the *Outrider*.

THE WORKING TITLE for this novel was *Holostar*. In 2010, readers of Del Rey's website chose the final title *Shadow Games* from a list of contenders that included *Pursuit* and *Shadow Play*.

THE HAN SOLO TRILOGY: REBEL DAWN

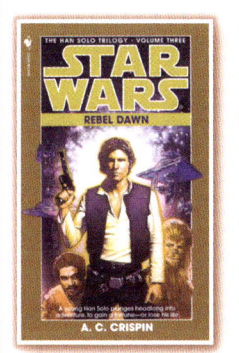

AUTHOR · A. C. Crispin
COVER ARTIST · Drew Struzan
PUBLICATION HISTORY · Novel, Bantam Spectra Books · Paperback, March 1998
TIME LINE PLACEMENT · c. 2 BBY–0
WORLDS VISITED · Bespin [K-18]; Corellia [M-11]; Kashyyyk [P-9]; Kessel (space near the Maw) [T-10]; Nal Hutta and Nar Shaddaa [S-12]; Ord Mantell [L-7]; Tatooine [R-16]; Teth [U-12]; Togoria [P-9]; Toprawa [P-5]; Ylesia [T-12]
MAIN CHARACTERS · Han Solo, smuggler (human male); Chewbacca, mechanic (Wookiee male); Jabba, crime lord (Hutt); Bria Tharen, Rebel agent

THE DARK TIMES
175

(human female); Lando Calrissian, gambler (human male); Boba Fett, bounty hunter (human male)

SUMMARY · While Han Solo has continued to make a name for himself as an incomparable pilot and smuggler, Bria Tharen has been working for the burgeoning Rebellion. She has been serving as a vital connection among scattered resistance groups, bridging freedom fighters on Corellia, Kashyyyk, and Alderaan. Still healing mental scars from her Exultation addiction, she has led raids against the slave camps of Ylesia.

Much has happened to Han in the interim. He has won the *Millennium Falcon* from Lando Calrissian in a heated sabacc tournament in Cloud City. His partner, Chewbacca, surprised him by marrying a Wookiee maiden, Mallatobuck, during a visit to Kashyyyk. And his principal employer, Jabba the Hutt, continues to grow more powerful in the criminal underworld.

The fledgling resistance needs funds to continue, and Bria decides to ask the Desilijic clan to help bankroll the strikes against the rival Besadii clan operations on Ylesia. On a starliner destined for Nar Shaddaa, Bria meets Lando Calrissian and recognizes him as one of Han's friends. She asks about Han, but her chance to reminisce is cut short when she narrowly avoids capture by Boba Fett, thanks to the intervention of Lando's pirate allies. She is impressed by the resourcefulness of underworld pilots and realizes they could be of great use in her fight against the Empire and Ylesia.

Despite their turbulent romantic history, Bria meets with Han and asks him to recruit smugglers to aid her mission. Bria promises a rich reward for their help, and Han ropes Lando into the assignment. Han and Bria rekindle their relationship during this brief reunion. Bria gets word that the Rebellion needs to prepare for a major Imperial initiative and cannot pay the smugglers. Lando and the other smugglers feel Han swindled them, leading to a major falling-out, while Han thinks Bria betrayed him.

Desperate for money, Han takes on a risky trip through the Kessel Run for Jabba. The unexpected appearance of an Imperial patrol forces Han to jettison his cargo, which puts him deeply in debt with the crime lord.

Meanwhile, Bria leads a Rebel team on Toprawa, which transmits the stolen Death Star plans to Princess Leia Organa's Alderaanian consular ship. Bria's Red Hand team is overrun by Imperials, and they are all killed or commit suicide to avoid capture.

Han lies low on Tatooine, eager to find a charter or any kind of business. He hears word of Bria's death from, of all people, Boba Fett.

Rebel Dawn begins with the fateful sabacc game that transfers ownership of the *Millennium Falcon* from Lando to Han. The book then incorporates deliberate gaps in the storytelling to allow for the Brian Daley novels to occur, before picking up the narrative after those events. The book leads directly into the events of *A New Hope*, specifically Han meeting with Obi-Wan Kenobi and Luke Skywalker in the Mos Eisley cantina.

"RINGERS"

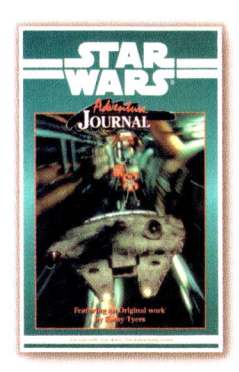

AUTHOR · Laurie Burns
COVER ARTIST · Lucasfilm
PUBLICATION HISTORY · Short story, West End Games · *Star Wars Adventure Journal* #6, May 1995
TIME LINE PLACEMENT · 0 BBY
WORLD VISITED · Stassia [K-10]
MAIN CHARACTERS · Zeck Tambell, Imperial investigator (human male); Aalia Duu-lang, crime madam (human female); Reye Sedeya, young gambler (human male); Valon Rizz, Imperial investigator (human male)

SUMMARY · A seemingly unnatural winning streak while betting on sporting events has drawn unwelcome attention to young Force-sensitive Reye Sedeya. Imperial investigator Sergeant Zeck Tambell, who doesn't particularly believe in the Force, wants to find out how the boy does it, while criminal Aalia Duu-lang also wants to find out the boy's secret of always picking winners. Though Reye ultimately escapes Imperial and criminal attention, Tambell is able to finally arrest his longtime adversary Duu-lang after catching her trying to fix a swoop race.

"MAZE RUN"

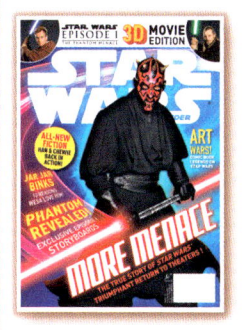

AUTHORS · David J. Williams and Mark S. Williams
PUBLICATION HISTORY · Short story, Titan Publishing · *Star Wars Insider* #131, January 2012
TIME LINE PLACEMENT · 0 BBY
WORLD VISITED · None, interstellar space in the Rishi Maze
MAIN CHARACTERS · Han Solo, smuggler (human male); Chewbacca, mechanic and copilot (Wookiee male)

SUMMARY · Han and Chewbacca take on a daring smuggling run transporting cargo into the heart of the chaotic Rishi Maze, to Firebase Alpha, a secret Rebel outpost. Han realizes almost too late that the delivery is a bomb arranged by the Empire. He and Chewbacca work feverishly to eject the bomb into a black hole before it detonates.

THE DARK TIMES

Wedge Antilles

Tash Arranda

Zak Arranda

Kell Tainer

Thune

X-7

CHAPTER 5

THE GALACTIC CIVIL WAR

Though *Star Wars* was created to be seen on the big screen, the public was first able to experience the story in print. In 1976, the *Star Wars* novelization appeared in bookstores six months before the movie premiered in theaters. The blockbuster success of the film catapulted the book onto bestseller lists, and *Star Wars* as literature has since been a mainstay.

Despite the 1978 follow-up book, *Splinter of the Mind's Eye*, also achieving bestseller status, the era in which the original trilogy of films—*A New Hope*, *The Empire Strikes Back*, and *Return of the Jedi*—was set has been sparsely explored in novels. Prose fiction has largely ceded this action-packed territory to comic books, meaning that in the vast library of *Star Wars* novels, a small fraction concern themselves with the classic struggle of Rebel Alliance versus Galactic Empire.

Marvel Comics was the first to expand the universe. The comic book company's six-issue adaptation of the first *Star Wars* film kicked off a 107-issue run of original tales set during (and immediately after) the classic trilogy. The *Los Angeles Times* Syndicate launched two *Star Wars* newspaper strips, the first in 1979 and the second in 1981, both set between *A New Hope* and *The Empire Strikes Back*. In more recent years, Dark Horse Comics also told stories set in this time frame, with titles such as *Star Wars: Empire* and *Star Wars: Rebellion*.

The editorial consensus is that Luke, Han, and Leia were *extremely* busy in the four years that span the destruction of the first and second Death Stars. Telling new stories featuring the storied trio proves challenging when taking the larger Expanded Universe continuity into account, because they've done *so much* in different media. On the other hand, because this is the era that launched the *Star Wars* saga, it means that stories featuring the Rebel Alliance battling Darth Vader and his minions are continually popular.

The most common form of fiction set in this era is the short story. From 1994 to 1997, West End Games published quarterly installments of the *Star Wars Adventure Journal*, a 280-page-plus trove of resources for players of the *Star Wars* Roleplaying Game. Among the materials were several short stories per issue, mostly focusing on new characters in the Galactic Civil War and early New Republic periods.

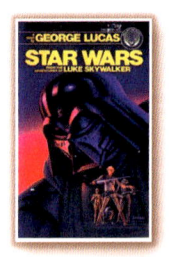

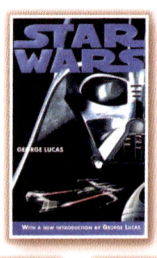

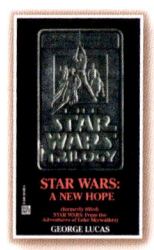

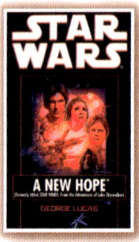

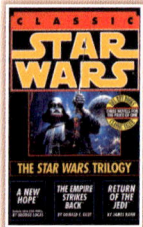

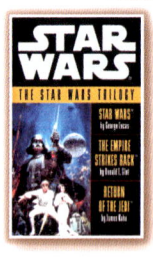

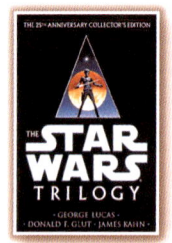

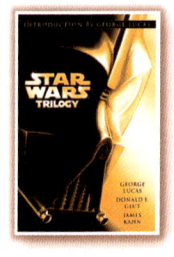

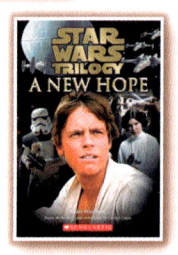

STAR WARS: EPISODE IV
A NEW HOPE

AUTHORS · George Lucas (adult novel); Ryder Windham (junior novelization), based on the story and screenplay by George Lucas

COVER ARTISTS · Ralph McQuarrie (first edition Ballantine novel and *Star Wars Trilogy* 25th Anniversary Edition); John Berkey (Ballantine movie tie-in novel, *Classic Star Wars* trilogy 1987, and *Star Wars Trilogy* 1993 and 1997); Tom Jung (*Classic Star Wars* 1994); Drew Struzan (*Star Wars: A New Hope* 1999); Lucasfilm Ltd. (*Star Wars* 1995, *Star Wars: Episode IV: A New Hope* 2004, *Star Wars Trilogy* 1987 and 2004, and Scholastic novel)

PUBLICATION HISTORY · Novel, Del Rey Books

- Paperback, December 1976 as *Star Wars: From the Adventures of Luke Skywalker* (first edition novel)
- Paperback, May 1977, and hardcover, October 1977, as *Star Wars: From the Adventures of Luke Skywalker* (movie tie-in novel)
- Paperback, October 1994 as *Classic Star Wars: A New Hope*
- Hardcover, September 1995 as *Star Wars*
- Paperback, January 1997 and August 1999 as *Star Wars: A New Hope*

THE GALACTIC CIVIL WAR

180

After defeating Obi-Wan Kenobi, Darth Vader recovers his former Master's lightsaber from the empty robes left behind.

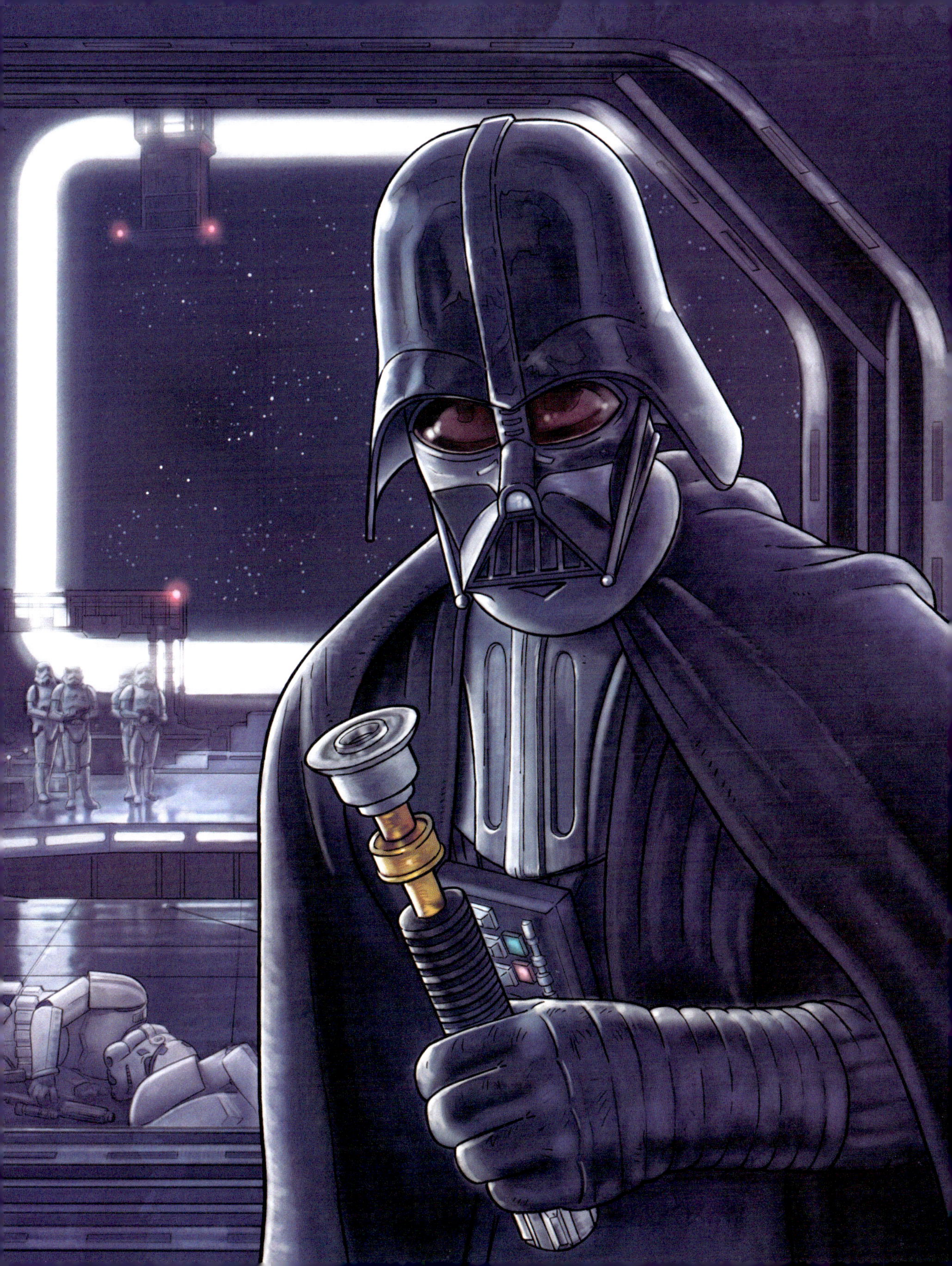

- Paperback, September 2004 as *Star Wars: Episode IV: A New Hope*

Compiled as part of *The Star Wars Trilogy*
- Trade paperback, May 1987 and September 2004
- Hardcover and trade paperback, May 1989 as *Classic Star War Trilogy*
- Paperback, March 1993 and January 1997

Compiled as part of *The Star Wars Trilogy*, The 25th Anniversary Collector's Edition
- Hardcover, June 2002

Junior novelization, Scholastic Inc.
- Paperback, October 2004

TIME LINE PLACEMENT · 0 BBY

WORLDS VISITED · Alderaan [M-10]; Tatooine [R-16]; Yavin (and its moon Yavin 4) [P-6]

MAIN CHARACTERS · Luke Skywalker, farmboy (human male); Princess Leia Organa, Imperial Senator (human female); Han Solo, smuggler (human male); Obi-Wan Kenobi, Jedi exile (human male); Darth Vader, Dark Lord of the Sith (human cyborg male); Wilhuff Tarkin, Imperial governor (human male); C-3PO, protocol droid; R2-D2, astromech droid; Chewbacca, mechanic/copilot (Wookiee male)

SUMMARY · Princess Leia's consular ship is captured by Darth Vader's Star Destroyer while smuggling stolen schematics of the Empire's Death Star battle station. Before being imprisoned, Leia hides the plans in the memory systems of R2-D2, then sends the droid and his counterpart, C-3PO, to Tatooine to find the old Jedi Knight Obi-Wan Kenobi.

The droids instead encounter Luke Skywalker. The farmboy discovers Leia's recorded plea for help and is persuaded by Obi-Wan to go to her aid. Obi-Wan and Luke secure passage to Alderaan from smuggler captain Han Solo aboard the *Millennium Falcon*. When they arrive at Alderaan's coordinates, however, they realize the planet has been destroyed by the Death Star.

After their ship is forcibly taken aboard the enormous battle station, the *Falcon*'s crew and passengers stage a daring and often reckless rescue of Princess Leia. To allow the *Falcon* time to escape, Obi-Wan duels with Darth Vader and is cut down by his former apprentice.

The liberated *Falcon* speeds to Yavin 4, site of the hidden Rebel base. There Rebel tacticians analyze the Death Star plans and launch a fighter assault against the Imperial superweapon. Luke, strong in the Force and guided by the spirit of Obi-Wan, launches a torpedo volley that strikes the Death Star's weak point, triggering a chain reaction that destroys the station. It is a crucial victory for the Rebellion, though Darth Vader lives on, having escaped aboard his TIE fighter.

The first *Star Wars* book published is credited to George Lucas, but the novel was ghostwritten by Alan Dean Foster based on Lucas's fourth-draft screenplay. The novel begins with a prologue describing the immediate history of the Old Republic and the rise of Emperor Palpatine. For decades, this 362-word introduction served as the only real insight into the events potentially covered in Episodes I, II, and III. Indeed, for years it was the only source to identify the Emperor by name.

In earlier printings, some specific terms were rendered with nonstandard spellings that have since been corrected: *Wookie, lightsabre,* and *'droids,* for example.

Though the first *Star Wars* movie spawned many adaptations published across different media—activity books, comics, radio dramas, and storybooks—the 2004 juvenile novel cited here was released by Scholastic Inc. to coincide with the *Star Wars* Trilogy DVD release.

STAR WARS JOURNALS

THE FIGHT FOR JUSTICE · CAPTIVE TO EVIL · HERO FOR HIRE

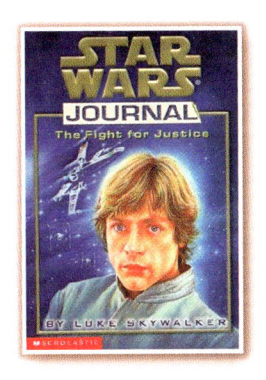

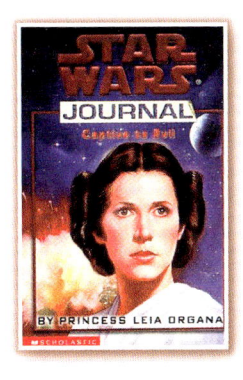

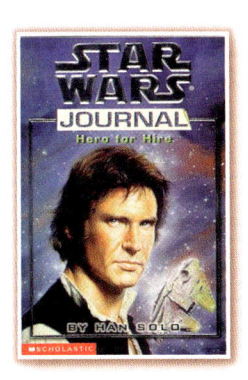

AUTHORS · Jon Peel (*The Fight for Justice*); Jude Watson (*Captive to Evil*); Donna Tauscher (*Hero for Hire*)

COVER ARTIST · Maren (all)

PUBLICATION HISTORY · Young reader novels, Scholastic Inc. · Paperback, July 1998

TIME LINE PLACEMENT · 0–3 ABY

WORLDS VISITED · Alderaan [M-10]; Tatooine (system) [R-16]; Yavin [P-6]

MAIN CHARACTERS · Luke Skywalker, farmboy (human male); Princess Leia Organa, Rebel leader (human female); Han Solo, smuggler (human male); Sai'da, B'omarr monk (human male)

SUMMARY · A retelling of major events in the Galactic Civil War from the perspective of those who experienced it.

T*HE FIGHT FOR JUSTICE* and *Captive to Evil* occur during the events of *A New Hope*, and are first-person narratives told by Luke Skywalker and Princess Leia Organa, respectively. These books include references to scenes created for the National Public Radio dramatization of *Star Wars* in 1981. The impulsive Han Solo was never one for introspection, so his story is not in the form of a personal journal but rather told through an intermediary—a B'omarr monk who interviews Solo during the Corellian's imprisonment in Jabba's palace after being released from carbonite. Though the Solo journal is included here for completeness' sake, those readers who want to preserve a chronological flow of storytelling are encouraged to read it after the *Return of the Jedi* novelization (1983).

Leia's journal is noteworthy as prolific author Jude Watson's first foray into *Star Wars* novels. She would go on to write the Jedi Apprentice, Jedi Quest, and Last of the Jedi series. In her journal, Leia references her aunts Tia, Rouge, and Celly. These characters were first mentioned in passing in *Children of the Jedi* (1995).

"WHEN THE DESERT WIND TURNS: THE STORMTROOPER'S TALE"

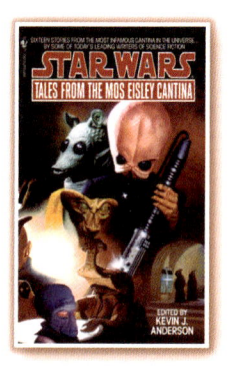

AUTHOR · Doug Beason
COVER ARTIST · Stephen Youll
PUBLICATION HISTORY · Short story, included in *Tales from the Mos Eisley Cantina* short-story anthology, Bantam Spectra
 · Paperback, August 1995
TIME LINE PLACEMENT · 0 BBY
WORLDS VISITED · Carida [M-9]; Tatooine [R-16]
MAIN CHARACTERS · Davin Felth, stormtrooper (human male); Maximilian Veers, Imperial major (human male)

SUMMARY · Cadet Davin Felth arrives at the Academy on Carida for six months of training as an Imperial stormtrooper. Piloting an AT-AT walker during a combat simulation, Davin devises a clever strategy to prevent Rebel speeders from attacking the walker's legs with cables. Rather than being commended by Major Veers, Davin is instead reassigned to an undesirable station on Tatooine, where he becomes part of the detachment scouring the desert planet for a missing escape pod and two Rebel droids. He is taken aback by the ruthlessness of fellow troopers when they destroy a Jawa sandcrawler and all those aboard, and then slaughter an innocent moisture farmer and his wife. During a shootout with a smuggler in Docking Bay 94, Davin has a change of loyalty and shoots his commanding officer in the back, using the confusion of the gunfight as cover. He then intends to help the Rebellion in whatever way he can from within the ranks of the Empire.

"WE DON'T DO WEDDINGS: THE BAND'S TALE"

AUTHOR · Kathy Tyers
PUBLICATION HISTORY · Short story, included in *Tales from the Mos Eisley Cantina* short-story anthology, Bantam Spectra
 · Paperback, August 1995
TIME LINE PLACEMENT · 0 BBY
WORLD VISITED · Tatooine [R-16]
MAIN CHARACTERS · Figrin D'an and the Modal Nodes, music band (Bith males); Lady Valarian, crime boss (Whiphid female)

SUMMARY · Although the Modal Nodes band has signed a contract to perform exclusively at Jabba the Hutt's palace, their reckless leader Figrin D'an commits them to play at the wedding of Lady Valarian, a rival to the Hutt gang lord. The wedding erupts in chaos when an attempt by Jabba's agents to collect the band coincides with an Imperial raid. Escaping the tumult, the band members instead lay low by playing a gig at the Mos Eisley cantina.

This story was adapted by Charles Potter as a full-cast audio dramatization and released on CD and cassette by Bantam Doubleday in 1995. Figrin D'an was originally spelled "Figrin Da'n" in

THE GALACTIC CIVIL WAR

Violence and chaos erupt at the wedding of Lady Valarian, and the members of the Modal Nodes band attempt to escape unscathed.

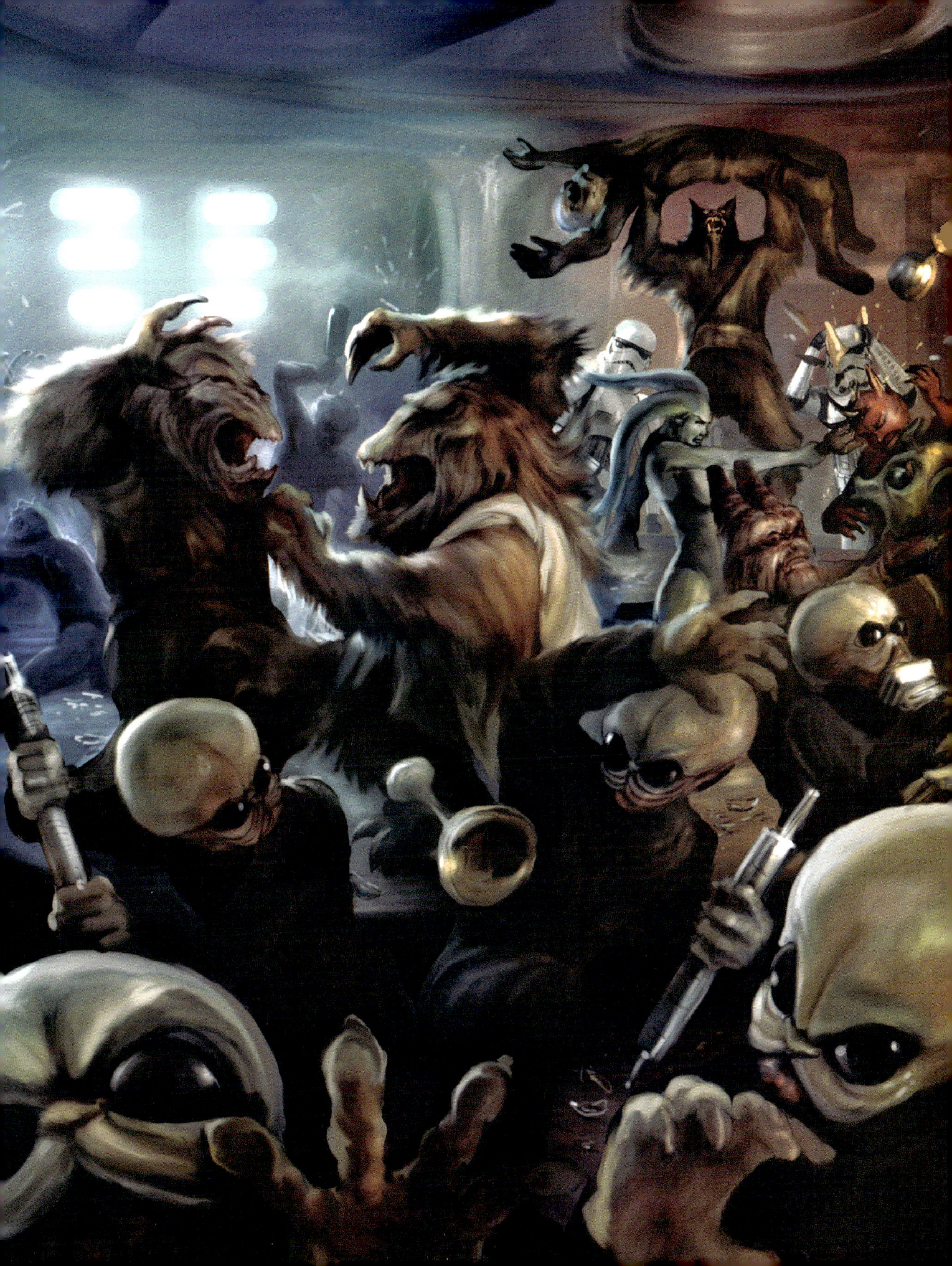

Galaxy Guide 1: A New Hope (1989), the roleplaying game supplement that first gave the Bith musician his name.

"A HUNTER'S FATE: GREEDO'S TALE"

AUTHORS · Tom Veitch and Martha Veitch

PUBLICATION HISTORY · Short story, included in *Tales from the Mos Eisley Cantina* short-story anthology, Bantam Spectra
· Paperback, August 1995

TIME LINE PLACEMENT · 4–0 BBY

WORLDS VISITED · Nar Shaddaa (moon of Nal Hutta) [S-12]; Tatooine [R-16]; U-Tendik [Q-16]

MAIN CHARACTERS · Greedo, bounty hunter (Rodian male); Spurch "Warhog" Goa, bounty hunter (Diollan male); Han Solo, smuggler (human male)

SUMMARY · Greedo and his family are part of a clan hunted by Rodian warlord Navik the Red. They seek refuge within the urban sprawl of Nar Shaddaa. When the Empire attacks Rebel cells hiding on Nar Shaddaa, many Rodian refugees are killed in the crossfire. Orphaned, young Greedo falls in with bounty hunters who steer him into a dangerous assignment on Mos Eisley: collaring Han Solo for the debt the smuggler owes Jabba the Hutt. Little does Greedo know he's been set up to fail by the hunters who want to collect the bounty Navik the Red has placed on Greedo's head.

THE STORY MAKES a number of assumptions regarding Greedo's history that have since been disproven in the canon established by George Lucas. In the story, the Rodian is nineteen years old at the time of his death. A deleted scene from *Star Wars: Episode I The Phantom Menace* (1999) shows Greedo as a child around the same age as Anakin Skywalker, and a denizen of Tatooine at the time, which would make him much older than nineteen at his death.

The New Essential Guide to Characters (2002) attempted to preserve both stories by presenting the Episode I Greedo as "Greedo the Elder," father to the younger Greedo depicted in "A Hunter's Fate." However, "Sphere of Influence," a Season Three episode of *Star Wars: The Clone Wars* (2010), made this fix impossible, as it is clear that Lucas intends Greedo to be an older, luckless hunter who has spent years on Tatooine trying to make a name for himself.

"HAMMERTONG: THE TALE OF THE TONNIKA SISTERS"

AUTHOR · Timothy Zahn

PUBLICATION HISTORY · Short story, included in *Tales from the Mos Eisley Cantina* short-story anthology, Bantam Spectra
· Paperback, August 1995

TIME LINE PLACEMENT · 0 BBY

WORLDS VISITED · Gorno [R-17]; Tatooine [R-16]

MAIN CHARACTERS · Shada D'ukal, Mistryl warrior (human female); Karoly D'ulin, Mistryl warrior

THE GALACTIC CIVIL WAR

SPOTLIGHT *Galaxy Guide 1: A New Hope*

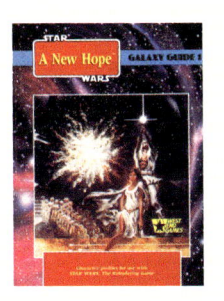

From 1987 to 1990, many regarded the *Star Wars* brand as dormant, but there was one publisher actively expanding the universe with new stories, characters, and lore. West End Games produced the original *Star Wars* Roleplaying Game and supplemented it with a vast series of sourcebooks, guides, adventure modules, and other media. In many ways, the foundations of the Expanded Universe were being quietly built by the roleplaying game before the relaunch of the novels in 1991.

One notable example is *Galaxy Guide 1: A New Hope* by Grant Boucher, published in 1989. This illustrated book took the story of *A New Hope* and broke it into character dossiers complete with roleplaying stats. This book was the first to officially name the Mos Eisley cantina denizens, as well as give them their backstories. The *Tales from the Mos Eisley Cantina* short-story anthology, published in 1995, owes a great debt to this guide and its establishment of the following characters: Momaw Nadon, Figrin D'an, the Tonnika sisters, Greedo, Dr. Evazan, Ponda Baba, Labria, Lak Sivrak, Muftak, and Kabe.

(human female); Riij Winward, Rebel agent (human male)

SUMMARY · The Mistryl Shadow Guard, an elite cadre of all-female mercenaries, are tasked with protecting a top-secret Imperial research project codenamed Hammertong. After an attack against the project leaves several of the Mistryls dead, Shada and Karoly decide to steal the Imperial Strike cruiser carrying Hammertong. They make it as far as Tatooine, where the ship crashes into the Dune Sea. Shada and Karoly know they must secure transport offplanet so they pose as twin criminals the Tonnika sisters and scout out the Mos Eisley cantina. Their disguises prove too convincing: an Imperial officer who believes they truly are the Tonnika sisters arrests them. In jail they meet Riij Winward, a guard who knows Shada's and Karoly's true identities. He offers to free them if they will lead him to the Strike cruiser and Hammertong. As they journey to the Dune Sea, Winward reveals that he is a Rebel agent and that Hammertong is part of the superlaser for the second Death Star.

THE STORY SERVES as an elaborate continuity fix regarding the appearance of the Tonnika sisters. *Galaxy Guide 1: A New Hope* (1989) first established the name and background of the Tonnika sisters, describing them as indistinguishably identical. However, the performers depicting the characters in Episode IV are distinctly different in appearance. To explain the discrepancy, this story describes the sisters seen in the film as imposters. Shada D'ukal, who first appeared in *The Last Command* (1993), would return in other Zahn-penned stories.

"PLAY IT AGAIN, FIGRIN D'AN: THE TALE OF MUFTAK AND KABE"

AUTHOR · A. C. Crispin

PUBLICATION HISTORY · Short story, included in *Tales from the Mos Eisley Cantina* short-story anthology, Bantam Spectra

· Paperback, August 1995

TIME LINE PLACEMENT · 0 BBY

WORLD VISITED · Tatooine [R-16]

MAIN CHARACTERS · Muftak, street urchin (Talz male); Kabe, thief (Chadra-Fan female)

SUMMARY · Muftak has long wondered about his origins, so when a passing Imperial identifies his species as Talz, the large furry biped's curiosity is piqued. Wanting to explore the galaxy beyond Tatooine, he agrees to his friend Kabe's long-repeated request to rob Jabba the Hutt's town house. The two ragamuffins infiltrate the building, where they find a captive Rebel agent who promises them credits if they deliver a datadot containing valuable Rebel intelligence. When security teams surround Muftak and Kabe and a house fire breaks out in the resulting gunfight, the two urchins leave the blaze without any riches, but pass on the datadot to a second Rebel agent. This secures them thousands of credits and passage offworld, allowing them to leave their lowly station.

"THE SAND TENDER: THE HAMMERHEAD'S TALE"

AUTHOR · Dave Wolverton

PUBLICATION HISTORY · Short story, included in *Tales from the Mos Eisley Cantina* short-story anthology, Bantam Spectra

· Paperback, August 1995

TIME LINE PLACEMENT · 0 BBY

WORLD VISITED · Tatooine [R-16]

MAIN CHARACTERS · Momaw Nadon, exile (Ithorian male); Captain Alima, Imperial captain (human male)

SUMMARY · Years ago, Momaw Nadon, High Priest of the Ithorian herdship *Tafanda Bay*, chose to share the secrets of Ithorian technology and agricultural ceremonies with the Empire to save his beloved people and planet from the ruthless Imperial captain Alima and his Star Destroyer's deadly laser cannons. Momaw's decision upset the Ithorian elders and led them to exile him. Many years have passed and Momaw Nadon now lives on Tatooine, where he manages his numerous farming ventures and tends to a lush greenhouse within Mos Eisley. It is in Mos Eisley that Captain Alima once again visits Momaw, this time to pressure him for information regarding missing Rebel droids. Though Momaw contemplates vengeance against Alima, it is simply not in his nature to kill. Instead, he later reports to the Imperial prefect that Alima failed to stop the missing droids from leaving Tatooine. The prefect impulsively kills Alima, an act Momaw was not expecting. As penance in keeping with the Ithorian tradition of planting after harvesting, Momaw takes a genetic sample of Alima to clone the officer.

188 | THE GALACTIC CIVIL WAR

The peaceful Momaw Nadon holds in his growing frustration in the obnoxious presence of Imperial officer Captain Alima.

"DRAWING THE MAPS OF PEACE: THE MOISTURE FARMER'S TALE"

AUTHOR · M. Shayne Bell

PUBLICATION HISTORY · Short story, included in *Tales from the Mos Eisley Cantina* short-story anthology, Bantam Spectra

· Paperback, August 1995

TIME LINE PLACEMENT · 0 BBY

WORLD VISITED · Tatooine [R-16]

MAIN CHARACTERS · Ariq Joanson, moisture farmer (human male); Eyvind, moisture farmer (human male); Ariel, moisture farmer (human female); Wimateeka, scavenger (Jawa male)

SUMMARY · Wishing to make peace with the indigenous species of Tatooine, moisture farmer Ariq Joanson shares his land with Jawas and Tusken Raiders. He even invites a Jawa clan to the wedding of his friends Eyvind and Ariel. A Tusken Raider hunting party attacks, resulting in bloodshed and chaos that is settled by stormtroopers. Ariq comes to realize that the Empire will never allow peaceful cohabitation of settlers and natives, since only the Empire can be the instrument of order on Tatooine. Ariq then joins the Rebel Alliance.

THE GALACTIC CIVIL WAR

"BE STILL MY HEART: THE BARTENDER'S TALE"

AUTHOR · David Bischoff

PUBLICATION HISTORY · Short story, included in *Tales from the Mos Eisley Cantina* short-story anthology, Bantam Spectra

· Paperback, August 1995

TIME LINE PLACEMENT · 0 BBY

WORLD VISITED · Tatooine [R-16]

MAIN CHARACTERS · Wuher, bartender (human male); C2-R4, multipurpose droid

SUMMARY · Wuher longs to concoct a beverage that will please Jabba the Hutt. When Han Solo blasts Greedo in the cantina, Wuher takes the Rodian's body and incorporates it into a cocktail using an odd Jawa-scavenged droid, C2-R4, as a blender. Jabba loves the drink, which causes Wuher to briefly soften his hostile attitude toward droids.

"NIGHTLILY: THE LOVERS' TALE"

AUTHOR · Barbara Hambly

PUBLICATION HISTORY · Short story, included in *Tales from the Mos Eisley Cantina* short-story anthology, Bantam Spectra

· Paperback, August 1995

TIME LINE PLACEMENT · 0 BBY

WORLD VISITED · Tatooine [R-16]

MAIN CHARACTERS · Feltipern Trevagg, tax collector (Gotal male); M'iiyoom Onith, traveler (H'nemthe female)

SUMMARY · Scheming lothario Feltipern Trevagg's lustful eye is caught by the beautiful M'iiyoom Onith, a naïve H'nemthe female who is stranded on Tatooine after she misses her flight offworld. Though M'iiyoom dreams of a deeper romantic relationship, Feltipern is only interested in a quick physical rendezvous. He seduces M'iiyoom with alcohol and an offer of marriage, only to learn the true meaning of commitment to such a tryst the hard way, as M'iiyoom ritually murders Feltipern with her razor-sharp tongue, per the mating custom of the H'nemthe.

The name M'iiyoom is derived from a white flower found on the planet H'nemthe. It translates from the local tongue to "nightlily" in Basic. This story was adapted by Andy Mangels as a full-cast audio dramatization and released on CD and cassette by Bantam Doubleday in 1995.

"EMPIRE BLUES: THE DEVARONIAN'S TALE"

AUTHOR · Daniel Keyes Moran

PUBLICATION HISTORY · Short story, included in *Tales from the Mos Eisley Cantina* short-story anthology, Bantam Spectra

· Paperback, August 1995

THE GALACTIC CIVIL WAR

TIME LINE PLACEMENT · 0 BBY

WORLDS VISITED · Devaron (flashbacks) [M-13]; Tatooine [R-16]

MAIN CHARACTER · Kardue'sai'Malloc, fugitive (Devaronian male)

SUMMARY · Kardue'sai'Malloc is a former Imperial army officer who committed atrocities on his home world of Devaron. Now he lives on Tatooine as a fugitive under the alias of Labria. He recalls his bloody past while also reflecting upon his true passion: music. When Labria hears that Figrin D'an and the Modal Nodes are playing at Lady Valarian's wedding, he arranges an Imperial crackdown at the nuptials and gives the band a refuge by setting them up at his favorite watering hole, the Mos Eisley cantina.

"SOUP'S ON: THE PIPE SMOKER'S TALE"

AUTHOR · Jennifer Roberson

PUBLICATION HISTORY · Short story, included in *Tales from the Mos Eisley Cantina* short-story anthology, Bantam Spectra
· Paperback, August 1995

TIME LINE PLACEMENT · 0 BBY

WORLD VISITED · Tatooine [R-16]

MAIN CHARACTER · Dannik Jerriko, bounty hunter (Anzati male)

SUMMARY · Dannik Jerriko, a thousand-year-old Anzati vampire, coolly eyes potential prey in the Mos Eisley cantina. His hungry gaze lingers on Luke Skywalker and Han Solo, but they depart before he can strike.

"SWAP MEET: THE JAWA'S TALE"

AUTHOR · Kevin J. Anderson

PUBLICATION HISTORY · Short story, included in *Tales from the Mos Eisley Cantina* short-story anthology, Bantam Spectra
· Paperback, August 1995

TIME LINE PLACEMENT · 0 BBY

WORLD VISITED · Tatooine [R-16]

MAIN CHARACTERS · Het Nkik, trader (Jawa male); Wimateeka, clan leader (Jawa male); Reegesk, trader (Ranat male); Obi-Wan Kenobi, Jedi Knight (human male)

SUMMARY · An unnaturally brave and vengeful Jawa, Het Nkik sets out to avenge the death of his clanmate Jek Nkik, whose sandcrawler was torched and gutted by Imperial stormtroopers. He is particularly emboldened by inspiring words from Obi-Wan Kenobi, whom he meets in passing at the destroyed sandcrawler. Armed with an illegal blaster rifle, Het travels to Mos Eisley to target Imperial stormtroopers. After a brief stop in the cantina, he confronts a squad of eight troopers in the streets.

"TRADE WINS: THE RANAT'S TALE"

AUTHOR · Rebecca Moesta

PUBLICATION HISTORY · Short story, included in *Tales from the Mos Eisley Cantina* short-story anthology, Bantam Spectra
· Paperback, August 1995

TIME LINE PLACEMENT · 0 BBY

WORLD VISITED · Tatooine [R-16]

MAIN CHARACTERS · Reegesk, trader (Ranat male); Het Nkik, trader (Jawa male)

SUMMARY · Reegesk, a shifty Ranat trader, barters with Het Nkik, the Jawa with a vendetta against the Empire. In the process of trading him a Tusken Raider battle talisman, Reegesk secretly lifts a power charge from Het's blaster, leaving the Jawa unarmed. This results in Het's death when he later attempts to blast some stormtroopers.

The short story "Swap Meet" ends with a cliffhanger that is not resolved until the reader completes "Trade Wins," as the stories are meant to be read back-to-back. Het Nkik's story also intersects with "When the Desert Wind Turns" and "At the Crossroads," and is referenced in "Drawing the Maps of Peace" and "Spare Parts."

"AT THE CROSSROADS: THE SPACER'S TALE"

AUTHOR · Jerry Oltion

PUBLICATION HISTORY · Short story, included in *Tales from the Mos Eisley Cantina* short-story anthology, Bantam Spectra
· Paperback, August 1995

TIME LINE PLACEMENT · 0 BBY

WORLD VISITED · Tatooine [R-16]

MAIN CHARACTER · BoShek, spacer (human male)

SUMMARY · Racing to Tatooine after breaking the Kessel Run record, spacer BoShek briefly meets Obi-Wan Kenobi in the Mos Eisley cantina. As a Force-sensitive, BoShek is particularly touched by this encounter with a former Jedi Knight. Later, when on the run from Imperials, BoShek instinctively taps into the Force to mind-trick his pursuers, perhaps guided by the unseen hand of Obi-Wan.

"SPARE PARTS"

AUTHOR · Pablo Hidalgo

COVER ARTIST · Lucasfilm Ltd.

PUBLICATION HISTORY · Short story, West End Games
· *Star Wars Adventure Journal* #11, November 1996

TIME LINE PLACEMENT · 0 BBY

WORLD VISITED · Tatooine [R-16]

MAIN CHARACTERS · Aguilae, trader (Jawa female); Macemillian Winduarté, trader (Squib male);

THE GALACTIC CIVIL WAR

The desperate Corellian spacer BoShek dons the robes of a street-corner preacher in Mos Eisley to avoid an Imperial patrol.

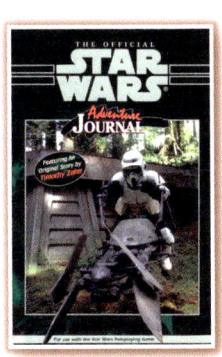

Opun "the Black Hole" Mcgrrrr, criminal (human male); Jabba, crime lord (Hutt male); CZ-3, business droid

SUMMARY · A pair of droid traders accidentally steal one of Jabba the Hutt's business droids, but it wanders free of their care. They search the desert for it, narrowly avoiding the stormtrooper attack that torches Jek Nkik's sandcrawler. In the end, the droid theft is a non-issue—the droid was deliberately set up to be stolen in a plot devised by Jabba to catch a business rival red-handed.

The Squib trader named Macemillian Winduarté—Mace Windu for short—first saw print in *Galaxy Guide 7: Mos Eisley* (1993). Therefore, this "Mace Windu" was established as a character years before the Jedi Master seen in Episode I, the result of the creators of the Squib character picking a name from an early *Star Wars* draft script written by George Lucas.

THE GALACTIC CIVIL WAR 193

DEATH STAR

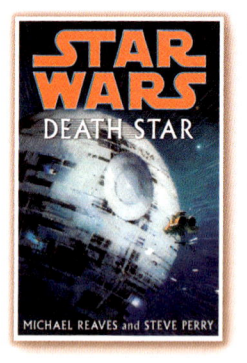

AUTHORS · Michael Reaves and Steve Perry
COVER ARTIST · John Harris
PUBLICATION HISTORY · Novel, Del Rey Books
- Hardcover, October 2007
- Paperback, November 2008

TIME LINE PLACEMENT · 3–0 BBY

WORLDS VISITED · Alderaan [M-10]; Despayre [L-5]; Tatooine (system) [R-16]; Yavin 4 [P-6]

MAIN CHARACTERS · Celot Ratua Dil, smuggler/thief (Zelosian male); Kornell "Uli" Divini, surgeon (human male); Memah Roothes, bartender (Twi'lek female); Villian "Vil" Dance, TIE fighter pilot (human male); Nova Stihl, Imperial guard (human male); Rodo, bouncer (Ragithian male); Teela Kaarz, architect (Mirialan female); Atour Riten, librarian (human male); Tenn Graneet, Imperial gunner (human male); Wilhuff Tarkin, Grand Moff (human male); Darth Vader, Dark Lord of the Sith (human cyborg male); Natasi Daala, Imperial admiral (human female); Conan Antonio Motti, Imperial admiral (human male)

SUMMARY · During the final phases of construction and activation of the first Death Star, several low-level crewers bond together in opposition to the battle station's monstrously destructive mission. Following the obliteration of the planets Despayre and Alderaan, this assortment of conscientious personnel from different walks of life arrange escape from the battle station during its approach to the Rebel base on Yavin 4. They flee the Death Star before it is annihilated and seek refuge with the Rebels.

Among these deserters are:

CELOT RATUA DIL: A convicted smuggler sentenced to imprisonment on the penal world of Despayre, which also served as a construction site for the Death Star, the crafty Ratua sneaks aboard a transport to escape confinement and manages to carve a survivable niche aboard the Death Star posing as a civilian contractor for two years. He falls in love with Memah Roothes, bartender at the onboard cantina, the Hard Heart.

KORNELL "ULI" DIVINI: An Imperial surgeon conscripted into service after the Clone Wars, Uli grows weary of wartime duty. While stationed aboard the Death Star, he tends to captive Princess Leia Organa's trauma after her Imperial interrogation and grows to sympathize with her cause. His research into Force sensitivity puts him on the Imperial wanted list just prior to the Battle of Yavin.

MEMAH ROOTHES: A bartender formerly based in the Southern Underground of Coruscant. When Memah's cantina on Coruscant, the Soft Heart, mysteriously burns down, the Empire recruits her to run a similar business aboard the Death Star. She brings with her Rodo, a hulking Ragithian bouncer. She develops feelings for Ratua despite his shady past.

VILLIAN "VIL" DANCE: A hotshot TIE fighter pilot always seeking a challenge, Vil grows to respect the Rebellion and is disturbed by the numerical superiority of the Empire. He falls in love with architect Teela Kaarz. When the Death Star obliterates Alderaan, it seals his commitment to leaving Imperial service. He pilots the escape shuttle away from the battle station, even briefly outflying Darth Vader during the Battle of Yavin.

TEELA KAARZ: An architect and political prisoner incarcerated on Despayre, Teela is conscripted to help

CHRONOLOGICAL NOTE | A Death Star Is Born

In much the same way the Death Star has no single architect, its fictional history has also undergone extensive revision and additions throughout *Star Wars* publishing. First appearing in *Star Wars*: Episode IV *A New Hope*, the Death Star's genesis was largely credited to Grand Moff Tarkin. Using this as a starting point, the Expanded Universe built upon Tarkin's role in such guidebooks as *The Imperial Sourcebook* (1989) and *The Death Star Technical Companion* (1991). *Galaxy Guide 5: Return of the Jedi* (1990) was the first to credit an engineer with the Death Star's design: Bevel Lemelisk.

With more and more *Star Wars* novelists wanting to add the specter of the Death Star to their works, more masterminds appeared who were in some way responsible for its construction. The 1994–95 Jedi Academy Trilogy introduced Maw Installation, an entire research facility of Imperial scientific geniuses who helped conceive the Death Star design. The *Dark Empire* comic series (1991–92) added scientist Umak Leth to the growing roster, while *Children of the Jedi* (1995) credited Nasdra Magrody as a key contributor.

With a project as big as the Death Star, such a sizable roster of masterminds does not stretch credibility too much—but this mid-1990s snapshot barely scratched the surface of the Death Star's history. *Rogue Planet* (2001) suggested that Tarkin may have cribbed the Death Star idea from Raith Sienar. *Star Wars: Episode II Attack of the Clones* (2002) had the biggest shocker: the Geonosians were chiefly responsible for the Death Star's construction. In George Lucas's canon history of the Death Star, it was the insectoid weaponsmiths who built the first battle station within the rings of their world, a fact verified by a visit to Geonosis in the Disney theme parks ride Star Tours: The Adventures Continue (2011).

If the Death Star's construction history seems convoluted, then the history of the theft of its plans is even more so. The first agent credited with ensuring the recovery of the Death Star plans was Keyan Farlander in LucasArts' **X-Wing: Space Combat Simulator** (1993). Then, in 1995's **Dark Forces**, Kyle Katarn is credited with stealing the plans. Other games like **Battlefront II** (2005), **Empire at War** (2006), **Lethal Alliance** (2006), and The Lost Jedi adventure game book series (1993) are all in some way part of continuity and yet all feature the stolen Death Star plans as objectives. **Empire at War** attempted to unify these disparate Death Star plans stories by suggesting that the plans, once stolen, were deliberately scattered in an attempt to prevent their recovery.

---

design and build interior spaces aboard the Death Star. Among the projects that passed by her desk was a certain thermal exhaust port that would later prove to be the Death Star's exploitable weakness. Teela falls in love with Vil Dance, TIE fighter pilot.

Nova Stihl: An Imperial guard and martial arts instructor, Nova is troubled by vivid dreams and flashes of vision into the future. Examined by Dr. Divini, Nova discovers that he is Force-sensitive. During the rush to escape the Death Star, Nova and the bouncer Rodo—a sparring partner—stay be-

SPOTLIGHT: The Farlander Papers

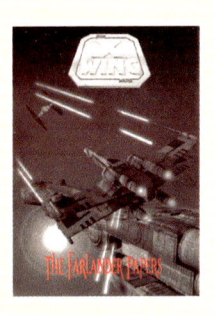

Boxed within the limited edition set of the 1992 LucasArts release **X-Wing: Space Combat Simulator** was the booklet titled *The Farlander Papers*. This ninety-six-page work by Russel DeMaria is part sourcebook, detailing information about the Rebellion, its allies, and its fighter craft. It is also a novella, a narrative told from the perspective of young Keyan Farlander, an activist on the planet Agamar. Orphaned by the Empire, Keyan is stirred by the speech given by Mon Mothma during one of her recruitment missions and joins the Rebel Alliance. Keyan trains aboard the Mon Calamari cruiser *Independence*, becoming fast friends with fellow pilot Hamo Blastwell. During a mission that targets a lone Imperial corvette, Keyan disables and boards the enemy craft and steals vital Imperial military data.

In this way, Keyan is presented as the player's proxy, since the assault on the corvette is one of the playable missions in the game. When Prima Publishing released *X-Wing: The Official Strategy Guide* in 1993, Rusel DeMaria continued the story of Keyan, making him the pilot who experiences the game missions and thus continuing his story in a narrative fashion with a novella that weaves its way through strategy-guide content. The game culminates with the attack on the Death Star at the Battle of Yavin. Since, historically, Luke Skywalker is the one to destroy the battle station, the strategy guide deviates from the game mission to place Keyan Farlander in a Y-wing fighter during the battle. Thus, it is Farlander who is the anonymous Y-wing pilot flying away from the doomed Death Star at the end of *Star Wars*: Episode IV *A New Hope*.

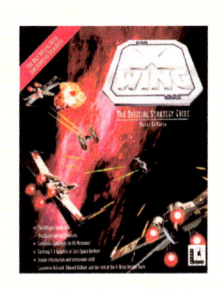

LucasArts expanded upon the **X-Wing** game with add-on content, offering new missions and new vessels in the expansion releases "Imperial Pursuit" and "B-Wing." These add-ons were given the strategy-guide treatment in 1995 when they were bundled as part of a collector's CD-ROM. Prima's expanded guide (credited to DeMaria, David Wessman, and David Maxwell) includes the content from the first edition, as well as new mission summaries, but no new novella content.

Keyan Farlander would be mentioned in the New Jedi Order books: first in Dark Tide I: *Onslaught* (2000), and then he would make an appearance as a New Republic fleet officer in the New Jedi Order novel *Destiny's Way* (2002). In 2008, Hasbro made an action figure of Farlander, based on an otherwise unnamed B-wing pilot from *Return of the Jedi*, thus retroactively making Farlander present in the film.

THE GALACTIC CIVIL WAR

A medical shuttle carrying defectors from the Death Star escapes the battle station in the thick of the Battle of Yavin.

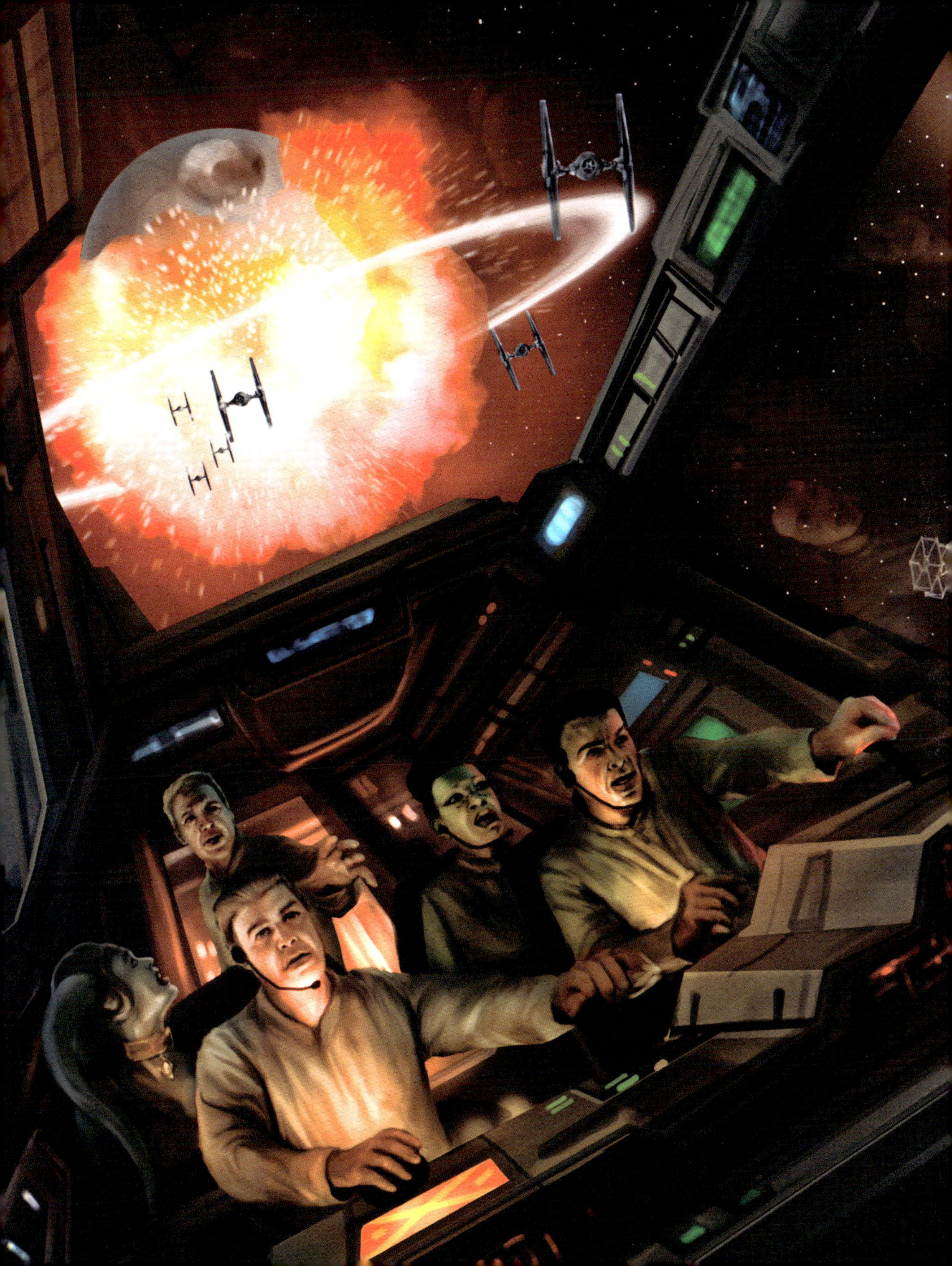

hind to hold off pursuing Imperial guards. Rodo and Nova are killed in the exploding Death Star.

Aside from this desertion, the final phases of the Death Star's life are marked by other dramas. Gunner Tenn Graneet struggles with his role in firing the battle station's devastating cannon against planets, but he nonetheless continues to serve the Empire loyally. Meanwhile, incidents of sabotage plague the Death Star's final phases. Grand Moff Tarkin instructs his secret lover, Admiral Daala, to investigate these incidents. She is injured during a Rebel attack and must undergo emergency brain surgery that wipes her memory of these events.

The *Death Star* novel spans the battle station's last three years, culminating with its destruction at the Battle of Yavin. It is placed here in the reading chronology so that the events of *Star Wars*: Episode IV are experienced first. Among the Imperial crewers given the spotlight is Admiral Motti, who was given the full name Conan Antonio Motti as a last-minute editorial change coinciding with George Lucas jokingly revealing the character's full name during a 2007 appearance on *Late Night with Conan O'Brien*.

Though this novel incorporates story threads from across the Expanded Universe, including nods to the Jedi Academy Trilogy (1994–95) and the short story "Interlude at Darkknell" (1999), noticeably absent is the Death Star's role as a location in The Force Unleashed (2008). This is because the game's story line would not be publicly disclosed until its launch a year after *Death Star*'s publication.

"BREAKING FREE: THE ADVENTURES OF DANNEN LIFEHOLD"

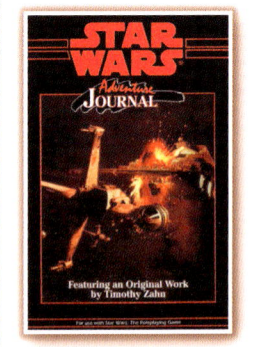

AUTHOR · Dave Marron

COVER ARTIST · Lucasfilm Ltd.

PUBLICATION HISTORY · Short story, West End Games · *Star Wars Adventure Journal* #1, February 1994

TIME LINE PLACEMENT · 0 BBY

WORLDS VISITED · Dohu VII [K-7]; Evas VI [I-7]

MAIN CHARACTERS · Dannen Lifehold, smuggler (human male); Purr, mechanic (Tinnell female); Linkaas, loan shark (Pliith male)

SUMMARY · Smuggler Dannen Lifehold is able to escape hired goons who want him dead. Dannen succeeds with the help of his new tagalong, the impressionable yet gifted mechanic named Purr, an affectionate feline alien.

"CHANGING THE ODDS: THE ADVENTURES OF DANNEN LIFEHOLD"

AUTHOR · Dave Marron

PUBLICATION HISTORY · Short story, West End Games · *Star Wars Adventure Journal* #3, August 1994

TIME LINE PLACEMENT · 0 BBY

THE GALACTIC CIVIL WAR

WORLDS VISITED · Alderaan [M-10]; Rafft [J-8]

MAIN CHARACTERS · Dannen Lifehold, smuggler (human male); Purr, mechanic (Tinnell female)

SUMMARY · Though he does not want to get involved with the Rebellion, Dannen Lifehold delivers medical supplies from Alderaan to a Rebel outpost on Rafft. A homing beacon hidden in the cargo alerts the Empire to the Rebel presence. Dannen helps evacuate the Rebels and, upon learning that Alderaan has been destroyed, commits himself fully to the Rebel Alliance.

"A CERTAIN POINT OF VIEW"

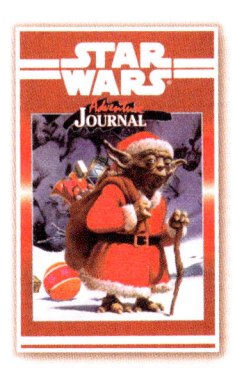

AUTHOR · Charlene Newcomb

COVER ARTIST · Ralph McQuarrie

PUBLICATION HISTORY · Short story, West End Games · *Star Wars Adventure Journal* #8, November 1995
Reprinted in *Tales from the Empire* short-story anthology, Bantam Spectra · Paperback, December 1997

TIME LINE PLACEMENT · 0 BBY

WORLDS VISITED · Maelstrom Nebula [K-5]; Mantooine [L-5]

MAIN CHARACTERS · Celia Durasha, navigation officer (human female); Detien Kaileel, security officer (Kabieroun male); Adion Lang, ISB agent (human male)

SUMMARY · Celia Durasha, the young navigation officer aboard the luxury liner *Kuari Princess*, is shocked to discover that her fellow crewmember, security officer Detien Kaileel, is a Rebel agent. Making this revelation especially difficult for her is news that Rebels killed her brother, an Imperial, on Ralltiir. Furthermore, her former boyfriend, Adion Lang, has been assigned by the Imperial Security Bureau (ISB) to arrest Kaileel. Following her conscience, Celia attempts to free Kaileel from shipboard detention, but Lang catches her red-handed, and shoots Kaileel. Celia attacks Lang, stabbing him with a blade, and escapes aboard a shuttle into the sensor-shrouding Maelstrom Nebula to start life anew.

Adventure Journal editor Peter Schweighofer asked Charlene Newcomb to develop a story around an existing piece of artwork, a painting by Daniel Horne that adorned the cover of the role-playing game adventure *Riders of the Maelstrom* (1989). It featured a human female playing a holographic chesslike game with a large alien. Celia would return in the short story "Crimson Bounty" (1997).

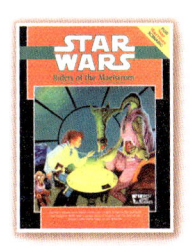

"DROID TROUBLE"

AUTHOR · Chuck Sperati

PUBLICATION HISTORY · Short story, West End Games · *Star Wars Adventure Journal* #3, August 1994

TIME LINE PLACEMENT · 0 ABY

WORLDS VISITED · Bothawui [R-14]; Tatooine [R-16]

THE GALACTIC CIVIL WAR | 199

MAIN CHARACTERS · Tereb Ab'Lon, politician (Bothan male); Nim Bola, investigator/hired gun (human male); R2-Z1, aka "Fweep," astromech droid

SUMMARY · An ambitious Bothan politician evades Imperial pursuit while trying to deliver an astromech droid loaded with sensitive Imperial military data to the Rebellion. His starship crashes into the deserts of Tatooine. Rather than help Tereb, the unscrupulous Nim Bola steals his droid and drops the Bothan into the Sarlacc pit.

"THE OCCUPATION OF RHAMALAI"

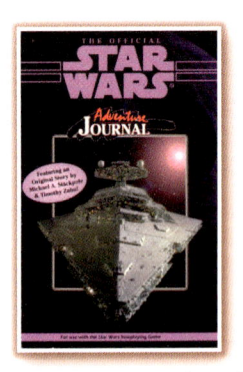

AUTHOR · M. H. Watkins

COVER ARTIST · Lucasfilm Ltd.

PUBLICATION HISTORY · Short story, West End Games · *Star Wars Adventure Journal* #13, May 1997

TIME LINE PLACEMENT · 0 ABY

WORLD VISITED · Rhamalai [I-19]

MAIN CHARACTERS · Denel Moonrunner (human male); Nadra Enasteri (human female); Charis Enasteri (human female); Naem Yrros, Imperial general (human male)

SUMMARY · The Empire subjugates the primitive, agrarian world of Rhamalai. Its human inhabitants have eschewed technology of any kind. The young men of Rhamalai are conscripted into the Imperial ranks. Young Nadra Enasteri must leave her ailing mother's side to work in the Imperial garrison base. The Empire, having no need for Nadra's infirm mother, Charis Enasteri, schedules her to be terminated. Denel Moonrunner, an adventurous youth being groomed as an Imperial trooper, decides to enlist the aid of his parents to help Nadra save her mother. The elder Moonrunners are actually Rebel agents who came to Rhamalai years ago, and have hidden technology in the countryside. Their astromech droid allows Denel and Nadra to bypass Imperial security and escape with Charis. The Imperials pursue, but Charis and Nadra hide in the countryside while the Moonrunners flee aboard their hidden starship.

"TO FIGHT ANOTHER DAY"

AUTHOR · Kathy Tyers

PUBLICATION HISTORY · Short story, West End Games · *Star Wars Adventure Journal* #6, May 1995

TIME LINE PLACEMENT · 0 ABY

WORLD VISITED · Silver Station, near the Dragonflower Nebula [P-15]

MAIN CHARACTERS · Tinian I'att, armaments heir (human female); Daye Azur-Jamin, wounded fugitive (human male); Una Poot, Rebel contact (human female); Chenlambec, bounty hunter (Wookiee male)

SUMMARY · Tinian I'att, fugitive from the Empire, arrives at Silver Station to hand over her prototype portable shielding technology to a Rebel Alliance contact, the elderly Una Poot. Tinian meets the Wookiee bounty hunter Chenlambec and asks to be apprenticed to him. She departs with the Wookiee aboard his starship, *Wroshyr*. Around the same time, Rebels carrying the wounded Daye Azur-Jamin also

THE GALACTIC CIVIL WAR

arrive at Silver Station. His bacta recovery is cut short when he and the Rebels are forced to flee the station as it comes under attack by an Imperial Star Destroyer.

This story takes place three weeks after "Tinian on Trial" (1995) and features the first meeting of Tinian and Chenlambec, who will appear in the short story "The Prize Pelt: The Tale of Bossk" (1996).

"SMALL FAVORS"

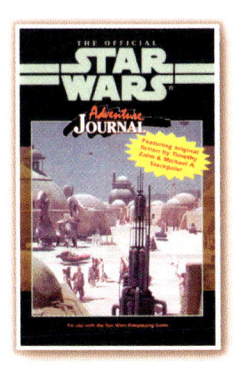

AUTHOR · Paul Danner
COVER ARTIST · Lucasfilm Ltd.
PUBLICATION HISTORY · Short story, West End Games · *Star Wars Adventure Journal* #12, February 1997
TIME LINE PLACEMENT · 0 ABY
WORLDS VISITED · Corulag [L-9]; Kuat [M-10]
MAIN CHARACTERS · Cryle Cavv, Rebel Special Ops agent (human male); Quillin Arkell, Rebel Special Ops agent (Velabri male); Sollaine, Imperial Security Bureau central commander (human male); Rivoche Tarkin, Imperial noble (human female); Finn Varatha, bounty hunter (human female); Darth Vader, Dark Lord of the Sith (human cyborg male)
SUMMARY · Rebel agent and master thief Cryle Cavv is sent to Corulag to extract a deep-cover Rebel agent, Rivoche Tarkin—niece of the late Grand Moff Tarkin—before her cover is blown. Complicating the rescue is the fact Cavv arrives during Rivoche's engagement party, which has drawn Imperial officers and nobles from across the sector. With his wits, daring, and luck, Cavv outruns the Empire, especially the maniacal ISB commander Sollaine.

That the *Executor*, Darth Vader's Super Star Destroyer, is just entering service in this story places it within six months of the Battle of Yavin, as the *Executor*'s blockade of the Rebels depicted in the *Classic Star Wars* newspaper strip has been pegged as happening six months ABY. Cavv makes an offhand comment about receiving wisdom from an odd acquaintance met after a crash landing on an uncharted swamp planet—a sly reference that points toward Yoda but is not elaborated upon.

"SANDBOUND ON TATOOINE"

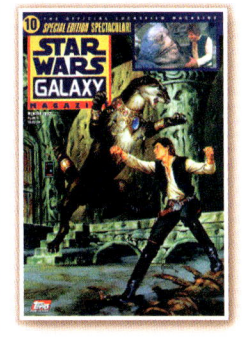

AUTHOR · Peter Schweighofer
PUBLICATION HISTORY · Short story, The Topps Company · *Star Wars Galaxy Magazine* #10, Winter 1997
TIME LINE PLACEMENT · 0 ABY
WORLD VISITED · Tatooine [R-16]
MAIN CHARACTER · Platt Okeefe, smuggler (human female)

THE GALACTIC CIVIL WAR 201

SUMMARY · Escaping bounty hunters, smuggler Platt Okeefe crashes her starship, *Pak's Demise*, into the Dune Sea on Tatooine. Avoiding a sandstorm, she rides into town atop a domesticated ronto.

SCOUNDRELS

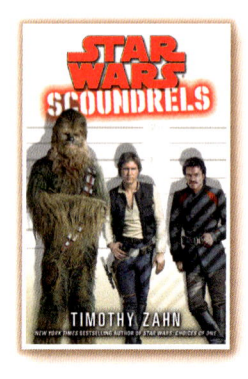

AUTHOR · Timothy Zahn
COVER ARTIST · Paul Youll
PUBLICATION HISTORY · Novel, Del Rey Books · Hardcover, December 2012
TIME LINE PLACEMENT · 0 ABY
WORLDS VISITED · Tatooine [R-16]; Wukkar [L-10]

MAIN CHARACTERS · Han Solo, smuggler (human male); Lando Calrissian, entrepreneur (human male); Dozer Creed, professional ship thief (human male); Chewbacca, mechanic/copilot (Wookiee male); Winter, observational detail (human female); Rachele Ree, intelligence (human female); Kell Tainer, demolitions and mechanics expert (human male); Bink Kitik, ghost burglar (human female); Tavia Kitik, electronics expert (human female); Zerba Cher'dak, pickpocket (Balosar male); Eanjer, funding and intelligence (human male); Qazadi, Black Sun official (Falleen male); Dayja, Imperial Intelligence agent (human male)

SUMMARY · After having his Rebel reward money stolen, Han Solo is so desperate to pay off Jabba the Hutt that he contemplates an offer from a stranger named Eanjer to steal a Black Sun official's riches from a very well-secured vault. The target is the estate of Villachor, a local Black Sun boss on Wukkar. Eanjer explains he is stealing back the credits that Villachor stole from his father. He also wants to avenge his father's death by Villachor. He cannot do it alone, so he asks if Han can assemble a team. Working with Villachor at the moment is Qazadi, another Black Sun gangster who has been instructed to lie low until Imperial scrutiny on criminal activity has cooled down.

Han gathers up a group of criminals with the necessary skills to pull off the heist. They include Rachele Ree, a low-level member of the Wukkar aristocracy who is plugged into the local bureaucracy; Dozer Creed, a professional ship thief with the bluff confidence and Corellian credentials to act as front man; Bink, a beautiful young ghost burglar, and Tavia, her disapproving but helpful identical twin sister; Winter, a somewhat shadowy figure who comes highly recommended for her photographic memory; Zerba Cher'dak, a Balosar pickpocket, sleight-of-hand master, and owner of a contraband (and slightly damaged) lightsaber; and Kell Tainer, an up-and-coming young demolitions expert. Chewie wants Han to recruit Lando Calrissian, but Han has had a falling out with the gambler. Despite not being included, Lando shows up to join the crew. He agrees to temporarily put aside his grudge because he also needs the credits.

As the team formulates a complex plan to work their way into Villachor's vaults, they risk running afoul of both Black Sun gangsters and Imperial Intelligence. They'll need all their complex and varied skills, as well as every ounce of Han Solo's famed luck, to pull off the heist.

HAN LOSES HIS REWARD MONEY to pirates in issue #7 of the Marvel Comics *Star Wars* se-

SHORT STORY — "Heist"

Published in *Star Wars Insider* #138 (December 2012) was a short story by Timothy Zahn that previewed characters who would later appear in *Scoundrels*. "Heist" focuses on the identical twin thieves Bink and Tavia Kitik, who are traveling aboard a starliner as it makes its way to Kailor V. Bink has been wooing Cristoff, an arrogant corporate baron, in order to work her way into the safe in his stateroom. Wearing a specially designed sensor-mesh hidden in her dress, Bink is able to electronically duplicate the keycard required to sneak into the room. As Tavia later distracts Cristoff by posing as Bink, Bink cracks the safe and steals gems that will keep the sisters solvent for at least another month.

ries (1977), the first issue to move beyond the events of Episode IV. In coming up with the idea for *Scoundrels*, Timothy Zahn was inspired by *Ocean's 11*, a 1960 heist film starring Frank Sinatra, remade in 2001 with George Clooney in the lead role.

REBEL FORCE: TARGET

AUTHOR · Alex Wheeler
COVER ARTIST · Randy Martinez
PUBLICATION HISTORY · Juvenile novel, Scholastic Inc.
· Paperback, December 2008
TIME LINE PLACEMENT · 0 ABY

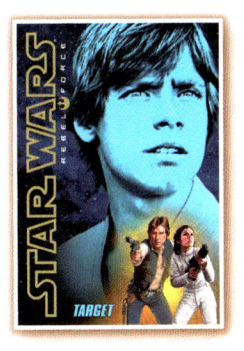

WORLDS VISITED · Coruscant [L-9]; Muunilinst [K-4]; Yavin (and its moon Yavin 4) [P-6]

MAIN CHARACTERS · Luke Skywalker, Rebel pilot (human male); Princess Leia Organa, Rebel leader (human female); X-7, spy (human male); Han Solo, smuggler (human male); Nal Kenuun, gambler (Muun male)

SUMMARY · In the weeks after the Battle of Yavin, the Emperor makes discovering the identity of the Rebel pilot who destroyed the Death Star of paramount importance. Imperial commander Rezi Soresh sends his secret agent X-7 to infiltrate the Rebel ranks. Posing as Tobin Elad, X-7 ingratiates himself with the Rebels during a mission to Muunilinst. Luke, Leia, and Han are there to secure funding for the Rebellion. To that end, Luke finds himself competing in a dangerous Podrace. He succeeds, and Tobin's continuing assistance throughout the mission earns the trust of the Rebels. X-7, having witnessed Luke's piloting skills, begins to suspect that Skywalker is the one the Emperor seeks.

Target is the first in the Rebel Force series of stories set during the "classic *Star Wars*" period of 0–3 ABY. These tales are some of the few from this point in the time line that benefit from full knowledge of the events of Episodes I through III. As such, Luke's Podrace competition is a deliberate nod to his father's Boonta Eve victory. C-3PO almost cites that historic race, but he is interrupted before he is able to refer to it.

THE GALACTIC CIVIL WAR

REBEL FORCE: HOSTAGE

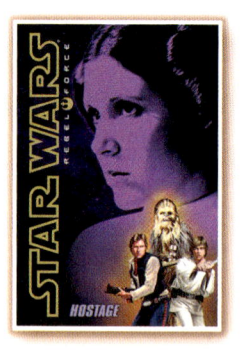

AUTHOR · Alex Wheeler
COVER ARTIST · Randy Martinez
PUBLICATION HISTORY · Juvenile novel, Scholastic Inc. · Paperback, December 2008
TIME LINE PLACEMENT · 0 ABY
WORLDS VISITED · Dagobah [M-19]; Delaya [L-9]
MAIN CHARACTERS · Princess Leia Organa, Rebel leader (human female); Luke Skywalker, Rebel pilot (human male); Ferus Olin, aka Fess Ilee, hidden guardian (human male); X-7, spy (human male); Han Solo, smuggler (human male); Halle Dray, Alderaanian survivor (human female); Kiro Chen, Alderaanian survivor (human male)
SUMMARY · Princess Leia makes a difficult journey to Delaya, sister world of Alderaan and home to many Alderaanians who were offplanet when Alderaan was destroyed and now find themselves refugees without a homeworld. She is shocked to discover the appalling overcrowded conditions faced by the refugees, as well as the outward hostility some of them show her. One woman, Halle Dray, feels the Organa house invited Imperial reprisal upon their world due to its involvement with the Rebel Alliance. Working with the Delayan government, Dray arranges for Leia's capture and handover to the Empire. Luke, Han, and a friend of the Organa family, Fess Ilee, work together to rescue her. Fess is in reality Ferus Olin, a Jedi who has watched over Leia since her infancy. X-7, still posing as Tobin Elad, frees Leia, but surreptitiously doses her with a truth serum that allows him to confirm the identity of the Rebel who destroyed the Death Star: Luke Skywalker.

At one point in this story, Han recalls Obi-Wan's quote regarding Alderaan's destruction, though he was not present to hear it said in *Star Wars*: Episode IV *A New Hope*. This story marks the reappearance of Ferus Olin, featured hero of the Last of the Jedi series.

REBEL FORCE: RENEGADE

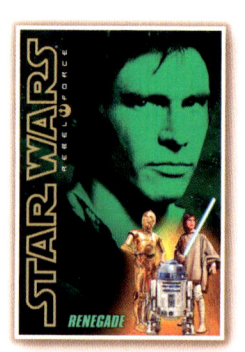

AUTHOR · Alex Wheeler
COVER ARTIST · Randy Martinez
PUBLICATION HISTORY · Juvenile novel, Scholastic Inc. · Paperback, May 2009
TIME LINE PLACEMENT · 0 ABY
WORLDS VISITED · Tythe [Q-16]; Yavin (and its moon, Yavin 4) [P-6]; Zoma system [S-17]
MAIN CHARACTERS · Han Solo, smuggler (human male); Princess Leia Organa, Rebel leader (human female); Luke Skywalker, Rebel pilot (human male); X-7, spy (human male); Jaxson, Tatooine youth (human male); Bossk, bounty hunter (Trandoshan male)
SUMMARY · Having discovered the identity of the Death Star's destroyer, X-7 attempts to assassinate Luke Skywalker by sabotaging his swoop bike while

204 THE GALACTIC CIVIL WAR

at the Rebel base on Yavin. Luke's Force abilities allow him to escape the deadly explosion. While Luke recovers in a medical center, Princess Leia leads an investigation into the murder attempts, and X-7's carefully planted evidence points the finger of guilt toward Han Solo. Han escapes a brief incarceration, and while picking up work in the Zoma system, uncovers the truth of Tobin Elad's identity.

Luke, meanwhile, lays low on Tatooine with Leia. Revisiting his friends at Tosche Station, Luke butts heads with Jaxson, a belligerent young farmer who doesn't agree with Skywalker's ideals. The two daredevils attempt to settle their differences by racing skyhoppers through Beggar's Canyon, but end up crashing in the desert wilderness. As Luke and Jaxson work together to survive the Tatooine desert the two begin to form a bond. They also outsmart and escape the bounty hunter Bossk, who has been tasked with capturing Skywalker by Jabba the Hutt because he is a known associate of Han Solo.

X-7 eventually tracks Luke to Tatooine, but his attempt to target young Skywalker is foiled by Han Solo, who arrives to rescue Luke as well as clear his name and reveal X-7's treachery. The Imperial agent escapes.

Although Luke Skywalker says in *Star Wars*: Episode IV *A New Hope* that he will never return to Tatooine, the Expanded Universe finds him coming back to the desert planet many times between Episodes IV and VI. Among the sources that show Luke returning to Tatooine are the newspaper strip *Tatooine Sojourn* (1979), Marvel Comics' *Star Wars* #31–33 (1980), the *Star Wars 3-D* #1 comic from Blackthorne Publishing (1987), and *Shadows of the Empire* (1996).

REBEL FORCE: FIREFIGHT

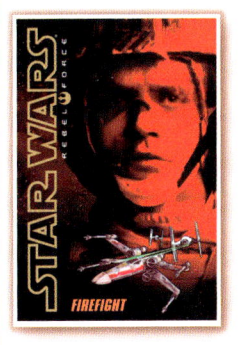

AUTHOR · Alex Wheeler
COVER ARTIST · Randy Martinez
PUBLICATION HISTORY · Juvenile novel, Scholastic Inc.
· Paperback, September 2009
TIME LINE PLACEMENT · 0 ABY
WORLDS VISITED · Kamino [S-15]; Rinn (and its moon Iope) [U-12]; Yavin (and its moon Yavin 4) [P-6]
MAIN CHARACTERS · Luke Skywalker, Rebel pilot (human male); Han Solo, smuggler (human male); Chewbacca, mechanic (Wookiee male); Princess Leia Organa, Rebel leader (human female)
SUMMARY · X-7 gathers mercenary pilots to target Luke Skywalker, among them Div—the new identity adopted by Lune Divinian. Meanwhile, Luke, Han, and members of Red Squadron are assigned by the Rebel Alliance to investigate reports of Imperial weapons development on Kamino. On the storm-drenched world, they find evidence of an Imperial program to genetically engineer monstrous beasts. The Rebels narrowly avoid these creatures, while Luke also avoids Div's assassination attempt. Div has a change of heart upon meeting Luke and learning of his Force sensitivity. Though he doesn't cooperate with Luke and refuses to reveal his benefactor, he nonetheless abandons his assignment to kill the young Rebel. Div is taken into Rebel custody.

THIS STORY BRINGS BACK Lune Divinian, now an adult. He was last seen as a child in the Last of the Jedi series. Aiwhas are repeatedly referred to as lizards in this story, even though most sources describe them as whales, and therefore mammals.

REBEL FORCE: TRAPPED

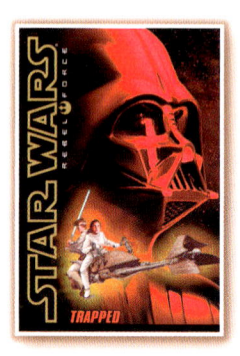

AUTHOR · Alex Wheeler
COVER ARTIST · Randy Martinez
PUBLICATION HISTORY · Juvenile novel, Scholastic Inc. · Paperback, January 2010
TIME LINE PLACEMENT · 0 ABY
WORLDS VISITED · Belazura [M-13]; Yavin (and its moon Yavin 4) [P-6]; unnamed dead moon [P-6]
MAIN CHARACTERS · X-7, spy (human male); Lune "Div" Divinian, mercenary pilot (human male); Luke Skywalker, Rebel pilot (human male); Han Solo, smuggler (human male); Princess Leia Organa, Rebel leader (human female); Ferus Olin, former Jedi apprentice (human male); Rezi Soresh, Imperial commander (human male)
SUMMARY · Lune "Div" Divinian, an uncooperative prisoner of the Rebel Alliance, is sprung from incarceration by Imperial agents. Luke Skywalker follows the kidnappers to their vessel and secretly boards it as it departs Yavin 4. The ship rendezvouses with an Imperial Star Destroyer, but Luke is able to retrieve Div thanks to the intervention of a TIE fighter piloted by Ferus Olin. On a dead moon, Ferus talks privately with Div, who is deeply resentful of the former Jedi apprentice for his failure to prevent the death of Div's family, including their mutual close friend Trever Flume. Div is further incensed by Ferus's bold plan to use Trever's identity to trick the assassin X-7 into becoming a weapon against the Empire.

Elsewhere, X-7 struggles with a profound identity crisis. The ordinarily implacable killer is overwhelmed by conflicting emotions. He confronts his master, Imperial commander Rezi Soresh, who explains that X-7 is the result of Project Omega, an Imperial program to create the perfect assassin from a person whose past is completely erased. Darth Vader, meanwhile, has learned of Soresh's plan to kill Luke Skywalker. The Dark Lord, wanting Skywalker alive, orders Soresh to abandon his plot.

The Alliance's next target is Belazura, Div's former home. The Rebels hope to destroy the Imperial garrison on the planet and thus stir the downtrodden populace into rebellion. As part of this assignment, Div and Ferus carry out the charade that X-7 was once Trever Flume. X-7, desperate for a connection to his past, comes to believe this. He seemingly aids the Rebels with access codes into the garrison, and information that Darth Vader will be visiting the installation, making it all the more tempting a target.

However, X-7's information and codes are faulty. He has engineered a trap for the Rebels, and for Div. Though X-7 tries to kill Div, he only wounds him with a blaster shot—perhaps testament to his true nature. Ferus has no choice but to kill X-7, who dies believing that he was once Trever Flume. The Rebels succeed in destroying the garrison.

———

IT IS SUGGESTED in the book that this story takes place about two months after the Battle of Yavin. Darth Vader is aware that Luke Skywalker is the Rebel who destroyed the Death Star. Vader's discovery of this fact is first established in Marvel Comics' *Star Wars* #35 (1980), and elaborated upon in *Vader's Quest* (1999), a comic series from Dark Horse.

ALLEGIANCE

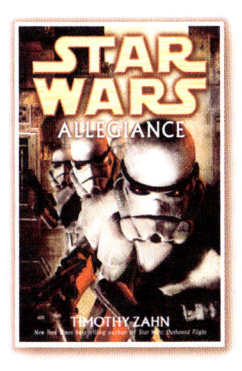

AUTHOR · Timothy Zahn

COVER ARTIST · John VanFleet

PUBLICATION HISTORY · Novel, Del Rey Books
- Hardcover, January 2007
- Paperback, December 2007

TIME LINE PLACEMENT · 0 ABY

WORLDS VISITED · Coruscant [L-9]; Crovna [L-17]; Drunost [M-9]; Gepparin [M-9]; Janusar [M-9]; Purnham [M-9]; Shelkonwa [M-9]; Teardrop [M-9]

MAIN CHARACTERS · Daric LaRone, Joak Quiller, Korlo Brightwater, Saberan Marcross, Taxtro Grave: stormtroopers (human males); Luke Skywalker, Rebel pilot (human male); Han Solo, smuggler (human male); Princess Leia Organa, Rebel leader (human female); Mara Jade, Emperor's Hand (human female); Barshnis Choard, Imperial governor (human male); Caaldra, mercenary (human male); Vilim Disra, administrator (human male)

SUMMARY · A stormtrooper unit led by Daric LaRone and attached to the Star Destroyer *Reprisal* refuses the orders of the Imperial Security Bureau (ISB) to fire upon civilians believed to be abetting members of the Rebel Alliance on the planet Teardrop. When the confrontation with the supervising ISB agent turns violent, LaRone kills the officer in self-defense. LaRone and his crew turn fugitive, fleeing in a stolen freighter. They dedicate themselves to battling corruption within the Imperial ranks, coming to the aid of beleaguered civilians on worlds such as Drunost and Janusar. The five troopers refer to themselves as the Hand of Judgment.

Elsewhere, the Emperor's Hand, Mara Jade—a highly trained assassin and Force-sensitive enforcer loyal to Palpatine—is rooting out corruption at the highest strata of the Imperial ranks. Her investigation into a Moff's embezzlement schemes puts her on the trail of the BloodScar pirate gang, a group of brigands operating in the Shelsha sector.

These same pirates have been raiding Rebel Alliance supply lines, prompting a mission to Drunost by Luke Skywalker, Han Solo, and Chewbacca aboard the *Millennium Falcon*. There they cross paths with the Hand of Judgment. Realizing their mutual goals, the fugitive stormtroopers and the Rebel heroes strike a tentative truce.

Princess Leia Organa is on a diplomatic mission to Shelkonwa, where she is attempting to unify disparate resistance groups and bring them into the Rebel Alliance fold. The entire Shelsha sector stands on the verge of seceding from the Empire under Governor Barshnis Choard. Choard's administrator, Vilim Disra, brokers an alliance with Leia, but in truth the ambitious Imperial plots to betray Choard and hand Leia over to the Empire. Disra locks down Shelkonwa to prevent Leia's escape and informs Coruscant of her presence.

Tracking down the connections between the BloodScar pirates and Imperial corruption leads the Hand of Judgment, the *Millennium Falcon*, and—separately—Mara Jade to Shelkonwa. Han, Luke, and Chewie rescue Princess Leia, while the Hand of Judgment aids Mara in defending against an attack by a pirate leader, Caaldra. Mara pieces together Governor Choard's traitorous bid for secession, which includes allying with the BloodScar pirates for security against Imperial reprisal. Now aware of the Hand of Judgment's story, Mara sympathizes with their crusade against Imperial corruption and pardons them, allowing them to leave Shelkonwa after securing a promise that she never see them again.

Capturing Choard, Mara hands the traitor over to Darth Vader, which is some consolation for the Dark Lord, who had arrived in hopes of apprehending Princess Leia.

This novel marks the first chronological account of Mara Jade, the popular anti-heroine whose first published appearance was in Timothy Zahn's *Heir to the Empire* (1991). In that novel, her mysterious past as the Emperor's Hand was revealed in pieces, meaning that readers undertaking a chronological journey through the Expanded Universe will know of her Imperial allegiance by the time she introduces herself to Luke Skywalker, Han Solo, and Princess Leia in stories set years after the Battle of Yavin.

REBEL FORCE: UPRISING

AUTHOR · Alex Wheeler
COVER ARTIST · Randy Martinez
PUBLICATION HISTORY · Juvenile novel, Scholastic Inc. · Paperback, May 2010
TIME LINE PLACEMENT · 0 ABY

WORLDS VISITED · Nyemari [R-6]; a moon in the Sixela system [P-18]; Yavin (and its moon Yavin 4) [P-6]

MAIN CHARACTERS · Luke Skywalker, Rebel pilot (human male); Rezi Soresh, Imperial commander (human male); Han Solo, smuggler (human male); Princess Leia Organa, Rebel leader (human female); Ferus Olin, former Jedi apprentice (human male); Lune "Div" Divinian, mercenary pilot (human male)

SUMMARY · Commander Rezi Soresh, outcast from the Empire, hides out on a barren moon in the Sixela system to plan his revenge against Luke Skywalker. During a covert Rebel mission on Nyemari, Luke receives a chilling holographic ultimatum from Soresh. The Imperial commander has captured an innocent passenger liner and threatens to kill those aboard unless Luke surrenders himself.

Despite being certain that the message is a trap, Luke cannot risk the lives of the captives. He becomes Soresh's prisoner and is subjected to the intensive brainwashing techniques that produced such assassins as X-7. Luke's will is strong, however, and he only pretends to be Soresh's servile subject.

Soresh's elaborate plan of vengeance involves both using Luke to lure Darth Vader to Sixela and disseminating reports of Imperial fleet movements to attract the attention of the Rebellion. With all parties drawn to Sixela, Soresh will then detonate an experimental resonance torpedo in the system's star, destroying them all and thus eliminating his rival and winning favor with the Emperor. Though Soresh launches the missile, he is shot dead by Han Solo. Princess Leia and Luke help evacuate everyone from the Sixela moon, and they warn both fleets of the impending cataclysm.

In the space battle over Sixela, Lune Divinian's ship is shot down and crashes. Ferus Olin stays behind on the moon when he detects the presence of Darth Vader. Determined not to let the Dark Lord threaten Leia, Ferus duels Vader, goading him by bringing up memories of his past as Anakin Skywalker. Vader kills Ferus and leaves Sixela before the entire system is wiped out by the star going supernova.

A MONTH HAS PASSED between this book and Rebel Force: *Trapped*, thus setting the conclusion of the Rebel Force series after a brief interruption by Timothy Zahn's *Allegiance*. The book offers finality to the remaining story threads of Jude Watson's series of Jedi-focused books, with Lune's death bringing an end to the Divinian family. Ferus's death also ends that story line, and as he passes away, he sees a vision of his old friend Roan Lands. The book ends with a coda set during *The Empire Strikes Back* (1980) told from the point of view of a spectral Obi-Wan Kenobi as he appears to Luke on Dagobah.

"THE MOST DANGEROUS FOE"

AUTHOR · Angela Phillips

PUBLICATION HISTORY · Short story, West End Games · *Star Wars Adventure Journal* #11, November 1996

TIME LINE PLACEMENT · 0 ABY (flashback c. 4000 BBY)

WORLDS VISITED · Teya IV (flashback) [M-10]; Yavin 4 [P-6]

The Emperor's Hand Mara Jade vouches for the loyalty and effectiveness of the fugitive stormtroopers known as the Hand of Judgment to Darth Vader.

THE GALACTIC CIVIL WAR

MAIN CHARACTERS · Deen Voorson, Rebel technician (human male); Vici Ramunee, Padawan learner (human female)

SUMMARY · As the Rebels evacuate their base on Yavin 4, technician Deen Voorson keeps the children of the Rebels occupied by telling them a story of the ancient Jedi. Voorson's story is of Padawan Vici Ramunee facing her Jedi trials in the Cave of Truth before becoming a Jedi Knight.

The frame story is set during this era, but the bulk of the tale is set about 4000 BBY, during the time of the *Tales of the Jedi* comic series. Because this story is presented as a tale told by Deen Voorson, handed down through the generations, the canonicity of its events may be subject to interpretation.

"DOCTOR DEATH: THE TALE OF DR. EVAZAN AND PONDA BABA"

AUTHOR · Kenneth C. Flint

PUBLICATION HISTORY · Short story, included in *Tales from the Mos Eisley Cantina* short-story anthology, Bantam Spectra
· Paperback, August 1995

TIME LINE PLACEMENT · 0 ABY

WORLD VISITED · Ando [Q-15]

MAIN CHARACTERS · Dr. Evazan, mad scientist (human male); unnamed Andoan Senator (Aqualish male); Ponda Baba, smuggler (Aqualish male); Gurion Silizzar, assassin (human male)

SUMMARY · On stormy Ando, the deranged Dr. Evazan meets with his patron, an ambitious Aqualish Senator. The politician is funding Evazan's research project to develop a medical breakthrough profitable enough to afford Ando independence from the Empire. Evazan's project: transference of consciousness as a means of practical immortality. Gurion Silizzar, a bounty hunter hoping to avenge the gruesome deaths of his family members at the hands of Evazan, infiltrates the doctor's gloomy castle. The assassin's attempt is thwarted by Rover, Evazan's pet meduza, a voracious bloblike creature.

"THE GREAT HERDSHIP HEIST"

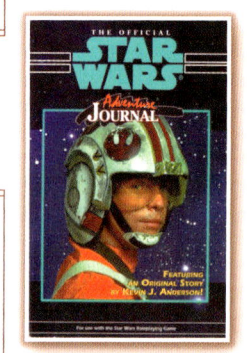

AUTHOR · Daniel Wallace

COVER ARTIST · Lucasfilm Ltd.

PUBLICATION HISTORY · Short story, West End Games
· *Star Wars Adventure Journal* #15, May 1997

TIME LINE PLACEMENT · 0 ABY

WORLD VISITED · Nar Shaddaa (moon of Nal Hutta) [S-12]

MAIN CHARACTERS · Cecil Noone, con man (human male); Kels Turkhorn, pickpocket (human female); Dawson, explosives expert (Tynnan male); Hass Sonax, slicer (Sluissi cyborg female)

SUMMARY · Cecil Noone is the leader of a quartet of thieves hired by Guttu the Hutt to infiltrate a private meeting of two rival crime lords and steal a lockbox desired by both. Posing as catering staff, the two human thieves—Cecil and Kels Turkhorn—make their way into the Ithorian herdship *Song of the Clouds*, the venue hosting the rendezvous of criminals Vop the Rodian and Ritinki the Bimm. The nonhuman thieves—the Tynnan Dawson and the Sluissi Hass Sonax—hide amid an ersatz delivery of food and bypass the security systems guarding the safe containing the lockbox, only to discover that the vault is empty. Ritinki's agents have already stolen it. Not willing to leave empty-handed, Dawson and Sonax sneak aboard Ritinki's starship, *Asaari Wind*. Just then, chaos erupts when other members of the catering staff prove to be assassins carrying out a mob hit against Vop and Ritinki. The crime bosses are killed in the crossfire, and Cecil and Kels narrowly escape aboard the *Asaari Wind*. They discover the lockbox aboard, and inside is a rare Hapan Gun of Command—an artifact that can compel a target to carry out the possessor's bidding. Thinking this too valuable an object to return to Guttu, Cecil instead decides to hold on to it, and to hold on to the *Asaari Wind* as well.

THE GUN OF COMMAND was first introduced in the novel *The Courtship of Princess Leia* (1994), when Han Solo uses it against Princess Leia. Whether the gun that Cecil steals is the same one that Han uses is not known.

"FAIR PREY"

AUTHOR · Daniel Wallace

PUBLICATION HISTORY · Short story, Wizards of the Coast · *Star Wars Gamer* #1, September 2000

TIME LINE PLACEMENT · 0 ABY

WORLD VISITED · Kabal [N-18]

MAIN CHARACTERS · Cecil Noone, con man (human male); Kels Turkhorn, pickpocket (human female); Dawson, explosives expert (Tynnan male); Hass Sonax, slicer (Sluissi cyborg female); Tyro Viveca, hunter (Krish male)

SUMMARY · Looking to fence the captured Gun of Command, Cecil Noone tries to strike a bargain with Krish hunter Tyro Viveca. Tyro instead steals the weapon and throws Cecil into his hunting grounds, where he will be stalked as game. Cecil desperately races to freedom, briefly assisted by a fellow prisoner, a vicious Florn Lamproid, before finally escaping with the aid of his fellow thieves.

BACKGROUND TEXT that accompanied this short story cited the 1924 short story "The Most Dangerous Game" by Richard Connell as inspiration. The same story inspired the 2011 episodes of *The Clone Wars* "Padawan Lost" and "Wookiee Hunt."

GALAXY OF FEAR: EATEN ALIVE

AUTHOR · John Whitman

COVER ARTIST · Steve Chorney

PUBLICATION HISTORY · Juvenile novel, Bantam Skylark · Paperback, February 1997

TIME LINE PLACEMENT · 0 ABY

WORLD VISITED · D'vouran [P-15] (location at the time)

MAIN CHARACTERS · Tash and Zak Arranda, siblings

(human female and male); Hoole, anthropologist (Shi'ido male); Smada, criminal (Hutt); DV-9, research droid; Chood, guide (Enzeen male)

SUMMARY · Tash and Zak Arranda—siblings orphaned by the destruction of Alderaan—travel with their "uncle" Hoole, a Shi'ido shape-shifter friend of the family who is their appointed guardian. Arriving at the mysterious planet D'vouran—a world only recently plotted on navigation charts—Tash and Zak have to outmaneuver not only a Hutt gangster, but also the planet itself. D'vouran is the bizarre result of an Imperial biological test program: a living planet that feeds on those who set foot upon it. The Arrandas and Hoole are able to escape being eaten alive with the help of Han Solo and the *Millennium Falcon*.

JUVENILE NOVELS in the vein of the smash hit Goosebumps series, Galaxy of Fear was a twelve-book series focusing on the travels of Zak and Tash Arranda as they repeatedly cross paths with a diabolical Imperial plot filled with chills and macabre twists. Major *Star Wars* characters have guest appearances in each story.

GALAXY OF FEAR: CITY OF THE DEAD

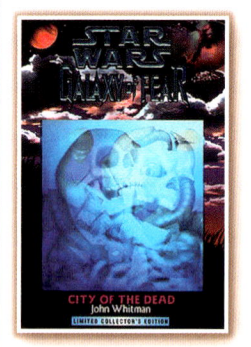

AUTHOR · John Whitman
COVER ARTIST · Steve Chorney
PUBLICATION HISTORY · Juvenile novel, Bantam Skylark · Paperback, February 1997
TIME LINE PLACEMENT · 0 ABY

WORLD VISITED · Necropolis [J-13]

MAIN CHARACTERS · Tash and Zak Arranda, siblings (human female and male); Hoole, anthropologist (Shi'ido male); Kairn, local (human male); Boba Fett, bounty hunter (human male); Dr. Evazan, mad scientist (human male); DV-9, research droid

SUMMARY · On the creepy world of Necropolis, Zak is kidnapped by the wanted criminal Dr. Evazan, who is working on bizarre experiments to reanimate the dead. Tash and Uncle Hoole are able to rescue Zak with the help of Boba Fett. Fett kills Evazan, and the Arrandas fly away with the criminal's ship, the *Shroud*.

GALAXY OF FEAR: PLANET PLAGUE

AUTHOR · John Whitman
COVER ARTIST · Steve Chorney

On the planet Necropolis, the evil Dr. Evazan sets a horde of zombies upon Boba Fett and the siblings Tash and Zak Arranda.

THE GALACTIC CIVIL WAR

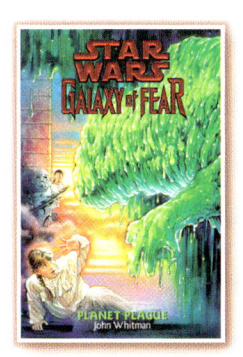

PUBLICATION HISTORY · Juvenile novel, Bantam Skylark · Paperback, April 1997

TIME LINE PLACEMENT · 0 ABY

WORLD VISITED · Gobindi [R-7]

MAIN CHARACTERS · Tash and Zak Arranda, siblings (human female and male); Hoole, anthropologist (Shi'ido male); Wedge Antilles, Rebel pilot (human male); Dr. Kavafi, scientist (human male); DV-9, research droid

SUMMARY · On Gobindi, the Arrandas uncover an Imperial biological weapons plot to unleash ancient viruses contained within the ziggurats of the jungle world. With the help of Wedge Antilles, they thwart the Imperial mastermind behind Project Starscream, a maniacal Shi'ido bent on developing further abominations of science.

GALAXY OF FEAR: THE NIGHTMARE MACHINE

AUTHOR · John Whitman

COVER ARTIST · Steve Chorney

PUBLICATION HISTORY · Juvenile novel, Bantam Skylark · Paperback, June 1997

TIME LINE PLACEMENT · 0 ABY

WORLDS VISITED · Hologram Fun World [S-7]; Koaan [N-8]

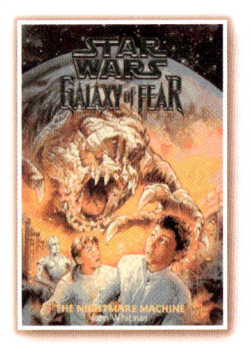

MAIN CHARACTERS · Tash and Zak Arranda, siblings (human female and male); Hoole, anthropologist (Shi'ido male); DV-9, research droid; Lando Calrissian, gambler (human male); Borborygmus Gog, scientist (Shi'ido male)

SUMMARY · What was to be a vacation on the carnival space station of Hologram Fun World turns to horror as the Arrandas are subjected to the Nightmare Machine, the latest stage in evil scientist Borborygmus Gog's nefarious Project Starscream. The machine incorporates a telepathic mutant creature that can read a subject's mind and uses advanced holography to create convincing terrifying images. With the help of Lando Calrissian, the Arrandas escape this trap.

"ONLY DROIDS SERVE THE MAKER"

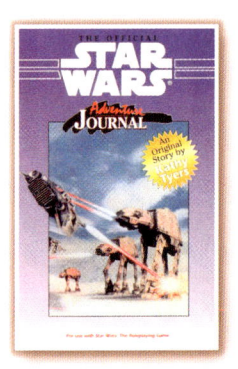

AUTHOR · Kathy Tyers
COVER ARTIST · Lucasfilm Ltd.
PUBLICATION HISTORY · Short story, West End Games · *Star Wars Adventure Journal* #10, May 1996
TIME LINE PLACEMENT · 0 ABY
WORLD VISITED · Monor II [P-15]

MAIN CHARACTERS · Daye Azur-Jamin, Rebel (human male); Tinian I'att, bounty hunter (human female); Chenlambec, bounty hunter (Wookiee male); Agapos the Ninth, inspirational leader (Sunesi male)

SUMMARY · Daye Azur-Jamin and his Rebel gunrunning crew are intercepted by an Imperial patrol while smuggling arms to the Sunesi revolutionaries on Monor II. Daye is thrown into a cell, and his prosthetic legs are disassembled, leaving him helpless. A Rebel agent planted among the Imperials arranges for Daye's escape, using the New Year celebration as cover.

Meanwhile, bounty hunters Tinian I'att and Chenlambec arrange the capture of the Sunesi leader, Agapos the Ninth. To end the Imperial pursuit of Agapos, Tinian and Chenlambec plant evidence that Agapos has been killed and quietly spirit him offplanet. They then drop him off at the Tekra Point colony ship.

Daye catches up with Agapos and learns of Tinian's survival and new career as a bounty hunter. While Agapos will live in hiding, transmitting his inspirational words to his followers, he agrees to mentor Daye in the Force techniques of Sunesi healing, which will help Daye rebuild his broken body.

"A BITTER WINTER"

AUTHOR · Patricia A. Jackson
PUBLICATION HISTORY · Short story, West End Games · *Star Wars Adventure Journal* #5, February 1995
TIME LINE PLACEMENT · 0 ABY

WORLDS VISITED · Redcap [Q-17]; Tatooine [R-16]

MAIN CHARACTERS · Drake Paulsen, smuggler (human male); Toob Ancher, smuggler (human male)

SUMMARY · Drake Paulsen is forced to make a difficult choice when one of his oldest smuggling mentors succumbs to debilitating dementia. Toob Ancher, suffering from the "bitter winter" disease, endangers himself and his friends, and Drake must shoot him down over the planet Redcap when Ancher flies a Z-95 Headhunter starfighter against an Imperial patrol.

SUMMARY · Looking for help against the Empire, Tash Arranda contacts her anonymous HoloNet friend Forceflow, who has helped her over the past year with information about the Force and the Jedi. She arranges a rendezvous in the ancient space station of Nespis VIII, a sprawling city frequented by treasure hunters seeking the fabled Jedi library of old. With the help of a Jedi spirit, Aidan Bok, Tash discovers she is Force-sensitive, and also that Forceflow is in fact the evil scientist Borborygmus Gog, who tries to lure Tash into one of his insidious experimental devices, an essence stealer that would extract her life force.

GALAXY OF FEAR: GHOST OF THE JEDI

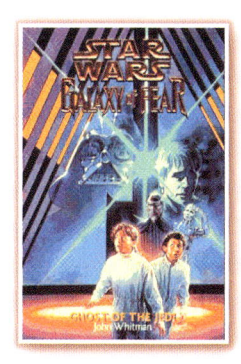

AUTHOR · John Whitman
COVER ARTIST · Steve Chorney
PUBLICATION HISTORY · Juvenile novel, Bantam Skylark · Paperback, August 1997
TIME LINE PLACEMENT · 0 ABY
WORLDS VISITED · Auril (system) [R-6]; Tatooine [R-16]
MAIN CHARACTERS · Tash and Zak Arranda, siblings (human female and male); Hoole, anthropologist (Shi'ido male); DV-9, research droid; Jabba the Hutt, crime lord (Hutt); Borborygmus Gog, scientist (Shi'ido male); Dannik Jerriko, bounty hunter (Anzati male)

GALAXY OF FEAR: ARMY OF TERROR

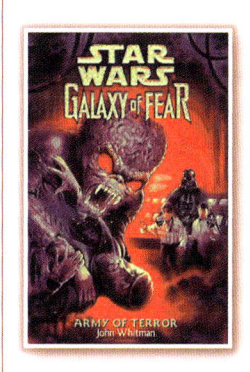

AUTHOR · John Whitman
COVER ARTIST · Steve Chorney
PUBLICATION HISTORY · Juvenile novel, Bantam Skylark · Paperback, October 1997
TIME LINE PLACEMENT · 0 ABY
WORLD VISITED · Kiva [O-7]
MAIN CHARACTERS · Tash and Zak Arranda, siblings (human female and male); Mammon Hoole, anthropologist (Shi'ido male); Borborygmus Gog, scientist (Shi'ido male); DV-9, research droid; Eppon, biological weapon (engineered male)

THE GALACTIC CIVIL WAR

SUMMARY · Determined to bring an end to Borborygmus Gog's Project Starscream, Hoole and the Arrandas journey to Kiva, site of the evil Shi'ido scientist's laboratory. There Hoole confronts his guilt-ridden past: years ago, he and Gog were research partners on an experiment gone awry that ravaged the planet, reducing its inhabitants to shadowy wraiths. Exploring on Kiva, the Arrandas find an infant named Eppon who quickly grows into an adult. Eppon is actually a bioengineered weapon—the culmination of Project Starscream. Tash tries to get Eppon to turn against Gog, but Gog destroys his creation. When the shadowy Kivans learn that it was, in truth, Gog who was responsible for their transformation, they kill the evil scientist.

GLAXY OF FEAR: THE BRAIN SPIDERS

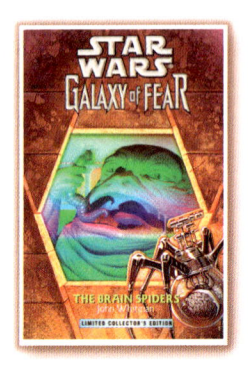

AUTHOR · John Whitman
COVER ARTIST · Steve Chorney
PUBLICATION HISTORY · Juvenile novel, Bantam Skylark · Paperback, December 1997
TIME LINE PLACEMENT · 0 ABY
WORLDS VISITED · Koda [I-18]; Tatooine [R-16]
MAIN CHARACTERS · Tash and Zak Arranda, siblings (human female and male); Mammon Hoole, anthropologist (Shi'ido male); Karkas, murderer (human male); Beidlo, B'omarr monk initiate (human male); Grimpen, B'omarr monk (human male)

SUMMARY · Still on the run from the Empire, Hoole and the Arranda siblings seek assistance from Jabba the Hutt. While at Jabba's palace, Zak uncovers Jabba's racket of using a treacherous B'omarr monk to surgically transplant the brains of wanted criminals into new bodies. Zak discovers that the brain of the murderous criminal Karkas was placed in Tash's body, while Tash's disembodied brain was placed in a spider-like droid. With the help of Uncle Hoole, the B'omarr monks reverse the process, and the Arrandas are on their way.

GALAXY OF FEAR: THE SWARM

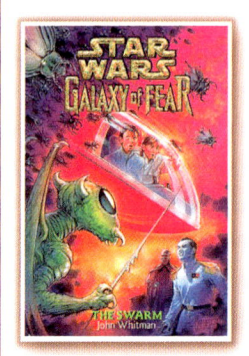

AUTHOR · John Whitman
COVER ARTIST · Steve Chorney
PUBLICATION HISTORY · Juvenile novel, Bantam Skylark · Paperback, February 1998
TIME LINE PLACEMENT · 0 ABY
WORLD VISITED · S'krrr [O-12]
MAIN CHARACTERS · Tash and Zak Arranda, siblings (human female and male); Mammon Hoole, anthropologist (Shi'ido male); Vroon, gardener (S'krrr male); Thrawn, Imperial captain (Chiss male); Sh'shak, poet-warrior (S'krrr male)

THE GALACTIC CIVIL WAR

SUMMARY · Zak fears that the accidental killing of a predatory shreev bat has upset the delicate ecological balance of the planet S'krrr. But the sudden explosion in the native drog beetle population can be pinned on Vroon, a native S'krrr who fanatically worships the beetles as descendants of the sentient insectoid life on the planet. The Arrandas and Hoole escape the ravenous swarms of beetles while avoiding the scrutiny of a visiting Imperial officer, Captain Thrawn.

The cover art for the book depicts Thrawn in the uniform of an Imperial Grand Admiral, though he only has the rank of captain in this book. At one point in the text, he is erroneously referred to as General Thrawn.

CHOICES OF ONE

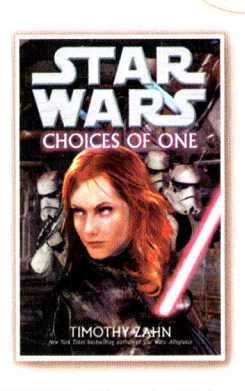

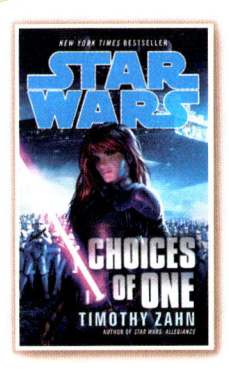

AUTHOR · Timothy Zahn

COVER ARTISTS · John VanFleet (hardcover); Daryl Mandryk (paperback)

PUBLICATION HISTORY · Novel, Del Rey Books
- Hardcover, July 2011
- Paperback, June 2012

TIME LINE PLACEMENT · 0 ABY

WORLDS VISITED · Elegasso [K-6]; Endor [H-16]; Pickerin [K-6]; Poln Major and Minor [J-5]; Teptixii [I-4]; Wroona [L-15]

MAIN CHARACTERS · Luke Skywalker, Rebel pilot (human male); Han Solo, smuggler (human male); Princess Leia Organa, Rebel leader (human female); Mara Jade, Emperor's Hand (human female); Daric LaRone, Joak Quiller, Korlo Brightwater, Saberan Marcross, Taxtro Grave: Hand of Judgment stormtroopers (human males); Nuso Esva, warlord (nonhuman male); Bidor Ferrouz, Imperial governor (human male); Vestin Axlon, Rebel leader (human male); Airen Cracken, Rebel leader (human male); Thrawn, Imperial senior captain (Chiss male); Gilad Pellaeon, Imperial captain (human male)

SUMMARY · The machinations of a mysterious alien warlord named Nuso Esva send ripples through the ranks of both the Rebellion and the Empire. Esva's strikes have unsettled Imperial governor Bidor Ferrouz of the outlying Candoras sector so much that he has turned to the Rebellion for assistance. In exchange, Ferrouz offers the Rebels a base on Poln Minor. The Rebels dispatch diplomat Vestin Axlon and Luke Skywalker to meet with Ferrouz, while others examine Poln Minor's suitability.

The Emperor's Hand Mara Jade also receives word of Ferrouz's treachery. She gathers the Hand of Judgment stormtrooper unit to assist her in infiltrating Ferrouz's palace on Poln Major. Mara confronts Ferrouz, and he reveals that he is being extorted by Esva to invite the Rebels to Poln. The warlord has kidnapped Ferrouz's wife and daughter and is holding them hostage.

Suddenly infiltrators attack the palace. Mara and the stormtroopers try to get Ferrouz and diplomat Axlon to safety. It's clear that this confrontation has been a setup: Mara was supposed to kill Ferrouz,

THE GALACTIC CIVIL WAR — 217

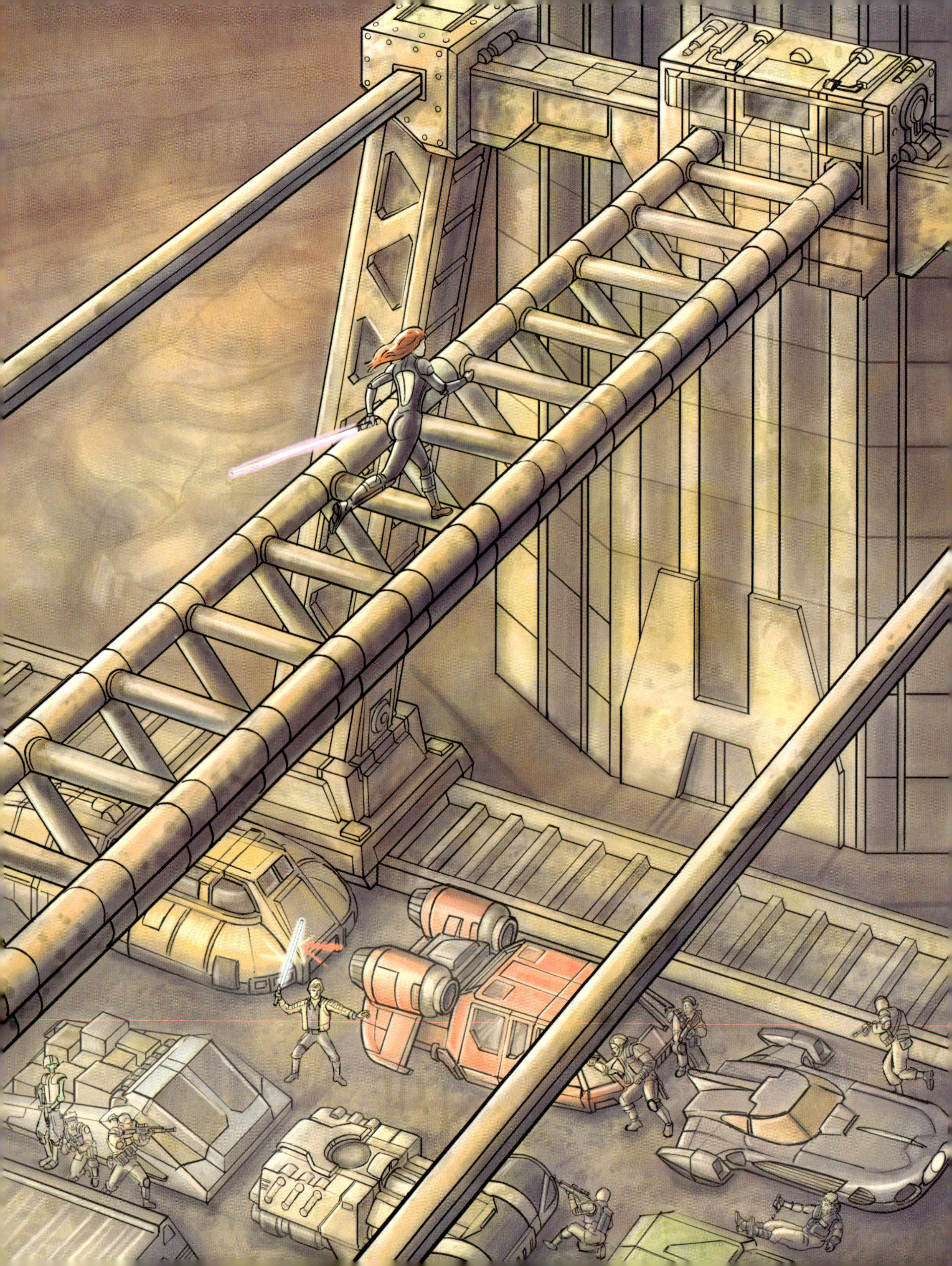

and now someone is trying to ensure that the governor dies. They escape the ambush, and Mara leaves a wounded Ferrouz in the stormtroopers' care while she returns to the palace to get some answers.

The Hand of Judgment troopers are surprised to learn that Luke Skywalker is outside the palace. Securing Ferrouz and Axlon in a hideout within the city, the troopers begin piecing together the evidence in the plot to discredit Ferrouz. Axlon is involved, colluding with Nuso Esva to extort Governor Ferrouz to make entreaties to the Rebel Alliance. This was all in a bid to have the governor targeted as a traitor by the Emperor's lightsaber-wielding agent, Mara Jade, so that Axlon could pin Ferrouz's death on Luke Skywalker. The mysterious Esva is evidently trying to engineer a battle for Poln Major between the Rebellion and the Empire. When the Hand of Judgment troopers confront Axlon about this plot, he attacks them, but they kill him in turn.

Mara's investigation in the palace uncovers more duplicity among Imperials who have conspired with Esva. A treacherous Imperial officer, Major Pakrie, arrives backed by some of Esva's alien soldiers. Mara has LaRone keep an eye on activity outside the palace, and LaRone in turn gets help from Luke Skywalker, who follows some of Esva's henchmen into the vast garage complex that also conceals their hostages. Luke and Mara both try to free the hostages, neither really seeing the other but nonetheless sharing the same objective. With the guards distracted by Luke, Mara frees the governor's wife and daughter.

Meanwhile, Han Solo and Princess Leia explore the spacious tunnel networks of mining planet Poln Minor. They discover a cache of military equipment and vessels being readied with Caldorf interceptor missiles for combat. The aliens gearing up for war appear to be agents of Esva. Han and Leia get caught snooping around, but with the help of Wedge Antilles and General Airen Cracken, they are able to lose their pursuers.

As violence erupts on Poln Major after the attack on Governor Ferrouz, General Cracken begins to surmise that the whole invitation to the system has been a charade to make the Rebel Alliance vulnerable. The Rebels plan an escape, with Wedge suggesting they use the T-47 airspeeders Han and Leia have discovered to cover their escape route. Han and Chewie orchestrate a foolhardy takeover of the orbital defense platform in order to target the planet's Dreadnought cruiser and cover the Rebel escape.

Elsewhere in the galaxy, the Star Destroyer *Chimaera*, under the command of Captain Drusan and Commander Pellaeon, has taken aboard a mysterious alien dignitary named Lord Odo. Lord Odo directs the *Chimaera* to distant Teptixii, where an Imperial task force belonging to Senior Captain Thrawn is waging war against Esva's forces. Thrawn, however, is not present. Odo offers unerring tactical advice in the battle before the assembled Imperial ships receive the distress call of insurrection on Poln Major.

The *Chimaera*, joined by Thrawn's cruisers, arrives at Poln. Drusan has been keeping secret the fact that a Mon Calamari freighter had been shadowing the cruisers with Senior Captain Thrawn aboard. As these various playing pieces are being amassed at the gameboard that is the Poln system, Lord Odo goes missing.

Pellaeon searches for the mysterious alien dignitary, when the *Chimaera* is suddenly rattled by explosions. Sabotage charges have gutted the ship's engine rooms, and debilitating vertigon gas floods the bridge. Pellaeon survives the attack by using a breath mask but finds Captain Drusan dying. Drusan's final breaths carry an admission of fatal misjudgment—Drusan had trusted Lord Odo to help defeat the Rebels, but was in turn betrayed by

Mara Jade dashes across a crane gantry, determined to rescue hostages, while far below Luke Skywalker also does battle with the hostage takers.

THE GALACTIC CIVIL WAR

the alien. A comlink transmission from Senior Captain Thrawn reaches Pellaeon. Thrawn reveals that Odo was in fact Nuso Esva.

Esva has placed the *Chimaera* on a collision course with the orbital defense platform, hoping that Thrawn will lose face by having to order the destruction of one of these key Imperial military assets. Aboard the platform, Han devises a plan to move it away from the path of the Star Destroyer by firing torpedoes to slightly change the station's position.

Esva has sprung an elaborate trap for his hated rival, Thrawn, as well as the Imperial and Rebel forces; however, his plan quickly unravels. The Rebels destroy his vessels hidden on Poln Minor, and Thrawn thwarts his attempt to scuttle the *Chimaera*. Esva escapes the battle, as do the Rebels.

Thrawn has long wanted to target Esva, but the Emperor has not given him the resources necessary to silence the warlord. Now Esva's forces have been shattered by the assembled Imperial fleet. Darth Vader arrives in system and is disappointed that the Rebels have fled, but Thrawn offers some consolation. By deliberately ensuring that the Rebels discovered a windfall of cold-weather gear and related supplies on Poln Minor, he can be certain that they will relocate to a planet that will make best use of such equipment. Vader will therefore be able to better focus his search for the Rebel fugitives.

A COMPLICATED TALE of move and counter move that would require a summary many times the size of this one to track all the threads adequately, *Choices of One* carefully manages several key character interactions in its plot. Mara Jade and Luke Skywalker, for example, work together to achieve the same goal of freeing hostages, but the necessities of continuity dictate that the two characters cannot meet until much later in the Expanded Universe time line. Similarly, Thrawn offers direct advice and guidance to Commander Pellaeon, via remote and faceless means, since the two cannot meet until just prior to the events of *Heir to the Empire* (1991).

Nuso Esva is a new character, though his introduction here makes it clear that he and Thrawn have had some sort of lengthy history. Whereas Thrawn has been likened by many—including author Zahn—to Sherlock Holmes for his precise methods of deduction, Esva exhibits similar craftiness and can be thought of as Moriarty to Thrawn's Holmes.

Jorj Car'das briefly appears in the novel, as a pilot and aide to Thrawn. He was last seen in the time line in *Outbound Flight* (2004) and will not be seen again until much later in the Hand of Thrawn duology. Car'das mentions a life-altering encounter. Avid readers will already know what this encounter is, but it won't be discussed in detail until *Vision of the Future* (1998).

GALAXY OF FEAR: SPORE

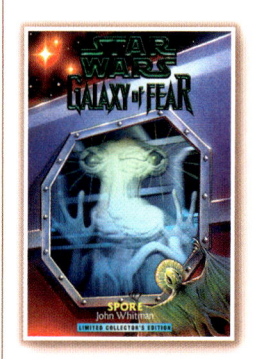

AUTHOR · John Whitman
COVER ARTIST · Steve Chorney
PUBLICATION HISTORY · Juvenile novel, Bantam Skylark · Paperback, April 1998
TIME LINE PLACEMENT · 0 ABY
WORLD VISITED · Ithor [M-6]

MAIN CHARACTERS · Tash and Zak Arranda, siblings (human female and male); Mammon Hoole, anthropologist (Shi'ido male); Fandomar Nadon, guide (Ithorian female); Jerec, Dark Jedi (Miraluka male)

SUMMARY · Needing raw materials to keep their starship running, Hoole and the Arrandas venture into an asteroid field near Ithor, with Fandomar Nadon as their guide. She is horrified to discover that Spore, an ancient biological threat, has been released from its asteroid tomb. Jerec, a dark servant of the Emperor, wishes to use Spore to give him control of the Empire. Spore is a genetically engineered hive-mind that can spread its consciousness through its hosts. Tash defeats it by exposing its original host to the vacuum of space.

Fandomar is the wife of Momaw Nadon, who was featured in "The Sand Tender: The Hammerhead's Tale" (1995). Jerec is the principal villain in the 1997 videogame **Jedi Knight: Dark Forces II**.

GALAXY OF FEAR: THE DOOMSDAY SHIP

AUTHOR · John Whitman
COVER ARTIST · Steve Chorney
PUBLICATION HISTORY · Juvenile novel, Bantam Skylark · Paperback, June 1998
TIME LINE PLACEMENT · 0 ABY
WORLD VISITED · None (story occurs in interstellar space)
MAIN CHARACTERS · Tash and Zak Arranda, siblings (human female and male); Mammon Hoole, anthropologist (Shi'ido male); Dash Rendar, smuggler (human male); SIM, intelligent program; Hajj, captain (human male); Malik, technician (human male)

SUMMARY · What was to be a relaxing stint aboard the passenger liner *Star of Empire* becomes a crisis for the Arrandas when SIM, an experimental Imperial computer program, takes control of the entire vessel. Simulating a reactor breach, SIM causes all the passengers to evacuate, save for Zak, Tash, Dash Rendar, and some crewmembers. Though Zak is duped into trusting SIM for a while, he eventually outsmarts it long enough to allow for their escape.

Dash Rendar's signature ship, the *Outrider*, is erroneously called the *Outrunner* in this book, which has since been retroactively declared another, earlier vessel in Dash's career.

"PRIORITY: X"

AUTHOR · George R. Strayton
PUBLICATION HISTORY · Short story, The Topps Company · *Star Wars Galaxy Magazine* #12, Summer 1997
TIME LINE PLACEMENT · 0 ABY
WORLD VISITED · Abo Dreth [S-3]
MAIN CHARACTERS · Fiolla of Lorrd, CSA inspector (Lorrdian female); Naven Crel, prisoner (human male)

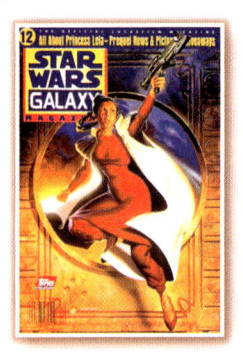

SUMMARY · While rooting out corruption in the Corporate Sector, Fiolla is surprised to learn that her prisoner, Naven Crel, is a deep undercover agent who sacrifices himself to save her life.

GALAXY OF FEAR: CLONES

AUTHOR · John Whitman

COVER ARTIST · Steve Chorney

PUBLICATION HISTORY · Juvenile novel, Bantam Skylark · Paperback, August 1998

TIME LINE PLACEMENT · 0 ABY

WORLD VISITED · Dantooine [L-4]

MAIN CHARACTERS · Tash and Zak Arranda, siblings (human female and male); Mammon Hoole, anthropologist (Shi'ido male); Maga, garoo/shaman (Dantari male); Eyal Shah, Rebel clone (human male); Darth Vader, Dark Lord of the Sith (human cyborg male)

SUMMARY · A visit to Dantooine causes Tash to reflect upon her Force sensitivity and fret about her tendency to embrace anger and the dark side. The Arrandas and Hoole make a bizarre discovery amid some ancient Jedi ruins—an entire camp of cloned Rebels living in the remains of a Rebel base led by a clone of Darth Vader. The ancient Jedi ruins conceal advanced cloning technology that can rapidly duplicate people, and Tash, Zak, and Hoole all must face copies of one another before they escape the nightmarish scenario, aided by the real Darth Vader who destroys his own doppelgänger. Though the trio escape, they have once again raised the ire of Vader.

One of the toughest stories to reconcile with ongoing continuity, *Clones* introduces an extremely advanced form of cloning that outpaces all others depicted elsewhere. The ruins of Dantooine are shown in active use in the *Tales of the Jedi* and *Knights of the Old Republic* comics, but there is no indication of any cloning technology in use during that era. Vader captures the cloning tech for the Emperor by the end of *Clones*, but it never surfaces again. Also unanswered is why a clone of Vader would resemble a man who is mostly artificial.

"UHL EHARL KHOEHNG"

AUTHOR · Patricia A. Jackson

PUBLICATION HISTORY · Short story, West End Games · *Star Wars Adventure Journal* #8, November 1995 Reprinted in *Tales of the Empire* short-story anthology, Bantam Spectra · Paperback, December 1997

TIME LINE PLACEMENT · 0 ABY

WORLDS VISITED · Iscera [R-17]; Trulalis [R-17]

MAIN CHARACTERS · Fable Astin, young Jedi/Rebel agent (human female); Adalric Brandl, former Inquisitor (human male); Jaalib Brandl, actor (human male); Vialco, Inquisitor (human male); Deke Holman, mercenary (human male)

SUMMARY · Haunted by terrifying visions of her nemesis Vialco, Rebel pilot and fledgling Jedi Fable Astin arrives on Trulalis, seeking training in self-defense. She tracks down the reclusive Adalric Brandl, an actor and former Imperial Inquisitor who has fallen out of favor with the Emperor. Fable trains under Adalric, learning difficult lightsaber skills while avoiding the temptations of the dark side of the Force. When Fable begins a romantic relationship with Adalric's son, Jaalib, however, the dark mentor becomes incensed and warns Fable to keep her distance.

Fable's enemy, the Inquisitor Vialco, confronts her on Trulalis, and with her newfound skills she is able to duel the dark warrior to a standstill. Using a Force illusion, Adalric tricks Fable into killing Vialco and then attempts to trap Fable on Trulalis by destroying her ship. He offers her power and even access to his son in exchange for her servitude on the dark side, but she refuses. Jaalib helps her escape Trulalis, even though he risks the wrath of his father.

The name of the short story is that of an Old Corellian play mentioned frequently in the text, which translates into "trickster king." The moody character Adalric Brandl previously appeared in *The Final Exit* (1994).

"FINDER'S FEE"

AUTHOR · Peter Schweighofer
PUBLICATION HISTORY · Short story, West End Games · *Star Wars Adventure Journal* #6, May 1995
TIME LINE PLACEMENT · c. 1 ABY
WORLD VISITED · Kelada [M-13]
MAIN CHARACTER · Loh'khar the Finder, procurement specialist (Twi'lek male)
SUMMARY · Loh'khar arranges transit for some Rebels on the run from his base of operations within Lorana's Labyrinth in exchange for a copy of their freshly acquired Imperial intelligence.

This very short story was presented as an introduction to the *DarkStryder Campaign* boxed set that West End Games was then publishing.

"THE BREATH OF GELGELAR"

AUTHOR · Jean Rabe
COVER ARTIST · Lucasfilm Ltd.
PUBLICATION HISTORY · Short story, West End Games · *Star Wars Adventure Journal* #14, August 1997
TIME LINE PLACEMENT · c. 1 ABY
WORLD VISITED · Gelgelar [M-20]
MAIN CHARACTER · T'laerean Larn, student of the Force (Sullustan male)

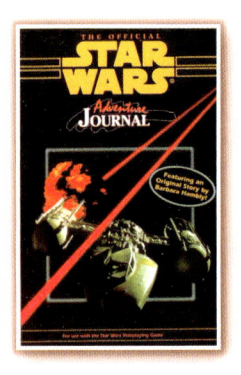

SUMMARY · T'laerean, a young Sullustan Force adept, has the ability to experience the senses of a wild reeho bird and occupy its mind as a "passenger," but he cannot break the Force connection without coming into physical contact with the bird. Thus, when the bird is captured, T'laerean begins to panic. The bird dies at the claws of a predator, and T'laerean nearly dies himself but is eased back into consciousness by his mentor, the Wise Man of Kooroo.

GALAXY OF FEAR: THE HUNGER

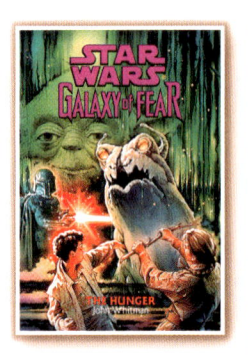

AUTHOR · John Whitman

COVER ARTIST · Steve Chorney

PUBLICATION HISTORY · Juvenile novel, Bantam Skylark · Paperback, August 1998

TIME LINE PLACEMENT · 1 ABY

WORLDS VISITED · Dagobah [M-19]; Koaan [N-8]; Nar Shaddaa (moon of Nal Hutta) [S-12]

MAIN CHARACTERS · Tash and Zak Arranda, siblings (human female and male); Mammon Hoole, anthropologist (Shi'ido male); Platt Okeefe, smuggler (human female); Boba Fett, bounty hunter (human male)

SUMMARY · Evading pursuit by Imperial bounty hunters, Hoole, Tash, and Zak hitch a ride with a smuggler crew led by Platt Okeefe to an uncharted planet where they can lie low. That world, Dagobah, is fraught with natural dangers—but it's the descendants of shipwrecked explorers who are the most unsettling. The small colony of Children—all gaunt adults—have turned to cannibalism, and they begin feasting on the smuggling crew. Compounding this danger, bounty hunter Boba Fett has tracked the Arrandas and Hoole to the swamp planet. With the help of the mysterious Yoda, the offworlders escape Dagobah along with the rehabilitated Children.

The Arrandas' adventures with Uncle Hoole are described as beginning "over a year ago," which suggests that this book takes place at least eighteen months after the Battle of Yavin. But the epilogue has Vader contacting Boba Fett to pursue the *Millennium Falcon*. This is too early to be the assignment seen in *The Empire Strikes Back* (1980), which takes place in 3 ABY.

STAR WARS GALAXIES: THE RUINS OF DANTOOINE

AUTHORS · Voronica Whitney-Robinson with Haden Blackman

COVER ARTIST · Lucasfilm Ltd.

PUBLICATION HISTORY · Novel, Del Rey Books · Paperback, January 2004

TIME LINE PLACEMENT · 1 ABY

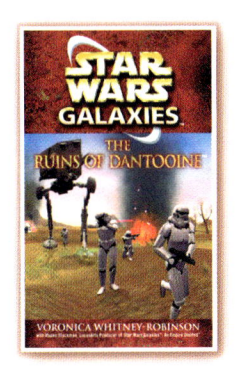

WORLDS VISITED · Corellia [M-11]; Dantooine [L-4]; Naboo (and its moons Rori and Lok) [O-17]

MAIN CHARACTERS · Dusque Mistflier, biologist (human female); Finn Darktrin, agent (human male); Tendau Nadon, biologist (Ithorian male); Nym, pirate (Feeorin male)

SUMMARY · Though Imperial bioengineer Dusque Mistflier has no love of the Empire, she has not joined the Rebel cause. She and her partner, the Ithorian Tendau Nadon, continue to catalog and study life-forms of diverse shapes and sizes. While on Naboo, Dusque meets a handsome yet overbearing man, Finn Darktrin, who reveals himself to be a Rebel sympathizer who needs her help leaving the planet. Rattled by the encounter, Dusque stews over Finn's request while carrying out a biological mission on Naboo's moon of Rori.

Returning to Naboo, Dusque is shocked to see Tendau coldly executed by stormtroopers who declared him a Rebel agent. Though Dusque didn't know everything about Tendau, she knows he did not deserve such a cruel fate. She chooses to help Finn—and by extension, the Rebel Alliance—to avenge Tendau's death.

Finn seeks a missing Rebel Alliance holocron that contains the names of high-level Rebel agents and sympathizers. This record was lost by the Rebels who abandoned the Dantooine outpost. Finn first voyages to the moon of Lok, where he hopes to cash in a favor owed to him by the pirate Nym. Nym gives Finn and Dusque a freighter, which they pilot to Corellia.

Their ship is shot down by Imperials and crash-lands into the surf on Corellia. Dusque and Finn are retrieved by Rebels, and at the temporary Alliance base on Corellia, they meet Princess Leia Organa and Luke Skywalker. The Rebels explain that the holocron is secreted somewhere among the ruins of Dantooine.

Finn and Dusque comb the remains of the ancient Jedi base on Dantooine, locating the holocron. Here, Finn reveals his true allegiance. He is an Imperial agent. Refusing to let the vital Rebel information reach Imperial hands, Dusque destroys the holocron before Finn is able to transmit it to the Empire. Finn and Dusque part ways, with Dusque returning to the Alliance.

Finn must report his failure to Darth Vader, but the Dark Lord does not slay him. Vader senses a powerful core of anger in Finn that may prove useful in the future.

SHORT STORY — **"Pearls in the Sand"**

Published in *Star Wars Insider* #74 (February 2004), "Pearls in the Sand" is a short story by Voronica Whitney-Robinson set shortly before the events of *The Ruins of Dantooine*. Dusque and Tendau follow rumors of a fabled krayt dragon graveyard into the wilderness of Tatooine and are nearly done in by Zabrak robbers. Left to die in the desert, the two scientists persevere and discover the krayt spawning ground—a place where the beasts die after laying their eggs. Dusque takes a krayt dragon egg for future study.

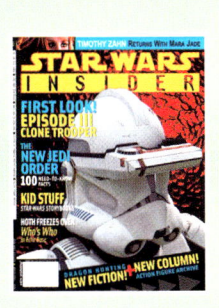

THE GALACTIC CIVIL WAR

THE RUINS OF DANTOOINE was the first tie-in novel specifically developed for a *Star Wars* videogame, complete with the LucasArts name and the **Star Wars Galaxies** logo on the cover. In 2003, LucasArts and Sony Online Entertainment released the first-ever *Star Wars* massively multiplayer online roleplaying game, and this tie-in book spotlights many of the game's features. The locations visited in the novel—Naboo, Lok, Rori, Corellia, and Dantooine—are all places featured in the game. The book's story includes "side quests," with Dusque undertaking zoological missions or looking for minor artifacts, in order to advance the plot. Much like **Star Wars Galaxies** itself, the book focuses on new characters but features guest appearances by such luminaries as Darth Vader, Luke Skywalker, Leia Organa, Han Solo, and Lando Calrissian.

"LANDO CALRISSIAN: IDIOT'S ARRAY"

AUTHOR · Rich Handley

PUBLICATION HISTORY · Short story, StarWars.com
· May 2008

TIME LINE PLACEMENT · 1 ABY

WORLDS VISITED · Bespin [K-18]; Quilken [R-15]

MAIN CHARACTERS · Lando Calrissian, baron administrator (human male); Lobot, aide (human cyborg male); Mungo Baobab, casino owner (human male); Thune, bounty hunter (human female)

SUMMARY · Just as Lando Calrissian is getting the hang of being the "respectable" administrator of Cloud City, he is targeted for assassination by Dominic Raynor, the city's former administrator. Lando escapes a bombing of his office, but allows the media to report on his death to prevent Raynor from striking again and endangering any more innocent lives. He and Lobot depart Cloud City aboard Lando's ship, *Cobra*, but are hounded by the tenacious bounty hunter Thune.

Lando voyages to Quilken, site of a casino operated by his old friend Mungo Baobab. Lobot, Lando, and Mungo are able to capture Thune when she strikes again, and Lando coerces her to drop her current target and hunt Raynor instead. After this caper, Lando briefly revels in the chance he had to be a scoundrel once more.

THE SHORT STORY MAKES several references to Lando's backstory as presented in the Expanded Universe, most notably the trilogy of novels by L. Neil Smith published by Del Rey Books in 1983, the "Lady Luck" comic book story published in *Star Wars Tales* #3 in 2000 by Dark Horse Comics, and "Sweetheart Contract" from Marvel Comics' *Star Wars* #83 in 1984.

SPLINTER OF THE MIND'S EYE

AUTHOR · Alan Dean Foster

COVER ARTIST · Ralph McQuarrie

PUBLICATION HISTORY · Novel, Del Rey Books
· Paperback, April 1978
Reprinted as *Classic Star Wars: Splinter of the Mind's Eye*
· Paperback, April 1994

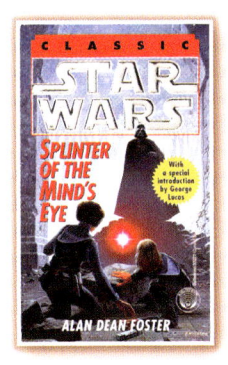

TIME LINE PLACEMENT · 2 ABY

WORLD VISITED · Mimban (Circarpous V) [O-12]

MAIN CHARACTERS · Luke Skywalker, Rebel pilot (human male); Princess Leia Organa, Rebel leader (human female); Halla, treasure seeker (human female); C-3PO, protocol droid; R2-D2, astromech droid; Grammel, Imperial supervisor (human male); Darth Vader, Dark Lord of the Sith (human cyborg male)

SUMMARY · Luke Skywalker and Princess Leia pilot separate Y-wing fighters to the Circarpous system to meet with a Rebel unit on the fourth planet. Leia's ship suddenly suffers mechanical failure and crash-lands on the fifth planet, Mimban. Luke, trying to steer Leia's ship to safety, also crashes.

Mimban is a swampy world and site of an Imperial mining operation. Luke, Leia, and the droids C-3PO and R2-D2 brave the savage jungles to reach the mining colony, where they attempt to pose as miners. In town, they meet an eccentric yet personable old woman named Halla. Luke is fascinated by her tales of a fabled crystal in one of the jungle temples that can amplify the powers of the Force. Indeed, Halla carries a splinter of the crystal, which appears to back her claims. Before Luke can investigate further, he and Leia get involved in an altercation with thuggish miners, and both land in Imperial custody.

Luke and Leia escape incarceration with the help of Halla and a pair of Yuzzem prisoners named Hin and Kee. The group treks into the jungle, but splits up when attacked by a massive swamp creature called a wandrella. Luke and Leia end up in a series of underground caves carved out by the ancient Mimban peoples. In these tunnels, Luke and Leia brave subterranean wildlife and the primitive Coway natives. They eventually arrive at the Temple of Pomojema, site of the Kaiburr crystal, meeting up again with the rest of their party.

Meanwhile, the local Imperial authority, Captain-Supervisor Grammel, realizes belatedly that he had two key Rebel agents in custody. This attracts the attention of Darth Vader, who arrives on Mimban and slays Grammel for his repeated failure to keep the Rebels captive. Vader follows the Rebels into the jungles and arrives at the Temple of Pomojema first. Vader kills Hin and Kee and deactivates the droids.

Luke is momentarily pinned underneath temple rubble, leaving Leia to fend off Vader with Luke's lightsaber. The Dark Lord toys with the Princess, wounding her repeatedly with his blade. Luke joins the battle, and as he duels with Vader he feels attuned to the Force, seemingly channeling the spirit of Obi-Wan Kenobi. Luke cuts off Vader's arm, and the Dark Lord stumbles into a deep well.

Luke uses the healing power of the Kaiburr crystal to save Leia from her injuries. They then leave Mimban with Halla, who joins the Rebellion.

THE FIRST *Star Wars* spin-off novel, *Splinter of the Mind's Eye* was written with the possibility of it being produced as a film. According to *Star Wars* producer Gary Kurtz, the novel took into account production budgets by being set in filmable locations (jungles, underground caverns) and avoiding costly visual effects sequences like space battles.

Even Han Solo's notable absence from the story is the result of a production reality—Harrison Ford was not contracted to appear in any *Star Wars* sequels at the time.

As an early Expanded Universe work, the novel does exhibit some dated inconsistencies in characterization and continuity. Luke is depicted as far more war-weary and cynical than he's ever been, and his feelings toward Leia are beyond brotherly affection. Darth Vader's villainy is far more arch and snarling, and his lightsaber duel with Luke doesn't match the level of skills displayed in *The Empire Strikes Back* (1980). Luke is shown as a capable swimmer, while Leia is unable to swim. This is the reverse of what is depicted in contemporary Marvel Comics, where Luke—hailing from a desert planet—is understandably unskilled in water. In 1996, Dark Horse Comics produced a four-part comics adaptation of *Splinter* by writer/inker Terry Austin and penciller Chris Sprouse. Aside from softening the aforementioned inconsistencies, the comic book version also made some minor deviations from the novel, and included continuity-enhancing elements such as Captain Piett and the *Executor* Star Destroyer.

The Kaiburr crystal as an artifact actually stems from early drafts of the *Star Wars* screenplay, where it was a Force-amplifying gem employed by the Sith Lords. It was largely forgotten in the Expanded Universe—aside from a reference in the Young Jedi Knights book *Lightsabers* (1996)—its insignificance explained away in nonfiction guides as a result of its effectiveness diminishing the farther it was taken from the Temple of Pomojema.

"CRIMSON BOUNTY"

AUTHORS · Charlene Newcomb and Rich Handley

PUBLICATION HISTORY · Short story, West End Games · *Star Wars Adventure Journal* #14, August 1997

TIME LINE PLACEMENT · 2 ABY

WORLDS VISITED · Ord Mantell [L-7]; Ord Simres [M-17]; Taskeed [S-7]

MAIN CHARACTERS · Celia "Crimson" Durasha, smuggler (human female); Kaj Nedmak, smuggler (human male); Thune, bounty hunter (human female); U-THR, protocol droid

SUMMARY · The smuggling duo of Celia Durasha and Kaj Nedmak is once again in trouble due to Kaj's wheeling and dealing and gambling. Rather than smuggling illegal weapons for Bwahl the Hutt, Kaj delivers them to another gangster to settle a debt. This sets bounty hunters on his trail, including the deceptive and tenacious Thune. Thune captures Kaj and nearly apprehends Celia, but she is betrayed by Uthre, a protocol droid in Thune's employ. Free of Thune's pursuit, Kaj and Celia are reunited.

"COMBAT MOON"

AUTHOR · John Whitman

COVER ARTIST · Ralph McQuarrie

PUBLICATION HISTORY · Short story, West End Games · *Star Wars Adventure Journal* #9, February 1996

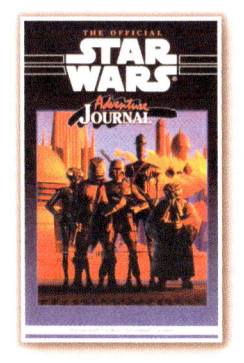

TIME LINE PLACEMENT · 2 ABY

WORLDS VISITED · Rabaan [O-12]; S'krrr [O-12]

MAIN CHARACTERS · Mika Streev, Rabaanite warrior (human male); Leda Kyss, Rabaanite warrior (human female); Sh'shak, S'krrr warrior (S'krrr male)

SUMMARY · Disputes between the neighboring Rabaanites and S'krrr are traditionally resolved through ritual duels on a satellite known as the Combat Moon. When tensions between the two cultures escalate, warrior champions Mika Streev and Sh'shak prepare for a match. Before their duel, however, they discover that the Empire has been secretly trying to spark open hostilities between the two worlds so they can enact martial law in a bid to expose a suspected Rebel enclave in the system. Joining with the Rebellion, the Rabaanites and S'krrr publicly broadcast the details of the Imperial plot.

"DO NO HARM"

AUTHOR · Erin Endom

PUBLICATION HISTORY · Short story, West End Games · *Star Wars Adventure Journal* #10, May 1996 Reprinted in *Tales of the Empire* short-story anthology, Bantam Spectra · Paperback, December 1997

TIME LINE PLACEMENT · c. 2 ABY

WORLD VISITED · Selnesh [K-6]

MAIN CHARACTER · Aurin Leith, doctor (female human)

SUMMARY · Doctor and Rebel agent Aurin Leith faces a moral quandary when she is assigned to a commando mission to liberate an important Rebel captive from Imperial custody. If Gebnerret Vibrion, the captured Rebel leader, cannot be extricated, then he must be silenced permanently at the medic's hand. Though Leith is not forced to commit an act that would violate her medical oath, she does kill a stormtrooper while escaping from the Imperial installation, an act that haunts her.

"THE CAPTURE OF IMPERIAL HAZARD"

AUTHOR · Nora Mayers

PUBLICATION HISTORY · Short story, West End Games · *Star Wars Adventure Journal* #10, May 1996

TIME LINE PLACEMENT · c. 2 ABY

WORLDS VISITED · Carosi XII [P-4]; Horob [I-8]

MAIN CHARACTERS · Sayer Mon Neela, Rebel war strategist (human female); Sergus Lanox, Imperial captain (human male)

SUMMARY · Vital Alliance war strategist and former Old Republic politician Sayer Mon Neela objects to being shuttled to safety when other Rebels risk their lives in their fight against the Empire. When the Victory Star Destroyer *Imperial Hazard* appears over the world of Horob, Neela decides to buy time for the evacuating Rebels below by brazenly demanding the Imperial warship surrender to her tiny star yacht. Intrigued and beguiled by the strong-

THE GALACTIC CIVIL WAR

willed woman, Imperial Captain Sergus Lanox invites her aboard. Neela uses experimental Rebel technology to disrupt the computer systems aboard the *Imperial Hazard*, jeopardizing the ship. She escapes in the confusion—surprisingly assisted by Captain Lanox, who deeply respects and admires her, and who snatches a quick kiss from her before she departs.

"IDOL INTENTIONS"

AUTHOR · Patricia A. Jackson

PUBLICATION HISTORY · Short story, West End Games · *Star Wars Adventure Journal* #12, February 1997

TIME LINE PLACEMENT · 2 ABY

WORLDS VISITED · Derora, a moon in the Birjis system [R-17]; Omman [S-6]

MAIN CHARACTERS · Drake Paulsen, smuggler (human male); Nikaede Celso, smuggler (Wookiee female); Padija Anjeri, anthropologist (human female); Colonel Tyneir Renz, Rebel leader and former Jedi (human male)

SUMMARY · Smuggler Drake Paulsen and his Wookiee partner Nikaede are hired by anthropologist Padija Anjeri for transport away from Omman and pursuing Imperials. Padija carries a crystal skull artifact greatly treasured by the Twi'leks and uses its return to secure the allegiance of an influential Twi'lek clan to the Rebel Alliance.

"THE LAST HAND"

AUTHOR · Paul Danner

PUBLICATION HISTORY · Short story, West End Games *Star Wars Adventure Journal* #13, May 1997 Reprinted in *Tales from the New Republic* short-story anthology, Bantam Spectra · Paperback, December 1999

TIME LINE PLACEMENT · 2 ABY

WORLDS VISITED · Morado [Q-11]; Nar Shaddaa (moon) [S-12]

MAIN CHARACTERS · Nyo, farmboy (human male); Kinnin Vo-Shay, legendary gambler (human male); Doune, gambler (Herglic male)

SUMMARY · Gambler Kinnin Vo-Shay wins a fortune off the ill-tempered Herglic Doune, while playing on the behalf of wide-eyed farmboy Nyo. Nyo aspires to be a Jedi Knight, so Vo-Shay agrees to transport him to the black markets of Nar Shaddaa to buy a lightsaber. A spiteful Doune buys the lightsaber from the dealer first and offers it up as a prize if Vo-Shay will once again play a single hand of sabacc with him. Vo-Shay loses and is forced to hand over a necklace believed to be the source of his incredible luck. Vo-Shay admits to Nyo that the necklace is merely a bauble; he lost the game on purpose to douse Doune's fiery vengeance. Feeling gleeful over his triumph, Doune gives the lightsaber to Nyo anyway.

Grand Admiral Thrawn (disguised as the bounty hunter Jodo Kast) and Captain Dagon Niriz toast a job completed as Darth Vader arrives.

"SIDE TRIP"

AUTHORS · Timothy Zahn and Michael A. Stackpole

PUBLICATION HISTORY · Short story, West End Games · Serialized over *Star Wars Adventure Journal* #12–13, February and May 1997
Reprinted in *Tales from the Empire* short-story anthology, Bantam Spectra · Paperback, December 1997

TIME LINE PLACEMENT · 2 ABY

WORLDS VISITED · Corellia [M-11]; Tramanos (system) [N-17]

MAIN CHARACTERS · Corran Horn, CorSec agent (human male); Hal Horn, CorSec agent (human male); Grand Admiral Thrawn, undercover Imperial (Chiss male); Zekka Thyne, Black Sun criminal (near-human male); Haber Trell, smuggler captain (human male); Riij Winward, Rebel agent (human male); Rathe Palror, Rebel agent (Tunroth male); Maranne Darmic, smuggler (human female); Dagon Niriz, Imperial captain (human male); Maximilian Veers, Imperial colonel (human)

SUMMARY · The freighter *Hopskip*, carrying Rebel Alliance contraband, is intercepted by the Imperial Star Destroyer *Admonitor*. Its smuggler crew is not subjected to inspection, but is rather forced by Captain Niriz to take aboard bounty hunter Jodo Kast, who supervises them on an Imperial assignment. They are to deliver a cargo to Corellia. Following Kast's bewildering instructions, the crew draws the attention of Black Sun criminals, as well as Corellian Security Force agents Hal and Corran

Horn. The Horns, posing as traders, agree to help the *Hopskip* crew, but Hal and half the crew—Captain Trell and Rathe Palror—are kidnapped by Black Sun. Kast agrees to help Corran free them.

Kast's mercurial actions are part of an elaborate plot to set up Black Sun mobster Zekka Thyne for a fall. Corran is able to free his father as well as the captive *Hopskip* crewers and capture Thyne. Imperial stormtroopers led by Colonel Veers, tipped off that Thyne is harboring Rebel contraband, attack Thyne's compound. The *Hopskip* crew, meanwhile, return to the space lanes, none the wiser that their original cargo has been fitted with Imperial tracking devices, which will lead the Empire to Derra IV.

The disruption in Black Sun operations is meant to create a distracting grievance for Prince Xizor—something that pleases Darth Vader. He thanks Kast—or, rather, the genius Imperial tactician hiding behind the Mandalorian armor: Grand Admiral Thrawn.

Between the events in this short story and the novel *Choices of One* (2011), it would appear that the Empire owes its triumph at the Battle of Hoth in *The Empire Strikes Back* (1980) to Grand Admiral Thrawn. It was his handiwork that narrowed the search for the Rebel base to ice planets, his intelligence that led to the disastrous defeat at Derra IV that ensured the Hoth Rebels would be ill equipped, and his recommendation to Vader to place Veers in command of his ground forces. In exchange, Thrawn is given access to Vader's Noghri death commandos, who are not described in this story but will figure prominently in the Thrawn Trilogy (1991–1993).

"COMMAND DECISION"

AUTHOR · Timothy Zahn

PUBLICATION HISTORY · Short story, West End Games · *Star Wars Adventure Journal* #11, November 1996

TIME LINE PLACEMENT · 2 ABY

WORLD VISITED · Unidentified world in Wild Space [H-7]

MAIN CHARACTERS · Thrawn, Imperial admiral (Chiss male); Dagon Niriz, Imperial captain (human male); Larr Haverel, Imperial general (human male); Creysis, pirate captain (Ebruchi male); Voss Parck, Imperial commander (human male)

SUMMARY · The Imperial Star Destroyer *Admonitor* voyages beyond the boundaries of charted space, commanded by Admiral Thrawn. Some of the ship's senior staff are wary of Thrawn's alien background and mysterious history. When Thrawn allows an Ebruchi captain to capture a TIE fighter as well as an Imperial shuttle crew, Imperial general Haverel believes the admiral has gone too far and tries to forcibly stop him in an attempted mutiny. Though he is skeptical of Thrawn, Captain Niriz refuses to go along with the sedition, and Thrawn soon reveals his true intentions. The Ebruchi's "captures" were merely calculated ruses to gauge enemy strength and lull the aliens into a false sense of superiority. His objectives achieved, Thrawn wipes out the Ebruchi space vessels.

THE GALACTIC CIVIL WAR

"LAUGHTER AFTER DARK"

AUTHOR · Patricia A. Jackson

PUBLICATION HISTORY · Short story, West End Games · *Star Wars Adventure Journal* #15, November 1997

TIME LINE PLACEMENT · 2 ABY (flashback to 5 BBY)

WORLDS VISITED · Aurea [M-11]; Corellia [M-11]; Elom [R-5]; Isamu [R-17]; Najiba [R-17]

MAIN CHARACTERS · Thaddeus Ross, smuggler (human male); Trep Winterrs, smuggler (human male); Saahir Ru'luv, entertainer (Twi'lek female); Reuther, tavern owner (Najib male)

SUMMARY · On the seventh anniversary of the death of his beloved Saahir Ru'luv, smuggler Thaddeus Ross visits Reuther's Wetdock tavern and has a lonely, sad drink. Ross remembers an unpleasant event when Saahir seduced him into transporting weaponry for the Rebel Alliance, a mission he wanted no part of. The mission turned sour when he discovered that Saahir was engaged to a Rebel commander. Though he was heartbroken and angry, his partner, Trep, convinced him to continue the mission for the credits. Tragedy followed when the Empire attacked the Rebel outpost just as they completed delivery of the cargo to Saahir and her fiancé. Saahir suffered mortal wounds and, with her dying breath, and in his arms, admitted she loved Ross all along and asked him to find the strength one day to forgive her. Seven years later Ross finally does, mourning her loss.

"THE DRAW"

AUTHOR · Angela Phillips

PUBLICATION HISTORY · Short story, West End Games · *Star Wars Adventure Journal* #15, November 1997

TIME LINE PLACEMENT · 2 ABY

WORLD VISITED · Vernet [N-14]

MAIN CHARACTERS · Mair Koda, trader (human female); Yuri Stonelaw, local boy (human male); Kristoff Stonelaw, Imperial conscript (human male)

SUMMARY · When freighter captain Mair Koda returns to the sleepy world of Vernet, she finds that the Empire has established a base and conscripted all the young men to serve in their ranks. This includes Kristoff, the older brother of Yuri Stonelaw, a big-hearted fifteen-year-old boy who enlists Mair's help in rescuing his brother from the Empire. Yuri is crushed to learn that Kristoff has become a loyal Imperial and does not want to leave. Mair and Yuri depart the planet together aboard her ship, *Blue Boy*.

"DOUBLE-CROSS ON ORD MANTELL"

AUTHOR · Michael Mikaelian

PUBLICATION HISTORY · Short story, The Topps Company · *Star Wars Galaxy* #5, Fall 1995

TIME LINE PLACEMENT · 3 ABY

WORLD VISITED · Ord Mantell [L-7]

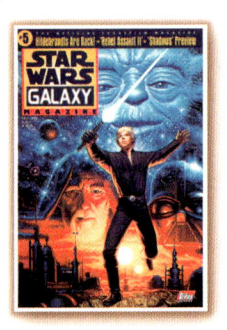

MAIN CHARACTERS · Cypher Bos, bounty hunter (Nalrithian male); Phoedris, Rebel agent (Nalrithian male)

SUMMARY · A Nalrithian Rebel agent named Phoedris is stalked and killed by his egg-mate, Cypher Bos, who then poses as him. Phoedris was arranging the capture of an Imperial shipment of credits to help fund the Rebel outpost on Hoth.

This short story expands upon *Rebel Mission to Ord Mantell*, an audio dramatization written by Brian Daley and released by Buena Vista Records in 1983. The audio drama was one of several stories attempting to explain who "the bounty hunter on Ord Mantell" was that Han Solo tangled with between the events of Episode IV and Episode V.

Other bounty hunters include Skorr, whom Han dealt with in the 1981 *Star Wars* newspaper strip distributed by the *Los Angeles Times* Syndicate and later released as *Classic Star Wars*. Han had to deal with bounty hunter Alfreda Goot in *Scoundrel's Luck*, a solitaire adventure written by Troy Denning and published by West End Games in 1989. There may be another bounty hunter—an unnamed thug whom Han blasts in a single panel in Marvel Comics' *Star Wars*, issue #37, from 1980.

It's a wonder Han keeps returning to Ord Mantell, given how often he ends up harassed by bounty hunters.

STAR WARS: EPISODE V THE EMPIRE STRIKES BACK

AUTHORS · Donald F. Glut, based on a story by George Lucas and the screenplay by Leigh Brackett and Lawrence Kasdan (adult novel); Ryder Windham (junior novelization)

COVER ARTISTS · Roger Kastel (first edition Ballantine novel and *Classic Star Wars: The Empire Strikes Back*); Drew Struzan (*Star Wars: The Empire Strikes Back* 1999); Lucasfilm Ltd. (*The Empire Strikes Back* 1995, *Star Wars: The Empire Strikes Back* 1997, *Star Wars: Episode V: The Empire Strikes Back* 2004, and Scholastic novel)

PUBLICATION HISTORY · Novel, Del Rey Books
- Paperback, May 1980, January 1997, and August 1999 as *Star Wars: The Empire Strikes Back*
- Paperback, October 1994 as *Classic Star Wars: The Empire Strikes Back*
- Hardcover, September 1995 as *The Empire Strikes Back*
- Paperback, April 2005 as *Star Wars: Episode V: The Empire Strikes Back*

Compiled as part of *The Star Wars Trilogy*
- Trade paperback, May 1987 and September 2004
- Hardcover and trade paperback, May 1989 as *Classic Star War Trilogy*
- Paperback, March 1993 and January 1997

Compiled as part of *The Star Wars Trilogy*, The 25th Anniversary Collector's Edition
- Hardcover, June 2002

Junior novelization, Scholastic Inc.
- Paperback, October 2004

234 THE GALACTIC CIVIL WAR

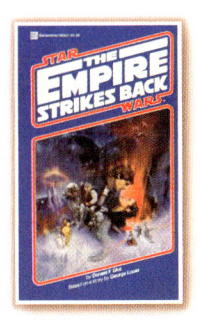

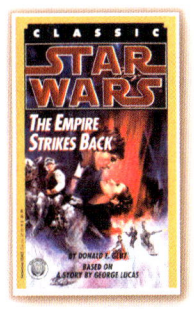

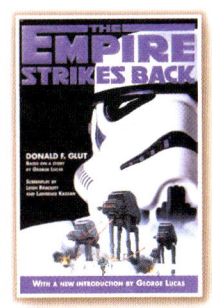

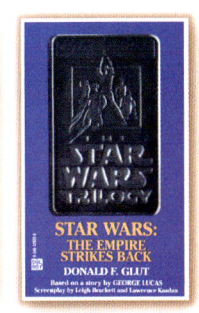

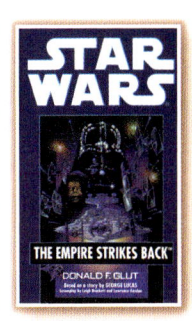

TIME LINE PLACEMENT · 3 ABY

WORLDS VISITED · Anoat (system) [K-18]; Bespin [K-18]; Dagobah [M-19]; Hoth [K-18]

MAIN CHARACTERS · Luke Skywalker, Rebel pilot (human male); Princess Leia Organa, Rebel leader (human female); Han Solo, smuggler (human male); Darth Vader, Dark Lord of the Sith (human cyborg male); Lando Calrissian, baron administrator (human male); Yoda, Jedi Master (alien male); C-3PO, protocol droid; R2-D2, astromech droid; Chewbacca, mechanic/copilot (Wookiee male)

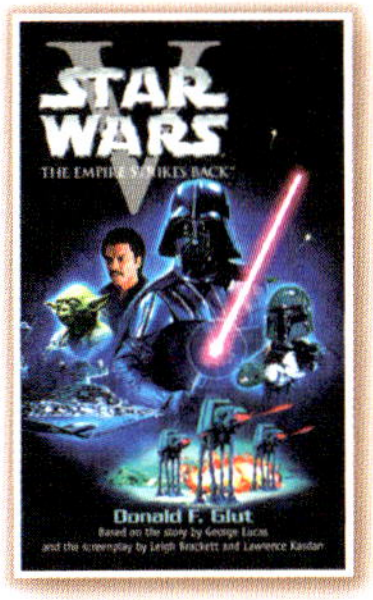

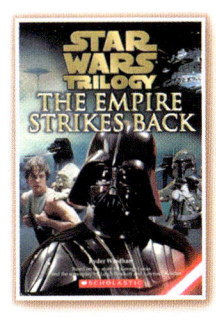

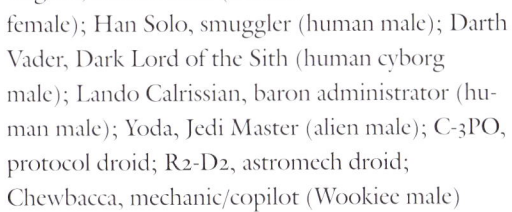

SUMMARY · An Imperial probe droid discovers the Rebel Alliance's newly established base on the ice planet Hoth and alerts Darth Vader's Star Destroyer fleet. The Rebels hurriedly evacuate their base as the Empire attacks with powerful AT-AT walkers. Han Solo and Chewbacca escape with Princess Leia and C-3PO aboard the *Millennium Falcon*. Following the instructions of a Force vision of Obi-Wan Kenobi, Luke Skywalker pilots his X-wing fighter to the mysterious world of Dagobah to find the Jedi Master Yoda.

The *Falcon* evades pursuit by diving into a chaotic asteroid field, but its unreliable hyperdrive prevents it from truly escaping the Imperial fleet. Darth Vader hires a motley assortment of bounty hunters, including Boba Fett, to find the *Falcon*. Fett tracks the vessel as it limps its way to the mining colony of Cloud City on Bespin, a refuge administered by Han's old friend Lando Calrissian. Along the journey, Han and Leia grow closer. When Lando is forced to betray Han and hand him over to the Empire, Leia proclaims her love for Han. Vader orders that Han be frozen in a slab of carbonite to test the procedure he intends to use on Luke Skywalker. Vader awards the frozen smuggler to Boba Fett, who plans to deliver him to Jabba the Hutt to collect the bounty Jabba has placed on his head.

On Dagobah, Luke studies the ways of the Force with Yoda, but he finds it hard to unlearn his impatience and impulsiveness. When he experiences visions of his friends in danger, Luke abandons his training to rescue them. He goes to Cloud City, where he stumbles into a trap set by Vader. The Dark Lord overpowers Luke in a lightsaber duel, severing the younger man's hand. Vader then stuns Luke by revealing the truth about Luke's father: the Dark Lord *is* Anakin Skywalker. Vader tries to lure Luke to the dark side, so that together they can overthrow the Emperor and rule the galaxy. Luke refuses the offer and drops into a massive chasm that runs the depth of Cloud City.

THE GALACTIC CIVIL WAR

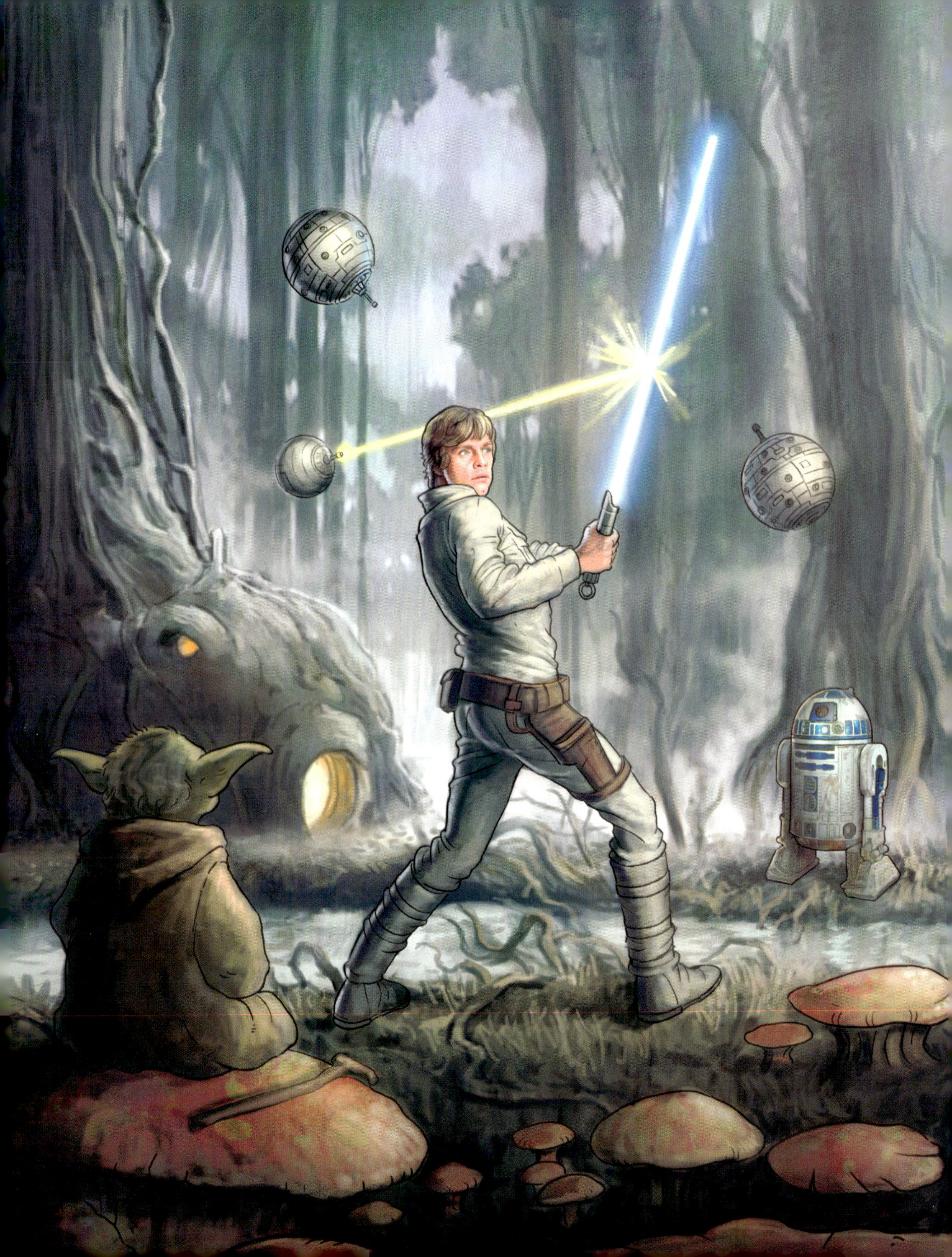

SPOTLIGHT *The Stele Chronicles*

Following the same format as *The Farlander Papers*, the 1994 videogame **Star Wars: TIE Fighter** included a ninety-six-page booklet entitled *The Stele Chronicles*, written by Rusel DeMaria. While some of the book was devoted to technical description of Imperial and Rebel spacecraft, much of it is a novella that describes the recruitment of Maarek Stele, a young man who grew up in the chaos of the decades-long civil war between the worlds Kuan and Bordal. The Empire subjugated both worlds, bringing an end to the civil war. Maarek undergoes indoctrination and finds himself in the technical repair bays of the Star Destroyer *Vengeance* working on TIE fighters.

While test-flying an Imperial TIE starfighter, Stele intercepts a distress call from Admiral Mordon's shuttle, which is under attack from Alliance starfighters. Maarek sweeps in, distracting the Rebel ships and allowing Mordon to escape. Impressed by his initiative, Mordon promotes Stele and transfers him from repair to starfighter pilot training.

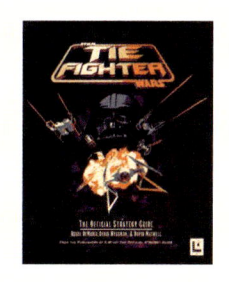

In the same way Keyan Farlander becomes the fictional counterpart of the player through this novella, Maarek Stele is the TIE fighter pilot carrying out the missions of the game in *The Stele Chronicles*. *Star Wars: TIE Fighter: The Official Strategy Guide* (1994, Prima Publishing) by Rusel DeMaria, David Wessman, and David Maxwell expands *The Stele Chronicles*, tracking Stele's service under Vice Admiral Thrawn, his recruitment into a secret order loyal to Emperor Palpatine, and his rooting out of treachery among the ranks of the Imperial admiralty. The guide was reissued for the Collector's CD-ROM release in 1995. While overviews of additional missions were added to the guide, it contains no new novella content.

As Leia and Chewbacca are being marched away by Imperial stormtroopers, Lando surprises them by freeing them. He regrets having to betray Han, but claims he had no choice. Lando broadcasts an evacuation order to the citizens of Cloud City and leads the Rebels to the *Millennium Falcon*. The ship blasts away from the city, but Leia senses the presence of an imperiled Luke through the Force. She guides the *Falcon* to the underside of Cloud City and rescues a wounded Luke. The ship then escapes into hyperspace, leaving Vader empty-handed.

Although much has been said about the lengths the movie producers went to in order to keep Vader's revelation to Luke a secret—closed sets, falsified script pages, false dialogue—anyone who picked up *The Empire Strikes Back* novelization when it arrived at bookstores on April 12, 1980,

---

On Dagobah, Luke Skywalker trains against seeker remotes under the stern instructions of Jedi Master Yoda.

could have found out the shocking truth over a month before the movie arrived in theaters.

The novel follows the screenplay closely, with some discrepancies that stem from an absence of visuals when author Donald F. Glut was preparing his manuscript. Yoda, a character closely guarded by Lucasfilm, is described as being long-haired and blue-skinned in the book, matching early concept art of the character. By keeping Boba Fett's percolating backstory out of the novel—he is described simply as "dressed in a weapon-covered, armored spacesuit, the kind worn by armored warriors defeated by the Jedi Knights during the Clone Wars"—Glut avoided the pitfall of Mandalorian continuity that would complicate later books. In fact, this description of Fett's suit aligns nicely with current Clone Wars canon.

receives word that the Empire has invited Loqesh to join the bounty hunters hired to track down the *Millennium Falcon*. Loqesh declines—he doesn't do work for the Empire—and goes into hiding to avoid Imperial reprisal.

THE BRIEF STORY SUGGESTS that it takes place on the planet Garnib without explicitly stating so, but Breil'lya comments that the planet is very hot—which is not a characteristic of frigid Garnib.

"THE PRIZE PELT: THE TALE OF BOSSK"

"HUNTING THE HUNTERS"

AUTHOR · Bill Smith
PUBLICATION HISTORY · Short story, The Topps Company · *Star Wars Galaxy* #6, Winter 1996
TIME LINE PLACEMENT · 3 ABY
WORLD VISITED · Garnib (possibly) [L-18]
MAIN CHARACTERS · Nariss Siv Loqesh, bounty hunter (Kerestian male); Crote, expeditor (Bimm male); Bie Breil'lya, quarry (Bothan male)
SUMMARY · Nariss Siv Loqesh apprehends a Bothan quarry when his expeditor, a Bimm named Crote,

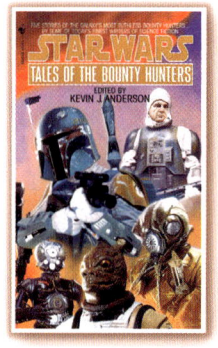

AUTHOR · Kathy Tyers
COVER ARTIST · Stephen Youll
PUBLICATION HISTORY · Short story, included in *Tales of the Bounty Hunters* short-story anthology, Bantam Spectra · Paperback, December 1996
TIME LINE PLACEMENT · 3 ABY
WORLDS VISITED · Aida [Q-13]; Hoth asteroid belt [K-18]; Lomabu III [Q-13]
MAIN CHARACTERS · Bossk, bounty hunter (Trandoshan male); Tinian I'att, bounty hunter apprentice (human female); Chenlambec, bounty hunter (Wookiee male)
SUMMARY · Bossk answers Darth Vader's call to capture the *Millennium Falcon* in the hope of skinning Chewbacca, his hated Wookiee foe. To that end, he reluctantly teams with the Wookiee hunter

THE GALACTIC CIVIL WAR

Chenlambec and his human apprentice, Tinian I'att, who promise to use their Wookiee contacts to find their prey. According to Chen and Tinian, Chewbacca has taken refuge with escaped Wookiee slaves on Lomabu III. Bossk flies his temporary allies to Lomabu III aboard his ship, *Hound's Tooth*, all the while plotting a betrayal. The bloodthirsty Bossk sees this as an opportunity to destroy an entire Wookiee colony. Unbeknownst to him, Chen and Tinian actually plan to betray Bossk—their sentient computer probe named Flirt helps them commandeer the starship. They redirect Bossk's destructive efforts into the Imperial weapons towers overlooking a Wookiee slave camp, thus freeing the captives. Bossk is trapped aboard his own vessel, and Chen and Tinian hand him over to Imperial governor Io Desnand. The governor plans to kill and skin the Trandoshan to make a gown for his female companion.

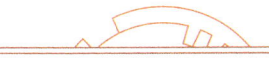

"OF POSSIBLE FUTURES: THE TALE OF ZUCKUSS AND 4-LOM"

AUTHOR · M. Shayne Bell

PUBLICATION HISTORY · Short story, included in *Tales of the Bounty Hunters* short-story anthology, Bantam Spectra · Paperback, December 1996

TIME LINE PLACEMENT · 3 ABY

WORLDS VISITED · Darlyn Boda [K-18]; Hoth [K-18]

MAIN CHARACTERS · Zuckuss, findsman (Gand male); 4-LOM, bounty hunter protocol droid; Toryn Farr, Rebel controller (human female)

SUMMARY · Zuckuss and 4-LOM are hesitant to answer Darth Vader's call for bounty hunters, for they have claimed a Rebel bounty on an Imperial official in the past. But they need the credits for a surgical procedure to restore Zuckuss's severely injured lungs. Hoping to curry favor with the Imperials en route to the summons, the bounty hunters blast apart a Rebel transport fleeing the Battle of Hoth.

After receiving the assignment to hunt the *Millennium Falcon*, Zuckuss's ancient Gand findsman rituals grant him a vision of the Rebel fleet rendezvousing at a point beyond the galactic periphery. He intuits that the *Falcon* could be found there, so Zuckuss and 4-LOM plan to infiltrate the Rebellion. To ingratiate themselves with the Alliance, they return to the battle wreckage above Hoth and rescue the stranded crew of the Rebel transport they had previously destroyed, the *Bright Hope*. Rebel controller Toryn Farr negotiates passage for all ninety survivors aboard Zuckuss's crowded ship to the planet Darlyn Boda.

Their time with the Rebels changes the outlook of the bounty hunters. Zuckuss comes to learn that Rebel medics can regrow his lungs. The hunters return the Rebels to the Alliance fleet and learn that Han Solo has already been captured by Boba Fett. Farr is promoted to commander, and the hunters receive special recognition from General Rieekan, who offers them positions in the Rebel Alliance Special Forces.

The story spans a month, from the Battle of Hoth to the reunion of the Rebel fleet seen at the end of *The Empire Strikes Back* (1980). This is unusual specificity about the length of time encompassed by that film, something Lucasfilm has been reticent to set down firmly. A writers' guide produced by West End Games in 1995 had an internal estimate of eight months covered by *Empire*, to account for Luke's training on Dagobah and what is presumably a very slow journey undertaken by the *Millennium Falcon*, but this length has never been backed up by published sources.

The character backgrounds of Zuckuss as a Gand findsman and 4-LOM as a former ship's purser come from *Galaxy Guide 3: The Empire Strikes Back* (1989) from West End Games. Gand physiology, including ammonia-breathing lungs, differs in this story from what is presented in the contemporary X-Wing novel series in 1996. In those books, the Gand Ooryl Qrygg does not have lungs and does not even need to breathe, drawing what nutrients and metabolic fuels he needs from his food. Subsequent sources explained the incongruity by stating that isolated pockets of evolution on the Gand home planet resulted in physiologically disparate subspecies. Zuckuss's quirk of referring to himself in the third person is echoed in Ooryl's speech patterns, but Zuckuss drops this characteristic in The Bounty Hunter Wars novels (1998) by K. W. Jeter. *The Essential Guide to Aliens Species* (2001) chalked up this discrepancy to Zuckuss suffering from multiple personality disorder.

This story spells the droid 2-1B's phonetically rendered name as "Two-Onebee," as opposed to the standard "Too-Onebee," and his partner is misnamed Effour-Seven, rather than Effex-Seven.

"THE EMPEROR'S TROPHY"

AUTHOR · Peter Schweighofer
PUBLICATION HISTORY · Short story, The Topps Company · *Star Wars Galaxy* #11, May 1997
TIME LINE PLACEMENT · 3 ABY

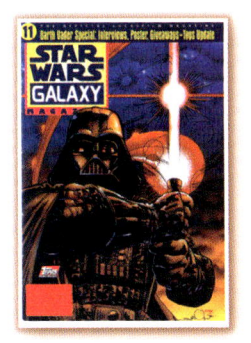

WORLD VISITED · Wayland [N-7]

MAIN CHARACTERS · Palpatine, Galactic Emperor (human male); Darth Vader, Dark Lord of the Sith (human cyborg male)

SUMMARY · Days after the fateful duel on Bespin, Vader delivers Luke Skywalker's severed hand and lost lightsaber to the Emperor's storehouse within Mount Tantiss on Wayland.

Just what the Emperor plans to do with this trophy will not be revealed until the events of *The Last Command* (1993), the third book of the Thrawn Trilogy, which was published before this short story.

"SLAYING DRAGONS"

AUTHOR · Angela Phillips

PUBLICATION HISTORY · Short story, West End Games · *Star Wars Adventure Journal* #9, February 1996 Reprinted in *Tales from the Empire* short-story anthology, Bantam Spectra · Paperback, December 1997

TIME LINE PLACEMENT · 3 ABY

WORLD VISITED · Kuat [M-10]

MAIN CHARACTERS · Shannon Voorson, child (human female); Deen Voorson, Rebel engineer (human male)

SUMMARY · Nine-year-old computer prodigy Shannon Voorson detests the Empire. When her cousin, Deen Voorson, receives no help from her parents in procuring a power generator from the Kuat Freight Port, Shannon takes it upon herself to help by using her computer-slicing skills. She then runs away from home to join Deen in the Rebellion.

Deen mentions that he helped the Rebellion convert airspeeders for subzero temperatures—a reference to the Rebel snowspeeders on Hoth—a few months prior to this story. That would set its events shortly after *The Empire Strikes Back* (1980).

"THE LONGEST FALL"

AUTHOR · Patricia A. Jackson

PUBLICATION HISTORY · Short story, West End Games · *Star Wars Adventure Journal* #11, November 1996 Reprinted in *Tales from the New Republic* short-story anthology, Bantam Spectra · Paperback, December 1999

TIME LINE PLACEMENT · 3 ABY

WORLD VISITED · Nharqis'I Nebula [K-2]

MAIN CHARACTER · Jovan Vharing, Imperial captain (human male)

SUMMARY · Aboard the Star Destroyer *Interrogator*, Senior Lieutenant Leeds intercepted a suspected Rebel transmission and ordered a strike that mistakenly resulted in the deaths of numerous Imperial officials. Now Captain Jovan Vharing reflects upon his career and missteps for he knows his punishment for his junior officer's mistake will most likely

---

Rebel escapee Toryn Farr monitors Zuckuss's debilitating cough with the assistance of 2-1B and 4-LOM.

be his own summary execution at the hands of Imperial High Inquisitor Tremayne.

"FIREPOWER"

AUTHOR · Carolyn Golledge

PUBLICATION HISTORY · Short story, West End Games · *Star Wars Adventure Journal* #8, November 1995

TIME LINE PLACEMENT · 3 ABY

WORLDS VISITED · Hargeeva [M-15]; Karatha [L-15]

MAIN CHARACTERS · Stevan "Mak" Makintay, X-wing squadron leader (human male); Ketrian Altronel, metallurgist (human female); Nial Pedrin, Imperial major (human male)

SUMMARY · After suffering repeated starfighter losses while raiding Imperial convoys, X-wing squadron leader Stevan Makintay proposes recruiting sympathetic manufacturing experts as a way to alleviate Rebel Alliance supply shortages. He undertakes a solo recruitment mission to his homeworld, Hargeeva, a planet he fled as a noble in exile. His embittered betrothed, the metallurgist Ketrian Altronel, is at first resistant to his invitation, but when she witnesses the cruelty of the Empire firsthand, she has a change of heart. She and Mak are captured by the Empire and shuttled to Coruscant for interrogation. En route, their transport is waylaid by pirates, allowing Mak and Ketrian to avoid Imperial imprisonment and rejoin the Rebellion. Ketrian brings with her a breakthrough alloy that can increase the firepower of the Rebel X-wings—but her veins carry a toxin injected by a nefarious Imperial, Nial Pedrin, who wants her dead before she can help the Rebellion.

"DESPERATE MEASURES"

AUTHOR · Carolyn Golledge

PUBLICATION HISTORY · Short story, West End Games · *Star Wars Adventure Journal* #10, May 1996

TIME LINE PLACEMENT · 3 ABY

WORLDS VISITED · Hargeeva [M-15]; Karatha [L-15]

MAIN CHARACTERS · Stevan "Mak" Makintay, X-wing squadron leader (human male); Ketrian Altronel, metallurgist (human female); Nial Pedrin, Imperial major (human male)

SUMMARY · Rebel medics are not able to find an antidote for the toxin threatening Ketrian Altronel, a brilliant metallurgist who has defected to the Alliance cause. Defying orders, her beloved Mak Makintay returns to Hargeeva to kidnap the Imperial who poisoned her. Mak captures Major Nial Pedrin, but will not stoop to torture to extract information from him. Pedrin bargains for his freedom in exchange for saving Ketrian's life. In truth, Pedrin does not know how to cure Ketrian, but he bluffs his way along hoping to escape later. At the Rebel base on Karatha, Mak and Pedrin discover the true cause of Ketrian's incapacitation—a rival within the Rebel medical staff has been secretly poisoning her. Pedrin realizes his deception is exposed, so he stabs Mak in a bid to flee, but is captured by Rebels. Mak and Ketrian make a full recovery.

"VADER ADRIFT"

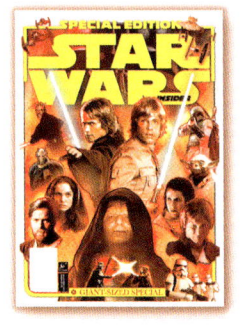

AUTHOR · Ryder Windham

PUBLICATION HISTORY · Short story, Titan Publishing
· *Star Wars Insider* Special Edition, 2012

TIME LINE PLACEMENT · 3 ABY

WORLD VISITED · Hockaleg [M-18]

MAIN CHARACTER · Darth Vader, Dark Lord of the Sith (human cyborg male)

SUMMARY · Darth Vader survives the destruction of the *Tarkin*, an experimental weapons platform battle station over the planet Hockaleg that had been sabotaged by Rebels. Adrift in his TIE fighter, he is rescued by a stormtrooper veteran of the Clone Wars, whom Vader recognizes as part of Shadow Squadron, a unit he commanded back when he was Anakin Skywalker.

The *Tarkin* story line is from Marvel Comics' *Star Wars*, issues #51–52, published in 1982.

SHADOWS OF THE EMPIRE

AUTHORS · Steve Perry (adult novel); Christopher Golden (junior novelization)

COVER ARTIST · Drew Struzan (both editions)

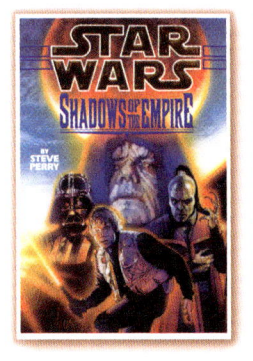

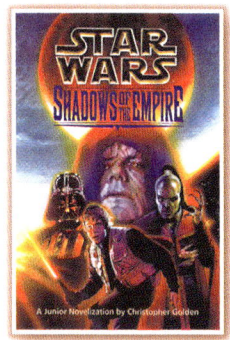

PUBLICATION HISTORY · Novel, Bantam Spectra
· Hardcover, May 1996
· Paperback, April 1997
Junior novelization, Bantam Doubleday Dell
· Paperback, October 1996

TIME LINE PLACEMENT · 3–4 ABY

WORLDS VISITED · Bothawui [R-14]; Coruscant [L-9]; Gall [P-17]; Kothlis [R-14]; Rodia [R-16]; Tatooine [R-16]; Vergesso asteroids [C-16]

MAIN CHARACTERS · Luke Skywalker, Rebel pilot (human male); Princess Leia Organa, Rebel leader (human female); Darth Vader, Dark Lord of the Sith (human cyborg male); Prince Xizor, Black Sun crime lord (Falleen male); Dash Rendar, smuggler (human male); Lando Calrissian, gambler (human male); C-3PO, protocol droid; R2-D2, astromech droid; Chewbacca, mechanic/copilot (Wookiee male)

SUMMARY · During the events surrounding the Battle of Hoth, the scheming Prince Xizor discovers that Luke Skywalker is Darth Vader's son, and that the Dark Lord has promised capture and delivery of the young Rebel to his Master, the Emperor. Having long hated Vader for his past sundering of the Falleen homeworld, Xizor plots to assassinate Luke and blame the death on Vader's incompetence, thereby causing the Dark Lord to lose favor with the Emperor. Xizor, the most powerful crime lord in the galaxy, seeks further advancement and

THE GALACTIC CIVIL WAR

sees Vader as the principal obstacle to his standing directly at the Emperor's side.

Following the trail of Boba Fett's ship *Slave I*, Luke, Leia, Chewbacca, and Lando venture to the planet Gall in the hope of intercepting the bounty hunter and freeing the carbon-frozen form of Han Solo. The heroes are guided to Gall by Dash Rendar, the cocksure smuggler captain of the souped-up *Outrider*. Wedge Antilles and the X-wing fighters of Rogue Squadron assist the Rebels in the space battle that erupts with Imperial forces over Gall. Luke narrowly avoids being shot down by friendly fire, as one of the Rogue Squadron astromech droids has been corrupted by a Black Sun assassin. While Luke neutralizes that threat, *Slave I* blasts away from Gall, outrunning the *Millennium Falcon* into hyperspace.

Luke returns to Tatooine and continues his Jedi studies in Obi-Wan's abandoned hut. He constructs a new lightsaber to replace the one lost in combat with his father. Skywalker is attacked by a swoop gang hired by Xizor, but escapes their efforts to kill him by commandeering a swoop bike and leading the gang into a harrowing chase through Beggar's Canyon. Soaring to Luke's help is Dash Rendar, who has been asked to protect Luke by a concerned Princess Leia as she continues to investigate the attempts on Luke's life.

Luke and Dash intercept an important message from the Bothans that their spies have uncovered key information regarding a huge new Imperial military project. A computer carrying vital intelligence is en route to Coruscant aboard the freighter *Suprosa*. Luke agrees to train a group of rookie Bothan fighter pilots on Bothawui to intercept the ship. The Bothans succeed in capturing the computer, but at the cost of many lives. As Luke travels with the Bothans to Kothlis, he dispatches Dash to find Leia and update her about this discovery.

Luke is attacked by persistent bounty hunters, but escapes with Lando's help. Vader had paid the hunters to capture Luke alive, but Xizor had paid hunters to kill Luke. When the Dark Lord arrives on Kothlis, disappointed to find his quarry vanished, he brutally interrogates a hunter and learns about Xizor's death warrant on Luke.

Leia's investigations into the criminal underworld lead her to a meeting with Prince Xizor on Coruscant. To facilitate travel into the Imperial capital, Xizor provides Leia and Chewbacca with false identities—they will travel as the bounty hunters Boushh and Snoova. In the company of Xizor, Leia is nearly overwhelmed by the Falleen's natural pheromones, which make him irresistible to humanoid females. Her strength of will allows her to reject Xizor's advances, and he imprisons her, hoping to lure Luke into a trap.

Luke and Lando arrive on Coruscant and sneak into the planet's labyrinthine underworld, where they reconnect with Chewbacca and Dash. Luke can sense Leia's presence in Xizor's palace through the Force. Luke leads the infiltration of the fortress through the building's underground accessways. They rescue Leia, then leave aboard a shakily piloted *Millennium Falcon* helmed by C-3PO and R2-D2.

A furious Prince Xizor commands his space forces from his orbital skyhook over Coruscant. He orders the destruction of the fleeing *Falcon*, foolishly naming Luke in an open transmission. Darth Vader, freshly returned to Coruscant, intercepts this message and has his Star Destroyer *Executor* destroy the skyhook. The *Falcon* weaves its way through the dense orbital traffic, joined by Dash Rendar's *Outrider* and Wedge's Rogue Squadron. Leia and Luke see Dash's ship apparently collide with space debris and presume him lost.

Having survived Xizor's assassination schemes, Luke returns to Tatooine to prepare for Boba Fett's eventual return to Jabba's palace and to carry out the rescue of Han Solo.

SHADOWS OF THE EMPIRE was a coordinated effort to tell a single, unified *Star Wars* story across multiple media. When it became apparent that a projected 1997 release date for Episode I wasn't feasible, and a planned re-release of *A New Hope* was consequently moved from 1996 to 1997, an opportunity arose to create some sort of *Star Wars* event for 1996 that would not only engage fans but continue the momentum of creative development already under way at Lucas Licensing and its partners.

It was accurately described as "a movie without a movie," because all the tie-in products one would expect from a *Star Wars* theatrical release were present . . . except a movie. At the core of the *Shadows* story was the novel from Bantam Spectra, which focused on the newly created Prince Xizor and his plot to assassinate Luke and discredit Darth Vader. A six-issue series from Dark Horse Comics, written by John Wagner with art by Kilian Plunkett and P. Craig Russell, explored Boba Fett's story as he faced rival hunters while trying to return to Tatooine with Han Solo. A videogame from LucasArts focused on Dash Rendar, a new smuggler character who served as the game player's proxy, and his various missions to help the Rebel Alliance.

Other *Shadows of the Empire* releases that year included toys, action figures, a behind-the-scenes book from Ballantine Books, trading cards, role-playing game supplements, pewter figures, ceramic mugs, Halloween costumes, T-shirts, baseball caps, posters and prints, sculptures, model kits, and even a full orchestral soundtrack CD from Varèse Sarabande.

The wily Prince Xizor, leader of the galaxy's criminal underworld, attempts to seduce Princess Leia Organa.

Talon Karrde

Cronal

Corran Horn

Mirax Terrik

Voort "Piggy" saBinring

Tendra Risant Calrissian

CHAPTER 6

THE NEW REPUBLIC

The Death Star exploded, Vader's armor burned on a pyre, and Ewoks danced the night away. In 1983, the *Star Wars* trilogy ended with a satisfying finale, and the attentions of many *Star Wars* fans wandered elsewhere. Lucasfilm's focus shifted briefly from galaxy-spanning epics to smaller, kid-targeted fare starring Ewoks and droids. By 1986, *Star Wars* was silent. There had not been a new novel to read since 1983, and the Marvel Comics story line dried up.

The Expanded Universe wasn't a complete desert. In 1987, West End Games began producing source material and roleplaying game products. Rather than telling stories, these works concentrated on giving players the *tools* to tell stories. It was successful enough for its audience, but did little to inject *Star Wars* back into the public consciousness.

Bantam Books' publication of *Heir to the Empire* in 1991 changed everything. Lucasfilm's licensing division embarked on a plan to create a publishing program, partnering with Bantam Books and Dark Horse Comics, to resurrect *Star Wars* storytelling. By this time, licensed *Star Wars* products were a rarity, and the level of potential interest in new *Star Wars* stories was unknown. Even George Lucas had his doubts, but he allowed the program to go forward with a few caveats: to ensure that the characters remained true (and intact), and to have each tale build upon and affect the others, so that the universe depicted in the books could expand with every story.

Heir to the Empire by Timothy Zahn debuted at number eleven on the *New York Times* bestseller list, and by its sixth week moved to the number one spot, pushing John Grisham's *The Firm* off the top of the charts. It stayed on the list for nineteen weeks. This success clearly proved that there was an audience hungry for more *Star Wars* storytelling. Also in 1991, *Star Wars* returned to comics, and within a few short years more licensees added to the growing drumbeat of excitement as *Star Wars* returned to the forefront of the pop-culture landscape. From 1991 to 1999, with the prequel era still roped off from exploration due to the impending theatrical release of Episode I, publishers such as Bantam, Dark Horse, and Berkley Books added to the opposite end of the *Star Wars* trilogy time line, filling out the years beyond *Return of the Jedi*.

Luke, Han, and Leia had renewed life, and they were joined by a rich cast of new heroes and villains who would set the foundation for future storytelling.

STAR WARS: EPISODE VI RETURN OF THE JEDI

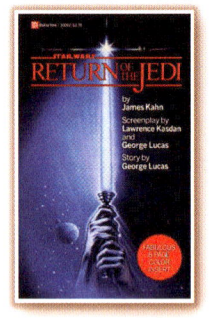

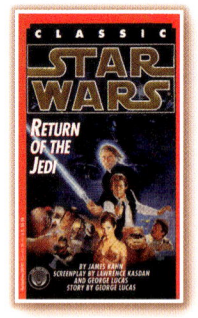

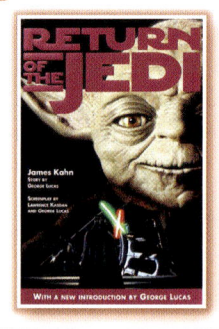

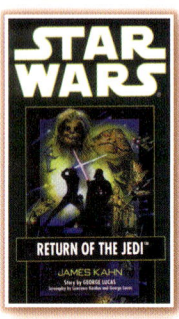

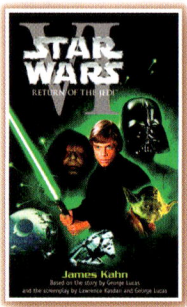

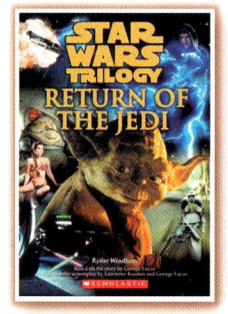

AUTHORS · James Kahn (adult novel); Ryder Windham (juvenile novel); based on the screenplay by Lawrence Kasdan and George Lucas and story by George Lucas

COVER ARTISTS · Kazuhiko Sano (*Classic Star Wars: Return of the Jedi*); Drew Struzan (*Star Wars: Return of the Jedi* 1999); Lucasfilm Ltd. (first edition Ballantine novel, *Return of the Jedi* 1995, *Star Wars: Return of the Jedi* 1997, *Star Wars:* Episode VI *Return of the Jedi* 2004, and Scholastic novel)

PUBLICATION HISTORY · Novel, Del Rey Books
- Paperback, May 1983, January 1997, and August 1999 as *Star Wars: Return of the Jedi*
- Paperback, October 1994 as *Classic Star Wars: Return of the Jedi*
- Hardcover, September 1995 as *Return of the Jedi*
- Paperback, April 2005 as *Star Wars:* Episode VI: *Return of the Jedi*

Compiled as part of *The Star Wars Trilogy*
- Trade paperback, May 1987 and September 2004
- Hardcover and trade paperback, May 1989 as *Classic Star War Trilogy*
- Paperback, March 1993 and January 1997

Compiled as part of *The Star Wars Trilogy*, The 25th Anniversary Collector's Edition
- Hardcover, June 2002

Junior novelization, Scholastic Inc.
- Paperback, October 2004

TIME LINE PLACEMENT · 4 ABY

WORLDS VISITED · Dagobah [M-19]; Endor [H-16]; Sullust (system) [M-17]; Tatooine [R-16]

THE NEW REPUBLIC

248

Luke Skywalker, Han Solo, and Chewbacca are marched to their prison skiff by Tamtel Skreej—Lando Calrissian in disguise.

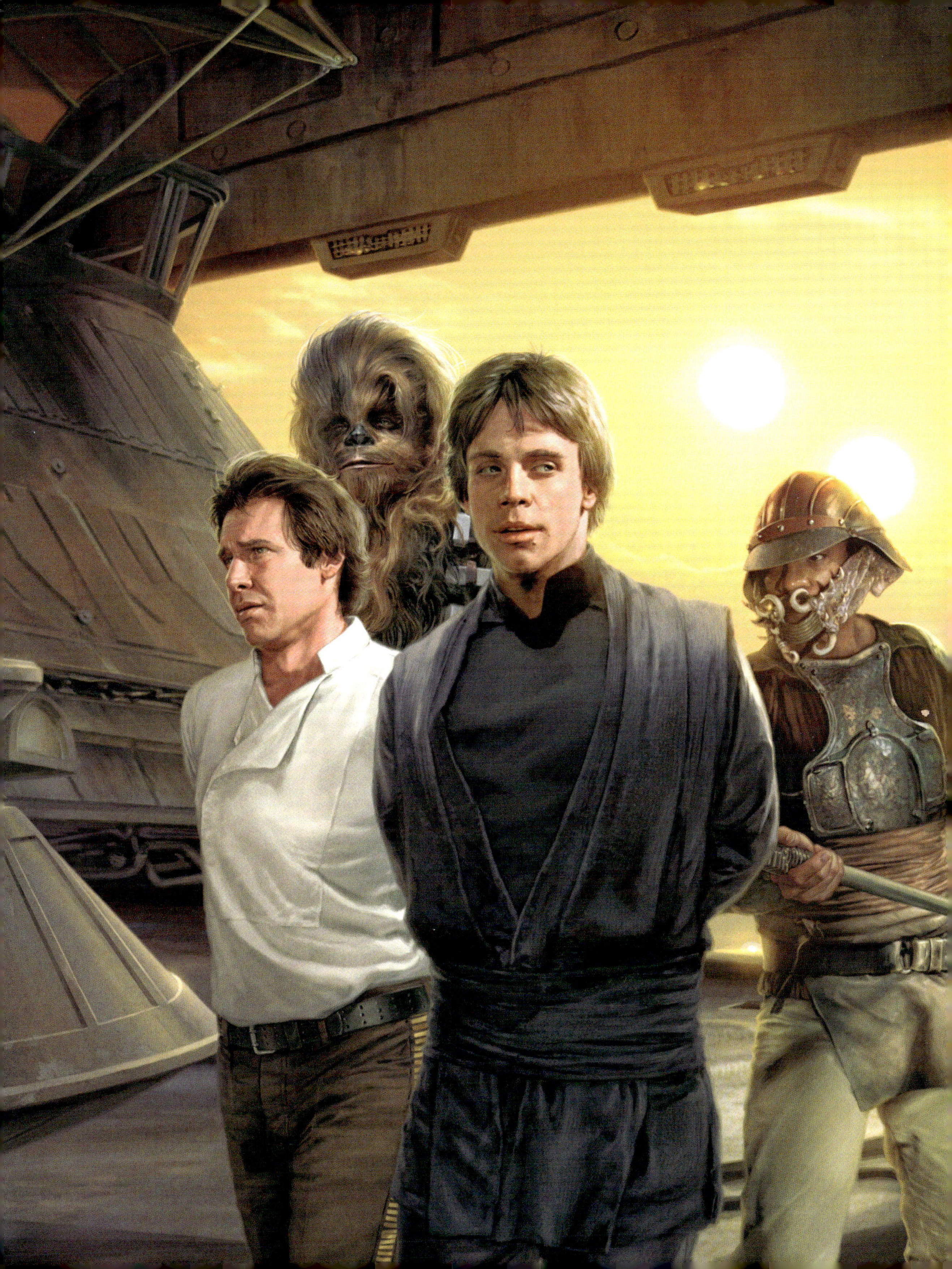

MAIN CHARACTERS · Luke Skywalker, Jedi Knight (human male); Princess Leia Organa, Rebel leader (human female); Han Solo, captain of the *Millennium Falcon* (human male); Darth Vader, Dark Lord of the Sith (human cyborg male); Palpatine, Galactic Emperor (human male); Lando Calrissian, Rebel general (human male); C-3PO, protocol droid; R2-D2, astromech droid; Chewbacca, mechanic/copilot (Wookiee male)

SUMMARY · Luke Skywalker, Leia Organa, Lando Calrissian, and Chewbacca daringly rescue Han Solo from his carbonite imprisonment in Jabba the Hutt's palace. The heroes escape Jabba's clutches by turning the execution he had ordered over the Sarlacc pit in the Dune Sea into a chaotic scramble for freedom. Princess Leia strangles Jabba with the very chains in which he had enslaved her, Han Solo knocks Boba Fett into the Sarlacc pit with an errant hit to his rocket pack, and Luke and Leia swing to an awaiting skiff piloted by Lando as Jabba's sail barge explodes in flames.

While his friends rendezvous with the Rebel Alliance, Luke returns to Dagobah to complete his Jedi training. An ailing Master Yoda's dying words reveal that there is another Skywalker. Luke talks to the spectral form of Obi-Wan Kenobi, learning the truth about Darth Vader. The Sith Lord is indeed Luke's father, Anakin Skywalker, a former Jedi hero corrupted by the Emperor. When Anakin succumbed to the dark side, he was unaware that he had twin children, Luke and Leia. Luke believes he can redeem his father, but Obi-Wan doubts any shred of his old friend remains within the villain.

Luke leaves Dagobah to join the Rebel fleet. He joins Han, Leia, and Chewbacca as they lead a Rebel strike team to the forest moon of Endor to disable the shield generator protecting a new Death Star. The Rebels befriend the indigenous Ewoks, and it is in the Ewok village that Luke reveals to Leia the truth about their relationship to each other and to Darth Vader.

Luke surrenders himself to Vader, who brings his son before the Emperor aboard the incomplete Death Star. Palpatine is eager to complete Luke's training and tries to goad him to the dark side in the hope of replacing Vader with Luke as his Sith apprentice.

Meanwhile, the Rebel strike team led by Han and Leia attempts to destroy the shield generator, but walks into a trap devised by the Emperor. They are captured by Imperials, then rescued by their newfound allies, the Ewoks. The resourceful forest-dwelling primitives are able to turn the tide against the more mechanically advanced Imperial military forces.

The Rebel fleet arrives over Endor to destroy the vulnerable Death Star. Outmaneuvered by the Imperial fleet, the Rebels suffer losses, but once Han's strike force succeeds in dropping the battle station's shields, Rebel starfighters led by Lando Calrissian fly into the superstructure and attack the station's exposed reactor core.

Luke refuses the Emperor's offer of dark side power, so the spiteful Sith Lord blasts young Skywalker with bolts of Force lightning. Unable to watch his son suffer at the Emperor's hand, Vader betrays his Master and hurls Palpatine into a vast shaft cutting into the heart of the battle station. Torrents of lightning ravage Vader's body, but his sacrifice saves his son. With this, Vader is freed of the dark side and dies as Anakin Skywalker, his body disappearing into the Force. Luke takes the dark armor that encased Anakin for decades and burns it on a funeral pyre fit for a Jedi.

The Rebels succeed in destroying the Death Star and defeat the Imperial fleet over Endor. It is a crucial victory for the Rebel Alliance, and a major step in the formation of a new galactic government free of tyranny.

Based on the third-draft screenplay of the film, the *Return of the Jedi* novelization retains dialogue carefully excised from the finished movie in which Obi-Wan describes taking an infant Luke to live with Obi-Wan's brother Owen Lars on Tatooine. This relationship would be proven apocryphal by *Star Wars: Episode II Attack of the Clones* (2002), though a remnant of it surfaced in the Jedi Apprentice novel *The Hidden Past* (1999). Another peculiar discrepancy involves Leia elaborating on the images she recalls of her mother "hiding in a trunk," a memory she could not possibly have of Padmé Amidala based on the events seen in *Star Wars: Episode III Revenge of the Sith*.

The novel's prologue describes Endor as "a moon whose mother planet had long since died of unknown cataclysm." This was contradicted in the Ewok-focused television movies and animated series that followed, which showed a gas giant visible in the skies of Endor.

"A BOY AND HIS MONSTER: THE RANCOR KEEPER'S TALE"

AUTHOR · Kevin J. Anderson

COVER ARTIST · Stephen Youll

PUBLICATION HISTORY · Short story, Bantam Spectra Included in *Tales from Jabba's Palace* · Paperback, January 1996

TIME LINE PLACEMENT · 0 BBY – 4 ABY

WORLD VISITED · Tatooine [R-16]

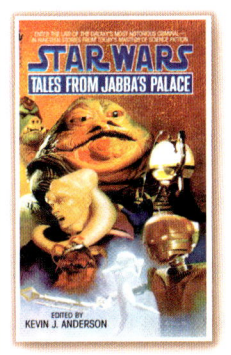

MAIN CHARACTER · Malakili, rancor keeper (human male)

SUMMARY · When the fearsome rancor monster is found in a shipwreck in Tatooine's Dune Sea, Jabba's underlings present it as a gift to the gangster. Jabba tasks Malakili with the care and feeding of his new pet. Malakili becomes quite fond of the beast and fears that the rancor will someday die of injuries suffered from Jabba's cruelty. Malakili conspires with Lady Valarian, a rival gangster, to transport the rancor to safety. Unfortunately, such hopes die when Luke Skywalker has no choice but to kill the creature.

The rancor's arrival on Tatooine was first described in *The Star Wars Sourcebook* (1987), a roleplaying gamebook published by West End Games. The date of the rancor's arrival is kept vague in that source, but has subsequently been pegged at about 0 BBY since Bidlo Kwerve, the rancor's first victim, is seen alive and well in *Rebel Dawn* (1997).

"THAT'S ENTERTAINMENT: THE TALE OF SALACIOUS CRUMB"

AUTHOR · Esther M. Friesner

PUBLICATION HISTORY · Short story, Bantam Spectra Included in *Tales from Jabba's Palace* · Paperback, January 1996

TIME LINE PLACEMENT · c. 4 ABY

WORLD VISITED · Tatooine [R-16]

MAIN CHARACTERS · Salacious Crumb, jester (Kowakian monkey-lizard male); Melvosh Bloor, academic (Kalkal male)

SUMMARY · Investigative politico-sociology professor Melvosh Bloor is intent on studying the criminal underworld of Jabba's palace. Unfortunately, Bloor mistakes the mischievous Salacious Crumb for his guide, and the little prankster leads the academic to his doom in an attempt to make Jabba laugh.

"A TIME TO MOURN, A TIME TO DANCE: OOLA'S TALE"

AUTHOR · Kathy Tyers

PUBLICATION HISTORY · Short story, Bantam Spectra · Included in *Tales from Jabba's Palace* · Paperback, January 1996

TIME LINE PLACEMENT · 4 ABY

WORLD VISITED · Tatooine [R-16]

MAIN CHARACTERS · Oola, slave girl (Twi'lek female); Sienn, slave girl (Twi'lek female)

SUMMARY · Oola reflects upon her enslavement to Jabba the Hutt. She and her younger friend and dancing companion, Sienn, were tricked into a life of servitude by the unscrupulous Bib Fortuna. During a brief stay in Mos Eisley, Oola and Sienn crossed paths with Luke Skywalker, who warned them to stay away from Jabba. Sienn fled with Skywalker, while Oola continued to Jabba's palace, selfishly believing she could become wealthy.

Now, chained to the loathsome gangster, Oola regrets her choices, but has some solace in knowing Sienn has been spared this fate. When Jabba's protocol droid, C-3PO, reveals that Skywalker is planning another rescue mission, Oola's hope is rekindled. She finds the energy to dance what she believes to be her best performance yet—not realizing it will be her last.

SIENN MAKES a brief appearance in X-Wing: *The Krytos Trap* (1996), set three years after her liberation from Jabba's palace.

"SLEIGHT OF HAND: THE TALE OF MARA JADE"

AUTHOR · Timothy Zahn

PUBLICATION HISTORY · Short story, Bantam Spectra · Included in *Tales from Jabba's Palace* · Paperback, January 1996

TIME LINE PLACEMENT · 4 ABY

WORLD VISITED · Tatooine [R-16]

MAIN CHARACTERS · Mara Jade, aka Arica, dancer/Emperor's Hand (human female); Melina Carniss, dancer (human female)

SUMMARY · Mara Jade, the Emperor's Hand, goes undercover as a dancer named Arica in Jabba's palace. Her mission is to kill Luke Skywalker for the Emperor. Her dark Master believes that Darth Vader may be courting Skywalker as an apprentice to unseat him. Another of the Hutt's dancers, Melina Carniss, suspects Mara of being more than meets the eye, so Mara quickly moves to neutralize

Mara Jade—as Arica the dancer—performs for the amusement of the dregs in Jabba the Hutt's throne room.

her. This distracts her from Luke's arrival, and she fails to intercept him before he faces and destroys the rancor. Luke is sentenced to execution in the Dune Sea, and Mara begs Jabba the Hutt to allow her to accompany the expedition, but he refuses her entreaties. Her mission to kill Luke will have to wait for another day.

Arranging Mara Jade's appearances in chronological order means readers will witness her failure to kill Luke first, prior to Luke actually meeting her in *Heir to the Empire* (1991), her first published appearance. As such, this reading order dispels the brief mystery surrounding her animosity toward Luke as presented in *Heir*. Mara would adopt the alias Celina Marniss in "First Contact" (1994), a short story published first but set much later in the time line.

Mara exhibits very articulate telepathic communication with the Emperor, a use of Force telepathy far more precise than shown elsewhere in the canon. Such a display of power needed to be vetted by George Lucas, as a July 19, 1994, memo indicates. Lucas specified that this telepathy is due to an innate difference in Mara Jade herself and should be limited to her alone.

A popular misconception around the time of this short story's publication was that Mara Jade could be spotted somewhere in *Return of the Jedi* (1983). Given that her character was conceived years after that film was produced and that no unnamed extras have been retroactively identified as "Arica," Mara is not actually in the movie.

"OLD FRIENDS: EPHANT MON'S TALE"

AUTHOR · Kenneth C. Flint

PUBLICATION HISTORY · Short story, Bantam Spectra
Included in *Tales from Jabba's Palace*
· Paperback, January 1996

TIME LINE PLACEMENT · 4 ABY

WORLD VISITED · Tatooine [R-16]

MAIN CHARACTER · Ephant Mon, mercenary (Chevin male)

SUMMARY · After encountering Luke Skywalker in Jabba's palace, Ephant Mon has a spiritual awakening that causes him to reconsider his life as a criminal. Ephant is convinced that Luke is capable of making good on his threats against Jabba and warns the Hutt out of a sense of loyalty and friendship. Jabba pays Ephant's warning no heed and heads off into the Dune Sea to execute Luke and his friends. Ephant decides to return to his home planet, Vinsoth, and begin his life anew.

"AND THE BAND PLAYED ON: THE BAND'S TALE"

AUTHOR · John Gregory Betancourt

PUBLICATION HISTORY · Short story, Bantam Spectra
Included in *Tales from Jabba's Palace*
· Paperback, January 1996

TIME LINE PLACEMENT · 4 ABY

WORLD VISITED · Tatooine [R-16]

MAIN CHARACTERS · Evar Orbus, bandleader (Letaki male); Max Rebo, keyboardist (Ortolan male); Sy Snootles, vocalist (Pa'lowick female); Snit, aka Droopy McCool, horn player (Kitonak male)

SUMMARY · When their bandleader, Evar Orbus, is killed by rival musicians, Max Rebo, Sy Snootles, and Droopy McCool secure a gig at Jabba's palace. The voraciously single-minded Max agrees to the band being paid in food. Sy agrees to spy on any conspirators plotting against Jabba. The band rides aboard the sail barge during the failed execution of Luke Skywalker and escapes the blast that consumes the floating pleasure craft. Max and Sy decide to carry on as the Max Rebo Duo, while Droopy wanders into the desert to find others of his kind.

Because this story was published before the release of the Special Edition of *Return of the Jedi* (1997), the expanded Max Rebo Band is absent from the tale, and the musical ensemble is merely a trio.

"OF THE DAY'S ANNOYANCES: BIB FORTUNA'S TALE"

AUTHOR · M. Shayne Bell

PUBLICATION HISTORY · Short story, Bantam Spectra
Included in *Tales from Jabba's Palace*
· Paperback, January 1996

TIME LINE PLACEMENT · 4 ABY

WORLD VISITED · Tatooine [R-16]

MAIN CHARACTERS · Bib Fortuna, majordomo (Twi'lek male); Nat Secura, prisoner (Twi'lek male)

SUMMARY · Bib Fortuna is one of the dozens of Jabba's underlings who scheme to kill the gangster and usurp his throne. Fortuna enlists the aid of the B'omarr monks in his conspiracy. When he learns that his old friend Nat Secura is to be executed by the Hutt, he has the monks surgically extract Secura's brain for safekeeping in a jar. Despite his repeated promises to secure his friend a new body, Fortuna never delivers as he is distracted by business, such as meeting with Luke Skywalker, who wants to arrange Han Solo's return. When Luke's rescue plan results in Jabba's destruction, Fortuna escapes the sail barge explosion in a skiff and returns to the palace. He is overpowered by the B'omarr monks, who disembrain him, leaving his gray matter in a jar.

Fortuna's brain would appear again in the comic series *X-Wing: Rogue Squadron: "Battleground: Tatooine"* (1996) and eventually be returned to a flesh-and-blood Twi'lek body. Nat Secura would appear in the *Star Wars: Republic* series story "Rite of Passage" (2002), set during his childhood. This character established the Secura clan name, from which the Jedi Knight Aayla also hails.

"A BAD FEELING: THE TALE OF EV-9D9"

AUTHORS · Judith and Garfield Reeves-Stevens
PUBLICATION HISTORY · Short story, Bantam Spectra
Included in *Tales from Jabba's Palace* · Paperback, January 1996

TIME LINE PLACEMENT · 4 ABY
WORLDS VISITED · Bespin [K-18]; Tatooine [R-16]
MAIN CHARACTERS · EV-9D9, administrator droid; 12-4C-41, traffic control droid; Lando Calrissian, baron administrator/gambler (human male)

SUMMARY · The deranged administrator droid EV-9D9 flees from Cloud City authorities, leaving a swath of mechanical mayhem in her wake. On Tatooine, she finds refuge among the droid pool in Jabba's palace. EV-9D9 becomes Jabba's chief administrator droid, delighting in torturing her subjects and modifying them with devices to ensure they feel pain. A vengeance-seeking traffic control droid from Cloud City, 12-4C-41, finds EV-9D9 after a lengthy hunt and blasts her, allowing the mangled droids in her torture chamber to tear her apart.

The droid 12-4C-41's name is a reference to a 1911 science fiction novel by Hugo Gernsback, *Ralph 124C 41+*, an alphanumeric pun meaning "one to foresee for one." Measuring all fictional accounts as equal, this is the *third* time the Expanded Universe has jeopardized Cloud City with wide-scale destruction during Lando's tenure as baron administrator. In the Marvel Comics series, Ugnaught insurrectionists detonate explosives that cause the city's antigravity generators to sputter in "Coffin in the Clouds," *Star Wars* #56 (1982). In the roleplaying game module *Crisis on Cloud City* (1989), the droid intelligence X0-X1 nearly succeeds with a mechanical coup that remarkably resembles Ninedenine's botched usurpation.

THE NEW REPUBLIC

"TASTER'S CHOICE: THE TALE OF JABBA'S CHEF"

AUTHOR · Barbara Hambly

PUBLICATION HISTORY · Short story, Bantam Spectra
Included in *Tales from Jabba's Palace*
· Paperback, January 1996

TIME LINE PLACEMENT · 4 ABY

WORLD VISITED · Tatooine [R-16]

MAIN CHARACTERS · Porcellus, chef (human male); Phlegmin, scullion (human male)

SUMMARY · The ever-fretful chef Porcellus hears that Jabba suspects him of putting *fierfek* in his food—a Huttese term that Porcellus takes to mean "poison." Porcellus knows that one bad meal would be a death sentence. When the dead body of a Weequay sail barge captain, Ak-Buz, turns up near the kitchen, a terrified Porcellus hides the corpse lest he be a suspect. In the midst of Luke Skywalker's rescue of his friends from Jabba's clutches, Porcellus learns the true definition of *fierfek* from Skywalker's droid, C-3PO. It translates not to "poison" but to "hex," and sure enough misfortune has followed many who have tasted Porcellus's wares.

"LET US PREY: THE WHIPHID'S TALE"

AUTHORS · Marina Fitch and Mark Budz

PUBLICATION HISTORY · Short story, Bantam Spectra
Included in *Tales from Jabba's Palace*
· Paperback, January 1996

TIME LINE PLACEMENT · 4 ABY

WORLD VISITED · Tatooine [R-16]

MAIN CHARACTER · J'Quille, hunter (Whiphid male)

SUMMARY · A Whiphid suitor to Lady Valarian, J'Quille is secretly on her payroll conspiring with Jabba's kitchen boy, Phlegmin, to slowly poison the gangster. Someone learns of this plot and tries to blackmail J'Quille. With Lady Valarian's remote assistance, J'Quille discovers it was Phlegmin himself. But when the boy is killed by a mysterious murderer who is loose in the palace, J'Quille's poisoning gambit evaporates, and he contemplates a more explosive way of eliminating the Hutt.

"AND THEN THERE WERE SOME: THE GAMORREAN GUARD'S TALE"

AUTHOR · William F. Wu

PUBLICATION HISTORY · Short story, Bantam Spectra
Included in *Tales from Jabba's Palace*
· Paperback, January 1996

TIME LINE PLACEMENT · 4 ABY

WORLD VISITED · Tatooine [R-16]

MAIN CHARACTERS · Gartogg, guard (Gamorrean male); Ortugg, guard (Gamorrean male)

SUMMARY · The dim-witted Gamorrean guard Gartogg dreams of one day serving aboard Jabba's barge. He attempts to curry favor with the Hutt by solving the mystery behind a rash of murders in the palace. Unfortunately, he is too stupid to find the killer or, indeed, to correctly identify dead bodies when he stumbles across them. Ironically, his idiocy saves his life, as the sail barge trip that day is doomed.

"GOATGRASS: THE TALE OF REE-YEES"

AUTHOR · Deborah Wheeler

PUBLICATION HISTORY · Short story, Bantam Spectra Included in *Tales from Jabba's Palace* · Paperback, January 1996

TIME LINE PLACEMENT · 4 ABY

WORLD VISITED · Tatooine [R-16]

MAIN CHARACTER · Ree-Yees, drifter (Gran male)

SUMMARY · The murderous fugitive Ree-Yees is secretly cobbling together a bomb to kill Jabba in return for a full pardon from the Empire. The bomb components come smuggled in shipments of goatgrass, a food favored by Gran. An encounter with a B'omarr monk grants Ree-Yees a vision of a fiery future, leading him to believe his bomb will be successful. But his vision presages a different outcome: Ree-Yees has been surgically implanted with a bomb by a distrustful Jabba. During the Hutt's death throes as he is strangled by Princess Leia, Jabba activates the device—an explosion rendered redundant by the fiery death of the sail barge moments later.

G*ALAXY GUIDE 5: RETURN OF THE JEDI* (1990), the same roleplaying supplement that provided Ree-Yees's basic backstory as a murderer, suggests that he survived the sail barge blast, though this explosives-laden story makes that claim extremely doubtful.

"THE GREAT GOD QUAY: THE TALE OF BARADA AND THE WEEQUAYS"

AUTHOR · George Alec Effinger

PUBLICATION HISTORY · Short story, Bantam Spectra Included in *Tales from Jabba's Palace* · Paperback, January 1996

TIME LINE PLACEMENT · 4 ABY

WORLD VISITED · Tatooine [R-16]

MAIN CHARACTERS · Barada, repulsorpool chief (Klatooinian male); Weequay guards (Weequay males)

SUMMARY · Barada uncovers the body of Ak-Buz stashed in the repulsor garage of the palace. There are no marks on the Weequay sail barge captain's body that would indicate the cause of death. The other Weequay, deranged and reverent toward a simple child's toy they regard as an avatar of their moon god, try to piece together the mystery behind the murder. They ask the toy—which they call a Quay—a series of simple yes-or-no questions, and the device answers at random in the affirmative, the negative, or with noncommittal deflection. Following a string of lucky questions and answers from the Quay, the Weequay discover and defuse a bomb aboard Jabba's sail barge, only to get blown up anyway when Luke Skywalker destroys the vessel while rescuing his friends.

T*HE QUAY IS* essentially an analog of the Magic 8 Ball toy manufactured by Mattel, and even uses the same "Reply hazy. Try again" response. Barada is described as a Klatooinan, but the spelling of that species name has been revised to "Klatooinian" in more recent materials.

THE NEW REPUBLIC

"A FREE QUARREN IN THE PALACE: TESSEK'S TALE"

AUTHOR · Dave Wolverton

PUBLICATION HISTORY · Short story, Bantam Spectra
Included in *Tales from Jabba's Palace*
· Paperback, January 1996

TIME LINE PLACEMENT · 4 ABY

WORLD VISITED · Tatooine [R-16]

MAIN CHARACTER · Tessek, accountant (Quarren male)

SUMMARY · The scheming Quarren businessman Tessek conspires with Barada to plant a bomb on Jabba's skiff and then encourages the gangster to take the skiff into the city, but the Hutt is preoccupied with Luke Skywalker's arrival at the palace. Tessek reluctantly accompanies Jabba aboard his sail barge for the execution of the Rebel interlopers at the Sarlacc pit and escapes the mayhem of the Rebel rescue on a swoop bike he had secreted aboard the craft. But when Tessek returns to the palace, eager to carve out a place for himself in the power vacuum left by the Hutt's death, he is instead assailed by B'omarr monks, who subdue him and transplant his brain into a jar.

"TONGUE-TIED: BUBO'S TALE"

AUTHOR · Daryl F. Mallett

PUBLICATION HISTORY · Short story, Bantam Spectra
Included in *Tales from Jabba's Palace*
· Paperback, January 1996

TIME LINE PLACEMENT · 4 ABY

WORLD VISITED · Tatooine [R-16]

MAIN CHARACTER · Bubo (male frog-dog)

SUMMARY · Bubo is yet another of the dregs within Jabba's palace plotting the gangster's demise. Bubo thinks he has an advantage over his adversaries in that many assume him to be an unintelligent creature—but his disadvantage is that he is in fact not very bright. After Jabba's death, the B'omarr monks disembrain Bubo.

"OUT OF THE CLOSET: THE ASSASSIN'S TALE"

AUTHOR · Jennifer Roberson

PUBLICATION HISTORY · Short story, Bantam Spectra
Included in *Tales from Jabba's Palace*
· Paperback, January 1996

TIME LINE PLACEMENT · 4 ABY

WORLD VISITED · Tatooine [R-16]

MAIN CHARACTER · Dannik Jerriko, bounty hunter (male Anzati)

SUMMARY · The ancient Anzati Dannik Jerriko is on the prowl on Tatooine, stalking prey so he can feed upon the blood, brains, and "soup" of his victims. He has had to make do with dregs and reprobates—not the refined meals of those truly gifted with luck or the Force. Skulking in Jabba's palace, he is responsible for the deaths of Ak-Buz (a Weequay sail barge captain) and the scullion Phlegmin, though no one suspects Jerriko is the true culprit in the murders. Jerriko longs to eat the soup of Jabba the Hutt—or, better yet, Han Solo and Luke Skywalker—but he misses their departure for the Dune Sea.

The tales of Phlegmin, J'Quille, Gartogg, Ree-Yees, Barada and the Weequay, Tessek, and Bubo form a weaving narrative of unsolved murders and a plot to bomb Jabba's sail barge. This story reveals Dannik Jerriko as the murderer.

"SHAARA AND THE SARLACC: THE SKIFF GUARD'S TALE"

AUTHOR · Dan'l Danehy-Oakes

PUBLICATION HISTORY · Short story, Bantam Spectra Included in *Tales from Jabba's Palace* · Paperback, January 1996

TIME LINE PLACEMENT · 4 ABY

WORLD VISITED · Tatooine [R-16]

MAIN CHARACTER · Anonymous skiff guard (male, species unknown)

SUMMARY · Assigned to escort Boba Fett to the Sarlacc pit, a skiff guard (whose name goes unmentioned) tells the story of his sister, Shaara, and how she narrowly avoided being eaten by the Sarlacc after she outran lecherous Imperials and crashed near the Pit of Carkoon.

In the film *Return of the Jedi*, Boba Fett is on the sail barge and not aboard a skiff at all, which raises the question of how a skiff guard engaged him in so lengthy a storytelling session. The skiff guard is never named in the story and has not been named in any other sources.

"SKIN DEEP: THE FAT DANCER'S TALE"

AUTHOR · A. C. Crispin

PUBLICATION HISTORY · Short story, Bantam Spectra Included in *Tales from Jabba's Palace* · Paperback, January 1996

TIME LINE PLACEMENT · 4 ABY

WORLD VISITED · Tatooine [R-16]

MAIN CHARACTERS · Yarna d'al' Gargan, dancer (Askajian female); Sergeant Doallyn, hunter (Geran male)

SUMMARY · Jabba's death means that dancer Yarna d'al' Gargan is now free of his employ. She is determined to journey to Mos Eisley, where her cubs are held as slaves. Sergeant Doallyn, a big-game hunter, helps her and accompanies her on the long trek into the city. In the Jundland Wastes, an enormous krayt dragon attacks them and smashes their landspeeder. Doallyn kills the beast, but with their vehicle scuttled and their supplies scattered, the remainder of the trek must be undertaken on foot. Doallyn requires cartridges of hydron-three in his breathing helmet to survive. Short on these vital gases, Doallyn collapses, but Yarna carries him the rest of the way to Mos Eisley. She sacrifices some of her meager funds to buy the necessary gases for Doallyn to live, even if it means she cannot buy her cubs out of slavery. Doallyn is touched by the gesture and reveals to Yarna that he cut an invaluable dragon pearl from the krayt's carcass. With such riches, the two can free Yarna's cubs and buy transport to leave Tatooine.

THE NEW REPUBLIC

| SPOTLIGHT | *Galaxy Guide 5: Return of the Jedi* |

Tales from Jabba's Palace (1996) heavily referenced *Galaxy Guide 5: Return of the Jedi*, a 1990 roleplaying game supplement written by Michael Stern and published by West End Games. This book featured histories for several characters that led to their stories in the anthology: Barada, Boba Fett, Tessek, Ree-Yees, and Ephant Mon. This book was also the first to detail a space battle between Fett and IG-88 high over Tatooine, which is recounted in Fett's story, "A Barve Like That," as well as the comic edition of *Shadows of the Empire* (1996).

"PAYBACK: THE TALE OF DENGAR"

AUTHOR · Dave Wolverton

PUBLICATION HISTORY · Short story, Bantam Spectra
· Included in *Tales of the Bounty Hunters*
· Paperback, December 1996

TIME LINE PLACEMENT · 3–4 ABY

WORLDS VISITED · Aruza [I-14]; Bespin [K-18]; Hoth (system) [K-18]; Tatooine [R-16]

MAIN CHARACTERS · Dengar, bounty hunter (human cyborg male); Manaroo, dancer (Aruzan female)

SUMMARY · The cold, cybernetically enhanced Imperial assassin Dengar has been targeting Imperial officers in a bid to infiltrate the Rebel Alliance so that he can exact vengeance on Han Solo. Decades earlier, Solo's reckless maneuver in a swoop race left Dengar with injuries so severe, only the Empire could restore him.

Dengar's plan succeeds and he receives an invitation to the Rebel base on Hoth, but when he arrives the base is under siege by the Empire. Dengar is taken aboard Darth Vader's Star Destroyer as a prisoner. Vader sees that Dengar is an effective bounty hunter and includes him in the hunt to find the *Millennium Falcon*. Boba Fett beats Dengar to the quarry, but Dengar does make it to Bespin, where he discovers Manaroo, a woman he once saved, working as a dancer in a casino.

Dengar and Manaroo flee Cloud City once it is taken over by the Empire. En route to Tatooine, the two share a cybernetic connection—Aruzans are

It is unclear as to whether Sergeant Doallyn is visible in the film *Return of the Jedi* (1983), as there are several helmeted warriors who match his description. A black-helmeted spacer in a black jumpsuit is tossed down a set of stairs by Chewbacca upon the Wookiee's arrival at Jabba's palace. Later, a gray-suited character wearing the same helmet is seen being cut down by Luke Skywalker in the skiff battle over the Sarlacc. A digitally manipulated image of the gray-suited character was used to visually depict Doallyn in a 1998 expansion to the *Star Wars* Customizable Card Game, but the black-suited version is the more accurate depiction. This black-suited character, though, invites confusion with another similarly outfitted hunter named Bane Malar.

Boba Fett finds a new definition of pain and suffering as he is slowly digested in the stomach of the Sarlacc.

technological empaths, beings who can use a device called an Attanni to link with one another and share emotions. This stirs the long-buried humanity and compassion in Dengar.

Arriving at Tatooine, Manaroo is kidnapped by one of Jabba's underlings and forced to dance in Jabba's palace. Dengar plots her escape by targeting Jabba for assassination, but the Hutt is on to Dengar's plan and orders Fett to drug the lovestruck hunter and stake him out in the desert to die in a sandstorm. Dengar survives, rescued by Manaroo.

THE SHORT STORY MAKES a point of establishing that Dengar was not present in Jabba's throne room when Luke Skywalker arrives, but ironically that is the one scene where Dengar is visible in *Return of the Jedi* (1983).

"A BARVE LIKE THAT: THE TALE OF BOBA FETT"

AUTHOR · J. D. Montgomery

PUBLICATION HISTORY · Short story, Bantam Spectra Included in *Tales from Jabba's Palace* · Paperback, January 1996

TIME LINE PLACEMENT · 4–5 ABY

WORLD VISITED · Tatooine [R-16]

MAIN CHARACTERS · Boba Fett, bounty hunter (human male); Susejo, personality within the Sarlacc

SUMMARY · Deep inside the Sarlacc, Boba Fett rouses. He is becoming integrated into the Sarlacc's biology—the bizarre system that sustains its victims for centuries as they are digested. In this way, Fett meets other personalities languishing within the beast's belly—including the Sarlacc's first victim, Susejo. Fett overloads his rocket pack, creating an explosion that rocks the Sarlacc. The badly wounded Fett crawls to the surface. A year later, he returns to Tatooine aboard *Slave II* and destroys the Sarlacc.

Taking into account all stories, this is the *second* time Fett has escaped the Sarlacc. The Marvel Comics story "Jawas of Doom!" in *Star Wars* #81 (1984) has Fett regurgitated by a dyspeptic Sarlacc. Despite a temporary bout of amnesia, he is relatively intact—armor and all. By tale's end, though, he once again falls into the same Sarlacc. This second round is much more debilitating, as this short story describes the burns and broken bones Fett sustains within the beast's gullet. The story of the Bounty Hunter Wars (1998–99) occurs in the yearlong gap found in this short story's finale.

J. D. Montgomery is actually a pseudonym that was used for this story by the author Daniel Keyes Moran.

"ONE LATE NIGHT IN THE MOS EISLEY CANTINA: THE TALE OF THE WOLFMAN AND THE LAMPROID"

AUTHORS · Judith and Garfield Reeves-Stevens
PUBLICATION HISTORY · Short story, Bantam Spectra Included in *Tales from the Mos Eisley Cantina* · Paperback, August 1995

TIME LINE PLACEMENT · 4 aby (with flashbacks to 0 bby and 3 aby)
WORLDS VISITED · Endor [H-16]; Hoth [K-18]; Tatooine [R-16]
MAIN CHARACTERS · Lak Sivrak, Rebel pilot (Shistavanen male); Dice Ibegon, Rebel soldier (Florn Lamproid female)
SUMMARY · During the Battle of Endor, Lak Sivrak's crippled X-wing fighter crashes into the Endor forests. Before he dies, he experiences time-bending flashbacks to the first time he met his beloved, a Florn Lamproid named Dice Ibegon. He recalls her death during the Battle of Hoth before realizing that these visions are part of becoming one with the Force.

This unique story has Lak reexperience the past with knowledge of the future, as well as the ability to alter his past. When he comes to understand these visions as part of the process of his death, he and the spirit of Dice join "three friends" awaiting them within the Force. The implication is that the trio consists of Yoda, Obi-Wan, and Anakin, the Force spirits from the end of *Return of the Jedi* (1983). It is now understood that such Force spirits are the results of lessons from the teachings of the Shaman of the Whills via Qui-Gon Jinn; thus it follows that Dice is also privy to such arcane knowledge.

"THEREFORE I AM: THE TALE OF IG-88"

AUTHOR · Kevin J. Anderson
PUBLICATION HISTORY · Short story, Bantam Spectra

THE NEW REPUBLIC

Included in *Tales of the Bounty Hunters*
· Paperback, December 1996

TIME LINE PLACEMENT · 3–4 ABY

WORLDS VISITED · Bespin [K-18]; Coruscant [L-9]; Endor [H-16]; Halowan [K-9]; Hoth (system) [K-18]; Mechis III [L-14]; Peridon's Folly [Q-11]; Tatooine [R-16]

MAIN CHARACTERS · IG-88, assassin droid; Gurdun, Imperial supervisor (human male)

SUMMARY · Upon activation within the Halowan Laboratories, the advanced assassin droid IG-88 wreaks havoc, killing the scientists responsible for his creation. IG-88 then copies his consciousness into several identical droids, forming a quartet of killing machines with a plan of galactic conquest. The droids surreptitiously conquer the vast droid factories of Mechis III by means of invasive programming, and IG-88 begins creating countless droids for distribution across the Empire that will ultimately be loyal to him.

To draw attention away from this vast cybernetic conspiracy, IG-88 becomes a notorious bounty hunter. He accepts Darth Vader's assignment to track down the *Millennium Falcon* after the Battle of Hoth, and his duplicates fight fellow hunter Boba Fett—in person near the industrial smelters of Cloud City and later in space over Tatooine when Fett returns with the carbon-frozen Han Solo. Though IG-88 fails to capture Solo, it is of no consequence to his master plan.

During his time working for the Empire, IG-88 learns of the second Death Star by snooping through classified Imperial computer networks. After intercepting delivery of the battle station's memory core, the droid inserts his own consciousness within it in a bid to become the most powerful machine in the galaxy.

The story ends with IG-88 as the second Death Star, and readers familiar with the outcome of *Return of the Jedi* (1983) understand what fate ultimately befalls the would-be conqueror droid. Throughout the story, there are descriptions of IG-88's physical form that are inconsistent with the rather spindly droid seen in *The Empire Strikes Back* (1980). For example, references are made to IG-88 having fingers and bulky armor, and weighing "several metric tons."

THE RISE AND FALL OF DARTH VADER

AUTHOR · Ryder Windham

COVER ARTIST · Drew Struzan

PUBLICATION HISTORY · Juvenile novel, Scholastic Inc.
· Hardcover, October 2007

TIME LINE PLACEMENT · 4 ABY (with flashbacks to 38 BBY, 32 BBY, 22 BBY, 19 BBY, 0 BBY, 2 ABY, and 3 ABY)

WORLDS VISITED · Bespin [K-18]; Coruscant [L-9]; Geonosis [R-16]; Mimban [O-12]; Mustafar [L-19]; Naboo [O-17]; Ord Mantell [L-7]; Tatooine [R-16]; Vjun (in a dream) [Q-6]

MAIN CHARACTER · Darth Vader, Dark Lord of the Sith (human cyborg male)

SUMMARY · As he prepares to confront his son for the last time, Darth Vader thinks back upon his life and the path that led him to this moment.

THE NEW REPUBLIC

The first in a series of biography-type novels that would also spotlight Obi-Wan Kenobi, Luke Skywalker, and Darth Maul, this book dramatizes Vader's role in the films from his point of view, but also makes mention of several major stories from the Expanded Universe, like *Splinter of the Mind's Eye* (1978). It includes new scenes, such as Anakin Skywalker's arrival on Tatooine at age three.

THE BOUNTY HUNTER WARS

THE MANDALORIAN ARMOR · SLAVE SHIP · HARD MERCHANDISE

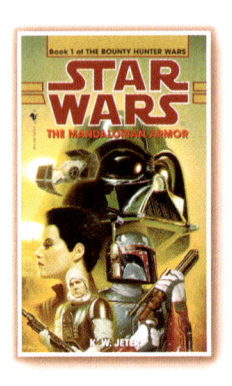

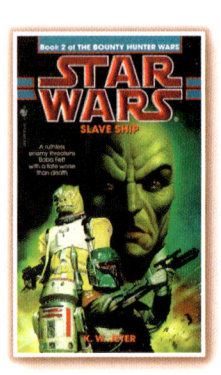

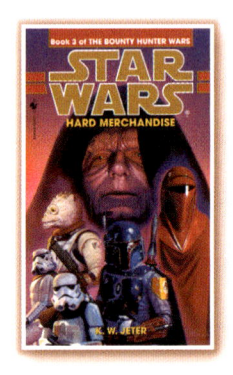

AUTHOR · K. W. Jeter

COVER ARTIST · Stephen Youll

PUBLICATION HISTORY · Novels, Bantam Spectra
The Mandalorian Armor · Paperback, June 1998
Slave Ship · Paperback, October 1998
Hard Merchandise · Paperback, July 1999

TIME LINE PLACEMENT · 0–4 ABY

WORLDS VISITED · Circumtore [S-12]; Coruscant [L-9]; Gholondreine-β [K-15]; Oran-μ [M-17]; Salaktori Anchorage (guild headquarters) [O-10]; Sarrish (site of Salla C'airmam's cantina) [K-16]; Tatooine [R-16]; Uhltenden [P-6]

MAIN CHARACTERS · Boba Fett, bounty hunter (human male); Dengar, bounty hunter (human male); Neelah/Kateel of Kuhlvult, Kuati noble (human female); Kuat of Kuat, head of the Kuat family (human male); Bossk, bounty hunter (Trandoshan male); Zuckuss, bounty hunter (Gand male); Prince Xizor, Black Sun crime lord (Falleen male); Kud'ar Mub'at, criminal go-between (Assembler male); Cradossk, Bounty Hunters' Guild master (Trandoshan male); D'harhan, bounty hunter (near-human cyborg male); Manaroo, dancer (Aruzan female)

SUMMARY · THE PAST: Prince Xizor, ruler of Black Sun, plots a purge of the Bounty Hunters' Guild to ensure that only the best in the dangerous trade survive. Working secretly through an intermediary—the scheming, methodically minded arachnid Kud'ar Mub'at—Xizor hires Boba Fett to infiltrate and destroy the guild. Fett's presence in the guild

THE NEW REPUBLIC

Boba Fett confers with Kud'ar Mub'at, the well-informed Assembler.

splits the organization along generational lines. When Bossk kills and consumes his father, the guild master Cradossk, the rivalries spill into all-out war.

To further splinter the factions into chaos, Xizor dangles a target that no hunter could resist. A huge bounty is posted on former Imperial stormtrooper commander Trhin Voss'on't, a highly skilled warrior. Fett captures Voss'on't, making a sworn enemy out of Bossk, Fett's former partner. Fett brings the dangerous quarry to Kud'ar Mub'at, just as the intermediary is overthrown by an alliance between Xizor and Balancesheet, one of Mub'at's treacherous underlings. Fett barely escapes a confrontation with Xizor, though the focus of Fett's ire is not the crime lord but rather Balancesheet, who executed the far more personal betrayal of pocketing half the bounty offered on Voss'on't.

THE PRESENT: Dengar and his beloved Manaroo, along with a former dancer at Jabba's court named Neelah, find the badly injured form of Boba Fett in the Tatooine sands in the aftermath of the battle over the Pit of Carkoon. Neelah is an enigma—a woman of obviously aristocratic heritage whose mind has been wiped of its history. Yet she knows of some past connection with Fett.

At Kuat Drive Yards, the industrial titan that manufactures the Empire's mightiest warships, the corporate and clan leader Kuat of Kuat is obsessed with the fallout from Jabba's destruction and whether or not Fett is truly dead. At great personal

THE NEW REPUBLIC

expense and risk, he arranges a bombing run on the Sarlacc pit to ensure the bounty hunter's death.

But Fett recovers and leaves Tatooine by tricking Bossk and stealing his ship, *Hound's Tooth*. Word begins to spread of Fett's survival. Bossk narrowly survives the theft of his ship, but finds a peculiar piece of evidence left behind by Fett aboard *Slave I*: a spy droid containing a record that Prince Xizor was involved in ordering the deaths of Owen and Beru Lars, Luke Skywalker's aunt and uncle.

Unbeknownst to Bossk, this recording was manufactured by Kuat of Kuat, and part of an incomplete plot to engineer Xizor's death through Skywalker's vengeance. That Xizor died at Vader's command made this particular gambit needless, but is indicative of Kuat's skulduggery. Kuat's vendettas and schemes greatly upset fellow members of his Kuhlvult clan, who question his commitment to their prosperity. Guarding against clan uprisings, Kuat installs Kodir of Kuhlvult as his security chief, but she is heavily enmeshed in conspiracy as well. Kodir plots Kuat's overthrow, and to ensure her success, she has already eliminated the one family member who disagreed with her methods: Kodir wiped the memories of her sister, Kateel of Kuhlvult, leaving her as Neelah.

Fett reveals the truth to Neelah upon returning to the grave site of Kud'ar Mub'at: Mub'at found Neelah aboard a derelict ship piloted by bounty hunter Ree Duptom, who died midtransit from radiation poisoning. Duptom had been partners with Fett and was in the midst of ferrying the mindwiped Neelah and the spy droid with the Lars family recording, thus tying both mysteries back to Kuat's plotting. Neelah begins to regain her memories as Kateel.

Meanwhile, Kodir secretly forges an accord with the Rebel Alliance to overthrow Kuat and secure control of the Kuat Drive Yards. She is confronted and defeated by Kateel. Kuat, not wanting his family heritage to fall into the hands of the Rebels, triggers the destruction of the yards—a move that results in his explosive death. Boba Fett thwarts Kuat's attempt at sabotage by piloting the Star Destroyer that contains most of Kuat's explosives away from the yards, sparing four-fifths of the facility.

Fett and Kateel part ways, and he gifts her with the Star Destroyer. Fett profits from the faked Xizor evidence by selling it to a faction of Black Sun. Also profiting is Dengar's beloved, Manaroo, who has wagered heavily on the outcome of this convoluted caper. Such a nest egg will furnish a more-than-comfortable start for their new life together.

THE TRUCE AT BAKURA

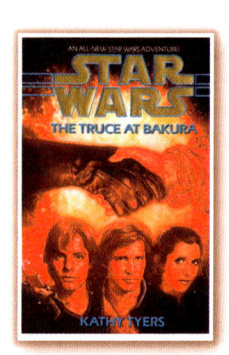

AUTHOR · Kathy Tyers
COVER ARTIST · Drew Struzan
PUBLICATION HISTORY ·
Novel, Bantam Spectra
· Hardcover, January 1994
· Paperback, December 1994
TIME LINE PLACEMENT · 4 ABY
WORLDS VISITED · Bakura [G-16]; Endor [H-16]
MAIN CHARACTERS · Luke Skywalker, Jedi Knight (human male); Princess Leia Organa, Rebel leader (human female); Han Solo, Rebel general (human male); Dev Sibwarra, brainwashed servant (human male); Wilek Nereus, Imperial governor

THE NEW REPUBLIC

(human male); Gaeriel Captison, Bakuran Senator (human female); Firwirrung, entechment specialist (Ssi-ruuvi male); Pter Thanas, Imperial commander (human male); Orn Beldon, Bakuran Senator (human male); Eppie Belden, Bakuran activist (human female)

SUMMARY · The day after the Death Star's destruction, a message intended for Emperor Palpatine arrives at Endor: the Imperial planet Bakura has been attacked by alien invaders, the Ssi-ruuk. Luke, Han, and Princess Leia lead a Rebel task force to Bakura to investigate the situation and help the otherwise unassisted Bakurans.

The Ssi-ruuk are a reptilian species who have mastered entechment—the process of powering technology through the captured life energies of sacrificed slaves. Alone among the Ssi-ruuk is a brainwashed Force-sensitive human servant, Dev Sibwarra. The Ssi-ruuk are fascinated with the Force and believe that by entechinga subject powerful in the Force, they can extend the field of effect of their entechment process even wider. This will greatly accelerate their plans to invade Imperial space.

Arriving at Bakura, the Rebels aid the beleaguered Imperial space forces led by Commander Pter Thanas. The Rebels meet with the assembled Bakuran Senate. Still under Imperial rule, the Bakurans nonetheless harbor currents of dissent that the Rebels hope to exploit to build sympathy for their cause, though Governor Nereus remains an Imperial to his core.

Luke is captivated by one Senator in particular, the lovely Gaeriel Captison, and she reciprocates his attraction, but her religious convictions cause her to reject him on the grounds of his Jedi Knighthood. Gaeriel is a devout adherent of the Cosmic Balance, and believes that for every being capable of remarkable ability another is diminished.

While on Bakura, Leia begins the lengthy process of accepting that Darth Vader was her father. She is visited by his spectral form as Anakin Skywalker but is not ready to talk to him or grant him the forgiveness he seeks.

Governor Nereus agrees to a truce to end Imperial and Rebel hostilities, but the Imperial has no intention of honoring the accord for long. He works out a secret deal with the Ssi-ruuk to capture Luke and deliver him to them in exchange for their retreat. Rather than hand the enemy a powerful ally, Nereus secretly infects Luke with a deadly pulmonary parasite in the hope of spreading the contagion among the Ssi-ruuk.

Luke is taken by the Ssi-ruuk and meets Dev aboard their flagship. Luke is a beacon in the Force that shines through the Ssi-ruuvi brainwashing, and Dev agrees to help Luke and become his apprentice. Luke rids himself of the parasites, sabotages the Ssi-ruuvi flagship, and escapes captivity, though Dev is mortally wounded in the flight.

Governor Nereus's unrestrained bid for control and power opens Gaeriel's eyes to the true nature of Imperial dominance. A planetwide uprising of disenfranchised Bakurans begins. Leia is arrested by Nereus for sedition, but Han rescues her from prison. As the joint Imperial–Rebel forces repulse the Ssi-ruuk, at Nereus's command the Imperial starships break the truce and begin attacking the Alliance forces. The Rebels suffer great losses at this betrayal, but manage to withdraw.

When Luke returns to Bakura, the beleaguered governor mistakenly believes him to still be infested with the parasites and opens fire on the Jedi. Luke deflects the blasts and kills Nereus. With Imperial control of the planet lost, Bakura agrees to join the Alliance.

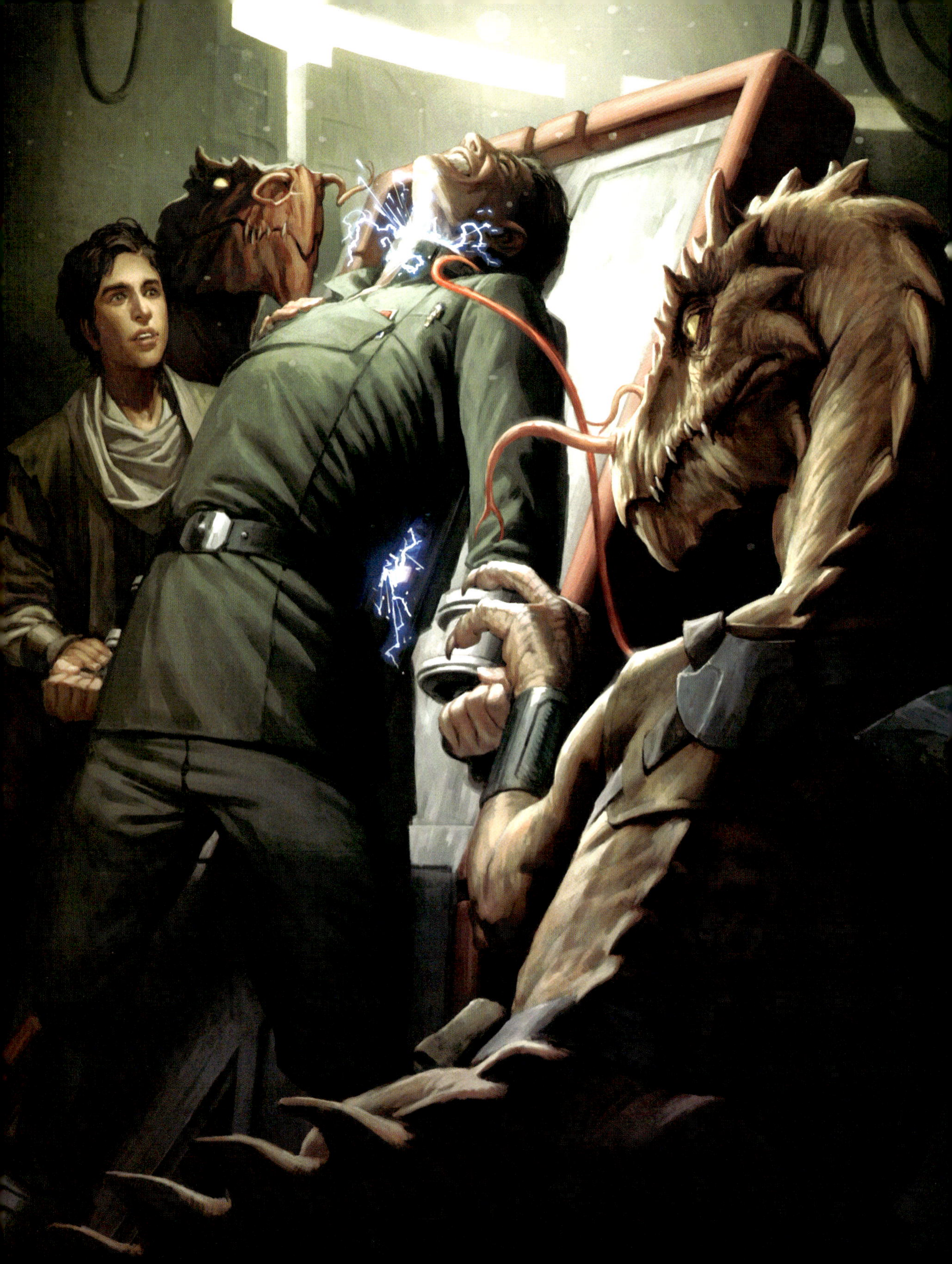

West End Games published *The Truce at Bakura Sourcebook* (1996), a guidebook co-authored by Kathy Tyers and Eric S. Trautmann that greatly expanded on the story, characters, and settings of this novel. The sourcebook integrated *Truce* with the surrounding stories in the time line by establishing that after Endor, the Rebel Alliance immediately became the Alliance of Free Planets, an interim government that would eventually become the New Republic established in the Thrawn Trilogy. That Alliance was an organization established after *Return of the Jedi* by Marvel Comics (1984–86) and had largely fallen into disuse in continuity, until the sourcebook explained that Marvel stories set after the Battle of Endor occupied about a month of chronology.

The fall of the Empire paved the way for several alien invasions. Marvel Comics told of the Nagai and the Tof, who were said to be extragalactic invaders. Bantam's *Truce* had the Ssi-ruuk. These incursions would be overshadowed by the epic Yuuzhan Vong invasion that formed the basis of the New Jedi Order novels that Del Rey published beginning in 1999.

Gaeriel Captison would return in the Corellian Trilogy (1995), while Bakura would be revisited in the Force Heretic trilogy (2004).

A NEW HOPE: THE LIFE OF LUKE SKYWALKER

AUTHOR · Ryder Windham

COVER ARTIST · Mike Butkus

PUBLICATION HISTORY · Juvenile novel, Scholastic Inc.
· Hardcover, September 2009

TIME LINE PLACEMENT · 4 ABY (with flashbacks to 15 BBY, 12 BBY, 6 BBY, 2 ABY, and 3 ABY)

WORLDS VISITED · Aridus [O-14]; Hoth (flashback) [K-18]; Seidhkona (flashback, S'ybll's base of operations) [T-5]; Spirador [Q-14]; Tatooine [R-16]

MAIN CHARACTERS · Luke Skywalker, farmboy become Jedi Knight (human male); Princess Leia Organa, Rebel leader (human female); S'ybll, mind witch (human female)

SUMMARY · As the Rebel Alliance brings aid to the ailing world of Aridus, Luke Skywalker tries to engage his sister, Princess Leia, in a discussion about their father, Darth Vader. Leia refuses to dwell upon her distressing lineage, but Luke thinks back to the events in his life that have shaped him and wonders what events shaped Anakin.

Luke's research uncovers Anakin's victorious Boonta Eve Podrace. Luke returns to Tatooine and visits the old Mos Espa Grand Arena, interviewing two of the surviving Podracer pilots, Teemto Pagalies and Ody Mandrell. Luke then visits Wald's junk shop (formerly Watto's) and learns that Anakin and Shmi Skywalker were once slaves.

Luke's personal mission is cut short when an emergency distress call from Tarnoonga reports of a woman wielding a lightsaber rescuing Rebel scouts. Luke rushes to a desolate island on the waterworld and encounters the mysterious woman—it is an old nemesis, the mind witch S'ybll, who has lured Luke into a trap. Luke kills S'ybll and reunites with his friends.

Dev Sibwarra eases the entechment process for an Imperial prisoner subjected to the administrations of his Ssi-ruuvi captors.

THE NEW REPUBLIC

This biography dramatizes as flashbacks scenes previously presented in other media and bridges the narrative with new scenes as well. Young Luke being stranded in the Tatooine desert with his friend Windy comes from a story told by Luke in the *Star Wars* National Public Radio dramatization (1981) by Brian Daley, which was later adapted as the comic "Luke Skywalker's Walkabout" by Phill Norwood, published by Dark Horse Comics (1999). It would also appear in *The Life and Legend of Obi-Wan Kenobi* (2008) by Ryder Windham.

A skyhopper race that nearly ends in tragedy is adapted from the Marvel Comics story "Crucible," published in *Star Wars* #17 (1978). Luke's daring skyhopper speed run, wherein he threads the stone needle—a natural monument in Beggar's Canyon—is from the first episode of the aforementioned radio drama.

The flashbacks set between Episode IV and Episode V are largely drawn from "Iceworld" and "The Paradise Detour," two installments of the daily *Star Wars* newspaper strip series (1981–84), written by Archie Goodwin and illustrated by Al Williamson. The latter is where S'ybll first appears.

"ESCAPE FROM BALIS-BAURGH"

AUTHOR · Paul Balsamo
PUBLICATION HISTORY · Short story, West End Games · *Star Wars Adventure Journal* #1, February 1994
TIME LINE PLACEMENT · 4 ABY
WORLDS VISITED · Balis-Baurgh [K-16]; Endor [H-16]
MAIN CHARACTERS · Grael, warrior (Ewok male); Junas Turner, Rebel scout (human male); Ponto, child (Ewok male)
SUMMARY · The adventurous Ewok Grael recounts a tale to his son, Ponto, of how he first met Rebel scout Junas Turner in the forests of Endor. They were both captured by an Imperial patrol and incarcerated at Balis-Baurgh, a fully automated prison facility. With his flute, Grael was able to re-create the acoustic signals of the droids at the prison, allowing him and Junas to escape.

"A CREDIT FOR YOUR THOUGHTS"

AUTHORS · Tish Eggleston Pahl and Chris Cassidy
PUBLICATION HISTORY · Short story, Wizards of the Coast · *Star Wars Gamer* #2, November 2000
TIME LINE PLACEMENT · 4 ABY
WORLD VISITED · Socorro [Q-17]
MAIN CHARACTERS · Fenig Nabon, smuggler (human female); Talon Karrde, smuggler (human male); Ghitsa Dogder, con artist (human female)
SUMMARY · With the deaths of Darth Vader, the Emperor, Boba Fett, and Jabba the Hutt, smugglers and information brokers Talon Karrde and Fenig Nabon exchange notes on the sudden changes in the galaxy while in a tavern on Socorro. Talon is cautious with word of the return of the Jedi, thinking ahead to a time when the Jedi Order may be ascendant. He needs a base of operations that Jedi will avoid. After surviving a sudden bar brawl, Fen partners with con artist Ghitsa Dogder to find a

world that fits Talon's bill—a planet said to be home to the ysalamiri, peculiar creatures rumored to have the ability to repel the Force.

Published nine years after *Heir to the Empire* (1991), this short story paves the way for Talon Karrde to find the planet Myrkr, his headquarters in that novel.

"DAY OF THE SEPULCHRAL NIGHT"

AUTHOR · Jean Rabe

PUBLICATION HISTORY · Short story, West End Games · *Star Wars Adventure Journal* #13, May 1997 Included in *Tales from the New Republic*, Bantam Spectra · Paperback, December 1999

TIME LINE PLACEMENT · c. 4 ABY

WORLD VISITED · Zelos II [N-16]

MAIN CHARACTERS · Solum'ke, bounty hunter (Weequay female); Diergu-Rea Duhnes'rd, bounty hunter (Weequay male); K'zk, treasure hunter (Qwohog male)

SUMMARY · A vacationing Weequay couple embarks on a treasure hunt on Zelos II during the Day of the Sepulchral Night, a tidal event that exposes any buried riches. Upon discovering some of the hidden wealth, the couple are betrayed by their employer, who strands them in the wilderness. The pair trust in their ability to survive, and they find the rest of the treasure.

"GATHERING SHADOWS"

AUTHOR · Kathy Burdette

PUBLICATION HISTORY · Short story, Bantam Spectra Included in *Tales from the New Republic* · Paperback, December 1999

TIME LINE PLACEMENT · 4 ABY

WORLD VISITED · Zelos II [N-16]

MAIN CHARACTERS · Dirk Harkness, mercenary (human male); Jai Raventhorn, New Republic Intel agent (human female); Platt Okeefe, smuggler (human female); Tru'eb Cholakk, smuggler (Twi'lek male)

SUMMARY · Mercenary Dirk Harkness and New Republic Intelligence agent Jai Raventhorn sit in a pitch-black Imperial prison cell recovering from interrogation. They are rescued by smugglers and Alliance sympathizers Platt Okeefe and Tru'eb Cholakk, who braved the eerie landscape of Zelos II to find the secret Imperial garrison. Jai, who is disillusioned by the New Republic, seriously considers Dirk's offer to become a mercenary and continue the fight against the Empire.

The quartet of protagonists featured in this story consists of recurring characters from role-playing game resource material published in the *Star Wars Adventure Journal* from West End Games. Their histories were previously detailed in a series titled *Star Wars* Stories (1994–95) that appeared in the first six issues of that periodical.

"HANDOFF"

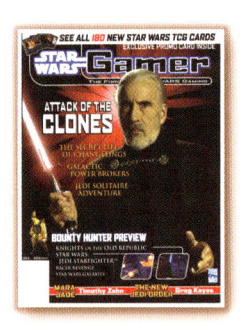

AUTHOR · Timothy Zahn
PUBLICATION HISTORY · Short story, Wizards of the Coast · *Star Wars Gamer* #10, April 2002
TIME LINE PLACEMENT · 4 ABY
WORLD VISITED · Chibias [K-17]

MAIN CHARACTERS · Mara Jade, former Emperor's Hand (human female); Zakarisz Ghent, slicer (human male); Markko, Rebel agent (human male); Egron, Imperial governor (human male)

SUMMARY · Now on the run from the Empire, Mara Jade witnesses a young slicer named Ghent get roped into a dangerous assignment and makes it her business to help him. Rebels led by an agent named Markko have hired Ghent, ostensibly to purge a captured Rebel computer of sensitive data before the Imperial governor Egron has time to examine it. Mara pieces together the true story: the computer is a Star Destroyer system containing sensitive Imperial data, and the treacherous Egron intends to sell it to the Rebels. Still inclined to dispense Imperial justice, Mara kills Egron, but allows Markko and Ghent to go their way. Ghent is intercepted by an up-and-coming smuggler baron named Talon Karrde, who is interested in his skills.

Filling out the backstory of the smuggler characters he created for *Heir to the Empire* (1991), Zahn introduces the slicer Ghent in this tale, making him the first of Karrde's organization to meet Mara Jade.

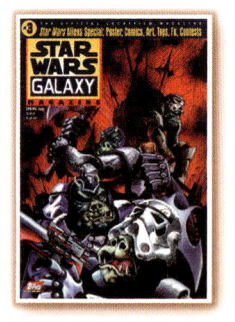

"LUMIYA: DARK STAR OF THE EMPIRE"

AUTHOR · Michael Mikaelian
PUBLICATION HISTORY · Short story, The Topps Company · *Star Wars Galaxy* #3, Spring 1995
TIME LINE PLACEMENT · 4 ABY
WORLD VISITED · Cron drift [R-6]

MAIN CHARACTER · Lumiya, Dark Lady of the Sith (human cyborg female)

SUMMARY · Lumiya leads an assault force to Epsilon 9, a secret Imperial research installation taken over by the New Republic. Her red-armored stormtroopers destroy the facility, killing all the Republic troops within.

This very short story published as part of the roleplaying game section of *Star Wars Galaxy* magazine is notable for bringing Lumiya back into "modern" continuity. Lumiya was developed as a post–*Return of the Jedi* villain for the Marvel Comics *Star Wars* series (1984–86), transforming a Rebel pilot and Imperial agent, Shira Brie, into a cyborg warrior dubbed the "Dark Lady of the Sith." In the mid-1990s, much of the material established by Marvel Comics had fallen by the wayside of continuity, but this *Galaxy* story was meant as a way of giving readers the ability to inject Lumiya into their roleplaying games. It anticipated a return of the character, who more than a decade later would figure prominently in the Legacy of the Force series.

"ONE OF A KIND"

AUTHOR · Paul Danner

PUBLICATION HISTORY · Short story, West End Games · *Star Wars Adventure Journal #5*, February 1995

TIME LINE PLACEMENT · c. 4 ABY

WORLD VISITED · Venaari [O-8]

MAIN CHARACTERS · Sienn Sconn, thief (human male); Shandria L'hnnar, New Republic operative (human female)

SUMMARY · Sienn Sconn, a down-on-his-luck charmer of a thief, cannot stand to see a beautiful woman in danger. So when Shandria L'hnnar is pursued by stormtroopers, he dares to rescue the New Republic agent. L'hnnar carries stolen Imperial data that could save the lives of millions if delivered to the New Republic. Sconn helps her stay a step ahead of the Imperials in a high-speed speeder chase, and delivers her to her Y-wing fighter, but refuses an invitation to join the New Republic.

"EASY CREDITS"

AUTHOR · Paul Danner

PUBLICATION HISTORY · Short story, West End Games · *Star Wars Adventure Journal #9*, February 1996

TIME LINE PLACEMENT · c. 4 ABY

WORLD VISITED · Rydonni Prime [M-11]

MAIN CHARACTERS · Sienn Sconn, thief (human male); Kalieva K'ntarr, princess (human female); Caerbellak, Imperial Moff (human male)

SUMMARY · Sienn Sconn finds himself reluctantly teaming up with the spoiled princess Kalieva K'ntarr to steal prototype Imperial technology right out from under the noses of the rulers of Rydonni Prime. In exchange for helping the thief, the temperamental royal demands to be taken offplanet—she wants to escape the life of a corporate baron. The theft turns complicated quickly, resulting in Sconn stealing an AT-AT walker and crashing the vehicle into an office building during a crowded parade. The spectacle covers the theft, but Princess Kalieva changes her mind, saying that a life of this much adventure is not for her. Little does Sconn realize that Kalieva abetted the theft to ensure that the trackable technology would be disseminated into New Republic research cells, allowing the villainous Moff Caerbellak to track them down while destroying his enemies.

LUKE SKYWALKER AND THE SHADOWS OF MINDOR

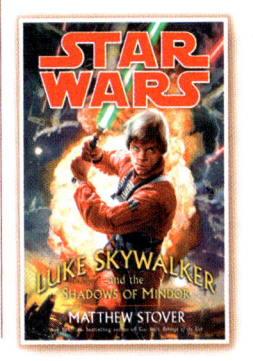

AUTHOR · Matthew Stover

COVER ARTIST · Dave Seeley

PUBLICATION HISTORY · Novel, Del Rey Books
· Hardcover, December 2008
· Paperback, November 2009

TIME LINE PLACEMENT · 5 ABY

WORLD VISITED · Mindor [M-8]

MAIN CHARACTERS · Luke Skywalker, Jedi Knight (human male); Cronal, aka Lord Shadowspawn, aka Blackhole, Imperial warlord (human male); Princess Leia Organa, Rebel leader (human female); Han Solo, New Republic general (human male); Nick Rostu, resistance fighter (human male); Aeona Cantor, pirate and resistance fighter (human female); Lando Calrissian, New Republic general (human male); Wedge Antilles, X-wing pilot (human male); Fenn Shysa, Mandalorian warrior (human male); Kar Vastor, warrior (human male).

SUMMARY · The Taspan system is a hellish cataclysm, the site of an Imperial gravitic weapons experiment gone awry that reduced the second planet into a chaotic asteroid field and showered the first planet, Mindor, with devastating debris. The cascade of shattered planetary material into the star has unsettled the system's primary, causing scorching solar flare activity and tipping the star inexorably toward nova. This apocalyptic system is a fitting base of operations for such a theatrical villain as Lord Shadowspawn, the latest Imperial tyrant to challenge the New Republic.

Shadowspawn has many names and faces. Often portrayed by proxies, he appears as a towering humanoid in flowing dark robes and moon-shaped helm. Shadowspawn is an alias of Lord Cronal, a former Emperor's Hand and an aged, decrepit man once also known as Blackhole. Force-sensitive, Cronal has transcended the dichotomy of dark side/light side that preoccupied the Sith and Jedi of old. Instead, he is devoted to a nihilistic ethos centered on the Dark, the inevitable, entropic force of destruction. Like other dark side devotees, he is also obsessed with immortality, and he has hatched a plan to seize it.

SPOTLIGHT Adventures of a Jedi Prince

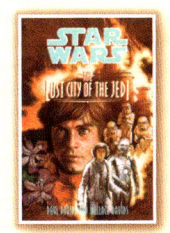

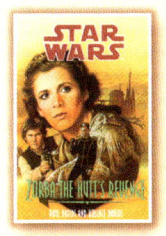

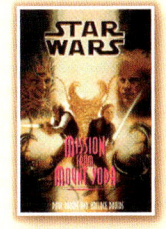

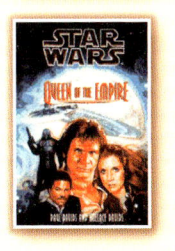

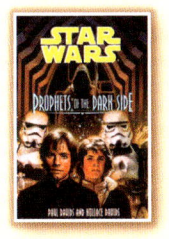

Illustrated children's books fall outside the scope of this *Reader's Companion*, but the six books published by Bantam Skylark from 1992 to 1993 deserve special mention. Written by Paul Davids and Hollace Davids, with interior art by Karl Kesel and covers by Drew Struzan, the series chronicles the story of Ken, a twelve-year-old Jedi prince raised by droids in the underground Lost City of the Jedi on Yavin 4, a hitherto unrevealed subterranean lair of advanced technology. Ken has adventures alongside the *Star Wars* heroes Luke, Han, Leia, Chewbacca, and the droids while facing new villains like the three-eyed Imperial slavemaster Trioculus, or Jabba the Hutt's bearded father, Zorba.

Geared toward younger readers, the stories are whimsical and often outlandish, particularly when compared with the timbre of the surrounding Expanded Universe. Highlights include Imperials scrambling to recover the indestructible glove of Darth Vader to ensure their rule of the Empire; Obi-Wan locking access to the vitally important Lost City of the Jedi under an indecipherable code of JE-99-DI-88-FOR-00-CE; Imperial Moffs holding convocations called Mofferences and bidding one another "dark greetings"; Palpatine having a three-eyed son named Triclops; and Han and Leia marrying each other earlier in the time line than the union depicted in *The Courtship of Princess Leia* (1994).

Nonetheless, the events of these stories were cited in reference books such as *A Guide to the Star Wars Universe,* Second Edition (1994), *The Star Wars Encyclopedia* (1998), and *The Essential Chronology* (2000) and are—for the most part—considered to have happened within continuity (though, perhaps, the specifics of their occurrence differ in tone and detail). Whereas some elements, including a Rebel base on Dagobah called Mount Yoda, the Lost City, and indeed the central characters of Ken and Triclops, have been forgotten in storytelling, other aspects—most notably the shadowy cult of the Prophets of the Dark Side—continue to play active roles in the expanding *Star Wars* story.

Book 1: *The Glove of Darth Vader* (July 1992)
Book 2: *The Lost City of the Jedi* (July 1992)
Book 3: *Zorba the Hutt's Revenge* (August 1992)
Book 4: *Mission from Mount Yoda* (February 1993)
Book 5: *Queen of the Empire* (March 1993)
Book 6: *Prophets of the Dark Side* (May 1993)

The hulking Kar Vastor grapples with Luke Skywalker on the hull of the *Millennium Falcon* while in the caverns of Mindor.

Repeated raids on New Republic ships have scored Shadowspawn legions of hostages. When reports trace his activities to Mindor, General Luke Skywalker leads a New Republic task force to the blighted world to confront the dark sider. A gravity bomb shreds Luke's flagship, but the Jedi successfully lands the tortured remains of the ship on the planet. There he surrenders himself to the Shadow Stormtroopers—black-armor-clad soldiers loyal to Shadowspawn.

Amid Shadowspawn's cultists, Luke Skywalker is oddly venerated by the brainwashed horde. They call him Emperor Skywalker and deem him to be the worthy successor to the Emperor's throne—an opinion apparently based on a pulpy holothriller, *Luke Skywalker and the Jedi's Revenge*. Luke sees firsthand the twisted machinations of Shadowspawn. He has used his Force ability as well as technology to mold an odd mineral on Mindor called meltmassif—a rock that can liquefy and also transmit energy. He has impregnated fibrous strands of meltmassif into the minds of his followers through shadow crowns, allowing him control of his pawns. Shadowspawn even subjects Luke's mind to a meltmassif invasion. He intends to use the mineral as a conduit to transfer his consciousness into Luke, who would then bodily inherit a legion of followers ready to proclaim him Emperor.

Luke's friends soon join him on Mindor—Leia follows impressions in the Force that tell her Luke is in danger. She brings Han and Chewie with her aboard the *Millennium Falcon* and convinces Rogue Squadron to come along against orders. When General Lando Calrissian learns of this, he redirects a task force to Mindor, bolstered by Fenn Shysa's Mandalorians, who are allied to the New Republic. They must battle Shadowspawn's space defenses as well as the volatile nature of the gravity-strained star system. For a time, the New Republic ships are trapped in the system, pinned in place by gravity projectors and threatened by the impending nova.

On Mindor, Leia and Han tangle with Aeona Cantor, the hardened leader of the local resistance. After a series of tense misunderstandings and fighting, they eventually recognize each other as allies and join forces to explore the depths of Mindor, seeking to free Luke and the pawns of Lord Shadowspawn.

Luke defends himself against Shadowspawn, but discovers the villain in the robe to be an imposter under the influence of a shadow crown. Luke tears the crown free, returning will to the thrall. It is Nick Rostu, a Clone Wars veteran, disguised by Shadowspawn to be his proxy. Luke brings Nick with him to the *Millennium Falcon*, where Nick reunites with his lover Aeona.

Through his meltmassif connection with Luke, Shadowspawn comes to understand that Leia is a more fitting receptacle for his consciousness. He dispatches the mighty Kar Vastor, one of his mind-controlled warriors, to kidnap Leia. Luke pursues Vastor into Mindor's depths and does battle with the hulking warrior. Rather than kill his opponent, Luke uses the Force and the meltmassif still contained in his body to free Vastor's mind.

The flood of light causes Shadowspawn to retreat from Vastor's body and back into his withered form. Shadowspawn escapes from Mindor in a rocky starship concealed in a volcano. Shadowspawn exhibits his ultimate control over his shadow stormtroopers by having them turn on Luke. In a great display of Force ability, Luke frees the troopers from their meltmassif influence, but trips a dead-man switch within their bodies that kills thousands of troopers. An act of liberation becomes a massacre, and Luke is haunted by what he will later describe as a mass murder.

Defeated, Shadowspawn retreats into hyperspace. Nick and Aeona agree to continue their search for him, with Kar Vastor as a surprising ally. Shaken by the experiences on Mindor, Luke has an old friend of Nick's, Lorz Geptun, investigate the mission to see if Skywalker is culpable of war crimes. Geptun's analysis paints Luke as a hero. Nonetheless, he is haunted by Mindor and considers this his last military campaign. He resigns his commission as a general in the New Republic military.

In addition to being a rousing adventure, *Shadows of Mindor* is a deliberately postmodern rumination on the authenticity of heroic accounts. The novel acknowledges that the *Star Wars* heroes live in a galaxy of stories, where their exploits are celebrated as legendary tales. The story's finale purposely suggests that the entire account may be a dramatized telling from a less-than-reliable, ultimately biased storyteller.

Cronal has a peculiar origin as a villain, as he was pieced together from three separate, unrelated accounts. He first appeared as Blackhole, an immaterial holographic foe in some of the earliest *Star Wars* newspaper comic strips by Russ Manning, published in 1979, and then was largely forgotten. West End Games' *Gamemaster Screen for Second Edition* (1992) included abbreviated story ideas for the role-playing game, such as a story that featured Lord Cronal, described as "one of the Emperor's most powerful dark-side servants" and "a powerful scientist and mystic." The *Dark Empire Sourcebook* (1993) by Michael Allen Horne, published by West End Games, makes a single mention of a Lord Shadowspawn among the early villains of the New Republic. In "The Emperor's Pawns," an article that appeared in *Star Wars Gamer* #5 (2001), author Abel G. Peña wove these histories together into a connected story that *Shadows of Mindor* would build upon.

DARK FORCES: REBEL AGENT

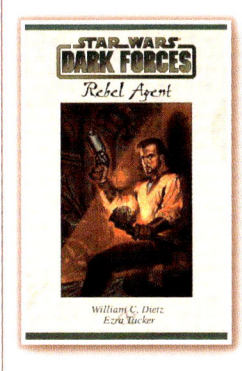

AUTHOR · William C. Dietz
COVER ARTIST · Ezra Tucker
PUBLICATION HISTORY ·
Illustrated novella, Dark Horse Comics and Boulevard Putnam Books
· Hardcover, March 1998
· Trade paperback, April 1999

TIME LINE PLACEMENT · 5 ABY (with flashback to 1 BBY)

WORLDS VISITED · Dorlo [L-19]; Nar Shaddaa (moon of Nal Hutta) [S-12]; Ruusan [P-11]; Sulon (moon of Sullust) [M-17]

MAIN CHARACTERS · Kyle Katarn, Rebel agent (human male); Jan Ors, Rebel agent (human female); Jerec, Dark Jedi (human male); 8t88, information broker (droid); Yun, Dark Jedi (human male)

SUMMARY · The Past: Morgan Katarn transplants a colony of farmers from Sulon to the distant, uncharted world of Ruusan to escape the scrutiny of the Empire. While on a trek through the wilderness, he encounters several native bouncers—a species of orblike beings—who describe to Morgan a prophecy of a Jedi Knight who will fight a battle on their world and free the tortured spirits found there. The bouncers lead Morgan to the fabled Valley of the Jedi, lost site of an ancient battle between the forces of light and darkness.

The Present: Years later, a band of Dark Jedi led by Jerec subjugates the planet Dorlo and captures

THE NEW REPUBLIC 277

Jedi survivor Qu Rahn. Jerec, eager to find the Valley of the Jedi, interrogates Rahn. Probing Rahn's mind, Jerec discovers that the late Morgan Katarn knew the Valley's location and passed this information on to his son, Kyle. Jerec slays Rahn and tasks 8t88, an information broker droid, to continue the search.

8t88 finds an encoded holodisc in Morgan's old residence on Sulon, but he cannot decrypt it. The droid later encounters Kyle Katarn on Nar Shaddaa and attempts to have his thugs extort information on the hidden Valley from him, but Kyle frees himself from the goons and steals the disc. In his frenzied escape from Nar Shaddaa, Kyle discovers that his latent Force abilities are growing.

The holodisc reveals that Morgan has left a map for Kyle at his Sulon farmhouse, as well as Rahn's lightsaber. With the blessing of Mon Mothma, Luke Skywalker, and Princess Leia, Kyle and Jan Ors undertake the quest for the Valley. On Sulon, Kyle finds the lightsaber, but the map—hidden in the tilework of the farmhouse ceiling—is missing. Jerec's lackeys have already found it, and 8t88 is on Sulon to decipher it. The droid destroys the map after recording an analysis of it and transmits that data to Jerec. Jerec's Dark Jedi minions betray the droid by severing its head, keeping the droid's memory module intact for their use.

On the trail of the map, Kyle fights Yun, one of Jerec's Dark Jedi followers. He defeats Yun, but spares his life. The Dark Jedi brothers Gorc and Pic attack Kyle, and he slays them. Retrieving 8t88's head, Kyle uncovers the data inside and locates the map to the Valley.

The story line of the second and third Dark Forces novellas expand upon the narrative of the **Jedi Knight: Dark Forces II** videogame from LucasArts. The story features a coterie of Dark Jedi villains—individual "bosses" who must be defeated to complete the game.

DARK FORCES: JEDI KNIGHT

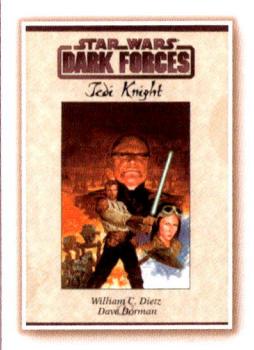

AUTHOR · William C. Dietz

COVER ARTIST · Dave Dorman

PUBLICATION HISTORY ·
Illustrated novella, Dark Horse Comics and Boulevard Putnam Books
· Hardcover, October 1998
· Trade paperback, October 1999

TIME LINE PLACEMENT · 5 ABY

WORLDS VISITED · Milagro [O-14]; Ruusan [P-11]

MAIN CHARACTERS · Kyle Katarn, Rebel agent (human male); Jan Ors, Rebel agent (human female); Jerec, Dark Jedi (human male); Alfonso Obota, Rebel lieutenant (human male); Yun, Dark Jedi (human male); Sariss, Dark Jedi (human female); Maw, Dark Jedi (Boltrunian male); Boc, Dark Jedi (Twi'lek male)

SUMMARY · Having found the planet that is home to the Valley of the Jedi, Jerec dispatches probe droids to Ruusan, followed by an envoy of Dark Jedi consisting of Boc, Sarris, and Yun. They destroy a fugitive settlement in their search for the ancient ruins, while Jerec's Star Destroyer, *Vengeance*, blockades the planet.

Kyle Katarn and Jan Ors continue their search for the Valley. The agents pose as Imperials aboard a captured transport to bypass the Ruusan blockade and take their ship, the *Moldy Crow*, to the surface of the planet.

On Ruusan, Jerec has begun an extensive excavation searching for powerful relics of the ancient Jedi battle. Kyle and Jan infiltrate Jerec's operation, but are separated. Imperials take Jan hostage.

Kyle battles his way through Jerec's defenses, treading dangerously close to the dark side as he aggressively defeats the Dark Jedi Maw in revenge for his father's death. When Kyle is knocked unconscious by Jerec after refusing to turn to the dark side, he experiences a vision of the Battle of Ruusan. Kyle witnesses the actions of Tal, a loyal follower of General Hoth, as the Army of Light confronts the Brotherhood of Darkness. Tal's consciousness, along with all the Jedi, is swept into the thought bomb weapon unleashed by the Brotherhood.

The evil Jerec unleashes the power of the dark side against Kyle Katarn amid the ancient ruins of Ruusan.

Awakening from this dream, Kyle battles Sariss. A conflicted Yun, who recalls how Kyle spared his life on Sulon, stops her blade. Sariss cuts down Yun, and Kyle picks up Yun's fallen blade as his own. With it, he defeats Sariss and, later, Boc. When he finally battles Jerec, Kyle disarms the Dark Jedi. Jerec demands that Kyle give in to dark temptation and slay him. Instead Kyle returns Jerec's lightsaber and strikes him down in combat.

With the villains defeated, Kyle frees the spirits contained in the thought bomb, dispersing the focus of Force energy beyond the Valley and finally bringing peace to these long-tortured souls.

Kyle's vision includes details of the final Battle of Ruusan that differ in this, its first printed account, compared with what is later chronicled in the Dark Horse Comics series *Jedi vs. Sith* (2000) and the Del Rey novel *Darth Bane: Path of Destruction* (2006). At no point is the Brotherhood of Darkness referred to as Sith—they are consistently called Jedi. Lord Kaan is described as having white hair, not the black mane he has in the later comics. The detonation of the thought bomb occurs in an open valley, while the comics have it happening deep inside some caves.

Leia is referred to throughout the story as "Leia Organa Solo," though she would not marry Han for another three years in the time line, according to *The Courtship of Princess Leia* (1994).

"BUYER'S MARKET"

AUTHOR · Timothy Zahn

PUBLICATION HISTORY · Short story, Titan Publishing · *Star Wars Insider* #126, May 2011

TIME LINE PLACEMENT · 5 ABY

WORLD VISITED · Vorrnti [L-8]

MAIN CHARACTERS · Lando Calrissian, entrepreneur (human male); Judder Page, New Republic commando (human male); Blackie, junk dealer (human male); Cravel, junk dealer (human male)

SUMMARY · Under the guise of being interested in heavy machinery, Lando Calrissian visits a junkyard in Vorrnti City. He recognizes it as a front for a sizable glitterstim deal and calls in Judder Page and his crack team of New Republic commandos. The commandos stop the drug dealers, and Lando helps himself to their vehicle of choice—an AT-AT walker. He has big plans for the walker—it will be one in a fleet of such vehicles he'll need to build a special mining operation on Nkllon.

"FISTS OF ION"

AUTHOR · Ed Erdelac

PUBLICATION HISTORY · Short story, StarWars.com · October 2008

TIME LINE PLACEMENT · c. 6 ABY

WORLD VISITED · Reuss VIII [P-18]

MAIN CHARACTERS · Lobar Aybock, shockboxer (Calian human male); Mygo Skinto, activist/recruiter (human female); Bren Derlin, NRI officer (human male)

SUMMARY · This story is presented as a magazine excerpt from an autobiography of champion shockboxer Lobar Aybock. Lobar recounts the night when en route to a shockboxing match with a Barabel champion, he is intercepted by a van full of New Republic Intelligence agents. The agents inform the boxer that a local gangster is rigging the fight so that Lobar will lose and he can sell the athlete's valuable organs. The NRI offers to counter-rig the match, so that Lobar can fight fairly. He wins the match, inspired by the opportunity to break the criminal hold on the planet that has kept so many impoverished.

The main character's name, Lobar Aybock, is an anagram of Rocky Balboa.

"DEADER THAN A TRITON MOON"

AUTHOR · Jason Fry

PUBLICATION HISTORY · Short story, StarWars.com · August 2008

TIME LINE PLACEMENT · 6 ABY

WORLD VISITED · Triton [M-18]

MAIN CHARACTERS · Shandy Fanaso, free trader (human male); Janzel Helot, ship's boy (human male)

SUMMARY · When he sees a youngster carrying a tract of Gactimus, a religious figure revered on the moons of Triton, an older Shandy Fanaso thinks back to his own particular dealings with the religion. The adherents of Gactimus's teachings preach intense asceticism, such that Triton's moons have a reputation for being "dead"—no fun at all. Young Shandy figured out a loophole in laws and scripture that let him open up a club on his ship while docked at Triton Besh. The followers of Gactimus revised their rules to end such offense, and Shandy's punishment was to spend years publicly reciting the hundreds of verses of the tracts of Gactimus.

"MISSED CHANCE"

AUTHOR · Michael A. Stackpole

PUBLICATION HISTORY · Short story, West End Games · *Star Wars Adventure Journal #7*, August 1995 Included in *Tales from the Empire*, Bantam Spectra · Paperback, November 1997

TIME LINE PLACEMENT · 6 ABY

WORLD VISITED · Garqi [K-5]

MAIN CHARACTERS · Corran Horn, fugitive pilot (human male); Mosh Barris, Imperial prefect (human male); Dynba Tesc, university student (human female); Whistler, astromech droid; Kirtan Loor, Imperial Intelligence officer (human male)

SUMMARY · Spirited university students are mistaken for full-fledged seditionists by the Imperial government of Garqi, prompting the arrest and interrogation of innocent Dynba Tesc. Fueling the Imperial crackdown are witnesses' accounts of a lone X-wing flying the night skies—the rash actions of Corran Horn, former CorSec agent on the run from the Empire, who is supposed to be keeping a low profile. Prefect Mosh Barris is determined to impress a visiting Imperial Intelligence officer with his hard-line actions against the Rebels. Advised by his aide Eamon Yzalli, Barris creates a larger trap for the Rebels by allowing Dynba to escape and arrange the freedom of other captive suspects. But when it comes time to spring his trap and round up all the would-be Rebels, Barris finds that Eamon has worked against him to ensure their safe passage. Eamon was, in truth, Corran Horn in disguise. Having fled Garqi, Corran is determined to join the New Republic as a pilot.

This story shared an issue of the *Adventure Journal* with Timothy Zahn's "Mist Encounter." Prefect Mosh Barris was the Imperial colonel whom Thrawn ran in circles in Zahn's story, and he is still nursing his wounded pride in Stackpole's tale, set a quarter century later.

captured, but is saved by a fellow freedom fighter named Chance.

This marks the first published appearance of Alex Winger, a character who would appear many times in the run of the *Star Wars Adventure Journal*.

"A GLIMMER OF HOPE"

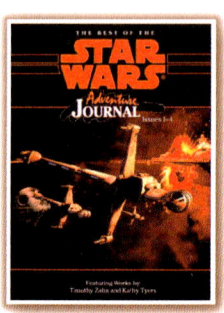

AUTHOR · Charlene Newcomb

COVER ARTIST · Lucasfilm

PUBLICATION HISTORY · Short story, West End Games · *Star Wars Adventure Journal* #1, February 1994 · Included in *The Best of the Star Wars Adventure Journal Issues 1–4*, West End Games, April 1996

TIME LINE PLACEMENT · 6 ABY

WORLD VISITED · Garos IV [P-7]

MAIN CHARACTERS · Alex Winger, underground freedom fighter (human female); Tork Winger, Imperial governor (human male); Brandei, Imperial Star Destroyer captain (human male)

SUMMARY · Alex Winger, adoptive daughter of the Imperial governor of Garos IV, is part of the local underground resistance, secretly supplying them with inside information from the governor's office. Unaware of his daughter's activities, Governor Tork Winger asks her to help host an event for a visiting Imperial captain. Before the party, Alex takes part in an attack against an Imperial convoy and is nearly

"WHISPERS IN THE DARK"

AUTHOR · Charlene Newcomb

PUBLICATION HISTORY · Short story, West End Games · *Star Wars Adventure Journal* #2, May 1994

TIME LINE PLACEMENT · 6 ABY

WORLD VISITED · Garos IV [P-7]

MAIN CHARACTERS · Alex Winger, underground freedom fighter (human female); Dair Haslip, Imperial lieutenant (human male)

SUMMARY · The Garosian resistance gets word that the Empire is stepping up security on Garos IV. Increased sentry patrols at the governor's mansion make Alex Winger's spy duties all the more difficult. The resistance does have an advantage in that they have a mole working within the Imperial ranks—Lieutenant Dair Haslip. Posing as lovers taking an evening stroll, Dair and Alex test the outer boundaries of the patrols on the mansion grounds. Alex later moves a valuable missile launcher from a hidden weapons cache so the Empire won't find it. The launcher proves essential in attacking an Imperial convoy carrying a shipment of advanced sensor equipment into the Garosian mines.

X-WING: ROGUE SQUADRON

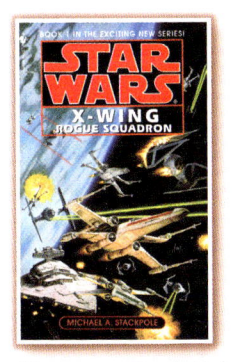

AUTHOR · Michael A. Stackpole

COVER ARTIST · Paul Youll

PUBLICATION HISTORY · Novel, Bantam Spectra · Paperback, February 1996

TIME LINE PLACEMENT · 6 ABY

WORLDS VISITED · Borleias [K-9]; Chorax [N-11]; Coruscant [L-9]; Folor (moon of Commenor) [N-10]; Hensara III [N-11]; Noquivzor [K-9]; Talasea [N-11]; Vladet [N-11]

MAIN CHARACTERS · Corran Horn, X-wing pilot (human male); Wedge Antilles, Rogue leader (human male); Tycho Celchu, New Republic captain (human male); Kirtan Loor, Imperial Intelligence agent (human male); Horton Salm, New Republic general (human male); Erisi Dlarit, X-wing pilot (human female); Mirax Terrik, smuggler (human female)

SUMMARY · Wedge Antilles is tasked with rebuilding the elite starfighter unit Rogue Squadron with expert pilots, including candidates appointed from worlds specifically chosen for their influence in the growing New Republic power structure. Wedge insists that Tycho Celchu be his executive officer, though some in the military object. Tycho previously escaped Imperial custody, and there are those who believe him to be a double agent. The new Rogue Squadron includes Lieutenant Corran Horn flying as Rogue Nine. Used to operating independently as a lawman, Corran initially finds it difficult to fit in with the team.

After a month of accelerated training, the unit is ready for its grand mission to retake the Core from the Empire. En route, Rogue Squadron rescues the Corellian freighter *Pulsar Skate* from an Imperial patrol. The *Skate* belongs to Mirax Terrik, an old friend of Wedge. She is, at first, cold toward Corran, whose father was responsible for the arrest and imprisonment of her own father, the smuggler Booster Terrik.

An Imperial spy informs Ysanne Isard, director of Imperial Intelligence and de facto ruler of the Empire, that Corran has joined the Rogues. Isard enlists the help of Corran's old enemy Kirtan Loor to destroy the squadron. Loor has obsessively been tracking Corran. Sifting through data from Rogue Squadron's operations, Loor deduces that their base of operations is located on Talasea. A squad of Imperial commandos raids the base. Though the commando mission to destroy the squadron is thwarted, many Rogues are injured, and one of the pilots dies in the raid.

After spearheading a reprisal attack on the Empire at Vladet, Rogue Squadron is next assigned to conquer Borleias, a crucial world on the path to Coruscant. New Republic Intelligence is unaware of the extent of bolstered defenses on the planet. The assault turns into a disaster, resulting in many New Republic casualties. The Rogues retreat from Borleias, but with new information they retry their assault. An attack strategy devised by Wedge Antilles and Horton Salm proves successful, and the Rogues secure Borleias as their next base.

ENVISIONED AS *"Top Gun* meets *Star Wars,"* the X-Wing novels proved very popular, numbering ten books by authors Michael A. Stackpole and Aaron Allston to date. The first four books represent a single story, focused on the conquering of Coruscant by the New Republic, an event estab-

SPOTLIGHT: *X-Wing: Rogue Squadron* in Comics

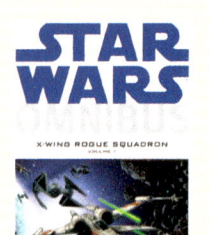

Concurrent with the publication of the X-Wing novels, Michael A. Stackpole penned an ongoing series of *X-Wing: Rogue Squadron* comics for Dark Horse Comics from 1995 to 1998, with cowriters Mike Baron, Darko Macan, Jan Strand, Scott Tolson, and artists Allen Nunis, Edvin Biukovic, John Nadeau, Jordi Ensign, Gary Erskine, Steve Crespo, Jim Hall, and Drew Johnson. The series ran for thirty-five issues and took place in the years 4–5 ABY, before the events of the novels. Since the novel series begins with a re-formation of Rogue Squadron, most of the pilots featured in the comic series do not appear in the books, but some supporting characters, locations, and events in the comics are referenced in the novels.

---

lished as history but never elaborated upon in *Heir to the Empire* (1991).

X-WING: WEDGE'S GAMBLE

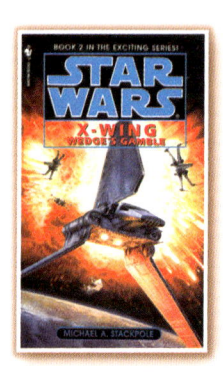

AUTHOR · Michael A. Stackpole

COVER ARTIST · Paul Youll

PUBLICATION HISTORY · Novel, Bantam Spectra · Paperback, June 1996

TIME LINE PLACEMENT · 7 ABY

WORLDS VISITED · Borleias [K-9]; Coruscant [L-9]; Kessel [T-10]; Noquivzor [K-9]

MAIN CHARACTERS · Corran Horn, X-wing pilot (human male); Wedge Antilles, Rogue leader (human male); Tycho Celchu, New Republic captain (human male); Erisi Dlarit, X-wing pilot (human female); Mirax Terrik, smuggler (human female); Kirtan Loor, Imperial Intelligence agent (human male); Gavin Darklighter, X-wing pilot (human male); Winter, New Republic procurement specialist (human female)

SUMMARY · Rogue Squadron rebuilds after their costly success in capturing Borleias. Their next assignment proves even more daunting: the conquest of Coruscant in a manner that spares needless civilian casualties and also allows the planet's defenses to remain intact to hold the capital under the New Republic banner. This mission requires the Rogues to be not only extraordinary pilots but undercover ground agents as well. A controversial part of the plan, proposed by New Republic councilor Borsk Fey'lya, involves freeing certain criminals from the spice mines of Kessel to act as insurgents on Coruscant, to keep the Imperials preoccupied as

THE NEW REPUBLIC

Rogue Squadron carries out their larger assignment.

Ysanne Isard readies her own diabolical plan in preparation for the New Republic invasion. She has concocted a virus to unleash on the nonhuman population of Coruscant. The deadly Krytos virus is specifically engineered to be curable—but only at great expense with large quantities of bacta. Isard hopes to bleed the Republic's coffers dry with this bioengineered disaster.

The Rogues arrive separately and undercover on Coruscant to reconnoiter the capital, with the help of New Republic Intelligence agents Iella Wessiri, Winter, and smuggler Mirax Terrik. Corran is paired with fellow pilot Erisi Dlarit, and with great difficulty resists the temptation to give in to their mutual attraction. Suspecting Tycho of treason based on intelligence gathering, Corran reports this to Wedge, who calls it an outright impossibility.

With their timetable of action accelerating, the Rogues launch their gambit. They infiltrate a computer control station that positions the orbital mirrors that warm Coruscant's colder latitudes. The Rogues aim a mirror at a massive water reservoir, destroying the structure with focused stellar energy and boiling away the huge quantities of water into vapor, creating an enormous storm front. The storm shorts out the power grid, which drops the planetary shields. During this phase of the plan, Corran pilots a Z-95 Headhunter and provides air cover for the Rogues on the ground.

As the New Republic fleet tangles with Imperial defenses over the capital, an unknown command signal overrides Corran's

Aboard Z-95-AF4 Headhunters, the ace pilots of Rogue Squadron fly air cover during the daring mission to liberate Coruscant from Imperial control.

control of his Z-95 Headhunter. He crashes into the city and is presumed dead. Based on Corran's accusations against Tycho, as well as other evidence gathered on the scene of the crash, Tycho is taken into custody on suspicion of arranging the crash of Corran's Z-95.

X-WING: THE KRYTOS TRAP

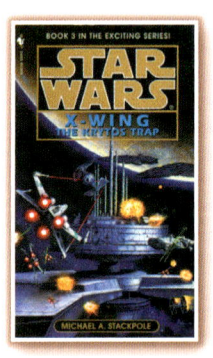

AUTHOR · Michael A. Stackpole

COVER ARTIST · Paul Youll

PUBLICATION HISTORY · Novel, Bantam Spectra · Paperback, October 1996

TIME LINE PLACEMENT · 7 ABY

WORLDS VISITED · Alderaan (system) [M-10]; Coruscant [L-9]; Ryloth [R-17]; Yag'Dhul [L-14]

MAIN CHARACTERS · Corran Horn, X-wing pilot (human male); Wedge Antilles, Rogue leader (human male); Tycho Celchu, New Republic captain (human male); Nawara Ven, X-wing pilot/lawyer (Twi'lek male); Diric Wessiri, former Imperial prisoner (human male); Kirtan Loor, Imperial Intelligence agent (human male); Halla Ettyk, prosecutor (human female); Jan Dodonna, captive (human male); Erisi Dlarit, X-wing pilot (human female)

SUMMARY · As the New Republic struggles to control the outbreak of the Krytos virus on newly conquered Coruscant, Wedge must bottle his outrage over Tycho Celchu's being placed on trial for the murder of Corran Horn. Nawara Ven, a fellow Rogue and former lawyer, serves as Tycho's defense lawyer, but evidence to remove suspicion is sparse. Serving as a further distraction, Wedge must now put aside his interest in Iella Wessiri when her husband, Diric, turns up alive and well after he was granted his freedom from Imperial custody by Alliance Intelligence.

As the case against Tycho speeds toward trial, the Rogues still carry out starfighter missions. Replenishing dwindling bacta supplies is of paramount importance, so the Rogues hit a cache of bacta plundered by the Imperial warlord Zsinj in a space station over Yag'Dhul. Later, they launch a mission to Ryloth to secure supplies of ryll, a medicinal agent that can alleviate the suffering caused by the Krytos virus.

Meanwhile the New Republic capital is under constant harassment from forces led by Kirtan Loor. He stokes antihuman resentment among the planet's beleaguered alien population and scuttles bacta supplies to ensure a shortage. The ambitious Loor seeks to unseat both Ysanne Isard and the local underworld's influence on Coruscant. Loor learns that his plans are known to Isard and realizes his days are numbered.

Unbeknownst to the Rogues, Corran Horn is alive and incarcerated at *Lusankya*, Isard's infamous prison facility where the Empire brainwashes its subjects into becoming potential sleeper agents. There, Corran meets and befriends an elder Alliance general named Jan. He also learns that Tycho was never a sleeper agent. While escaping from the facility, Corran discovers that *Lusankya* is actually a Super Star Destroyer hidden beneath the surface of Coruscant. Returning to Coruscant's surface, Corran detours through a sealed Galactic Museum exhibit about the Jedi Order. Here he picks up a lightsaber and begins to learn the truth of his heritage: he is a descendant of Jedi Knight Nejaa Halcyon.

A desperate Loor tries to broker a deal with Nawara Ven. In exchange for proving Tycho's innocence, Loor wants immunity and sanctuary within the New Republic. Before Loor can be taken into custody, however, word of a high-ranking defection reaches Isard. She has a sleeper agent—Diric Wessiri—eliminate the traitor. Diric kills Loor and is in turn killed by return fire from his wife, Iella. Loor's testimony is not required as Corran returns to the Rogues and clears Tycho's name. He discovers the identity of the true traitor in the squadron: Erisi Dlarit.

Isard launches the hidden Star Destroyer from beneath Coruscant's surface, and the *Lusankya* retreats from the capital to Thyferra. Erisi joins her in escape. Though the Rogues briefly celebrate the return of Corran and the reinstatement of Tycho, they are ordered by the New Republic to stay away from Thyferra for political reasons. Corran begins a tide of defection by resigning his commission, and the other Rogues follow his example. The squadron leaves the New Republic so that they can pursue Isard, stop her control of the bacta cartel on Thyferra, and free the captives aboard her prison warship.

THOUGH HIS LAST NAME is never mentioned in this book, the old Alliance general whom Corran meets at the *Lusankya* prison is Jan Dodonna, the Rebel officer who led the briefing prior to the attack on the first Death Star. His presence helps solve a continuity error. The original *Star Wars* newspaper comic strips distributed by the *Los Angeles Times* Syndicate from 1981 to 1984 depicted Dodonna sacrificing his life to set explosives as the Rebels evacuated their base on Yavin 4 while escaping Imperial pursuit. But in 1992, the *Dark Empire* comic book series depicted Dodonna alive and well, serving as a general in the New Republic, years after the events of *Return of the Jedi*. West End Games' *Star Wars: The Movie Trilogy Sourcebook* (1993) established that he was captured on Yavin 4 and later freed by a Rebel special mission. *The Krytos Trap* and *Isard's Revenge* (1999) would dramatize this in storytelling.

X-WING: THE BACTA WAR

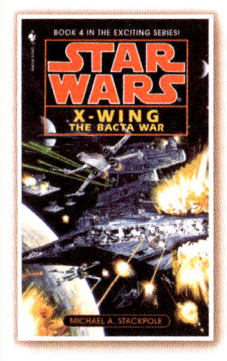

AUTHOR · Michael A. Stackpole

COVER ARTIST · Paul Youll

PUBLICATION HISTORY ·
Novel, Bantam Spectra
· Paperback, February 1997

TIME LINE PLACEMENT · 7 ABY

WORLDS VISITED · Alderaan (system) [M-10]; Chorax [N-11]; Coruscant [L-9]; Elshandruu Pica [O-18]; Halanit [N-11]; Qretu 5 [L-15]; Rishi [S-15]; Tatooine [R-16]; Thyferra [L-14]; Yag'Dhul [L-14]

MAIN CHARACTERS · Corran Horn, X-wing pilot (human male); Wedge Antilles, Rogue leader (human male); Tycho Celchu, New Republic captain (human male); Ysanne Isard, ruler of Thyferra (human female); Mirax Terrik, smuggler (human female); Booster Terrik, retired smuggler (human male)

THE NEW REPUBLIC

SUMMARY · Thyferra is the galaxy's principal source of bacta. Production and distribution of the healing agent has traditionally been managed by two ruling corporations—Xucphra and Zaltin. Zaltin has staged a coup on the planet and installed Ysanne Isard as its ruler. Politically, the New Republic cannot intervene in a strictly Thyferran matter. Determined to oust Isard, Rogue Squadron resigns from active duty.

Basing their operations on a space station over Yag'Dhul, the Rogues call in favors and scour the black market to supply their mission. Corran meets Mirax's father, the legendary smuggler Booster Terrik. Aided by Zaltin rebels, sympathetic Twi'leks, and mercenary allies, the Rogues begin raiding bacta convoys and redistributing the captured medicine freely to planets. Isard retaliates by targeting the worlds benefiting from Rogue Squadron's vigilantism. These violent exchanges culminate in Isard attacking Thyferra directly to eliminate the rebellious factions there, which costs her several key allies. By luring Isard's forces to their Yag'Dhul base, the Rogues provoke a confrontation with the *Lusankya* Super Star Destroyer. When New Republic reinforcements suddenly arrive, the Imperials retreat, surrendering the Star Destroyer *Virulence* as the *Lusankya* returns to Thyferra.

In a final battle over Thyferra, Corran shoots down the traitorous Erisi Dlarit. Overwhelmed by superior tactics, the Imperials aboard the *Lusankya* surrender, and Tycho blasts the shuttle believed to be ferrying Ysanne. The Rogues are disappointed to discover that the prisoners aboard the *Lusankya* have been secreted elsewhere.

Rogue Squadron's original resignation is conveniently lost in a bureaucratic mishap. Wedge Antilles assumes command of the *Lusankya*, and the grand warship is the setting for the wedding of Mirax Terrik and Corran Horn. Booster Terrik now owns the captured Star Destroyer *Virulence*, and this great prize helps to offset any misgivings he may have about his daughter marrying a former lawman.

"CONFLICT OF INTEREST"

AUTHOR · Laurie Burns
PUBLICATION HISTORY · Short story, West End Games · *Star Wars Adventure Journal* #13, May 1997 Included in *Tales from the New Republic*, Bantam Spectra · Paperback, December 1999
TIME LINE PLACEMENT · 7 ABY
WORLD VISITED · Verkuyl [H-17]
MAIN CHARACTERS · Selby Jarrad, New Republic Intelligence operative (human female); Daven Quarle, Imperial aide (human male)
SUMMARY · New Republic Intelligence agent Selby Jarrad goes undercover as a businesswoman on the bacta-producing planet of Verkuyl. She intends to meet and sway Imperial governor Parco Ein into surrendering control of the planet to its populace, which stands at the brink of revolt. Her aims run counter to Daven Quarle's, the governor's aide and her supposedly sympathetic contact within the government. A native of the planet, Quarle believes the Imperial presence stabilized Verkuyl, and that its populace is not ready for self-determination. His attempts to scuttle the operation fail, and the New Republic ultimately arrives and backs the revolt, though Jarrad has doubts if the planet truly is in better hands.

STAR WARS STORIES

"CHESSA'S DOOM" · "BIG QUINCE" · "EXPLOSIVE DEVELOPMENTS" · "STARTER'S TALE" · "VENGEANCE STRIKE"

AUTHOR · Peter Schweighofer

PUBLICATION HISTORY · Illustrated short stories, West End Games
· Serialized in *Star Wars Adventure Journal* #1–5 February 1994–February 1995

TIME LINE PLACEMENT · 7 ABY (with flashbacks to c. 0 ABY)

WORLDS VISITED · Bespin [K-18] (flashback); Kelada [M-13] (flashback); Romar [T-13] (flashback); Wroona [L-15]

MAIN CHARACTERS · Dirk Harkness, mercenary (human male); Tru'eb Cholakk, smuggler (Twi'lek male); Platt Okeefe, smuggler (human female); Jai Raventhorn, outlaw (human female); Starter, X-wing pilot (human male)

SUMMARY · A group of New Republic agents swap old stories at a bar on Wroona. The ordinarily laconic Dirk Harkness tells his tale of joining the Rebellion after witnessing Chessa, a girl he loved, gunned down by stormtroopers during a botched smuggling run for the Alliance. Platt Okeefe recounts her first meeting with her smuggling partner Tru'eb Cholakk, when they were both slaves escaping from the Sludir gangster Big Quince. Jai Raventhorn recalls her failed attempt to assassinate Moff Jellrek, and how it resulted in a near-fatal brawl with the bounty hunter Belyssa. Starter tells a tall tale of battling elite bounty hunters on Bespin before escaping interrogation by Darth Vader.

The next day, Dirk and Jai successfully carry out a daring undercover mission to destroy the Star Destroyer *Vengeance* while it sits in Wroona Stardock.

These short stories were a mix of prose fiction and pages of sequential, wordless comic-book-style art by John Paul Lona. The Star Destroyer *Vengeance* portrayed here is a different vessel from the *Vengeance* used by the Dark Jedi Jerec in the Dark Forces stories.

"KELLA RAND, REPORTING..."

AUTHOR · Laurie Burns
PUBLICATION HISTORY · Short story, West End Games · *Star Wars Adventure Journal* #6, May 1995
TIME LINE PLACEMENT · c. 7 ABY
WORLD VISITED · Indu San [Q-7]
MAIN CHARACTER · Kella Rand, GNN journalist (human female)
SUMMARY · Journalist Kella Rand uncovers a plot to discredit the New Republic just as the Indu San system is about to take a historic vote of alliance with the new galactic government. Rand's holographic footage proves that agents loyal to the Empire planted a deadly explosive that took the life of an Indu councilor.

X-WING: WRAITH SQUADRON

AUTHOR · Aaron Allston
COVER ARTIST · Paul Youll
PUBLICATION HISTORY · Novel, Bantam Spectra · Paperback, February 1998
TIME LINE PLACEMENT · 7 ABY
WORLDS VISITED · Belthu [O-7]; Borleias [K-9]; Coruscant [L-9]; Doldrums system [L-9]; Ession [S-4]; Folor (moon of Commenor) [N-10]; Gravan VII [O-8]; M2398-3 [P-7]; Obinipor [P-7]; Talasea [N-11]; Viamarr (system) [N-7]; Xartun [O-7]; Xobome 6 [N-10]
MAIN CHARACTERS · Wedge Antilles, Rogue leader (human male); Wes Janson, pilot (human male); Derek "Hobbie" Klivian, pilot (human male); Myn Donos, pilot/sharpshooter (human male); Voort "Piggy" saBinring, pilot (Gamorrean male); Kell Tainer, pilot/demolitions expert (human male); Garik "Face" Loran, pilot/actor (human male); Apwar Trigit, Imperial admiral (human male)

SUMMARY · Wedge Antilles creates a bold new experimental starfighter squadron comprising cross-trained commando/pilots who were once washouts and castaways from other units. Wedge believes he can shape such misfits into an effective special missions team for the New Republic's campaign to stop the destruction waged by Imperial Warlord Zsinj. Among the new pilots are sniper Myn Donos, sole survivor of Talon Squadron; Voort "Piggy" saBinring, a biologically modified Gamorrean whose unnatural skills are a result of Imperial experimentation; and Kell Tainer, a demolitions expert whose father, Kissek Doran, was killed by fellow pilot Wes Janson after Doran's panic attacks jeopardized a crucial Rebel mission.

The new Wraith Squadron's training base on Folor comes under attack from Imperial admiral Trigit and his Star Destroyer *Implacable*. The Wraiths use unorthodox tactics to delay and distract Trigit, allowing for the base's successful evacuation. Regrouping at Xobome 6, the Wraiths commandeer one of Zsinj's corvettes, the *Night Caller*. Posing as the *Night Caller*'s crew, the squadron uses the ship in secret missions against the warlord's scattered outposts and business ventures. Facilitating this deception are the acting skills of Wraith pilot Garik "Face" Loran, who poses as the corvette's captain.

Despite their actions against Zsinj, the warlord does not suspect the true nature of the *Night Caller*'s crew—he mistakenly believes the corvette to be shadowed by New Republic agents. Zsinj informs the *Night Caller* of his plan to attack New Republic forces on Ession. With the New Republic prepared for the assault, they defeat Admiral Trigit's Star Destroyer. Myn Donos exacts justice on Trigit for the destruction of Talon Squadron by shooting him down in his attempted escape.

Gara Petothel, Trigit's mistress and an Imperial Intelligence agent secretly loyal to Zsinj, escapes the fallout in an escape pod after carefully crafting an alias for herself for the purposes of infiltrating the New Republic.

Though their victories prove costly, the Wraith Squadron experiment is nonetheless successful, and Wedge is determined to continue his hunt for Warlord Zsinj.

X-WING: IRON FIST

AUTHOR · Aaron Allston
COVER ARTIST · Paul Youll
PUBLICATION HISTORY · Novel, Bantam Spectra · Paperback, July 1998
TIME LINE PLACEMENT · 7 ABY
WORLDS VISITED · Aldivy [Q-4]; Coruscant [L-9]; Halmad [N-6]; Kuat [M-10]; Lavisar [M-7]

MAIN CHARACTERS · Wedge Antilles, Rogue leader (human male); Gara Petothel/Lara Notsil, undercover spy (human female); Ton Phanan, pilot/medic (human cyborg male); Garik "Face" Loran, pilot/actor (human male); Tyria Sarkin, pilot/infiltrator (human female); Castin Donn, pilot/slicer (human male); Dia Passik, pilot (Twi'lek female); Zsinj, Imperial warlord (human male)

SUMMARY · Wraith Squadron rebuilds, adding such newcomers as Tyria Sarkin, an infiltrator whose service record was blemished by a corrupt New Republic officer; Castin Donn, a slicer; Dia Passik, a vehicle and criminal underworld specialist; and Lara Notsil, who is Imperial agent Gara Petothel in disguise. The Wraiths continue their hunt for Zsinj, posing as a pirate crew called the Hawk-bats in the hope of drawing Zsinj's attentions. Since Wedge is so well known, he opts out of direct involvement in this charade.

The Hawk-bats use captured TIE interceptors as their vehicles, and harass Halmad, a world loyal to Zsinj. A swift reprisal attack by Zsinj's Super Star Destroyer *Iron Fist* results in the death of Wraith pilot Ton Phanan. Zsinj offers the Hawk-bats an ultimatum to join his ranks or be destroyed, and thus the Wraiths enfold themselves into Zsinj's command. Castin slices a tracing program into the *Iron Fist* that will allow the New Republic to track Zsinj's movements, though his treachery is discovered by Zsinj. In a test of the Hawk-bats' loyalty, Zsinj orders the pirates to kill the treacherous slicer—keeping secret the fact that Castin is already dead, killed by Zsinj's enforcers. Dia Passik does what Zsinj demands. Although it keeps the Wraiths in good standing with the warlord, the act will continue to haunt her.

Zsinj covets the *Razor's Kiss*, a Super Star Destroyer nearing completion at the Kuat Drive Yards. He launches an assault, tasking the Hawk-bats with the theft of the massive warship. The warship is secretly loaded with the Wraiths' tracking program. The *Razor's Kiss* is intercepted by General Han Solo's New Republic task force just as it rendezvouses with the *Iron Fist*. In the battle that ensues, Zsinj scuttles the *Razor's Kiss* and flees aboard his flagship.

X-WING: SOLO COMMAND

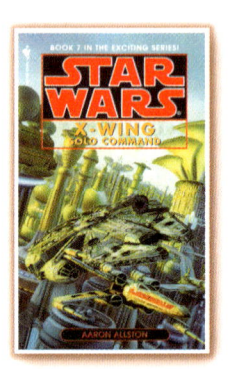

AUTHOR · Aaron Allston
COVER ARTIST · Paul Youll
PUBLICATION HISTORY · Novel, Bantam Spectra · Paperback, February 1999
TIME LINE PLACEMENT · 7 ABY
WORLDS VISITED · Comkin V [N-7]; Coruscant [L-9]; Jussafet IV [N-6]; Kidriff 5 [M-8]; Levian II [N-8]; Saffalore [S-4]; Selaggis (system) [N-6]; Vahaba asteroid belt [N-6]
MAIN CHARACTERS · Wedge Antilles, Rogue leader (human male); Gara Petothel/Lara Notsil, undercover spy (human female); Myn Donos, X-wing pilot (human male); Voort "Piggy" saBinring, X-wing pilot (Gamorrean male); Edda Gast, scientist (human female); Garik "Face" Loran, X-wing pilot (human male); Han Solo, New Republic general (human male); Zsinj, Imperial warlord (human male)
SUMMARY · Wraith Squadron is formally incorporated into the fleet commanded by General Han Solo to hunt down Warlord Zsinj, a task force that includes Rogue Squadron and the Mon Calamari cruiser *Mon Remonda*.

After narrowly surviving an attack by Zsinj's forces at Levian II, the Wraiths attempt to lure Zsinj into a trap using a fake *Millennium Falcon* (the *Millennium Falsehood*) as bait. The Wraiths target the Binring Biomedical Product facilities on Saffalore, the laboratory that altered Piggy. The same medical research, now under the supervision of Dr. Edda Gast aboard Zsinj's flagship *Iron Fist*, is creating sleeper agents among aliens in the New Republic. The Saffalore outpost is a trap, and the Wraiths barely escape with Rogue Squadron's assistance.

The sleeper agent program, dubbed Project Minefield, targets influential New Republic officials for assassination and is meant to sow dissent between human and alien allies in the fledgling government. Dr. Gast is captured by the New Republic, and she offers intelligence on Project Minefield in exchange for sanctuary.

Myn Donos and Lara Notsil begin a relationship, but the Wraiths become overly curious about her shrouded past. Face discovers her to be Gara Petothel, an Imperial double agent, and Myn is particularly hurt by this revelation as Gara, when working for Admiral Trigit, was an accessory to the destruction of his original unit. Gara flees her squadmates and rejoins Zsinj's forces. Determined to clear her name and her conscience, she plots to sabotage Zsinj's plans and the *Iron Fist* from within.

The honor-minded Admiral Teren Rogriss of the Star Destroyer *Agonizer* secretly contacts Han Solo to assist him in the battle against Warlord Zsinj. Rogriss supplies Solo with an interdictor cruiser that Solo uses to ambush Zsinj in the Vahaba system. The slippery Zsinj escapes this trap, fleeing to the Selaggis system where another confrontation takes place.

The *Iron Fist*'s hyperdrive is ruined by Gara, momentarily stranding the ship in the Selaggis system. As she escapes the Imperial warship, Gara

SPOTLIGHT **The DarkStryder Campaign**

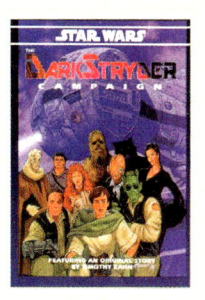

In 1995, West End Games added The DarkStryder Campaign to its expansive library of *Star Wars* roleplaying products. The boxed set was intended to give players a starting point with new characters, locations, and technology in a finite yet expansive setting and a gritty story line. Author Timothy Zahn worked with the West End Games editorial staff to flesh out the setting and penned the short story "The Saga Begins," which kicks off the Campaign.

Eight years after the Battle of Yavin, the New Republic launches an assault on the capital of the distant Kathol sector, Kal'Shebbol, to capture the Imperial warlord Moff Kentor Sarne. Lieutenant Page's commando team storms Sarne's fortress, but the wily Moff escapes, using the power of strange alien artifacts known as DarkStryder technology to cover his hasty retreat. The New Republic conquers the planet and launches a ragtag team made up of commandos, freed Imperial captives, and civilians aboard Sarne's discarded corvette, the *FarStar*, into the wilds of the Kathol sector to pursue Sarne and bring him to justice.

The Campaign would encompass three more gamebooks, the last of which, *Endgame* (1996), would start with the short story "The Saga Nears Its End" by George R. Strayton. Though mostly self-contained as its own chapter in the *Star Wars* Expanded Universe, elements of the DarkStryder mythology—particularly the Aing-Tii monks and its distant setting in the Kathol Rift—would figure notably in the novels *Vision of the Future* (1998) and *Omen* (2009).

---

frees as many of the Project Minefield patients as she can. She alerts the New Republic to the *Iron Fist*'s position, drawing Solo's task force in for the kill.

But in another act of deception, Zsinj escapes, using nightcloak technology and the carefully laid debris of the Super Star Destroyer *Razor's Kiss* to disguise his massive ship's departure. The hunt for the warlord will continue, though Wraith Squadron is dissolved as a fighter unit, its agents absorbed into New Republic Intelligence.

"FIRST CONTACT"

AUTHOR · Timothy Zahn
PUBLICATION HISTORY · Short story, West End Games · *Star Wars Adventure Journal* #1, February 1994
Included in *Tales from the Empire*, Bantam Spectra · Paperback, November 1997
TIME LINE PLACEMENT · 8 ABY
WORLD VISITED · Varonat [K-18]

THE NEW REPUBLIC   293

MAIN CHARACTERS · Talon Karrde, smuggler (human male); Quelev Tapper, smuggler (human male); Gamgalon, smuggler (Krish male); Celina Marniss, aka Mara Jade, mechanic (human female)

SUMMARY · Smuggling partners Talon Karrde and Quelev Tapper adopt pseudonyms to inspect a suspiciously profitable safari operation run by a lowlife named Gamgalon in the jungles of Varonat. Wealthy and adventurous hunters stalk large creatures called Morodins for sport. Talon learns the true nature of the scheme—the intelligent and endangered Morodins are being exploited by Gamgalon, because they secrete a slime that turns an innocuous native berry into a potent catalytic component in blaster gas. With his operation exposed, Gamgalon kills Quelev and targets Talon, but a mysterious hyperspace mechanic comes to his rescue. The mechanic, the highly skilled Mara Jade, recognizes Talon Karrde as an opportunity for her to return to the galactic mainstream after years on the run. She requests a job from him, and an intrigued Karrde is happy to offer one.

In his last assignment before resigning his commission, General Han Solo leads the crew of the *Mon Remonda* in the hunt for Warlord Zsinj.

T HIS SHORT STORY RELATES the first meeting of Mara Jade and Talon Karrde. Mara's alias of Celina Marniss is a nod to a former coworker in Jabba's court, as revealed in *Tales from Jabba's Palace* (1996). In X-Wing: *The Bacta War* (1997), Talon Karrde employs Melina Carniss, but in "First

THE NEW REPUBLIC

Contact," set after that novel, he shows no recognition of what would therefore be an obvious pseudonym used by Mara.

"CRISIS OF FAITH"

AUTHOR · Timothy Zahn

PUBLICATION HISTORY · Novella, Del Rey Books
Included in *Heir to the Empire: The 20th Anniversary Edition* · Hardcover, September 2011

TIME LINE PLACEMENT · 8 ABY

WORLD VISITED · Quethold [I-5]

MAIN CHARACTERS · Thrawn, Grand Admiral (Chiss male); Nuso Esva, warlord (alien male); Voss Parck, senior captain (human male); Soontir Fel, TIE squadron commander (human male); Trevik, royal servant (Quesoth male); Nyama, council liaison (Stromma male); Balkin, stormtrooper commander (human male)

SUMMARY · Thrawn's nemesis, Nuso Esva, has allied himself with the insectoid queen of the Quesoth. Thrawn plans an assault against him with the aid of his temporary partners the Stromma, a species formerly allied with the Quesoth. The Stromma are doubtful of his ability and withdraw their support, but not before translating some essential Quesoth phrases for him to use to his advantage in the upcoming battle.

Holographic intelligence gathered from the Quesoth, particularly imagery of the artwork with which Esva has decorated his quarters, appears to give Thrawn the insight he needs to properly strategize. But Esva has purposely arranged an intelligence breach—and also arranged the art on display to trick Thrawn into planning his attack to Esva's expectations.

Thrawn, however, has predicted this ploy by Esva and outmaneuvers the warlord. Esva's gambit on Quethold has involved corrupting the queen into a bid for power that makes the alliance inherently untrustworthy. When the battle begins to turn against Esva, he kills the queen out of suspicion of betrayal and is in turn killed by the soldiers under her command.

Thus Thrawn defeats his longtime archrival. He then concentrates on his next great plan—the restoration of the Empire to power over the New Republic.

Reading through the Expanded Universe in chronological order means that this story will be the first time readers are exposed to the Empire of the Hand faction, Soontir Fel's TIE squadron, and a 501st Stormtrooper Legion consisting of human and nonhuman soldiers. None of these elements are introduced in a manner to properly explain their origins in *Crisis of Faith*, as they had appeared in print in other sources first, such as *Specter of the Past* (1998) and *Fool's Bargain* (2004).

"CROSSROADS"

AUTHOR · Christopher Cerasi

PUBLICATION HISTORY · Short story, StarWars.com · August 2008

TIME LINE PLACEMENT · 8 ABY

WORLDS VISITED · None (story takes place in hyperspace transit)

MAIN CHARACTER · Princess Leia Organa, New Republic councilor (human female)

SUMMARY · As Leia returns from an extensive diplomatic mission to the normally reclusive Hapes Cluster, she reflects on how busy her life is and how she has had to continually set aside personal concerns for the good of the New Republic.

THE COURTSHIP OF PRINCESS LEIA

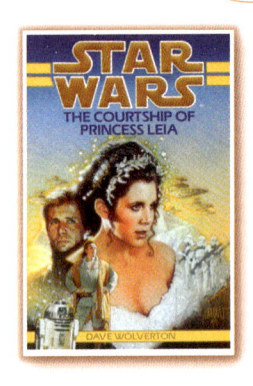

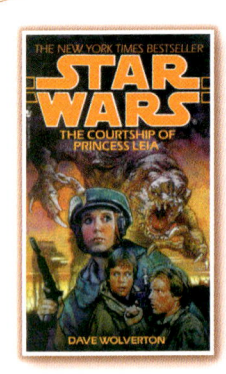

AUTHOR · Dave Wolverton

COVER ARTIST · Drew Struzan

PUBLICATION HISTORY · Novel, Bantam Spectra
 · Hardcover, May 1994
 · Paperback, May 1995

TIME LINE PLACEMENT · 8 ABY

WORLDS VISITED · Coruscant [L-9]; Dathomir [O-6]; Roche [Q-8]; Toola [S-5]

MAIN CHARACTERS · Princess Leia Organa, New Republic councilor (human female); Han Solo, New Republic general (human male); Luke Skywalker, Jedi Knight (human male); Isolder, Hapan prince (human male); Threkin Horm, Alderaanian politician (human male); Teneniel Djo, Witch of Dathomir (human female); Gethzerion, Nightsister (Dathomirian female); Zsinj, Imperial warlord (human male); C-3PO, protocol droid

SUMMARY · With immense pageantry, the sixty-three worlds of the reclusive Hapes Cluster send a fleet to Coruscant in a gesture of rare diplomacy to the government of the New Republic. As part of the envoy, the royal prince Isolder proposes marriage to Princess Leia Organa, thus bringing the much-needed wealth and military power of Hapes to the fledgling government. Such an alliance would also provide a new world for the many Alderaanian refugees left homeless by the first Death Star. Mon Mothma and Alderaanian politician Threkin Horm advise Leia to take the matter under serious consideration.

Han Solo has other ideas. In true Corellian scoundrel fashion, he ventures into the seamy underworld of Coruscant and enters into a high-stakes sabacc game, emerging as the winner of an obscure planet, Dathomir. He then kidnaps Leia and takes her to this world, all in a desperate effort to impress upon her how important she is to him. The harebrained gesture takes him into the heart of Imperial space controlled by Warlord Zsinj. Warships including Zsinj's flagship, *Iron Fist*, blockade the planet. A brief but intense space battle erupts, and Han bypasses the blockade by landing the *Falcon* on Dathomir using a crashing Imperial frigate as cover.

Luke Skywalker, meanwhile, is on a quest for information that will help him rebuild the Jedi Order. On frigid Toola, he uncovers a partial recording of Jedi Master Yoda from a damaged four-hundred-year-old holographic cylinder. In it, Yoda describes

Aboard the ruins of the *Chu'unthor*, Luke Skywalker defends himself from attack by the Dathomirian warrior Ieneniel Dju.

296 · THE NEW REPUBLIC

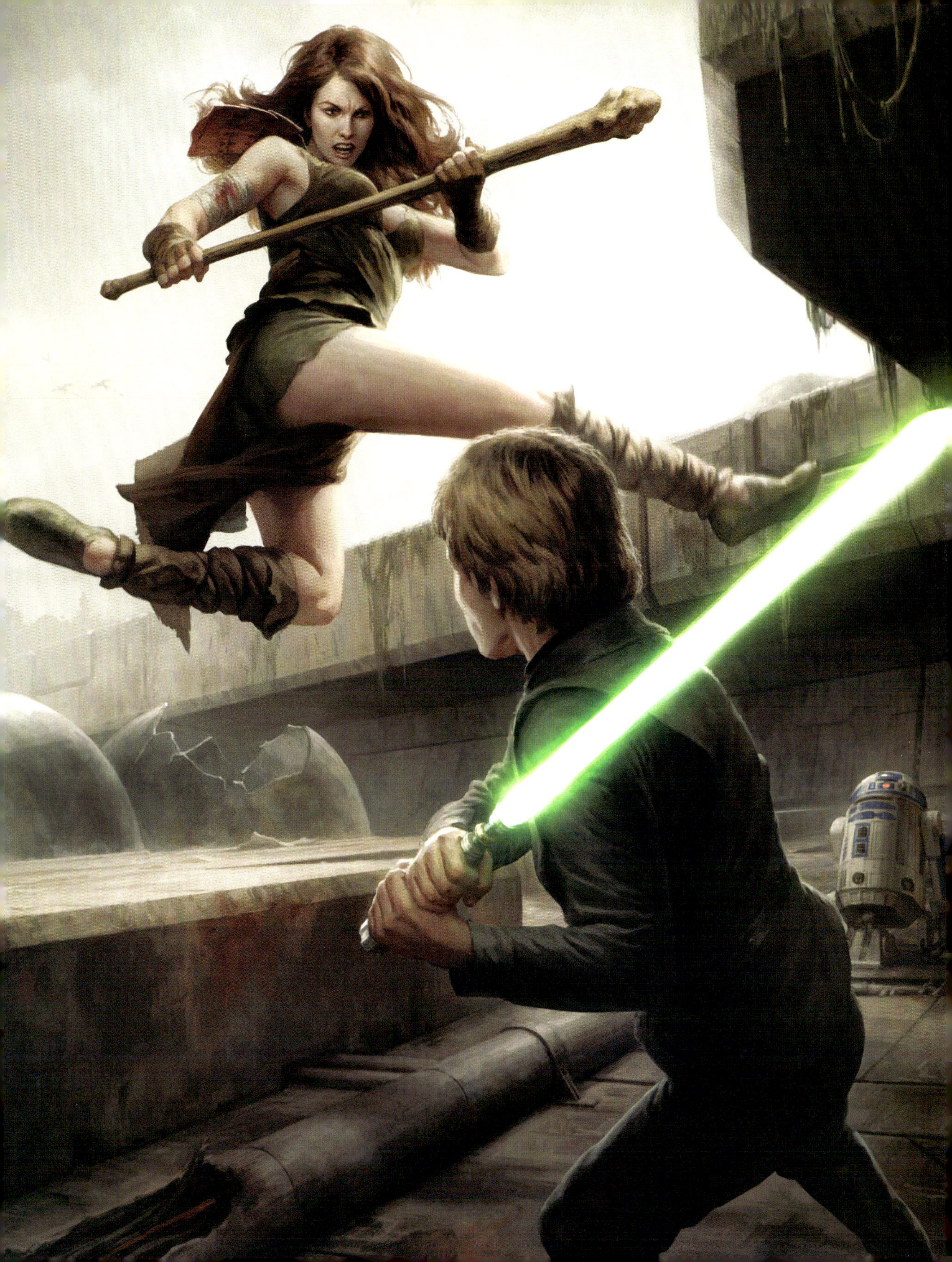

the Jedi training vessel *Chu'unthor*, stranded on Dathomir. Luke joins with Isolder to venture to Dathomir. Luke looks to find the vessel as well as his friends, while Isolder seeks to rescue Leia and reclaim her as his potential betrothed.

The newcomers to Dathomir promptly encounter the Witches of the planet. The warriors of the Singing Mountain Clan are noble and fearless females who enslave males as breeding stock and ride atop trained rancor beasts. The Witch named Teneniel Djo at first wants to enslave Luke and Isolder, but she later comes to respect them. Such is not the case with the wicked Nightsister clan ruled by Gethzerion. They are cruel and evil magic wielders who long to escape the blockaded world. Years earlier, Palpatine was alarmed by their growing power and purposely stranded them on Dathomir.

Zsinj wants Han as his prisoner and orders Gethzerion to deliver him. To ensure her compliance, Zsinj threatens to plunge the entire planet into darkness using an orbital nightcloak. Solo surrenders himself to Gethzerion to spare the world. This act of self-sacrifice causes Leia to realize that she is still in love with Han. Gethzerion hands Han over to Zsinj, demanding transit offworld. Though Zsinj supplies Gethzerion with a shuttle carrier, he has no intention of loosing the Nightsisters upon the galaxy. Zsinj's Star Destroyers blast the carrier, bringing a fiery end to Gethzerion and her coven.

Luke rescues Han with the *Millennium Falcon* before Han becomes Zsinj's prisoner. Han then orchestrates an attack run directly at the bridge of the *Iron Fist*, coming in under its shields and blasting the bridge with concussion missiles, killing Zsinj. The *Falcon* also blasts apart the orbital nightcloak satellites, and the arrival of the Hapan fleet overwhelms Zsinj's remaining forces.

In the aftermath, Luke secures the remains of the *Chu'unthor* on Dathomir. With the knowledge contained therein, he begins to form the solid foundation required to train a new generation of Jedi. Han Solo and Leia Organa are married at a formal ceremony on Coruscant. Isolder's worthy heroics have caught the attentive eye of Teneniel Djo.

THE COURTSHIP OF PRINCESS LEIA is important for the introduction of two cultures that would continue to play major roles in the Expanded Universe and beyond: the Hapans and the Witches of Dathomir.

Dathomir and its magical inhabitants would influence George Lucas directly in the creation of his canonical *Star Wars* universe. In 2008, the videogame Clone Wars: Jedi Alliance used abandoned Episode I concept art in its striking creation of animated Nightsisters, which caught Lucas's attention. He used this incarnation of the Nightsisters to forge backstories for Asajj Ventress, Savage Opress, and Darth Maul in the *Star Wars: The Clone Wars* television series, elevating Dathomir and its Witches to a higher status in the canon than their Expanded Universe origins. The fourth-season episode "Massacre" (2012) sees the Nightsisters wiped out, though their continued presence in the Expanded Universe later in the time line clearly suggests that other clans did survive.

In *Courtship*, Luke is repeatedly described as wielding a blue-bladed lightsaber, though at this point in time he is still using his green-bladed weapon.

"HUTT AND SEEK"

AUTHORS · Chris Cassidy and Tish Pahl, with special thanks to Timothy Zahn

THE NEW REPUBLIC

PUBLICATION HISTORY · Short story, Bantam Spectra Included in *Tales from the New Republic* · Paperback, December 1999

TIME LINE PLACEMENT · 8 ABY

WORLDS VISITED · Nal Hutta [S-12]; Naps Fral Cluster [S-16]; Ryloth [R-17]

MAIN CHARACTERS · Fenig Nabon, smuggler (human female); Ghitsa Dodger, con artist (human female); Shada D'ukal, Mistryl Shadow Warrior (human female); Dunc T'racen, Mistryl Shadow Warrior (human female); Durga, gangster (Hutt)

SUMMARY · The smuggling-and-con-artist duo of Fenig Nabon and Ghitsa Dodger hire a pair of Mistryl Shadow Warriors, Shada D'ukal and Dunc T'racen, to help them transport a cargo of Twi'lek slave girls to Nal Hutta. The proud warrior women are put off by this unsavory assignment. The Shadow Warriors hijack the vessel, eject Fenig and Ghitsa from the ship in an escape pod, and return the Twi'lek slaves to Ryloth—all of which is exactly what Ghitsa had hoped for when she hired them. With their cargo now stolen, Ghitsa is able to report to her client and benefactor, Durga the Hutt, that the Karazak Slavers Cooperative has stolen the Twi'leks. This allows Fenig and Ghitsa to leave Durga's employ and stir up trouble among slaving criminals while sparing the Twi'leks from slavery.

A NEWS REPORT WITHIN the story makes it clear that it occurs during the events of *The Courtship of Princess Leia* (1994), though early in the tale, Fenig reflects on her two years of partnership with Ghitsa. That estimate should be closer to four years given the timing of the story "A Credit for Your Thoughts" (2000).

"CORPHELION INTERLUDE"

AUTHOR · Troy Denning

PUBLICATION HISTORY · Short story, official Del Rey website · February 2003 Compiled in *Tatooine Ghost*, Del Rey Books · Paperback, January 2004

TIME LINE PLACEMENT · 8 ABY

WORLD VISITED · Corphelion [M-7]

MAIN CHARACTERS · Han Solo, captain of the *Millennium Falcon* (human male); Princess Leia Organa Solo, New Republic councilor (human female)

SUMMARY · On their honeymoon, Han takes Leia to witness the spectacle of the Corphelion comets. Upon arriving at the viewing platform, the couple is frustrated by the bustling crowds of tourists who have also come to see the comets. The spectators are scared away when a piece of one breaks off and tracks toward the viewing station. Han, stubborn as always, convinces Leia they are safe, and the two begin to enjoy their moment alone. Leia begins to seductively tease Han into admitting that he arranged this beautiful moment for them. Han, on the other hand, grows more nervous as the comet gets closer and closer. Just as he's about to swallow his pride and admit he had nothing to do with arranging this and that they should flee for safety, the comet veers off and the happy couple are left to enjoy the moment in each other's arms.

A FOREST APART: A CHEWBACCA ADVENTURE

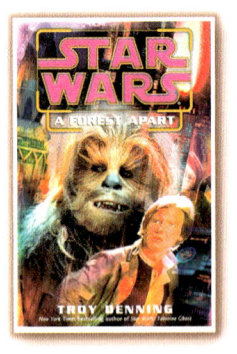

AUTHOR · Troy Denning
COVER ARTIST · Steven D. Anderson
PUBLICATION HISTORY · EBook novella, Del Rey Books
 · February 2003
Included in *Tatooine Ghost*, Del Rey Books
 · Paperback, January 2004
TIME LINE PLACEMENT · 8 ABY
WORLD VISITED · Coruscant [L-9]
MAIN CHARACTERS · Chewbacca, hero (Wookiee male); Lumpawarrump, preadolescent (Wookiee male); Mallatobuck, honor wife (Wookiee female)
SUMMARY · Mallatobuck, Chewbacca's wife, brings their eleven-year-old son Lumpawarrump to Coruscant to spend some time with his father. Lumpy pursues a burglar who attempts to rob the Solos' apartment. Despite his parents' words of caution, the young Wookiee dives after the gaunt, agile thief, following the robber into a service run that cuts deep into the Coruscant underworld. Though Chewbacca is proud of his son's courage, he is dismayed by Lumpy's defiance.

Too large to fit into the hole themselves, Chewbacca and Malla rush to the bottom of the service run, where they discover that Lumpy is already gone, pursuing the burglar into Coruscant's dangerous underlevels. The Wookiees track their son to a secret Imperial detention center concealed in the seamy undercity.

The Wookiees discover that a wayward advanced Imperial IT-3 interrogator droid has been masterminding a plot to assassinate New Republic Provisional Councilors, enlisting underdwellers to do the dirty work programmed into it years earlier by Ysanne Isard. Chewbacca dismantles the droid, ending the surprise threat and teaching Lumpawarrump a valuable lesson about obedience.

Though Lumpy is said to be eleven years old in this story, *Rebel Dawn* (1997) specifies he was born in 1 BBY, meaning he should be about eight or nine here.

TATOOINE GHOST

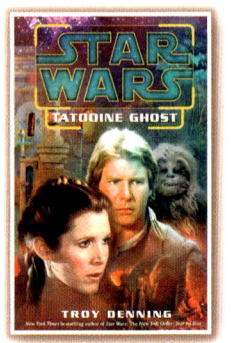

AUTHOR · Troy Denning
COVER ARTIST · Steven D. Anderson
PUBLICATION HISTORY · Novel, Del Rey Books
 · Hardcover, March 2003
 · Paperback, January 2004
TIME LINE PLACEMENT · 8 ABY
WORLD VISITED · Tatooine [R-16]
MAIN CHARACTERS · Princess Leia Organa Solo, New Republic councilor (human female); Han Solo, captain of the *Millennium Falcon* (human male); Kitster Banai, thief (human male); Wald, salvage shop owner (Rodian male); Chewbacca, first mate and mechanic (Wookiee male); C-3PO, protocol droid

Traveling incognito at a bazaar, Han Solo and Leia Organa Solo examine a holocube that contains an image of young Anakin Skywalker.

SUMMARY · Han, Leia, Chewbacca, and C-3PO travel aboard the *Millennium Falcon*, outrunning the Star Destroyer *Chimaera* to arrive on Tatooine. Their objective is to surreptitiously enter an art auction to win *Killik Twilight*, an Alderaanian moss painting. Though impressive enough as a work of art and artifact of the sundered world Alderaan, the painting actually hides a communicator used by Rebel Alliance spies. For this reason, the New Republic does not want it to end up in Imperial hands.

Little do the New Republic heroes know that the Empire now has a military tactical genius in command—a cunning admiral with an affinity for art.

While on Tatooine, Leia comes across an image of nine-year-old Anakin Skywalker and must reconcile the horrible thoughts she carries of her father with the tales of his days as a goodhearted boy. Leia has harbored doubts about parenthood, fearing that her offspring might succumb to the dark side as Anakin once did. Compelled to research Anakin's past, Leia meets Kitster Banai, a childhood friend of Anakin's, and reads a journal once kept by Shmi Skywalker.

The quest for *Killik Twilight* takes a violent turn when Imperials ambush the auction to collect the painting. With the help of shrewd art dealers, a trio of Squibs named Sligh, Emala, and Grees, Leia and Han recover the communications device, while the Imperial forces recover the painting.

THE NEW REPUBLIC

SHORT STORY: The Trouble with Squibs

The Squib hucksters featured in *Tatooine Ghost* would soon make a return appearance in "The Trouble with Squibs," a short story by Troy Denning published in *Star Wars Insider* #67 by Paizo Publishing in May 2003. The story begins with Han and Leia traveling incognito to the underwater casinos of Pavo Prime, following a tip that a criminal is selling off Alderaanian sculptures. They discover Emala and Sligh—two-thirds of the Squib trio—who insist that the New Republic heroes also try to secure a piece of art called *Second Mistake*. That sculpture turns out to be the third Squib, Grees, frozen in carbonite.

Del Rey Books published *Tatooine Ghost* in the midst of producing the New Jedi Order series. It was a step back in the time line, being set during the time frame dominated by the Bantam Spectra novels of the 1990s. Coming as it did after Episodes I and II, *Tatooine Ghost* was able to reference the prequels as the Bantam books never could and extrapolated that Leia was able to overcome her resistance to having children by learning more of Anakin Skywalker's past. Playing a role in the book is Grand Admiral Thrawn, who goes unnamed since the main New Republic heroes do not know of his existence until after the events of the Thrawn Trilogy.

"MISSION TO ZILA"

AUTHOR · Charlene Newcomb
PUBLICATION HISTORY · Short story, West End Games · *Star Wars Adventure Journal* #3, August 1994
TIME LINE PLACEMENT · 8 ABY
WORLD VISITED · Garos IV [P-7]
MAIN CHARACTERS · Alex Winger, underground freedom fighter (human female); Tork Winger, Imperial governor (human male); Chance, underground freedom fighter (human male)
SUMMARY · Alex Winger has moved from the governor's mansion to live at the university, though she still visits her father from time to time. She serves as his pilot when he visits the nearby city of Zila, and she recons the Imperial activity in the area. The underground Garosian resistance movement discovers that the Empire is garrisoning Zila and building a planetary ion cannon to better protect Garos IV from an inevitable New Republic invasion. Guerrillas led by Chance strike at the Imperial supplies, destroying them before they can be put to use.

The chronology of the story is difficult to pin down. Alex is twenty years old, making it two years after her first introduction, which would suggest a chronological setting of 8 ABY. However, the Garosians discuss reports that Coruscant is about to fall to the New Republic, an event described as happening in 7 ABY in *X-Wing: Wedge's Gamble* (1996). Though it would be easiest to assume the Coruscant rumors to be very out of date, the Garosians also have very timely reports that a new Grand Admiral has taken over the Imperial fleet. This suggests a date of 8 ABY.

THE NEW REPUBLIC

"SHADOWS OF DARKNESS"

AUTHOR · Charlene Newcomb

PUBLICATION HISTORY · Short story, West End Games
· *Star Wars Adventure Journal* #4, November, 1994

TIME LINE PLACEMENT · 8 ABY

WORLD VISITED · Garos IV [P-7]

MAIN CHARACTERS · Alex Winger, underground freedom fighter (human female); Carl Barzon, professor and underground leader (human male)

SUMMARY · The Empire begins moving against suspected dissidents on Garos IV, kidnapping the son of Dr. Carl Barzon, a scientist the Empire is pressing into researching cloaking technology. Using the cover of an inspection tour at the Imperial garrison, Alex plants explosives to damage the base's shuttle platform. A mistiming in the detonation results in the death of Dr. Barzon's son, but the Empire does not inform him of the tragedy. Instead, they continue to use the idea of his captive son as leverage against him as they transport Barzon offplanet.

THE THRAWN TRILOGY

HEIR TO THE EMPIRE · DARK FORCE RISING · THE LAST COMMAND

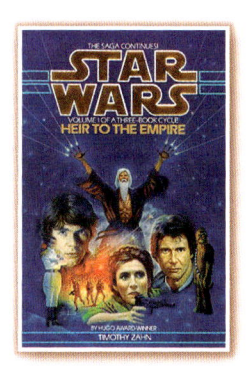

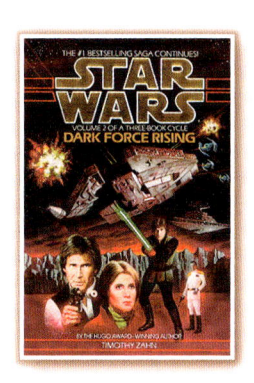

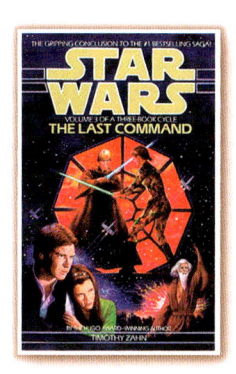

AUTHOR · Timothy Zahn

COVER ARTISTS · Tom Jung (series); Scott Biel (20th anniversary edition)

PUBLICATION HISTORY · Novels, Bantam Spectra

Heir to the Empire
· Hardcover, June 1991
· Paperback, June 1992

20th Anniversary Edition
· Hardcover, September 2011

Dark Force Rising
· Hardcover, June 1992
· Paperback, April 1993

The Last Command
· Hardcover, May 1993
· Paperback, February 1994

THE NEW REPUBLIC

TIME LINE PLACEMENT · 9 ABY

WORLDS VISITED · Abregado-rae [K-13]; Berchest [N-8]; Bilbringi [J-8]; Bimmisaari [R-9]; Bpfassh [M-19]; Chazwa [N-8]; Coruscant [L-9]; Dagobah [M-19]; Endor [H-16]; Hijarna [M-8]; Jomark [R-7]; Kashyyyk [P-9]; Myrkr [N-7]; New Cov [P-14]; Nkllon [L-16]; Obroa-skai (system) [N-8]; Pantolomin [K-9]; Peregrine's Nest [P-14]; Poderis [M-8]; Rishi [S-15]; Sluis Van [M-19]; Tatooine [R-16]; Trogan [R-7]; Ukio [S-15]; Wayland [N-7]; Xa Fel [K-9]

MAIN CHARACTERS · Luke Skywalker, Jedi Knight (human male); Han Solo, captain of the *Millennium Falcon* (human male); Princess Leia Organa Solo, New Republic councilor (human female); Thrawn, Grand Admiral (Chiss male); Mara Jade, former Emperor's Hand (human female); Joruus C'baoth, mad Jedi clone (human male); Talon Karrde, smuggler chief (human male); Lando Calrissian, entrepreneur (human male); Borsk Fey'lya, New Republic councilor (Bothan male); Ackbar, New Republic councilor (Mon Calamari male); Rukh, bodyguard/assassin (Noghri male); Gilad Pellaeon, Imperial captain (human male); Garm Bel Iblis, Corellian general (human male); Winter, councilor aide (human female)

SUMMARY · The Empire has withered to a quarter of its former size as the New Republic continues to consolidate its hold on the galaxy. From the Unknown Regions emerges a new Imperial commander, a mysterious tactical genius named Grand Admiral Thrawn, with an elaborate and grandiose plan to de-

Chewbacca carries Princess Leia Organa Solo to safety by climbing the wroshyr trees of Rwookrrorro.

stroy the New Republic. Commanding the Star Destroyer *Chimaera* with Captain Pellaeon, Thrawn begins an intricate stratagem built from pieces of information gleaned from across the galaxy. From a data raid in the Obroa-skai system, he obtains the location of one of the Emperor's secret storehouses: Mount Tantiss on Wayland. From the forests of Myrkr, he procures a peculiar Force-repelling creature called an ysalamir.

With an ysalamir carried in a specialized backpack, Thrawn arrives on Wayland immune to the Force abilities of Joruus C'baoth, the mad Jedi clone guarding the Emperor's storehouse. C'baoth figures into Thrawn's plans—the loyal Force-sensitive can help coordinate Thrawn's fighting forces to a supernatural degree. The Grand Admiral offers the insane Jedi the promise of new apprentices, since Luke Skywalker endeavors to rebuild the Jedi Order.

On a New Republic diplomatic mission to Bimmisaari, shadowy alien assailants—Thrawn's Noghri death commandos—attack Luke and Leia in a failed kidnapping attempt. Wary of such near misses, a pregnant Leia hides out on Kashyyyk with Chewbacca and his fellow Wookiees as protectors. They defend her from another strike, capturing one of the Noghri, Khabarakh, in the process. Leia is stunned when the Noghri proclaims fealty to her upon discovering—through his powerful sense of smell—that she is biologically related to Darth Vader. The Noghri venerate Vader as a savior.

Elsewhere in the galaxy, when Luke narrowly escapes an Imperial ambush, he is found stranded in space by smugglers Talon Karrde and Mara Jade. Mara is a tight-lipped, intensely focused woman who has been with Karrde's organization for only six months. She seemingly sensed Luke's presence in interstellar space and exhibits an intense hatred of the Jedi. Talon, realizing that Luke may be of great value, keeps him locked up in a supply shed at his headquarters on Myrkr, using the Force-blocking power of the ysalamiri against him.

Han Solo and Lando Calrissian attempt to connect with Karrde's organization, and the courteous smuggler hosts them at Myrkr, all the while keeping Luke's imprisonment a secret from them. Luke escapes, however, and Mara gives pursuit. The two are forced to work side by side to survive the dangers of the forests. Here Luke discovers that Mara was once an Emperor's Hand and that the death of Palpatine destroyed Mara's life.

Thrawn's next major move in his campaign against the New Republic is an attack on the bustling shipyards of Sluis Van. Using specially modified mining equipment stolen from a complex owned by Lando Calrissian, Thrawn's intent is not to destroy the New Republic fleet—but rather to *steal it*. The mining equipment cuts into the control systems of the undercrewed ships, allowing Thrawn's troops to commandeer the vessels. Though the New Republic manages to thwart Thrawn's theft before he can complete it, the victory is costly as it leaves many vessels inoperable.

Compounding the New Republic's difficulties are feats of political overreach and backstabbing from New Republic councilor Borsk Fey'lya. Hoping to more firmly entrench Bothan political power at the expense of the rival Mon Calamari, Fey'lya pounces upon evidence planted by the Empire asserting that Admiral Ackbar was guilty of embezzlement.

Solo and Calrissian embark on a private investigation into these Bothan affairs, which leads them to New Cov. There allies of Fey'lya have been helping Garm Bel Iblis fight his own private war against the Empire. Bel Iblis, a former Corellian Senator and cofounder of the Rebel Alliance, had a falling-out with Mon Mothma. He never joined the New

Republic, opting to wage war on his own. He has gradually come to realize that his pride and his refusal to cooperate have kept him from better helping the cause of freedom in the galaxy.

While with Bel Iblis, Han and Lando find evidence that some of the Corellian Senator's warships were Dreadnoughts from the fabled *Katana* fleet. The two-hundred-ship-strong task force vanished into hyperspace on its maiden voyage during the final decades of the Galactic Republic and has been the subject of treasure-seeking spacer legends ever since. Finding the fleet's heavily armed and armored warships would represent a huge boon to either the Empire or the New Republic. The ever-resourceful Talon Karrde has a lead on the ships. He was once a protégé of Jorj Car'das, a well-informed smuggler who knew of the fleet's location.

Leia voyages to Honoghr, the poisoned homeworld of the Noghri, with her captive would-be assassin, Khabarakh. The honor-bound Noghri keep her hidden on the planet, despite visiting Imperials. Leia learns of the Noghri history: how their planet was poisoned during the Clone Wars by a starship crash, and how Darth Vader engineered a plan to save the planet's crippled agriculture to keep it habitable. Leia's inspection of the decon droids tasked with maintaining Honoghr's crops reveals a deep betrayal—the droids are poisoning the planet just enough to keep the Noghri subservient to the Empire.

Meanwhile, Luke follows rumors of a Jedi Knight ruling on distant Jomark and finds Joruus C'baoth there. C'baoth takes Skywalker under his wing, teaching Luke his distressing authoritarian view of Jedi in society. Luke comes to realize that Joruus is not just touched by the dark side, but also insane.

The hunt for the Katana fleet leads to a standoff between New Republic and Imperial forces in the depths of space. The Empire succeeds in capturing most of the Dreadnoughts, while the New Republic discovers something just as disturbing—the stormtroopers who attacked them during the battle were freshly produced clones. Thrawn has the technology to build an army, and a new era of clone wars may fall upon the galaxy.

At Mount Tantiss, Thrawn uses captured Spaarti cloning cylinders to rapidly produce clones. He uses ysalamiri in the cloning process to prevent the "clone madness" inherent in such fast production. Thrawn has also recovered a prototype cloaking device, which he uses to cleverly place Coruscant under siege. Thrawn has cloaked an unknown number of asteroids and released them above the planet's surface, thus preventing the capital from lowering its shields for fear of a devastating asteroid strike.

While the New Republic is pinned beneath their own shields, Leia Organa gives birth to twins—Jacen and Jaina Solo. Even as infants, they exhibit strength in the Force.

Rallying against Thrawn, and with intelligence offered up by Mara Jade, the New Republic heroes infiltrate the Mount Tantiss storehouse on Wayland. Within a throne room built for the Emperor inside the mountain, the heroes are attacked by Joruus C'baoth. The Jedi madman releases a horrible weapon against Luke—a clone created from Skywalker's severed hand, recovered from Bespin years ago. In the end, Mara strikes down this duplicate. In killing an avatar of Skywalker, Mara releases some of her long-standing animosity toward Luke. Mara also succeeds in killing C'baoth, and explosives tear through the mountain, destroying Thrawn's cloning facility.

At Bilbringi, site of an assault by Thrawn, his fleet is opposed by a coalition of smuggler vessels organized by Talon Karrde as well as New Republic space forces, including Rogue Squadron. Though Thrawn's tactical cunning once again gives him the advantage, he fails to predict one crucial attack. His

In the heart of the Mount Tantiss storehouse, the insane Joruus C'baoth unleashes the cloned Luke Skywalker against the original Luke and Mara Jade.

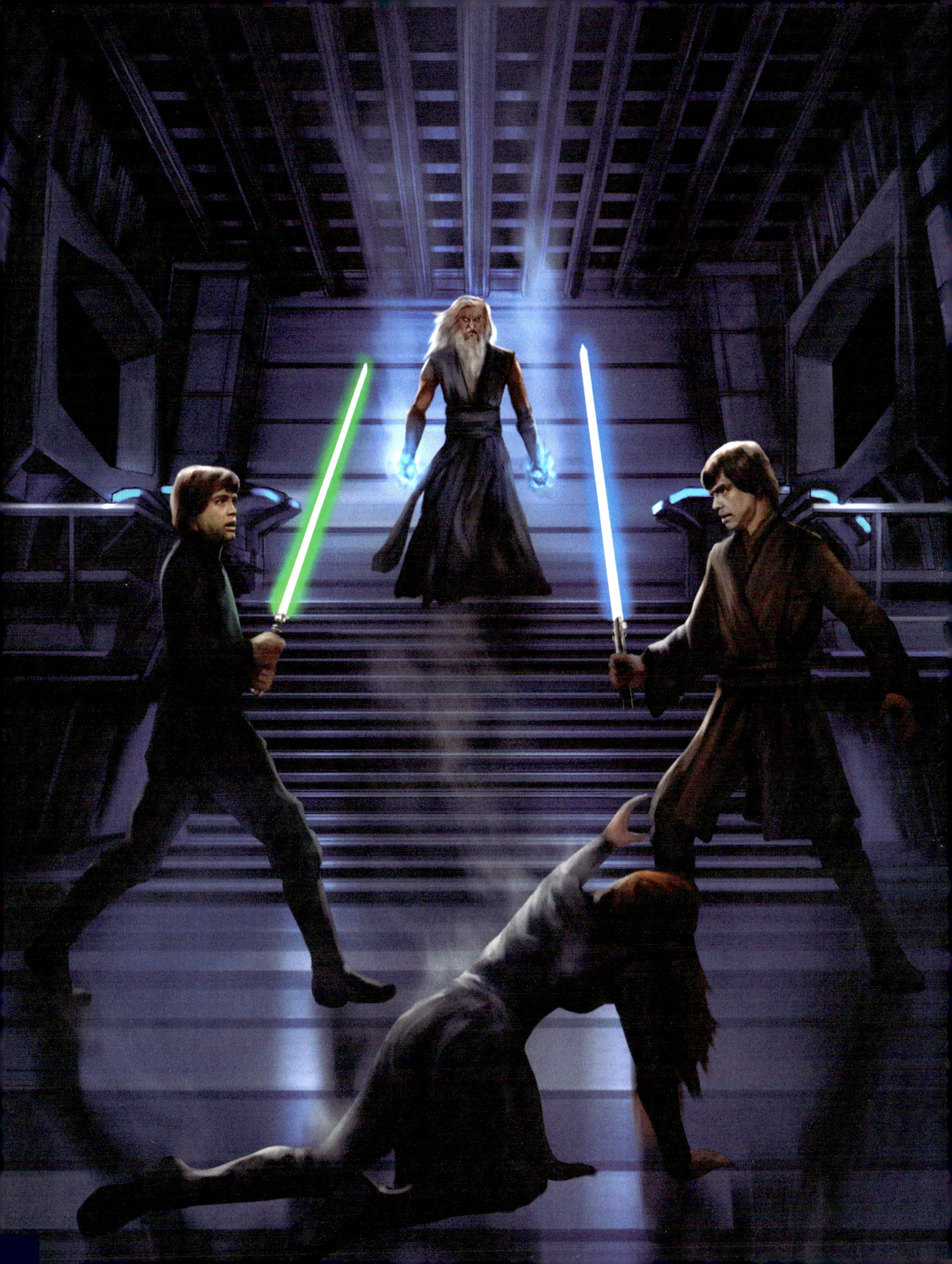

Noghri bodyguard, Rukh, is now aware of the Imperial deception on his homeworld. He stabs Thrawn in the chest, killing the Imperial warlord. Without Thrawn to steer the assault, the Imperial advance collapses, and Pellaeon calls for a retreat.

Perhaps the most influential work of the Expanded Universe, the Thrawn Trilogy successfully relaunched *Star Wars* published storytelling in 1991 and introduced characters such as Grand Admiral Thrawn, Talon Karrde, Mara Jade, Garm Bel Iblis, Borsk Fey'lya, Jacen and Jaina Solo, and Gilad Pellaeon into the *Star Wars* pantheon. These heroes and villains would have long careers in the books that followed.

The first novel of the cycle, *Heir to the Empire*, was honored with a twentieth-anniversary edition in 2011, which included many behind-the-scenes annotations about the creation of the story. It was *Heir* that truly began building the Expanded Universe. Before that, *Star Wars* storytelling was spread across different media, without a determined mandate to construct a consistent setting. As a result, works published from 1977 to 1990 would often contradict one another. With *Heir*, Lucasfilm asked Zahn to coordinate his story with the worldbuilding being undertaken by the *Star Wars: The Roleplaying Game* publisher West End Games, thus ensuring his work fit into a larger whole.

The collective title The Thrawn Trilogy did not come into effect until 1996. Before that, these three books were simply an untitled "3-Book Cycle," and for a time were branded as the Empire Trilogy. This trilogy underwent comic book adaptations by Dark Horse in 1995–98, resulting in three six-issue series devoted to this story.

THE LIFE AND LEGEND OF OBI-WAN KENOBI

AUTHOR · Ryder Windham

COVER ARTIST · Hugh Fleming

PUBLICATION HISTORY · Juvenile novel, Scholastic Inc. · Hardcover, September 2008

TIME LINE PLACEMENT · 9 ABY epilogue, with "present" story taking place in 3.5–4 ABY (with flashbacks to 44 BBY, 32 BBY, 22 BBY, 19 BBY, 17 BBY, 7 BBY, and 0 ABY)

WORLDS VISITED · Coruscant [L-9]; Dagobah [M-19]; Endor [H-16]; Farquar III [Q-11]; Geonosis [R-16]; Ilum [G-7]; Kamino [S-15]; Mustafar [L-19]; Ord Sigatt [N-6]; Tatooine [R-16]

MAIN CHARACTERS · Obi-Wan Kenobi, Jedi Knight (human male); Luke Skywalker, Jedi Knight (human male); A'Sharad Hett, Jedi Knight (human male); Owen Lars, moisture farmer (human male)

SUMMARY · After his devastating duel with Darth Vader on Bespin's Cloud City, Luke Skywalker returns to Obi-Wan Kenobi's hut on Tatooine, where he finds an old journal referencing Kenobi's past. Tales include Obi-Wan finding the crystal that would power his lightsaber while apprenticed to Qui-Gon Jinn, and his first meeting with a colorful prospector named Dexter Jettster. The story recounts Kenobi's introduction to Anakin Skywalker, and how the youngster came to be his apprentice. When Anakin was a boy, he met A'Sharad Hett in the Jedi Temple, a fellow Tatooine denizen who was

THE NEW REPUBLIC

raised by a Jedi Master who adopted the Tusken Raider culture as his own.

Other reflections include moments from the Clone Wars, as well as Obi-Wan's exile as "Old Ben" Kenobi on Tatooine, keeping a vigilant watch on young Luke Skywalker. Obi-Wan encounters A'Sharad Hett leading Tusken Raider attacks on the settlers on Tatooine and challenges him to a duel. Obi-Wan defeats Hett and makes him swear to leave Tatooine and never return.

Skywalker completes his lightsaber, and later helps redeem his father during a fateful confrontation with the Emperor on the second Death Star. Anakin's restored spirit meets with Obi-Wan in the afterlife.

Years later, a vision of Obi-Wan comes to Luke in a dream and tells him that he will no longer be able to visit him. Obi-Wan declares that Luke is the first in a new Order of Jedi Knights.

A TIME-HOPPING flashback-filled story, this installment of the Scholastic biography series has as its framing device Luke reading through an old journal kept by Obi-Wan. The chronological "present" in the story is the time Luke spent in Ben's old hut between Episode V and Episode VI, as depicted in *Shadows of the Empire* (1996). It is placed here in the *Reader's Companion* because the epilogue is from *Heir to the Empire* (1991), meaning the latest chronological point of the story is 9 ABY.

A'Sharad Hett was a character introduced in the *Outlander* story arc of the *Star Wars: Republic* comics from Dark Horse Comics, published in 1999. His future would be revealed in the *Star Wars Legacy* comics (2006–10).

X-WING: ISARD'S REVENGE

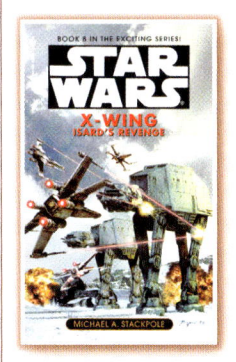

AUTHOR · Michael A. Stackpole
COVER ARTIST · Paul Youll
PUBLICATION HISTORY ·
Novel, Bantam Spectra
· Paperback, April 1999
TIME LINE PLACEMENT · 9 ABY
WORLDS VISITED · Bilbringi [J-8]; Brentaal [L-9]; Ciutric [N-5]; Commenor [N-10]; Coruscant [L-9]; Corvis Minor (system) [N-5]; Liinade III [N-5]

MAIN CHARACTERS · Corran Horn, X-wing pilot (human male); Wedge Antilles, New Republic general (human male); Delak Krennel, Prince-Admiral (human cyborg male); Ysanne Isard, former head of Imperial Intelligence (human female); Ysanne Isard, clone (human female); Gavin Darklighter, X-wing pilot (human male); Asyr Sei'lar, X-wing pilot (Bothan female); Captain Page, New Republic commando (human male); Iella Wessiri, New Republic Intelligence agent (human female); Booster Terrik, smuggler (human male); Mirax Terrik, smuggler (human female); Whistler, astromech droid

SUMMARY · Wedge Antilles finally accepts a promotion to general, and Rogue Squadron is given its new assignment: the liberation of the Ciutric Hegemony from the iron hand of Prince-Admiral Delak Krennel, an Imperial warlord. This mission is also an opportunity for Corran Horn to locate the lost prisoners of the *Lusankya* prison complex, hidden by Ysanne Isard after her retreat from Coruscant. When a former prisoner surfaces at a Rogue

THE NEW REPUBLIC 309

Squadron gathering only to die a bloody death from a surgically implanted booby trap inadvertently triggered by Corran, two disturbing facts become clear: the New Republic is infiltrated by spies, and someone is deliberately trying to goad Rogue Squadron into a trap.

Chasing down leads to Commenor lets Rogue Squadron uncover more prisoners from the *Lusankya*, who report that Ysanne Isard is still alive. She appears to be allied with Prince-Admiral Krennel, attempting to elevate him to Emperor. Krennel is careful to present himself to the HoloNet media as a benevolent man, subject to unreasonable persecution by the New Republic.

Pursuing ultimately spurious rumors of Krennel devising a superweapon draws Rogue Squadron into a deadly trap in the Corvis Minor system. The Rogues lose two members, but the rest of the squadron is saved by a TIE defender squadron answering to Ysanne Isard. She reveals that she is attempting to topple Krennel from power. The Prince-Admiral holds the *Lusankya* prisoners on Ciutric and has been colluding with a clone of Ysanne Isard. The Rogues reluctantly agree to help her in her mission.

Posing as defecting TIE fighter pilots, the Rogues infiltrate Krennel's forces, spearheading an attack that is backed by the New Republic fleet. The Rogues free the Ciutric prisoners, including Jan Dodonna, and destroy Krennel and Isard's clone. The real Isard, duplicitous as ever, uses the New Republic's focus on Ciutric to launch a mission to liberate and steal back the *Lusankya* Star Destroyer. Iella Wessiri, Booster Terrik, and Mirax Terrik see through Isard's plan and stop her. Iella shoots her dead.

Though the Rogues succeed, for Gavin Darklighter, this victory is overshadowed. His beloved Asyr Sei'lar was apparently lost in battle. She in truth survived to work undercover to reform Bothan society to stop abuses of power such as those exhibited by the conniving Borsk Fey'lya.

"RENDEZVOUS WITH DESTINY"

AUTHOR · Charlene Newcomb

PUBLICATION HISTORY · Short story, West End Games · *Star Wars Adventure Journal* #6, May 1995

TIME LINE PLACEMENT · 9 ABY

WORLDS VISITED · Coruscant (in a vision) [L-9]; Garos IV [P-7]; Sarahwiee [P-7]

MAIN CHARACTERS · Alex Winger, underground freedom fighter (human female); Tere Metallo, freighter captain (Riileb female); Carl Barzon, professor and underground leader (human male); Luke Skywalker, Jedi Knight (human male)

SUMMARY · Following visions granted to her by the Force, Alex Winger stows away on the starship *Star Quest*, a freighter operated by Tere Metallo, an independent pilot carrying out a mission for the New Republic. Metallo plans to insert a crippling computer virus into the systems of an Imperial research base on Sarahwiee. This coincides with a strike carried out by Page's Commandos. At the research base, Alex finds and frees Carl Barzon from imprisonment and meets Luke Skywalker—the subject of repeated Force visions she has been having. Luke is part of the commando mission to destroy the base. The commandos succeed, and Luke offers Alex guidance in using her natural Force sensitivity.

"BLAZE OF GLORY"

AUTHOR · Tony Russo

PUBLICATION HISTORY · Short story, West End Games
· *Star Wars Adventure Journal* #8, November 1995
Included in *Tales from the Empire*, Bantam Spectra
· Paperback, November 1997

TIME LINE PLACEMENT · 9 ABY

WORLD VISITED · Gabredor III [K-4]

MAIN CHARACTERS · Brixie Ergo, mercenary combat medic (human female); Sully Tigereye, mercenary leader (Trunsk male); Lex "Mad Vornskr" Kempo, mercenary pathfinder (human male); Hugo Cutter, mercenary demolitions expert (human male); Greezim Trentacal, slave master (human male)

SUMMARY · The Red Moons mercenary team was originally aligned with the New Republic but went independent when its members grew impatient with the new government's pace of bringing freedom to those still under the oppression of the Empire. The Red Moons crash-land in the jungle of Gabredor III on their mission to liberate slaves held by the Karazak Slavers Guild. It is Brixie Ergo's first assignment with the tough-as-nails merc group, and she experiences their skills and devotion firsthand as they storm the slavers' camp and free the captives. Lex Kempo sacrifices himself in the course of the mission.

"BETRAYAL BY KNIGHT"

AUTHORS · Patricia A. Jackson and Charlene Newcomb

PUBLICATION HISTORY · Short story, West End Games
· *Star Wars Adventure Journal* #12, February 1997

TIME LINE PLACEMENT · 9 ABY

WORLD VISITED · Garos IV [P-7]

MAIN CHARACTERS · Alex Winger, underground freedom fighter (human female); Jaalib Brandl, actor/Imperial Dark Jedi (human male); Tork Winger, Imperial governor (human male)

SUMMARY · The Empire prepares to evacuate Garos IV as a New Republic invasion force approaches. Leading the Imperial efforts is Jaalib Brandl, Dark Jedi, actor, and son of Adalric Brandl. Jaalib is intrigued by Alex Winger, the governor's daughter, and recognizes Force sensitivity within her. The shocking bombing of a pub near the Imperial headquarters prompts Jaalib to sequester Governor Winger and Alex in a safehouse. Alex does not want to leave Garos and finally admits to her father that she has been a member of the resistance for five years.

Alex leaves the safehouse to collect her thoughts. Encountering Jaalib, she realizes that he was responsible for the bombing. He reveals his dark agenda: he wishes to decisively break his ties with the Empire, and to that end he will assassinate the loyal Governor Winger. The safehouse explodes with Governor Winger still inside.

Alex rushes to her injured father and touches the power of the dark side to stabilize his fading life signs. Governor Winger will live, while Alex has learned to beware the power of the dark side. Jaalib respects her, and he leaves the Imperial service to vanish into the galaxy.

"RETREAT FROM CORUSCANT"

AUTHOR · Laurie Burns
PUBLICATION HISTORY · Short story, West End Games · *Star Wars Adventure Journal #7*, August 1995 Included in *Tales from the Empire*, Bantam Spectra · Paperback, November 1997
TIME LINE PLACEMENT · 10 ABY
WORLD VISITED · Coruscant [L-9]
MAIN CHARACTERS · Taryn Clancy, courier (human female); Jak Bremen, New Republic Security officer (human male); Del Sato, courier (human male); Garm Bel Iblis, New Republic Security officer (human male); Mara Jade, Smugglers' Alliance representative (human female)
SUMMARY · Courier freighter captain Taryn Clancy and her ship, the *Messenger*, are trapped beneath the planetary shields of Coruscant when the reinvigorated Imperial forces attack the capital. The New Republic signals a full-scale evacuation of the city planet. General Garm Bel Iblis commandeers Taryn's ship, appointing Colonel Jak Bremen to serve aboard as Taryn must deliver vital information to the New Republic fleet. Avoiding Imperial pursuit and bluffing her way past an Imperial inspection, Taryn succeeds in delivering a secure message regarding a new rendezvous point to the fleet.

"NO DISINTEGRATIONS, PLEASE"

AUTHOR · Paul Danner
PUBLICATION HISTORY · Short story, West End Games · *Star Wars Adventure Journal #14*, August 1997 Included in *Tales from the New Republic*, Bantam Spectra · Paperback, December 1999
TIME LINE PLACEMENT · c. 10 ABY (with flashback to 1 ABY)
WORLDS VISITED · Ladarra [P-5]; Vryssa (in flashback) [K-19]
MAIN CHARACTERS · Boba Fett, bounty hunter (human male); Rivo Xarran, slicer/fugitive (human male)
SUMMARY · A storyteller spins a tale about Boba Fett for urchins. In the story, Fett is hired to track down a fugitive slicer for Jabba the Hutt. His quarry, Rivo Xarran, is being harbored by his brother, Imperial General Gaege Xarran in a garrison base. Fett decimates the Imperial forces. Fett allows Rivo to barter for his life but also promises to one day finish the job. As the storyteller finishes his tale, he is visited by Boba Fett. Jabba, and thus the bounty placed on Rivo Xarran, is long dead. Fett gives the storyteller, who is revealed to be Rivo, credits equal to his bounty before departing.

Beyond Jabba the Hutt already being dead, there is no specific indication as to when the story is being told. The *Companion* estimates it occurs around the time of Fett's return to public activity in the *Dark Empire* comics.

THE NEW REPUBLIC

SPOTLIGHT   Meanwhile in Comics: The *Dark Empire* Saga

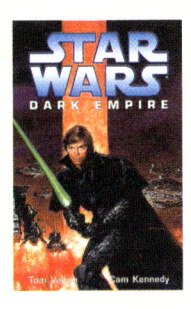

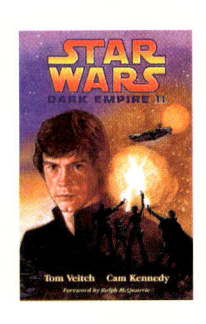

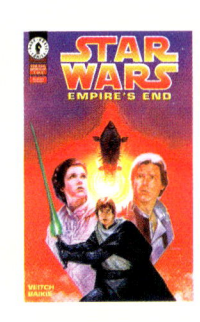

By the mid-1990s, one of the questions most commonly asked by *Star Wars* novel readers who had never perused the rich universe of *Star Wars* comics was "Which novel was it when Luke fell to the dark side?"

The answer was the *Dark Empire* comics series published by Dark Horse Comics in 1991–92. The series was as influential and important to the world of *Star Wars* sequential art storytelling as *Heir to the Empire* was to prose fiction. Written by Tom Veitch and illustrated by Cam Kennedy, *Dark Empire* depicted seismic events that would be folded into the Expanded Universe fabric of the novels. *Dark Empire* was originally envisioned as taking place immediately after the events of *Return of the Jedi*, its story developed before the mandate of an all-encompassing continuity. Timothy Zahn, in the midst of developing the Thrawn Trilogy, found the events of *Dark Empire* incompatible with his story, so the comics tale was moved after the novels, to 10 ABY.

This led to some complications. In *Dark Empire*, Coruscant is devastated by warfare, and the New Republic is based out of Da Soocha V. Text pages that accompanied the individual issues of *Dark Empire* elaborated that Imperial factions, emboldened by Thrawn's progress, launched an attack on the capital that pushed the New Republic off the planet. *The Dark Empire Sourcebook* (1993) from West End Games would make great strides in smoothing over the transition from the Thrawn Trilogy to the events of the comics.

And what events they were: Luke Skywalker discovers that Emperor Palpatine had transferred his life essence into a clone after his corporeal death, attaining a state of immortality accessible through the dark side. Luke gives in to the dark side to learn how to stop the Emperor. Han and Leia encounter Boba Fett, alive and well and back on the hunt, while on the smugglers' moon, Nar Shaddaa. And Leia carries a third child, Anakin Solo, in her womb.

Dark Empire would be followed by *Dark Empire II* (1994–95) and *Empire's End* (1995), tales that would see the Emperor's final death and the defeat of his campaign.

THE NEW REPUBLIC

THE JEDI ACADEMY TRILOGY

JEDI SEARCH · DARK APPRENTICE · CHAMPIONS OF THE FORCE

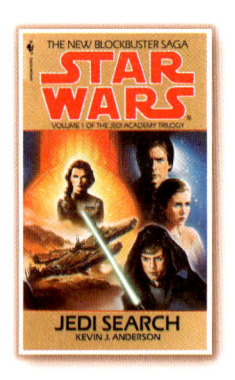

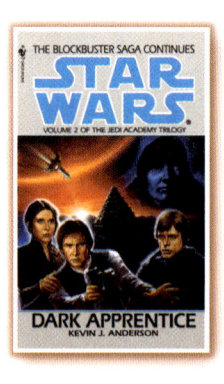

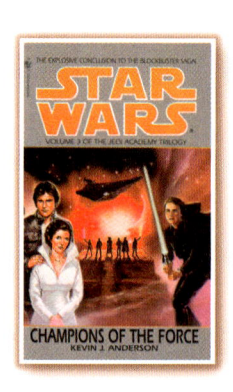

AUTHOR · Kevin J. Anderson

COVER ARTIST · John Alvin

PUBLICATION HISTORY · Novels, Bantam Spectra

Jedi Search
 · Paperback, March 1994

Dark Apprentice
 · Paperback, July 1994

Champions of the Force
 · Paperback, October 1994

TIME LINE PLACEMENT · 11 ABY

WORLDS VISITED · Anoth [J-20]; Bespin [K-18]; Carida [M-9]; Cauldron Nebula [P-3]; Coruscant [L-9]; Dantooine [L-4]; Eol Sha [P-3]; Kessel [T-10]; Mon Calamari [U-6]; Umgul [N-16]; Vortex [K-7]; Yavin 4 [P-6]

MAIN CHARACTERS · Luke Skywalker, Jedi Master (human male); Han Solo, captain of the *Millennium Falcon* (human male); Kyp Durron, Jedi apprentice (human male); Princess Leia Organa Solo, New Republic Minister of State (human female); Natasi Daala, Imperial admiral (human female); Chewbacca, copilot and mechanic (Wookiee male); Qwi Xux, scientist (Omwati female); Moruth Doole, Kessel administrator (Rybet male); Furgan, ambassador (Caridan male); Mon Mothma, Chief of State (human female); Ackbar, New Republic admiral (Mon Calamari male); Cilghal, Jedi healer (Mon Calamari female)

SUMMARY · On a diplomatic mission for the New Republic, the *Millennium Falcon* is shot down over Kessel, and Han Solo and Chewbacca are imprisoned within the grueling spice mines of the forsaken world. Moruth Doole, paranoid administrator of the mines, is afraid the new government will take control of his operations. While imprisoned, Han and Chewie befriend Kyp Durron, a young Force-sensitive who helps them escape the pitch-black tunnels and commandeer an Imperial shuttle. Fleeing Kessel, Kyp uses the Force to navigate a path to safety through the black holes of the Maw and stumbles upon the Maw Installation, a secret Imperial research facility under the command of Admiral Daala. Han, Chewie, and Kyp once again find themselves prisoners.

Young Jacen Solo, guided in the Force by the incapacitated Luke Skywalker, defends his uncle's body from creatures of the dark side.

THE NEW REPUBLIC

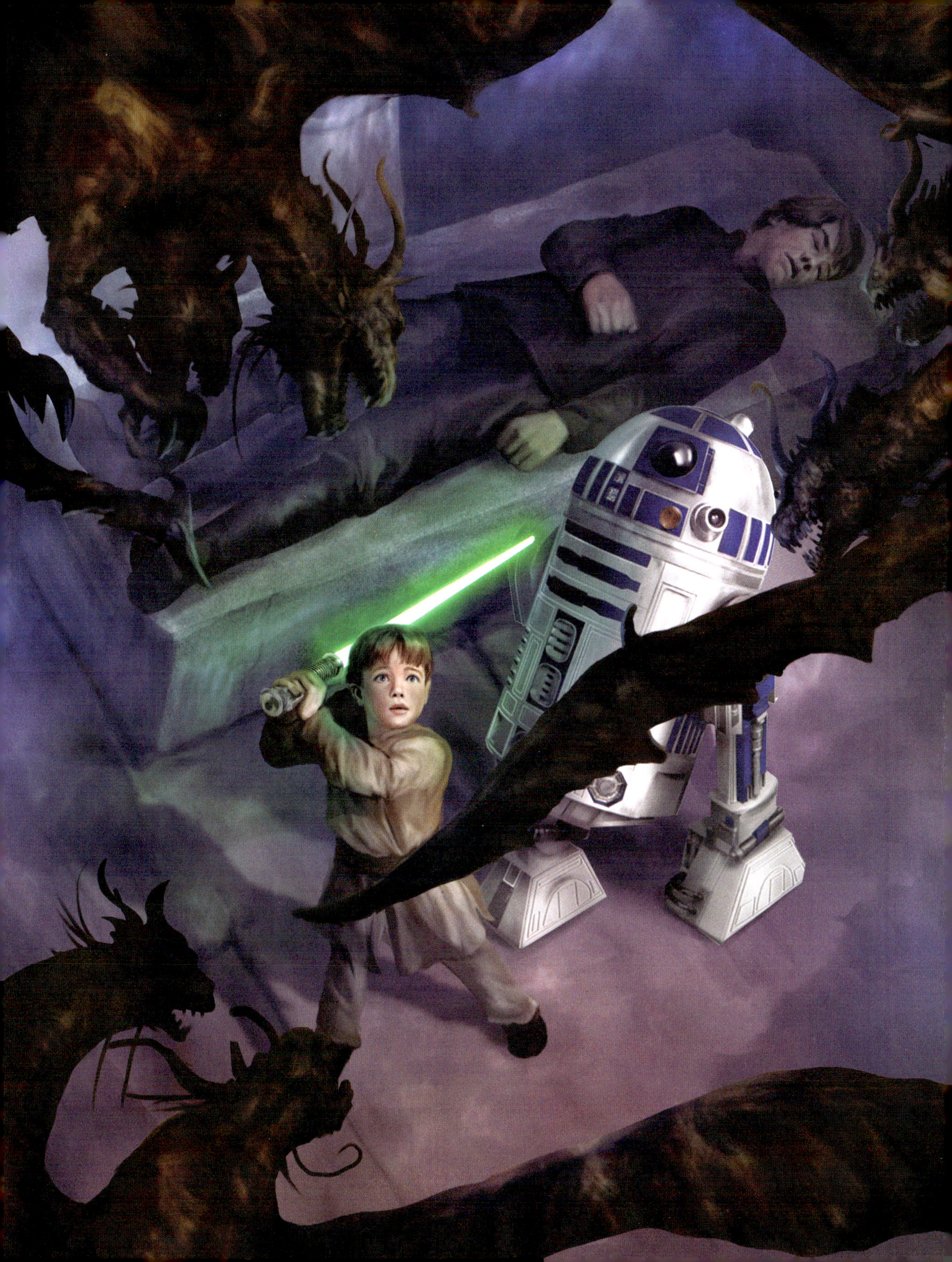

At the Maw Installation, they befriend Qwi Xux, a brilliant but naïve Imperial scientist who was part of the team that helped engineer the Death Star. Han explains to her how her scientific breakthroughs were used for massive destruction. Qwi is shocked by this, and in a conscientious effort to redeem her work she helps the new prisoners escape aboard a new experimental weapon, the Sun Crusher. The weapon is a small vessel protected by nigh-indestructible quantum-crystalline armor and armed with resonance torpedoes that can provoke a supernova in a targeted star, thus wiping out entire star systems. Rather than let such a potent weapon fall into irresponsible hands, the New Republic sinks the Sun Crusher into the depths of the gas giant Yavin.

Luke Skywalker sets out to establish a Jedi academy to begin training a new generation of Jedi Knights. Using partial records captured from scattered sources, Luke finds twelve Force-sensitive candidates to train, including Gantoris of Eol Sha, Streen of Bespin, Kirana Ti of the Dathomirian Witches, the cloned Dorsk 81, and Kyp Durron, who exhibits enormous Force potential. Luke sets up his training center in the abandoned temples of Yavin 4, where the Rebels previously hid their headquarters.

The New Republic suffers a series of tragedies and setbacks. Mon Mothma falls ill with a mysterious wasting disease and asks for Leia to serve in her stead. Admiral Ackbar, while visiting the planet Vortex, suffers inexplicable mechanical failure in his modified B-wing fighter, crashing the vessel and killing hundreds of innocents. Inconsolable, Ackbar resigns his command. Admiral Daala, now aware of the state of the galaxy outside the Maw Cluster, begins a battery of attacks against the New Republic, striking at Dantooine and Mon Calamari.

On Yavin 4, the spirit of Exar Kun—a long-dead Sith Lord—begins to corrupt Luke's students. First, Gantoris falls to the dark side and attempts to attack Luke and then is utterly destroyed by the Sith spirit. Then Kun possesses Kyp. Doing Kun's bidding, Kyp attacks and incapacitates Luke, then steals the Sun Crusher vessel, resurrecting it from the heart of Yavin. He wipes Qwi Xux's memories to ensure that the technological knowledge required to build such devices is lost. In a strike of vengeance against Admiral Daala, Kyp uses the Sun Crusher to ignite the stars of the Cauldron Nebula, causing a devastating explosion that Daala narrowly avoids. Kyp, an instrument of destruction, adopts the mantle of Dark Lord of the Sith.

Luke's Jedi students band together to protect his body from the dark side and do battle with the spirit of the Sith Lord. Even young Jacen Solo, just three years old, picks up a lightsaber—guided by Luke's spirit—to defend his uncle. Luke is revived, but the threat of Exar Kun remains.

The possessed Kyp next targets the Carida system in his swath of vengeance-fueled destruction.

SHORT STORY "Firestorm"

Published in *Star Wars Adventure Journal* #15 (1997), "Firestorm" is a short story by Kevin J. Anderson set during his Jedi Academy Trilogy. As Luke Skywalker establishes his Jedi praxeum on Yavin 4, he follows a lead that brings him to Exis Station, an ancient space station in the Teedio system once used as an outpost by the Jedi. There he encounters Tionne, a scholar of Jedi lore. Tionne and Luke uncover the ancient Jedi records of Nomi Sunrider and leave the station before Teedio's stellar eruptions prove too dangerous. Luke extends an invitation to Tionne to join his Jedi academy.

He comes to the horrific realization that his brother, Zeth, is stationed on Carida. Kyp fails to rescue him before the world is eradicated by the star's explosion.

Mon Mothma's illness is a nanovirus engineered by Ambassador Furgan of Carida, who has been using such deceptive measures to unsettle the New Republic. His agent, Terpfen, was subjected to mind control and sabotaged Ackbar's fighter. Luke's student Cilghal uses her Force healing abilities to remove the virus from Mothma's body, but Furgan continues his strikes, this time attacking the planet Anoth, where the youngest Solo child, Anakin, resides. Ackbar and Winter defend the child, and Terpfen, shaking off his programming, kills Furgan.

Han Solo is able to reach out to Kyp and get him to surrender. New Republic officials call for Kyp's execution for punishment of his crimes, but he instead takes up arms against Admiral Daala's renewed campaign. She has returned to the Maw and unleashed another experimental weapon against the New Republic—a prototype Death Star. In a final battle over Kessel, adjacent to the Maw Cluster, Kyp uses the Sun Crusher to destroy the Imperial weapon, then drops the Sun Crusher into a black hole before escaping within a messenger capsule.

The Kessel operation is in shambles after Daala's attack, but Lando Calrissian sees an opportunity to rebuild it. The spirit of Exar Kun is exorcised from Kyp, and he heals from the ordeal of Sith possession. Daala escapes aboard the Star Destroyer *Gorgon* and flees into space.

Though Mon Mothma is regaining her

Possessed by the spirit of ancient Sith Lord Exar Kun, Jedi apprentice Kyp Durron readies the Sun Crusher superweapon.

health, she nonetheless relinquishes her title of Chief of State, bestowing it upon Leia as her successor.

THE ORIGINAL OUTLINE for the Jedi Academy Trilogy had Mon Mothma die as a result of her infection. Lucasfilm rejected the idea, keeping Mothma alive in books through the end of the New Republic era.

I, JEDI

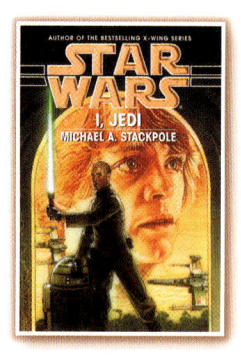

AUTHOR ·
Michael A. Stackpole

COVER ARTIST ·
Drew Struzan

PUBLICATION HISTORY ·
Novel, Bantam Spectra
· Hardcover, May 1998
· Paperback, June 1999

TIME LINE PLACEMENT · 11 ABY

WORLDS VISITED · Corellia [M-11]; Coruscant [L-9]; Khuiumin (system) [O-18]; Kerilt [P-15]; K'vath (system) [M-16]; Suarbi (system) [O-19]; Xa Fel [K-9]; Yavin 4 [P-6]

MAIN CHARACTERS · Corran Horn, Jedi apprentice (human male); Leonia Tavira, pirate leader (human female); Luke Skywalker, Jedi Master (human male); Elegos A'Kla, Trustant (Caamasi male); Mirax Terrik Horn, pilot (human female); Rostek Horn, retired CorSec (human male)

SUMMARY · After returning from a Rogue Squadron mission against the Invid pirates, Corran Horn finds his wife, Mirax, missing from their Coruscant apartment. He feels a disturbance in the Force and seeks counsel from Luke Skywalker, who is setting up his Jedi academy on Yavin 4. Corran accepts Luke's invitation to train as a Jedi. He adopts the alias Keiran Halcyon during his studies, the name of his Jedi ancestor. Corran is witness to the spirit Exar Kun's attempts to corrupt Jedi students. Kun offers him a gift of power—enough to find his wife and destroy his enemies—but Corran refuses.

After the threat of Exar Kun is dispelled, Corran is disgusted that Kyp Durron is not brought to justice for his crimes while possessed. Corran resigns from the academy, returning to Corellia to seek advice from his stepgrandfather, Rostek Horn. Corran decides to rely more on his CorSec training than his Jedi gifts as he adopts an alias to infiltrate the Invid pirates.

He begins at Courkrus, flying with the Khuiumin Survivors pirate gang, working his way up the ranks with his daring and crack piloting skills. Corran draws the amorous eye of Leonia Tavira, pirate leader and ex-Moff. He resists her advances, staying loyal to Mirax. He surreptitiously constructs his own lightsaber. Corran joins the Invid raid on a Caamasi colony on Kerilt. There he meets Elegos A'Kla, a nephew of a Caamasi who was friends with Nejaa Halcyon, Corran's grandfather. Corran comes to realize that to have the best chance at finding his wife, he must embrace all aspects of himself—including his Jedi heritage.

To protect her group against Jedi reprisals, Leonia Tavira recruits a team of Jedi-like Jensaarai, mercenaries from a splinter order of Force-sensitives. Corran gets help from Luke Skywalker and Ooryl Qrygg, and together they are able to finally track Mirax to Susevfi, where Corran rescues her. With Mirax now safe, Corran uses a Force technique to plant an image in Tavira's mind of the Sun Crusher pursuing her ship. The image strikes terror in her, and she flees the system, leaving her Jensaarai mercenaries behind to reconcile with the Jedi and the New Republic.

I, Jedi and the Jedi Academy Trilogy have chapters that occur simultaneously and tell the same story from different vantage points. It is this *Companion*'s recommendation that the Jedi Academy Trilogy be read first and then *I, Jedi*, since the latter novel reveals the surprises of the former books.

The Jedi Academy Trilogy describes in detail only a few members of Luke's initial class of Jedi apprentices, leaving room for the anonymous few to be filled in afterward. Such is the case with Corran Horn, who was not yet developed when the trilogy was published in 1995.

CHILDREN OF THE JEDI

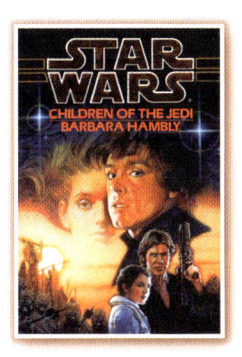

AUTHOR · Barbara Hambly

COVER ARTIST · Drew Struzan

PUBLICATION HISTORY · Novel, Bantam Spectra
- Hardcover, May 1995
- Paperback, July 1996

TIME LINE PLACEMENT · 12 ABY

WORLDS VISITED · Belsavis [L-18]; Ithor [M-6]; Moonflower Nebula [U-16]; Pzob [T-15]

MAIN CHARACTERS · Luke Skywalker, Jedi Master (human male); Callista Masana, Jedi Knight (disembodied human female); Princess Leia Organa Solo, New Republic Chief of State (human female); Han Solo, captain of the *Millennium Falcon* (human male); C-3PO, protocol droid; Cray Mingla, Jedi student (human female); Nichos Marr, Jedi student (human male transferred into droid body)

SUMMARY · At a diplomatic reception on Ithor, Leia and Han are accosted by Drub McKumb, a delirious, bedraggled smuggler who in fits of raging incoherence rails about an old Jedi sanctuary on Belsavis. Luke, along with his Jedi students Cray Mingla and Nichos Marr and the droid C-3PO, follows a separate lead into the depths of the Moonflower Nebula, where their ship is attacked by an automated, asteroid-like construct and they are taken aboard.

The vessel is the *Eye of Palpatine*, a pre-programmed battlemoon that has been reactivated and is carrying out its decades-old mission to collect stormtroopers from secret billets across scattered worlds and attack the Belsavis refuge. In its attempt to gather the troops, the dreadnaught instead draws natives from the worlds it visits and subjects them to brainwashing, amassing a mismatched army of Gamorreans, Tusken Raiders, Kitonaks, Talz, and Affytechans who believe themselves to be Imperial troops. Aboard the *Eye of Palpatine*, Luke discovers the disembodied consciousness of Callista, a Jedi of the Galactic Republic. Years earlier, in an attempt to stop the battlemoon, Callista and her lover Geith sacrificed themselves. Geith died and Callista shed her corporeal form to stop the computerized intelligence that operated the battlemoon.

At Belsavis, Han and Leia's investigations uncover Roganda Ismaren, a former concubine of the Emperor whose son, Irek, is a powerful Force-sensitive who has been surgically enhanced with a transmitter that allows him to control machinery. It was Irek, carrying out his mother's commands, who reactivated the *Eye of Palpatine*.

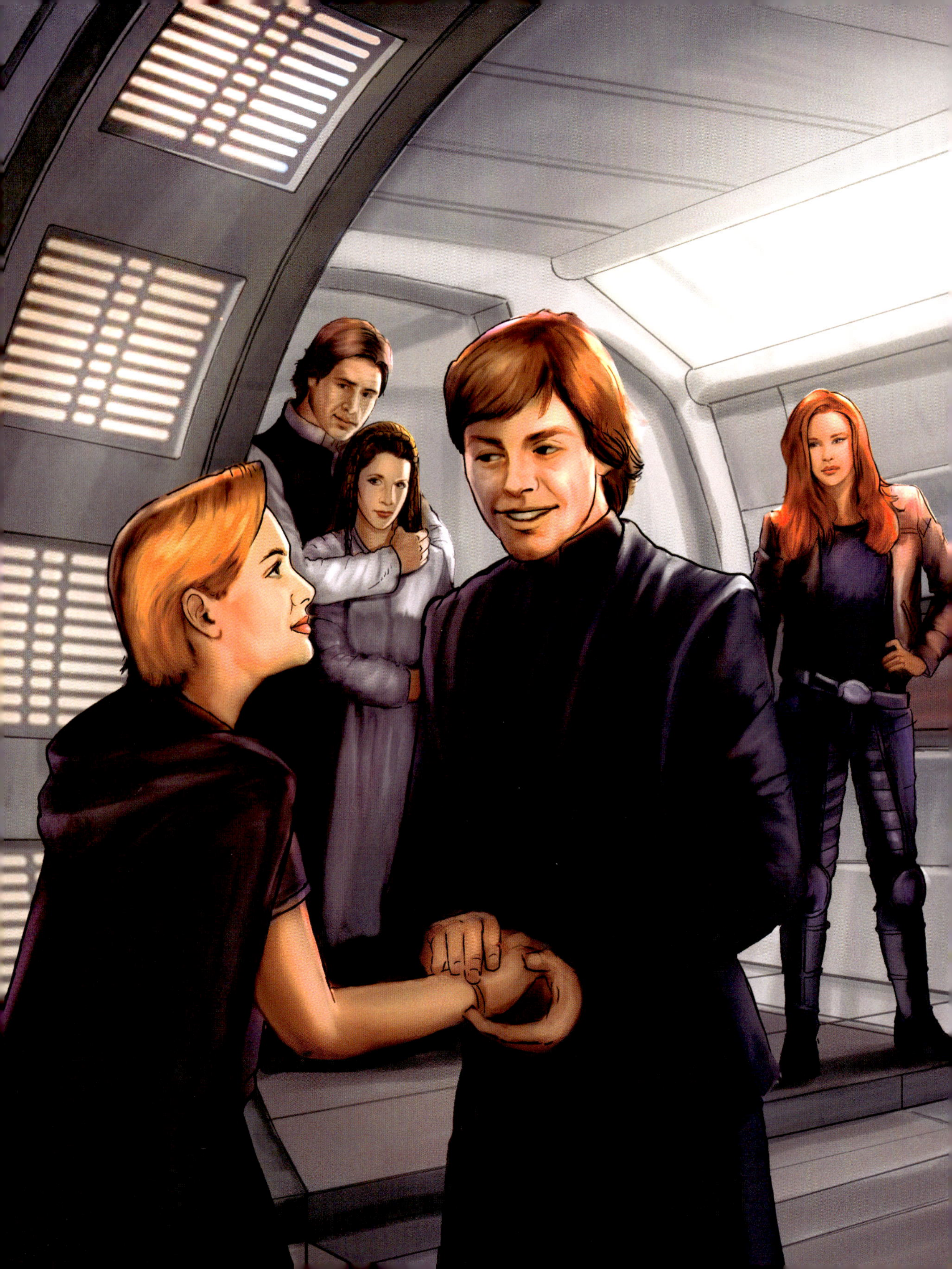

In surviving the traps and dangers aboard the *Eye* and stopping the weapon with Callista's help, Luke comes to admire her, and the two grow closer. Nichos and Cray do not survive the travails of the battlemoon, and in a final gesture Cray allows Callista to transfer her consciousness into her body before she dies. Callista awakens as flesh and blood, but she cannot touch the Force.

"SIMPLE TRICKS"

AUTHORS · Chris Cassidy and Tish Pahl
PUBLICATION HISTORY · Short story, Bantam Spectra Included in *Tales from the New Republic* · Paperback, December 1999
TIME LINE PLACEMENT · 12 ABY
WORLD VISITED · Prishardia [R-7]
MAIN CHARACTERS · Fenig Nabon, smuggler (human female); Ghitsa Dogder, con artist (human female); Kyp Durron, Jedi Knight (human male); Gibb, mechanic (human male); Ral, Hutt councilor (human male)
SUMMARY · A faulty hyperdrive has left the smuggling duo of Fenig Nabon and Ghitsa Dogder stranded on Prishardia, but Ghitsa makes the most of the situation by posing as a Jedi Knight to bilk gullible locals out of goods. Ghitsa's act attracts some unwelcome attention—an underworld businessman kidnaps her due to her past dealings with the Hutts. Ghitsa's Jedi act has also brought Kyp Durron to Prishardia, and though Fen at first has serious misgivings about Kyp—she knows about his utter destruction of the Carida system—the two work together to rescue Ghitsa. Fen comes to see Kyp as a tortured, broken soul still healing from his past misdeeds. After her rescue, Ghitsa decides to drop the Jedi act from her repertoire, while Fen chooses to forward interesting information about Hutt dealings to her friend and colleague Talon Karrde.

"SHADES OF GRAY: FROM THE ADVENTURES OF ALEX WINGER"

AUTHOR · Charlene Newcomb
PUBLICATION HISTORY · Short story, StarWars.com · December 2009
TIME LINE PLACEMENT · 12 ABY
WORLD VISITED · Janara III [L-14]
MAIN CHARACTERS · Alex Winger, X-wing pilot (human female); Brandei, Star Destroyer captain (human male); Dair Haslip, undercover operative (human male)
SUMMARY · X-wing pilot Alex Winger is shot down and captured by Captain Brandei of the Star Destroyer *Adjudicator*. She is imprisoned in a cell on her birth planet, Janara III. Brandei has the Imperial interrogators tell her that her father, Tork, and her friend Dair Haslip are also imprisoned and will undergo torture unless she offers him valuable information. This is a ruse, as Alex discovers when Dair rescues her. Dair, disguised as a stormtrooper, reveals to Alex that her father died three months earlier. The two escape Janara III with the help of X-wing fighter reinforcements. Alex decides it is time to undergo Jedi training and sets Yavin 4 as her destination.

Aboard Mara Jade's yacht, *Hunter's Luck*, Luke Skywalker welcomes his student Cray Mingla.

THE NEW REPUBLIC 321

During her escape from prison, Alex loses a few fingers when shot by a blaster. This serves to explain why she has cybernetic fingers in her cameo appearance in *Vision of the Future* (1998).

DARKSABER

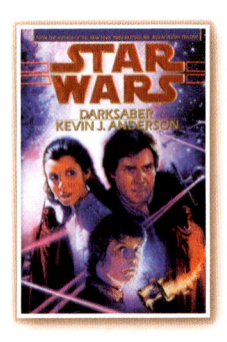

AUTHOR · Kevin J. Anderson
COVER ARTIST · Drew Struzan
PUBLICATION HISTORY ·
Novel, Bantam Spectra
· Hardcover, November 1995
· Paperback, November 1996
TIME LINE PLACEMENT · 12 ABY

WORLDS VISITED · Chardaan [N-13]; Coruscant [L-9]; Dagobah [M-19]; Hoth [K-18]; Kampe (Delvardus's base of operations) [L-11]; Khomm [L-12]; Mulako Corporation comet [N-14]; Nal Hutta [S-12]; Porus Vida [O-9]; Tatooine [R-16]; Tsoss Beacon [L-11]; Yavin 4 [P-6]

MAIN CHARACTERS · Luke Skywalker, Jedi Master (human male); Callista Masana, former Jedi Knight (human female); Durga, crime lord (Hutt); Bevel Lemelisk, engineer (human male); Natasi Daala, Imperial admiral (human female); Princess Leia Organa Solo, Chief of State (human female); Han Solo, captain of the *Millennium Falcon* (human male); Gilad Pellaeon, Imperial vice admiral (human male); Crix Madine, New Republic general (human male)

SUMMARY · Luke Skywalker quests to reconnect his beloved Callista to the Force. He first travels to Tatooine, along with Han Solo who is investigating a suspicious increase in Hutt activities. Luke hopes that the spirit of Obi-Wan might appear again to give him guidance, but it is not to be. Luke and Callista's journey also includes visits to a water quarry comet, the swamps of Dagobah, and the ice planet Hoth before finally returning to Yavin 4. Callista discovers that she is not completely cut off from the Force. She can seemingly only tap into its dark side, however—a disturbing prospect.

The Hutts, led by Durga, embark on an ambitious plan to build their own planet-shattering superweapon. Using schematics stolen from a Coruscant mainframe, Durga tasks Bevel Lemelisk, one of the Death Star's engineers, with constructing a kilometers-long superlaser-equipped battle station called the Darksaber. Durga bases this project in the Hoth asteroid belt. New Republic officer Crix Madine leads a commando mission to sabotage the station, but he is discovered by Durga and killed. A New Republic task force attacks, prompting Durga to move the Darksaber deeper into the asteroid field. The shoddily made weapon's primary cannon fails to activate, and asteroids smash the station into pieces.

Elsewhere, Admiral Daala ruthlessly wipes out a coterie of squabbling Imperial warlords in a single strike and assumes control of the Empire. Daala, with Vice Admiral Pellaeon as her ally, makes the Super Star Destroyer *Night Hammer* her flagship, renaming the massive warship the *Knight Hammer*. She leads an assault against the Jedi academy on Yavin 4. Jedi Knights Kyp Durron and Dorsk 81 bring word of warning to the Jedi, and Dorsk 81 sacrifices himself to become a conduit of collimated Force energy exerted by all the Jedi Knights in defense of their world. The blast of energy scatters the Imperial fleet. In an act of sacrifice, Callista commandeers a TIE bomber and infiltrates the *Knight Hammer*, critically damaging the craft. Though Daala escapes again, Callista is briefly presumed dead in the explosion that consumes the enormous Star Destroyer. The former Jedi instead continues the search for the Force on her own, leaving Luke a heartbreaking promise to return once she is worthy of his love.

Disgusted by the ineffectiveness of the many squabbling Imperial warlords, Admiral Daala gases them to death to assume control of the Empire.

X-WING: STARFIGHTERS OF ADUMAR

AUTHOR · Aaron Allston
COVER ARTIST · Paul Youll
PUBLICATION HISTORY · Novel, Bantam Spectra · Paperback, August 1999

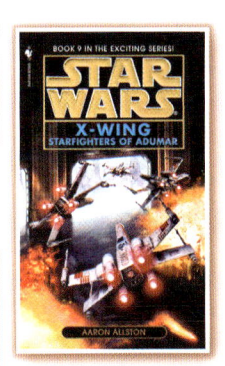

TIME LINE PLACEMENT · 13 ABY
WORLDS VISITED · Adumar [J-6]; Coruscant [L-9]
MAIN CHARACTERS · Wedge Antilles, New Republic general (human male); Iella Wessiri, New Republic Intelligence agent (human female); Tycho Celchu, X-wing pilot (human male); Wes Janson, X-wing pilot (human male); Derek "Hobbie" Klivian, X-wing pilot (human male); Hallis Saper, historian (human female); Tomer

Darpen, New Republic diplomat (human male); Pekaelic ke Teldan, perator (human male); Teren Rogriss, Imperial admiral (human male)

SUMMARY · After generations of isolation, Adumar is seeking to join the galactic community, but has yet to decide whether to ally with the New Republic or the Empire. The planet's militaristic culture idolizes fighter pilots, prompting General Cracken to request that Wedge Antilles lead the diplomatic mission to Adumar. A treaty with Adumar would benefit the New Republic with new warriors and a significant industrial capacity to produce proton torpedoes.

In the largest Adumari nation-state of Cartann, Wedge and his fellow Rogues are greeted as heroes. The Empire has also sent an envoy of fighter pilots, led by Tur Phennir of the legendary 181st TIE squadron. Perator Pekaelic ke Teldan, ruler of the nation, wants to scrutinize both parties before committing his planet's allegiance. The honor-bound Adumari have a rigid code, and duels are common, both in the air and on the ground. Wedge, finding such bloodshed wasteful and saying as much, drops in Teldan's estimation, and the perator begins leaning toward the Empire. Wedge insists on carrying out only simulated duels, while the Imperial envoy takes no such lifesaving precautions.

At a tavern, Wedge coincidentally meets with Admiral Teren Rogriss, an Imperial also stewing over such matters of honor. He seems disenchanted with the Empire and its ways. Rogriss had sworn to the Adumari that should they side with the New Republic, he would leave peacefully, but he knows in his heart that his Imperial commanders would order him to break his word and attack the planet. Wedge later offers an invitation to Rogriss to join the New Republic, including providing sanctuary for his family. Rogriss refuses, however.

Emboldened by the offworld presence, Perator Teldan declares Cartann the dominant nation and government on Adumar. He invites the Imperial and New Republic envoys to help him wage a war of conquest against the nations that do not comply. The Empire agrees, but Wedge refuses, essentially dissolving the New Republic's diplomatic bid. Branded enemies by Teldan, Wedge and his party flee to the nation of the Yedagon Confederacy, a rival state to Cartann. A coalition of Adumari nations opposed to Cartann asks Wedge to lead a strike against the ambitious state. Wedge agrees, and with his experience, the combined militaries break Cartann's rule.

The new Adumari Union government allies with the New Republic. Though the Empire attempts a reprisal strike, its forces are repulsed by the forces of the New Republic and the Adumari. Admiral Rogriss agrees to lead the defenses of the Cartann state and its new government.

Wedge feels increasingly drawn to Iella Wessiri, who was on the planet as part of New Republic Intelligence. The two have long had feelings for each other, though timing and circumstances worked against any pursuit of a relationship. Now, however, the time is right to begin.

"MURDER IN SLUSHTIME"

AUTHOR · Barbara Hambly
PUBLICATION HISTORY · Short story, West End Games · *Star Wars Adventure Journal* #14, August 1997
TIME LINE PLACEMENT · 13 ABY
WORLD VISITED · Gamorr [T-14]

MAIN CHARACTERS · Callista Ming, former Jedi Knight (human female); Guth, boar (Gamorrean male); Ugmush, captain of the *Zicreex* (Gamorrean female); Kufbrug, clan matron (Gamorrean female)

SUMMARY · Callista, now using the name Callista Ming and serving Captain Ugmush aboard the Gamorrean freighter *Zicreex*, comes to Gamorr. Guth, the captain's brother, is framed for the murder of a rival for the attentions of a Gamorrean sow, Kufbrug. Callista investigates the death and finds that a shapeshifting creature, a kheilwar, was used in the murder. The creature instinctively adopts a form that points to the real murderers. Callista clears Guth's good name, allowing the Gamorrean to marry his beloved.

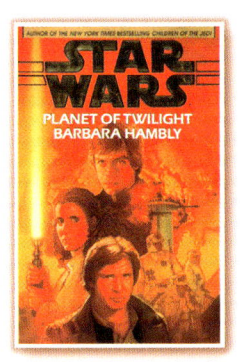

PLANET OF TWILIGHT

AUTHOR · Barbara Hambly

COVER ARTIST · Drew Struzan

PUBLICATION HISTORY ·
Novel, Bantam Spectra
· Hardcover, May 1997
· Paperback, May 1998

TIME LINE PLACEMENT · 13 ABY

WORLDS VISITED ·
Brachnis Chorios [R-7]; Coruscant (and its moon Hesperidium) [L-9]; Damonite Yors-B [R-7]; Durren [R-7]; Nam Chorios [R-7]; Nim Drovis [R-7]

MAIN CHARACTERS · Luke Skywalker, Jedi Master (human male); Princess Leia Organa Solo, Chief of State (human female); Seti Ashgad, politician and conspirator (human male); Dzym, would-be conqueror (mutated Droch male); Beldorian the Splendid, warlord and conspirator (Hutt); Liegeus Vorn, pilot and programmer (human male); C-3PO, protocol droid; R2-D2, astromech droid; Han Solo, captain of the *Millennium Falcon* (human male)

SUMMARY · The Rationalist Party of Nam Chorios asks the New Republic to intervene in the burgeoning conflict with the planet's traditional-minded Theran Listeners, whose devotion to superstition and prohibitions against technology have kept the world cloistered from interstellar trade. Seven centuries earlier, Nam Chorios was settled as a prison colony, with powerful gun stations meant to secure the skies. The fanatical Therans have commandeered these guns and use them to blast any large vessel on approach, dooming the world to isolation.

Though Leia is personally sympathetic to the party's position and empathizes with its leader Seti Ashgad, she cannot intervene in this affair. After Ashgad visits Leia aboard her flagship accompanied by his aide, Dzym, and a pair of humanoid synthdroid bodyguards, he knocks Leia unconscious and kidnaps her, taking her to Nam Chorios. The synthdroids unleash the Death Seed plague aboard the New Republic vessels, killing all aboard.

Luke Skywalker is drawn to Nam Chorios for other reasons. Prior to Leia's meeting with Ashgad, she had received a scrawled message of warning from Callista to stay away. The former Jedi had been to the world, prompting Luke to search for her there. Despite his cautious piloting, Luke's B-wing fighter is shot from the skies, and he crashes into the crystalline landscape. It is a bleak setting, infested with parasitic drochs—tiny bloodsucking insects. Despite this desolation, the Force flourishes, and Luke is alarmed at how powerful it is on Nam Chorios.

Leia awakens within Ashgad's fortress and sees that his co-conspirators include Dzym, the Force-sensitive Hutt Beldorian the Splendid, and the kind-hearted programmer Liegeus Vorn. Vorn does what he can to make Leia's stay more comfortable, for he is very much a prisoner of the conspirators as well.

Leia begins to piece together Ashgad's plot, a complex web of alliances joined in parallel goals. Ashgad is spreading the Death Seed plague across the Meridian sector to destabilize it. Backing Ashgad's plan is Moff Getelles of the adjacent Antemeridian sector, who intends to annex the Meridian. Ashgad also has the support of the Loronar Corporation, which seeks mineral rights on Nam Chorios. In exchange, the corporation has offered up automated needle fighters that can be enhanced with Chorian crystals to Ashgad's cause of destroying the stalwart Therans. Leia's kidnapping is part of an attempt to derail and deadlock the New Republic government.

With the help of local settlers, Luke follows Callista's trail and confirms that she was once on the planet. He discovers that the so-called Spook-crystals in the planet are sentient transmitters and amplifiers of the Force. They are the source of the Therans' supernatural healing abilities and deeply rooted spirituality. He also meets an aged Jedi, Taselda, a member of the old Order who has been kept alive by consuming drochs, though the hardships of Nam Chorios have stripped her of her reason. She claims to have trained Callista during her visit. Taselda tries to manipulate Luke into carrying out her dreams of vengeance against Beldorian, the Hutt who wounded her and stole her lightsaber.

Luke and Leia discover a more disturbing layer to the plot—the true mastermind of all this chaos. The tiny drochs are the source of the Death Seed plague, and one of their members—Dzym—has been mutated to the point of sentience. He scarcely resembles his insectoid origins. He has ambitions to take over the galaxy by spreading the plague off-world. Ashgad and Beldorian are under his sway since Dzym offers them vitality and longevity through the transfer of life energy. To succeed, Dzym needs a starship filled with drochs to escape Nam Chorios, past the gun stations.

In their desperate race to stop Dzym, Leia must first defeat the corrupt Beldorian, which she does in a lightsaber duel with her well-muscled larger foe. Through the Force, Luke compels the crystal-driven needle fighters to shoot down Ashgad's ship. Luke comes to understand that the crystals knew that the drochs were the source of the plague, and so—acting through the Therans—they purposely kept Nam Chorios isolated.

Moff Getelles's invasion fleet is thwarted by a New Republic task force arranged by Han Solo and Lando Calrissian and bolstered by a surprise ally: Admiral Daala. She was disgusted with how low Getelles would stoop to secure territory and power. Daala's arrival happily reunites her with Liegeus Vorn, a former lover whom she hadn't seen in years.

Luke is likewise reunited with Callista, who was captured by Ashgad in her attempt to stop him. The two have a wordless exchange, but each recognizes that their time together has come to an end.

THE DESCRIPTION of the plot on the inside flap of the hardcover misnames Nam Chorios as Renat Chorios and Seti Ashgad as Seti Draconis, the only place where those versions of these names appear.

THE CRYSTAL STAR

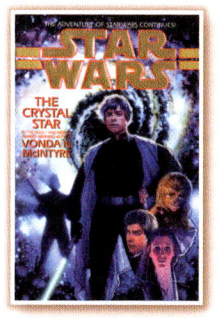

AUTHOR · Vonda M. McIntyre
COVER ARTIST · Drew Struzan
PUBLICATION HISTORY ·
Novel, Bantam Spectra
· Hardcover, December 1994
· Paperback, December 1995
TIME LINE PLACEMENT · 14 ABY
WORLDS VISITED · Crseih research station [T-6]; Munto Codru [T-6]
MAIN CHARACTERS · Luke Skywalker, Jedi Master (human male); Princess Leia Organa Solo, New Republic Chief of State (human female); Han Solo, ship captain (human male); Jaina, Jacen, and Anakin Solo, children (female and male humans); Hethrir, Lord of the Empire Reborn (Firrerreo male); Tigris, servant (Firrerreo male); Xaverri, informant (human female); Rillao, escaped prisoner (Firrerreo female); Waru, healer/charlatan (extradimensional alien male)
SUMMARY · While Chief of State Leia Organa Solo is on a diplomatic mission to Munto Codru, unknown kidnappers abscond with her children, Jacen, Jaina, and Anakin. Against diplomatic protocol, Leia gives pursuit aboard her personal vessel, *Alderaan*, with R2-D2 and Chewbacca aboard. Using the Force as her guide, Leia finds several sleeper ships floating in interstellar space, filled with Firrerreo slaves in hibernation. Leia resuscitates one of them, a torture victim named Rillao, who reveals that the slaves are the property of Lord Hethrir of the Empire Reborn, a movement hitherto unknown to the New Republic.

Leia Organa Solo defends herself against the ruthless Hutt Beldorian the Splendid.

Anakin, Jacen, and Jaina are held captive by Hethrir aboard his worldcraft, a small planetoid starship made of experimental technology. Hethrir was the former procurator of justice for the Empire, and once a student of Darth Vader. He proved his loyalty to his Imperial masters by sacrificing his people and condemning Firrerre to destruction. To fund his resurgent movement, Hethrir sells slaves to the wealthy.

The Empire Reborn is made up of Force-imbued students who are subservient to Hethrir. Hethrir's Force-sensitive child-prisoners have their abilities tested and are subjected to the cruel ministrations of the bullying proctors. Jaina in particular is defiant, and Jacen cooperates with her in small rebellions against the mean overseers. Anakin, though, is separated from his siblings and watched by Tigris, a sensitive youth who has failed to measure up to the level of a proctor. Though seemingly loyal to Hethrir, Tigris is gentle with Anakin.

Elsewhere, at distant Crseih Station, Luke Skywalker, Han Solo, and C-3PO travel incognito. The space station is in precarious orbit around a black hole and a crystallizing star—a tortured expanse of gravity-twisted space–time where the barriers between dimensions are stretched taut. The radiation-drenched installation is a former research base transformed into a lively way station and bazaar. Luke investigates strange rumors of Jedi activity.

Xaverri, Han's former girlfriend, has contacted them with word of Waru—a mysterious healer worshipped at the station. Waru appears as a bizarre alien resembling an enormous towering slab of meat covered in golden scales. Supplicants bring their ailing family members to Waru. Waru "consumes" them in his scales, oftentimes returning the subjects in good health. But sometimes Waru fails, and the subject dies. Han immediately suspects something evil at the heart of Waru.

Trusting the Force, Leia finds her children on Hethrir's worldcraft. Jaina has been leading a child rebellion against their keepers. Though Leia is reunited with Jaina and Jacen, Anakin has been taken from the worldcraft to Crseih Station. Hethrir has struck up an alliance with Waru. In exchange for the sacrifice of a Force-strong child, Waru has promised Hethrir untold power.

Waru was plucked from another dimension to Crseih Station by the experiments of Hethrir and his scientists during Palpatine's Empire. Waru had inestimable abilities—he could heal any disease and grant the power of the Force. Growing disgusted with Hethrir's ways, Tigris saves Anakin from this sacrifice. In an effort to stop Waru, Luke plunges *into* the strange creature. Leia and Han follow, breaking through the creature's form and emerging with Luke intact. Angered and deprived of his meal, Waru consumes Hethrir instead and then recedes into his dimension, leaving reality altogether.

With Anakin safe, the Solo family is reunited. Rillao is likewise reunited with Tigris, the son she bore to Hethrir.

The crystal star fragments and explodes. Crseih Station escapes into safety under its own hyperdrive engines. With Hethrir dead, the worldcraft and all of its prisoners are now in the hands of the New Republic. Xaverri commits herself to finding a home for all the children aboard.

T*HE CRYSTAL STAR* was the first book to develop the characters of Jaina, Jacen, and Anakin Solo. Jaina is depicted as headstrong, rebellious, and technically inclined, while Jacen is more introspective and sensitive. At three years old, Anakin's personality is still being defined, and at this point he is mostly just reactive to his environment.

THE BLACK FLEET CRISIS

BEFORE THE STORM • SHIELD OF LIES • TYRANT'S TEST

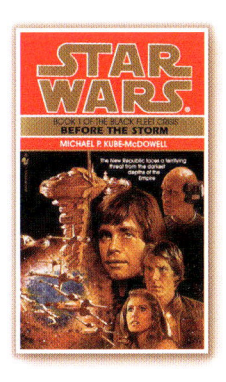

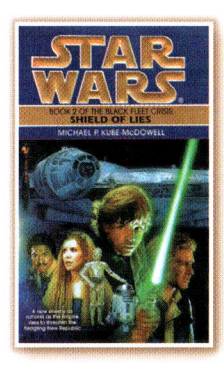

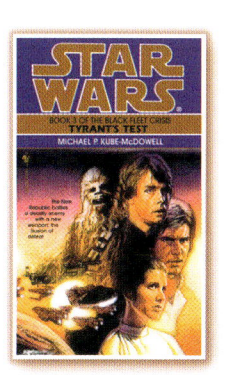

AUTHOR · Michael P. Kube-McDowell

COVER ARTIST · Drew Struzan

PUBLICATION HISTORY · Novels, Bantam Spectra
Before the Storm · Paperback, April 1996
Shield of Lies · Paperback, September 1996
Tyrant's Test · Paperback, January 1997

TIME LINE PLACEMENT · 16–17 ABY (with flashbacks to 4 ABY)

WORLDS VISITED · Atzerri [M-13]; Bespin [K-18]; Bessimir [L-9]; Coruscant [L-9]; Doornik-319 (aka Morning's Bell) [K-10]; Doornik-1142 [K-10]; Gmar Askilon [L-14]; J't'p'tan [K-10]; Kashyyyk [P-9]; Lucazec [Q-6]; Maltha Obex (aka Brath Qella) [O-3]; New Brigia [K-10]; N'zoth [K-10]; Pirol-5 [K-10]; Polneye [K-10]; Prakith [K-10]; Prildaz [K-10]; Rathalay [R-9]; Teyr [L-13]; Tholatin [P-10]; Utharis [K-10]; Yavin 4 [P-6]

MAIN CHARACTERS · Luke Skywalker, Jedi Master (human male); Han Solo, captain of the *Millennium Falcon* (human male); Princess Leia Organa Solo, New Republic Chief of State (human female); Nil Spaar, viceroy and crusader (Yevethan male); Hiram Drayson, New Republic Intelligence (human male); Akanah Norand Pell, Fallanassi (human female); Lando Calrissian, entrepreneur (human male); C-3PO, protocol droid; R2-D2, astromech droid; Lobot, aide (human cyborg male)

SUMMARY · THE PAST: Eight months after the Battle of Endor, Yevethan dockworkers who had been indentured by the Empire on N'zoth rise up against their outnumbered Imperial masters, conquering the Black Fleet warships stationed there and claiming the vessels as their own. The xenophobic species spends years mastering starship technology, killing many Imperials and enslaving crewers to ready the ships for strikes against their neighbor worlds.

THE PRESENT: Years later, during a rare moment of peace in the galaxy, Chief of State Leia Organa Solo proposes bolstering New Republic defenses with new warships, a politically unpopular stance during such tranquil times.

THE NEW REPUBLIC

329

Nil Spaar, leader of the Duskhan League, meets with New Republic Chief of State Leia Organa Solo.

Meanwhile, an introspective Luke Skywalker leaves his Jedi academy in the care of his most experienced students as he adopts the life of an anchorite, retreating from society to contemplate the nature of the Force. Despite his desire for solitude, he is visited by Akanah Pell. She claims to be a Fallanassi, a member of a religious sect able to tap into the Force—or, as they call it, the White Current—to unique effects. Akanah pleads for Luke to help her find her missing people, appealing to him by revealing that Luke's mother might have been Nashira, a member of the Fallanassi order. Skywalker has long wondered about his mother, but knows nothing of her. Compelled by her request, Luke agrees to help Akanah.

Prompted by a spirit of adventure, Lando Calrissian leads a xenoarchaeological search—accompanied by Lobot, R2-D2, and C-3PO—to track the movements of the mysterious Teljkon vagabond, a "ghost ship" of unknown origins spotted sporadically throughout the galaxy. Lando finds and boards the strange alien vessel, which then disappears into hyperspace.

Unaware of Yevethan history, and against the counsel of her advisers, Leia meets with Nil Spaar, leader of the Duskhan League of the Yevethan Protectorate, to discuss a political alliance. New Republic Intelligence suspects Spaar of hiding something, and Admiral Hiram Drayson has an unarmed scout ship perform a recon of the Yevethan

THE NEW REPUBLIC

territory, the Koornacht Cluster. Spaar destroys the scout, then publically excoriates Leia and the New Republic for such aggressive and provocative trespassing. As he engages in this highly volatile political theater, Leia's opponents in the government harp on her blood relation with Darth Vader to suggest she is building a new Empire.

Spaar's fanatical followers attack neighboring worlds with their captured Imperial warships, embarking on a genocidal swath of destruction they gloriously proclaim as the Great Purge. Although a survivor from the Purge brings news of this violence to the New Republic, Leia is too politically hobbled to effectively counter it. The New Republic citizenry has grown comfortable with peace; they will shed no blood in a distant foreign war.

Luke and Akanah follow the tenuous trail of the Fallanassi to scattered worlds such as Lucazec, Teyr, and Atzerri. After an extended period alone, Luke finds his weeks of travel with Akanah invigorating, and the two share the stirrings of a kindling relationship. Akanah is not what she seems, however, and Luke begins to have his doubts about the veracity of her story. He soon comes to realize that Akanah has been using him to find her people and that the tales of Nashira are unfounded.

Leia demands that Nil Spaar surrender the worlds he has conquered or face New Republic reprisal, but the smug Yevethan warlord does not back down. A battle erupts over Doornik-319, where Spaar callously uses New Republic hostages as a shield. Once again, Leia's political enemies turn this against her, characterizing the danger to New Republic citizens as Leia's fault, rather than Spaar's. Opposition Senators rally, calling for Leia to step down or face impeachment.

Exacerbating an already terrible situation, Han Solo—temporarily given command of a New Republic task force—is captured by the Yevetha.

Han is beaten, humiliated, and used as a pawn against Leia, but she refuses to surrender or abandon her office on claims she is too involved in the situation. Spaar underestimates his opponent, and his cruelty toward his captive unites the New Republic behind Leia's declaration of war against the Duskhan League.

Luke and Akanah finally find the Fallanassi hiding in plain sight on J't'p'tan, a world sundered by the Yevethan purges. The followers of the White Current use their unique illusory abilities to conceal their presence—a power that could be employed to great advantage against the New Republic's enemies.

Learning of Han's capture, Chewbacca returns from a pilgrimage to Kashyyyk aboard a newly upgraded *Millennium Falcon* and launches a Wookiee mission to rescue his beloved friend. This harrowing task—the infiltration of a Super Star Destroyer and the successful extraction of a prisoner—becomes a successful rite of passage for Chewbacca's son, Lumpawarrump. Lumpy adopts the name Waroo upon being accepted as an adult.

The New Republic begins a concerted attack against the Yevethan Black Fleet. The alien aggressors are momentarily stymied by the appearance of an illusory fleet, conjured by Luke's newfound Fallanassi allies. Then Spaar faces a long-overdue betrayal from his Imperial slaves, who retake their ships and flee into the depths of the galactic core. Spaar is ejected into hyperspace in an escape pod, left to die as his plans of conquest crumble.

Finally, after weeks of hopscotching around the galaxy, the alien Teljkon vagabond arrives at the seemingly dead world of Maltha Obex—its point of origin. The ship was launched by the long-extinct Qella in anticipation of a catastrophic ice age and contains the technology necessary to thaw and return life to the planet.

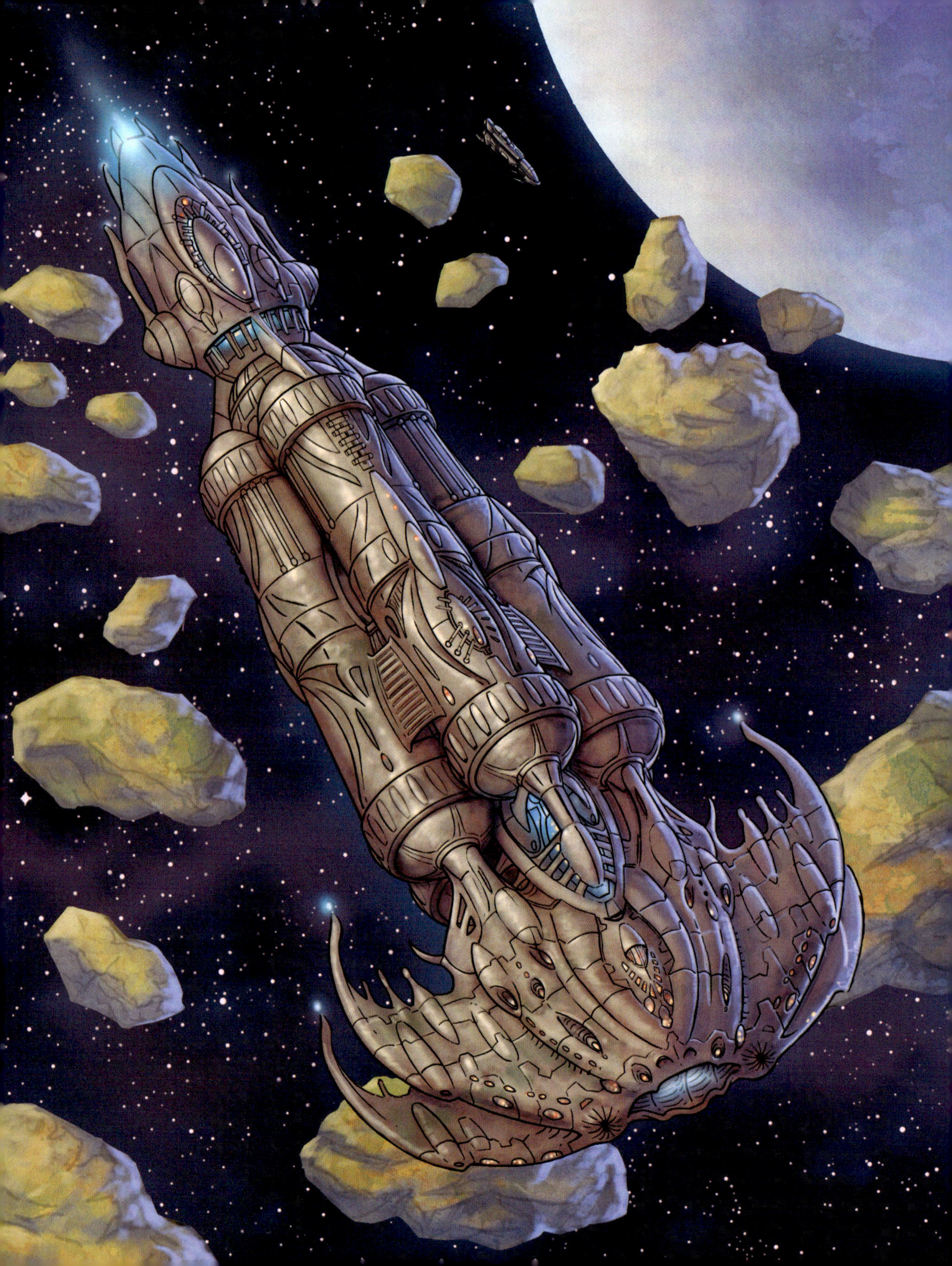

Luke and Leia's heritage as Darth Vader's children is known to the public at this point in the time line—enough so that it is used as the foundation of political attacks against Leia. The public revelation of their bloodline has never been depicted in a story. The original Marvel Comics set after *Return of the Jedi* portrayed Leia and Luke vowing to keep their ancestry a secret at the time. The Thrawn Trilogy only works if this fact is not known—the well-informed Thrawn would never have risked sending Noghri after Luke and Leia if he knew they were Vader's offspring.

At the time the Black Fleet Crisis series was published, nothing was known of Luke and Leia's mother. The story of Padmé Amidala was still being developed by George Lucas and was a closely guarded secret to be properly unveiled through the course of Episodes I–III. As such, the plot line of finding Nashira was always intended to be a red herring, and in the galaxy of the New Republic, Luke and Leia have no access to records that would connect Amidala to Anakin Skywalker. Indeed, it would not be until 35–36 ABY that they learn anything tangible about their mother, in the pages of the Dark Nest Trilogy (2005).

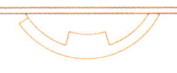

THE NEW REBELLION

AUTHOR · Kristine Kathryn Rusch

COVER ARTIST · Drew Struzan

PUBLICATION HISTORY · Novel, Bantam Spectra
- Hardcover, December 1996
- Paperback, October 1997

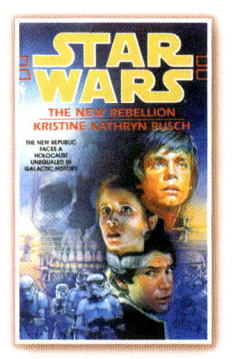

TIME LINE PLACEMENT · 17 ABY

WORLDS VISITED · Almania [S-5]; Coruscant [L-9]; Smuggler's Run [S-18]; Telti [N-10]; Yavin 4 [P-6]

MAIN CHARACTERS · Luke Skywalker, Jedi Master (human male); Princess Leia Organa Solo, New Republic Chief of State (human female); Han Solo, captain of the *Millennium Falcon* (human male); Kueller, warlord (human male); Brakiss, fallen Jedi (human male); Cole Fardreamer, technician (human male); Nandreeson, crime lord (Glottalphib male); Lando Calrissian, entrepreneur (human male); R2-D2, astromech droid; C-3PO, protocol droid

SUMMARY · While Leia Organa Solo is preoccupied with a controversial move in the New Republic Senate granting former Imperials the right to hold office, villainy strikes. Coordinated terrorists' bombs kill more than a million sentients on Pydyr—sending ripples of disturbance through the Force—and an explosion rips apart the Senate Hall. Leia survives the deadly blast, but in the political turmoil that follows more former Imperials are voted into the Senate by frightened constituents. The antagonistic Imperials point to Leia's administration as responsible for the devastation.

Han Solo and Chewbacca journey to the Smuggler's Run asteroid field to investigate a strange rash of deaths and disappearances suffered by suddenly wealthy smugglers. Fearing for Han's safety, Lando Calrissian joins his old friend and is nearly killed by Nandreeson, an old foe and crime lord. Lando and Han discover that the Smuggler's Run is a delivery route for bombs intended for Coruscant—the smugglers, well compensated at the start, were silenced to ensure the secrecy of the attack.

The mysterious vessel known as the Teljkon vagabond sends a New Republic research team on a strange, erratic journey through the galaxy.

THE NEW REPUBLIC

Luke suspects that his former student Brakiss is in some way responsible for the bombings. He tracks his fallen apprentice to Telti, a world of immense droid factories. Brakiss reluctantly tells Luke to head to Almania, where Brakiss's dark master, Kueller, awaits. Luke flies to Almania, crashing to its surface when his X-wing suffers sabotage.

Meanwhile, Cole Fardreamer—a New Republic technician—discovers a plot to bomb new model X-wings such as Luke's. Inspection of the found bombs reveals they were manufactured on Telti, so Fardreamer and the droids R2-D2 and C-3PO head to the factory world to learn more. The devastation on Pydyr and to the Senate was the result of millions of sabotaged droids assembled on Telti and secretly disseminated throughout the New Republic.

On Almania, Luke faces Kueller, a Dark Jedi warrior who was once a student at his Jedi academy. Kueller sends Leia an ultimatum: surrender the New Republic or he will slay Luke and unleash another explosive cataclysm. Burdened by the growing unrest in the Senate and aware she can no longer remain objective in the face of the Almanian threat, Leia recuses herself and turns over her administration to Mon Mothma.

Leia and Han journey to Almania to help Luke, who is not faring well in his battle with Kueller. Luke's despair over the damage wrought by his former apprentice only fuels Kueller's power. Luke realizes that in order to defeat the dark warrior, he must sacrifice himself as Obi-Wan did when facing Vader. But Kueller is suddenly cut off from the Force by ysalamiri brought to the battlefield—a gift to Luke from Talon Karrde and Mara Jade, delivered by Han and Leia.

Desperate, Kueller tries to activate his bombs, but C-3PO and R2-D2 have neutralized the explosives at the source. With Kueller rendered powerless by the ysalamiri, Leia is able to kill him with her blaster. The Almanian threat counteracted, Leia reclaims her title as Chief of State.

In THE BLACK FLEET CRISIS (1996–97), threatening Han only reinforced Leia's dedication to the office of the Chief of State, and she refused to back down in the face of allegations that she was too personally invested in the threat to the New Republic. Here, she surrenders her office when Luke is threatened. The inconsistency is the result of two stories in near-concurrent development, but hindsight suggests that perhaps Leia was indeed worn down by the time she faced the Almanian crisis. She does, after all, temporarily step down from office in 19 ABY.

"TWO FOR ONE"

AUTHOR · Paul Danner

PUBLICATION HISTORY · Short Story, West End Games · *Star Wars Adventure Journal* #15, November 1997

TIME LINE PLACEMENT · 17 ABY

WORLDS VISITED · Soullex [P-3]; Vohai [O-18]

MAIN CHARACTERS · Sienn Sconn, thief (human male); Cryle Cavv, thief (human male); Gaen Drommel, Imperial admiral (human male); Shandria L'hnnr, New Republic operative (human female)

SUMMARY · The New Republic hires the uncle-and-nephew team of thieves Cryle Cavv and Sienn Sconn to capture the damaged Super Star Destroyer

Guardian. Tracking the movements of repair parts, the thieves commandeer an Imperial shuttle and fly to the crippled warship's secret location. Aboard *Guardian*, Sconn and Cavv disguise themselves as stormtroopers and free several New Republic prisoners held in the ship's hold, including Sconn's estranged beloved, Shandria L'hnnr. The thieves are outmaneuvered and captured by the *Guardian*'s commander, Admiral Drommel. But before their capture the duo successfully tampered with the warship's navicomputer, the results of which deposit the ship in the midst of a New Republic ambush. The Imperials surrender, Shandria and Sienn are reunited, and the New Republic finds itself one Super Star Destroyer richer.

This story takes place as the New Republic is investigating Kueller's rash of bombings in *The New Rebellion* (1996). General Cracken says to the thieves that "taking a Super Star Destroyer intact would be one of the greatest coups in New Republic history," though at this point in the time line, the New Republic would have already captured the *Lusankya*. It's possible he was appealing to their sense of glory.

"JADE SOLITAIRE"

AUTHOR · Timothy Zahn

PUBLICATION HISTORY · Short story, Bantam Spectra Included in *Tales from the New Republic* · Paperback, December 1999

TIME LINE PLACEMENT · 18 ABY

WORLD VISITED · Torpris [K-9]

MAIN CHARACTERS · Mara Jade, trader (human female); Sansia Bardrin, captive (human female); H'sishi, scavenger (Togorian female); Ja Bardrin, corporate baron (human male); Chay Praysh, pirate (Drach'nam male)

SUMMARY · With the crew of the *Wild Karrde* taken hostage, Mara Jade is forced to carry out a dangerous errand for corporate heavyweight Ja Bardrin. His daughter, Sansia, is being held captive, forced to toil in the slime pits beneath the fortress of his evil nemesis, Chay Praysh. Mara deliberately allows herself to be captured by Praysh's guards—the sick pirate enjoys enslaving women to carry out such humiliating tasks as sifting through slime to pluck prize larvae from the ooze. With the timely assistance of a Togorian scavenger, H'sishi, Mara liberates Sansia as well as Bardrin's yacht, *Winning Gamble*. Returning to Bardrin, Mara finds him outmaneuvered by Talon Karrde, who exacts upon him a heavy toll for using his people in this manner. For her role in rescuing Sansia, Mara is gifted the yacht, which she renames *Jade's Fire*, the first starship she has ever truly owned.

THE NEW REPUBLIC

THE CORELLIAN TRILOGY

AMBUSH AT CORELLIA · ASSAULT AT SELONIA · SHOWDOWN AT CENTERPOINT

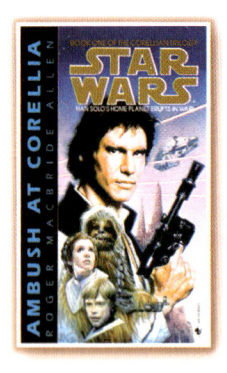

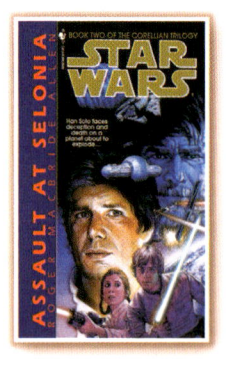

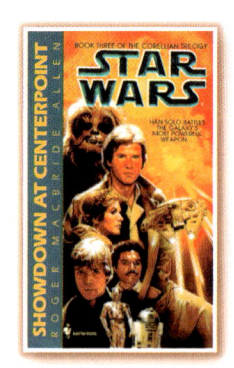

AUTHOR · Roger MacBride Allen

COVER ARTIST · Drew Struzan

PUBLICATION HISTORY · Novels, Bantam Spectra
Ambush at Corellia · Paperback, March 1995
Assault at Selonia · Paperback, July 1995
Showdown at Centerpoint · Paperback, October 1995

TIME LINE PLACEMENT · 18 ABY

WORLDS VISITED · Bakura [G-16]; Bovo Yagen [O-13]; Corellia [M-11]; Coruscant [L-9]; Drall [M-11]; Leria Kerlsil [M-10]; Sacorria [M-11]; Selonia [M-11]; Talfaglio (system) [M-11]; Talus and Tralus [M-11]; TD-10036-EM-1271 [J-15]; Thanta Zilbra [Q-3]

MAIN CHARACTERS · Han Solo, captain of the *Millennium Falcon* (human male); Leia Organa Solo, Chief of State (human female); Lando Calrissian, entrepreneur (human male); Thrackan Sal-Solo, Human League insurrectionist (human male); Mara Jade, Smugglers' Alliance trader (human female); Luke Skywalker, Jedi Master (human male); Anakin, Jacen, and Jaina Solo, children (human males and female); Ebrihim, tutor (Drall male); Q9-X2, tutoring droid; Dracmus, rebel (Selonian female); Gaeriel Captison, Bakuran plenipotentiary (human female); Belindi Kalenda, NRI agent (human female); Tendra Risant, businesswoman (human female)

SUMMARY · Chief of State Leia Organa Solo travels to Corellia for a trade summit in the hope of opening up the insular and distrustful sector to the New Republic. The Solo family intends to turn the trip into a vacation, though Han is put on edge when a New Republic Intelligence agent, Belindi Kalenda, warns him of the dangerous unrest percolating in the sector. The five worlds of the Corellian system are inhabited by three primary species—humans, Drall, and Selonians. Years of isolationism have greatly withered the Corellian economy, exacerbating historic tensions among its native cultures, and there are rumors of the sector separating from the New Republic.

Kalenda also travels to Corellia, using the Solo delegation as cover, but is shot down by an unknown enemy who clearly knew of her secret plans. She survives a crash landing.

Once on Corellia, Leia selects Ebrihim, an elderly

male Drall, to serve as a tutor for Jacen, Jaina, and Anakin during their stay. The scholar takes the family on a tour of an archaeological site, where young Anakin spots suspicious soldiers. His attunement to the Force leads the children to discover an immense and complex machine of unknown origin or purpose buried beneath the guarded location.

Elsewhere, Luke Skywalker accompanies Lando Calrissian on his latest business venture. Lando is determined to find a wife—it's good business, after all—and asks Luke to come along to make him appear more reputable. Their search leads to near disaster on Leria Kerlsil, where Lando almost weds a vampiric life-witch. Then the wife hunt brings them to Sacorria, where Lando meets the charming Tendra Risant, but heavy-handed local authorities chase the offworlders from the planet before Calrissian and Risant can build a true connection.

As the trade summit begins on Corellia, Leia encounters a visiting Mara Jade, who delivers a message from Pharnis Gleasry of the Human League. The spokesman of the humanocentric ideological group issues an astounding ultimatum—to heed the word of the league lest entire stars explode. The message includes a map of stars in the Corellian sector, with countdowns to their destruction highlighted. One of the stars has already exploded.

Han alerts Luke to this astonishing Starbuster plot in the hope of preventing cataclysm among other star systems. Just then, the Human League sets a match to the growing tinderbox of racial tensions in the Corellian system, as coordinated riots erupt across the five worlds. Ebrihim, his droid Q9-X2, Chewbacca, and the children flee aboard the *Millennium Falcon* to nearby Drall.

Accompanying this unrest is the inexplicable shutdown of communications and even hyperspace transit within the system. This prevents Luke and Lando from entering the Corellian system, prompting them to return to Coruscant. Lieutenant Kalenda escapes just prior to the mysterious interdiction, likewise bound for Coruscant. At this time, the mastermind leader of the Human League reveals himself—it is Han Solo's unscrupulous cousin, Thrackan Sal-Solo.

For his twisted amusement, Sal-Solo forces Han to fight with a captive Selonian revolutionary named Dracmus. Dracmus believes there may be more to the Starbuster plot than the Human League. After they are imprisoned together, Dracmus helps Han escape into a tunnel network created by the Selonians. They leave the planet aboard a rickety Selonian coneship bound for Selonia.

At the trade center, Leia, Mara, and the rest of the delegates are held by Human League hostage takers. Using the Force to distract the guards, Leia reclaims her lightsaber from her quarters and uses it to slash into Mara's room, where Mara uses a remote-control device to summon her starship, *Jade's Fire*. The two women flee Corellia, heading toward Selonia as well.

On Drall, Ebrihim leads the children and Chewbacca to the home of his aunt, Marcha. She informs Ebrihim of an archaeological dig on the planet. Examining imagery from the dig, the children are able to confirm that the Drall site contains mysterious machinery that is identical to machinery found on Corellia. Ebrihim quietly arranges for the children to explore the excavation. Anakin, with a precocious combination of Force ability and a supernatural affinity for machinery, is able to activate the device at the site, revealing it to be an enormous, ancient repulsor. Ebrihim and Marcha explain that each world in the Corellian system must have one, for it has long been speculated that an ancient, highly advanced culture made possible the peculiar assortment of worlds in the system by artificial means.

After Mon Mothma is briefed on the Corellian crisis, she suggests that Luke, Lando, and Kalenda contact Gaeriel Captison of Bakura to assemble a

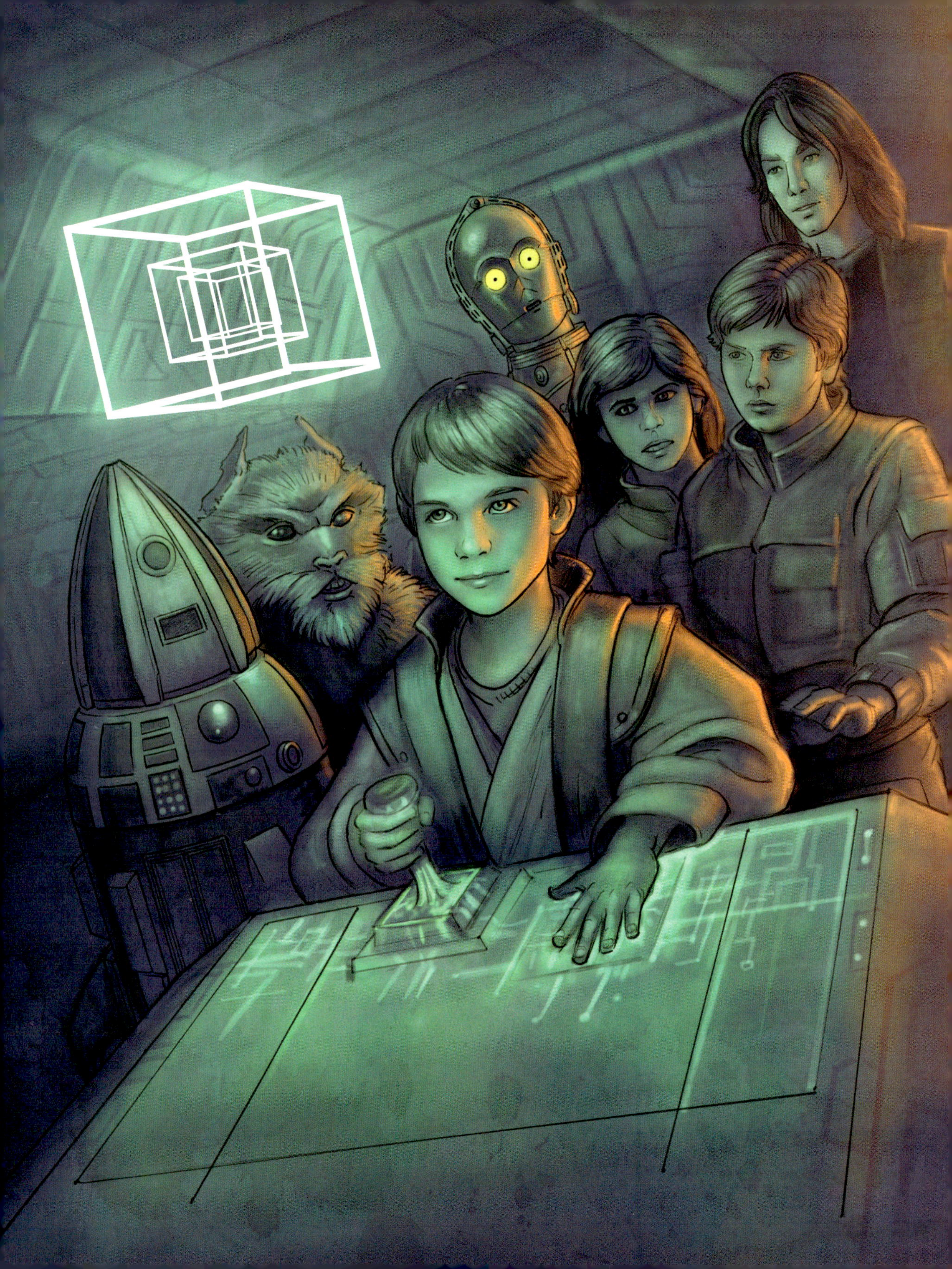

specialized fleet of four ships that can bypass the enormous interdiction field barricading the system. The task force plans a diversionary raid on Selonia before moving toward the real target: Centerpoint Station. A gargantuan space station of unknown origins that occupies the gravitational fulcrum between the twin worlds of Talus and Tralus, Centerpoint appears to be the source of the interdiction field.

The Bakuran task force emerges in Selonia, arriving to encounter enemy insurrectionist vessels, as well as *Jade's Fire* and Han's rapidly failing coneship. Mara and Leia rescue Han and Dracmus from the doomed vessel. One of the four Bakuran warships is crushed by a sudden blast of repulsor energy emerging from Selonia. To help out in the battle, Lando boards his ship *Lady Luck* and discovers a message of warning from Tendra: a huge fleet is amassing in the Sacorrian system, destined for Corellia.

The crisis escalates as the second star on the Starbuster hit list detonates. The New Republic is able to relocate most of the populace to safety in time. The third star listed, Bovo Yagen, is orbited by worlds with populations in the millions. There will not be enough time to evacuate the system.

Han, Leia, and Mara set down on Selonia and are taken captive by the ruling Overden. The Overden speaker, Kleyvits, demands that the Chief of State grant her world independence.

The battered Bakuran fleet arrives at Centerpoint, finding the station abandoned. It becomes clear Centerpoint is the weapon being used as the Starbuster, sending gravitic bursts through hyperspace at targeted stars. Lando realizes that the way to stop advanced alien technology is with *more* advanced alien technology. A blast from one of the planetary repulsors could offset the pulse from Centerpoint Station. It becomes imperative to capture one of the planetary repulsors.

Anakin's activation of the Drall repulsor alerts Thrackan Sal-Solo and prompts him to send his Human League troops to secure the device. Sal-Solo's soldiers capture Ebrihim, Chewbacca, and the children. Sal-Solo drops the systemwide communication blackout to issue a villainous announcement that he controls the Drall repulsor, and that he has taken Han and Leia's children captive. This turns the sentiments of the family-focused Selonians in the Solos' favor, and with Dracmus's help they are able to overthrow Kleyvits and secure the captives' release.

Thrackan Sal-Solo's true masters are the Sacorrian Triad, a secretive council made up of representatives from the human, Drall, and Selonian species. The opportunistic Sal-Solo has overstepped his bounds by seeking to secure power for himself. In an effort to rein him in, the Triad drops the systemwide interdiction field to bring their vessels onto the scene. The New Republic takes advantage of the newfound mobility to launch a rescue mission to Drall, where they are able to secure the hostages and the repulsor, as well as capture Sal-Solo.

In a space battle for Centerpoint Station, the vessels of the Sacorrian Triad tangle with the Bakuran fleet. Gaeriel Captison's flagship is critically damaged, and she heroically sacrifices herself and the ship to punch a hole in the Triad formation. New Republic reinforcements commanded by Admiral Ackbar outmaneuver the Triad vessels, but Centerpoint Station is still counting down to its next detonation.

On Drall, Anakin intuitively activates the planetary repulsor and uses it to jam Centerpoint Station, thus sparing Bovo Yagen. The Triad insurrection founders.

In the aftermath of the crisis, Aunt Marcha is appointed governor of the Corellian sector. Lando and Tendra, each impressed by the other in the face of crisis, begin to make wedding plans.

Young Anakin Solo activates the ancient technology of the Drall planetary repulsor.

Though Corellia was part of George Lucas's original roster of planetary names during the development of *Star Wars*, it was not depicted in the Expanded Universe until the publication of the Corellian Trilogy. Author Roger MacBride Allen offered the high concept of a system mysteriously engineered by an advanced, vanished race, and introduced Centerpoint Station—constructs that would later be attributed to advanced aliens who may have also constructed the Maw. Centerpoint Station would figure prominently in the New Jedi Order and the Legacy of the Force novel series.

The Corellian Trilogy shines more of a spotlight on the Solo children, continuing their development as characters. These books gave Anakin Solo a knack for technology as well as a tendency to follow his own instincts.

"THE LAST ONE STANDING: THE TALE OF BOBA FETT"

AUTHOR · Daniel Keyes Moran

PUBLICATION HISTORY · Short story, Bantam Spectra Included in *Tales of the Bounty Hunters* · Paperback, December 1996

TIME LINE PLACEMENT · 19 ABY (with prologue set in 12 BBY, 3 ABY, and 4 ABY)

WORLDS VISITED · Concord Dawn [O-7]; Coruscant [L-9]; Devaron [M-13]; Hoth (system) [K-18]; Jubilar [T-7]; Peppel [P-5]; Tatooine [R-16]

MAIN CHARACTERS · Boba Fett, bounty hunter (human male); Han Solo, captain of the *Millennium Falcon* (human male); Kardue'sai'Malloc, fugitive war criminal (Devaronian male)

SUMMARY · THE PAST: Journeyman Protector Jaster Mereel of Concord Dawn—also known as Boba Fett—is sentenced for the murder of a fellow Journeyman Protector. Fett is unrepentant for administering justice to a corrupt lawman. Years later, under the mantle of Boba Fett, he targets the spice dealer Hallolar Voors on Jubilar. While there, Fett witnesses a young Han Solo fight and acquit himself well in the All-Human Free-for-All brawl. Later, during the Galactic Civil War, Fett captures Han Solo and delivers him to Jabba the Hutt. Fett has a brief discussion of morals and allegiances with a captive Princess Leia on the eve of the botched execution that sees her escape with Luke and Han, Jabba killed, and Fett fall into the Sarlacc.

THE PRESENT: Fett tracks down the notorious war criminal Kardue'sai'Malloc and delivers him to Devaron for the hefty bounty of five million credits. He receives a message from the Bounty Hunters' Guild that Han Solo is on Jubilar. A restless Han, chafing under the role of first husband and diplomat, has come to Jubilar looking to stir up trouble by taking on a smuggling run. Fett chases him, and the two end up in a standoff, where neither can kill the other without dying himself.

The story presents an outdated backstory for Boba Fett, identifying him as a lawman named Jaster Mereel. This history would prove apocryphal with the release of *Star Wars*: Episode II *Attack of the Clones* (2002). The comic series *Jango Fett: Open Seasons* (2002) would attempt to salvage part of the Jaster Mereel story by presenting a character with that name as a contemporary of Jango and suggest that Jango would on occasion adopt that identity.

Han Solo and Boba Fett point blasters at each other in a tense standoff on Jubilar.

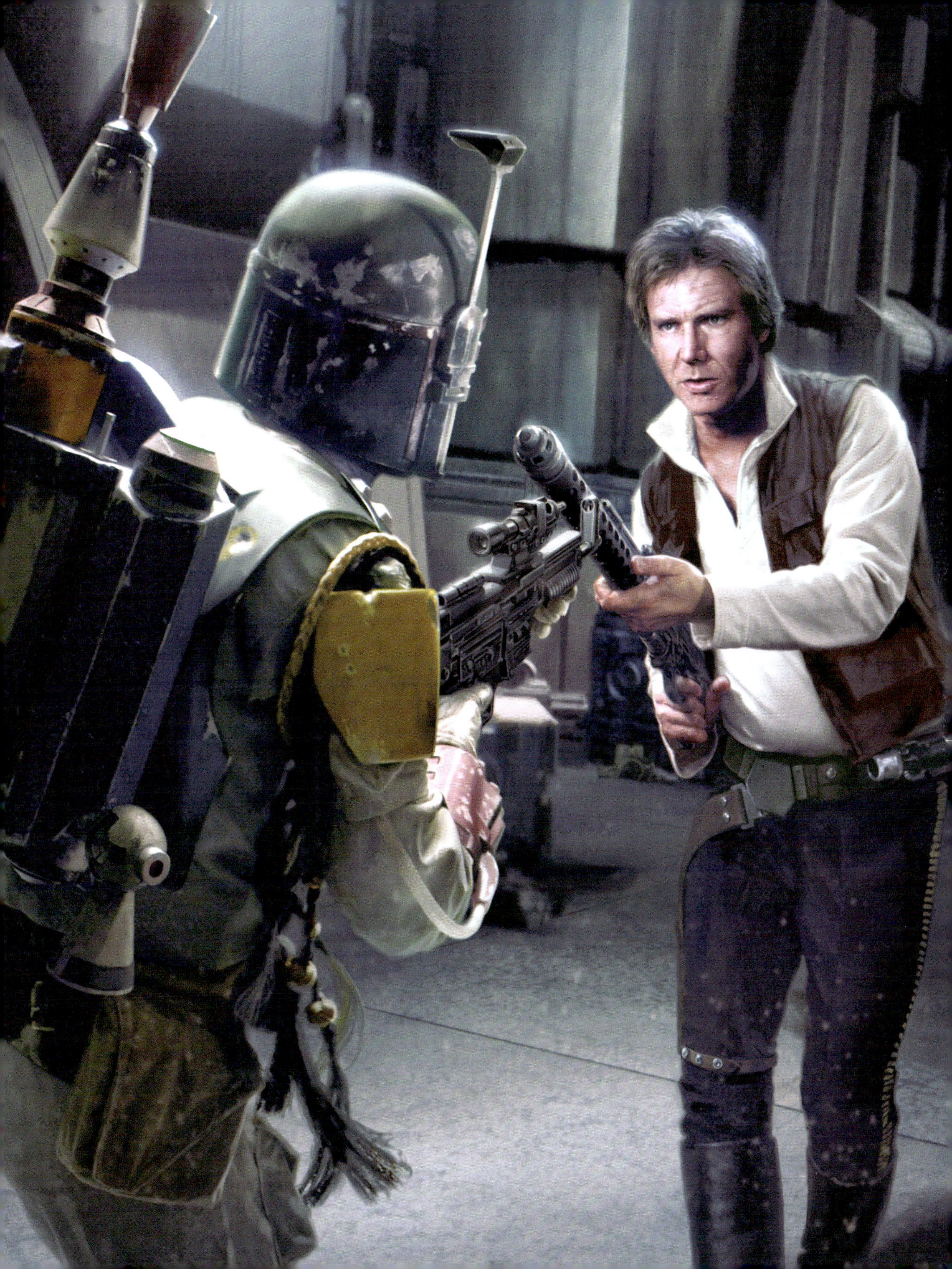

Apart from the outdated history, the story makes certain claims about Fett—a chaste prudishness, and that he *never* talks to himself—that don't stack up well with the wealth of Fett storytelling that came both before and after this tale.

The story ends with no resolution, though the implication is that Fett and Han agree to a truce and walk away from the confrontation, older, wiser, and very much alive.

THE HAND OF THRAWN

SPECTER OF THE PAST · VISION OF THE FUTURE

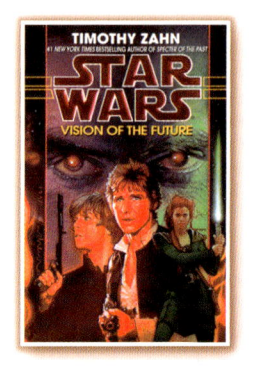

AUTHOR · Timothy Zahn

COVER ARTIST · Drew Struzan

PUBLICATION HISTORY · Novels, Bantam Spectra

Specter of the Past
- Hardcover, December 1997
- Paperback, September 1998

Vision of the Future
- Hardcover, September 1998
- Paperback, September 1999

TIME LINE PLACEMENT · 19 ABY

WORLDS VISITED · Bastion [K-3]; Borcorash [N-6]; Bothawui [R-14]; Cejansij [R-9]; Cilpar [L-13]; Di'tai'ni [R-14]; Dordolum [K-13]; Episol [M-21]; Exocron [M-21]; Iphigin [L-13]; Jangelle [M-21]; Kauron [O-4]; Morishim [K-5]; Muunilinst [K-4]; Nirauan [I-5]; Nosken system [J-6]; Pakrik Minor and Major [K-9]; Rimcee (system) [J-3]; Sif'kric [M-7]; Wayland [N-7]; Yaga Minor [K-5]

MAIN CHARACTERS · Luke Skywalker, Jedi Master (human male); Han Solo, captain of the *Millennium Falcon* (human male); Princess Leia Organa Solo, New Republic councilor (human female); Mara Jade, trader (human female); Gilad Pellaeon, Imperial Supreme Commander (human male); Vilim Disra, Imperial Moff (human male); Talon Karrde, smuggler chief (human male); Grodon Tierce, Imperial Guard (human male); Flim, con artist (human male); Borsk Fey'lya, New Republic minister (Bothan male)

THE NEW REPUBLIC

SUMMARY · The Empire is a dwindling fragment of its former power and glory: only eight sectors encompassing a thousand worlds and a scant two hundred Star Destroyers remain. Supreme Commander Pellaeon laments how fortunes have turned since the days of Grand Admiral Thrawn. On the Imperial capital world of Bastion, Pellaeon proposes to the council of Moffs that the Empire should deliver terms of surrender to the New Republic in the hope of preserving what little they have.

Han Solo and Luke Skywalker pursue a Cavrilhu pirate force that ambushed a New Republic transport. Luke, from his X-wing, senses that there are Spaarti-produced clones aboard the pirate ships and follows the brigands back to their base in the Kauron system.

On Wayland, Leia Organa Solo—who has taken a leave from her position as Chief of State—learns of data cards uncovered near the ruins of the Emperor's storehouse on Mount Tantiss. Among the cards is one with the mysterious title "The Hand of Thrawn," as well as a damning, if incomplete, document that reveals the Bothans were complicit in the destruction of Caamas decades earlier. Recognizing the incendiary nature of this data, Leia rushes back to Coruscant with it.

Leia confronts Borsk Fey'lya with this revelation, and he admits that the Bothans were indeed involved, and that this knowledge was kept secret. This shame was what prompted many Bothans to join the Rebellion. Fey'lya does not know which clan colluded with Palpatine to betray Caamas. Word of the Bothan involvement in the Caamas genocide begins to spread through the New Republic, prompting outrage and calls for retribution.

In the Imperial Remnant, Vilim Disra refuses to go along with Pellaeon's plan of capitulation, but he does not openly rebel. He surreptitiously sends one of his Star Destroyers to intercept and capture Pellaeon's envoy to the New Republic. While Pellaeon waits patiently and futilely to make contact with General Garm Bel Iblis to discuss terms, Disra crafts a devious plot to unsettle the New Republic. Disra holds in his possession many of Grand Admiral Thrawn's personal documents—documents that assured the loyalty of Major Grodon Tierce, former Imperial Guard. Another of Disra's allies is the con man Flim, who with some cosmetic alteration becomes the spitting image of Grand Admiral Thrawn. Disra intends to plant rumors of Thrawn's return, adding fuel to the fires of tension, fear, and anti-Bothan sentiment racking the New Republic. Disra's agents in the New Republic begin sparking riots on various worlds.

Leia and New Republic President Gavrisom meet with Fey'lya to determine a possible settlement of the Caamasi controversy. Fey'lya shoots down suggestions that the Bothans pay restitution to the Caamasi, citing a weak Bothan economy. To verify this claim, Leia, Han, and C-3PO depart for Bothawui to comb through financial records. They get caught in the thick of an Imperial-fueled riot, and Han is briefly implicated in the murder of a Bothan official, all part of Disra's plan to undermine the New Republic.

Luke's pursuit of the pirates leads to an asteroid base in the Kauron system. He is pinned by a trap designed to ensnare Jedi Knights but is rescued by Mara Jade, who was investigating the Cavrilhu on Karrde's behalf. Mara and Luke reunite with Karrde aboard Booster Terrik's Star Destroyer, *Errant Venture*. As Luke recovers from his injuries, he receives visions from the Force of Mara endangered, possibly dead in a chamber filling with water.

The *Errant Venture* is suddenly buzzed by a peculiar ship, an alien craft that appears to be a hybrid of a TIE fighter and unknown technology. The mystery ship skims past the Star Destroyer before vanishing into hyperspace. The *Errant Venture* communications crew is able to intercept a signal transmitted by the ship—"Mitth'raw'nuruodo," the full name of Grand Admiral Thrawn. Mara decides to pursue this mystery and vanishes on Nirauan, a planet on the edge of Unknown Space.

Luke, concerned about his visions of Mara, follows her to Nirauan with R2-D2 accompanying him. The small, telepathic avian-like natives of the distant world lead Luke to Mara, who has discovered a mighty five-spired fortress on the planet filled with Chiss soldiers. As Mara and Luke work together to penetrate the fortress, they grow closer in trust and cooperation, coming to plainly realize how much they complement each other's abilities and outlooks.

On Pakrik Minor, Han and Leia discover a cell of clones living as farmers. Duplicates of Imperial fighter pilot legend Baron Soontir Fel, the clones were intended to be part of a contingency sleeper cell created by Grand Admiral Thrawn, but a decade after Thrawn's death they simply want to continue their lives as farmers (their original cover story) and not become entangled with the war. Leia offers them amnesty, and with some reluctance the clone leader—Carib—agrees to help them find the secret location of Bastion, the code-named Imperial capital world.

With many in the galaxy clamoring for Bothan blood, it becomes imperative to find the complete Caamas Document. Several attempts are launched simultaneously. Han, Lando, and Lobot voyage to Bastion. When Pellaeon finally makes contact with Leia, he puts the search for the Caamas Document on the table as a negotiating point. Talon Karrde reasons that his old mentor, Jorj Car'das, would have a record, so he searches for Car'das in the distant Kathol sector. General Bel Iblis offers a more martial solution: launching a mission to raid the Imperial records vault on Yaga Minor.

On the distant planet Exocron, Talon Karrde and his partner Shada D'ukal find old Car'das. He explains his disappearance, years earlier, when his starship was commandeered by a Dark Jedi and taken to Dagobah. There, Car'das was physically and mentally traumatized when caught in the middle of a battle between the Dark Jedi and Master Yoda. Yoda nursed Car'das to health and opened his mind to the Force. Car'das has spent years wandering the galaxy, coming to study the ways of the mystic Aing-Tii monks in the Kathol sector. He gives Karrde a copy of the Caamas Document from his extensive files.

On Nirauan, Mara and Luke discover more of Thrawn's origins and legacy. He had been dispatched by the Emperor to secure a base of power in the Unknown Regions to prepare against an incoming, extragalactic threat. To that end, Thrawn created the Empire of the Hand, an alliance of worlds governed by Imperial and Chiss philosophies. Their command is the Hand of Thrawn, the fortress on Nirauan, led by such men as Admiral Voss Parck and Baron Fel in Thrawn's stead. Fel offers Mara a role in this new Empire, but she refuses.

Bothawui hovers on the brink of destruction as a cell of Imperial saboteurs drops the planet's shields, allowing for retribution to come raining down from fleets of anti-Bothan factions. The New Republic scrambles to defend the world. Aboard the *Millennium Falcon*, Han Solo inadvertently uncovers a cloaked trio of Moff Disra's Star Destroyers monitoring the fray. The sudden appearance of Imperials binds the factions, and Lando Calrissian leads the united New Republic charge to repulse the Imperials.

At Yaga Minor, Moff Disra's heavy defenses overpower Garm Bel Iblis's invading task force. Disra's charlatan, Flim, gloats as Grand Admiral Thrawn to his conquered foes, but Disra's plan unravels with the unexpected arrival of Pellaeon.

Luke Skywalker and Mara Jade work together to escape the rising waters within a cave on Nirauan.

Pellaeon, the Imperial officer with the most direct experience with Thrawn, inspects Flim and denounces him as a sham. This brings an end to Disra's campaign against the New Republic.

As Mara and Luke make their way out of the Hand of Thrawn, they are shocked to discover a Spaarti cloning cylinder containing a clone of Thrawn, another of the Grand Admiral's contingencies. An attack by guard droids forces them to retreat into a chamber that is filling with water. Luke recognizes his vision of Mara imperiled. As they face death by drowning, Luke asks Mara to marry him should they survive. Mara agrees. With a slash of her lightsaber, she breaches their dead-end chamber and causes the rising waters to flood the chamber holding Thrawn's clone, destroying the equipment keeping the duplicate alive.

Escaping Nirauan, Luke and Mara return to New Republic space with a full copy of the Caamas Document that R2-D2 has retrieved from the Hand of Thrawn computers. The list identifies the Bothan saboteurs, allowing the New Republic to defuse tensions by trying those specifically involved in the genocide.

With the crisis averted, delegates from the New Republic and the Empire can finally convene to sign a peace treaty bringing an end to the Galactic Civil War.

AFTER THE SUCCESS of the Thrawn Trilogy, Bantam Books' initial plan for 1994 and beyond was for twelve additional *Star Wars* novels. These were initially mapped out to be *The Truce at Bakura* by Kathy Tyers, *The Courtship of Princess Leia* by Dave Wolverton, the Jedi Academy Trilogy by Kevin J. Anderson, *The Crystal Star* by Vonda M. McIntyre, a paperback trilogy by Roger MacBride

Allen (which became the Corellian Trilogy), hardcover novels by Margaret Weis (which never came to pass) and Barbara Hambly, and a final book by Timothy Zahn. This roster flexed as the popularity of the *Star Wars* publishing program grew, but it was always intended that Zahn would have the last book of Bantam's contract with *Star Wars*, allowing him to close the era of storytelling he started.

By the time this plan coalesced, Zahn knew several points he wanted to address in this book. Mara Jade and Luke Skywalker would end up together, and the Empire and the New Republic would sign a peace accord.

Known for a time as *Hand of Thrawn*, the single-novel finale expanded into two books, published a year apart. Early in development, there was a plan to bridge the two novels with a comics series, *Specter of Thrawn*, written by Zahn and Michael A. Stackpole, focusing on Wedge Antilles's efforts to contain an outbreak of violence during the Caamas Document Crisis.

During his search for Jorj Car'das, Talon Karrde encounters Entoo Needaan E-elz, "a short, slender man with short hair," who says, "Oddly enough, people do sometimes mistake me for a droid . . . I can't imagine why." The name, if read aloud, is clearly a nod to Anthony Daniels, the actor who plays C-3PO.

SPOTLIGHT: The Marriage of Luke and Mara

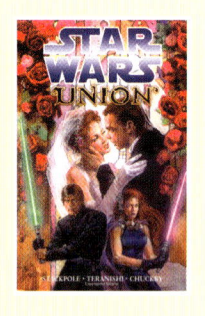

Though *Vision of the Future* ends with Luke and Mara intending to marry, their actual wedding would not be depicted in a novel. Instead, writer Michael A. Stackpole and artist Robert Teranishi did the honors with Dark Horse Comics in 1999–2000. The four-part miniseries *Star Wars Union* is set in 19 ABY, right after the events of the Hand of Thrawn duology.

The Young Jedi Knights novels, published years before Hand of Thrawn and *Union*, were set after the wedding, but no mention is made of Luke and Mara being married. In fact, Mara is conspicuously absent from those books set in 23–24 ABY. This was a deliberate omission by the authors of those works, who knew Luke would be married at this point in the chronology, but could not make mention of it until after Hand of Thrawn was published.

"RED SKY, BLUE FLAME"

AUTHOR · Elaine Cunningham

PUBLICATION HISTORY · Short story, Wizards of the Coast
· *Star Wars Gamer* #7, December 2001

TIME LINE PLACEMENT · 19 ABY

WORLD VISITED · Rhigar [E-9]

MAIN CHARACTERS · Jagged Fel, cadet (human male); Shankyr Nuruodo, cadet commander (Chiss female)

SUMMARY · Fourteen-year-old Jagged Fel attends a Chiss military academy on the frozen world of Rhigar. The academy is attacked by pirates. Fel uses his clawcraft, *Blue Flame*, to

THE NEW REPUBLIC

lure the pirates into a clever trap of his devising, earning the respect and admiration of his Chiss peers, who would not usually consider treating a human outsider as an equal.

This story describes how Jag (here in his first chronological appearance) earns the distinctive scar on his face. It is complicated by time line errors: Jagged Fel's birth date was established in other sources to be 7 ABY, which would mean this story should occur at 21 ABY if Jag is indeed fourteen. Stent, a Chiss warrior who first appeared in *Vision of the Future* (1998), apparently dies in this story, but he is alive and well in *Survivor's Quest* (2004), set later in the time line. *The Complete Star Wars Encyclopedia* (2008) would reconcile this inconsistency by making it clear that Stent had survived the attack on Rhigar.

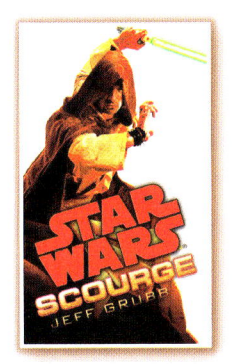

SCOURGE

AUTHOR · Jeff Grubb
COVER ARTIST · Larry Rostant
PUBLICATION HISTORY ·
Novel, Del Rey Books
· Paperback, April 2012
TIME LINE PLACEMENT · 19 ABY
WORLDS VISITED · Bosph moon [Q-3]; Budpock [R-7]; Dennogra [S-8]; Endregaad [S-5]; Makem Te [S-5]; Nal Hutta (and its moon, Nar Shaddaa) [S-12]; Rhilithan [S-5]; Varl [S-11]

MAIN CHARACTERS · Mander Zuma, Jedi Knight (human male); Reen Toro, smuggler (Pantoran female); Eddey Be'ray, mechanic (Bothan male); Popara Anjiliac, Hutt lord (Hutt); Mika Anjiliac, businessbeing (Hutt); Angela Krin, CSA lieutenant commander (human female); Vago Gejalli, adviser (Hutt); Zonnos Anjiliac, businessbeing (Hutt); Koax, Spice Lord agent (Klatooinian female)

SUMMARY · The mysterious circumstances surrounding the death of novice Jedi Knight Toro Irana on the world of Makem Te bring his former mentor, Jedi Knight Mander Zuma, to the planet. Toro apparently overdosed on a variety of hard spice called Tempest. In his search for answers, Mander meets Toro's sister, Reen, who is seeking justice for her brother's death. She is wary of the Jedi Order, thinking that they led her brother to ruin. She believes Toro was not suddenly poisoned one night but had become an abuser of Tempest. Reen's Bothan friend, the laconic Eddey Be'ray, also joins the hunt for answers.

Mander explains that Toro was in the midst of brokering a deal for vital astrogation coordinates from the relatively benevolent Hutt Popara Anjiliac. Mander, Reen, and Eddey continue that mission, which has been expanded by Popara to now include a journey to the quarantined world of Endregaad to deliver medicinal spice and check on the status of Popara's son Mika, with whom he has lost contact since the outbreak of plague on the planet. Popara's other offspring, the surly Zonnos, makes it clear to Mander that he cares little for the well-being of his brother.

Mander, Reen, and Eddey are granted their own starship (freshly christened *New Ambition* by Reen) for the journey to Endregaad. Corporate Sector Authority official Lt. Commander Angela Krin commands a blockade around the planet, but Mander pilots past the cordon regardless, coming

THE NEW REPUBLIC 347

Jedi Knight Mander Zuma seeks an audience with the mighty and benevolent Popara the Hutt.

in for a bumpy landing on the barren world. There Mander finds Mika, along with evidence that a delivery of Tempest may have brought the plague to the planet.

By returning Mika to his father, Popara, Mander and his companions have earned the trust of a powerful Hutt. Mika is peculiar for a Hutt—polite, erudite, relatively slim, and comfortable speaking Basic. He is puzzled by the outbreak of Tempest and wishes to get to the bottom of it. Mander, Reen, and Eddey are brought before Popara for an audience with the appreciative Hutt at his lavish estate on Nar Shaddaa. The ceremony is cut short when Popara violently explodes. Mander and his associates are framed as the perpetrators of the assassination, and they are forced to flee.

Zonnos takes advantage of the chaos to make a bid for power. Mander and his allies scurry deeper into Nar Shaddaa's layered city, narrowly avoiding Hutt pursuers, such as the well-armored hunter Parella the Hutt. Angela Krin, surprisingly, comes to the rescue of Mander and his crew; she's been on detached duty, attempting to track down the source of the Tempest scourge. Her contact—Mika the Hutt—has somehow convinced her to take up the cause and led her to Nar Shaddaa. Mander reasons that given the biochemical expertise required to create Tempest, as well as engineer the explosive death of Popara, both incidents are related. Whoever is developing the drug is attempting to cover his or her tracks. Before Mander can act on this hunch, however, Zonnos's mercenaries strike, knocking

THE NEW REPUBLIC

SHORT STORY — "Hunting the Gorach"

Published in *Star Wars Insider* #133 (June 2012), "Hunting the Gorach" by Jeff Grubb focuses on the armored Hutt hunter Parella. He voyages to the forests of Lowick, hunting the legendary Gorach creature for sport. A Pa'lowick guide, Kashina Furt, leads Parella into the wilderness. Parella reflects on the tales of the ancient Gorach, who ruled with merciless cruelty before degenerating into jungle savages. Parella tracks down a Gorach and, after a mighty fight, kills the beast. In the process of the hunt, the Hutt and his guide discover the Gorach's lair. Inside they find evidence that the Gorach was a great artist, who created many fine works. Distressed with that knowledge, Parella erases the notes of this expedition from his personal log.

---

both Mika and Reen unconscious and kidnapping them.

Mander stages a foolhardy rescue of his comrades by crashing an airspeeder into the Anjiliac clan spire and shooting Reen at point-blank range with a stun blast. Mander is forced to kill Zonnos, who proves to be infected by Tempest. The newly rescued Mika is installed as the new leader of the Anjiliac clan.

Reen returns to consciousness and is outraged by Mander's rescue—he has proven far more unpredictable than she presumed the Jedi archivist to be. Mander is determined to track down the source of the Tempest spice and bring an end to its scourge. Mander, Reen, Eddey, and Angela shake down pushers and middlemen on various worlds before coming across evidence that the spice is mutated on the radiation-drenched world of Varl, the long-abandoned homeworld of the Hutts. Journeying to the blighted world, they discover that the mysterious Spice Lord manipulating events is Mika the Hutt.

Mika is Force-sensitive. Frustratingly, he can sense the Force but has real difficulty mastering it. He sought to coerce a Jedi—Toro Irana—into training him, getting Toro hooked on spice as a means of controlling him. Mika used mind tricks to ensure his safety and manipulate others, and also used deception to great effect, since few would predict the diminutive Hutt to be the real mastermind. Mander defeats Mika, killing the Hutt. Vago, an adviser to Popara, becomes ruler of the Anjiliac clan and agrees to end the Tempest trade as long as she can continue her business without Jedi interference.

The story for *Scourge* first appeared in *Tempest Feud*, a roleplaying game adventure module published by Wizards of the Coast in 2002 and written by Jeff Grubb and Owen K. C. Stephens. The novel follows the same plot, but casts the new characters of Mander Zuma, Reen Toro, and Eddey Be'ray in the roles that would have been filled by players of the game. Working titles for *Scourge* included *Huttstorm* and *A Rage of Hutts*.

"JUDGE'S CALL"

AUTHOR · Timothy Zahn
PUBLICATION HISTORY · Short story, Del Rey Books · Posted on the Del Rey website, February 2004
TIME LINE PLACEMENT · 21 ABY
WORLD VISITED · Maicombe [K-7]
MAIN CHARACTERS · Luke Skywalker, Jedi Master (human male); Mara Jade Skywalker, Jedi Knight (human female)
SUMMARY · Mara accompanies Luke as he spends a long day arbitrating disputes on an alien world. She laments how little time they have together. Luke suddenly gets an emergency summons off site by an agricultural minister. It turns out to be a special arrangement by Luke for Mara. At a mountain retreat, Luke treats Mara to a second honeymoon furnished with all her favorite comforts.

JUNIOR JEDI KNIGHTS #1: THE GOLDEN GLOBE

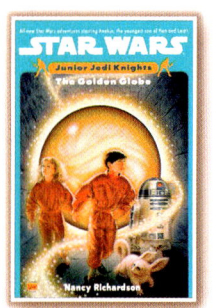

AUTHOR · Nancy Richardson
COVER ARTIST · Eric J. W. Lee
PUBLICATION HISTORY · Juvenile novel, Boulevard Books · Paperback, October 1995
TIME LINE PLACEMENT · 22 ABY
WORLD VISITED · Yavin 4 [P-6]
MAIN CHARACTERS · Anakin Solo, Jedi student (human male); Tahiri Veila, Jedi student (human female); Ikrit, Jedi Master (Kushiban male)
SUMMARY · Anakin Solo, eleven years old, begins training at the Jedi academy on Yavin 4, where he meets his new friend Tahiri Veila. Sharing strange visions in the Force through their dreams, the two children explore the jungles and discover the Palace of the Woolamander, an ancient temple. Inside, they awaken an ancient, sleeping Jedi Master named Ikrit, who stands guard over a large golden globe. Ikrit explains that the globe contains the trapped spirits of Massassi children, imprisoned millennia ago by Exar Kun.

Published in the mid-1990s, the Junior Jedi Knights and Young Jedi Knights series never use the term *Padawan* for the apprentices studying at the academy, as that word did not become common in lore until after *Star Wars*: Episode I *The Phantom Menace* (1999). Instead, they are simply called "Jedi students."

JUNIOR JEDI KNIGHTS #2: LYRIC'S WORLD

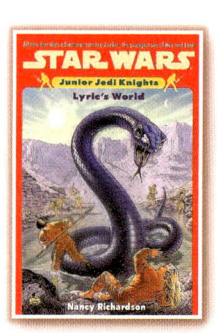

AUTHOR · Nancy Richardson
COVER ARTIST · Eric J. W. Lee
PUBLICATION HISTORY · Juvenile novel, Boulevard Books · Paperback, January 1996
TIME LINE PLACEMENT · 22 ABY
WORLDS VISITED · Yavin 4 [P-6]; Yavin 8 [P-6]; Yavin 13 [P-6]

Luke and Mara Jade Skywalker enjoy a romantic retreat on the planet Maicombe.

THE NEW REPUBLIC

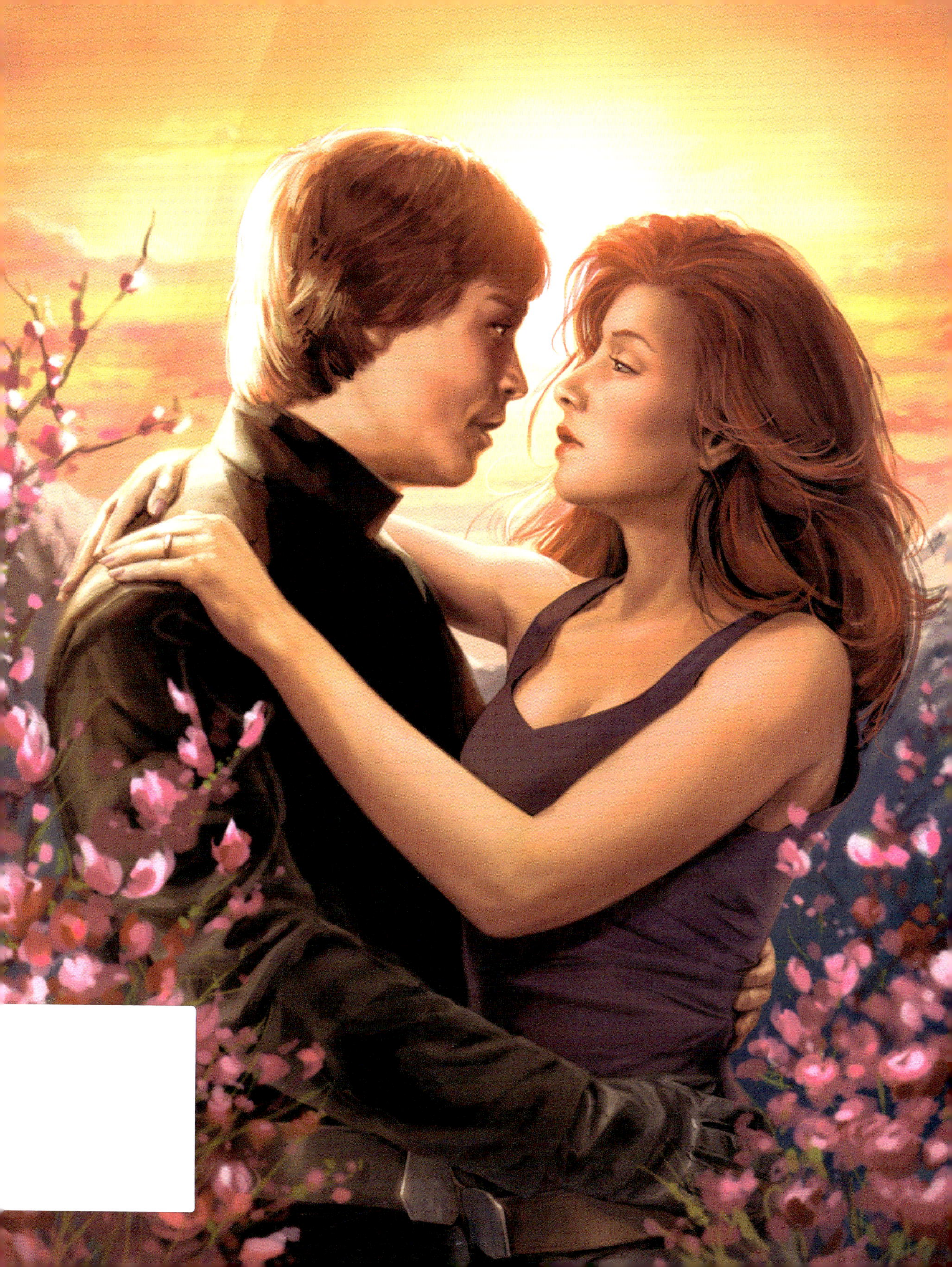

MAIN CHARACTERS · Anakin Solo, Jedi student (human male); Tahiri Veila, Jedi student (human female); Lyric, Jedi student (Melodie female); Ikrit, Jedi Master (Kushiban male)

SUMMARY · Anakin and Tahiri accompany their friend Lyric to her home on Yavin 8. She is a Melodie and is undergoing a major life stage change, from terrestrial biped to finned water dweller. During her metamorphosis, Lyric is vulnerable to external dangers, and Anakin and Tahiri repel many predators while Lyric transforms. A grateful Lyric leads Anakin and Tahiri to the grotto where the Melodie elders live, and they find a translation for the glyphs that appear in the Temple of the Woolamander near the golden globe. It speaks of an ancient prophecy that children, powerful in the Force, will free the Massassi spirits.

Anakin Solo is mistakenly referred to as "Anakin Skywalker" in the first sentence of the first chapter in this book.

JUNIOR JEDI KNIGHTS #3: PROMISES

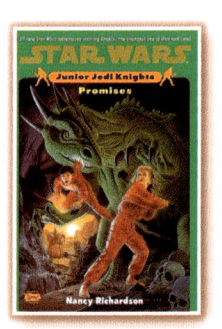

AUTHOR · Nancy Richardson
COVER ARTIST · Eric J. W. Lee
PUBLICATION HISTORY · Juvenile novel, Boulevard Books · Paperback, April 1996
TIME LINE PLACEMENT · 22 ABY
WORLDS VISITED · Tatooine [R-16]; Yavin 4 [P-6]
MAIN CHARACTERS · Anakin Solo, Jedi student (human male); Tahiri Veila, Jedi student (human female); Sliven, Tahiri's adoptive father (Tusken Raider male); Ikrit, Jedi Master (Kushiban male)

SUMMARY · Tahiri, accompanied by Anakin, returns home to Tatooine, where she was raised by the Tusken Raiders after her parents were inadvertently killed in a raid. Her adoptive father, Sliven, tells her of an important Tusken rite of passage she must undergo. She must survive being stranded in the Jundland Wastes to prove her worthiness as a Tusken. If she fails, Sliven will be killed. Anakin accompanies Tahiri on her desert trek, encountering dangerous animals, Jawas, and eventually finding Tahiri's bantha, who helps lead them back to the tribe.

Having completed the ritual and saved the life of her adoptive father, Tahiri returns to Yavin 4. Together she and Anakin concentrate through the Force and penetrate the golden globe, freeing the spirits within. Luke Skywalker meets Master Ikrit, welcoming the ancient Jedi into the Order.

JUNIOR JEDI KNIGHTS #4: ANAKIN'S QUEST

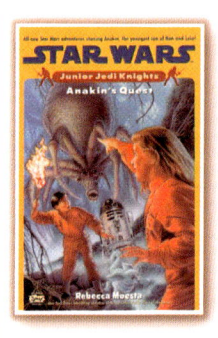

AUTHOR · Rebecca Moesta
COVER ARTIST · Eric J. W. Lee
PUBLICATION HISTORY · Juvenile novel, Boulevard Books · Paperback, April 1997
TIME LINE PLACEMENT · 22 ABY
WORLDS VISITED · Dagobah [M-19]; Yavin 4 [P-6]
MAIN CHARACTERS · Anakin Solo, Jedi student (human male); Tahiri Veila, Jedi student (human female); Ikrit, Jedi Master (Kushiban male); Uldir Lochett, stowaway (human male)

THE NEW REPUBLIC

SUMMARY · Troubled by visions of the dark side, Anakin seeks counsel from his uncle Luke. Anakin wishes to go to Dagobah and visit the strange cave as Luke did, to experience insight from the Force. Luke allows this as long as Master Ikrit and R2-D2 go along, so Anakin and Tahiri are shuttled to the swamp planet by Peckhum, a courier pilot of the *Lightning Rod*. Stowing away aboard the craft is Uldir, a teenager who longs to be a Jedi Knight. On Dagobah, Ikrit continues to teach Anakin and Tahiri, and they avoid the various dangers of the swamp planet. Anakin and Tahiri go into the cave, each experiencing a vision, but when Uldir enters he experiences nothing. Anakin emerges, having confronted visions of his doubts and understanding that he is the master of his choices.

JUNIOR JEDI KNIGHTS #5: VADER'S FORTRESS

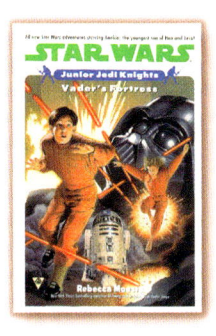

AUTHOR · Rebecca Moesta
COVER ARTIST · Eric J. W. Lee
PUBLICATION HISTORY · Juvenile novel, Boulevard Books · Paperback, July 1997
TIME LINE PLACEMENT · 22 ABY
WORLDS VISITED · Vjun [Q-6]; Yavin 4 [P-6]
MAIN CHARACTERS · Anakin Solo, Jedi apprentice (human male); Tahiri Veila, Jedi apprentice (human female); Tionne, Jedi scholar (human female); Ikrit, Jedi Master (Kushiban male); Uldir Lochett, Jedi hopeful (human male)
SUMMARY · The Jedi researcher Tionne brings news that Darth Vader might have sent Obi-Wan Kenobi's captured lightsaber to Bast Castle on Vjun prior to the Battle of Yavin. Tionne believes it is vital to recover this important artifact. Tionne travels to Vjun accompanied by Anakin, Tahiri, Ikrit, and Uldir. Avoiding the many traps set throughout the castle, the group eventually finds the lightsaber as well as a Jedi Holocron, which they bring back with them to Yavin 4.

THE FATE of Obi-Wan Kenobi's lightsaber was previously explored in the roleplaying game module *Scavenger Hunt* (1989) from West End Games. In it, a Rebel player character would have found it hidden within a fragment that was hurled free of the exploded Death Star. Though this contradicts *Vader's Fortress*'s account of how it came to Vjun, it is possible that Vader or agents of the Dark Lord retrieved it from the Rebels sometime after the events of *Scavenger Hunt*.

Tionne describes her ship, the *Lore Seeker*, as newly acquired in this book, but she had it as far back as 11 ABY, as it appears in the short story "Firestorm" (1997), set during the Jedi Academy Trilogy.

JUNIOR JEDI KNIGHTS #6: KENOBI'S BLADE

AUTHOR · Rebecca Moesta
COVER ARTIST · Eric J. W. Lee
PUBLICATION HISTORY · Juvenile novel, Boulevard Books · Paperback, September 1997
TIME LINE PLACEMENT · 22 ABY
WORLDS VISITED · Teedio system [R-7]; Yavin 4 [P-6]

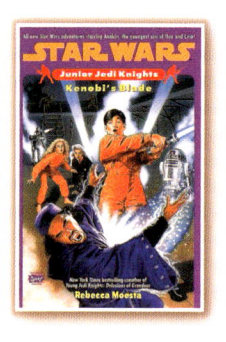

MAIN CHARACTERS · Anakin Solo, Jedi apprentice (human male); Tahiri Veila, Jedi apprentice (human female); Tionne, Jedi scholar (human female); Ikrit, Jedi Master (Kushiban male); Uldir Lochett, Jedi hopeful (human male); Orloc, fraud (human male)

SUMMARY · The Holocron contains information about Exis Station, an ancient space city in the Teedio system that once housed a Jedi library. Believing he could become a Jedi Knight if he only had a fair chance, Uldir absconds with Obi-Wan's lightsaber and the Holocron and travels to Exis Station. Uldir encounters pirates led by a con man, the Mage Orloc, who claims to be powerful in the Force. Anakin, Tahiri, Tionne, and Ikrit follow Uldir and expose Orloc for the fraud he is.

SURVIVOR'S QUEST

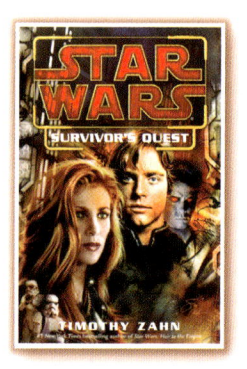

AUTHOR · Timothy Zahn
COVER ARTIST · Steven D. Anderson
PUBLICATION HISTORY ·
Novel, Del Rey Books
- Hardcover, February 2004
- Paperback, January 2005

TIME LINE PLACEMENT · 22 ABY
WORLDS VISITED · Brask Oto [H-7]; Crustai [H-8]; Nirauan [I-5]; Redoubt (planetoid) [H-7]

MAIN CHARACTERS · Luke Skywalker, Jedi Master (human male); Mara Jade Skywalker, Jedi Knight (human female); Dean Jinzler, ambassador (human male); Chak Fel, stormtrooper leader (human male); Bearsh, delegate ("Geroon" male); Chaf'orm'bintrano, aka Formbi, Aristocra (Chiss male)

SUMMARY · Dean Jinzler, a mysterious man newly employed by Talon Karrde, intercepts a priority message from the Empire of the Hand intended for Luke and Mara Jade Skywalker. Talon informs Luke and Mara of this odd development, prompting the Jedi couple to visit Admiral Parck at Nirauan. Parck tells them that the Chiss have discovered the remains of Outbound Flight, the intergalactic Jedi-led expedition launched fifty years ago. In penance for Thrawn's destruction of Outbound Flight, the Chiss extend an invitation to Jedi delegates to meet so they can turn over the remains of the massive vessel to them.

The Chiss diplomatic ship *Chaf Envoy* voyages into an occluded area of the Unknown Regions known to the Chiss as the Redoubt, where Outbound Flight's grave rests. Luke and Mara join the voyage as representatives of the Jedi. The *Chaf Envoy* carries a diverse assortment of passengers. Led by a Chiss potentate, Aristocra Chaf'orm'bintrano, the group is joined by Bearsh, leader of the Geroon, a near-extinct species that Thrawn saved from slavery during the battle for Outbound Flight against the Vagaari, decades earlier. Luke and Mara are surprised to find Dean Jinzler aboard, posing as a New Republic ambassador. The Jedi confront Jinzler. He remains tight-lipped, but admits to a deeply personal reason for needing to be on this voyage to see the remains of Outbound Flight.

Also aboard the vessel are security forces from the Empire of the Hand: crack Imperial stormtroopers from the 501st Legion, led by Chak Fel, son of the legendary Baron Fel. They were assigned by Admiral

Aboard the wreckage of Outbound Flight, Luke and Mara Jade Skywalker defend themselves against a still-active destroyer droid.

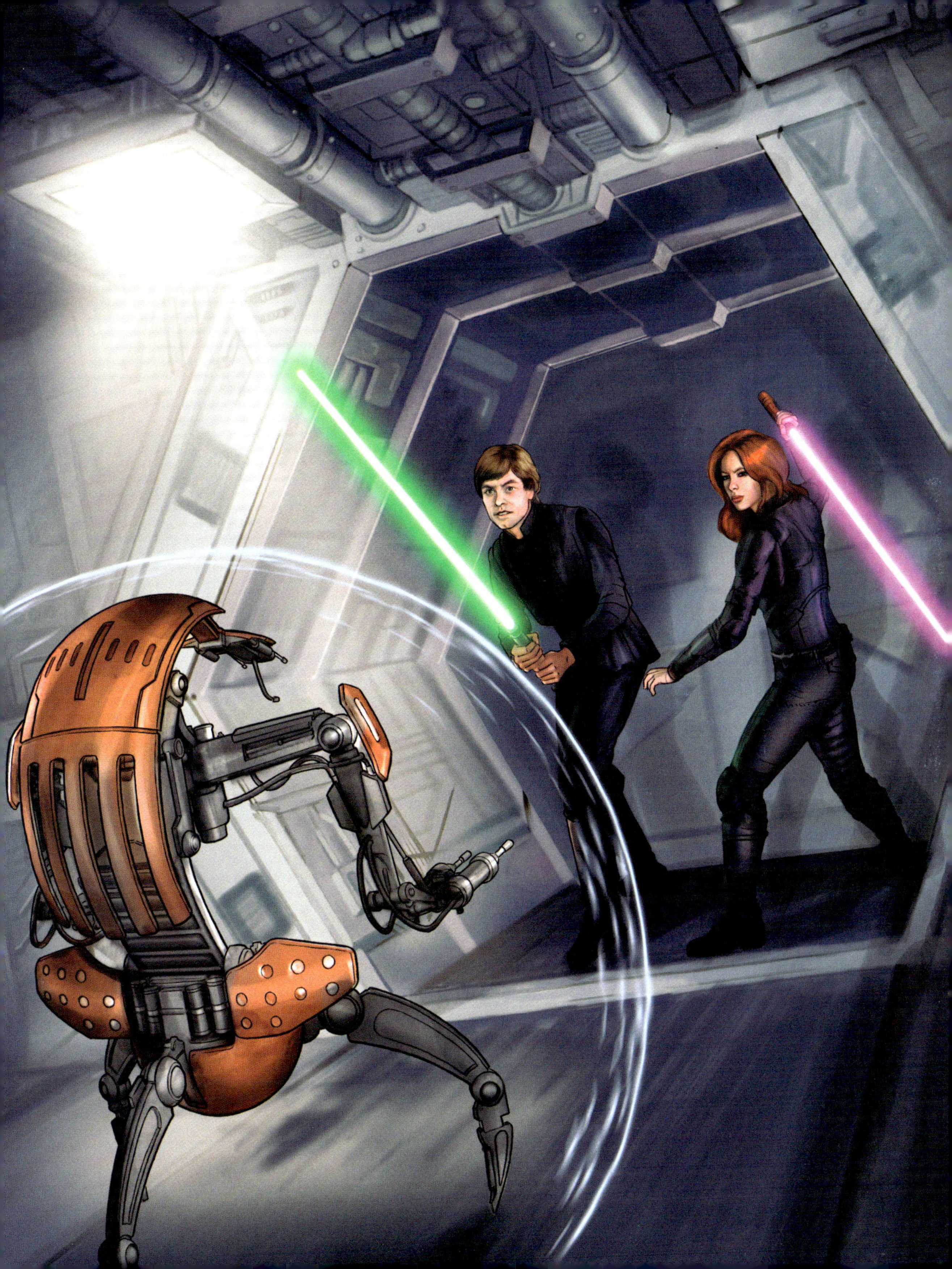

SPOTLIGHT   Fool's Bargain

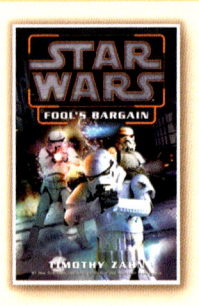

Fool's Bargain was an eBook novella by Timothy Zahn released in December 2004 by Del Rey Books. The paperback edition of *Survivor's Quest* includes a reprint of the story. Set before the events of *Survivor's Quest*, the tale focuses on unit Aurek-Seven of the 501st Legion, consisting of troopers Whistler, Cloud, Shadow, Watchman, and Twister. They are helping the native Eickaries of Kariek overthrow a brutal warlord on their planet.

Parck to protect the Jedi. Fel and the Jedi work together to investigate a strange series of accidents aboard the *Chaf Envoy* indicating that someone is trying to sabotage the mission, but they arrive at the crash site before they can uncover any solid evidence.

The *Chaf Envoy* reaches the planetoid where Outbound Flight rests. An interlinked cluster of six Dreadnought cruisers surrounding a storage core, Outbound Flight lies mostly buried in the scree, with only the topmost cruiser (designated D-4) on the surface. The delegates enter the vessel, finding survivors aboard who have lived there for five decades. The survivors foster a deep distrust of Jedi, based on the circumstances surrounding their ill-fated voyage. Jinzler reveals that he sought Outbound Flight to pay respects to his sister, Lorana, who died aboard the vessel. Jinzler's presence aboard the *Chaf Envoy* was facilitated by the ever-mysterious Jorj Car'das, who told Jinzler only that he was trying to fulfill a promise he made long ago. Jinzler hated his sister but comes to terms with her upon learning that she sacrificed herself to save the Outbound Flight passengers.

Bearsh and the Geroons reveal their true intent. They are not Geroon penitents, but rather Vagaari bent on vengeance. They launch an attack, releasing hundreds of Vagaari warriors who were hidden in suspended animation aboard their ship. Mara, Luke, and the 501st stormtoopers defend against the Vagaari, destroying many of the attacking warriors, eventually turning the tide of battle against the aggressors. Formbi is wounded in the battle, and it becomes apparent that he was aware of the Geroon deception. He purposely used the Outbound Flight wreckage as a lure to prompt the Vagaari attack, since the Chiss cannot launch preemptive attacks on would-be threats. With the Vagaari proven to be hostile, however, the Chiss are able to declare war.

Survivor's Quest was the first official *Star Wars* work to use the 501st Legion name. The 501st began in 1997 as a fan organization of stormtrooper and Imperial costumers and has been a mainstay at *Star Wars*, sci-fi, and comic book conventions. Members are lauded by Lucasfilm for their charitable work, particularly with children's hospitals. Author Timothy Zahn had met fans from the 501st on his many book tours and convention appearances and honored them by including them as part of the *Star Wars* canon.

Published after the release of Episodes I and II, but set amid stories originally written in the 1990s, *Survivor's Quest* benefits from lore revealed in the prequels. For example, Luke reflects on Yoda's teachings of the Jedi restrictions against marriage—something Luke is not depicted as knowing in the stories that led to his union with Mara, since no author would have been privy to that revelation made in *Attack of the Clones* (2002). *Survivor's Quest* clarifies that Luke did know the Jedi edicts of old, but thought that they no longer applied in this new era.

A chronological reading of Expanded Universe works means that readers would have read *Outbound Flight* (2006) first, which dispels a number of mysteries present in *Survivor's Quest*, particularly the nature of Dean Jinzler's history.

YOUNG JEDI KNIGHTS: HEIRS OF THE FORCE

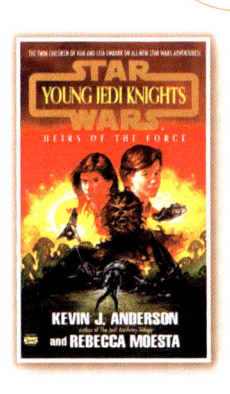

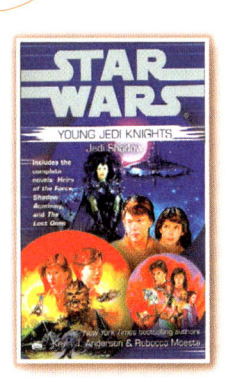

AUTHORS · Kevin J. Anderson and Rebecca Moesta

COVER ARTIST · Dave Dorman (both)

PUBLICATION HISTORY · Novel, Boulevard Books
· Paperback, June 1995
Compiled as part of Young Jedi Knights: *Jedi Shadow*
· Paperback, April 2002

TIME LINE PLACEMENT · 23 ABY

WORLD VISITED · Yavin 4 [P-6]

MAIN CHARACTERS · Jacen Solo, Jedi student (human male); Jaina Solo, Jedi student (human female); Lowbacca, Jedi student (Wookiee male); Qorl, TIE fighter pilot (human male)

SUMMARY · Jacen and Jaina along with their Wookiee friend Lowbacca (Chewbacca's nephew) discover a TIE fighter crashed in the jungles of Yavin 4. It had been there for twenty-three years, since the Battle of Yavin. Jaina, envious of Lowbacca's skyhopper, decides to refurbish the craft, making it better than ever before. She repairs it and even installs a hyperdrive. Her work is closely watched by Qorl, the TIE fighter's pilot, who has been surviving in the wilderness for nearly a quarter of a century. Qorl holds the young Jedi students at gunpoint and reclaims his craft, escaping into hyperspace so he can rejoin the Empire.

YOUNG JEDI KNIGHTS was a very popular series of novels geared to teens and was instrumental in developing the characters of Jacen and Jaina. Jaina truly takes after her father, being more brash and mechanically inclined, while Jacen is more contemplative, attuned to nature, and has a corny sense of humor. The series would last fourteen books and introduce a supporting cast of young Jedi characters—Tenel Ka, Lowbacca, Zekk, Raynar Thul—who would play important roles later in the time line, starting with the New Jedi Order novels.

Qorl's pilot designation of CE3K-1977 is a nod to Steven Spielberg's *Close Encounters of the Third Kind*, a 1977 motion picture contemporary of *Star Wars*. In a 2002 installment of *The Official Star Wars Fact File*, a weekly periodical published by De Agostini, Qorl's character was combined with a stranded TIE fighter pilot first depicted in "The Day After the Death Star," a comic strip published in *Star Wars Weekly* #97–99 (1980) by Marvel's UK office.

THE NEW REPUBLIC

YOUNG JEDI KNIGHTS: SHADOW ACADEMY

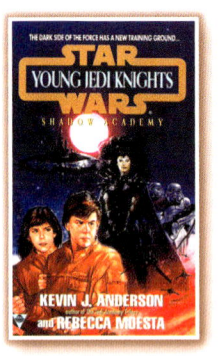

AUTHORS · Kevin J. Anderson and Rebecca Moesta

COVER ARTIST · Dave Dorman

PUBLICATION HISTORY · Novel, Boulevard Books
· Paperback, September 1995
Compiled as part of Young Jedi Knights: *Jedi Shadow*
· Paperback, April 2002

TIME LINE PLACEMENT · 23 ABY

WORLDS VISITED · Borgo Prime [M-6]; Dathomir [O-6]; Yavin and its moon Yavin 4 [P-6]

MAIN CHARACTERS · Jacen Solo, Jedi student (human male); Jaina Solo, Jedi student (human female); Lowbacca, Jedi student (Wookiee male); Luke Skywalker, Jedi Master (human male); Tenel Ka, Jedi student (human female); Brakiss, Shadow Academy headmaster (human male); Tamith Kai, Dark Jedi (human female); Qorl, TIE fighter pilot (human male)

SUMMARY · Jaina, Jacen, and Lowbacca are kidnapped by Imperial raiders during a tour of Lando Calrissian's GemDiver Station over the gas giant Yavin. The raiders hail from the Shadow Academy, a dark institute deep inside the Core Systems where Brakiss, a fallen disciple of Luke Skywalker, hopes to train Dark Jedi to restore the Empire's former glory. As the Shadow Academy tries to break Jaina's, Jacen's, and Lowie's wills, Luke Skywalker and student Tenel Ka search for the kidnapped students. The trail of clues from the GemDiver raid leads them to Borgo Prime, then Dathomir, where they find the Nightsister clan involved in gathering recruits for the Shadow Academy. Luke and Tenel use a Shadow Academy transport to travel from Dathomir to the academy, where they reunite just in time with the escaped Jaina, Jacen, and Lowbacca and flee the Imperials to return to Yavin 4.

YOUNG JEDI KNIGHTS: THE LOST ONES

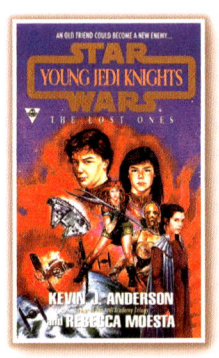

AUTHORS · Kevin J. Anderson and Rebecca Moesta

COVER ARTIST · Dave Dorman

PUBLICATION HISTORY · Novel, Boulevard Books
· Paperback, December 1995
Compiled as part of Young Jedi Knights: *Jedi Shadow*
· Paperback, April 2002

TIME LINE PLACEMENT · 23 ABY

WORLDS VISITED · Coruscant [L-9]; Yavin 4 [P-6]

MAIN CHARACTERS · Jacen Solo, Jedi student (human male); Jaina Solo, Jedi student (human female); Zekk, undercity urchin (human male); Tenel Ka, Jedi student (human female); Lowbacca, Jedi student (Wookiee male)

SUMMARY · Jaina and Jacen return to Coruscant, on leave from the Jedi academy for a month. Back on the city-planet, Jaina reconnects with her friend Zekk, a scamp from the undercity who frequently travels with old Peckhum, the shuttle pilot for the academy. Zekk is most at home in the lower levels, despite such dangers as the Lost Ones gang, and un-

At the Jedi academy on the moon Yavin 4: Jaina Solo, Jacen Solo, Em Teedee, Tenel Ka, Lowbacca, Anakin Solo, Zekk, and Tahiri Veila.

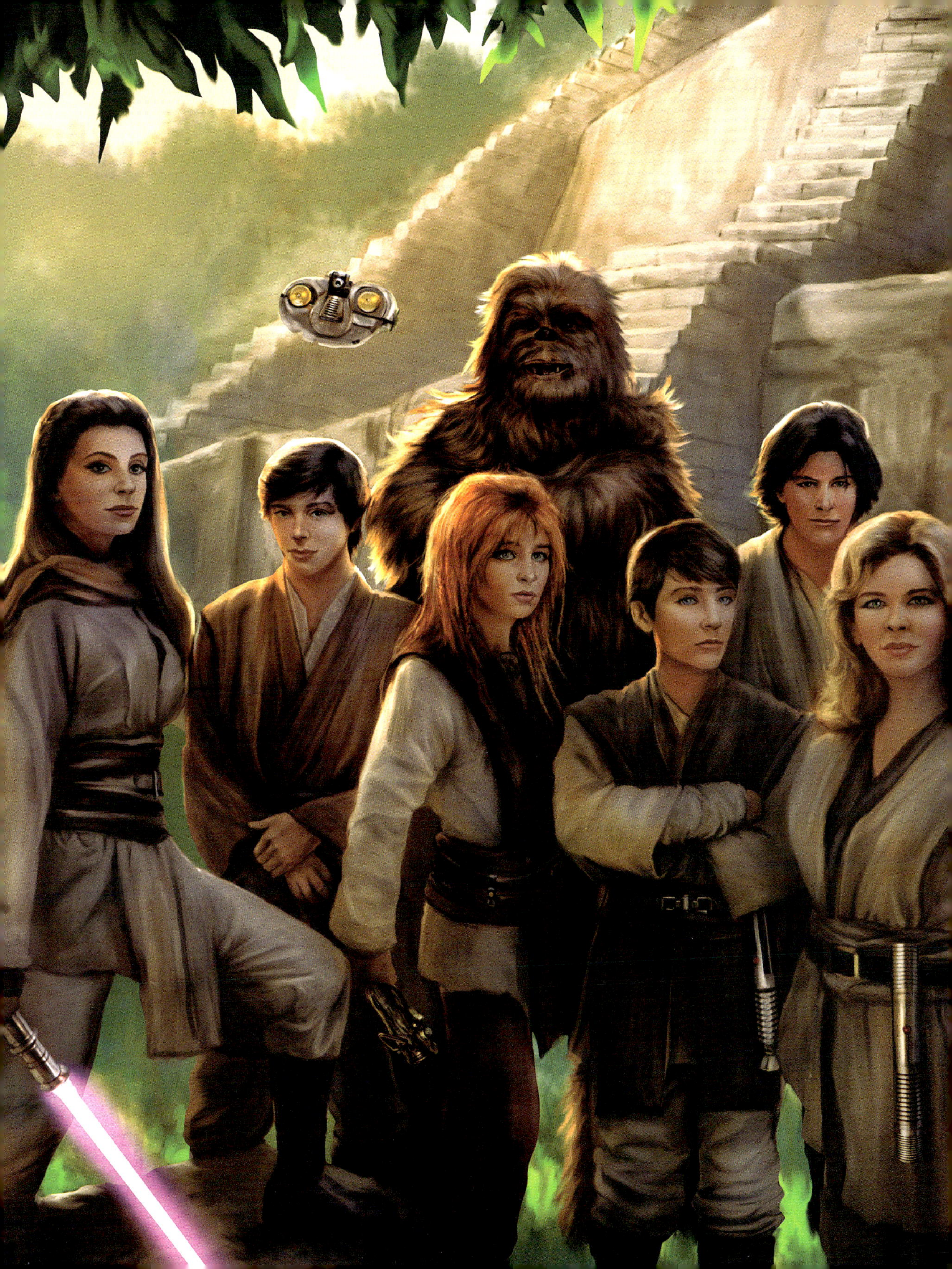

comfortable in the polished upper strata that Jaina calls home. Though he attends a diplomatic dinner with Jaina, Zekk's unfamiliarity with proper etiquette results in him embarrassing himself. His pride wounded, Zekk runs off. He is intercepted by Tamith Kai of the Shadow Academy, who reveals to him that he has Jedi potential.

Jaina worries about Zekk. She and Jacen look for him in the undercity, believing the Lost Ones to be responsible for his disappearance. What they find instead is Zekk recruiting Lost One members to join the Second Imperium. He has joined the dark side and departs aboard the cloaked Shadow Academy Station that has been hiding in orbit over Coruscant.

YOUNG JEDI KNIGHTS: LIGHTSABERS

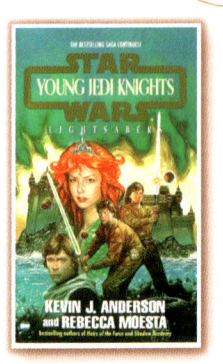

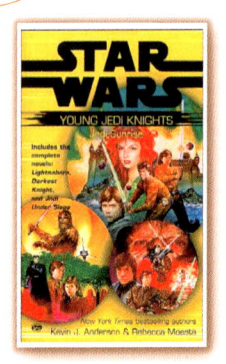

AUTHORS · Kevin J. Anderson and Rebecca Moesta
COVER ARTIST · Dave Dorman (both)
PUBLICATION HISTORY · Novel, Boulevard Books
· Paperback, March 1996
Compiled as part of Young Jedi Knights: *Jedi Sunrise*
· Paperback, December 2003

TIME LINE PLACEMENT · 23 ABY

WORLDS VISITED · Denarii Nebula [P-6]; Hapes [O-9]; Yavin 4 [P-6]

MAIN CHARACTERS · Jacen Solo, Jedi student (human male); Jaina Solo, Jedi student (human female); Tenel Ka, Jedi student (human female); Zekk, Dark Jedi student (human male); Lowbacca, Jedi student (Wookiee male); Luke Skywalker, Jedi Master (human male)

SUMMARY · With the growing threat of the Second Imperium, Luke has his Jedi academy students construct their own lightsabers. Unfortunately, Tenel Ka has hastily constructed an inferior weapon. During a sparring session with Jacen Solo, her blade dissipates, causing Jacen to accidentally sever her left arm just above the elbow. Jacen is horrified that he has maimed his friend. Tenel is spirited back to her homeworld of Hapes to recover. Tenel Ka is watched over by her grandmother, Ta'a Chume, who is determined to keep her safe amid court intrigue and assassination attempts by a treacherous ambassador. After the ambassador is exposed and arrested, Tenel Ka decides to return to the academy to continue her studies, as well as build a new lightsaber.

Meanwhile, Zekk trains under Tamith Kai, becoming one of the top students at the Shadow Academy. The Shadow Academy is devoted to rebuilding the Empire to power under its leader, the inexplicably alive and well Emperor Palpatine. To prove his skills, Zekk engages the other top student, Vilas, in a lightsaber duel and kills him.

THE NEW REPUBLIC

YOUNG JEDI KNIGHTS: DARKEST KNIGHT

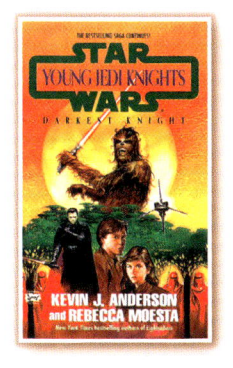

AUTHORS · Kevin J. Anderson and Rebecca Moesta
COVER ARTIST · Dave Dorman
PUBLICATION HISTORY ·
Novel, Boulevard Books
· Paperback, June 1996
Compiled as part of Young Jedi Knights: *Jedi Sunrise*
· Paperback, December 2003

TIME LINE PLACEMENT · 23 ABY

WORLDS VISITED · Kashyyyk [P-9]; Yavin 4 [P-6]

MAIN CHARACTERS · Jacen Solo, Jedi student (human male); Jaina Solo, Jedi student (human female); Lowbacca, Jedi student (Wookiee male); Zekk, Dark Jedi student (human male); Tenel Ka, Jedi student (human female)

SUMMARY · Lowie is concerned for his sister, Sirra, who is about to undergo a dangerous Wookiee rite of passage. Lowie returns to Kashyyyk, accompanied by Jacen, Jaina, and Tenel Ka. When the Second Imperium learns of this, Master Brakiss dispatches Zekk and a team of Dark Jedi to the Wookiee homeworld to steal vital computer parts. As a test of his loyalty, Zekk is also tasked with slaying his former friends should they cross paths. The Second Imperium attacks Kashyyyk, and the young Jedi are chased through the lower levels of the treacherous jungles. Zekk and Jaina confront each other, but Zekk cannot bring himself to harm her. He lets her go, warning her that Yavin 4 will soon be under attack. Zekk informs his colleagues that he killed Jaina.

Meanwhile, the Emperor arrives at the Shadow Academy. Much to the consternation of Brakiss, he is not allowed to see or speak to Palpatine. But the Emperor remotely orders Brakiss to set course for Yavin 4.

YOUNG JEDI KNIGHTS: JEDI UNDER SIEGE

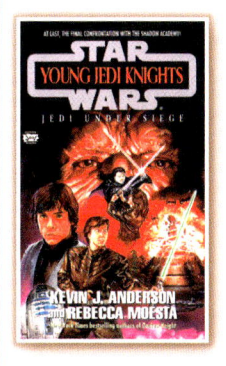

AUTHORS · Kevin J. Anderson and Rebecca Moesta
COVER ARTIST · Dave Dorman
PUBLICATION HISTORY ·
Novel, Boulevard Books
· Paperback, September 1996
Compiled as part of Young Jedi Knights: *Jedi Sunrise*
· Paperback, December 2003

TIME LINE PLACEMENT · 23 ABY

WORLD VISITED · Yavin 4 [P-6]

MAIN CHARACTERS · Jacen Solo, Jedi student (human male); Jaina Solo, Jedi student (human female); Zekk, Dark Jedi student (human male); Lowbacca, Jedi student (Wookiee male); Tenel Ka, Jedi student (human female); Luke Skywalker, Jedi Master (human male); Brakiss, Shadow Academy headmaster (human male)

SUMMARY · The Second Imperium attacks the Jedi academy on Yavin 4. Zekk leads his Dark Jedi troops into battle, while Tamith Kai leads teams of stormtroopers. The Jedi defend their school. Jacen joins Peckhum in attempting to fly his shuttle, *Lightning Rod*, beyond the jamming of the Shadow Academy

THE NEW REPUBLIC

Station to call for reinforcements. Second Imperium troopers led by Zekk and Tamith Kai land on the jungle surface and plant explosives on the Great Temple of the Jedi academy.

Brakiss and Luke confront each other once more. In a duel, Luke destroys Brakiss's lightsaber but refuses to kill Brakiss, who escapes. Tenel Ka defeats Tamith Kai in a duel. New Republic reinforcements led by Lando Calrissian eventually defeat the Imperial forces, and Qorl is once again shot down into the Yavin 4 wilderness.

Brakiss rushes back into the Shadow Academy Station and confronts the Emperor, only to discover he is a holographic sham carried out by the ersatz Royal Guards protecting him. One of the guards detonates the station's self-destruct systems, and the Shadow Academy is engulfed in a huge explosion.

Zekk tries to keep Jaina away from the Great Temple. The two duel, and Jaina defeats Zekk. She does not want to kill him, and Zekk, overcome with emotion, begins to surrender. The bomb at the Great Temple detonates, gravely injuring Zekk. As he recovers, Zekk rejects the dark side and instead pledges loyalty to his friends.

YOUNG JEDI KNIGHTS: SHARDS OF ALDERAAN

AUTHORS · Kevin J. Anderson and Rebecca Moesta
COVER ARTIST · Dave Dorman
PUBLICATION HISTORY · Novel, Boulevard Books
· Paperback, January 1997
TIME LINE PLACEMENT · 23–24 ABY

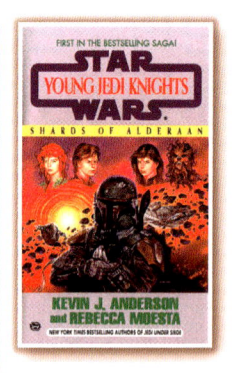

WORLDS VISITED · Alderaan (system) [M-10]; Ennth [Q-18]; Yavin 4 [P-6]
MAIN CHARACTERS · Jaina Solo, Jedi student (human female); Jacen Solo, Jedi student (human male); Boba Fett, aka Ailyn Vel in disguise (human female); Zekk, bounty hunter (human male); Raynar Thul, Jedi student (human male); Tenel Ka, Jedi student (human female); Lowbacca, Jedi student (Wookiee male)

SUMMARY · The Jedi academy rebuilds after the devastating battle against the Second Imperium. As Zekk recovers from his injuries, he returns to his home planet of Ennth to seek new direction.

An arrogant noble named Raynar Thul is a student at the Jedi academy. His father is missing. The Diversity Alliance, an anti-human/pro-alien extremist group interested in Bornan Thul's disappearance, hires Boba Fett to investigate.

Jaina and Jacen, meanwhile, decide to go to the graveyard of Alderaan, the asteroid field left behind by the planet's destruction. They travel aboard the *Rock Dragon*, Tenel Ka's new ship which she received as a gift from her parents. Raynar and Lowie are also aboard. The Solo twins seek a shard of the planet to give as a gift to their mother for her birthday. The *Rock Dragon* is attacked by Boba Fett in *Slave IV*; he demands the location of Bornan Thul. Zekk comes to the rescue, piloting the *Lightning Rod*. After Fett retreats, Zekk decides to become a bounty hunter, thinking that his Force abilities would be a great advantage.

THE AUTHORS FULLY INTENDED for the bounty hunter pursuing the Jedi kids to be

THE NEW REPUBLIC

Boba Fett, the famous bounty hunter from the saga. But the evolving Expanded Universe since the book's publication necessitated changing the character well after the fact. An article in *Star Wars Insider* #80 (2005) revealed that beneath Boba Fett's helmet in this story is a woman, Fett's daughter, Ailyn Vel. In *A Practical Man* (2006), Fett would later be established as building up Mandalore in advance of the Yuuzhan Vong invasion and would be unavailable at this point in the time line.

YOUNG JEDI KNIGHTS: DIVERSITY ALLIANCE

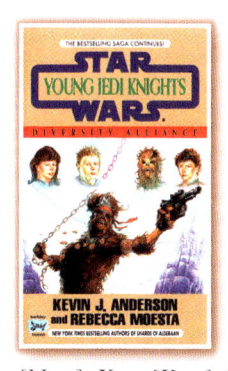

AUTHORS · Kevin J. Anderson and Rebecca Moesta

COVER ARTIST · Dave Dorman

PUBLICATION HISTORY · Novel, Boulevard Books · Paperback, April 1997

TIME LINE PLACEMENT · 24 ABY

WORLDS VISITED · Borgo Prime [M-6]; Gammalin [N-16]; Kuar [K-10]; Ryloth [R-17]; Yavin 4 [P-6]

MAIN CHARACTERS · Jacen Solo, Jedi student (human male); Jaina Solo, Jedi student (human female); Raynar Thul, Jedi student and noble (human male); Lowbacca, Jedi student (Wookiee male); Zekk, bounty hunter (human male); Tenel Ka, Jedi student (human female)

SUMMARY · Concerned for Raynar's safety in the face of his father's kidnapping, his mother, Aryn, requests that he return to the family flagship, the *Tradewyn*. Her plan backfires when a treacherous crewmember attempts to kidnap Raynar. Raynar's fellow Jedi students defend him. They then set off for Kuar, the last known destination of Bornan Thul.

Following his own leads regarding Bornan Thul's disappearance brings Zekk to Gammalin, where he is shocked to discover that the world's populace has been wiped out by a plague. Zekk encounters Boba Fett, who considers Zekk an honorable rival. The two work together and discover that the plague was introduced by command of Nolaa Tarkona, leader of the Diversity Alliance. Only Bornan Thul knows how to stop the deadly contagion that targets humans.

On Kuar, the Jedi find Raaba, a Wookiee and friend of Lowbacca's from Kashyyyk. She has joined the Diversity Alliance and invites Lowie to do so as well. The group finds Tyko Thul, Raynar's uncle and Bornan's brother, who is hunted by the assassin droid IG-88. The droid kidnaps Tyko, leaving the Jedi no further avenues but to return to the academy.

YOUNG JEDI KNIGHTS: DELUSIONS OF GRANDEUR

AUTHORS · Kevin J. Anderson and Rebecca Moesta

COVER ARTIST · Dave Dorman

PUBLICATION HISTORY · Novel, Boulevard Books · Paperback, July 1997

TIME LINE PLACEMENT · 24 ABY

WORLDS VISITED · Borgo Prime [M-6]; Kashyyyk [P-9]; Kuar [K-10]; Mechis III [L-14]; Ryloth [R-17]; Tatooine [R-16]; Yavin 4 [P-6]; Ziost [R-4]

THE NEW REPUBLIC

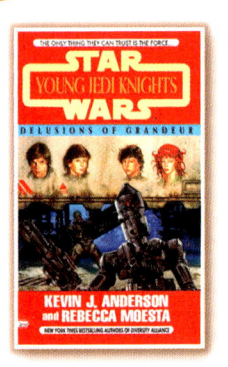

MAIN CHARACTERS · Jacen Solo, Jedi student (human male); Jaina Solo, Jedi student (human female); Raynar Thul, Jedi student and noble (human male); Lowbacca, Jedi student (Wookiee male); Zekk, bounty hunter (human male); Tenel Ka, Jedi student (human female); Dengar, bounty hunter (human male)

SUMMARY · After seeing his uncle kidnapped, Raynar decides to take over Tyko Thul's droid-manufacturing operation on Mechis III. He is shocked to find Tyko there. Tyko explains that he reprogrammed IG-88 to create the illusion that he was kidnapped, in the hope that word of such a fate might provoke Bornan Thul to reveal himself.

Tyko is right. Bornan Thul does surface, as an anonymous, disguised man who hires Zekk to find Tyko and pass a message on to the Thul family. Zekk's search brings him to Ziost, where he is chased by the bounty hunter Dengar; to Tatooine, where he seeks advice from Boba Fett; and finally to Mechis III, where he joins with his friends in the search for Bornan.

Nolaa Tarkona—leader of the Diversity Alliance—continues her plot against humanity. The plague she used on Gammalin was part of a sample created for the Emperor. Only Bornan Thul knows where further supplies of the toxin can be found, making it imperative that the Diversity Alliance find him.

Raaba the Wookiee arrives on Yavin 4, imploring Lowbacca to return with her to meet with Tarkona.

YOUNG JEDI KNIGHTS: JEDI BOUNTY

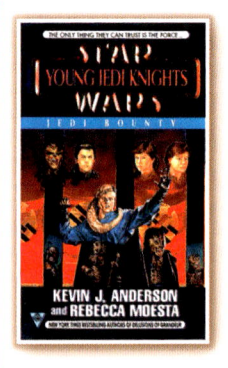

AUTHORS · Kevin J. Anderson and Rebecca Moesta
COVER ARTIST · Dave Dorman
PUBLICATION HISTORY ·
Novel, Boulevard Books · Paperback, October 1997
TIME LINE PLACEMENT · 24 ABY
WORLDS VISITED · Coruscant [L-9]; Ryloth [R-17]; Yavin 4 [P-6]

MAIN CHARACTERS · Jacen Solo, Jedi student (human male); Jaina Solo, Jedi student (human female); Raynar Thul, Jedi student and noble (human male); Lowbacca, Jedi student (Wookiee male); Zekk, bounty hunter (human male); Tenel Ka, Jedi student (human female); Nolaa Tarkona, Diversity Alliance leader (Twi'lek female); Luke Skywalker, Jedi Master (human male); Lusa, Jedi student (centauriform female)

SUMMARY · Jacen, Jaina, Tenel Ka, and Raynar Thul voyage to Ryloth to learn what they can about the Diversity Alliance, hoping to stop the organization. They see that Nolaa Tarkona is stockpiling supplies, gearing up for full war against the New Republic. The young Jedi are discovered and captured, and Tarkona sentences them to toil in the ryll mines.

Zekk finds Bornan Thul, saving him from pursuit by Dengar the bounty hunter. Bornan reveals to Zekk details about the Emperor's plague and provides him coordinates to the storehouse where supplies of the pathogen can be found. Bornan hopes Zekk can stop Tarkona before it is too late. Zekk

THE NEW REPUBLIC

passes word of Tarkona's plan to Luke on Yavin 4, and Luke leads a mission to Ryloth to rescue the captive Jedi with the help of Lowbacca and Sirra.

YOUNG JEDI KNIGHTS: THE EMPEROR'S PLAGUE

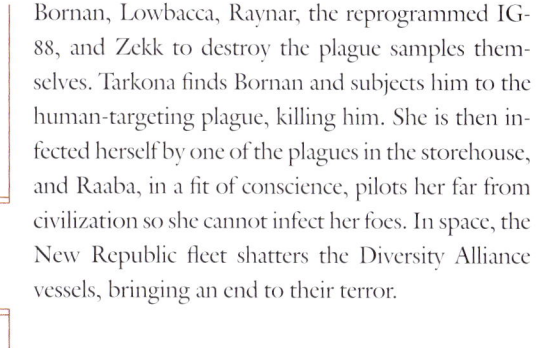

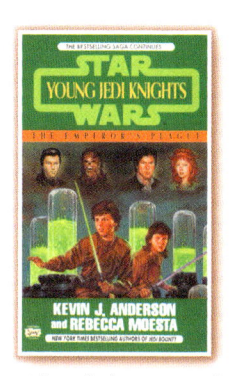

AUTHORS · Kevin J. Anderson and Rebecca Moesta
COVER ARTIST · Dave Dorman
PUBLICATION HISTORY · Novel, Boulevard Books
 · Paperback, January 1998
TIME LINE PLACEMENT · 24 ABY
WORLDS VISITED · Coruscant [L-9]; a Deep Core asteroid (site of plague warehouse) [L-11]; Ryloth [R-17]; Yavin 4 [P-6]
MAIN CHARACTERS · Jacen Solo, Jedi student (human male); Jaina Solo, Jedi student (human female); Raynar Thul, Jedi student and noble (human male); Lowbacca, Jedi student (Wookiee male); Zekk, bounty hunter (human male); Tenel Ka, Jedi student (human female); Nolaa Tarkona, Diversity Alliance leader (Twi'lek female); Bornan Thul, noble (human male)
SUMMARY · Boba Fett tracks Bornan Thul's location and secures the coordinates to the Emperor's plague storehouse from Bornan's computer, delivering the data to Nolaa Tarkona. She departs Ryloth, destined for the Deep Core. The Jedi arrive first, planting explosives throughout the depot to destroy it. Inside is a huge variety of devastating plague toxins. Tarkona's forces arrive and begin defusing the bombs, forcing Bornan, Lowbacca, Raynar, the reprogrammed IG-88, and Zekk to destroy the plague samples themselves. Tarkona finds Bornan and subjects him to the human-targeting plague, killing him. She is then infected herself by one of the plagues in the storehouse, and Raaba, in a fit of conscience, pilots her far from civilization so she cannot infect her foes. In space, the New Republic fleet shatters the Diversity Alliance vessels, bringing an end to their terror.

YOUNG JEDI KNIGHTS: RETURN TO ORD MANTELL

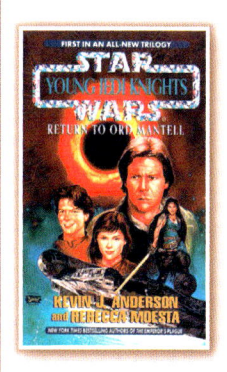

AUTHORS · Kevin J. Anderson and Rebecca Moesta
COVER ARTIST · Dave Dorman
PUBLICATION HISTORY · Novel, Berkley Jam Books
 · Paperback, May 1998
TIME LINE PLACEMENT · 24 ABY
WORLDS VISITED · Anobis [L-7]; Ord Mantell [L-7]; Yavin 4 [P-6]
MAIN CHARACTERS · Jacen Solo, Jedi student (human male); Jaina Solo, Jedi student (human female); Anja Gallandro, reluctant Black Sun agent (human female); Han Solo, captain of the *Millennium Falcon* (human male); Tenel Ka, Jedi student (human female); Zekk, Jedi student (human male)
SUMMARY · Jedi studies are briefly interrupted when Han Solo arrives on Yavin 4 and invites his kids and their friends to accompany him to Ord Mantell, where he's been named Grand Marshal of the Blockade Runners Derby. During the event, a young

woman brandishing a lightsaber confronts Han, claiming that he killed her father. It is Anja Gallandro, daughter of the late, infamous gunslinger. Han tries to explain he didn't kill Gallandro, but the bitter Anja doesn't believe him. She has grown up an orphan on the war-ravaged world of Anobis, and Han tries to improve her lot by voyaging to the beleaguered planet to help settle the conflict. Little does Han know that Anja is working for Czethros, a Black Sun agent who wants Han dead. Czethros keeps Anja strung out on andris, an addictive spice that can boost one's senses and reflexes to Jedi-like levels.

ANJA GALLANDRO IS the daughter of the gunslinger featured in Brian Daley's *Han Solo's Revenge* (1979) and *Han Solo and the Lost Legacy* (1980). The bounty hunter Czethros was originally intended to be Skorr, the titular antagonist from the 1981 comic strip *The Bounty Hunter of Ord Mantell* by Archie Goodwin and Al Williamson. At the eleventh hour, however, editors realized Skorr dies at the end of the newspaper strip in 1984, so Skorr was hastily rewritten as new character Czethros.

YOUNG JEDI KNIGHTS: TROUBLE ON CLOUD CITY

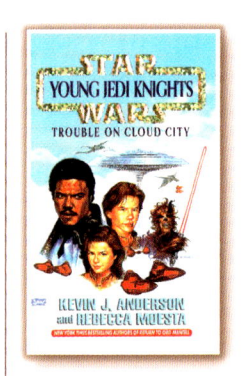

MAIN CHARACTERS · Jacen Solo, Jedi student (human male); Jaina Solo, Jedi student (human female); Anja Gallandro, reluctant Black Sun agent (human female); Lando Calrissian, entrepreneur (human male); Tenel Ka, Jedi student (human female); Zekk, Jedi student (human male); Lowbacca, Jedi student (Wookiee male); Czethros, Black Sun leader (humanoid male)

SUMMARY · At the invitation of the Solos, Anja Gallandro studies at the Jedi academy, but she is too short-tempered and distracted to make much progress. Lando Calrissian invites the kids to visit his newest business venture: the SkyCenter Galleria amusement park on Cloud City. There, the Jedi investigate the strange death of Lando's business partner, Cojahn, who was secretly murdered by Czethros of Black Sun. Lando, Jaina, and Zekk follow leads to Clak'dor VII, while Tenel Ka, Lowie, Jacen, and Anja stay on Bespin. Anja warns her benefactor, and Czethros dispatches Black Sun assassins to kill the Jedi. With Czethros's involvement discovered, and all traitorous Galleria employees exposed, the threat seems abated. But Anja frets that since she is now cut off from Czethros, she is also cut off from her badly needed andris spice.

AUTHORS · Kevin J. Anderson and Rebecca Moesta
COVER ARTIST · Dave Dorman
PUBLICATION HISTORY · Novel, Berkley Jam Books · Paperback, August 1998
TIME LINE PLACEMENT · 24 ABY
WORLDS VISITED · Bespin [K-18]; Clak'dor VII [M-18]; Yavin 4 [P-6]

YOUNG JEDI KNIGHTS: CRISIS AT CRYSTAL REEF

AUTHORS · Kevin J. Anderson and Rebecca Moesta
COVER ARTIST · Dave Dorman

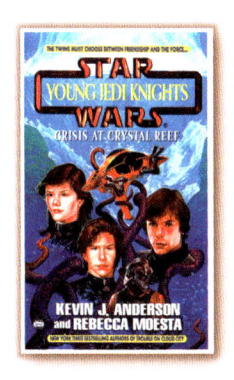

PUBLICATION HISTORY · Novel, Berkley Jam Books · Paperback, December 1998

TIME LINE PLACEMENT · 24 ABY

WORLDS VISITED · Kessel [T-10]; Mon Calamari [U-6]; Yavin 4 [P-6]

MAIN CHARACTERS · Jacen Solo, Jedi student (human male); Jaina Solo, Jedi student (human female); Anja Gallandro, reluctant Black Sun agent (human female); Cilghal, ambassador and Jedi Knight (Mon Calamari female); Tenel Ka, Jedi student (human female); Zekk, Jedi student (human male); Lowbacca, Jedi student (Wookiee male); Czethros, Black Sun leader (humanoid male)

SUMMARY · Racked by spice withdrawal, Anja steals Zekk's ship. Upon discovering that Czethros was behind the long, terrible war on Anobis, she vows to strike back against her former master. Anja voyages to Mon Calamari to scuttle Czethros's spice-smuggling operation there. Jacen and his friends, concerned over Anja's behavior, find her on Mon Calamari with the help of Jedi Knight and Mon Calamari ambassador Cilghal. Cilghal uses her Force-healing abilities to clear Anja of her addiction. Meanwhile, Jaina and Lowbacca corner Czethros in the spice mines of Kessel. Rather than be captured, Czethros throws himself into a vat of carbonite, where he is flash-frozen.

Returning to Yavin 4, the young Jedi are honored in a graduation ceremony that sees them promoted to the rank of Jedi Knights.

Because the details of the Padawan–Master apprenticeship were not known to *Star Wars* book authors at this time, the graduation of the students to Jedi Knights does not signify the end of their training. Although the students are described as "fully trained Jedi Knights" at this point in the time line, Jacen, Jaina, and Anakin begin the New Jedi Order series apprenticed to other Masters.

"THE CRYSTAL"

AUTHOR · Elaine Cunningham

PUBLICATION HISTORY · Short story, Wizards of the Coast · *Star Wars Gamer* #5, August 2001

TIME LINE PLACEMENT · 24 ABY

WORLDS VISITED · Mon Calamari [U-6]; Yavin 4 [P-6]

MAIN CHARACTER · Jaina Solo, Jedi Knight (human female)

SUMMARY · After graduating from the Jedi academy, Jaina Solo asks her aunt, Mara Jade Skywalker, to be her mentor. Han Solo gives Jaina a graduation gift: a modified Z-95 Headhunter. During her inaugural flight, Jaina is attacked by a deranged cyborg piloting an X-wing fighter, who misidentifies her as his enemy. Despite suffering some damage in the dogfight, Jaina destroys the enemy fighter while sparing the pilot's life. She decides to call her Z-95 the *Crystal*.

Mara is described as suffering from a mysterious ailment in her appearance here, a story point that continues through to the New Jedi Order novels.

THE NEW REPUBLIC

Anakin Solo

Nom Anor

Saba Sebatyne

Tahiri Veila

Cal Omas

Raynar Thul

CHAPTER 7

THE NEW JEDI ORDER

AFTER DOZENS OF *Star Wars* novels from Bantam Spectra, the license to produce adult fiction shifted from Bantam to Del Rey—the original publishers of *Star Wars* books—offering an opportunity for a fresh perspective. Del Rey's editorial team would work with LucasBooks to build upon the vast universe of characters, history, and settings established in the Bantam novels. Rather than isolated trilogies and stand-alone works, Del Rey would embark upon an expansive multibook series that told an epic story.

The original plan was ambitious: twenty-nine books plotted over the course of five years—a number that would be whittled down to a more manageable nineteen as development began. The story arc was to hew closely to the mythic structure of the Hero's Journey as outlined by Joseph Campbell, a huge influence on the creation of the *Star Wars* films. With that as its basic framework, the plot underwent much evolution and exploration. Its earliest descriptions had Luke Skywalker sending the three Solo children on an epic quest, during which they encounter a female character from an invading species sent to infiltrate the galaxy. This unnamed female corrupts Anakin, nearly turning him to the dark side, but instead she falls in love with him and Anakin redeems her. In a fit of intense sibling rivalry, Jacen and Jaina turn on Anakin, and the resulting conflict tragically ends with Jacen's death.

As readers of the series know, very little of this outline survived subsequent reworking. Early ideas for the invading aliens proposed that they were perhaps the source of the original Sith, the ones who gave the Sith their dark side powers. They were described as being predisposed to using the powers of the dark side, but more out of necessity and for survival than with evil intent. As per a working 1998 outline, this society would have observed the brightness of "our" galaxy for a thousand generations, fearing an ancient prophecy that foretold they would be brought down by a "light-bringer." They watched the galaxy dim as Palpatine launched his regime, and saw the return of the light as the Jedi were rebuilt, prompting their strike.

George Lucas commented on the story overview, making a number of specific changes. Among them, he disapproved of the idea that the invaders were dark side users. Per Lucas, such dark siders would ultimately vie for power, which would be their undoing as a group. Thus no Sith or proto-Sith appear in the series.

With Lucas's feedback and a framework of an epic told through five yearly hardcovers and with several mass market paperbacks filling out the plot in between, The New Jedi Order began with a bang: its shocking first book would include one of the most polarizing moments in Expanded Universe history, heralding a level of gravitas that would dominate *Star Wars* novels for years to come.

VECTOR PRIME

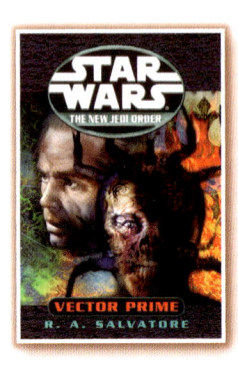

AUTHOR · R. A. Salvatore
COVER ARTIST · Cliff Nielsen
PUBLICATION HISTORY · Novel, Del Rey Books
- Hardcover, October 1999
- Paperback, July 2000

TIME LINE PLACEMENT · 25 ABY
WORLDS VISITED · Belkadan [L-1]; Coruscant [L-9]; Dubrillion-Destrillion [K-3]; Helska IV [L-2]; Reecee [J-8]; Rhommamool-Osarian [N-13]; Sernpidal [L-3]

MAIN CHARACTERS · Luke Skywalker, Jedi Master (human male); Leia Organa Solo, New Republic diplomat (human female); Han Solo, captain of the *Millennium Falcon* (human male); Chewbacca, copilot/mechanic (Wookiee male); Jacen Solo, Jedi (human male); Jaina Solo, Jedi (human female); Anakin Solo, Jedi (human male); Danni Quee, ExGal researcher (human female); Nom Anor, executor (Yuuzhan Vong male); Wurth Skidder, Jedi Knight (human male); Miko Reglia, Jedi Knight (human male); Yomin Carr, advance agent/saboteur (Yuuzhan Vong male); Lando Calrissian, entrepreneur (human male); Kyp Durron, Jedi Master (human male); Mara Jade Skywalker, Jedi Master (human female)

SUMMARY · Rising tensions between the neighboring Osarians and Rhommamoolians are fanned by an inscrutable agitator named Nom Anor. Leia Organa Solo, Jaina Solo, and Mara Jade Skywalker arrive as a New Republic diplomatic delegation to settle the peace, but Anor ends the talks abruptly. The presence of a reckless Jedi Knight, Wurth Skidder, who impulsively engages Osarian starfighters in his X-wing only exacerbates the tense situation. After Leia, Mara, and Jaina leave, Anor orders the destruction of Osa-Prime.

On Coruscant, Luke Skywalker realizes that the Jedi Knights maintaining law and order in the Outer Rim have been working too independently—and perhaps too enthusiastically—in chasing smugglers. These loose cannons have riled several New Republic councilors. Luke proposes to the government the reinstitution of the Jedi Council to act as an authority over the Jedi Knights. Interested in gathering solid intelligence from the Outer Rim, Luke voyages to the Dubrillion system with Han, Jacen, and Anakin Solo aboard the *Millennium Falcon*. Mara, Jaina, and Leia soon join them.

Jacen and Anakin have differing opinions when it comes to the role of the Jedi in the galaxy. Anakin has an assertive perspective, believing that it is the duty of the Jedi to protect those who cannot protect

Mara Jade Skywalker deflects incoming thud bugs thrown by Yomin Carr, a Yuuzhan Vong advance agent who has orchestrated the destruction of a scientific outpost on Belkadan.

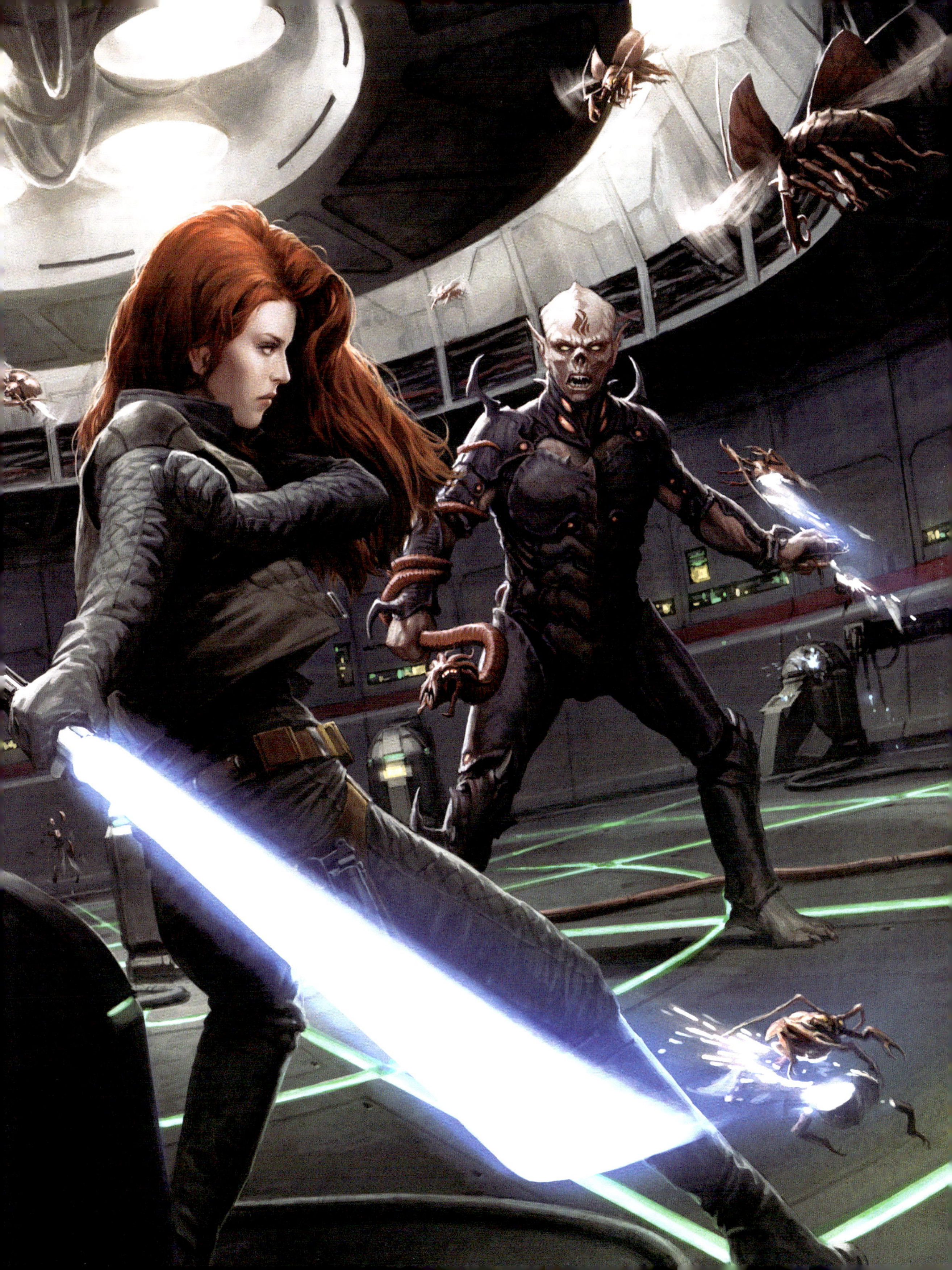

SPOTLIGHT: Meanwhile, in Comics

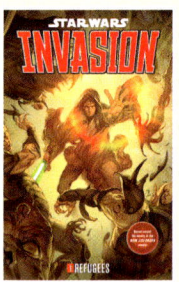

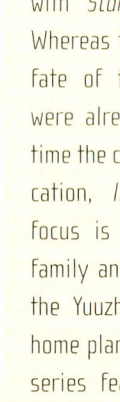

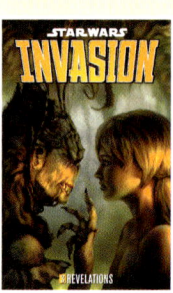

In 2009, well after the completion of the New Jedi Order novel series, Dark Horse Comics began telling stories set during this era, starting with *Star Wars: Invasion*. Whereas the overall arc and fate of the Yuuzhan Vong were already known by the time the comics began publication, *Invasion*'s primary focus is on the Galfridian family and the incursion by the Yuuzhan Vong on their home planet of Artorias. The series features cameos by Luke Skywalker, Jaina Solo, Anakin Solo, and Jacen Solo. The *Invasion* series comprises a number of miniseries, including *Refugees* (2009), *Rescues* (2010), and *Revelations* (2011).

---

tific team suspect that one of their members is an advance scout from an extragalactic civilization: Yomin Carr is a Yuuzhan Vong alien in disguise. Carr awaits the arrival of his people's invasion force and communicates remotely with Nom Anor, who is another disguised Yuuzhan Vong. At Anor's command, Carr destroys the station's communications systems and proceeds to kill the ExGal scientists, though a small research team has already left the planet to track an incoming asteroid headed for the ice planet Helska IV. Carr also unleashes a plague of rapidly breeding beetles with a biochemistry toxic to the planet's ecosystem. In time, the creatures transform Belkadan into a world suitable for Yuuzhan Vong military needs.

The approaching asteroid from beyond the galaxy is the vanguard vessel of the Yuuzhan Vong invasion force. The aliens are masters at engineering organic technology, and they reject lifeless machinery as anathema to their deeply held beliefs. The worldship impacts on the surface of Helska IV. Beneath the ice, the aliens deploy a yammosk, an immense brainlike coordinating intelligence that will manage the creation of their new foothold in the galaxy. On Helska IV, the Yuuzhan Vong capture Danni Quee, a member of the ExGal research team who had avoided the slaughter on Belkadan.

Lando Calrissian runs a mining operation on the twin worlds of Dubrillion-Destrillion. The reunion of the Solos, Skywalkers, and Lando includes a thrilling interlude of competitive piloting as Jaina Solo clocks record-breaking speeds while "running the belt"—flying a specially equipped TIE ship through an asteroid obstacle course. Such skill draws the envious admiration of Kyp Durron, who is in system with his apprentice, Miko Reglia, and their maverick squad of fliers, the Dozen-and-Two Avengers.

Kyp and his squadron depart and stumble upon the Yuuzhan Vong invasion force. The X-wings are

themselves, while Jacen believes meditation and mediation are the Jedi mandates. This disagreement represents in microcosm the philosophical rift worming its way through the Jedi Order.

Light-years away on the galactic frontier world of Belkadan, an ExGal science station scans intergalactic space for any sign of life. Little does the scien-

cut apart by alien coralskippers, bio-engineered ships that use directed singularities created by creatures called dovin basals to not only absorb incoming blasts but also strip the shields off enemy starships. Other weaponized creatures known as grutchins are insects that gobble their way through X-wing hulls. Kyp survives the battle and limps his ship to nearby Sernpidal. The Yuuzhan Vong capture Miko and imprison him with Danni Quee. The Jedi is subjected to telepathic torture by the yammosk.

At Lando's behest, Han, Anakin, and Chewbacca depart aboard the *Millennium Falcon* to ferry supplies to nearby Sernpidal. The planet is in chaos as its moon, Dobido, is inexplicably dropping out of orbit. The Yuuzhan Vong have secreted a powerful dovin basal beneath Sernpidal's surface, which uses its gravity-altering powers to draw the moon closer. With time ticking away, the *Falcon*'s crew crowds as many desperate refugees as possible within its holds. When Chewbacca is left behind, Anakin makes the difficult decision that the *Falcon* cannot rescue the Wookiee in time without jeopardizing all aboard. The *Falcon* departs, and Chewbacca dies in the cataclysmic collision of Dobido and Sernpidal. Han is devastated by the death of his friend, and in his anger and grief blames Anakin for abandoning Chewbacca. The *Falcon* intercepts Kyp and tows his battle-worn X-wing behind as the ship heads back to Dubrillion.

Luke and Mara investigate ruined Belkadan, finding ExGal reports of the mysterious asteroid that impacted on Helska IV. Yomin Carr attacks the Jedi, proving to be a formidable opponent—especially since, as Luke and Mara discover, Yuuzhan Vong are invisible to the Force. Despite the fact that Mara has been afflicted by a mysterious infection, she slays the infiltrator. Her illness is inflamed by the destruction on Belkadan, suggesting some sort of connection. Luke and Mara follow the lead to Helska IV, where they are attacked by Yuuzhan Vong ships.

Those at Dubrillion prepare to defend themselves against these strange invaders. Leia requests New Republic reinforcements, but the nearest Star Destroyer is days away. Anakin helps coordinate a defense using the belt-running racing vessels. The Solo children are able to meld their piloting skills through the Force, giving them an edge in combat. In their victory, they capture a Yuuzhan Vong coralskipper, which Luke studies upon his arrival.

Luke launches an attack that targets the sunken Yuuzhan Vong base on Helska IV. In the battle, Jacen lands one of Lando's ice-boring mining machines on the planet and rescues Danni. Miko sacrifices himself in combat. With firsthand knowledge of the yammosk supplied by Danni, the New Republic succeeds in destroying the war coordinator in an assault that tears apart Helska IV. Though this Yuuzhan Vong foothold is destroyed, it is just the beginning of a much larger invasion.

THE DEATH OF CHEWBACCA was a seismic event designed to mark a bold new era of storytelling—and it drew an outpouring of grief and shock from longtime readers and *Star Wars* fans. The idea of sacrificing Chewie was initially suggested by Dark Horse editor Randy Stradley, citing the impact his death would have on other characters.

In the developing story, the invading aliens were given the working name of the Adzakans, and then the Vici-Vicians, which later was supplanted by the Yunnan Vong before finally becoming the Yuuzhan Vong. They were first said to be tribal-minded humans, transformed by ritual tattooing and the use of the dark side into yellow-eyed zealots. Later versions did away with the dark side influence, and the aliens were described as resembling humans but taller, heavier, and with less hair. It was author R. A. Salvatore who came up with the bio-organic technology angle to give the invaders a suitably distinctive hook.

In a testament to the times when the series was envisioned, the story overview describes something akin to a sense of "millennialism" sweeping through parts of the galaxy, wherein some of its citizens sense an impending war or disaster on the horizon.

According to the Campbellian mythology structure cited during the series' conception, this book is Jacen's "Call to Adventure," when he enters into the enemy's first stronghold to rescue Danni Quee.

Mara Jade Skywalker is described as suffering a mysterious alien disease—a coomb spore infestation planted by Nom Anor at a previous encounter. Readers looking for that story will not find it; it is an event intended to have happened between books, prior to the events of *Vector Prime*.

DARK TIDE

ONSLAUGHT

RUIN

AUTHOR · Michael A. Stackpole

COVER ARTIST · John Harris

PUBLICATION HISTORY · Novels, Del Rey Books
Onslaught · Paperback, February 2000
Ruin · Paperback, June 2000

TIME LINE PLACEMENT · 25 ABY

WORLDS VISITED · Agamar [M-5]; Bastion [K-3]; Belkadan [L-1]; Bimmiel [N-4]; Coruscant [L-9]; Dantooine [L-4]; Dubrillion-Destrillion [K-3]; Garos IV [P-7]; Garqi [K-5]; Ithor [M-6]; Sernpidal [L-3]; Vortex [K-7]; Yavin 4 [P-6]

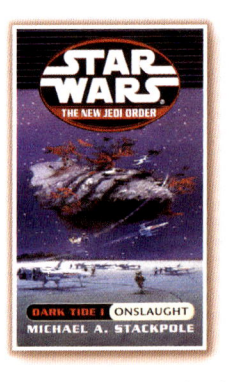

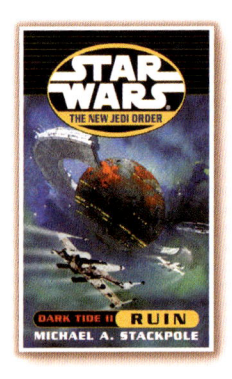

MAIN CHARACTERS · Luke Skywalker, Jedi Master (human male); Corran Horn, Jedi Knight (human male); Shedao Shai, commander (Yuuzhan Vong male); Mara Jade Skywalker, Jedi Master (human female); Elegos A'Kla, New Republic Senator (Caamasi male); Jacen Solo, Jedi (human male); Jaina Solo, Jedi and Rogue Squadron pilot (human female); Anakin Solo, Jedi (human male); Leia Organa Solo, New Republic diplomat (human female); Ganner Rhysode, Jedi Knight (human male); Danni Quee, scientist (human female); Lando Calrissian, entrepreneur (human male); Gavin Darklighter, New Republic colonel (human male); Borsk Fey'lya, Chief of State (Bothan male)

SUMMARY · Two months have passed since the destruction of Sernpidal and Helska IV. A lack of overt Yuuzhan Vong activity since then has led many in the New Republic government, including Chief of State Borsk Fey'lya, to doubt the severity of the alien threat. As such, the New Republic military cannot adequately mobilize for defense, though Gavin Darklighter, leader of Rogue Squadron, keeps his fighter pilots vigilant. Leia Organa Solo takes her warnings directly to the worlds on the predicted path of the invasion, beginning with Agamar.

Still reeling from the loss of his fighter squadron, Kyp Durron wants to take the fight to the

Yuuzhan Vong, but Luke Skywalker disagrees with such an aggressive response. Luke instead assigns teams of Jedi to conduct careful scouting missions to gather more intelligence. Corran Horn and the arrogant, headstrong Jedi Knight Ganner Rhysode reconnoiter Bimmiel, site of an endangered xenoarchaeological expedition. Scientists there have uncovered the mummified remains of a Yuuzhan Vong, proof that the invaders probed the galaxy before. These remains have also brought the Yuuzhan Vong to Bimmiel. Corran and Ganner work together to defend the scientists from the aliens and escape with the remains. In doing so, Corran makes a blood enemy of Yuuzhan Vong commander Shedao Shai.

Luke and a disillusioned Jacen Solo travel to Belkadan, a planet conquered by the Yuuzhan Vong and transformed into a shipbuilding resource. Jacen has difficulty accepting that the Yuuzhan Vong exist apart from the Force, blaming instead a shallowness to Jedi perception that renders the aliens invisible and untouchable. Moved by a dream, Jacen rushes to free the slaves laboring under the command of the Yuuzhan Vong, but he is defeated by the aliens and captured briefly before Luke is able to rescue him.

Leia voyages to Dubrillion and, with the help of Rogue Squadron and Admiral Kre'fey of the New Republic fleet, begins to evacuate the world. The beleaguered populace intends to retreat to nearby Agamar, but a Yuuzhan Vong attack diverts them to Dantooine instead. Mara Jade Skywalker, accompanied by Anakin Solo, is sojourning on the tranquil planet in the hope of recuperating from her mysterious illness. She finds that such inactivity does not become her, though, and when the Yuuzhan Vong arrive on the planet she springs back into action.

New Republic and Yuuzhan Vong forces converge on Dantooine. The Yuuzhan Vong disguise their warriors within the human refugee camps and reveal themselves in deadly surprise attacks. The aliens launch waves of slave soldiers into an immense battle along the grasslands. It becomes evident that these attacks are merely tests, enabling the Yuuzhan Vong to gauge the New Republic's response.

The New Republic begins to fray under such strains and retreats from Dantooine. Bloodied by the assault but carrying undeniable proof of the ongoing invasion, Kre'fey, Leia, and Gavin demand that Fey'lya act against the threat, lest he lose the allegiance of the military. The government sends Leia to Bastion to seek an alliance with the Imperial Remnant to defend against this common foe. Her efforts bring Imperial forces led by Grand Admiral Pellaeon and Chiss forces led by Baron Soontir Fel's son, Jagged, to help. An adherent of peace and diplomacy, Elegos A'Kla of the New Republic Senate offers to become an envoy to the Yuuzhan Vong, to learn more of this strange new culture.

Elegos allows himself to be captured by Shedao Shai. The Yuuzhan Vong, amused and intrigued by the pacifist Senator, establish a rapport with A'Kla before coldly murdering the Caamasi upon discovering that he is a good friend of Corran Horn.

The Jedi continue their scouting missions, venturing deeper into enemy territory. Corran, Ganner, and Jacen visit Garqi, a world besieged by the Yuuzhan Vong. While helping the local resistance battle the aliens, Corran discovers that the living Yuuzhan Vong armor exhibits a crippling allergy to the pollen of the bafforr trees, plants native to Ithor. Meanwhile, Anakin and Luke voyage to Garos IV, following the path of Daeshara'cor, a Jedi driven rogue by fear of the Yuuzhan Vong.

Shedao Shai learns of the bafforr pollen threat and attacks Ithor, clashing with the New Republic forces in space and within the sacred jungles of the planet. Corran Horn, now also on Ithor, recognizes that Shai has a personal vendetta against him and challenges Shai to one-on-one combat to determine the fate of the planet. Though Corran is able to kill his opponent, the Yuuzhan Vong do not honor the agreement the Jedi made. Shai's subordinate Deign Lian orders the Yuuzhan Vong forces to bombard Ithor.

The remaining Vong retreat when faced with New Republic reprisal, but with Ithor reduced to a lifeless husk, the New Republic has lost the battle. Corran shoulders the blame for the loss of the planet, and the Jedi lose credibility in the eyes of New Republic politicians for taking so foolhardy a risk, even though such destruction was inevitable.

The Dark Tide series was first outlined as three books, under the working title the Jedi Retreat Trilogy. These included *Onslaught*, *Siege*, and *Ruin*, which told largely the same story except spread out over three novels. *Siege* would have included Leia's efforts to recruit help from the Imperial Remnant, and a disillusioned Jacen would briefly apprentice himself to Corran. In the *Ruin* outline, Luke and Mara would be drawn to Ithor to search for a cure to Mara's illness, which would turn the planet into a target—the bafforr tree allergy was not present in early outlines. The allergy would surface again as a prime ingredient in a biological weapon introduced in *Destiny's Way* (2002).

AGENTS OF CHAOS

HERO'S TRIAL
JEDI ECLIPSE

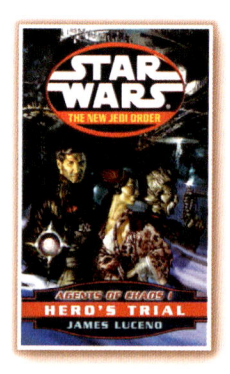

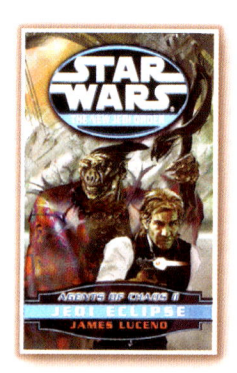

AUTHOR · James Luceno
COVER ARTISTS · Rick Berry/Braid Media Arts
PUBLICATION HISTORY · Novels, Del Rey Books
Hero's Trial · Paperback, August 2000
Jedi Eclipse · Paperback, October 2000
TIME LINE PLACEMENT · 25 ABY
WORLDS VISITED · Ando [Q-15]; Anobis [L-7]; Bilbringi [J-8]; Commenor [N-10]; Corellia [M-11]; Coruscant [L-9]; Drall [M-11]; Gyndine [O-12]; Hapes [O-9]; Kalarba [P-15]; Kashyyyk [P-9]; Kuat [M-10]; Myrkr [N-7]; Nal Hutta [S-12]; Nim Drovis [R-7]; Obroa-skai [N-8]; Ord Mantell [L-7]; Ruan [K-10]; Sriluur [S-8]; Talus and Tralus [M-11]; Tholatin [P-10]; Tynna [N-14]; Vortex [K-7]; Wayland [N-7]; Yavin 4 [P-6]
MAIN CHARACTERS · Luke Skywalker, Jedi Master (human male); Han Solo, captain of the *Millennium Falcon* (human male); Leia Organa Solo, New Republic diplomat (human female); Nom Anor, executor (Yuuzhan Vong male);

Droma, spacer (Ryn male); Elan, priestess (Yuuzhan Vong female); Vergere, familiar (Fosh female); Harrar, priest (Yuuzhan Vong male); Viqi Shesh, Senator (human female); Reck Desh, Peace Brigade mercenary (human male); Roa, retired smuggler (human male); Nas Choka, Supreme Commander (Yuuzhan Vong male)

SUMMARY · For six months, the Yuuzhan Vong have inexorably advanced into the galaxy, conquering many worlds as they head toward the Core. The New Republic government has failed to mount an effective defense, as squabbling and self-interest among its Senators undercut the necessary unity. In the absence of leadership from the New Republic, opportunistic elements arise, such as the Peace Brigade, mercenaries who would sell out their own and aid the enemy to ensure their protection.

The Yuuzhan Vong have identified the Jedi Knights as their most dangerous foes within the Republic. Nom Anor and the priest Harrar hatch a scheme to use Elan, a Yuuzhan Vong priestess, to infiltrate the Jedi ranks. She deliberately allows herself to be captured by the New Republic as part of a calculated plan that will provide her access to release a deadly, infectious spore among the Jedi. Accompanying Elan in this assignment is her familiar, an odd avian being known as Vergere. For Nom Anor, the success of this plan is particularly important—the defeat at Helska IV has reflected poorly upon him, and he longs to regain his status.

After a funeral for Chewbacca on Kashyyyk, Han Solo ventures out on his own, hit hard by the death of his best friend. He reunites with his old smuggling mentor Roa, who tells of a past friend, Reck Desh, who has sided with the Peace Brigade. Han and Roa journey to Ord Mantell, and at the Jubilee Wheel orbital station they learn more about the Peace Brigade from gangster Big Bunji, who feels indebted to Han for his role in the death of Jabba the Hutt.

Suddenly the Yuuzhan Vong attack Ord Mantell, and the Jubilee Wheel is engulfed by an immense wormlike creature. Yuuzhan Vong invaders capture Roa, but Han is able to scramble to freedom aboard the fleeing starliner *Queen of Empire* with the help of Droma, a well-traveled Ryn vagabond with combat reflexes, a keen sense of intuition, and a strong survival instinct. Though Solo finds Droma irksome at first, he soon grows to appreciate the resourcefulness of his new acquaintance.

Also aboard the *Queen of Empire* are Elan and Vergere, in New Republic Intelligence custody. An informant within the ranks of the New Republic tips off the Peace Brigade to the Yuuzhan Vong defector—unaware of the ultimate gambit to use Elan against the Jedi. Desh's mercenaries attack the liner. Han briefly helps NRI defend Elan, but soon figures out and thwarts her plan. Elan releases her deadly spores in an attempt to stop Han, but she dies a failure. Before fleeing, the mysterious Vergere gives Han a vial of her tears, claiming the liquid will slow the disease crippling Mara Jade Skywalker.

Han returns to his family to deliver Vergere's peculiar cure, but the reunion is brief and tense. Still haunted by the loss of his friend, he refuses to let his loved ones help. The Yuuzhan Vong's relentless advance has displaced millions of Republic citizens, among them the Ryn. Han returns to the life of a spacer, determined to help Droma find his missing people. Leia Organa Solo works tirelessly with the Senate Select Committee for Refugees (SELCORE), an aid organization headed by Senator Viqi Shesh. Ever the diplomat, Leia reaches out to the Hapes Consortium for help with the refugees and military assistance in fighting the extragalactic invaders.

SPOTLIGHT Meanwhile, in Comics

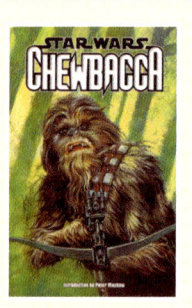

While Chewbacca's memorial appears in the novel *Hero's Trial*, it is more fully explored in a four-part comic series, *Chewbacca*, released by Dark Horse Comics in 2000. The anthology-like series consists of stories of Chewbacca's past as recounted by those paying their respects to the fallen Wookiee, including Luke, Han, Leia, Lando, Wedge, Chewie's wife Mallatobuck, his father Attichitcuk, a Trandoshan slaver, and a bounty hunter. For novel readers, the comics not only provide some emotional closure but also visually depict the heroes at the time of The New Jedi Order, and present Chewie's death at Sernpidal as a flashback.

The Yuuzhan Vong have found unlikely allies in the Hutts, striking a treaty with the gangsters that allows the invaders to accelerate their advance through Hutt space by sparing the Hutt worlds. The Yuuzhan Vong don't trust the Hutts, and in fact purposely use the loathsome gangsters to spread disinformation to the New Republic, knowing that the Hutts will sell such intelligence to the highest bidder.

Suspecting that the Yuuzhan Vong might attack Corellia, the New Republic prioritizes its defense. Jacen and Anakin Solo rush to Centerpoint Station, the ancient space station used as a weapon during the Corellian insurrection. The two Solo teens reluctantly work with Thrackan Sal-Solo, their father's cousin, who attempted to kidnap them six years earlier. During that event, Anakin imprinted himself on the space station, and it is believed that only he can activate it. Jacen disagrees with the use of such a device in war.

At the Battle of Gyndine, the impulsive Jedi Knight Wurth Skidder lets himself be captured by the Yuuzhan Vong in the hope of getting to study the enemy up close. Aboard the clustership *Crèche*, Skidder is forced to toil alongside fellow prisoners tending a growing yammosk, a brainlike war coordinator. While Skidder attempts to keep his Jedi identity a secret, he befriends Roa, who is also imprisoned aboard the vessel.

The Yuuzhan Vong attack is *not* directed at Corellia, but rather at the starship yards of Fondor. Han and Droma are in system searching for the Ryn. Kyp Durron leads his starfighter squadron in an attack on the *Crèche*, penetrating the vessel and rescuing many prisoners, including Roa. Skidder, though, does not make it—he has been tortured to death by the nascent yammosk, who was able to determine Skidder's agenda. Ganner Rhysode slays the yammosk, causing the *Crèche* to destroy itself.

The New Republic is able to rally support from the Hapans, whose fleet arrives at Fondor just as the impulsive Thrackan Sal-Solo activates Centerpoint Station. Unfortunately, the massive blast is poorly aimed, and wipes out not only half the Yuuzhan Vong fleet at Fondor, but also three-quarters of the Hapan warships as well.

In the aftermath of the battle, Nom Anor makes contact with a secret ally deep in the folds of New Republic politics: Senator Viqi Shesh, who is working for the Yuuzhan Vong.

THE WORKING TITLES for the books of the Agents of Chaos series were *Solo Crusade* and *The Crooked Sky*. In the original outline of the first novel, the information broker on the Ord Mantell space station was to be Boba Fett, but concerns that the book was adding too many characters caused Fett to be written out and replaced with Big Bunji, an incidental character mentioned in Brian Daley's Han Solo novels. Fett would not appear in the New Jedi Order series until the final book, *The Unifying Force* (2003).

A longtime friend of the late Daley, author James Luceno included many nods to Daley's influential trilogy, including the reappearance of Roa, first seen in *Han Solo's Revenge* (1979). In the outline, Roa was to die during the Yuuzhan Vong attack on the Jubilee Wheel, but his fate changed as the novel developed. A detour in Han and Roa's search for the Ryn takes them to Ruan, where they meet a droid who looks and acts an awful lot like the labor droid Bollux from Daley's Han Solo trilogy, but the text is deliberately vague as to the droid's identity.

In the initial story outline for the New Jedi Order series, the refugee plot was described as a means of supplying the point of view of the underclasses, as the droids did in the first *Star Wars* movie.

BOBA FETT: A PRACTICAL MAN

AUTHOR · Karen Traviss
COVER ARTIST · Steven D. Anderson
PUBLICATION HISTORY · Novella, Del Rey Books · eBook novella, August 2006
Included in *Sacrifice*, Del Rey Books · Paperback, April 2008

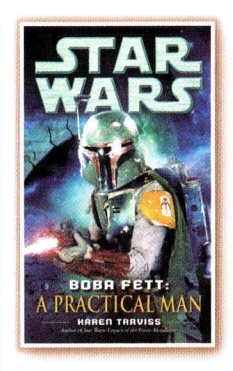

TIME LINE PLACEMENT · 24–25 ABY

WORLDS VISITED · Coruscant [L-9]; Mandalore [O-7]; Nar Shaddaa (moon of Nal Hutta) [S-12]; New Holgha [N-5]; Vorpa'ya [O-7]

MAIN CHARACTERS · Boba Fett, Mandalore and bounty hunter (human male); Nom Anor, executor (Yuuzhan Vong male); Goran Beviin, Mandalorian mercenary (human male); Briika Jeban, Mandalorian mercenary (human female)

SUMMARY · Nom Anor, disguised as a human named Udelen, recruits a Mandalorian mercenary to carry out an assassination on the industrial world of Ter Abbes. Impressed by the Mandalorians, Anor meets with Boba Fett, who is now Mandalore, leader of his people. Anor arranges for the Mandalorians to meet with the encroaching Yuuzhan Vong fleet. Anor lays out the invasion plans to Fett, asking the Mandalorians to help by acting as saboteurs and commandos. Fett agrees, provided that the Yuuzhan Vong spare the Mandalore sector.

Fett doesn't trust the Yuuzhan Vong—nor is he forthcoming or trustworthy. He intends to carefully maintain the illusion of collaboration, all the while studying these new extragalactic enemies with an eye toward defeating them. Fett slips the New Republic information about the Yuuzhan Vong but refuses to become an ally. The Mandalorians are fighting for their own side in the war.

An eBook novella published well after the New Jedi Order series had wrapped, *A Practical Man* sought to describe Fett's activity during the invasion and set up his role as Mandalore as revealed in the Legacy of the Force novels, starting in 2006. The novella also serves to explain why Fett is depicted as working for the Yuuzhan Vong in the comic story "Revenants," an installment in the quasi-canonical *Star Wars Tales* series, published by Dark Horse in 2003.

BALANCE POINT

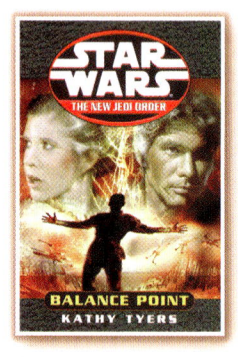

AUTHOR · Kathy Tyers
COVER ARTIST · Cliff Nielsen
PUBLICATION HISTORY ·
Novel, Del Rey Books
· Hardcover, November 2000
· Paperback, July 2001
TIME LINE PLACEMENT · 26 ABY
WORLDS VISITED · Coruscant [L-9]; Duro [M-11]; Kalarba [P-15]; Rodia [R-16]
MAIN CHARACTERS · Luke Skywalker, Jedi Master (human male); Leia Organa Solo, New Republic diplomat (human female); Han Solo, captain of the *Millennium Falcon* (human male); Jacen Solo, Jedi (human male); Jaina Solo, Jedi (human female); Anakin Solo, Jedi (human male); Nom Anor, executor (Yuuzhan Vong male); Mara Jade Skywalker, Jedi Master (human female); Randa Besadii Diori, refugee (Hutt); Tsavong Lah, warmaster (Yuuzhan Vong male); Viqi Shesh, Senator (human female)
SUMMARY · Two months after the Battle of Fondor and ten months since the fall of Sernpidal, Rogue Squadron pilot Lieutenant Jaina Solo is shot down, injured, and blinded at the Battle of Kalarba and must take medical leave as she recovers. She joins the rest of her family on Duro, the site of extensive refugee relief efforts by SELCORE. The world's orbital cities as well as the erected shelters on its toxic surface have become home to thousands of citizens displaced by the ongoing Yuuzhan Vong invasion.

Jacen Solo, helping his father organize Ryn refugees at Settlement 32, experiences intense and apocalyptic Force visions. He sees an image of himself failing to catch a lightsaber tossed to him by his uncle Luke, as well as the galaxy tipping toward fiery destruction. He believes that by withdrawing from the Force, he can prevent such a cataclysmic future from coming to pass. Though Jacen turns his back on his Jedi heritage, the visions continue.

At the Gateway dome, Leia, now a Jedi Knight, meets with the Duro reclamation project team, although one team member, Dr. Dassid Cree'Ar, has been suspiciously absent. Cree'Ar is actually an alias adopted by Yuuzhan Vong infiltrator Nom Anor, who is working under the noses of the New Republic. He cultivates a strain of destructive mothlike creatures that he intends to unleash on Duro. He secretly contacts his superiors with word that Leia, Jacen, and Jaina are on Duro.

The New Republic believes the Yuuzhan Vong invasion will not reach Coruscant. However, under the bold command of the bellicose warmaster Tsavong Lah, the aliens intend to target Duro, as the planet is the perfect launching point for an attack against the New Republic capital world. On Coruscant, the covert collaborator, SELCORE leader Viqi Shesh, conspires against the New Republic, communicating with Tsavong Lah via villip, an organic communications device.

Luke Skywalker continues his efforts to form a governing Jedi Council. As Mara recovers from her ailment, she senses a presence within her body through the Force. Initially fearing it to be another

380 THE NEW JEDI ORDER

Jacen Solo defends his fallen mother, Leia Organa Solo, against the monstrous Yuuzhan Vong warmaster Tsavong Lah.

Yuuzhan Vong infection, she soon realizes she is pregnant. Mara and Luke agree to keep this development a secret. Joined by Anakin Solo, they depart for Duro to investigate the suspicious disappearance of a Jedi who was investigating misappropriated relief supplies. They travel incognito, arriving at the space city of Bburru, and inspect the CorDuro shipping company.

Randa the Hutt, a refugee at Settlement 32, entertains thoughts of handing Jacen over to the Yuuzhan Vong for the sake of his homeworld. Changing his mind, he instead tries to inform the New Republic that a Yuuzhan Vong presence has infiltrated Duro. He contacts Viqi Shesh, who now counts Randa as an enemy of the Yuuzhan Vong.

Jacen discovers the destructive mothlike creatures infesting Settlement 32. The hungry pests can chew through the containment dome, threatening the settlement's inhabitants. The refugees must evacuate to Gateway. Following the exodus, Jacen, Jaina, and Han are reunited with Leia. Tensions are high, and Jaina's resentment of her mother, for her abandonment of family to tend to duties elsewhere, grows.

At Gateway, Jaina finds and confiscates Shesh's villip—her means of communicating with the Yuuzhan Vong. Mara goes to Gateway and meets with Leia, and Jaina joins in the search for Dr. Cree'Ar. When they find him, Mara and Jaina expose the scientist as Nom Anor. Before the Jedi can capture him, Anor escapes after triggering a rockslide atop Mara and Jaina.

THE NEW JEDI ORDER

The Jedi extricate themselves and take the *Jade Shadow* back to the orbital city Bburru, where they reunite with Luke and Anakin. With the help of R2-D2, they gather evidence indicating an imminent Yuuzhan Vong attack on Duro. Leia and Han prepare the refugees, hoping to find some way to get them offworld before the invaders strike, but it is too late. Nom Anor captures Leia and brings her before Tsavong Lah.

Leia is held prisoner alongside Randa the Hutt, and they are forced to watch as refugees are marched to their death in a gruesome fire pit. Jacen returns to Settlement 32 to rescue his mother. Randa futilely sacrifices himself by attacking the Yuuzhan Vong. Tsavong Lah tortures and cripples Leia with red garrote-like creatures until Jacen arrives. Though Jacen has attempted to devote himself to a more peaceful understanding of the Force through passivity, knowing that his mother will die if he fails to act moves him to action. Jacen attacks, injuring Lah. Escaping, Jacen and Leia rendezvous with Jaina and Han aboard the *Millennium Falcon*. The freighter escorts refugee ships off Duro's surface.

In space, an overwhelming force of Yuuzhan Vong battlegroups arrives. With a renewed hatred of the Jedi, and Jacen Solo in particular, Tsavong Lah addresses the New Republic and promises to suspend hostilities provided the New Republic turn over all Jedi to the Yuuzhan Vong.

In the initial plot outline, the second New Jedi Order hardcover was to feature Luke and Mara journeying to a new world to meet with the invading leader, an example of the common mythological motif of entering into the "heart of darkness." With Tsavong Lah's ultimatum issued at story's end, one of the points in the initial outline is covered: the alien invaders would use the Jedi to pit factions within the New Republic against one another. Notes regarding Tsavong Lah say, "He is Darth Vader to Supreme Overlord Shimrra's emperor; Jacen is Luke, without the blood tie."

Again mirroring the Hero's Journey as detailed by Joseph Campbell, this book casts Jacen as the Reluctant Hero archetype as he struggles to reconcile the need for aggression against the invaders with his idealistic philosophies.

RECOVERY

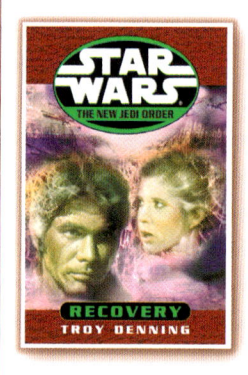

AUTHOR · Troy Denning

COVER ARTIST · Steven D. Anderson

PUBLICATION HISTORY · Novella, Del Rey Books
· eBook, October 2001
Reprinted as part of *Star by Star*
· Paperback, July 2001

TIME LINE PLACEMENT · 26 ABY

WORLDS VISITED · Cinnabar Moon [M-11]; Corellia [M-11]; Coruscant [L-9]

MAIN CHARACTERS · Leia Organa Solo, New Republic diplomat (human female); Han Solo, captain of the *Millennium Falcon* (human male); Eelysa, Jedi Knight (human female); Saba Sebatyne, Jedi Knight (Barabel female); Viqi Shesh, Senator (human female)

SUMMARY · After being tortured at the hands of Warmaster Tsavong Lah, Leia is in need of immediate medical attention. Han Solo rushes her to Corellia, where they enter a medcenter under assumed names and she is tended to by a Jedi-sympathetic doctor. After Tsavong Lah's ultimatum to the galaxy—turn over the Jedi in exchange for a cease in the terrible Yuuzhan Vong hostilities—Peace Brigade thugs infiltrate the medcenter to attack Leia. Han fends them off with the help of Eelysa, another Jedi there for medical treatment.

Leia and Han worm their way past Han's opportunistic cousin, Thrackan Sal-Solo, who has ridden a tide of popularity for his role in defending Corellia and now leads the Centerpoint Party, a political entity that has no qualms over striking deals with the Yuuzhan Vong. Han, Leia, and Eelysa depart Corellia aboard the *Millennium Falcon*, aided by the Wild Knights, a Jedi fighter squadron led by Eelysa's apprentice, Saba Sebatyne. As Leia continues her recuperation at the Wild Knights' secret headquarters at Cinnabar Moon, she also mends her strained relationship with Han. The two piece together evidence from the Duro debacle and realize Viqi Shesh is collaborating with the Yuuzhan Vong.

Han and Leia return to Coruscant to accuse the Senator as Shesh leads a movement in the Senate to officially appease the Yuuzhan Vong. Shesh's vote fails, and Han and Leia are unable to make their evidence stick due to the untimely death of Shesh's chief of staff. His ersatz deathbed confession absolves Shesh of all guilt and allows her to stay in power.

The Jedi are left with few friends in the galaxy, but Luke Skywalker begins planning an underground network of safe passage for the beleaguered Jedi Knights, which he dubs "the Great River."

EDGE OF VICTORY

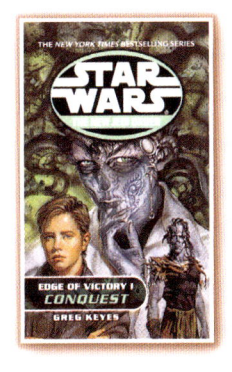

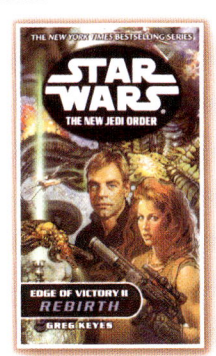

CONQUEST
REBIRTH

AUTHOR · Greg Keyes

COVER ARTIST · Terese Nielsen

PUBLICATION HISTORY · Novels, Del Rey Books
Conquest · Paperback, April 2001
Rebirth · Paperback, August 2001

TIME LINE PLACEMENT · 26 ABY

WORLDS VISITED · Ando [Q-15]; Chandrila [L-9]; Cha Raaba (system) [T-12]; Clak'dor VII [M-18]; Coruscant [L-9]; Eriadu [M-18]; Sernpidal [L-3]; Shelter [T-10]; Yag'Dhul [L-14]; Yavin 4 [P-6]

MAIN CHARACTERS · Luke Skywalker, Jedi Master (human male); Mara Jade Skywalker, Jedi Master (human female); Anakin Solo, Jedi (human male); Tahiri Veila, Jedi (human female); Vua Rapuung, Shamed One (Yuuzhan Vong male); Mezhan Kwaad, master shaper (Yuuzhan Vong female); Nen Yim, shaper (Yuuzhan Vong female); Talon Karrde, smuggler baron (human male); Corran Horn, Jedi Master (human male); Jaina Solo, Jedi and X-wing pilot (human female); Jacen Solo, Jedi (human male); Kyp Durron, Jedi Master (human male); Han Solo, captain of the *Millennium Falcon* (human male); Leia Organa Solo, New Republic diplomat (human female)

SUMMARY · Six weeks after Warmaster Tsavong Lah's ultimatum, several worlds of the New Republic betray their Jedi protectors, colluding with nefarious agencies, including the Peace Brigade, to hand over Jedi Knights to the Yuuzhan Vong in exchange for a lessening of hostilities. These grim developments continue to split the Jedi Order, as some Jedi such as Kyp Durron push for an aggressive response. Luke Skywalker favors a more measured course of action, concentrating on defending the most vulnerable of Jedi.

Anakin Solo voyages to the Jedi academy on Yavin 4 to ensure the safety of the young Jedi stationed there. Peace Brigade mercenaries attack the Temple, killing Anakin's old mentor, Ikrit, and capturing his dear friend Tahiri Veila. The Yuuzhan Vong destroy the ancient edifice, building new camps out of the rubble. Anakin survives in the jungle, trekking toward the Yuuzhan Vong damutek buildings to rescue Tahiri.

Smuggling baron Talon Karrde arrives on Yavin 4 aboard the *Wild Karrde* to wage a war of wits and firepower against the Peace Brigade. Karrde frees Masters Kam and Tionne Solusar and their Jedi students from captivity and sends them to Coruscant while he continues his search for the missing Anakin. When word of his nephew's predicament reaches Luke on Coruscant, the Jedi Master finds little help from the New Republic government. Instead he assigns Jaina and Jacen to contact Booster Terrik aboard his Star Destroyer, *Errant Venture*.

Battling Yuuzhan Vong scouts, Anakin damages his lightsaber. He is saved by Vua Rapuung, a mysterious Yuuzhan Vong of the lowliest caste. The Shamed Ones' bodies have rejected the ritual organic grafting of implants and modifications, and they are deemed worthless in Yuuzhan Vong society. Vua was a great warrior whose fall from grace was orchestrated by his former lover, Mezhan Kwaad. Mezhan is Tahiri's captor. Once Vua and Anakin realize they have a common foe, they band together. To fix his lightsaber, Anakin uses a lambent crystal grown by the Yuuzhan Vong. Attunement of the crystal within his Jedi weapon allows Anakin to rudimentarily sense the aliens in the Force.

Mezhan Kwaad and her apprentice, Nen Yim, are from the shaper caste, devoted to biological alterations. Mezhan reshapes Tahiri's memories through intensive brainwashing, causing her to believe she is Riina Kwaad, a Yuuzhan Vong Jedi. Mezhan wants to create a hybrid warrior able to touch the Force, unlike the rest of the Yuuzhan Vong, and in her pursuit she pushes past the boundaries of sacred protocols, courting heresy in favor of scientific progress.

Anakin and Vua arrive at the alien base just as Yuuzhan Vong warriors attempt to apprehend the shapers for heresy. The pursuit of Tahiri culminates in a confrontation that neither Vua nor Mezhan survives, but Vua acquits himself well in combat and publicly exposes Mezhan's betrayal of him. In this way, he earns back some level of redemption with his death. Anakin escapes with Tahiri, with cover from the *Wild Karrde*, the *Errant Venture*, and Jacen and Jaina Solo's X-wing fighters.

On Coruscant, Jedi Master Kenth Hamner warns Luke that Borsk Fey'lya has issued a warrant for his arrest. Mara's illness has returned, and she grows weaker by the moment. These concerns distract Luke from his ambitious Great River project. Han and Leia help secure routes for the Jedi to Shelter, a rebuilt refuge within the old abandoned Maw Installation. Luke and Mara flee the capital aboard the *Errant Venture*.

Booster Terrik's modified Star Destroyer becomes the temporary traveling refuge of the Jedi

Sealed in a storage locker for their own safety, Anakin Solo and Tahiri Veila exchange their first kiss.

children. Anakin watches over Tahiri's recovery. The ship must be covertly resupplied, so Anakin and Corran Horn pilot the freighter *Lucre* to Eriadu, accompanied by a restless Tahiri. They cross paths with Kelbis Nu, a Jedi attacked by the Peace Brigade. The dying Nu passes on word of an impending assault that will target the planet Yag'Dhul.

With Mezhan Kwaad dead, Nen Yim is reassigned to the dying worldship *Baanu Miir*. Following in Mezhan's footsteps, she explores the frontiers of Yuuzhan Vong knowledge. According to doctrine, the Yuuzhan Vong were gifted with their shaping abilities by the gods, as communicated via their mortal intermediary, the Supreme Overlord. The current Overlord, Shimrra, parceled out the latest of this knowledge to the shapers during their exodus from their native galaxy.

Nen Yim discovers the shocking truth that this knowledge store is bare. She decides to begin developing her own protocols, goaded into action by a peculiar master shaper named Kae Kwaad. Making matters all the more intriguing, Kae Kwaad reveals himself to be Onimi, the twisted jester and Shamed One in service to Shimrra.

Hoping to bring much-needed decisiveness to the Jedi, Jaina seeks out Kyp Durron's help. Kyp surprises her by requesting *her* help, and that of Rogue Squadron, to take out a superweapon being developed by the Yuuzhan Vong at Sernpidal. Kyp also asks Jaina to be his apprentice.

Investigating the Yag'Dhul lead, the *Lucre* emerges in the midst of a Yuuzhan Vong fleet. Anakin, Tahiri, and Corran recognize that the Yuuzhan Vong truce has evidently been broken. Nom Anor, posing as a native Givin, has infiltrated the Yag'Dhul command structure. Anor leads the Jedi into a trap aboard a space station over Yag'Dhul.

Elsewhere in the galaxy, the *Millennium Falcon* begins a brief career as a privateer vessel, raiding Peace Brigade convoys. Han has renamed the ship

Princess of Blood and is aided by Leia and Jacen. Warmaster Tsavong Lah, still holding a smoldering grudge against Jacen, learns of this deception from Vergere, the former familiar to the late priestess Elan, who has returned to the Yuuzhan Vong fold. Armed with this knowledge, Lah springs a trap for the *Falcon* with a particularly tempting Peace Brigade convoy.

Lah offers Han a cease-fire in exchange for handing over Jacen. Han refuses. Jacen develops a clever plan for escape, releasing a cargo of liquid hydrogen against the Yuuzhan Vong defenses. The Vong ships use miniature black holes as shields, and the acceleration of hydrogen into these singularities reacts explosively, allowing the Solos to escape.

At Yag'Dhul, Anakin battles against the Yuuzhan Vong. He calls out Nom Anor for a duel, warrior-to-warrior, but Anor declines. With the Givin poised to expel the atmosphere of the space station to stymie the invaders, Corran equips Anakin and Tahiri with an oxygen tank and shoves them into a storage locker for safety. In such cramped quarters, and with death at every corner, Anakin and Tahiri exchange their first kiss and resolve to figure out their relationship after the Yuuzhan Vong have been defeated. Meanwhile, a fleeing Nom Anor murders a trio of Yuuzhan Vong warriors who judge him to be a disgrace for refusing a challenge posed by the Jedi. Corran, Anakin, and Tahiri make their escape aboard a Givin transport.

At Sernpidal, after the New Republic forces destroy the Vong "superweapon," Jaina realizes it was not a military target but rather the site of a shipwomb—a production facility filled with noncombatants who were developing new Yuuzhan Vong worldships and transports. Incensed at Kyp's deception, she slaps the Jedi Master in the face. Jaina swears that she will never help Kyp again.

Aboard the *Errant Venture*, Luke is at Mara's side, concerned about her worsening condition and her impending childbirth. Tapping into the Force and drawing strength from Luke and her unborn child, Mara not only rids her body of all remaining traces of the Yuuzhan Vong illness but gives birth to a healthy baby boy: Ben Skywalker. Luke then receives a message from Borsk Fey'lya, welcoming his return to Coruscant.

Nen Yim is brought to Supreme Overlord Shimrra, who decrees that Yim is now his personal master shaper and is to continue her work exploring the secrets of shaping beyond current Yuuzhan Vong understanding.

BALANCE POINT (2000) was originally to be followed up by the Knightfall trilogy of paperback novels by Michael Jan Friedman: *Jedi Storm*, *Jedi Fire*, and *Jedi Blood*. A change in Del Rey's publishing program resulted in these books being canceled early in development, with the Edge of Victory duology by Greg Keyes taking their place. The canceled trilogy was to feature Danni Quee and focus on Peace Brigade actions against the Jedi.

EMISSARY OF THE VOID

AUTHOR · Greg Keyes

PUBLICATION HISTORY · Novella, Wizards of the Coast; originally serialized in six parts
- "Battle on Bonadan," *Star Wars Gamer* #8 (January 2002)
- "Dark Tidings," *Star Wars Gamer* #9 (March 2002)
- "The War on Wayland," *Star Wars Gamer* #10 (April 2002)
- "Relic of Ruin," *Star Wars Insider* #62 (October 2002)

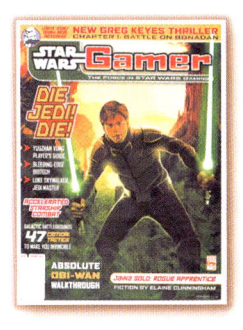

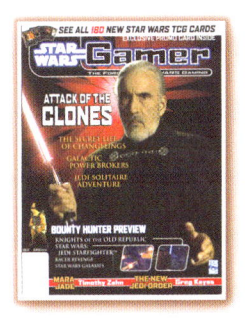

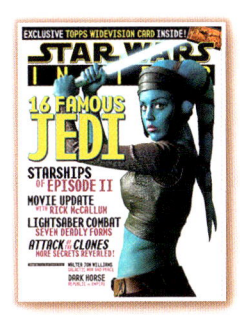

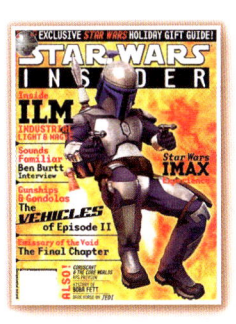

SUMMARY · Though Uldir Lochett failed to become a Jedi Knight, he serves the galaxy as the leader of the Catchhawks, a unit of the Space Rescue Corps. On Bonadan, Lochett crosses paths with Klin-Fa Gi, a Jedi being pursued by the Corporate Sector Authority on behalf of the Yuuzhan Vong. With the help of Lochett and his crew, Klin-Fa escapes aboard the Rescue Corps freighter *No Luck Required*. Destined for Wayland, Klin-Fa claims to be on a secret assignment for Luke Skywalker, but the Catchhawks cannot verify his claim.

Klin-Fa reveals to Uldir that she and her partner, Bey Gandan, had uncovered reports that the Yuuzhan Vong were developing a terrible weapon on Wayland that could wipe out the Jedi. With the Catchhawks' help, Klin-Fa rescues Bey from imprisonment on Wayland and uncovers the nature of the Yuuzhan Vong plot: a potentially devastating resequencing of bacta that would transform the lifesaving salve into a poison.

Uldir, Klin-Fa, Bey, and the Catchhawks rush to Thyferra, site of bacta production, only to discover the shocking truth that Bey is the agent who intends to sabotage the bacta. Bey had fallen to the dark side as a result of his spurned feelings for Klin-Fa. Uldir cuts down Bey with Klin-Fa's lightsaber before the scorned Jedi can cause any more harm.

T**HE SIX-PART** *Emissary of the Void* story began in *Star Wars Gamer* magazine, but that title ceased publication with only half the story told. The remaining three parts were published in *Star Wars Insider*. To help out readers who hadn't read *Gamer*, StarWars.com reprinted parts 1 through 3.

- "A Perilous Plan," *Star Wars Insider* #63 (November 2002)
- "Emissary of the Void," *Star Wars Insider* #64 (December 2002)

TIME LINE PLACEMENT · 26 ABY

WORLDS VISITED · Bonadan [S-3]; Thyferra [L-14]; Wayland [N-7]; Yag'Dhul [L-14]

MAIN CHARACTERS: Uldir Lochett, rescue worker (human male); Klin-Fa Gi, Jedi Knight (human female); Bey Gandan, Jedi Knight (human male)

THE NEW JEDI ORDER

387

STAR BY STAR

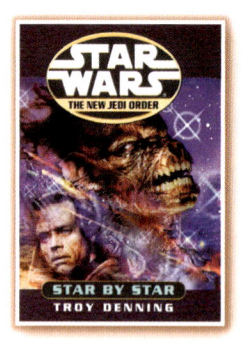

AUTHOR · Troy Denning
COVER ARTIST · Cliff Nielsen
PUBLICATION HISTORY ·
Novel, Del Rey Books
· Hardcover, November 2001
· Paperback, October 2002
TIME LINE PLACEMENT · 27 ABY
WORLDS VISITED · Arkania [M-8]; Bilbringi [J-8]; Borleias [K-9]; Carida (system) [M-9]; Coruscant [L-9]; Eclipse [M-11]; Froz [M-11]; Myrkr [N-7]; Obroa-skai [N-8]; Reecee (system) [J-8]; Talfaglio [M-11]

MAIN CHARACTERS · Anakin Solo, Jedi (human male); Jacen Solo, Jedi (human male); Jaina Solo, Jedi (human female); Luke Skywalker, Jedi Master (human male); Leia Organa Solo, New Republic diplomat (human female); Han Solo, captain of the *Millennium Falcon* (human male); Mara Jade Skywalker, Jedi Master (human female); Nom Anor, executor (Yuuzhan Vong male); Tsavong Lah, warmaster (Yuuzhan Vong male); Lando Calrissian, entrepreneur (human male); Vergere, adviser (Fosh female); Viqi Shesh, Senator (human female); Borsk Fey'lya, Chief of State (Bothan male); C-3PO, protocol droid; R2-D2, astromech droid; Danni Quee, scientist (human female); Cilghal, Jedi Master (Mon Calamari female); Ben Skywalker, infant (human male)

SUMMARY · The Yuuzhan Vong have unleashed a new weapon in their war against the Jedi: the voxyn. Genetically engineered eight-legged ferocious beasts, these creatures have a rudimentary connection to the Force that allows them to effectively hunt Jedi. The slobbering, acid-blooded monsters stalk Jedi sisters Numa and Alema Rar, killing Numa—a tragedy that emotionally scars Alema.

The Yuuzhan Vong have done what many in the New Republic Senate loudly declared impossible—but what most privately feared was inevitable: they have come within striking distance of the galactic capital. Warmaster Tsavong Lah continues to demand the surrender of the Jedi, this time targeting helpless refugees should the Order not comply. Leia Organa Solo entreats the Senate for support but finds only political paralysis. Framing the war as being chiefly between the Jedi and the Yuuzhan Vong, Senator Viqi Shesh polarizes the Senate by labeling the standoff as a Jedi affair and insists the New Republic does not have the resources to intervene. This sets off a quagmire of debate in the government. Borsk Fey'lya shrewdly avoids taking a stance until he can better assess which way the winds of political fortune are blowing.

Under Luke Skywalker's leadership, the Jedi have erected a new secret base, code-named Eclipse, hidden deep in the Galactic Core. Jedi scientists Cilghal and Danni Quee research the Yuuzhan Vong yammosk, trying to determine a weakness in the bio-engineered telepathic combat coordinator. Without a live yammosk sample, however, their progress is stalled. Luke prioritizes these studies, as well as analysis of a voxyn carcass. Cilghal determines that the voxyn is cloned from a primary template—a voxyn queen—and that its natural Force attunement comes from its genetic roots as a vornskr from Myrkr.

Nom Anor grows increasingly irritated by Tsavong Lah's command, especially now that the warlord has taken Vergere as his trusted adviser. The mysterious Vergere offers unerring advice on how to challenge the Jedi, and Anor's past failures continue to tarnish his reputation. Lah dispatches Anor to Coruscant to address the Senate in a diplomatic bid that Lah knows will fail. When Anor arrives at the capital, Borsk Fey'lya sees Lah's intent—by sending an inflammatory speaker, it's evident the Yuuzhan Vong seek to split the Senate. This galvanizes Fey'lya's resolve, and he speaks out against the invaders in support of the Jedi. Viqi Shesh, eyeing Fey'lya's post as Chief of State, quietly suggests to Tsavong Lah that the Bothan must be assassinated.

As voxyn strikes become more common, Luke worries that the Jedi children carried aboard the *Errant Venture* may be vulnerable. He recalls the ship to Eclipse, but does not trust broadcast communications—he instead sends Han and Leia to contact the ship and supply travel coordinates.

With more and more Jedi falling to the voxyn threat, Anakin suggests a special mission to Myrkr to hunt down and destroy the queen. The plan involves a "concerned citizen" handing over young Jedi to a Yuuzhan Vong ship, which the Jedi will then commandeer. Anakin argues that Luke cannot participate: any indication of Luke's involvement would raise Yuuzhan Vong defenses beyond their ability to breach. Jacen has deep misgivings about such an aggressive approach—he fears the protracted war against a brutal enemy is tipping the Jedi to the dark side. Anakin has no time for introspective philosophizing, but he needs Jacen to help forge a battle-meld among the Jedi team assembled in order to give them an edge against an overwhelming foe.

As Anor leaves Coruscant, he hears word that Jacen and Jaina Solo are twins—something with great religious ramifications among the Yuuzhan Vong. When Anor communicates this to Tsavong Lah, the warmaster realizes he must tread carefully, for the presence of twins may erode Yuuzhan Vong morale and sway the priest caste to the belief that the Jedi are favored by the gods. Already an undercurrent of Jedi worship is weaving its way through heretics among the Shamed Ones. Lah does not need the Jedi further deified. He intends to capture the twins.

Lando pilots the insertion mission, with extra firepower provided by his latest entrepreneurial venture: YVH combat droids. Developed by Tendrando Arms, a company founded by Lando and his wife Tendra Risant, the droids are skeletal humanoids with a passing resemblance to the Yuuzhan Vong to inspire hatred and insult among their targets. A team of seventeen Jedi—including leader Anakin, Jaina, Jacen, Lowbacca, Tenel Ka, Raynar Thul, Tahiri Veila, and Ganner Rhysode—readies for an undoubtedly deadly assignment: to destroy the voxyn research site aboard the *Baanu Rass*, an ailing worldship in the Myrkr system.

Upon their approach to the target site, the Jedi are surprised when they sense the presence of other Jedi held captive by the Yuuzhan Vong. This leads to an intense disagreement regarding a change in plans. Anakin weighs his options and agrees with Jacen's impassioned pleas to risk the mission to save the lives of the prisoners. The liberated Jedi turn out to be dark siders, Lomi Plo the Nightsister and Welk of the Shadow Academy. They strike an uneasy alliance with the Jedi in an effort to survive.

In the Talfaglio system, the rallied forces of the New Republic and the Jedi attack a Yuuzhan Vong flotilla en route to destroy a refugee convoy. In the attack, Tsavong Lah comes to learn of the Jedi interest in yammosks, and he warns his forces to be especially vigilant in the protection of their war coordinators. Lah launches "Battle Plan Coruscant," a pincer assault with Yuuzhan Vong ships attacking from Reecee and Borleias. Jedi Saba Sebatyne succeeds in capturing a live yammosk at Reecee. The organism refuses to emit signals for Danni and Cilghal to study, but they eventually are able to cobble together a successful yammosk jammer.

Aboard the *Baanu Rass*, the Jedi strike team, continuing its pursuit of the voxyn queen, is waylaid by casualties and a deadly running defense by hordes of Yuuzhan Vong led by Nom Anor. Anakin valiantly sacrifices himself while wiping out a store of genetic material vital in the production of voxyn. His death reverberates through the Force, hitting Luke and Leia hard. The strike force, devastated by the demise of their leader, is momentarily split as Jacen and Jaina argue over differing courses of action. Jaina treads perilously close to the dark side in her anguish as she recovers her brother's body. Jacen takes command, ordering the strike force to secure a ship and escape while he proceeds to stalk and kill the queen. Though successful, Jacen is captured by the Yuuzhan Vong.

Mara instinctively realizes that her child, presently on Coruscant under the Solos' care, may be in danger if Han and Leia are consumed by the death of their youngest son. She and Luke rush to Coruscant, but they run headlong into the advancing Yuuzhan Vong conquest. Their vessel is shot down, and they crash intact into the city-planet's artificial Western Sea.

The New Republic shatters with the arrival of the Yuuzhan Vong forces. Senators are the first to flee the besieged planet, taking control of whatever slices of the navy and security forces they can appropriate. Viqi Shesh attempts to kidnap Ben Skywalker, who is being protected by Noghri at the Solos' apartment. The assault exposes her as a traitor. When Shesh rushes the fleeing Solos, Leia wounds her with her lightsaber. Shesh survives to escape the chaos of invasion. Ben Skywalker, meanwhile, is rescued and shuttled safely off Coruscant by Lando Calrissian. Surprising his closest colleagues and longtime political opponents, Borsk Fey'lya stays behind as the Yuuzhan Vong arrive. He detonates a proton bomb in the capital building in a final sacrifice that takes out over twenty-five thousand Yuuzhan Vong soldiers.

The survivors flee Coruscant, seeking what little safe harbor exists in the galaxy. The New Republic is no more, but a means must still be found to defeat an emboldened enemy.

The theme of the third New Jedi Order hardcover was sketched out in the early story line as "Occupation." Development notes state, "By Hardcover #3, we should have about 75% Jedi left, 25% having been captured or killed by the [Yuuzhan Vong]."

In the original story pitch, Jacen was the Solo child to die, killed by invaders who were certain he was the prophesied one who could be their undoing—which in actuality was a reference to Anakin Solo. Feeling that it trod too closely to the beats being covered in the Prequel Trilogy, George Lucas requested that the prophecy be removed altogether and the central Solo changed from Anakin to Jacen, thus sparing Jacen's life but ensuring Anakin's demise.

DARK JOURNEY

AUTHOR · Elaine Cunningham
COVER ARTIST ·
Steven D. Anderson
PUBLICATION HISTORY ·
Novel, Del Rey Books
· Paperback, February 2002

TIME LINE PLACEMENT · 27 ABY

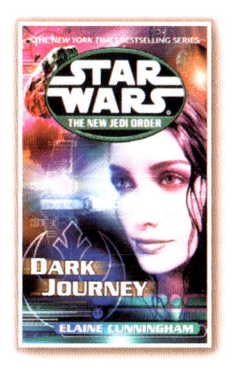

WORLDS VISITED · Cherith base [I-6]; Coruscant (system) [L-9]; Gallinore [O-9]; Hapes [O-9]; Ithor [M-6]; Myrkr [N-7]

MAIN CHARACTERS · Jaina Solo, Jedi (human female); Kyp Durron, Jedi Master (human male); Jagged Fel, pilot (human male); Ta'a Chume, former Hapan Queen Mother (human female); Leia Organa Solo, New Republic diplomat (human female); Han Solo, captain of the *Millennium Falcon* (human male); Lowbacca, Jedi (Wookiee male); Zekk, Jedi (human male); Tenel Ka, Jedi (human female); Harrar, priest (Yuuzhan Vong male); Khalee Lah, warrior (Yuuzhan Vong male)

SUMMARY · Jaina Solo and the surviving members of Anakin Solo's strike team retreat from Myrkr in a stolen Yuuzhan Vong frigate, *Ksstarr*. Jaina is still reeling from the death of Anakin and the capture of Jacen. She does not want to give up on her brother, but she cannot feel him through the Force. The other Jedi must drag her away from Myrkr. She only relents upon seeing the ever implacable Tenel Ka similarly devastated by the loss of Jacen. Collecting herself, Jaina flies the *Ksstarr* toward Coruscant.

The Yuuzhan Vong reinforcements do not attack the frigate. When the priest Harrar learns that Jaina has escaped, he calls off pursuit. The Yuuzhan Vong hope to entice Jaina back within reach so they can claim both twins as captives.

Arriving at Coruscant, the *Ksstarr* is immediately identified as an enemy vessel by the retreating New Republic forces. Jaina hastily pilots the frigate through some signature maneuvers that Han Solo, aboard the *Millennium Falcon*, recognizes. Leia confirms Jaina's presence aboard the frigate through the Force, but the dark, vengeful intensity she senses in her daughter gives her pause. The fleeing starships escape to the Hapes Cluster.

Hapes is greatly unsettled by turmoil from both within and without. The world has become a haven for refugees, which in turn makes it a viable target for the Yuuzhan Vong. The area of space is also rife with pirates who, like the Peace Brigade, would rather help the Yuuzhan Vong. The *Ksstarr* and *Millennium Falcon* land there, as does Kyp Durron. Seeing the suffering of the refugees firsthand helps blunt Kyp's more aggressive nature as he begins to better appreciate the consequences of the war. Jagged Fel and two squadrons of Chiss clawcraft also arrive. Fel is determined to fight in the war against the Yuuzhan Vong, despite the misgivings of his Chiss and Imperial masters. After the Hapans request Jag's assistance, Kyp accompanies him to escort the Jedi team down to the planet. Jaina narrowly avoids crashlanding the Yuuzhan Vong vessel, now renamed *Trickster*.

Jaina brings Anakin's body to Han and Leia for a proper Jedi funeral. Leia worries about Jaina's state of mind and is convinced that Jacen still lives, even though Jaina believes otherwise. Jaina thinks that Leia is so shaken by the loss of Anakin that she is desperate to believe her other son still lives.

Relations with the Hapans are severely strained following the tremendous losses they incurred on behalf of the New Republic at Fondor. There is great animosity among the Hapans toward the Queen Mother Teneniel Djo and Prince Isolder, who bear the brunt of responsibility for committing their fleet in the debacle. Extremely Force-sensitive, Teneniel was devastated by the loss of the Hapan fleet, which resulted in a miscarriage of her second child. Ta'a Chume, the scheming former Queen Mother, views Teneniel's grief as self-indulgent weak-

SHORT STORY — "The Apprentice"

Set during the events of *Dark Journey*, this short story was written by Elaine Cunningham and published in January 2002 in *Star Wars Gamer* #8 from Wizards of the Coast. Jaina, Kyp, Lowbacca, and Tenel Ka voyage to the scientific research labs of Gallinore, where Jaina hopes to find a way of using biotechnology against the Yuuzhan Vong. Unbeknownst to their fellow Jedi, Kyp and Jaina have smuggled a pirate prisoner into the facility who bears a fragment of a Yuuzhan Vong coral slave implant. They deliver the prisoner to a scientist for research. To cover her tracks, Jaina uses Kyp's Force technique of memory erasure to wipe Lowbacca's mind of the incident, a stark indication of how far she is willing to go to defeat the enemy.

ness. She cannot help but contrast her daughter-in-law with the newly militant Leia, or the intensely focused Jaina.

Jaina finds herself juggling a multitude of emotions and personal challenges. Jagged is attracted to her, but their histories are very different, and the extremely reserved Fel is not one to prioritize personal matters in the face of so many crises. Kyp and Jaina mend some of their differences as they both share brushes with the dark side. Jaina even reconsiders Kyp's offer of apprenticeship, something that alienates Jaina from some of her closest friends. Her friends, meanwhile, are increasingly concerned by her intense desire to strike back at the Yuuzhan Vong. She wants decisive action, feeling that dithering by the Jedi is what has led to their current losses.

As Jaina isolates herself, she is sought out by Ta'a Chume. The former Queen Mother privately tells Jaina that Isolder needs to divorce Teneniel and find a new wife, someone suitable to rule during wars. Jaina presumes Ta'a Chume is trying to maneuver Leia into that role, based on rumors of tensions in the Solo marriage.

Jaina and Lowbacca thoroughly examine the *Trickster* to better understand the enemy's technology. She and Lowie determine a way to jam the ship's signature so that yammosks cannot properly track it. Ta'a Chume abets this research by giving Jaina access to some of the best—and most unscrupulous—scientists under her command.

Harrar now fears that Jaina's escape might validate the heretical beliefs that she is in some way connected to the Yuuzhan Vong Trickster goddess, Yun-Harla. Khalee Lah, the warrior attending Harrar, finds the idea of an infidel piloting a Yuuzhan Vong vessel infuriating. Jaina discovers that the ship belongs to Nom Anor and contains tribute to the Trickster goddess. She activates a villip aboard the ship that connects her directly to Warmaster Tsavong Lah. Jaina goads the Yuuzhan Vong by renaming the ship the *Trickster*, playing her role as the goddess incarnate.

Jaina's modifications include finding a way to send baffling gravity signals among Yuuzhan Vong ships to confuse enemy vessels. When Harrar and Khalee Lah finally surmise that Jaina is in the Hapan system, they launch an attack. However, Jaina has led them into a trap, using her modified dovin basal technique to trick the Yuuzhan Vong ships into firing on one another.

After their victory over the Yuuzhan Vong, Jaina is called aside by Ta'a Chume. The former Queen Mother shocks Jaina by making clear her intentions: she wants Jaina to wed Prince Isolder and rule as Queen Mother. Jaina rejects the offer and discovers the extent of Ta'a Chume's machinations:

to make way for a new Queen Mother, Teneniel Djo has been poisoned and is now dead. Tenel Ka, who had previously committed herself to the Jedi Order, claims her place on the Hapan throne.

ENEMY LINES

REBEL DREAM
REBEL STAND

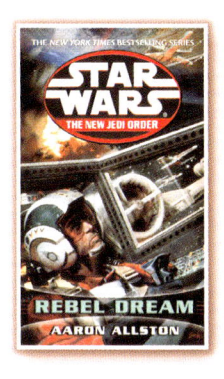

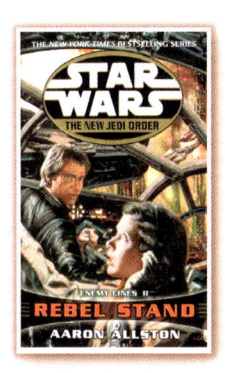

AUTHOR · Aaron Allston

COVER ARTIST · David Seeley

PUBLICATION HISTORY · Novels, Del Rey Books
Rebel Dream · Paperback, April 2002
Rebel Stand · Paperback, June 2002

TIME LINE PLACEMENT · 27 ABY

WORLDS VISITED · Aphran IV [K-8]; Borleias [K-9]; Coruscant [L-9]; Shelter [T-10]; Vannix [M-10]

MAIN CHARACTERS · Luke Skywalker, Jedi Master (human male); Mara Jade Skywalker, Jedi Master (human female); Leia Organa Solo, New Republic diplomat (human female); Han Solo, captain of the *Millennium Falcon* (human male); Jaina Solo, Jedi (human female); Wedge Antilles, New Republic general (human male); Czulkang Lah, legendary military commander (Yuuzhan Vong male); Tam Elgrin, holocam operator (human male); Tsavong Lah, warmaster (Yuuzhan Vong male); Viqi Shesh, traitor (human female); Tahiri Veila, Jedi (human female); Lord Nyax, abomination (human male)

SUMMARY · As the Yuuzhan Vong conquer Coruscant, Wedge Antilles commands the Star Destroyer *Mon Mothma* and leads a New Republic fleet to strike at the invaders' overextended flank on Borleias. Bolstered by the Twin Suns starfighter squadron commanded by Luke Skywalker with Mara Jade Skywalker and Corran Horn, as well as Han and Leia Organa Solo in the *Millennium Falcon* and the massive firepower of the Super Star Destroyer *Lusankya*, Wedge takes back the planet. New Republic troops and YVH battle droids, courtesy of Lando Calrissian, help secure the victory.

Warmaster Tsavong Lah asks his father, Czulkang Lah, to lead a retaliatory strike. The traitorous Viqi Shesh avoids execution at the hands of the Yuuzhan Vong for her failures by planting an insidious notion in the warmaster's head—that his body's suspicious rejection of biological implants is the result of sabotage by the shaper and priest sects. This causes Tsavong to suspect the shaper Ghithra Dal, whom he kills once Nen Yim confirms the treachery.

Upon arrival at Borleias, Jaina assumes command of the Twin Suns at Luke's request. Compelled by dark impressions in the Force, Luke is determined to return to Coruscant. He will receive assistance behind enemy lines from Wraith Squadron. Well versed in deceptive tactics, the Wraiths begin training Jaina in how best to live up to her growing reputation among the Yuuzhan Vong as the living manifestation of the Trickster goddess. When Yuuzhan Vong intelligence confirms Jaina's presence on Borleias, Czulkang Lah makes her capture a priority. Jaina grows distant from her loved ones, deter-

THE NEW JEDI ORDER

mined to avoid the grief of any future losses, but Jagged Fel chips away at her emotional armor.

With the New Republic weakening under the command of the conciliatory Councilor Pwoe, Wedge comes to realize they had best rely on the tried-and-true methods of the old Rebel Alliance. Working only with those he trusts most—allies such as Booster Terrik, the Solos, and the Skywalkers—he creates an information network dubbed the Insiders, focused on undermining the Yuuzhan Vong. To that end, Han and Leia depart for Vannix, where they will help ensure that the planet's election yields leadership more strongly opposed to the Yuuzhan Vong. Later, they try to unsettle the Peace Brigade operations on Aphran IV.

Fully embracing smokescreen tactics, Wedge confuses the Yuuzhan Vong with an elaborate but fake superweapon program dubbed Operation Starlancer. Supposedly a laser that could fire through hyperspace and destroy a Yuuzhan Vong worldship, the ersatz weapon is principally a means to keep the aliens distracted from other New Republic operations. Czulkang Lah's ground assault manages to surround the New Republic base but is decimated by orbital bombardment from the *Lusankya*, which forces Czulkang into a full retreat.

Lando pilots the freighter *Record Time* to Coruscant and deposits Luke, Mara, Tahiri, and several Wraiths on the besieged capital. The Yuuzhan Vong have ravaged the world's surface through a program of Vongforming—extensive reformatting of the lifeless urban cityscape with organic matter. Luke follows the fragmented tales of terrified Coruscant survivors that de-

Amid the turmoil of the Yuuzhan Vong war, Jaina Solo finds comfort and love with Jagged Fel.

scribe Lord Nyax, a monster from Corellian legend. Luke discovers that Nyax is the rebuilt, rampaging form of Irek Ismaren, a failed Dark Jedi son and protégé of an Emperor's Hand, Roganda Ismaren. Nyax is attempting to uncover a Force nexus buried in the Coruscant rubble—the site of the old Jedi Temple. This effort is the source of the disturbance Luke senses in the Force.

Upon learning that there are Jedi on Coruscant, Tsavong Lah sends Viqi Shesh and a group of Yuuzhan Vong with the last of the voxyn breed to hunt them down. After her Yuuzhan Vong escorts are killed by Lord Nyax, Shesh tries to flee the capital, but her path is blocked by the Wraiths. Rather than be captured, Shesh hurls herself out a viewport, committing suicide. Luke, Mara, and Tahiri confront Lord Nyax, a hulking cyborg humanoid fitted with an unbelievable *eight* lightsabers jutting from his limbs. Through her Yuuzhan Vong conditioning, Tahiri can make herself invisible in the Force, giving the Jedi the advantage they need to stop Nyax.

At Borleias, Wedge reveals the truth of Operation Starlancer—the *Lusankya* has been stripped down to a skeleton crew and transformed into an immense ramship that lances through Czulkang Lah's worldship. The destruction covers the evacuation of the New Republic ships from Borleias. The Yuuzhan Vong reel from such a massive defeat and the loss of their legendary military figure.

TRAITOR

AUTHOR · Matthew Stover
COVER ARTIST · Steven D. Anderson
PUBLICATION HISTORY · Novel, Del Rey Books · Paperback, August 2002

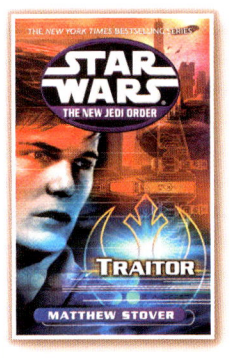

TIME LINE PLACEMENT · 27 ABY
WORLD VISITED · Coruscant (and its moons) [L-9]
MAIN CHARACTERS · Jacen Solo, Jedi (human male); Vergere, enigma (Fosh female); Nom Anor, executor (Yuuzhan Vong male); Ganner Rhysode, Jedi Knight (human male)

SUMMARY · Jacen Solo survives his capture by the Yuuzhan Vong and is tortured by the enigmatic Vergere. He is at her mercy as he is placed within the Embrace of Pain, a bio-engineered torture rack that closely monitors Jacen's life signs, keeping him enmeshed in pain but away from the release of death. A cruel teacher, Vergere advises Jacen to accept the pain.

Nom Anor watches the appalling process carefully. He intends to convert Jacen to the True Way, so that Jacen will forget his past ideals and be pitted against his sister in a duel to the finish that will satisfy the demands of Yuuzhan Vong scripture.

Jacen is released from the Embrace to toil aboard a seedship ferrying organic building blocks to Coruscant for its transformation into Yuuzhan'tar, a re-creation of the invaders' homeworld. Aboard, he tends to a dhuryam, a nascent yammosk-like organism that may one day grow to coordinate the transformation of the city-planet as its "World Brain." Jacen's natural affinity with living creatures serves him well as he allies with the dhuryam. He is able to influence the living organisms that make up his environs. Jacen conspires with his dhuryam ally to kill all rival dhuryams.

Though Jacen intends to kill his ally, the remaining dhuryam, Vergere stops him by knocking him out. He awakens on Coruscant to discover the Vongforming under way. Dovin basals have altered

Coruscant's orbit, making the planet warmer. One of its moons has been crushed into a glittering ring that circles the planet. Jacen hides in the increasingly lush undercity, avoiding Yuuzhan Vong patrols.

Guided by Vergere, Jacen makes his way to the remains of the Jedi Temple. There Vergere reveals to Jacen her radical understanding of the Force: There is no dark side. The Force defies alignment—the light side and dark side are artificial lenses placed on it by the morality espoused by its most indoctrinated users. As Vergere describes it, the Force simply *is*, and it is what a user would make of it.

A shaken Jacen follows what appears to be a spectral image of Anakin Solo into the maw of a massive creature. He avoids being devoured by the beast and then wanders into the old Solo apartment, where Vergere and Nom Anor find him. Anor is still intent on converting Jacen to suit his ends. Jacen claims loyalty to the True Way, and Anor marches him into the Well of the World Brain (as the dhuryam from the seedship is now called) for a test of his convictions.

The old Senate Rotunda has been converted into a fluid-filled chamber holding the World Brain. There Jacen is to sacrifice Ganner Rhysode, a Jedi captive. Jacen instead spares Ganner's life and runs to the dhuryam. Ganner buys Jacen time by holding the Yuuzhan Vong guards at bay, whirling a lightsaber in a furious display of combat. Though Ganner eventually falls under the crushing advance of dozens of Yuuzhan Vong, Jacen succeeds in mentally transmitting a command that resonates in the lobes of the World Brain. Ganner's spectacular sacrifice draws the attention of many Yuuzhan Vong, who have slowly come to respect—and in some cases revere—the power of the Jedi Knights.

With Vergere's help, Jacen finds an escape route out of the Well of the World Brain. Together they depart Yuuzhan'tar using Nom Anor's commandeered coralcraft. Jacen's command to the World Brain was to introduce imperfections into the Vongforming process, to force the Yuuzhan Vong to confront the flaws in their orthodoxy and deal with the concept of compromise.

The only installment in The New Jedi Order to not feature the principal heroes Luke, Han, and Leia at all, *Traitor* is a novel filled with challenging philosophies that elaborates upon Vergere and her divergent teachings about the Force. The initial story outline for the New Jedi Order series had Anakin Solo encounter a female mentor "seemingly sprung from the dark side." Later versions would describe her as a Jedi sleeper agent, dispatched just prior to Palpatine and Vader's extermination campaign. She is described as a member of a long-lived alien species, "cute in a Yodalike manner," which would lead the Yuuzhan Vong to underestimate her. Her philosophies are called "aikido-like" in the outline, and the plan was for her to teach Jacen how to reflect an opponent's hostile energy back at him without expending his own energy.

DESTINY'S WAY

AUTHOR · Walter Jon Williams
COVER ARTIST · Cliff Nielsen
PUBLICATION HISTORY · Novel, Del Rey Books
 · Hardcover, October 2002
 · Paperback, August 2003
TIME LINE PLACEMENT · 28 ABY

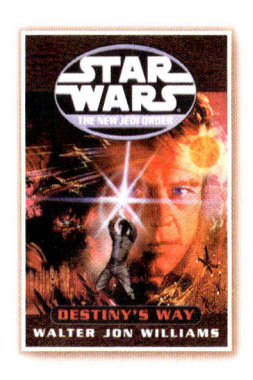

WORLDS VISITED · Bastion [K-3]; Coruscant [L-9]; Duro [M-11]; Ebaq 9 [M-11]; Kashyyyk [P-9]; Mon Calamari [U-6]; Obroa-skai [N-8]; Tarkin's Fang [L-11]

MAIN CHARACTERS · Jacen Solo, Jedi Knight (human male); Jaina Solo, Jedi Knight (human female); Luke Skywalker, Jedi Master (human male); Leia Organa Solo, New Republic diplomat (human female); Han Solo, captain of the *Millennium Falcon* (human male); Mara Jade Skywalker, Jedi Master (human female); Cal Omas, politician (human male); Nom Anor, executor (Yuuzhan Vong male); Tsavong Lah, warmaster (Yuuzhan Vong male); Dif Scaur, director of Intelligence (human male); Onimi, Shamed One (Yuuzhan Vong male); Shimrra, Supreme Overlord (Yuuzhan Vong male); Danni Quee, scientist (human female); Gilad Pellaeon, Imperial Grand Admiral (human male)

SUMMARY · En route to recruit help from the Imperial Remnant in the battle against the Yuuzhan Vong, Leia Organa Solo senses through the Force that Jacen lives. It is a small moment of hope shared by the Solos, quickly interrupted by a Yuuzhan Vong coralskipper ambush. Han Solo is able to outfly the aliens, aided by Jag Fel arriving with E-wing starfighters and Chiss clawcraft reinforcements. Elsewhere, over Obroa-skai, Jaina Solo leads an assault against a Yuuzhan Vong worldship. With her forces bolstered by Hapan warships commanded by Queen Mother Tenel Ka, Jaina's efforts destroy the massive enemy vessel. Jaina, too, senses flickers of Jacen's presence in the Force.

The New Republic has transplanted its command and government personnel to the ocean planet Mon Calamari. Finally settling into a framework after the death of Borsk Fey'lya, the New Republic readies an election among its Senators to install new leadership. Luke Skywalker gets an unwelcome taste of politics as he supports Senator Cal Omas, a politician sympathetic to the Jedi Order who would back Luke's bid to create a Jedi Council.

Aboard Jacen and Vergere's commandeered coralcraft, Vergere reveals more about her mysterious past. She was once a Jedi Knight who investigated strange reports of alien invaders known as Far Outsiders—in actuality the Yuuzhan Vong—attacking the verdant world of Zonama Sekot. Vergere concealed her Jedi abilities from the Yuuzhan Vong by attributing them to the living planet and accompanied the aliens as they returned to their own kind to prepare a massive invasion of the galaxy.

Arriving at Mon Calamari, Vergere is questioned by New Republic Intelligence (NRI) while Jacen is reunited with his loved ones. Luke senses that the war against the Yuuzhan Vong is at a turning point.

Narrowly avoiding Yuuzhan Vong assassins dispatched by Nom Anor, Cal Omas wins the election as Chief of State. He begins strengthening the relationships that nearly collapsed under the strain of the invasion. He earns the faith of the New Republic military command. He presides over the creation of a new Jedi Council, with half its members comprising Jedi Masters and the other New Republic officials. He honors the sacrifice and duty of the Jedi Knights involved in the Myrkr mission by fully Knighting them in a very public ceremony. Jaina Solo draws the special distinction of being named the Sword of the Jedi by Luke.

The New Republic research into the Yuuzhan Vong has unlocked the secrets of their genetic code and revealed vulnerabilities that could be exploited. Collaborating with Chiss researchers, NRI commander Dif Scaur has masterminded Alpha Red, a secret project to engineer a virus that would kill all

Yuuzhan Vong life as well as their bio-engineered technology. When Vergere discovers this, she uses her unique chemical-altering abilities (the same she used to concoct a cure for Mara Jade Skywalker) to neutralize the viral agent. Vergere then flees New Republic custody.

An aged and ailing Ackbar, retired admiral, returns to duty to help devise a plan to destroy the Yuuzhan Vong, using an old Imperial fortress in the Deep Core as bait to lure the invaders into a closed-off area of space. Knowing that there are Yuuzhan Vong spies in their midst, the New Republic is careful to sow enough disinformation to keep their trap at Ebaq 9 looking genuine.

On the defaced surface of Coruscant, Supreme Overlord Shimrra grows impatient with the delays and malfunctions in the errant World Brain's transformation. The misfortunes and setbacks suffered by the Yuuzhan Vong have added fuel to the fires of heresy growing in the Coruscant underworld. Some among the Shamed Ones point to Yuuzhan'tar's imperfections as evidence that the gods no longer favor the Supreme Overlord. Nom Anor is intrigued by these reports and disguises himself as a Yuuzhan Vong worker so he can look into them further. His investigations begin to point to the fact that Shimrra's crusade, which led the Yuuzhan Vong into this galaxy at the behest of the gods, has no foundation. The store of shaping knowledge—the very gift of the gods—is barren. Shimrra has tasked heretical shapers with expanding it for him.

Returning to Shimrra with a report from spies within the New Republic, Anor assures the Overlord that the target at Ebaq 9 is genuine. He stakes his life on it. The Yuuzhan Vong mobilize a fleet under the command of Tsavong Lah. They are ultimately defeated by a coalition of New Republic, smuggler, and Imperial Remnant forces. Jacen leads a Jedi mission on Ebaq 9 against overwhelming Yuuzhan Vong odds. Fearing that he will not survive, Vergere sacrifices herself by crashing a captured A-wing fighter into the moon's air supply, a maneuver that wipes out the enemy forces. Tsavong Lah, having survived Vergere's suicide attack, ambushes the Jedis Jaina Solo, Lowbacca, and Tesar Sebatyne. Tsavong injures Lowbacca, but Jaina stands strong and in the end takes the warmaster's life.

Realizing he has spectacularly failed the Overlord, Anor disappears into the Coruscant underworld. The New Republic enjoys its victory, but Cal Omas restructures the failed government under the banner of the Galactic Federation of Free Alliances.

DESTINY'S WAY includes an elaborate Knighting ritual for Jacen and Jaina, though they were Knighted at the end of the Young Jedi Knights novel *Crisis at Crystal Reef* (1998). The delineations of Jedi ranks seem much hazier in Luke's Jedi Order than those of the past; even after that first promotion, Jacen and Jaina still sought out Masters to apprentice themselves to.

Admiral Ackbar was once slated to die at the Battle of Ebaq 9, though his life was spared to better ensure the spirit of a New Republic victory. His fate is resolved in *The Unifying Force* (2003), where he dies "offscreen," succumbing to illness and old age. The new government created by story's end, the Galactic Federation of Free Alliances, was a subtle nod to the fan-coined term *GFFA*, which describes the *Star Wars* setting of a "galaxy far, far away. . . ."

YLESIA

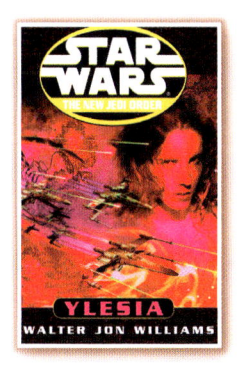

AUTHOR · Walter Jon Williams

COVER ARTIST · Cliff Nielsen

PUBLICATION HISTORY · Novella, Del Rey Books · eBook, September 2002 Reprinted as part of *The Joiner King* · Paperback, July 2005

TIME LINE PLACEMENT · 28 ABY

WORLDS VISITED · Coruscant [L-9]; Kashyyyk [P-9]; Ylesia [T-12]

MAIN CHARACTERS · Jacen Solo, Jedi Knight (human male); Jaina Solo, Jedi Knight (human female); Thrackan Sal-Solo, Governor-General (human male); Pwoe, Senator (Quarren male)

SUMMARY · The Yuuzhan Vong assign Corellian Governor-General Thrackan Sal-Solo to run the Peace Brigade out of Ylesia. The world becomes the target of a retaliatory strike by the New Republic, with a small Jedi team including Jacen and Jaina Solo landing first to liberate prisoners. The Jedi succeed and capture Sal-Solo and Senator Pwoe, the erstwhile acting Chief of State of the New Republic, who shows his true colors as an enemy collaborator. The Jedi escape before the Yuuzhan Vong can rally their forces, thus breaking the back of the Peace Brigade movement.

This eBook was originally intended to be included in the 2003 paperback edition of *Destiny's Way*, but was left out due to an oversight. As recompense, Del Rey and LucasBooks made it available in August 2003 as a free eBook download on StarWars.com. It was later included as bonus content in *The Joiner King* (2005).

FORCE HERETIC

REMNANT · REFUGEE · REUNION

AUTHORS · Sean Williams and Shane Dix

COVER ARTIST · Jon Foster

PUBLICATION HISTORY · Novels, Del Rey Books
Remnant · Paperback, February 2003
Refugee · Paperback, May 2003
Reunion · Paperback, July 2003

TIME LINE PLACEMENT · 28 ABY

WORLDS VISITED · Bakura [G-16]; Barab I [U-12]; Borosk [K-5]; Coruscant [L-9]; Csilla [F-8]; Esfandia [I-6]; Galantos [K-10]; Mobus [F-9]; Mon Calamari [U-6]; Munlali Mafir [G-5]; N'zoth [K-10]; Onadax [M-20]; Yaga Minor [K-5]; Zonama Sekot [F-9]

THE NEW JEDI ORDER

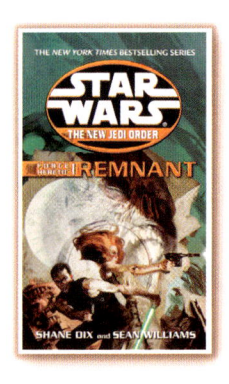

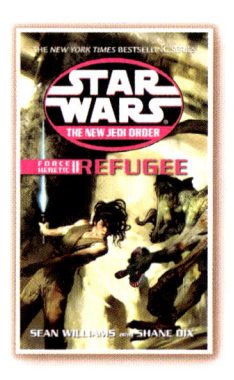

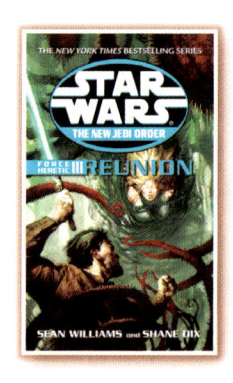

MAIN CHARACTERS · Luke Skywalker, Jedi Master (human male); Mara Jade Skywalker, Jedi Master (human female); Leia Organa Solo, Galactic Alliance diplomat (human female); Han Solo, captain of the *Millennium Falcon* (human male); Jaina Solo, Jedi Knight (human female); Jacen Solo, Jedi Knight (human male); Tahiri Veila, Jedi Knight (human female); Nom Anor, aka Prophet Yu'shaa (Yuuzhan Vong male); Danni Quee, scientist (human female); Jagged Fel, Chiss squadron leader (human male); Saba Sebatyne, Jedi Knight (Barabel female); Tekli, Jedi Knight (Chadra-Fan female); Shimrra, Supreme Overlord (Yuuzhan Vong male); Jabitha, Magister of Zonama Sekot (Ferroan female); Zonama Sekot, living planet; Gilad Pellaeon, Imperial Grand Admiral (human male); Droma, vagabond (Ryn male); Arien Yage, captain of the *Widowmaker* (human female); Malinza Thanas, revolutionary (human female); Molierre Cundertol, Prime Minister (human male)

SUMMARY · Bloodied by their defeat at Ebaq 9, the Yuuzhan Vong have become more unpredictable in their attacks. Barab I is ravaged by the invaders, much to the heartache of Barabel Jedi Knight Saba Sebatyne. Recognizing Zonama Sekot as a potential key to finally ending Yuuzhan Vong aggression, Luke Skywalker arranges an expedition to seek out the mysterious rogue planet. Joined by Mara, Jacen, Tekli, and Danni Quee, Luke pilots the *Jade Shadow* into the Unknown Regions, inviting Saba along to help her deal with the loss of her people. Jacen hopes the planet will provide answers to the many questions Vergere's views presented about the Jedi and their duty in the Force.

Han and Leia Solo, aboard the *Millennium Falcon* and accompanied by the Twin Suns Squadron (which includes Jaina and Jag), set out on their own mission to contact the worlds cut off from the Galactic Alliance. Leia invites Tahiri to accompany them so she can better deal with the demons haunting her: the loss of Anakin and the scrambling of her identity by the Yuuzhan Vong shapers. On Galantos, the group discovers that the native Fia have collaborated with the Yuuzhan Vong to wipe out the aggressive Yevethan species. Tahiri and the Solos find Ryn spies who have been monitoring the Yuuzhan Vong activities on the fringes of the galaxy. The Ryn advise them to make Bakura their next stop.

As the *Jade Shadow* voyages toward the Unknown Regions, it makes a stop within the Imperial Remnant. Luke hopes to convince Grand Admiral Pellaeon to join the newly formed Galactic Alliance. Skywalker is surprised to find the Imperial Remnant in retreat from Yuuzhan Vong warships—the war has reached the Empire. Though Luke cannot add much firepower to the fray, his seasoned tactics against the enemy prove invaluable to the Imperials, allowing them to escape intact.

Luke meets with a war-wounded Pellaeon, who explains that the Remnant has drawn Yuuzhan Vong attention since supplying the navigational data that resulted in the victory over the aliens at Ebaq 9. The proud Imperials have not asked for assistance as they face a war of attrition against this merciless enemy. Luke offers what help he can, providing vital tactical aid in routing the alien forces at Borosk. This convinces even the hard-line isolationist Moffs to join the larger galactic community. The grateful Imperials provide Luke with an escort, the frigate *Widowmaker* and its crew, along with the latest rumors of Zonama Sekot's movements, which help the Jedi focus their search.

On Coruscant, Nom Anor hides in the lower ruins of the city and earns the trust of the Shamed Ones, who are spreading a heretical new faith that questions Yuuzhan Vong doctrine. The Jedi are said to be the true instrument of the Yuuzhan Vong gods, and the only heroes who would fight on behalf of the Shamed Ones. Anor adopts the alias Prophet Yu'shaa and amasses many followers with his powerful message.

After narrowly escaping dangerous natives on Munlali Mafir, Luke and his team are intercepted by a Chiss vessel. Chiss commander Irolia assesses their intent and the nature of their character before allowing them to proceed deeper into the cloistered Chiss territories. On Csilla, the icy Chiss homeworld, they are coldly met by Chiss delegates and a few human hosts (including Peita Aabe and Baron Soontir Fel). The Chiss begrudgingly allow the Jedi limited access to their extensive library to research the whereabouts of Zonama Sekot.

The *Millennium Falcon* arrives on Bakura to find a world in turmoil. The planet has become very insular since the loss of Gaeriel Captison and several warships during the Corellian insurrection. A surprising overture of peace from the P'w'eck—the slave race of the Ssi-ruuk—has split the populace. Some are leery of anything to do with the Ssi-ruuk, since the invasion of a quarter century earlier. Others, though, recognize that the P'w'eck bring with them technology and inside knowledge of a former enemy. Prime Minister Cundertol, known for anti-alien sentiment, unexpectedly favors accepting the P'w'eck, but he is briefly kidnapped by a rebellious movement.

Tahiri is warned by the Ryn underground that not everything is what it seems on Bakura. Jaina seeks more information regarding the Bakuran strife, questioning the imprisoned Malinza Thanas, a leader in the underground movement and the teenage daughter of Gaeriel Captison. Thanas claims to be innocent of kidnapping. She escapes when a conveniently timed power shortage unlocks her prison door. Malinza returns to her rebel camp, inadvertently leading government troops to her friends.

During his stay on Csilla, Jacen befriends Syal and Wynssa Fel, Soontir Fel's wife and daughter. Jacen saves Wyn's life when she is attacked by Peita Aabe, one of several extremists who want to ensure that the Chiss stay out of the Galactic Alliance. For Jacen's help, the Chiss allow him extended access to their records, where he finds evidence that Zonama Sekot is orbiting around Mobus in the Klasse Ephemora system.

On Yuuzhan'tar, the rebuilt Coruscant, Nom Anor's heretical movement gains a potent follower in Ngaaluh, a Yuuzhan Vong priestess of the deception sect, which Anor plans to exploit to infiltrate the highest ranks of Shimrra's court. When Shimrra's suspicions lead to the death of some of Anor's most highly placed allies, the former executor worries how long he can maintain his dangerous ruse.

On Bakura, Prime Minister Cundertol arranges a consecration ceremony that would make their planet safe for their newfound P'w'eck allies. In

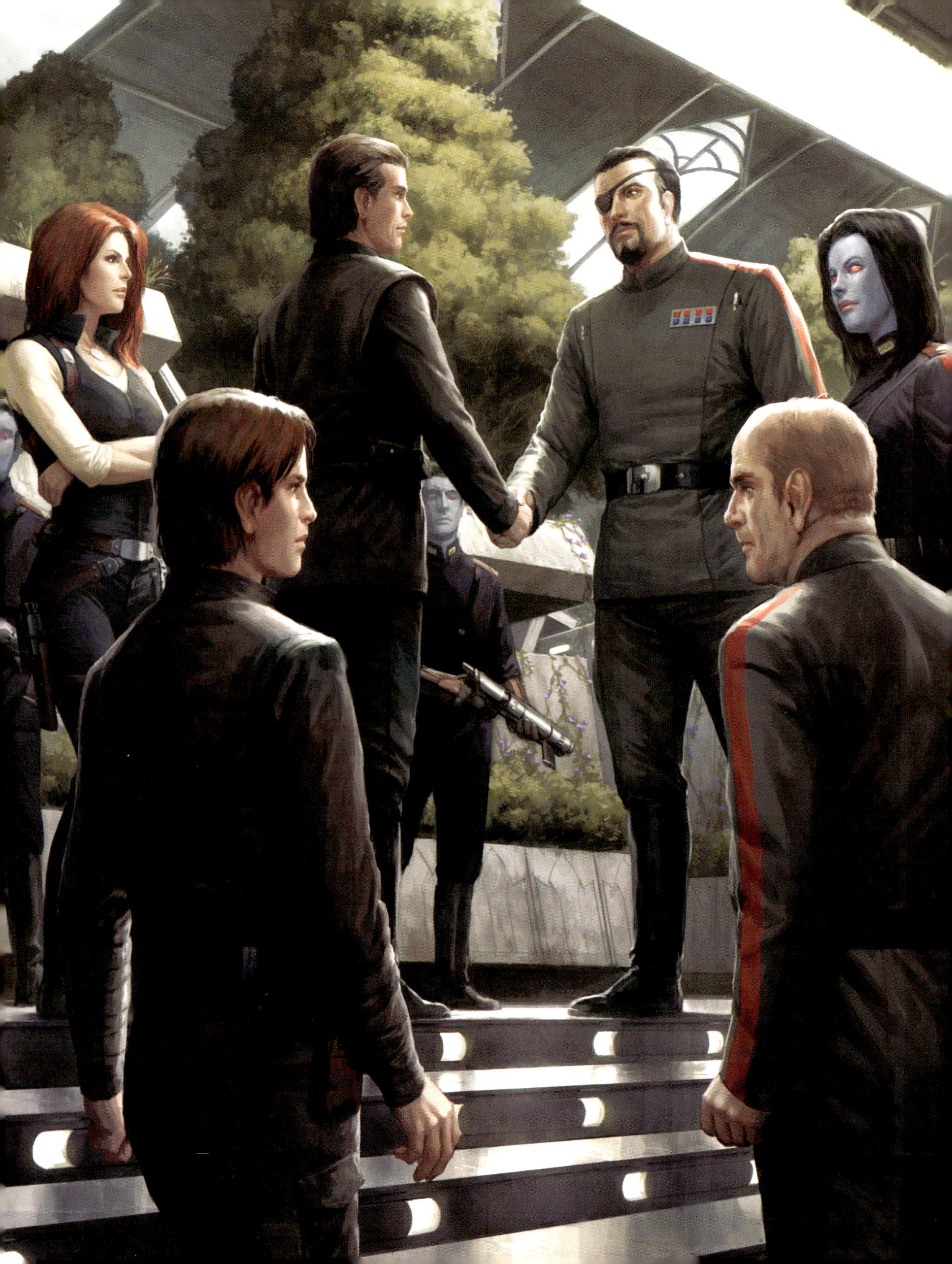

truth, the ceremony is meant for the benefit of the Ssi-ruuk, who wish to once again attack Bakura. Cundertol has sold out his planet in exchange for promised immortality—he is in fact a convincing human replica droid that has been "entenched" with his living soul. The Solos and Tahiri unravel this plot, preventing the consecration. The P'w'eck, finally given a taste of freedom as part of this conspiracy, truly do turn on their masters, joining with the Bakurans in repulsing the would-be invaders. When the Ssi-ruuk retreat, they punish Cundertol for his failure by letting his life energy bleed from his robotic body.

With further tips from the Ryn network—including a reunion with its founder, Droma—the *Falcon* ventures to the remote Minos Cluster, arriving eventually at the planetoid Esfandia, site of a crucial New Republic communications hub that connects the galaxy to the Unknown Regions. The Yuuzhan Vong target Esfandia to deter searches for Zonama Sekot. A small Galactic Alliance battlegroup defends the planetoid, bolstered by Imperial reinforcements commanded by Grand Admiral Pellaeon. The assistance of Ryn vessels helps the Galactic Alliance win this battle, though Jaina sustains some injuries. Jag stands by her side as she recuperates, declaring his love for her.

Aboard the *Falcon*, another far more personal battle takes place. Tahiri enters a comalike state, in which she envisions a duel between her two conflicting halves: the Jedi Tahiri Veila and the Yuuzhan Vong Riina Kwaad. Through the Force, Jaina tries to help Tahiri, but this challenge is Tahiri's alone. Tahiri puts aside the conflict and integrates the two sides of her personality, emerging as a stronger individual.

Finally, Luke and his party arrive at Zonama Sekot, which has taken up position around a large gas giant. The effects of its flights through hyperspace, decades earlier, caused great injury, and the planet is still healing from its efforts. Its inhabitants, the Ferroans, were hard-hit by the enforced moves, but they have survived and rebuilt. They do not welcome Luke's mission. They want nothing more to do with the rest of the galaxy. Luke and the Jedi converse with the current Magister—the previous Magister's daughter, Jabitha. She knew Anakin Skywalker when he visited Zonama Sekot as a boy and remembers both him and Obi-Wan Kenobi well. Her experiences with them have left her sympathetic to the Jedi cause, although she is still cautious of any outside involvement.

Jabitha's willingness to listen alarms the more isolationist Ferroans, who fear a return of the strife and cataclysm that accompanied Zonama Sekot's last encounter with offworlders. This group kidnaps Danni Quee and Jabitha, prompting a confrontation with the Jedi. Jacen's repeated insistence on finding a solution that averts any bloodshed impresses Zonama Sekot. The planet's consciousness appears simultaneously to Luke and Jacen in the avatars of twelve-year-old Anakin Skywalker and Vergere, respectively. Sekot offers its service in battle against the Yuuzhan Vong to both Jedi. Luke accepts, while Jacen declines. Nonetheless, the planet commits itself to the cause.

WITH THE RETURN of Zonama Sekot and Jabitha, the Force Heretic trilogy connects the New Jedi Order series to the prequel-era novel *Rogue Planet* (2000), creating a story that spans decades. In the original outline of the third novel, it was to be Zonama Sekot's younger moon (called, simply, Zonama X as a placeholder name) that helped convince its elder, weary planet to join the war against the Yuuzhan Vong, appearing as an avatar of Anakin Skywalker.

Luke Skywalker and his Jedi delegation receive a frosty welcome from Baron Soontir Fel and the Chiss on Csilla.

SHORT STORY "Or Die Trying"

Published after the New Jedi Order series had concluded, "Or Die Trying" is a short story by Sean Williams and Shane Dix that appears in *Star Wars Insider* #75 (May 2004), published by Paizo Publishing. "Or Die Trying" bridges the gap between *Refugee* and *Reunion*. Following the revelation that Prime Minister Cundertol had become a human replica droid (HRD) through the entchment process, Jaina Solo traces the droid maker who made this possible to the ODT company on Onadax. She is confronted by an HRD of Stanton Rendar (the brother of Dash Rendar), who reveals the process for creating mechanical repositories for life energies as a form of immortality. Before Jaina can apprehend Stanton, she is attacked by combat droids. She escapes, and the droid-manufacturing facility is destroyed.

In the original outline for *Remnant*, Cilghal was to be the science-minded Jedi on Luke's expedition. She was replaced by her apprentice, Tekli, in the final book. Baby Ben was also to be part of the expedition, and Jacen would take it upon himself to act as a guardian in the Force toward his cousin, Ben, warding any darkness or disturbances from the infant, an act that Mara would grow to resent. Though this story thread might have set up events in the Legacy of the Force series nicely, it was discarded from the Force Heretic trilogy.

THE FINAL PROPHECY

AUTHOR · Greg Keyes
COVER ARTIST · Terese Nielsen
PUBLICATION HISTORY · Novel, Del Rey Books · Paperback, October 2003

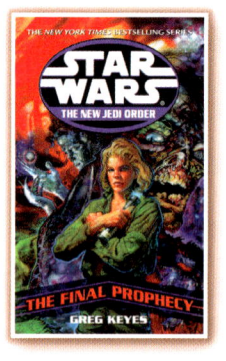

TIME LINE PLACEMENT · 28 ABY

WORLDS VISITED · Bilbringi [J-8]; Coruscant [L-9]; Dagobah [M-19]; Duro [M-11]; Mon Calamari [U-6]

MAIN CHARACTERS · Tahiri Veila, Jedi Knight (human female); Corran Horn, Jedi Knight (human male); Harrar, priest (Yuuzhan Vong male); Nom Anor, aka Prophet Yu'shaa (Yuuzhan Vong male); Jaina Solo, Jedi Knight (human female); Leia Organa Solo, Galactic Alliance diplomat (human female); Han Solo, captain of the *Millennium Falcon* (human male); Onimi, Shamed One (Yuuzhan Vong male); Shimrra, Supreme Overlord (Yuuzhan Vong male); Nen Yim, shaper (Yuuzhan Vong female); Zonama Sekot, living planet; Wedge Antilles, Galactic Alliance general (human male)

SUMMARY · Supreme Overlord Shimrra fears Zonama Sekot. Piecing together snippets overheard by spies

THE NEW JEDI ORDER

near the throne, Nom Anor capitalizes on those fears by weaving together a prophecy of a living planet unanchored by a star, whose presence will spell an end to Shimrra's rule. Anor, as the prophet Yu'shaa, stirs the thousands of Shamed Ones who follow his heresy, though he himself does not believe his own words.

On Dagobah, Tahiri Veila has come to meditate and heal her strained psyche. She is sought out by Shamed Ones who have mistaken the bog planet as the world of prophecy and are convinced that Tahiri—the one-who-was-shaped—will be instrumental in their redemption.

Deep inside Shimrra's headquarters citadel, Master Shaper Nen Yim is given a most intriguing subject to dissect: a captured Sekotan starship. She reports to Shimrra that the starship's biotechnological components share much in common with Yuuzhan Vong technology. Shimrra tries to simultaneously convince Yim that the ship's world of origin, Zonama Sekot, is of no concern to the Yuuzhan Vong and that it is imperative that she continue the heretical research into weapons that could counter such vessels. These conflicting commands give Yim pause, for she fears that the Overlord is mad, misguided, or both.

Nen Yim conspiratorially meets with Harrar, who has also grown suspicious of Shimrra. Harrar believes the Overlord is revising history and deleting accounts regarding his ascent to power and the launching of his crusade into the galaxy. As Yim relates her own discoveries, Harrar shares what he's learned of Zonama Sekot through heretical prophecies spread by Yu'shaa. Yim is determined to visit Zonama Sekot to learn more of the world, and Harrar believes Yu'shaa could facilitate such a voyage.

Yu'shaa smuggles out a message to the Galactic Alliance, making clear his desire to find Zonama Sekot and explaining that he sees it as a world vital to the Shamed Ones' crusade of redemption. He requests that the Jedi rescue him from Coruscant and bring him to the planet. Although suspicious of a trap, Tahiri Veila and Corran Horn take on the assignment. They enter Coruscant aboard a captured Yuuzhan Vong vessel and depart aboard the Sekotan ship, with Yu'shaa, Harrar, and Nen Yim aboard. Tahiri recognizes Yim as one of her torturers, adding to the tensions and distrust already inherent in the group. The animosity between Tahiri and Yim subsides once Tahiri learns her Riina Kwaad personality was built from Nen Yim's memories.

The ailing Sekotan vessel arrives at Zonama Sekot. The Yuuzhan Vong are enervated by the world, stunned by its power and resemblance to their homeworld of legend. Nen Yim confirms a biological connection between Yuuzhan Vong technology and the Zonama Sekot ecosphere. Tahiri postulates that Zonama Sekot *is* the Yuuzhan Vong homeworld. Yu'shaa takes advantage of access to Yim's scientific files and purloins information on how to cripple the planet. Armed with this information, and allied with two highly placed Yuuzhan Vong turncoats, the treacherous Anor contacts Supreme Overlord Shimrra, hoping to parlay this into a reinstatement into Yuuzhan Vong command. Anor crushes Nen Yim's skull with a rock, sabotages Zonama Sekot's hyperdrives, and flees to Coruscant with Yim's research. With her dying breath, Yim reveals Yu'shaa's true identity. The planet, reeling from Nom Anor's attack, instinctively retreats into hyperspace.

Meanwhile, the Galactic Alliance concentrates its efforts on Operation Trinity: a three-pronged attack on Bilbringi, commanded by Wedge Antilles from the Star Destroyer *Mon Mothma*. Wedge leads one prong, while Grand Admiral Pellaeon and Admiral Traest Kre'fey command the other two. The attack is thwarted by a Yuuzhan Vong campaign that targets the HoloNet relays tying the

Alliance communications network together. Unable to communicate with the other two fleets, Wedge's fleet is ambushed by the Yuuzhan Vong and suffers heavy losses before it is able to retreat.

THE UNIFYING FORCE

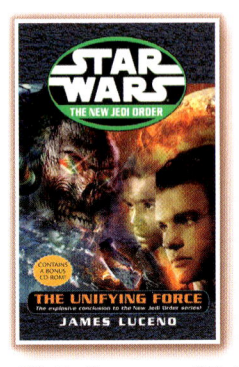

AUTHOR · James Luceno
COVER ARTIST · Cliff Nielsen
PUBLICATION HISTORY ·
Novel, Del Rey Books
· Hardcover, November 2003
· Paperback, August 2004
TIME LINE PLACEMENT · 29 ABY
WORLDS VISITED · Caluula [T-6]; Contruum [O-8]; Corulag [L-9]; Coruscant [L-9]; Denon [N-13]; Kashyyyk [P-9]; Mon Calamari [U-6]; Mon Eron [U-6]; Muscave [L-9]; Selvaris [I-9]; Sep Elopon [U-6]; Stentat [L-9]; Vandor-3 [L-9]; Zonama Sekot [L-9]

MAIN CHARACTERS · Jacen Solo, Jedi Knight (human male); Luke Skywalker, Jedi Master (human male); Jaina Solo, Jedi Knight (human female); Leia Organa Solo, Galactic Alliance diplomat (human female); Han Solo, captain of the *Millennium Falcon* (human male); Mara Jade Skywalker, Jedi Master (human female); Shimrra, Supreme Overlord (Yuuzhan Vong male); Onimi, Shamed One (Yuuzhan Vong male); Nom Anor, prefect (Yuuzhan Vong male); Harrar, priest (Yuuzhan Vong male); Cal Omas, politician (human male)

SUMMARY · The Ryn network has smuggled vital information into a Yuuzhan Vong camp that holds Galactic Alliance prisoners. Escapees risk their lives to deliver this data to Han and Leia Solo aboard the *Millennium Falcon*. Decoding the message, the Galactic Alliance discovers the Yuuzhan Vong's shocking plan to sacrifice hundreds of their war prisoners in an immense ceremony at Supreme Overlord Shimrra's citadel on Yuuzhan'tar. The Alliance prioritizes their rescue, not only to liberate so many essential personnel, but also to drive a thorn into the side of the Supreme Overlord during the important ritual.

Shimrra grows increasingly unhinged at this crucial point in the war. He has greatly overextended his military might and knows how fragile his control of the galaxy truly is. Shimrra openly courts heresy, revealing that his shapers have mixed genetic traits from across the Yuuzhan Vong castes to create ten elite warriors called slayers. Shimrra has also welcomed back the blasphemous Nom Anor into his court, absolving the false prophet of his transgressions due to Anor's sabotage of Zonama Sekot. Anor is now prefect of Coruscant, and in private discourse with Shimrra he learns that the Overlord has cast aside any fear or reverence of the Yuuzhan Vong gods.

On the devastated Zonama Sekot, the Jedi discover that Harrar survived Anor's treachery. Harrar speaks to the Jedi, and to the intelligence of Sekot, revealing and in turn learning much of the Yuuzhan Vong history. A scouting party, decades earlier, had returned to then–Supreme Overlord Quoreal with word of Zonama Sekot's existence. Believing the world to be the undoing of the Yuuzhan Vong, Quoreal had no intention of entering the galaxy that had harbored it, but Shimrra had other plans, usurping the throne and ordering the invasion. In discussing the history of the Yuuzhan Vong, Harrar reveals that ages ago, his people were threatened by a technological menace and turned to their connection to the natural world to repulse their enemy. But over time, this symbiosis was corrupted into something unwholesome, and their living homeworld banished them for their barbarous ways, stripping the Force from them altogether.

The Galactic Alliance ambush on the Yuuzhan Vong prisoner convoy proceeds, with numerous starfighter groups harrying the Yuuzhan Vong and Peace Brigade transports. Han Solo's *Millennium Falcon* rescues officers Judder Page and Pash Cracken but must divert to Caluula, only to find more combat. As Han and his family defend themselves from Yuuzhan Vong attacks, he is surprised to find himself fighting side by side with Boba Fett, who leads a new cadre of Mandalorian supercommandos.

On Coruscant, Shimrra's sacrificial ceremony continues, despite the interception of some of its intended victims. As hundreds of prisoners are marched to their doom, the pathways erupt with Shamed Ones emerging from the Coruscant underworld. Chaos breaks out as the Shamed One uprising foils Shimrra's plans. Even his reprisal—the public execution of hundreds of captured heretics—is a hollow victory for the Overlord, as the Shamed Ones fail to live up to their name and instead die proudly, defiantly decrying Shimrra with their last words.

The botched sacrifice was intended as a blessing to a forthcoming offensive against the Galactic Alliance's capital on Mon Calamari. Shimrra amasses thousands of warships, readying for a strike. The Alliance, tipped off about this in advance, commits only half of its forces to defend the waterworld—for it intends to secretly commit its other half to retake the capital. For this counteroffensive to work, the Alliance will stage from multiple worlds. Han and Leia return to Caluula aboard the *Falcon* to be part of the attack and are shocked to discover evidence that the Alliance has somehow re-created and used Alpha Red on the Yuuzhan Vong. The Yuuzhan Vong on Caluula and their biotechnology die wretched deaths, but the toxin also appears to affect native life: insects on Caluula have succumbed to Alpha Red, proving that the pathogen can jump species. A sole surviving Yuuzhan Vong escapes Caluula and brings the plague to Coruscant.

Zonama Sekot emerges from hyperspace near Coruscant, its passing sundering the planet's new asteroidal rings and scattering its moons. As the living planet eclipses the sun, the Shamed Ones see it as a portent of the time of reckoning. The planet settles in the outer system, still visible in the Coruscant night sky. Shimrra recalls his warships to the system, but holds off from attacking the planet. The *Millennium Falcon* journeys to Zonama Sekot, where the Solos regroup with Luke and his team. Zonama Sekot agrees to build ships for the Jedi. Traveling to Mon Calamari, Luke meets with the Alliance military command and requests that they hold off on their strike against Coruscant. Luke would rather let the revolution on Yuuzhan'tar run its course, in the hope that Shimrra is deposed. He fears a full-scale military engagement will only end once all the Yuuzhan Vong are exterminated.

Shimrra calls Nom Anor before him and tasks him as his special envoy to get the Yuuzhan Vong priests to begin venerating the Trickster goddess rather than Yun-Yuuzhan and Yun-Yammka. He hopes to create a war among the gods. Baffled by this command, Anor realizes that Shimrra must truly be deranged. The Alpha Red–afflicted ship arrives in the system from Caluula, and Shimrra sees it as a way to strike back at Zonama Sekot. He orders it to be sent to the living planet so that the plague will kill the world.

The Galactic Alliance fleet arrives at Yuuzhan'tar, and battle erupts in space. Shimrra commands the World Brain to render the planet uninhabitable as the ultimate contingency, making it clear to Nom Anor that allegiance to the Supreme Overlord is a dead end. Anor instead resumes his mantle as the Prophet Yu'shaa, hoping to find refuge among the Shamed Ones. Jedi piloting Sekotan ships, reinforced by Smugglers' Alliance vessels, create a defensive blockade to protect Zonama Sekot from the incoming plague ship.

A Jedi strike team that includes Luke, Mara, Jacen, Jaina, Tahiri, and Kenth Hamner lands on Yuuzhan'tar. Leia and Han accompany Harrar in a mission to convince the World Brain to call off its cataclysm, a task that ultimately falls to Jacen, who reconnects with the commanding organism and calms its destructive fits. Mara chases Nom Anor, intending to strike the deceiver down for subjecting her to coomb spores, but the conniving Yuuzhan Vong pleads for mercy and Mara spares his life. Anor slinks away.

Luke and the twins breach Shimrra's citadel—which also becomes a spacebound vessel—where they are nearly overwhelmed by slayers. Luke gives himself fully to the Force, becoming a whirlwind of devastation, slashing through Yuuzhan Vong guards. Shimrra engages Luke in a duel, his amphistaff of command against Skywalker's paired lightsabers. Though Luke is poisoned by amphistaff venom, the Jedi Master decapitates Shimrra, bringing an end to his reign.

But it turns out Shimrra was never the true power behind the Yuuzhan Vong. The real mastermind was the twisted, snickering jester who sat at Shimrra's feet: Onimi. Jaina chases the Shamed One into the upper passages of the citadel. The twisted Yuuzhan Vong hides Force abilities—a former shaper, Onimi discovered how to reconnect to the Force when in his experiments he grafted yammosk tissue to his brain. Able to manipulate the minds of others, Onimi made Shimrra his puppet as he commanded the invasion of the galaxy.

Jacen confronts Onimi and taps into the unifying Force, letting its power flow through him. He briefly becomes a luminous being whose power overwhelms Onimi, destroying the Yuuzhan Vong mastermind. The Jedi escape aboard the *Millennium Falcon* as Onimi's escape vessel disintegrates, an explosion that apparently takes Nom Anor with it. Without their leader, the Yuuzhan Vong are finally defeated.

In the aftermath, the Galactic Alliance commits to rebuilding Coruscant. The Yuuzhan Vong survivors are banished to Zonama Sekot, which is revealed to be a seed of the original Yuuzhan'tar. The world welcomes them back, provided the Yuuzhan Vong turn their back on their destructive ways. Danni Quee, Tekli, and Tahiri agree to remain on the living planet to help the Yuuzhan Vong settle as it makes its journey to a new, remote home.

The Galactic Alliance sets up a provisional headquarters on nearby Denon as Coruscant recuperates. It will be a long time before the scars of this long, bloody war begin to fade.

THE EPIC FINALE of The New Jedi Order reveals Onimi's true nature—an element that existed even in the initial storyline. When the invaders were still described as dark siders, they were to be led by a "god-king and his dwarfish adjutant." The adjutant's relationship with the king was described as symbiotic, and in this early form, Onimi was "Iago-like." He would be destroyed by Anakin Solo. From the outline:

> Forged by Luke, by his dark side mentor, by his very ancestry as the grandson of Darth Vader, Anakin *is* the Sword of Righteousness.

As the outline underwent revision with George Lucas's feedback, and Anakin was replaced by Jacen, Jacen's defeat of Onimi became more specific. Vergere had been identified as someone who could use the Force on a molecular level—as evidenced by her healing tears. Jacen learns this ability and applies a version of it when he destroys Onimi. From the revised outline:

> And this is when Jacen uses what he has learned: he connects with the Living Force to

Luke Skywalker along with Jaina and Jacen Solo are surrounded by Yuuzhan Vong slayers as they confront Supreme Overlord Shimrra.

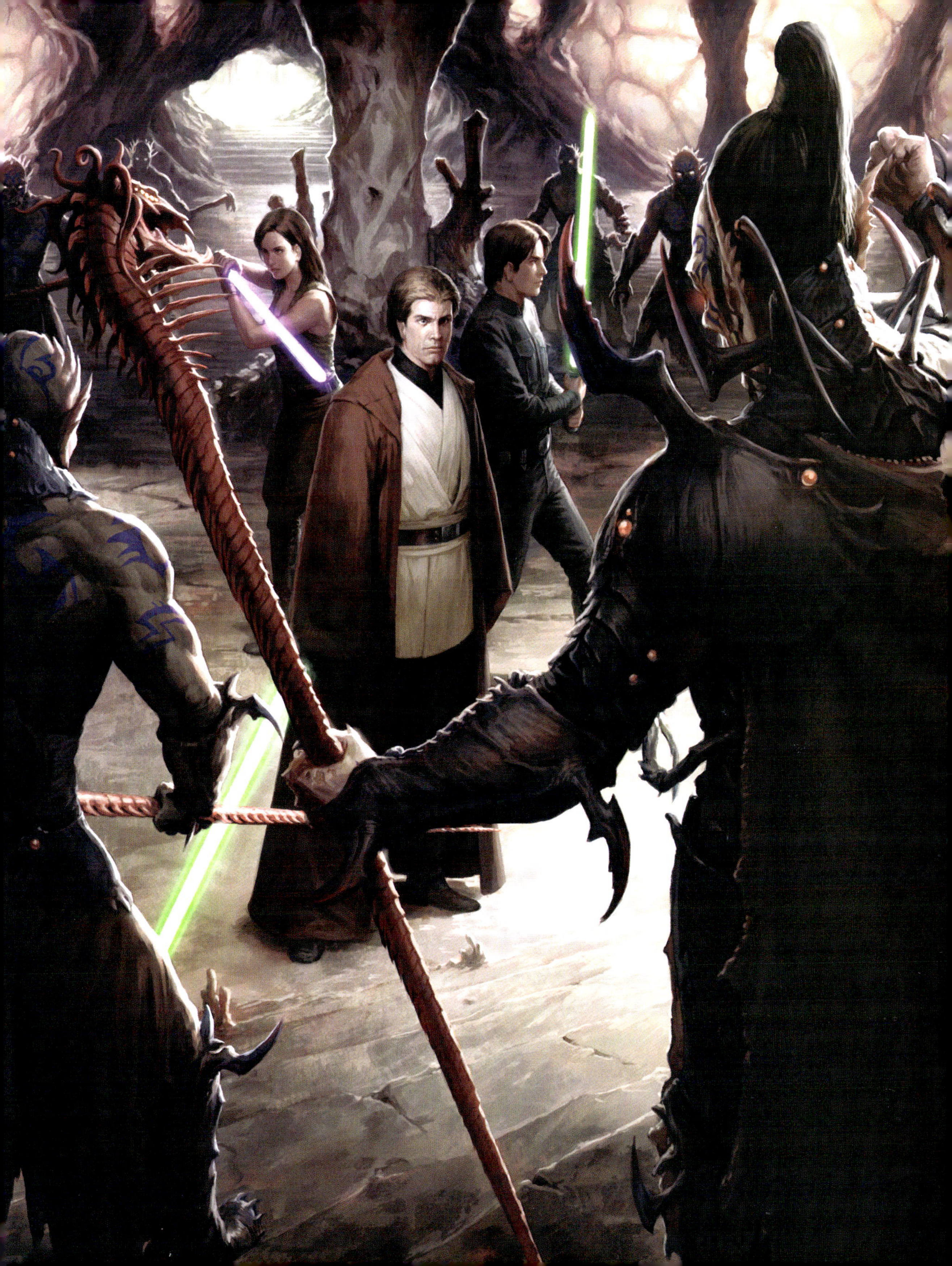

analyze the attack on a cellular level, and then turn it back on his attacker . . . and the minion is consumed horribly.

The final book retains some of this cellular transmutation—as Jacen uses the Force to neutralize toxins secreted by Onimi—but layers it with metaphysical transformation as Jacen becomes a conduit to the Force. The original description of Vergere as an aikido-like Jedi resonates in this passage, as Jacen essentially uses Onimi's power against him.

The Unifying Force also sheds more light on the history of the Yuuzhan Vong. A fleeting mention of a technological foe deeply imprinting a hatred of technology among the ancient Vong was expanded upon in *The New Essential Guide to Droids* (2006), which connects the Silentium—the enormous mechanical beings at the end of The Lando Calrissian Adventures (1983)—to the backstory of The New Jedi Order.

The hardcover edition of the novel came packaged with a CD-ROM of supplemental materials, including the full text of *Vector Prime* (1999) as an eBook, a round-robin interview with members of the New Jedi Order development team, a description of the Yuuzhan Vong from the series planning documents, and select illustrations of relevant starships from *The New Essential Guide to Vehicles and Vessels* (2003). The paperback edition of *The Unifying Force* included the round-robin interview.

THE DARK NEST

THE JOINER KING · THE UNSEEN QUEEN · THE SWARM WAR

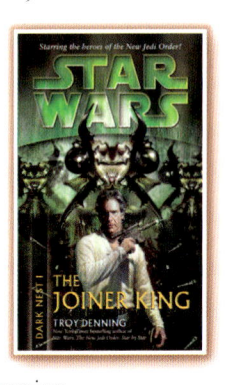

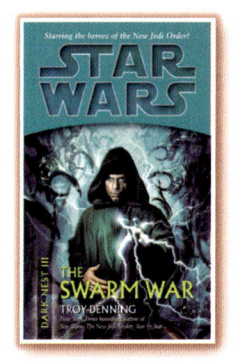

AUTHOR · Troy Denning
COVER ARTIST · Cliff Nielsen
PUBLICATION HISTORY · Novels, Del Rey Books
The Joiner King · Paperback, July 2005
The Unseen Queen · Paperback, September 2005
The Swarm War · Paperback, December 2005

TIME LINE PLACEMENT · 35–36 ABY
WORLDS VISITED · Bespin [K-18]; Borao [M-14]; Coruscant [L-9]; Hapes [O-9]; Ossus [R-6]; Qoribu and its moons [H-7]; Roche system [Q-8]; Sarm [I-8]; Snevu [H-7]; Sullust [M-17]; Tenupe [I-8]; Thrago [H-8]; Woteba [I-8]; Yoggoy [H-7]; Zonama Sekot [F-9]

THE NEW JEDI ORDER
410

MAIN CHARACTERS · Luke Skywalker, Jedi Master (human male); Leia Organa Solo, Jedi Knight (human female); Han Solo, captain of the *Millennium Falcon* (human male); Mara Jade Skywalker, Jedi Master (human female); Jaina Solo, Jedi Knight (human female); Jacen Solo, Jedi Knight (human male); Jagged Fel, Chiss task force commander (human male); Zekk, Jedi Knight (human male); Raynar Thul, Jedi Knight/UnuThul (human male); Saba Sebatyne, Jedi Master (Barabel female); Alema Rar, Jedi Knight (Twi'lek female); Tenel Ka, Hapan Queen Mother (human female); Ben Skywalker, child (human male); C-3PO, protocol droid; R2-D2, astromech droid; Cilghal, Jedi Master (Mon Calamari female); Cal Omas, Galactic Alliance Chief of State (human male); Jae Juun, smuggler captain (Sullustan male); Tarfang, smuggler (Ewok male); Welk, crash survivor (human male); Lomi Plo, Gorog queen (mostly human female); Nek Bwua'tu, admiral (Bothan male)

SUMMARY · Six years have passed since the Yuuzhan Vong War ended. Jacen has journeyed throughout the galaxy to study the Force and its many different followers. He and his fellow veterans of the Myrkr strike team are suddenly compelled through the Force to follow an unidentified call for help emanating from the Unknown Regions.

A Chiss diplomat complains to Luke Skywalker's Jedi Council that these rogue Jedi have intruded upon their space and are assisting alien trespassers in violating Chiss borders. Unable to contact these Jedi, Luke and Mara leave for the Unknown Regions to investigate, bringing their son, Ben, with them. The *Millennium Falcon* escorts the *Jade Shadow*, with Leia, Han, and Saba Sebatyne aboard.

With the help of the smuggling duo Jae Juun and Tarfang, the Solos and Skywalkers find Yoggoy, a planet dominated by insectile Killiks, an ancient hive-minded species long thought to be extinct. The Skywalkers and Solos are stunned to discover that Raynar Thul is the spokesman and leader of the hive. Presumed dead, Raynar is alive, but he is a very changed man.

Part of the Myrkr strike team, Raynar was feared lost when he was taken captive by two dark side survivors, Lomi Plo and Welk. His face is extensively burned from the crash of the shuttle that ferried him away from Myrkr to Yoggoy. His speech and thoughts seem altered by his exposure to the insects. His Force sensitivity has reshaped the disparate hives into a single consciousness: the Colony. He is UnuThul, and his connection to the Force has allowed other beings, noninsectile life, to become Joiners in the collective mind. UnuThul explains that the Colony needs the contested worlds claimed by the Chiss to feed itself.

On one of the moons of Qoribu, the summoned Jedi Knights become Joiners. They fight on the Colony's behalf, engaging in battles with Chiss patrols in disputed space. This puts Jaina and Jag Fel on opposite sides of the conflict. The *Falcon* and *Shadow* fight their way past a swarm of insect dart-fighter ships to arrive at Qoribu, where they are reunited with Jaina, Jacen, and the others. The hive refuses to believe that they were attacked, offering up outlandish explanations and bewildering leaps in logic to account for the damage to the two family ships. Luke insists that the Jedi Joiners return with him. Jaina and Zekk refuse, however, committing themselves to help the Colony.

Before the vessels depart Qoribu, Saba is savagely assaulted by Welk, who is backed by blue-skinned Killiks. She is wounded, but Welk escapes. When pressed, UnuThul cannot offer any explanation for the assault and simply cannot believe it happened.

The *Millennium Falcon* departs to bring Saba back to the Temple so she can recover. Alema Rar accompanies the Solos and secretly sabotages the ship, forcing it to briefly touch down on a paradise world within the Utegetu Nebula. Saba subdues Alema when it becomes clear the Twi'lek is reacting far more dangerously to the Killik influence than any of the other Joiners.

The Jedi Joiners reach out to interstellar allies to aid the Killik cause. Tesar Sebatyne enlists the help of Lady Aryn Dro Thul, Raynar's mother, who commits her supply fleet to help her son's crusade. Jacen seeks help from Tenel Ka, who resisted UnuThul's call by sequestering herself in the royal palace at Hapes. In their private time together, Jacen and Tenel discover their romantic feelings for each other are still strong.

As the *Jade Shadow* returns to the new Jedi Temple on Ossus, Mara notices that young Ben has been eating far more than usual. The boy explains he's been sharing food with his new friend, Gorog. Mara later discovers that Gorog is not some imaginary friend of Ben's, but rather a blue Killik who has stowed away aboard the *Shadow*. She subdues the creature, delivering it to Cilghal for study.

Cilghal examines the Jedi Joiners as well as Gorog and confirms a unique form of telepathy born of their exposure to the Killik Colony. Cilghal notes that Alema's link is to Gorog, a separate consciousness from that shared by the other Joiners. The reason Raynar did not know of the attacks is because they were coming from another hive, a subconscious part of the collective he could not know about. The Jedi describe this entity as the Dark Nest. It is doubtlessly controlled by Welk or Lomi Plo and was able to latch onto Alema due to the dark emotions she has harbored since the Yuuzhan Vong War, when the voxyn killed her sister, Numa.

The Jedi free Alema to follow her to Qoribu's moon of Kr. There they discover the horrible secret of the Gorog nest: the hive's larvae feast upon Chiss prisoners. This was the motive behind the hostilities against the Chiss; prisoners and casualties provide fertile breeding grounds for the Dark Nest. The Skywalkers and the Solos, backed by Jedi Masters from Ossus and heavily armed YVH droids, storm the Dark Nest. Luke battles Welk, killing the dark sider, and maims Alema, cutting off her arm, but Alema manages to escape.

With the Dark Nest exposed, the Colony ceases its hostilities. Leia offers the hive access to the worlds of the Utegetu Nebula in exchange for a promise to avoid the Chiss territories. No longer needing their aid, UnuThul severs his ties to the Joiners. Jaina and Zekk, however, discover they are still intimately linked.

The Killiks continue to be a headache for the Galactic Alliance, as Han and Leia investigate claims that they are harboring pirates and smugglers. Complicating matters is the strange outbreak of an epidemic that targets the Killiks within the Utegetu Nebula: a destructive froth called the Fizz. UnuThul believes the Galactic Alliance is somehow responsible, or at the very least complicit in this genocidal attack against the Colony. Investigating the dissolving agent on Woteba, Luke and Han theorize that it is some sort of defensive mechanism that targets anything that threatens the planet. Cilghal's examination of the substance proves it to be some sort of nanotechnological terraforming agent created by a culture far more advanced than any known. Evidence suggests that the worlds within the Utegetu Nebula were specifically engineered to flourish.

Queen Mother Tenel Ka summons Jacen to Hapes, and he brings young Ben with him. Tenel Ka surprises Jacen by revealing that she has given birth to Allana, Jacen's daughter. Tenel has kept it a secret for as long as she could, since Hapan customs prohibit a child born out of wedlock. Suddenly the Dark Nest attacks the palace—an attack that Ben can sense due to his previous connection to the

Gorog. Jacen and Tenel defend their daughter, and Tenel believes that it was her grandmother, Ta'a Chume, who somehow arranged the assassination attempt.

Furious, Jacen interrogates Ta'a Chume, showing uncharacteristic ferocity toward the former Queen Mother. She reveals that the Gorog had approached her seeking navigation technology, and she brokered a deal to deliver it in exchange for them killing Tenel Ka's heir. Jacen uses the Force to mentally attack the former Queen Mother, plunging her into a coma. He also uses the Force to erase knowledge of his daughter from Ben's memories.

Jacen is chilled by another Force vision: Killik fecundity will prevail over Chiss battle prowess, spreading the Colony across the galaxy to establish an eternal empire of assimilated Joiners. Realizing the Jedi must prevent the war he foresaw at any cost, Jacen leads Jaina and the other strike team survivors back into Colony space. It is not long before Jaina finds herself skirmishing with Jag Fel, trying to prevent the Chiss from establishing a staging base that would inevitably lead to full-scale war.

These compounding crises cause Cal Omas to lose faith in the ability of the Jedi to settle affairs. He intervenes by establishing a blockade around the nebula. Han learns that Jae Juun and Tarfang have been delivering glass replicas of famous Rebel starships as souvenirs to members of the Galactic Alliance Fifth Fleet. These replicas actually contain tiny Gorog assassins, now disseminated throughout the fleet. Leia works with Admiral Nek Bwua'tu, commander of the blockade, to deal with this threat. In the chaos that ensues, Alema infiltrates the flagship and attacks Leia. Leia, having been apprenticed to Saba Sebatyne with a renewed focus on her Jedi abilities, defends herself in a lightsaber duel that results in one of Alema's lekku being severed. The tenacious Twi'lek escapes once again.

Luke tracks down the true leader of the Dark Nest, Lomi Plo, the unseen queen. She uses doubt to fuel her mental abilities. Throughout the Dark Nest crisis, she has been planting suggestions to try to cause Luke to doubt Mara Jade's integrity. But Luke trusts Mara, and Lomi's abilities cannot diminish Luke's resolve. She escapes the encounter, but has succeeded in pushing the Alliance and Chiss into war against the Killiks.

As the Swarm War escalates, Jaina again finds herself in active combat against Jag. Her feelings for him permeate through the Joiner link she shares with Zekk, which makes Zekk jealous.

Luke convenes a grand Jedi assembly, sending out a Force summons so powerful that all Jedi in the galaxy attend—except for Zekk and Jaina, who remain Joiners. Declaring it has fallen to the Jedi to prevent another terrible war from engulfing the galaxy, he invites those who cannot place their allegiance to the Force above other considerations to leave. A handful of Jedi, including Danni Quee and Tenel Ka, do just that, but the majority remain. Luke decides the Order needs true leadership, and he adopts the mantle of Grand Master.

Jacen suggests a radical course of action: ending the Swarm War by assassinating Raynar. Luke agrees that UnuThul will have to be neutralized, but he believes in alternatives to killing and deems that such a course of action must be a last resort. At Sarm, Luke, Mara, and Jacen lead a Jedi assault on the Gorog nest ship, targeting Lomi Plo. The Gorog queen proves to be a formidable adversary, grievously injuring both Jacen and Mara before escaping the Jedi. As Mara and Jacen recover, Luke vows to eliminate Lomi in their next encounter.

Using his underworld contacts, Han finds that Jaina and Zekk are at the battlefront on Tenupe. There the Chiss intercept the *Millennium Falcon* and interrogate Han and Leia to discover what their in-

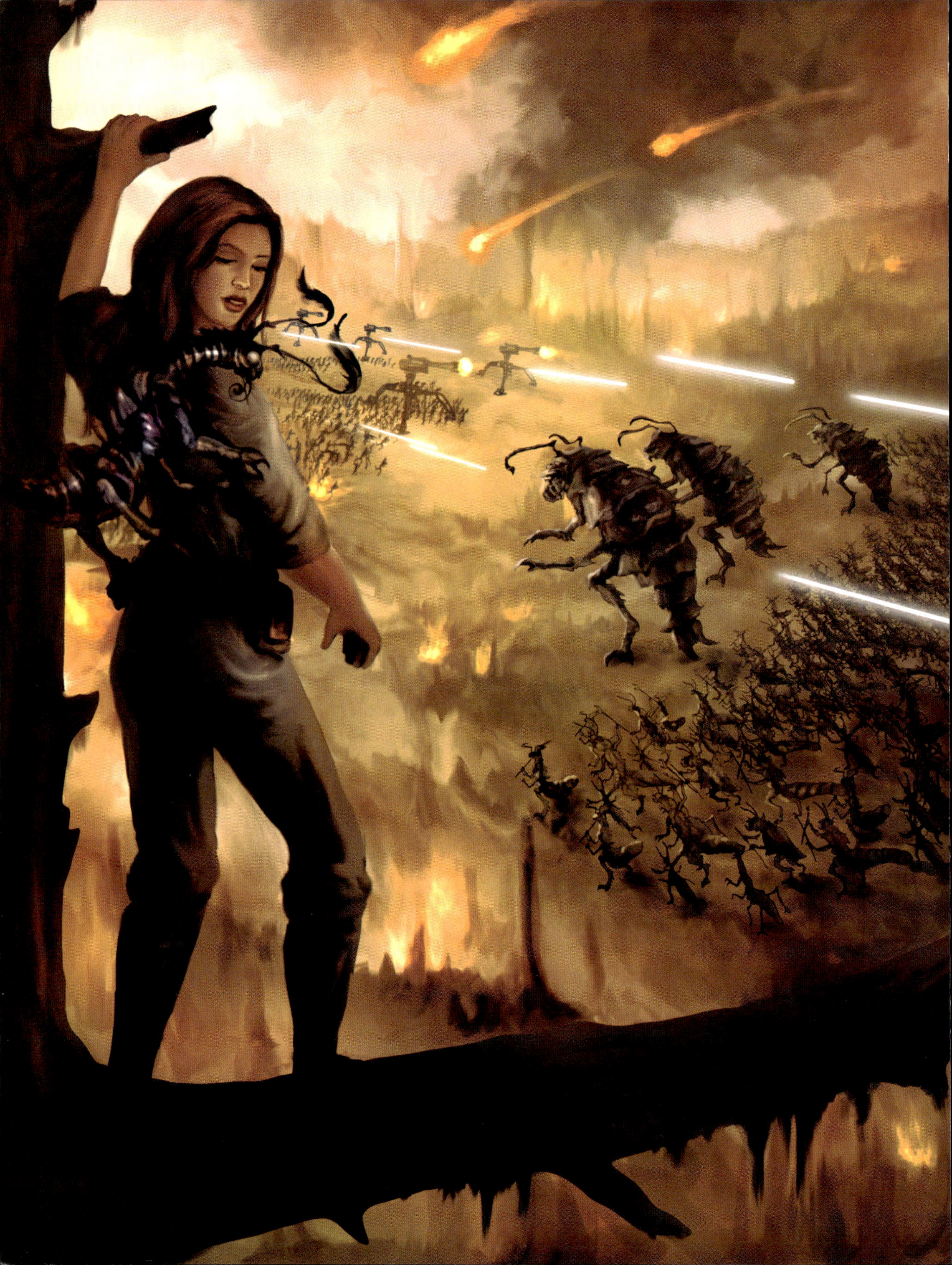

tentions are and where their true loyalties lie. Leia discovers that the Chiss intend to release a bioweapon against the Killiks. Appalled, Leia warns Jaina, and Alema Rar defends the Colony by shooting down the Chiss carriers. Leia and Saba search the Tenupe landscape for the downed bioweapon, as do the Killiks, who want to destroy it, and the Chiss, who want to reclaim it. Leia once again crosses paths with Alema Rar, defeating Alema in a lightsaber duel and presuming her to be dead.

Luke confronts UnuThul, dueling the former Jedi. He severs UnuThul's arm and entreats him to abandon his allegiance to the Killiks so that he can properly heal as a Jedi. Doing so releases his control over the insects, returning them to the scattered, unthreatening beings they were prior to Raynar's joining. Enraged, Lomi attacks Luke, but he defeats the queen. With their masterminds neutralized, the Killik threat is abated and the Swarm War ends.

THE SWARM WAR is a transitional trilogy that bridges the New Jedi Order series and the Legacy of the Force series that would follow. Given author Troy Denning's role in developing the latter story line, he was able to plant story threads that would build into the events covered in that series, especially the role of Jacen Solo.

Indicative of when these books were written—after the Prequel Trilogy had concluded in 2005 and the remaining holes of the cinematic *Star Wars* saga had finally been filled in, these were the first latter-era books to include mention of Padmé Amidala and her fate. A subplot involving a malfunctioning R2-D2 sees Luke and Mara uncover holographic data secretly recorded and saved by Artoo, meaning that Luke was essentially able to watch key scenes from *Revenge of the Sith* (2005) in holographic form, finally learning more about his mother and father so many decades after the events that sealed their fates.

On the battlefields of Tenupe, Jaina Solo commands the Killik army that advances on the Chiss forces.

IMPRINT

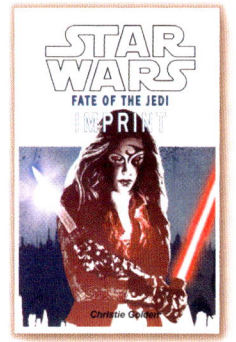

AUTHOR · Christie Golden
COVER ARTIST · Ian Keltie
PUBLICATION HISTORY · Short story, The Official *Star Wars* Fan Club
· Paperback, July 2009
TIME LINE PLACEMENT · 37 ABY
WORLD VISITED · Kesh [U-10]
MAIN CHARACTERS · Vestara Khai, Sith Tyro (human female); Ahri Raas, Sith Tyro (Keshiri male)

SUMMARY · At a festival on Kesh, the youngsters of the lost Sith tribe, known as Tyros, compete to secure an uvak familiar—a winged creature used by the Sith as mounts. Ten-year-old Vestara Khai competes with other Tyros to imprint her will on a newborn hatchling and bonds with an uvak that she names Tikk.

THE LOST TRIBE OF THE SITH was developed for the Fate of the Jedi series and was the focus of the eBook novella series by John Jackson Miller set in 5000 BBY. This short story, included as a small booklet in the Official *Star Wars* Fan Club Kit for 2009, is the first story to focus on the Lost Tribe in the modern era. It was written as a prelude to *Omen* (2009), the second Fate book and first of the novels in the series to feature an older Vestara Khai.

Mirta Gev

Jagged Fel

Allana "Amelia" Solo
(with Anji)

Natasi Daala

Wynn Dorvan
(with Pocket)

Bhindi Drayson

CHAPTER 8

LEGACY

When the heroes of the Rebellion first created the New Republic, their primary villains were stalwart Imperial holdouts. As the final embers of the Galactic Civil War were snuffed out, the galaxy was shaken apart by the Yuuzhan Vong. With such titanic threats defeated, the next era of *Star Wars* storytelling would bring back an ancient menace reborn: the Sith.

With Episode III, the conclusion of the cinematic *Star Wars* saga brought the shadowy Sith into the spotlight and to the top of the public's mind. Dark villains in previous works were usually called dark siders, Dark Jedi, dark adepts, or some other descriptor that set them apart from true Sith Lords. As long as Darth Vader and Darth Sidious lived, no other villain could capably don the Sith Lord mantle. Comics and videogames dived deep into the past to tell stories of ancient Sith Lords, but novels forged ahead without the Sith as featured players.

Starting in 2006, the Sith became featured villains across the Expanded Universe. Del Rey Books gave the ancient Sith new life with the bestselling novel Darth Bane: *Path of Destruction*, and Dark Horse Comics introduced a future in which an entire order of Sith would control the galaxy in the *Star Wars: Legacy* comic series. This series significantly advanced the time line, forging into uncharted territory 130 years after *A New Hope*. These comics gave their name to the next era of *Star Wars* stories, the Legacy era, which was unveiled at the 2005 *Star Wars* fan convention Celebration III with the following introduction:

LEGACY (37+ ABY) This is the era of Luke Skywalker's legacy: the Jedi Master has unified the Order into a cohesive group of powerful Jedi Knights. However, as this era begins, planetary interests threaten to disrupt this time of relative peace and Luke is plagued by visions of an approaching darkness.

The Sith would cast a shadow on the novels of this era. The working title for what became the nine-book Legacy of the Force series was in fact Sith Rising. And the Fate of the Jedi nine-book series that would follow would reveal a long-forgotten Lost Tribe of the Sith.

BETRAYAL

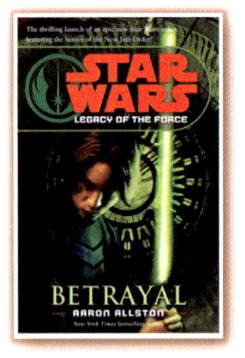

AUTHOR · Aaron Allston

COVER ARTIST · Jason Felix

PUBLICATION HISTORY ·
Novel, Del Rey Books
· Hardcover, May 2006
· Paperback, May 2007

TIME LINE PLACEMENT ·
40 ABY

WORLDS VISITED · Adumar [J-6]; Corellia [M-11]; Coruscant [L-9]; Kuat (system) [M-10]; Lorrd [N-4]; MZX32905 [N-4]; Tralus [M-11]

MAIN CHARACTERS · Jacen Solo, Jedi Knight (human male); Luke Skywalker, Grand Master of the Jedi Order (human male); Mara Jade Skywalker, Jedi Master (human female); Ben Skywalker, Jedi apprentice (human male); Han Solo, captain of the *Millennium Falcon* (human male); Leia Organa Solo, Jedi Knight (human female); Jaina Solo, Jedi Knight (human female); Lumiya, Dark Lady of the Sith (human cyborg female); Zekk, Jedi Knight (human male); Cal Omas, Chief of State (human male); Nelani Dinn, Jedi Knight (human female); Wedge Antilles, retired pilot (human male); Syal Antilles, pilot (human female); Aidel Saxan, Corellian Prime Minister (human female); Thrackan Sal-Solo, Corellian Head of State (human male)

SUMMARY · Having spent his formative years exposed to a galaxy at war, Ben Skywalker was for a time hesitant to use the Force. Now apprenticed to Jacen Solo, the thirteen-year-old has become more outgoing, learning much from the older, well-traveled Jedi Knight. He accompanies Jacen on an inspection tour of a missile-manufacturing company on Adumar, to ensure that Galactic Alliance weapons regulations are being met. When the Jedi discover the company attempting to produce black-market weapons, they crack down on the manufacturers in spectacular fashion.

Such are the travails of the Galactic Alliance as it tries to flex its authority over its member worlds. It seeks to centralize a galactic military for security, but its attempts to curb the militarization of sovereign worlds such as the fiercely independent-minded Corellia are met with controversy. Han Solo complains loudly about it at a family gathering on Coruscant. He sides with the Corellians, who have been negotiating in bad faith and encouraging other worlds to resist the Alliance.

Chief of State Cal Omas intends to put on a provocative show of naval power at Corellia to enforce the centralization efforts. Omas's biggest concern is reports that the Corellians are coming close to reactivating Centerpoint Station, a weapon far too powerful to fall into autonomous hands. Luke asks Jacen to lead a mission to infiltrate Centerpoint and commandeer the station for the Alliance. Though Han and Leia know none of this, they suspect an Alliance crackdown on Corellia. Favoring the idea of Corellian independence, Solo takes the *Millennium Falcon* back to his homeworld to give the Corellians fair warning.

Galactic Alliance military agents request an audience with Wedge Antilles, ostensibly to seek his seasoned military advice. In truth, they are detaining him to ensure he cannot assist the Corellians in the coming conflict. This rift between the Alliance and Corellia is particularly personal for Wedge—he's Corellian, but his eldest daughter, Syal, is a fighter pilot in the Alliance. The resourceful Wedge soon escapes his captors.

Han and Leia arrange an audience with Prime Minister Aidel Saxan, who insists Corellia is well

A normally tranquil dinner gathering of the Solo and Skywalker families instead becomes a tense argument over galactic politics.

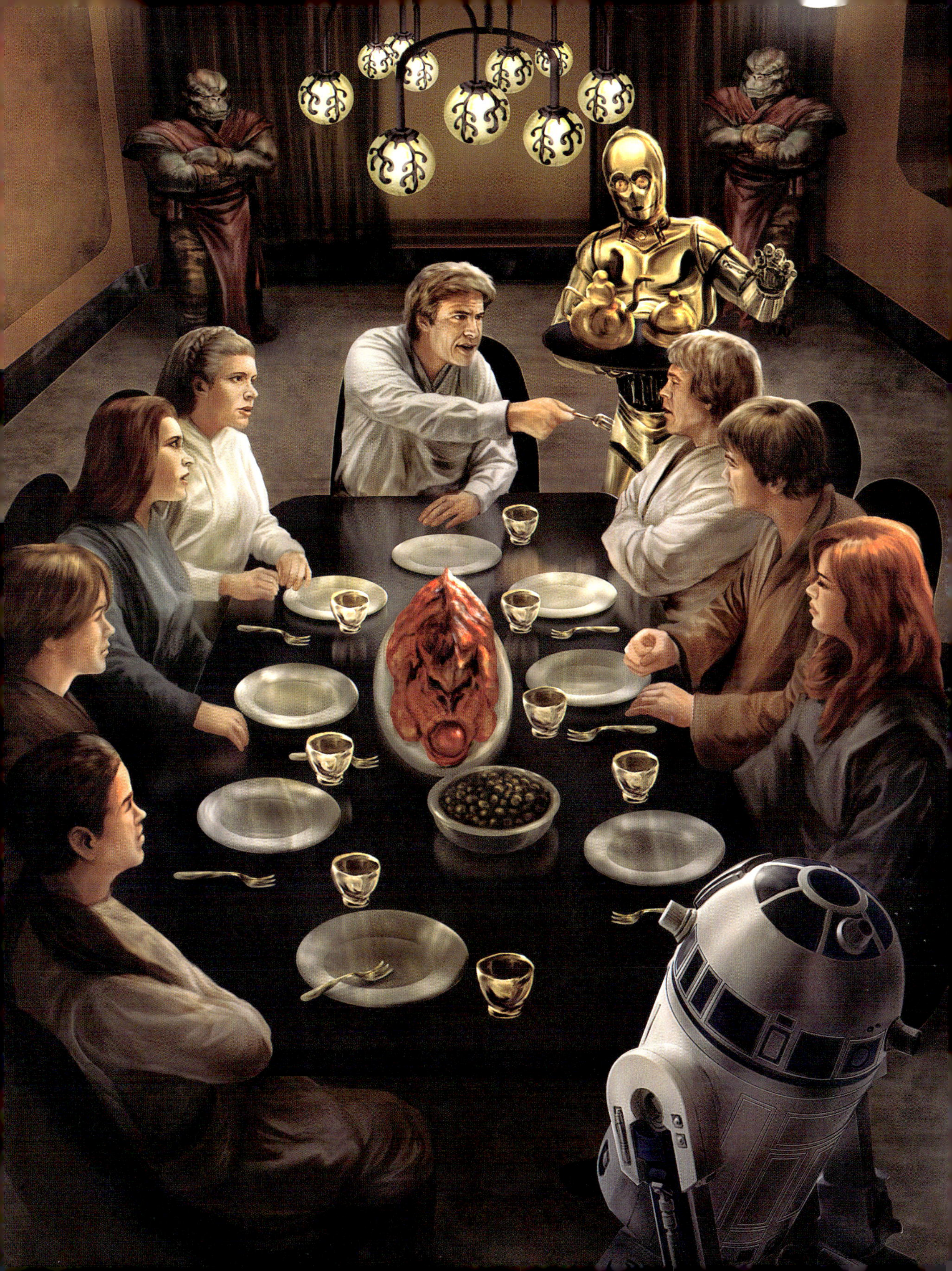

prepared. Saxan and Thrackan Sal-Solo have been readying their defenses for this day. The Galactic Alliance fleet is met by stiff Corellian resistance. Ben and Jacen infiltrate Centerpoint Station. While Ben deactivates the station, Jacen corners Sal-Solo. Even though the Corellian is unarmed, Jacen seriously contemplates killing him. Another Jedi mission to apprehend Saxan fails, as she has reinforced her retinue with modified YVH droids.

The Alliance's attempt at intimidating Corellia utterly fails. Proposed diplomatic talks between Supreme Commander Pellaeon of the GA and Prime Minister Saxan disintegrate before they start when black-armored assassins ambush the negotiation site, killing Saxan. The assassins die with no indication of their origins. Wedge investigates the attack site and finds a strange tasseled artifact, which he passes on to the Jedi. It eventually finds its way into Jacen's hands, and he is fascinated by the object.

An expert recognizes some of the patterns in the braided tassel as a form of writing, with the cryptic message, "He will strengthen himself through pain." To find out more, Jacen voyages to Lorrd, bringing Ben with him. There he encounters the Jedi Knight Nelani Dinn, who introduces him to a specialist in tactile writing. This expert translates more of the tassel, revealing additional seemingly prophetic phrases.

A disturbance of the peace demands the attention of the Jedi. A crazed civilian threatens to fire missiles from an armed starfighter unless he is allowed to speak to the Jedi. Jacen uses the Force to reposition the fighter so it can't safely fire its missiles. The man fires anyway, killing himself in the resulting explosion. Over the next few days, more incidents like this occur—events seemingly engineered by crazed beings to force the Jedi into an ethical choice of sacrifice for the greater good.

Ben discovers a shuttle on Lorrd that departed from the assassination site in the Corellian system. It is registered to a Force-sensitive woman named Brisha Syo, held prisoner by the Lorrd Security Force for suspicious acts. She tells the Jedi she has been afflicted by nightmares that correspond to the recent rash of deadly incidents on Lorrd. Brisha reveals she is responsible for the tassel and cryptically offers Jacen answers.

Brisha brings Jacen, Ben, and Nelani to her asteroid base near Bimmiel. After separating Jacen from Ben she reveals her true identity: she is the Dark Lady of the Sith, Lumiya, a former nemesis of Luke Skywalker from the Galactic Civil War era. Lumiya inundates Jacen with visions from the dark side, which purport to show that Vergere had already begun Jacen's training in the Sith ways during the Yuuzhan Vong War, for she and Lumiya are architects of the Sith rebirth. Lumiya seduces Jacen to the dark side by revealing that the power of the Sith would be capable of stopping the impending war between the Alliance and the Corellians. Convinced she speaks the truth, Jacen kills Nelani with his lightsaber and later uses the Force to erase any memories of her from Ben's mind. His path to the dark side has begun.

WITH LESSONS LEARNED from the sprawling New Jedi Order series, Del Rey Books and LucasBooks focused the follow-up series into nine books divided among three authors: Aaron Allston, Karen Traviss, and Troy Denning. The working title for this first book was *Control*. Among the earliest concepts to surface in brainstorming was to begin with a small conflict—a local dispute with the Corellian system that could then spiral out of control.

From the onset, it was known that Jacen would succumb to the dark side, but what would tip him over the brink would evolve in early story planning. In his Dark Nest Trilogy, author Troy Denning added years of flexible padding to Jacen's chronology, sending him on a vision quest among the galaxy's Force-users and widening his viewpoint beyond the traditional doctrines of the Jedi. As this first book came together, Allston at first proposed a more literal interpretation of Vergere's continued influence on Jacen: an actual "seedling" of Vergere's mind had been planted within Jacen's mind to act as a controlling influence. This direction was excised at the outline stage, in order to keep Jacen fully accountable for his transgressions later on in the series.

In preparation for the Legacy of the Force story, Denning wrote *The Vergere Compendium*, a twenty-seven-page outline of Vergere's master plan to transform Jacen into a Sith, complete with an examination of all her previous appearances, with detailed commentary on her overt actions and subtle implications.

In the earliest story meetings, the role of Lumiya was defined only as a "wizard" who would push Jacen along the dark path. A look at *Star Wars* characters with unresolved fates revealed that Lumiya, a villainess from the original Marvel Comics series, was unaccounted for in the galaxy.

BLOODLINES

AUTHOR · Karen Traviss

COVER ARTIST · Jason Felix

PUBLICATION HISTORY · Novel, Del Rey Books
· Paperback, August 2006

TIME LINE PLACEMENT · 39 ABY (prologue flashback); 40 ABY

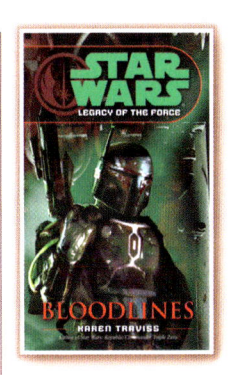

WORLDS VISITED · Atzerri [M-13]; Corellia [M-11]; Coruscant [L-9]; Drall [M-11]; Kamino [S-15]; Roonadan [S-3]; Taris [N-7]; Vohai [O-18]

MAIN CHARACTERS · Jacen Solo, Jedi Knight (human male); Mara Jade Skywalker, Jedi Master (human female); Luke Skywalker, Grand Master of the Jedi Order (human male); Ben Skywalker, Jedi apprentice (human male); Boba Fett, Mandalore (human male); Han Solo, captain of the *Millennium Falcon* (human male); Leia Organa Solo, Jedi Knight (human female); Jaina Solo, Jedi Knight (human female); Lumiya, Dark Lady of the Sith (human cyborg female); Cal Omas, Chief of State (human male); Cha Niathal, admiral (Mon Calamari female); Goran Beviin, Mandalorian soldier (human male); Mirta Gev, bounty hunter (human female); Thrackan Sal-Solo, Corellian Head of State (human male)

SUMMARY · After so many decades of close calls in his dangerous career as a bounty hunter, it is Boba Fett's clone origins that may finally kill him. Ten years after the end of the Yuuzhan Vong War, a doctor diagnoses Fett with a defect in his genes that will give him at most a year to live. Fett begins a search for any clues that may unlock genetic secrets that will prolong his life.

The tensions between the Galactic Alliance and Corellia have put Coruscant on edge as Corellia rallies support from independent-minded worlds that believe the Alliance is overstepping its bounds. Jacen thinks a stronger hand is needed to maintain order, but Chief of State Cal Omas disagrees. Jacen strikes up an alliance with the hawkish Admiral Cha Niathal to push an agenda beyond Omas's reservations.

LEGACY 421

Protected by Mandalorian armor, Han Solo joins Boba Fett and Mirta Gev on a mission to eliminate Thrackan Sal-Solo.

Han and Leia continue their rogue and incognito operations on Corellia, attempting to subvert the more provocative actions taken by the Alliance. Despite their efforts, Thrackan Sal-Solo still views them as the enemy. Sal-Solo, hardly a political idealist, sees the conflict as an opportunity to accrue more power and influence. Sal-Solo still intends to reactivate Centerpoint Station. He enlists a number of black-op teams to target Han, Leia, and their children for assassination. Among Sal-Solo's hired guns is the mercenary Ailyn Habuur—who is actually Boba Fett's estranged daughter Ailyn Vel.

Goran Beviin, one of Boba Fett's close Mandalorian confidants, brings him word that Fett's daughter has taken up the contract on the Solos. With his time running out, Fett hopes to make amends with Ailyn. A young female Mandalorian bounty hunter named Mirta Gev finds Fett and offers to help him track Ailyn down, promising information that can help.

Luke Skywalker is troubled by the conflict that has befallen the Galactic Alliance after actions he believes to be just. Furthermore, he is plagued by recurring visions of a mysterious dark man who threatens the galaxy. Luke senses a darkness on Coruscant, but he cannot identify the source. Though Luke has reservations about Ben's attachment to Jacen—and his obvious hero worship—Mara thinks Jacen is a good influence.

With each success against the enemy, Jacen gains more authority from the Alliance. He is offered command of the Galactic Alliance Guard (GAG), a

LEGACY

secret police force meant to ensure security. Supreme Commander Gilad Pellaeon steps down from his position, citing differences with the direction the Alliance is heading. Admiral Niathal assumes Pellaeon's command, extending Jacen's influence over the military.

It is not an easy mantle Jacen wears, but he is buoyed by the public support for his actions. Jacen is increasingly convinced that the dark side is not evil—in the hands of the right person, it's the necessary application of force and action—sentiments once espoused by Vergere. For reassurance, Jacen flow-walks, a time-twisting Force ability that allows him to experience past events firsthand, to witness the actions of his grandfather, Anakin Skywalker, during the rise of the Empire. Jacen sees Anakin's assault on the Jedi Temple and judges his grandfather to have been misguided; Anakin simply was not strong enough to resist the destructive power of the dark side. Jacen believes he can do better. Under his command, the Alliance escalates the tense blockade around Corellia, pushing the conflict into open war.

Jacen has Ben serve in the GAG. One of Jacen's first orders is imprisoning the Corellians on Coruscant to defend against terrorist strikes that have threatened peace on the capital. In rounding up suspects, the Guard arrests Ailyn Vel. Jacen brutally interrogates her using the Force, killing Ailyn in the process.

Dur Gejjen, a political rival of Thrackan Sal-Solo, wants the dangerous Corellian eliminated and proposes that Han assassinate his cousin. Fett also approaches Han, wanting to use him as bait to lure Ailyn Vel. In return, Fett will kill Sal-Solo for Han. Donning Mandalorian armor, Han accompanies Mirta and Fett as they track down Sal-Solo. Mirta kills the Corellian Head of State. Han discovers that Ailyn was a captive of the GAG and died in custody, though he remains unaware that Jacen is to blame.

Contacting Jacen, Han arranges for Ailyn's body to be delivered to Mandalore for a proper burial. In a surprising turn, Fett discovers that Mirta is in truth Ailyn's daughter, and therefore his granddaughter.

During an assault on Corellian forces, Jaina refuses a direct order from Jacen to destroy a defenseless target. For punishment, Jacen removes her from duty. His hard-line stance and ruthless actions further distance him from his family. Ben is the sole exception; he continues to admire his cousin's decisive victories, shielded from the more gruesome truths behind them. Lumiya, who still guides Jacen through the ways of the Sith, tells him this is but the start. Turning against his loved ones is part of a process that demands sacrifice. Jacen is chilled to realize that sacrifice may one day demand the deaths of Tenel Ka and his daughter, Allana.

When Fett learns from Beviin that Jacen Solo was in fact responsible for the death of Ailyn, he does not spring into action. Fett decides watching the Solo family disintegrate from within is suitable revenge.

EVEN FOR MANY avid *Star Wars* readers of novels and comics, the appearance of Boba Fett's daughter came as a surprise. She originates in a single story in *Star Wars Tales,* an anthology series that sometimes overtly separated itself from the established expectations of continuity, both retrospective and prospectively, to allow the talents at Dark Horse Comics leeway to tell a lively mix of stories. Issue #7, published in 2001, carried the story "Outbid But Never Outgunned" by writer Beau Smith and artists Mike Deodato Jr. and Neil Nelson. The sixteen-page tale had Boba Fett and Sintas Vel both chasing down a holographic recording that was being auctioned off by a mobster. The recording shows Fett and Vel standing together as husband and wife, holding their infant daughter.

LEGACY 423

Though this story could have been chalked up as noncontinuity, Sintas and her daughter were later referenced in "Unusual Suspects," an article by Andrew Hind that appeared in *Star Wars Gamer* #6 (2001), and "The History of the Mandalorians," an article by Abel G. Peña in *Star Wars Insider* #80 (2005). Their mention in *Bloodlines* was their first appearance within a prose story, as well as the first appearance of the next generation in Fett's family, Mirta Gev (who was originally named Vessin Ghif in the outline).

The working title for *Bloodlines* was *Necessary Evils*. Like Karen Traviss's other *Star Wars* novels, it heavily features the Mandalorian culture she helped develop for the Republic Commando series.

TEMPEST

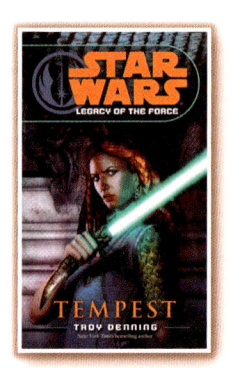

AUTHOR · Troy Denning
COVER ARTIST · Jason Felix
PUBLICATION HISTORY ·
Novel, Del Rey Books
· Paperback, November 2006
TIME LINE PLACEMENT · 40 ABY
WORLDS VISITED · Corellia [M-11]; Coruscant [L-9]; Hapes [O-9]; Kiris Asteroid Cluster [M-11]; Relephon [O-9]; Roqoo Depot [M-11]; Telkur Station [M-11]; Terephon [O-9]
MAIN CHARACTERS · Jacen Solo, Jedi Knight and Galactic Alliance Guard colonel (human male); Ben Skywalker, junior Galactic Alliance Guard member (human male); Luke Skywalker, Grand Master of the Jedi Order (human male); Han Solo, captain of the *Millennium Falcon* (human male); Leia Organa Solo, Jedi Knight (human female); Jaina Solo, Jedi Knight (human female); Mara Jade Skywalker, Jedi Master (human female); Lumiya, Dark Lady of the Sith (human cyborg female); Alema Rar, fallen Jedi (Twi'lek female); Allana, Hapan princess (human female); Aurra Sing, aka Nashtah, bounty hunter (female); Tenel Ka, Hapan Queen Mother (human female); Zekk, Jedi Knight (human male); Dur Gejjen, Five Worlds Prime Minister/Corellian Chief of State (human male); Jagged Fel, bounty hunter (human male)

SUMMARY · In the depths of Coruscant, Jacen Solo confers with the Yuuzhan Vong World Brain. The entity helps Jacen track the activities of criminals and terrorists who hide in the capital. Jacen is unaware that he is stalked by Alema Rar, his former Jedi strike team member, left maimed and unhinged in the Swarm War. Alema burns with hatred against the Skywalker/Solo clan and attempts to assassinate Jacen. Her poison dart misses him, killing the World Brain instead. Alema escapes into the shadows.

The besieged Corellians are desperate for allies, but few in the galaxy will openly support their contentious bid for independence. Queen Mother Tenel Ka of Hapes has taken an unpopular pro-Alliance stance, but a strong undercurrent of dissent threatens her rule. Would-be usurpers have struck a covert alliance with the Corellians—in exchange for weapons and funds, they would depose Tenel Ka and promise to bring the Hapes Consortium into the war on the side of Corellia. Though Han and Leia have done much to help the Corellian cause, the new Corellian leadership excludes the Solos from this plan due to their close friendship with Tenel Ka. The Solos go to Hapes, hoping to convince Tenel Ka to support Corellia.

On Coruscant, Alema spies Lumiya and Jacen together and recognizes Lumiya as a threat to Luke Skywalker, so she aims to ally herself with this dark woman. Luke, meanwhile, has tasked Jedi Master Tresina Lobi with spying on Jacen. Hoping to curry favor with Lumiya, Alema attacks and kills Tresina, then asks to help Lumiya in her dark plans.

After Han and Leia arrive on Hapes, assassins led by bounty hunter Aurra Sing strike in an attempt to kill the Queen Mother. Han and Leia defend the Queen Mother, but in the erupting chaos the Hapan guards mistake their intent and believe them to be in collusion with the assassins. The Solos flee, forced to take Sing with them. As the *Millennium Falcon* hastily departs, Jaina and Zekk arrive and begin investigating the attack. The Solos trick Sing into revealing the coup's leader, Ducha AlGray of the Heritage Council. The Solos pass on this information to the Hapans.

At a brief touchdown on Telkur Station, Han and Leia find Jagged Fel, who claims to have been exiled from the Chiss following failures in the Swarm War. Fel has been hunting down Alema, hoping to reinstate his honor by apprehending her.

Jacen hears that Allana has been threatened and rushes to Hapes with Ben in tow and a full contingent of the Galactic Alliance Guard aboard the Star Destroyer *Anakin Solo*. Under the belief that his parents not only are helping the Corellians but were also involved in the attempted assassination of Tenel Ka, Jacen issues a high-priority arrest warrant for Han and Leia and takes Allana aboard his Star Destroyer.

Luke and Mara investigate the death of Tresina, which leads them to discover Lumiya's hideout on Coruscant. They find evidence that Lumiya has access to GAG files and is possibly colluding with the Guard. Luke's concern for Ben grows, and he and Mara voyage to Hapes to bring their son back under closer supervision. Luke questions Jacen about Lumiya, but Jacen claims no knowledge of her or her involvement with the GAG. This does not alleviate Luke's suspicions.

Jacen sends Luke and Mara to retrieve Ben on Roqoo Depot. The Skywalkers are unaware that Jacen is sending them into a trap: he has dispatched Lumiya there as well, hoping they will eliminate each other while making it appear that Lumiya's plot consisted solely of targeting Ben. A duel erupts, with the Skywalkers facing Lumiya and Alema. The sly villainesses in the end are unable to kill either Luke or Mara but elude capture themselves.

The Corellian-backed Heritage Council fleet launches its attack on Hapes, where it is squarely met by Tenel Ka's loyalist fleet and the Galactic Alliance forces. The *Millennium Falcon* is caught in the middle, still targeted and fired upon by Jacen's command. Han picks up Jaina, Zekk, and Ben. In a misguided attempt, Ben tries to carry out Jacen's orders to arrest Han. Luke insists that Ben return with him to Coruscant, more certain than ever that Jacen has fallen into darkness.

BY THIS POINT in the story, it is clear Jacen is heading to a future as a Sith Lord. The outline to the Legacy series gave Jacen the Sith name Darth Kallus, but that was only a placeholder moniker. For his final name, LucasBooks and Del Rey turned to the fan community. In conjunction with StarWars.com, the temporary website DarthWho.com began accepting submissions for possible Sith names in October 2006. By November, over eighty-five hundred entries were received. Del Rey reviewed and cut the list down to a manageable five hundred before passing them on to the three series authors.

EXILE

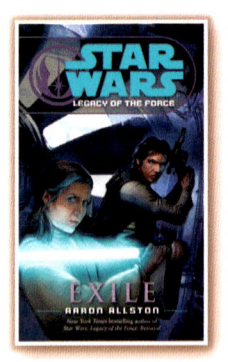

AUTHOR · Aaron Allston
COVER ARTIST · Jason Felix
PUBLICATION HISTORY ·
Novel, Del Rey Books
· Paperback, February 2007
TIME LINE PLACEMENT · 40 ABY
WORLDS VISITED · Bothawui [R-14]; Commenor [N-10]; Corellia [M-11]; Coruscant [L-9]; Drewwa [S-5]; Gilatter VIII [I-7]; Gyndine [O-12]; Kuat [M-10]; MZX32905 [N-4]; Ziost [R-4]

MAIN CHARACTERS · Luke Skywalker, Grand Master of the Jedi Order (human male); Ben Skywalker, Jedi apprentice (human male); Mara Jade Skywalker, Jedi Master (human female); Jacen Solo, Jedi Knight and Galactic Alliance Guard colonel (human male); Lumiya, Dark Lady of the Sith (human cyborg female); Han Solo, captain of the *Millennium Falcon* (human male); Leia Organa Solo, Jedi Knight (human female); Jaina Solo, Jedi Knight (human female); Jagged Fel; bounty hunter/operative (human male); Zekk, Jedi Knight (human male); Alema Rar, fallen Jedi (Twi'lek female); Booster Terrik, captain of the *Errant Venture* (human male); Cha Niathal, Galactic Alliance Supreme Commander (Mon Calamari female); Kiara, child (human female); Lando Calrissian, entrepreneur (human male); Corran Horn, Jedi Master (human male); Wedge Antilles, Corellian admiral (human male); Iella Antilles, intelligence operative (human female)

SUMMARY · Disagreeing with the dishonorable turns of the Corellian government, Wedge Antilles resigns from his position as Supreme Commander of their military forces. This puts him in the crosshairs of the capricious Corellian leaders, who are considering drastic tactics to counter the extreme measures undertaken by Jacen Solo in his command of the Galactic Alliance Guard.

Han and Leia want to get to the bottom of the assassination attempt on Tenel Ka, but first must acquire a new vessel while the *Millennium Falcon* undergoes repair. Lando Calrissian offers his port facilities in the Gyndine system, as well as the temporary loan of a ship, *Love Commander*. Lando accompanies them to Corellia, where they are able to confirm from Corellian Justice Minister Denjax Teppler that the Corellians backed the failed coup. The Solos, Calrissian, and Wedge find refuge aboard Booster Terrik's private Star Destroyer *Errant Venture*, now operating as a lucrative bazaar, casino, and listening post. Also skulking aboard the *Venture* is Alema Rar.

Continuing his search for Alema, Jag Fel offers his services to Luke, who teams the exiled pilot with Jaina and Zekk to hunt her down. It's an awkward partnership, given Jaina's complicated feelings toward both men. Tipped off by a smuggler, the Solos learn of Alema's presence aboard the *Errant Venture* and try to trap her. The elusive Twi'lek once again escapes.

Jacen's military successes prompt Chief of State Cal Omas and Supreme Commander Cha Niathal to request that Luke Skywalker elevate him to the rank of Jedi Master, as a show of unity between the Galactic Alliance and the Jedi Order. Luke refuses, but Jacen gives it little thought, for he is concerned with Sith mastery instead.

Lumiya decrees it is time Jacen test whether or not Ben Skywalker is a suitable apprentice. Should

---

The holographic form of Turr Phennir witnesses Jedi siblings Luke Skywalker and Leia Organa Solo battle the Dark Lady Lumiya and Alema Rar aboard the resort satellite over Gilatter VIII.

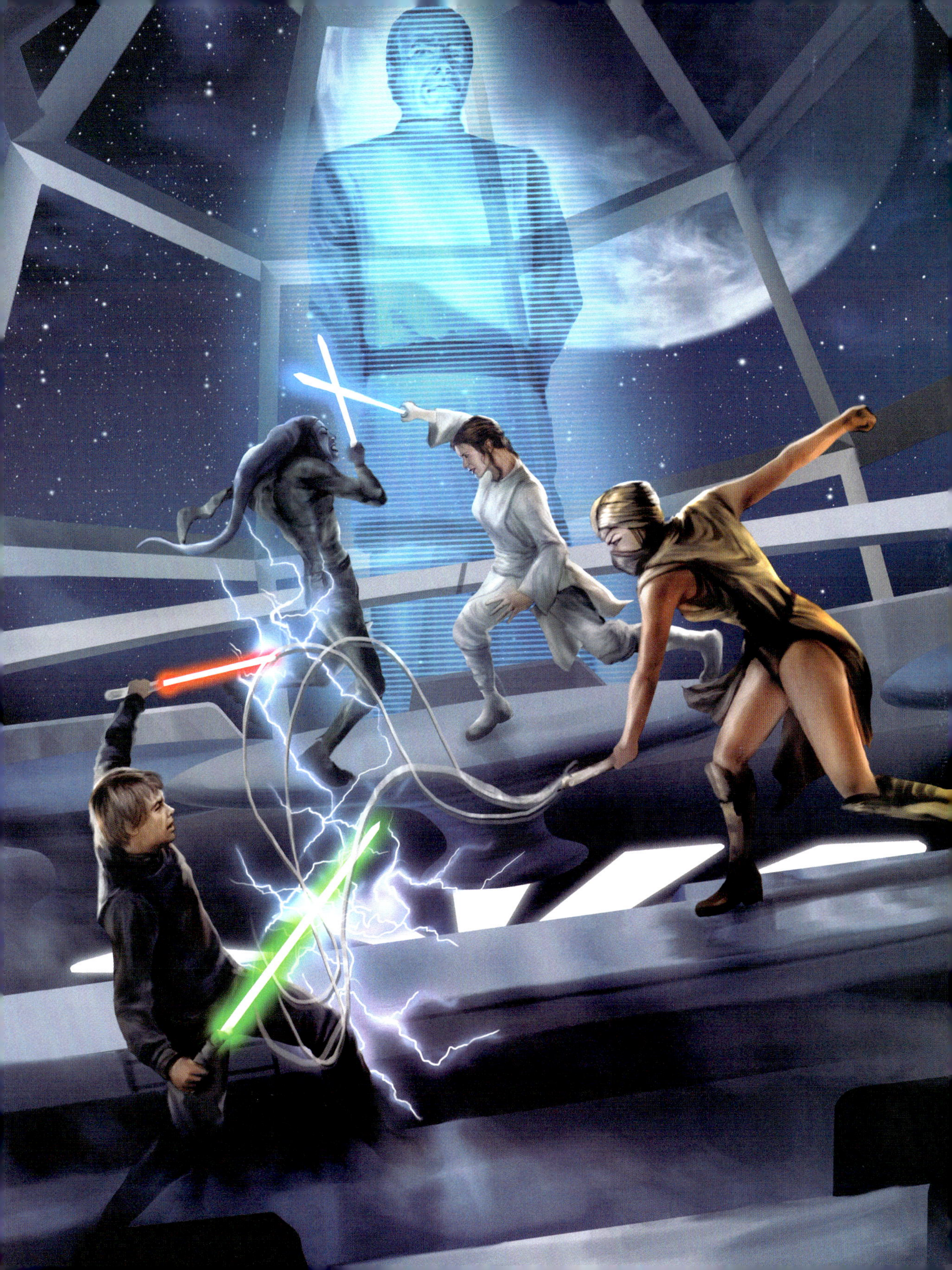

Ben fail, then perhaps his death is the sacrifice Jacen must make on his path into the depths of the dark side. To gauge his cousin's abilities, Jacen sends Ben on a mission to retrieve the Amulet of Kalara, a Force-imbued relic reputed to turn its wearer invisible in the Force. Ben's search for the artifact leads him to the ancient Sith world of Ziost, to hunt a thief named Faskus who already has the Amulet.

While Ben tracks his quarry, he must contend with agents tracking him on Lumiya's behalf. Ben subdues an injured Faskus, who is traveling with his young daughter, Kiara. Faskus claims that Lumiya's trackers forced him to steal and hide the talisman. After Faskus succumbs to his wounds, Ben brings Kiara with him as he continues his search for the Amulet. Ben is alarmed to discover that the ancient dark side presence of Ziost plants unnatural suggestions in his head, such as killing and devouring the little girl. Remaining resolute, Ben uncovers ruins housing a working Sith meditation sphere, a bizarre ancient spacecraft seemingly alive in the Force and possessing intelligence. Ben learns to pilot the vessel, and he flies it and Kiara off the evil planet.

Lumiya conspires to escalate the interstellar conflict by supplying vital Galactic Alliance intelligence to the Bothans and the world of Commenor. Allying with Corellia, this triad becomes the nucleus of the Corellian Confederation. Waging open war against the Alliance and breaking the choke-hold blockade of Corellia turns the Confederation–Alliance showdown into the Second Galactic Civil War. Fondor, Adumar, and Bespin join the battle against the Alliance as well.

On Gilatter VIII, the leadership of the growing Confederation gathers to select Turr Phennir of Corellia as Supreme Commander. Jacen is undercover at the convocation—which is a trap set to ensnare him. Also in attendance are Luke, Mara, Han, and Leia, who come to Phennir's aid despite their differences. Lumiya and Alema are there as well, adding to the chaos. The dark warriors keep the Solos and Skywalkers occupied as Jacen escapes to his Star Destroyer.

THE SITH MEDITATION SPHERE was first introduced as a type of starship in the *Tales of the Jedi: The Fall of the Sith Empire* comic series in 1997. This vessel, called Ship, would figure prominently not only in the remainder of the Legacy of the Force series, but also the Fate of the Jedi series that follows.

The next stage in the search for Jacen's Sith name accompanied the release of *Exile*. Of the potential names submitted by readers, authors Aaron Allston, Troy Denning, and Karen Traviss selected five finalists: Darth Acheron, Darth Caedus, Darth Judicar, Darth Paxis, and Darth Taral. These were put to a vote from late January through February 2007, with the winner to be revealed with the publication of *Sacrifice* in May.

SACRIFICE

AUTHOR · Karen Traviss

COVER ARTIST · Jason Felix

PUBLICATION HISTORY · Novel, Del Rey Books
- Hardcover, May 2007
- Paperback, April 2008

TIME LINE PLACEMENT · 40 ABY

WORLDS VISITED · Contruum (system) [O-8]; Coruscant (and its moon Hesperidium) [L-9]; Drall [M-11]; Hapes [O-9]; Kavan [O-9]; Kuat [M-10]; Mandalore [O-7]; MZX32905 [N-4]; Taanab [O-8]; Terephon [O-9]; Vulpter [L-10]; Ziost [R-4]

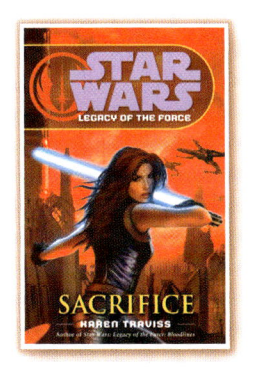

MAIN CHARACTERS · Jacen Solo, Jedi Knight and Galactic Alliance Guard colonel (human male); Mara Jade Skywalker, Jedi Master (human female); Ben Skywalker, junior Galactic Alliance Guard (human male); Luke Skywalker, Grand Master of the Jedi Order (human male); Boba Fett, Mandalore (human male); Lumiya, Dark Lady of the Sith (human female); Leia Organa Solo, Jedi Knight (human female); Han Solo, captain of the *Millennium Falcon* (human male); Jaina Solo, Jedi Knight (human female); Jori Lekauf, GAG corporal (human male); Lon Shevu, GAG captain (human male); Cal Omas, Chief of State (human male); Cha Niathal, Alliance Supreme Commander (Mon Calamari female); Dur Gejjen, Corellian Prime Minister (human male); Ghes Orade, Mandalorian soldier (human male); Goran Beviin, Mandalorian soldier (human male); Medrit Beviin, Mandalorian soldier (human male); Mirta Gev, bounty hunter (human female); Alema Rar, fallen Jedi (Twi'lek female)

SUMMARY · Ben Skywalker delivers the Amulet of Kalara to Jacen Solo. From the shadows, Lumiya is intensely interested in the Sith meditation sphere Ben has uncovered, which Jacen secretly secures aboard his flagship. Within the Galactic Alliance command structure, Chief of State Cal Omas grows wary of Jacen and Cha Niathal's aggressive tactics—he wants a peaceful end to hostilities. Word that the Mandalorians may be mobilizing puts the Alliance on edge, since it is very likely they would ally with the Confederation, given Jacen killed Boba Fett's daughter.

Ben returns home, but avoids the disappointed gaze of his father. Mara, concerned for Ben, does not suspect that Jacen is the ultimate source of danger. She is determined to investigate the tenuous leads on Lumiya, but also wants to keep Ben safe. She gifts him with a vibroblade in which she has secretly concealed a tracking device.

Boba Fett continues his search for a cure to his bodily deterioration. He and Mirta Gev set out to find Jaing, a rumored Clone Wars–era Null ARC trooper who has lived long past the age his accelerated genes should allow. Though Jaing initially refuses to hand over tissue samples for research, a man named Venku—Darman's son, born at the end of the Clone Wars—helps change Jaing's mind. Venku knows of a Mandalorian of Kiffar heritage who has the psychometric ability to pull impressions from inanimate objects. He handles an artifact owned by Mirta's mother and sees that Ailyn Vel was once hunting for a gangster named Rezodar, who had in his possession a carbonite block with Sintas Vel sealed within. Boba Fett is stunned—Sintas, his former lover and Ailyn's mother, has been presumed dead for a long time.

Hearing of frustrations from inadequately supplied Alliance troops on the front lines, Jacen works with a legal droid, HM-3, to cut through the choking bureaucracy and discovers gaping loopholes that allow him to sidestep regulations and Senate approval. In this way, Jacen has determined how to subvert the political machinery to obtain the power he needs to effectively command the Alliance.

Jacen gives Ben the difficult mission of assassinating the Corellian Prime Minister, Dur Gejjen, in order to quickly end the war. Ben goes undercover with fellow GAG agents Jori Lekauf and Lon Shevu and targets Gejjen on Vulpter. Gejjen has been secretly engaging Cal Omas in correspondence to settle the conflict, in which Omas gives thought to eliminating Niathal and Jacen in return for peace.

When Ben learns of this, it galvanizes his convictions. When Omas returns to the capital, the GAG arrests him, allowing Jacen and Niathal to assume joint command.

Ben kills Gejjen with a shot from a sniper rifle. As the GAG team tries to leave Vulpter, security forces block their path and Jori Lekauf sacrifices himself, making his suicide and the assassination appear to be the acts of a lone Corellian dissident. Shevu and Ben escape, and young Ben is rattled by Jori's death. When he returns to Coruscant, Mara knows Ben was involved in the assassination, since the tracking device in his dagger indicated he was on Vulpter. Mara, having been trained as an assassin from a young age, sympathizes with her son's predicament.

Mara's search for Lumiya uncovers the Dark Lady hiding on Coruscant, but her attempt to apprehend the cyborg Sith fails when Mara is knocked aside by the ancient Sith meditation sphere that comes to Lumiya's rescue. Mara affixes a tracking device to the sphere as it departs. Ben reveals to Mara that he has just overheard Jacen talking with Lumiya and naïvely assumes that Jacen has fallen under Lumiya's influence as opposed to actively plotting with the Sith. Mara confronts Jacen about Lumiya, and he denies any knowledge of the woman. Mara doesn't believe him and realizes that Jacen must be stopped. Jacen, likewise, begins to see his aunt as a grave threat.

Recognizing that his journey is at a turning point, Jacen travels to Hapes to visit with Tenel Ka and his daughter, possibly for the last time. Lumiya shadows Jacen to the throneworld aboard the Sith meditation sphere, unwittingly also drawing Mara (via her tracking device) and Ben (via his attunement to Ship). Jacen senses Lumiya's presence and fears that his child's safety is endangered. As he tries to track down his Sith mentor, he instead tangles with Mara in a confrontation in the caves of Kavan. As Mara and Jacen duel, Ben forces the meditation sphere to land to apprehend Lumiya.

The duel between Jacen and Mara is an exhausting, no-limits display of acrobatics and Force power. Mara comes to truly comprehend how far Jacen has fallen to the dark side. Jacen uses the Force to distract Mara with a vision of Ben before closing in to stab her with a poison dart. The fast-acting toxin kills Mara, and her death reverberates through the Force, hitting Luke and Ben as if it were a physical blow. Using the echoes of Mara's death as a distraction, Lumiya escapes to nearby Terephon.

Jacen has reached a threshold in his Sith potential. He has sacrificed a loved one and the bond of trust between himself and Ben. Lumiya senses this shift in power and decides a further sacrifice is needed to cement Jacen's rule. She allows herself to be found on Terephon by a vengeful Luke Skywalker, who attacks the Dark Lady. Lumiya claims credit for killing Mara, and an enraged Luke, tipping toward the dark side, decapitates the Sith. It is a hollow victory, for Luke soon learns from Ben that it could not have been Lumiya who was responsible, as she was with Ben at the time of Mara's death.

Jacen consoles Ben about Mara's death, coldly feigning innocence in the murder and suggesting that it was an unseen agent of Lumiya who was responsible. Jacen feels his power in the dark side swell, unlocking new powers, including an unparalleled ability to command and coordinate fighting forces as the former Emperor once did. Fully committed to the Sith path, Jacen assumes the title Darth Caedus.

The winning entry for Jacen's Sith name, Darth Caedus, was submitted by Tawnia Poland, who is acknowledged at the front of the book.

INFERNO

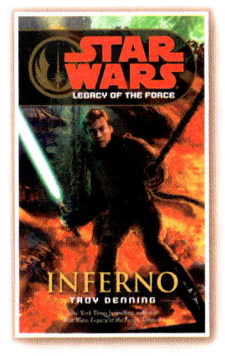

AUTHOR · Troy Denning
COVER ARTIST · Jason Felix
PUBLICATION HISTORY ·
Novel, Del Rey Books
· Paperback, August 2007
TIME LINE PLACEMENT · 40 ABY
WORLDS VISITED · Balmorra [M-10]; Coruscant [L-9]; Hapes [O-9]; Kashyyyk [P-9]; Korriban [R-5]; Kuat [M-10]; MZX32905 [N-4]; Ossus [R-6]

MAIN CHARACTERS · Jacen Solo/Darth Caedus, Sith Lord (human male); Luke Skywalker, Grand Master of the Jedi Order (human male); Ben Skywalker, Galactic Alliance Guard member (human male); Tahiri Veila, Jedi Knight (human female); Tenel Ka, Hapan Queen Mother (human female); Cal Omas, former Chief of State (human male); Jagged Fel, bounty hunter (human male); Jaina Solo, Jedi Knight (human female); Zekk, Jedi Knight (human male); Alema Rar, fallen Jedi (Twi'lek female); Han Solo, captain of the *Millennium Falcon* (human male); Leia Organa Solo, Jedi Knight (human female); Saba Sebatyne, Jedi Master (Barabel female)

SUMMARY · As acting Joint Chief of State, Jacen attends Mara Jade Skywalker's funeral. The police state he has created on Coruscant has raised the security alerts so high that Han and Leia cannot attend, lest they be arrested. Ben helps a despondent Luke deal with his grief, while he continues his search for Mara's killer. Ben suspects Jacen, but he needs evidence. Jacen tries to throw Ben off the trail by suggesting that Cal Omas had ordered the killing. Jacen orders Ben to kill Omas.

Omas is, of course, innocent. Omas shares Ben's belief that Jacen is the culprit and has faith that Ben, and only Ben, can expose Jacen's treachery and bring him to justice. To ensure that Ben appears loyal to Jacen, Omas sacrifices himself upon Ben's blade, dying secure in the knowledge that Ben will succeed.

Jacen Solo compels his friend and Jedi Knight Tahiri Veila to spy for him, earning her loyalty by exploiting her desire to revisit Anakin Solo through his time-bending ability of flow-walking. Jacen also convinces Tenel Ka to lend him the Hapan Home Fleet, stripping Hapes's defenses, so he can ambush the Confederation's fleet and end the rebellion once and for all.

Under the guise of security, Jacen has the GAG forces seize the Jedi academy on Ossus. An overzealous commander, Major Salle Serpa, leads the occupation, essentially taking the Jedi present at Ossus hostage. Jaina, Jag, and Zekk arrive there on the trail of Alema Rar and discover this outrage, but initially do not confront Serpa. When he moves against the Jedi and brutally tortures Kam and Tionne Solusar in front of the young apprentices, however, they swiftly overpower the GAG forces.

Alema Rar, having absconded with the Sith meditation sphere, takes it to Lumiya's asteroid base. There she uncovers evidence that Lumiya has concealed a resurgent Sith presence on Korriban. Voyaging to the ancient Sith world, Lumiya learns of Darth Krayt's dormant One Sith movement. The burgeoning Sith are reluctant to help her, claiming that Lumiya acted on her own and was not part of their plan.

When word reaches Luke that Ben killed Omas, he holds Jacen responsible. Luke ends his commitment to the Galactic Alliance, taking with him his contingent of Jedi StealthX fighters, abandoning

Jacen's fleet. Luke reunites with Han and Leia on Kashyyyk, where they have spearheaded an opposition against Jacen's command, convincing the Wookiees to support Corellia and her allies.

Jacen retaliates by attacking Kashyyyk. Much of the forest-covered world burns under his assaults. Luke and Jaina lead StealthX fighters against Jacen's flagship, *Anakin Solo*. Aboard the massive vessel, Ben attempts to strike at Jacen but fails, falling captive. Jacen holds his young cousin in the last known surviving Embrace of Pain, a Yuuzhan Vong torture device that he believes will strengthen Ben's character and reshape the young Jedi as Jacen was reshaped by Vergere during the Yuuzhan Vong War.

Luke sneaks aboard the *Anakin Solo* and frees his son, engaging Darth Caedus in a duel. Both Luke and Caedus are injured in the fight, but Luke has the upper hand. Once freed Ben tries to kill Jacen. Luke prevents it, fearing such aggression may turn his son to the dark side.

Han and Leia rush to Hapes to get aid from Tenel Ka. The Solos convince the Queen Mother that Jacen must be stopped, then sneak her back to Kashyyyk. Tenel Ka retakes command of the Hapan fleet and drives Jacen's fleet away. Jacen realizes that his entire family has turned against him.

ALEMA'S TRIP to Korriban offers a direct connection to the future spelled out in the *Star Wars: Legacy* comic series. In that series, a mysterious Sith Lord named Darth Krayt has built the Sith anew and done away with the infighting that had plagued the ancient Sith by elevating the very concept of the Order above the desires of any one Lord. Thus, the Rule of Two was supplanted by the One Sith, with all the Sith adherents identifying as one. As Darth Krayt would eventually be revealed to be a character preexisting in the lore, preserved into the future by slumbering in stasis, he cannot appear as a character in this era. Instead, other intermediaries represent the One Sith cult in Luke Skywalker's age, as seen in *Inferno* and later in *Crosscurrent* (2010) and *Riptide* (2011). The novel *Apocalypse* (2012) finds a unique way of including Darth Krayt in this era of storytelling.

FURY

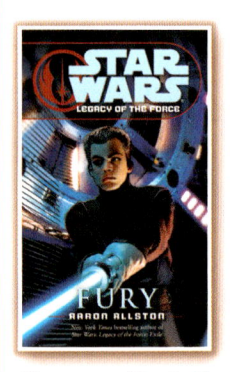

AUTHOR · Aaron Allston

COVER ARTIST · Jason Felix

PUBLICATION HISTORY · Novel, Del Rey Books
· Paperback, November 2007

TIME LINE PLACEMENT · 40 ABY

WORLDS VISITED · Commenor [N-10]; Corellia [M-11]; Coruscant [L-9]; Endor (forest moon) [H-16]; Gyndine [O-12]; Hapes [O-9]; Kashyyyk [P-9]; Korriban [R-5]; MZX32905 [N-4]; Talus and Tralus [M-11]

MAIN CHARACTERS · Jacen Solo/Darth Caedus, Sith Lord (human male); Luke Skywalker, Grand Master of the Jedi Order (human male); Ben Skywalker, Galactic Alliance Guard member (human male); Alema Rar, fallen Jedi (Twi'lek female); Han Solo, captain of the *Millennium Falcon* (human male); Leia Organa Solo, Jedi Knight (human female); Jaina Solo, Jedi Knight (human female); Tenel Ka, Hapan Queen Mother (human female); Jagged Fel, pilot/mercenary

432 LEGACY

(human male); Zekk, Jedi Knight (human male); Allana, Hapan princess (human female); Denjax Teppler, Corellian Minister of Information (human male); Sadras Koyan, Corellian Five Worlds Prime Minister (human male)

SUMMARY · Under the mistaken assumption that Alema Rar, not Jacen Solo, killed Mara Jade Skywalker, the Jedi prioritize the capture of the mad Twi'lek. While Jaina, Zekk, and Jag ready themselves for the inevitable confrontation with Alema, Jag forces Jaina to consider if she is training so hard she is losing touch with her humanity. Also hunting for Alema are agents of the One Sith movement on Korriban, who want to know the secrets of the Sith power she has uncovered in Lumiya's asteroid base.

Jacen returns to Hapes, abducts his daughter, Allana, and holds her hostage, forcing Queen Tenel Ka to return her fleet to the Galactic Alliance cause. Jacen uses Allana as a shield against reprisal strikes from the Hapans and the Jedi. He transports the young girl within an armored container carried by a modified YVH droid. A Jedi strike team that includes Kyle Katarn, Valin Horn, and Seha Dorvald launches an assault against him on Coruscant, succeeding in affixing a tracking device on him. Katarn is gravely injured in the attack.

The Second Galactic Civil War continues to escalate, with the Alliance dropping meteors onto Commenor's surface, pounding the world with indiscriminate devastation. The Confederation strikes back with biological weapons on Coruscant. The Five Worlds Prime Minister, Sadras Koyan, sends a message of parley to Jacen Solo to end the war. Leia, likewise, seeks a diplomatic—and familial— discussion with Jacen, meeting him aboard his flagship *Anakin Solo*. Leia is in actuality stalling while a Jedi insertion team boards the *Anakin Solo* to uncover the location of Alema Rar. Though the Jedi have a chance to strike at Jacen, they will not risk Allana's life as long as Jacen keeps the innocent girl in the potential crossfire.

As the *Anakin Solo* approaches the Corellian system, Prime Minister Koyan and Minister of Information Denjax Teppler spring a trap, firing at Jacen's fleet with Centerpoint Station. The blast eradicates most of Jacen's ships, but the *Anakin Solo* survives unscathed. Turr Phennir, Supreme Commander of the Confederation military forces, berates his two partners within the Confederation triumvirate for acting so foolishly. Teppler and Phennir consider removing Koyan from his position. Aware that Centerpoint has now been reactivated, Jacen and Cha Niathal target it for destruction.

Jaina, Jagged, and Zekk arrive at Lumiya's asteroid base, as does the *Poison Moon*, a vessel dispatched on behalf of the One Sith. Jag kills Alema while the Sith followers destroy the base. The Sith meditation sphere, Ship, escapes the conflict, retreating into space.

At the new Jedi sanctuary on Endor's forest moon, Luke is comforted to hear that Alema— Mara's supposed killer—is dead. Ben still harbors doubts that Alema was the murderer, but he is relieved to see his father begin to emerge from his grief. Father and son grow closer when Luke begins training Ben directly, instructing him on how to construct a lightsaber.

As the Alliance closes in on Centerpoint, Han Solo launches a strike team that includes Leia and Iella Wessiri, who board the *Anakin Solo* and successfully rescue Allana. A Jedi team infiltrates Centerpoint Station, delivering technician Toval Seyah to sabotage the massive weapon so that it explodes and destroys itself with its next blast, which is intended for Coruscant.

With his family's honor restored and his duty to the Jedi satisfied by Alema's death, Jag discusses his future with Jaina. When she assures him she wants him in her life after she fulfills her own duty, he agrees to continue to fight alongside the Jedi. Jaina decides her victory will come only by turning to a surprising teacher.

A WORKING TITLE for *Fury* was the synonymous *Rage*. The destruction of Centerpoint would unleash calamitous repercussions that would haunt the heroes in the Fate of the Jedi series that follows. A happier development in *Fury* is Lando Calrissian learning that his wife, Tendra, is pregnant. Their son would feature as a character in *Millennium Falcon* (2008) and *Outcast* (2009). Ship, the Sith meditation sphere, would reappear in *Omen* (2009), the second book of the Fate of the Jedi series, in flashback chapters that pick up immediately from the events in *Fury*.

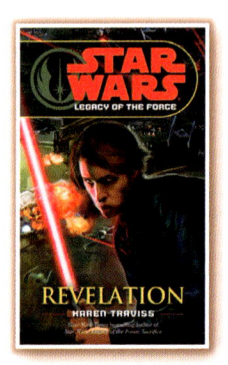

REVELATION

AUTHOR · Karen Traviss
COVER ARTIST · Jason Felix
PUBLICATION HISTORY ·
Novel, Del Rey Books
· Paperback, February 2008
TIME LINE PLACEMENT · 41 ABY
WORLDS VISITED · Bastion [K-3]; Coruscant [L-9]; Endor (forest moon) [H-16]; Fondor [L-13]; Kavan [O-9]; Mandalore [O-7]; N'zoth [K-10]; Phaeda [L-6]; Shedu Maad [O-9]
MAIN CHARACTERS · Jacen Solo/Darth Caedus, Sith Lord (human male); Luke Skywalker, Grand Master of the Jedi Order (human male); Ben Skywalker, Galactic Alliance Guard member (human male); Boba Fett, Mandalore (human male); Jaina Solo, Jedi Knight (human female); Leia Organa Solo, Jedi Knight (human female); Han Solo, captain of the *Millennium Falcon* (human male); Tahiri Veila, Sith apprentice (human female); Gilad Pellaeon, Imperial Remnant admiral (human male); Cha Niathal, Joint Chief of Staff (Mon Calamari female); Mirta Gev, bounty hunter (human female); Sintas Vel, former bounty hunter (human female)

SUMMARY · Seeking any possible advantage in her quest to defeat her twin brother, Darth Caedus, Jaina Solo requests training from Boba Fett and his Mandalorian forces. Fett agrees; helping bring about Jacen's death will provide a measure of justice for his murder of Fett's daughter Ailyn. Jaina sees a new side of Fett as he deals with the return of his wife, Sintas Vel, from decades of carbonite imprisonment. Jaina grows to understand the tradition-bound ways of the Mandalorians, becoming friends with Fett's granddaughter, Mirta Gev.

Darth Caedus has taken on a new apprentice: Tahiri Veila. He has corrupted her with promised contact with Anakin Solo—his dead brother and her beloved—through his flow-walking techniques. Caedus sends Tahiri as his envoy to the Imperial Remnant to secure the allegiance of Grand Admiral Pellaeon and the Imperial forces. Tahiri believes she must kill the veteran fleet officer if he refuses. Pellaeon has been watching the conflict from the sidelines since stepping down from Alliance command, and he is wary of Jacen's motives and actions. Though he agrees to allow the Imperial Remnant fleet to accompany the Alliance's reprisal strike against Fondor, Pellaeon keeps a card up his sleeve by secretly contacting a surprise ally.

LEGACY 434

Ben Skywalker continues his investigation into his mother's death. He works with his former GAG partner Lon Shevu to piece together evidence, operating true to the methodical training he received as Jacen's protégé within the Guard. He eventually compiles enough proof that Jacen was responsible for Mara's death to make the case to Luke.

Jacen Solo launches the attack on Fondor, but is incensed to find it protected by Luke Skywalker and his Jedi. Luke was alerted to the attack by Cha Niathal, who has soured on Jacen's methods and has plotted with Captain Kral Nevil of the *Anakin Solo* to overthrow Jacen. Niathal refuses Jacen's order to bombard Fondor for its disloyalty. She openly betrays Jacen, taking much of the Alliance fleet with her. Pellaeon sides with Niathal, prompting Tahiri Veila to shoot him dead. As Pellaeon expires, he taps out a secret code to his emergency contact.

Suddenly a task force of Imperial vessels—the Maw Irregulars—led by Admiral Natasi Daala arrives. She has contracted the Mandalorians to fight at her side. The Mandalorians, including Jaina, board Pellaeon's flagship *Bloodfin* and per Daala's orders kill the most treacherous of the Imperial Moffs aboard. Jaina and Mirta try to secure Tahiri, knowing that Jacen will try to extract her, but they fail to stop the Sith Lord from rescuing his apprentice.

Returning to Mandalore, Jaina discovers that two of the Mandalorians are Force-sensitive. One is Venku, son of Darman and Etain Tur-Mukan, and the other is Bardan Jusik, a former Jedi who defected to the Mandalorian cause during the Clone Wars. She trains with them to master a fighting technique that folds in Mandalorian combat with Force-sensitive ability. Bardan uses the Force to help Sintas Vel heal, and she regains her vision and her memories.

INVINCIBLE

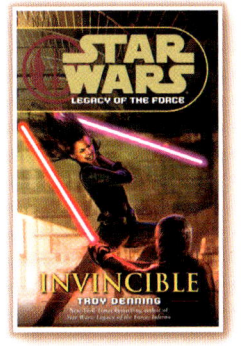

AUTHOR · Troy Denning
COVER ARTIST · Jason Felix
PUBLICATION HISTORY ·
Novel, Del Rey Books
· Hardcover, May 2008
· Paperback, December 2008
TIME LINE PLACEMENT ·
41 ABY

WORLDS VISITED · Carbos Thirteen [Q-8]; Carida Nebula [M-9]; Coruscant [L-9]; Roche system [Q-8]; Shedu Maad [O-9]

MAIN CHARACTERS · Jacen Solo/Darth Caedus, Sith Lord (human male); Luke Skywalker, Grand Master of the Jedi Order (human male); Ben Skywalker, Galactic Alliance Guard member (human male); Boba Fett, Mandalore (human male); Jaina Solo, Jedi Knight (human female); Leia Organa Solo, Jedi Knight (human female); Han Solo; captain of the *Millennium Falcon* (human male); Tahiri Veila, Sith apprentice (human female); Cha Niathal, Joint Chief of Staff (Mon Calamari female); Mirta Gev, bounty hunter (human female); Natasi Daala, former Imperial officer (human female)

SUMMARY · After weeks of training with Boba Fett, Jaina Solo accompanies the Mandalorians on a mission to defend the Verpine munitions factories of the Nickel One asteroid from an Imperial invasion. The Empire employs an aerosol-delivered nanovirus that targets the Verpine soldier caste, destroying their defenses. Though the Mandalorians acquit themselves well, they must tactically retreat to restage an attack.

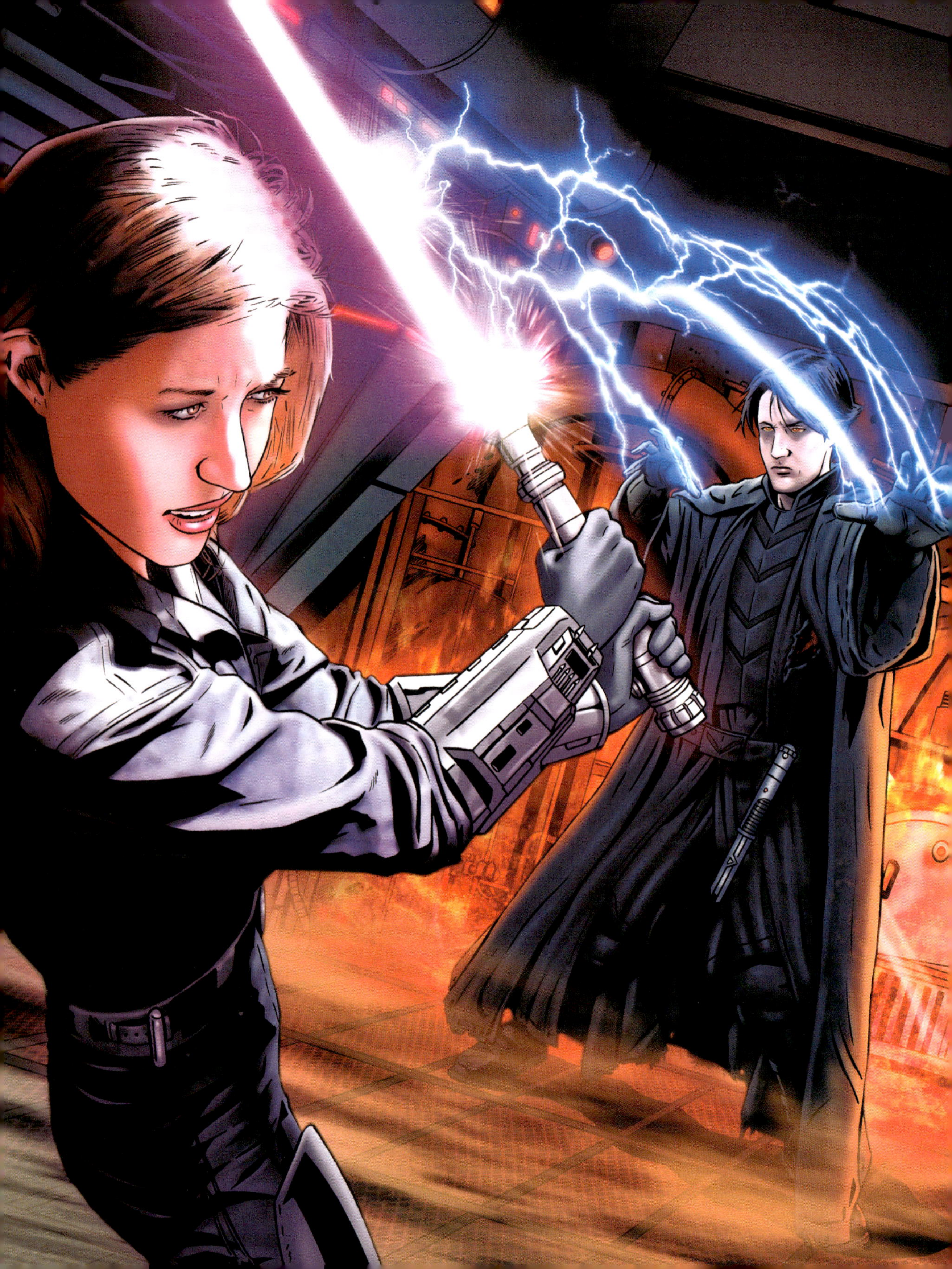

Fett tells Jaina he has taught her all he can and she is ready to face Darth Caedus.

At their new secret headquarters on Shedu Maad, Jaina requests permission from the Jedi Order to confront her brother. Luke agrees that Jaina, the Sword of the Jedi, is the ideal person to stop Jacen, since he worries any action on his own part might further lead to the dark side.

On Coruscant, Ben Skywalker learns of Jacen's whereabouts from his GAG ally Lon Shevu. Their interaction is spotted by Alliance spies, and a GAG force led by Tahiri captures Ben and Lon. Ben senses uncertainty in Tahiri, suggesting that she hasn't fully fallen to the dark side. Tahiri interrogates Ben to determine the location of the secret Jedi outpost, but Ben resists, all the while trying to turn Tahiri away from the dark side. Torturing Lon to get Ben to talk, Tahiri accidentally kills Lon, an act she instantly regrets. Ben escapes with the aid of Hapan intelligence agents, returning to the Jedi sanctuary on Shedu Maad.

Caedus travels to Nickel One to reprimand the Imperial Moffs for their unauthorized attack on the Verpines. The Mandalorians return to the asteroid to target the Imperials and carry out their hired duty on the Verpines' behalf. Arriving at the same time to pursue Caedus, Jaina accompanies them. Mirta Gev is wounded and captured by Imperial troops. As Jaina duels Caedus, Luke uses the Force to project his likeness, confusing Caedus into thinking he is dueling his uncle. Jaina overpowers Caedus by slicing off his arm. As Caedus retreats, he uses a Nightsister technique to mark Jaina with his blood.

Jaina returns to Shedu Maad, unknowingly leading Darth Caedus to the Jedi by way of his blood trail. Meanwhile, Caedus learns that the Empire has captured Prince Isolder of Hapes and has derived a nanokiller virus from his genetic makeup that will target the Hapan royal family. The Moffs have released the virus aboard Tenel Ka's flagship, *Dragon Queen*, without Caedus's permission. Caedus realizes that his daughter, Allana, will be susceptible to such an attack and tries to broker a deal with Isolder to save Allana and Tenel Ka. Isolder does not believe Caedus and refuses to help. Caedus kills Isolder in anger.

Jaina and Zekk try to lure Jacen's flagship *Anakin Solo* into a trap. Jaina loses contact with Zekk and boards the ship alone. In a final, grueling duel with her brother, Jaina wears Caedus down. Knowing he is about to die, Caedus lowers his lightsaber and tries to use the Force to warn Tenel Ka of the deadly virus. Jaina strikes her brother down before he can complete the warning.

On Shedu Maad's surface, Ben continues to insist that there is good in Tahiri as they battle. She surrenders her attack, and Ben invites her back to the Jedi Order, though her fate has yet to be determined.

The destruction of Caedus blunts the Alliance and Imperial Remnant aggression. Leaderless, the Moff Council is rounded up by the Jedi. Luke offers the Moffs an ultimatum—allow Jagged Fel to preside over the Imperial Remnant, or be left to answer to the Hapans for their crimes. Jag is shocked—he has never aspired to political power. Luke reasons that this alone makes him the best candidate for the job.

In the aftermath of the battle, the Galactic Federation of Free Alliances stands unified in its rejection of Darth Caedus's extreme actions. Ironically, it was Jacen Solo who did unify the galaxy. Natasi Daala becomes Chief of State of the Alliance. Zekk has disappeared in the fighting, and the search for him begins. Many royal Hapans die in the nanovirus attack, and the Hapans mourn the loss of Allana Solo. The daughter of Jacen and Tenel Ka secretly lives, though, perhaps as the last living remnant of Jacen Solo's legacy. To protect her daughter, Tenel Ka sends Allana into hiding; Allana assumes the

Jaina Solo battles her twin brother, Darth Caedus, to the finish.

name Amelia and is taken in by her grandparents Han and Leia as an adopted war orphan.

As a reminder of how far Jacen has fallen to the dark side, each chapter of *Invincible* begins with a corny joke told by the teenage Jedi, quoted from the Young Jedi Knight series (1995–98), or newly crafted in the style of quips and puns found in these books.

Working titles for *Invincible* included *Maelstrom* and *Descent*. In its outline form, author Troy Denning initially proposed an ending that included an element designed to offset the otherwise extremely dark fare in the novel. The outline describes Jacen's continued flow-walking to the time of Anakin Solo's final mission in *Star by Star* (2001) for the purposes of corrupting Tahiri to be his underling. In his final fight with Jaina, he conjures the image of a mortally stricken Anakin to vex Jaina and erode her focus. But in his reaching into the past, Jacen makes contact with Anakin, and the two switch places. In this manner, the time line of past events is not altered—a body that perfectly resembles Anakin falls on the *Baanu Rass* mission, but it is, in fact, a disguised future Jacen. The dying Anakin is transported to the future of 41 ABY, where he is saved by Jaina and resuscitated. This ending was not explored beyond being suggested in the novel outline.

Zekk's fate was to be resolved in a follow-up novel, *Blood Oath*, slated to be written by Elaine Cunningham and published in 2010, but this work was canceled. Cover art by Dave Seeley was posted on StarWars.com prior to the book's cancellation, and a brief synopsis promised to have Zekk face "a pirate captain with an unknown agenda and allegiance to none but herself."

CROSSCURRENT

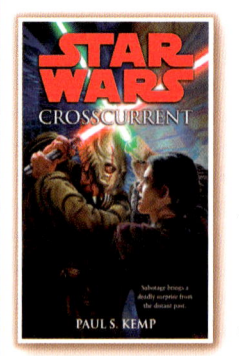

AUTHOR · Paul S. Kemp
COVER ARTIST · Dave Seeley
PUBLICATION HISTORY · Novel, Del Rey Books · Paperback, January 2010
TIME LINE PLACEMENT · 5000 BBY (flashbacks); 41 ABY (present)
WORLDS VISITED · Coruscant [L-9]; Fhost [H-7]; Korriban [R-5]; Phaegon III (and its moon) [N-17]; unidentified star system and moon (UR-2212-GR) [H-6]
MAIN CHARACTERS · Jaden Korr, Jedi Knight (human male); Khedryn Faal, salvager (human male); Relin Druur, Jedi Master (human male); Saes Rrogon, Sith Lord (Kaleesh male); Kell Douro, assassin (Anzati male); Marr Idi-Shael, salvager (Cerean male)

SUMMARY · THE PAST: During the Great Hyperspace War, the Sith warship *Harbinger* roasts the living moon of Phaegon III, searing its surface to expedite extraction of Lignan crystal deposits. The mineral, essential for the Sith war effort, enhances the power of the dark side of the Force. Leading the harvest is Sith Lord Saes Rrogon.

A Master–Padawan team tracking the *Harbinger* feels the effects of Phaegon III's death, as well as the power of the Lignan. The Master, Relin Druur, infiltrates the *Harbinger*, intent on stopping the Sith. He cuts his way past Massassi guards to sabotage the *Harbinger*'s hyperdrive with explosives and is confronted by Saes, who is his former Padawan. Relin

The Anzati assassin Kell Douro attempts to consume the "soup" of a badly beaten Jedi Knight, Jaden Korr.

LEGACY

loses an arm in the duel and is poisoned by exposure to radiation from the *Harbinger*'s engine core.

Meanwhile, Drev Hassin, Relin's current Padawan, distracts the *Harbinger* with strafing runs. The *Harbinger* continues its jump into hyperspace despite a damaged drive. Drev plows his ship into the dreadnought's bridge in a futile effort to stop it. Crushed at the loss of his Padawan and driven to rage by the Lignan, Relin nonetheless makes it to an escape pod to flee the stricken vessel. The pod is swept up in the Sith dreadnought's wash as the *Harbinger* shakily jumps into hyperspace.

The Present: Jedi Knight Jaden Korr is compelled by dark dreams and Force visions to venture to the remote world of Fhost. Jaden is troubled by the ease with which he can summon the dark side. At Farpoint outpost, Jaden hires the services of salvager Khedryn Faal, his navigator/partner Marr Idi-Shael, and their ship *Junker*. They are to transport him to the place of his visions—a distant moon orbiting an unknown world. Jaden's premonitions correspond with Khedryn's recent find, a signal emanating from the moon repeating the message "*Help us.*"

The One Sith of Korriban are also intrigued by the moon, but are not yet ready to act. The Sith Lord Darth Wyyrlok hires an intermediary, the Force-sensitive Anzati assassin named Kell Douro. Douro shadows Jaden as he leaves Fhost, drawn to the Jedi. He hopes to feed on the intriguing mix of dark side and light-side potentials that he senses in Jaden.

At the unknown system, the *Junker* encounters the *Harbinger*. The Sith ship's faulty hyperdrive jump has transported it across time and space. Jaden instantly feels the Lignan—as does Marr, who is a bur-

SHORT STORY — "A Fair Trade"

Set some time prior to the events of *Crosscurrent*, the short story "A Fair Trade" by Paul S. Kemp, printed in *Star Wars Insider* #129, was published in October 2011 between the releases of *Crosscurrent* and *Riptide*. In the story, Khedryn Faal and Marr Idi-Shael operate the salvage vessel *Seeker* out of Fhost, and during a deep-space salvage operation outwit the deadly gangster Reeges out of his ship, *Blackstar*. With the salvagers taking over Reeges's vacant ship, and Reeges stuck on Khedryn's dilapidated *Seeker*, Khedryn bargains for the *Blackstar* in exchange for Reeges's life. Khedryn and Marr then decide to rechristen the *Blackstar* the *Junker*.

geoning Force-sensitive. The salvagers intercept Relin's escape pod, bringing the ancient Jedi aboard. *Junker* hides in an asteroid field to avoid the Sith. Khedryn, Marr, and Jaden meet Relin. Tainted by the dark side, and knowing his death from radiation exposure is inevitable, Relin is driven by vengeance. He is single-minded in his determination to stop Saes.

Jaden believes it is no coincidence that they have been brought to this moon as the ancient Sith have emerged from hyperspace. Khedryn and Marr agree to help him: Khedryn will pilot Jaden aboard the *Junker*'s shuttle to the moon outpost, while Marr and Relin will board the *Harbinger* to finish Relin's mission. Douro, in his stealthy modified CloakShape fighter *Predator*, follows Jaden to the moon's icy surface.

Jaden and Khedryn find an abandoned cloning facility dating back to Grand Admiral Thrawn's campaigns. It is a site of carnage, evidence of a botched experiment to clone Jedi and Sith subjects into a hybrid warrior. Jaden and Khedryn separate, and Khedryn encounters and is badly beaten by Douro. Rather than kill Khedryn, Douro continues obsessively stalking Jaden as prey. Reaching the heart of the facility, Jaden finds a Spaarti cloning cylinder filled with butchered, decomposing bodies. Alpha, one of the hybrid clones, evidently grown from Kam Solusar's DNA, confronts Jaden. Jaden duels with Alpha, and though he loses three of his fingers to the clone's lightsaber, Jaden defeats the insane warrior. Exhausted and wounded, Jaden is then set upon by Douro and nearly becomes a victim of the Anzati. Despite his injuries, Khedryn has followed Douro and blasts the Anzati, saving Jaden.

Aboard the *Harbinger*, Relin once more cuts his way past Massassi warriors to confront Saes. The doomed Jedi tells Marr to return to the *Junker*, leaving him to his fate. Relin battles his former apprentice in a lightsaber duel, as well as through intense contests of Force power. He eventually slays Saes and directs an intense wave of the Force to detonate the stores of Lignan aboard the dreadnought. Relin is consumed by the explosion, and the dying *Harbinger* tumbles into the moon's atmosphere.

As Jaden and Khedryn emerge from the outpost to return to their shuttle, they witness the final death of the *Harbinger*. Douro's ship is missing, and Jaden surmises that the surviving clones must have stolen it. As the *Harbinger* erupts, the *Predator* intersects with its expanding cloud of Lignan remnants—exposing the fleeing clones to the dark power of the crystals before the ship leaves the moon.

Jaden Korr was created for the videogame *Jedi Knight: Jedi Academy* (2003), an entry in the series that began with *Dark Forces* (1995). He was Kyle Katarn's apprentice and studied at Luke Skywalker's Jedi academy. Jaden was the player's character and was subject to customization that could allow male, female, human, Rodian, Twi'lek, Zabrak, or Kel Dor interpretations. The novel *Abyss* (2009) has a passing reference to Jaden Korr, canonizing his gender as male, and the following year Jaden became the central figure in *Crosscurrent*. Though Jaden reflects upon his experience as part of the Jedi mission to destroy Centerpoint Station during the recent war with the Corellian Confederation, he does not actually appear in the Legacy of the Force novels.

The *Harbinger* was a sister ship to *Omen*, the vessel that crashes on Kesh in the first installment of the *Lost Tribe of the Sith* stories (2009), meaning that the story thread that began more than five thousand years earlier comes to fruition here in the time line, in 41 ABY, though only a year separates the publication of each source.

RIPTIDE

AUTHOR · Paul S. Kemp

COVER ARTIST · Dave Seeley

PUBLICATION HISTORY · Novel, Del Rey Books
· Paperback, October 2011

TIME LINE PLACEMENT · 41 ABY

WORLDS VISITED · Fhost [H-7]; Korriban [R-5]; unidentified pulsar star system, site of the Rakatan space station (UR-6572-AK) [G-8]; unidentified star system and moon with cloning facility (UR-2212-GR) [H-6]; unidentified red dwarf star system with two gas giants and asteroid belt (UR-5292-FH) [H-7]

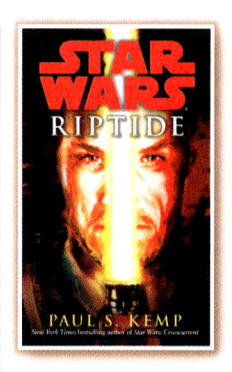

MAIN CHARACTERS · Jaden Korr, Jedi Knight (human male); Khedryn Faal, salvager (human male); Marr Idi-Shael, salvager (Cerean male); Soldier, clone (human male); Seer, clone (human female); Grace, offspring of clones (human female); Nyss Nenn, agent of the Sith (Umbaran male); Syll Nenn, agent of the Sith (Umbaran female); Mother, Rakatan technology entity

SUMMARY · With his sensitivity to the Force opened up by the recent effort to stop the *Harbinger*, Marr Idi-Shael begins to study the Force as Jaden Korr's apprentice. The crew of the *Junker* seeks out the escaped clones before they can wreak havoc on the galaxy.

Aboard their stolen ship, the hybrid clones experience accelerated deterioration of their physical and mental health due to exposure to the Lignan cloud. Rallied by a mystically minded clone named Seer, they hope their faith in an entity called Mother will be their salvation. Soldier, the most able-bodied clone, has no use for their superstitions. But Mother is not a figment of the faithful—she is real and awaits the arrival of the clones. The clones journey to Fhost, the last point of departure for their ship, in the hope of securing medicine that can ease their genetic ailments.

By the time the clones arrive at Farpoint outpost on Fhost, most of their number have died. Soldier, Seer, Runner, Hunter, and young Grace survive. Jaden, too, arrives on Fhost, seeking out the hybrids, as do the Umbaran twins Syll and Nyss Nenn, agents of the One Sith tasked with tracking the clones and Jaden. Encountering the clones, Jaden is shocked to see familiar faces—Seer is a clone of Lumiya, Runner of his former mentor Kyle Katarn, and Soldier of Jaden. Jaden fails to stop them, and the clones capture Khedryn, taking the salvager with them as they escape aboard a hijacked medical shuttle. Unknown to the clones, Nyss has slipped aboard the ship.

Jaden tracks the shuttle with a homing device he has affixed on the ship. He is disturbed and puzzled by the existence of a clone of himself generated by a Thrawn-era facility, as he did not discover his Force sensitivity and enroll in Skywalker's Jedi academy until four years after Thrawn's death.

The clones interrogate Khedryn, hoping to find out how Jaden tracked them to Fhost. He has no satisfying answers—it was happenstance or through the mysteries of the Force that the *Junker* arrived at the same time as the clones. The clones plan to execute the salvager as he has served his purpose. Khedryn's life is inadvertently saved by Nyss, who just then cuts the shuttle's lights and attacks the clones. Nyss has the peculiar ability to disrupt the Force powers of his opponents, and he uses it to surprise and kill Runner and Hunter. Nyss captures Khedryn, figuring he can use Jaden's friend against him. He shackles Khedryn before moving on to attack the clones. Young Grace, the daughter of Hunter and Alpha, befriends Khedryn and cuts him free.

When he battles Soldier, Nyss finds that the clone of Jaden is not as susceptible to his Force-blocking ability. Nyss instead relies on his combat skills to subdue Soldier. Calling Soldier "the Prime," he intends to bring the clone back to his Sith masters.

The supply ship emerges in an unnamed star system, as does *Junker*. Nyss hails the *Junker*, demanding that Jaden surrender himself in exchange for Khedryn's life. Jaden has no choice but to accept; he dons a space suit to transfer to the shuttle. With few options, Khedryn cuts Soldier free, and the clone once again battles the Umbaran. Khedryn takes advantage of this distraction to flee the shuttle aboard an escape pod. Nyss is at a disadvantage: he must not kill Soldier, since Darth Wyyrlok wants him alive. Though it galls him, Nyss also boards an escape pod, jettisoning it to be intercepted by his sister, who has tracked the shuttle. Syll fires at Khedryn's escape pod. Jaden, floating in space toward Khedryn, uses his lightsaber to deflect the blast back at Syll, killing her. Marr rescues his shipmates aboard the *Junker*.

The remaining clones journey aboard the shuttle to a pulsar star system, site of an ancient space station constructed by the Rakatans in pre-Republic times. Aboard is Mother, an intelligence that emerged from the dark side that powers the ancient Rakatan technology. Seer leads Soldier and Grace aboard the station to commune at long last with the revered Mother. But Mother is no benevolence—she has drawn Seer here in the hope of freeing herself from such ancient, immobile technology by transferring her consciousness into another's body.

Nyss, having lost his beloved sister and tasted defeat at the hands of both Soldier and Jaden, will take no chances. Aboard his vessel, he frees a cloned body he kept in stasis as a contingency plan. It is the Iteration, another clone of Jaden, developed by the One Sith as a means of infiltrating an agent into the Jedi Order. Nyss uses navigational data he had pulled from the medical shuttle to also arrive at the Rakatan space station. Nyss confronts Jaden and his apprentice, Marr. Though Nyss incapacitates Marr, he cannot defeat Jaden, who strangles the Umbaran to death.

Spent from the battle with the Umbaran, Jaden collapses. The Iteration appears and kills Jaden with a Rakatan transference device called a mindspear, which draws Jaden's consciousness out of his body and into the apparatus. Marr witnesses the death of his master and friend and attacks the Iteration.

LEGACY

Though still an apprentice and not as powerful as the Iteration, Marr nonetheless defeats the clone and uses the mindspear to download Jaden's disembodied consciousness into the duplicate body. Jaden awakens, unaware of what has transpired.

Marr and the revived Jaden encounter Soldier. He is focused on simply escaping the station and ensuring Grace's safety. He explains that he was the most stable of the clones, being the last one produced, and not one of the raving maniacs who slaughtered the scientists at the cloning facility. Jaden and Marr ally with Soldier to fend off Mother, who has possessed Seer's body and desperately wants to leave the station. At Jaden's command, Khedryn sabotages the medical shuttle so that its power core erupts, damaging the station and sending it crashing to the irradiated world below. Jaden, Marr, and Khedryn escape in the *Junker*.

When Jaden later discovers that a small scar he has had since adolescence is now gone, he begins to question his identity. Elsewhere, Soldier and Grace fly into the Unknown Regions aboard Nyss's abandoned ship. Soldier is determined to keep her safe.

MILLENNIUM FALCON

AUTHOR · James Luceno

COVER ARTIST · John VanFleet

PUBLICATION HISTORY · Novel, Del Rey Books
- Hardcover, October 2008
- Paperback, November 2009

TIME LINE PLACEMENT · 60 BBY, 19 BBY, 10 BBY, 5 BBY (flashbacks); 43 ABY (present)

WORLDS VISITED · Carcel [O-8]; Corellia [M-11]; Coruscant [L-9]; Epica [L-15]; Fondor [L-13]; Holess [R-14]; Lujo [L-12]; Lutrillia [J-18]; Nar Shaddaa (moon of Nal Hutta) [S-12]; New Balosar [K-15]; Nilash III [M-17]; Obroa-skai [N-8]; Oseon VII [T-8]; Sriluur [S-8]; Tandun III [P-5]; Taris [N-7]; Tungra [K-18]; unnamed Tion planetoid (Xifal) [S-6]; Vaced [J-7]; Yarith (system) [J-18]; Zamael Archipelago [K-12]

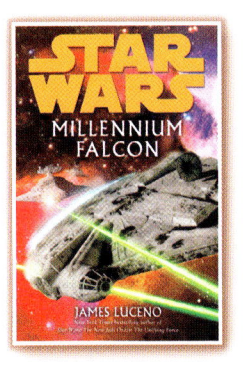

MAIN CHARACTERS · Han Solo, captain of the *Millennium Falcon* (human male); Leia Organa Solo, copilot and Jedi Knight (human female); Allana "Amelia" Solo, child (human female); Tobb Jadak, treasure seeker (human male); Lestra Oxic, collector (human male); Lando Calrissian, entrepreneur (human male); Flitcher Poste, treasure seeker (human male); Seff Hellin, Jedi Knight (human male)

SUMMARY · THE PAST: Like a wild stallion refusing to be corralled, an errant YT-1300 freighter breaks from its assembly line and soars free, creating havoc to the amazement and consternation of Corellian Engineering Corporation factory workers, who remark that the ship is truly one in a hundred million.

Decades later, during the Battle of Coruscant near the end of the Clone Wars, this ship, now known as the *Stellar Envoy*, saves the lives of its crew, Captain Tobb Jadak and Reeze Duurman, who navigate through the space battle and land safely on the capital. Jadak and Duurman take on an assignment from the underground Republic Group to seek out a treasure that will help in the efforts to oust Supreme Chancellor Palpatine. Republic Intelligence catches wind of the seditious activity, prompting another hasty escape by the *Stellar Envoy*. Their harried flight is cut short after a collision with another freighter. Duurman dies in the

LEGACY 443

crash, and Jadak falls into a coma. Later, the salvaged *Envoy* is sold to a crime boss, Rej Taunt, who renames it *Second Chance*. Taunt runs afoul of deadly Colicoids during an underworld deal and flees headlong into an Imperial patrol.

THE PRESENT: Aboard the *Millennium Falcon*, young Allana Solo discovers a previously unknown transponder affixed to the ship since the time of the Clone Wars. Puzzled by this, Han Solo launches an adventure to uncover more of the *Falcon*'s past, starting with Lando Calrissian. The quest takes the Solos to Oseon VII, where they learn of Cix Trouvee, who lost the *Falcon* to Lando in a sabacc game. On Taris, they seek the owner before Trouvee, a former circus employee named Vistal Purn.

On Obroa-skai, Tobb Jadak awakens from a coma after sixty-two years. His recuperation was made possible by an insurance policy taken out by the Republic Group, but he cannot fathom why they would bother with such a contingency. His memory gradually returns and he recalls piloting the *Stellar Envoy* until it collided over Nar Shaddaa. With that as a starting point, he attempts to piece together his own history.

Monitoring Tobb's progress is Lestra Oxic, a collector of Republic-era artifacts who has secretly paid for Tobb's recovery. Lestra hopes that Tobb will lead him to the lost Republic Group treasure.

Prior to their arrival on Taris, Lando warns Han of an odd encounter with Seff Hellin, a Jedi Knight on the planet investigating criminal activity. Lando believes Hellin was asking, in a roundabout way, for Tendrando Arms to develop combat droids to counter the Mandalorian mercenaries that Chief of State Daala hired as her guards. On Taris, the Solos run afoul of terrorists who attempt to kidnap Allana, but Hellin saves the little girl. He exhibits Force abilities at a level he should not yet have access to, an achievement that Leia remarks as odd. Allana confides in Leia that something about Hellin's Force display reminded her of Jacen Solo. For his rogue actions in unsanctioned territory, Hellin is branded as a danger by the Galactic Alliance authorities, and Daala's Mandalorians attempt to stop him. This crisis underscores the tensions and distrust between Daala's government and the Jedi Order.

On Nar Shaddaa, Tobb hires a local named Flitcher Poste to help him find the *Stellar Envoy* and its treasure. The streetwise Flitcher acts as Tobb's guide through the Nar Shaddaa underworld, eventually leading him to Quip Fargil, a member of the early Rebellion who had piloted the *Falcon*.

Solo's interview with Vistal Purn also eventually points back through several generations of the *Millennium Falcon*'s provenance to Quip Fargil. This leads the Solos and Jadak on parallel paths to Vaced, where Quip resides. Jadak reaches him first, learning of Quip's history with the *Falcon*. Quip named the ship *Millennium Falcon* and was supposed to destroy the vessel in a Rebel mission to sabotage the shipyards of Fondor. Quip could not bring himself to sacrifice the *Falcon*, however, so he abandoned his assignment, giving up the ship.

Jadak eventually comes to tell Han of his past history with the *Falcon*, and aboard the ship recalls a mnemonic he memorized prior to his crash. He uses the phrase to reactivate the transponder, a device placed aboard the ship by Jedi Master J'oopi Sheé. The transponder reveals their next destination to be Tandun III, a planet transformed by the Yuuzhan Vong during their invasion.

There the *Falcon*'s crew and passengers find the "treasure"—an Insignia of Unity, a seal formerly found on the Senate Rotunda. The Republic Group had hoped to use the symbol as a means of rallying resistance to Palpatine's regime. Oxic arrives to claim the artifact for his collection, but is outraged

LEGACY

to find that it is a counterfeit. Still determined to find the original, Oxic hires Jadak and Poste on the spot to continue their search. Jadak, still looking for direction in life after being out of commission for so long, accepts.

The *Falcon* departs the planet as it falls apart from the strain of Vongforming. As the Solos return to Coruscant, they receive word that the Galactic Alliance government is attempting to file charges against Luke Skywalker for dereliction of duty.

Del Rey Books invited James Luceno to explore the *Falcon*'s history when his developing *Darth Plagueis* novel (2012) was momentarily shelved for further review. The *Millennium Falcon* concept was plucked from a growing list of internal ideas developed at LucasBooks for possible future novels. The pitch paragraph read as follows:

> A novel about the most famous hunk of junk in the galaxy. It can be a series of episodic vignettes connected by a through-line, or a more traditional sequential narrative. [Start] off late in the time line, with an aging Han getting ready to finally retire the old bird. But then something happens that sheds light on the *Falcon*'s history. Some sort of prompt that forces the heroes to find out about the *Falcon*'s pedigree. No galaxy-shattering events. No tragedy or atrocities. Just a love letter to *Falcon* fans and a trip through galactic history.

Given the novel's place after the events of Legacy of the Force, *Millennium Falcon* also became a bridge novel into the Fate of the Jedi series that was in development at the time of its writing.

OUTCAST

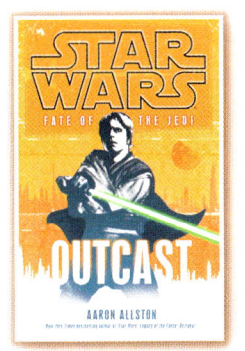

AUTHOR · Aaron Allston
COVER ARTIST · Ian Keltie
PUBLICATION HISTORY ·
Novel, Del Rey Books
 · Hardcover, March 2009
 · Paperback, April 2010
TIME LINE PLACEMENT ·
43 ABY
WORLDS VISITED · Coruscant [L-9]; Dorin [J-8]; Kessel [T-10]

MAIN CHARACTERS · Luke Skywalker, Grand Master in exile of the Jedi Order (human male); Ben Skywalker, Jedi apprentice (human male); Natasi Daala, Galactic Alliance Chief of State (human female); Han Solo, captain of the *Millennium Falcon* (human male); Leia Organa Solo, copilot and Jedi Knight (human female); Allana "Amelia" Solo, child (human female); Lando Calrissian, entrepreneur (human male); Jaina Solo, Jedi Knight (human female); Jagged Fel, Imperial Head of State (human male); Valin Horn, Jedi Knight (human male); Corran Horn, Jedi Master (human male); Cilghal, Jedi Master (Mon Calamari female)

SUMMARY · Imperial diplomats arrive on Coruscant for a unification summit intended to strengthen the strained relations within the Galactic Alliance caused by the recent Second Galactic Civil War. Imperial Head of State Jagged Fel and Jedi Knight Jaina Solo snatch what romantic moments they can.

At the Horn family residence, Valin Horn is suddenly seized by the mad realization that everyone

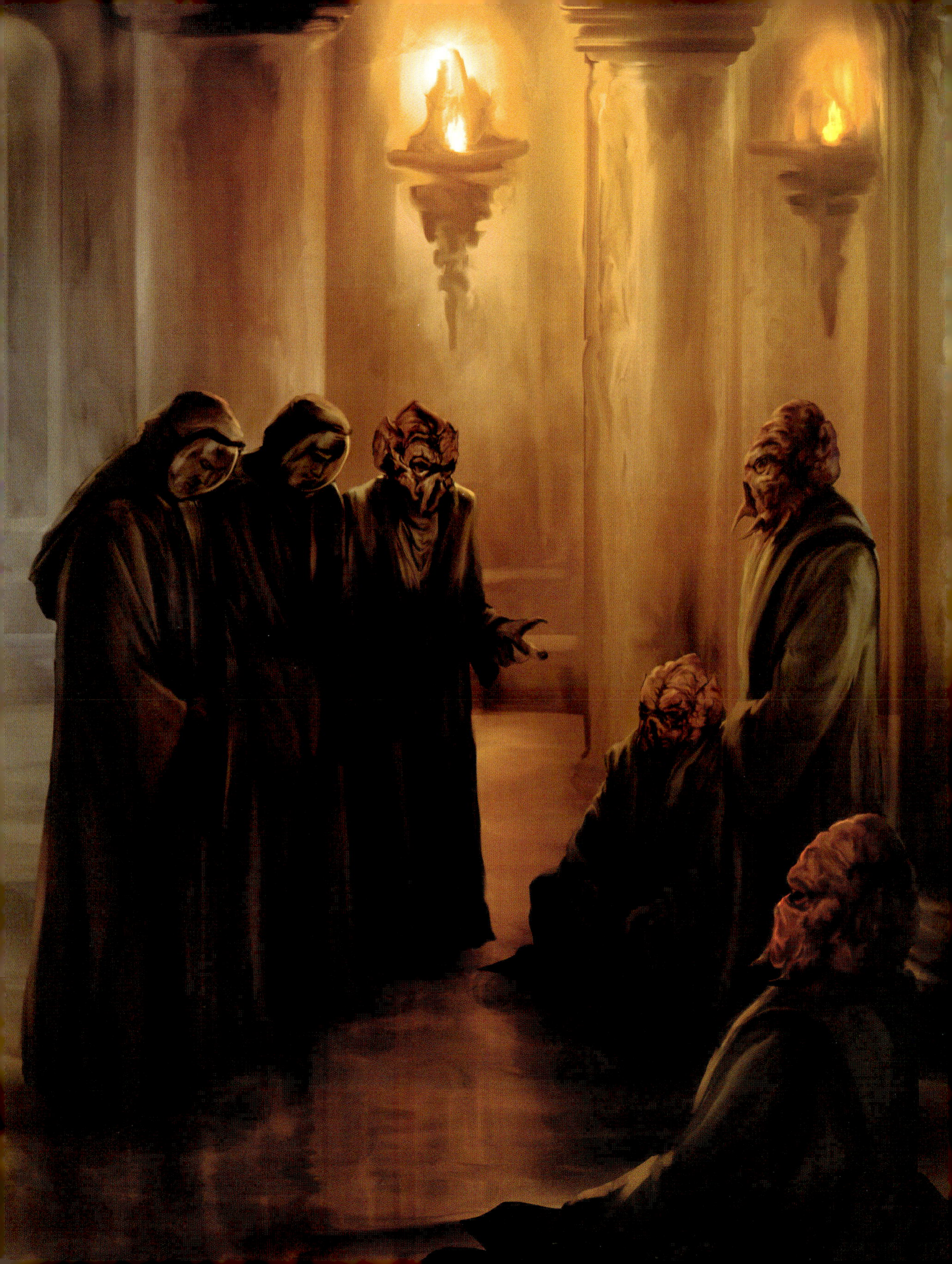

around him has inexplicably been replaced by an imposter. In frenzied delusion, Valin tries to escape this overwhelming conspiracy. His parents, Mirax and Corran, attempt to stop him before he hurts anyone or himself. Corran even crosses lightsaber blades with Valin, and Mirax has no choice but to stun-blast her son. Valin is taken to the Jedi Temple for examination by Cilghal. When Valin briefly escapes custody, the Jedi are able to stop him—but not before a very public display of Jedi madness is captured by the unblinking eye of the Coruscant media.

Grand Master Luke Skywalker is arrested by Alliance security forces and incarcerated for dereliction of duty for allowing Jacen Solo to fall to the dark side. Chief of State Daala explains to Luke that his trial is a crucial step in holding the Jedi Order accountable for their actions. Luke pleads guilty to reckless endangerment of a population; he is sentenced to exile from Coruscant for ten years and is prohibited from leading the Jedi. Kenth Hamner will serve as Grand Master in his stead. Luke hopes the sentence can end early if he finds the reasons why Jacen turned. To that end, Luke plans to retrace Jacen's five-year vision quest to see if he can learn what influences Jacen was exposed to that may have set him along the path to the dark side. Luke's son, Ben, accompanies his father aboard the *Jade Shadow*.

Kenth, eager to prove responsive to Daala's concerns, reveals to the Jedi Council his steps to demystify the Order to the general public by allowing government observers to shadow the Jedi. This is met with apprehension among the Jedi. Tahiri, in self-imposed exile from the Order, flatly refuses to cooperate. Later, bounty hunters arrive at the Temple to apprehend Valin. Kenth agrees to turn over the Jedi to the government, a capitulation that some, like Jaina, disagree with. The Coruscant courts find Valin unfit for trial, and he is frozen in carbonite to prevent him from being a danger.

Meanwhile, Lando Calrissian calls Han Solo to help investigate a rash of quakes that are hitting his operations on Kessel. Han and Leia agree to help and bring their seven-year-old adopted granddaughter Allana on a family trip aboard the *Millennium Falcon*. Investigating xenoarchaeological ruins beneath the planet's surface, Leia postulates that Kessel may be somehow related to Centerpoint Station, and that the destruction of the ancient Corellian relic may be responsible for Kessel's troubles. Han develops and executes a risky plan to detonate a series of controlled explosives deep within Kessel to relieve the seismic pressure and prevent the planet from tearing itself apart. A restless Allana, meanwhile, is spooked by a strange sense of longing emerging from deep within the Maw.

Dorin is the first stop in Luke's quest. While learning from the Baran Do sages, he and Ben uncover a misguided plot by the leaders of the sect to hide deep within the underworld of the planet in order to avoid any future purges like the devastating Order 66. By defeating the closed-minded and fearful Hidden One who led the Baran Do, Luke is able to convince the Kel Dor to return to the surface. Luke and Ben learn from them Jacen's next destination on his epic journey and thus continue their quest.

On Coruscant, Jaina and Jag create a covert team of Jedi and allies called Darkmeld to move against the overreaching actions of the Galactic Alliance in their handling of the afflicted Jedi. When Darkmeld learns that a similarly afflicted Seff Hellin is plotting to rescue Valin Horn, the group intercepts and captures him for further study in the Jedi Temple.

TAKING A DELIBERATE DEPARTURE from the arch darkness that dominated the last two epic novel series, Fate of the Jedi intersperses scenes of relative domestic tranquillity amid a growing sense

Luke and Ben Skywalker bow reverently as they visit the Baran Do sages of Dorin.

of dreadful confrontation brewing between the Jedi Order and the Galactic Alliance. The series also set out to mend the relationship between Luke and Ben, sending them off on an interstellar journey together inspired by Homer's epic poem *The Odyssey*.

OMEN

AUTHOR · Christie Golden
COVER ARTIST · Ian Keltie
PUBLICATION HISTORY ·
Novel, Del Rey Books
· Hardcover, June 2009
· Paperback, May 2010
TIME LINE PLACEMENT ·
41 ABY (flashbacks);
43 ABY (present)

WORLDS VISITED · Aing-Tii homeworld [M-21]; Coruscant [L-9]; Kesh [U-10]; unnamed Kathol Rift moon [M-21]

MAIN CHARACTERS · Luke Skywalker, Grand Master in exile of the Jedi Order (human male); Ben Skywalker, Jedi apprentice (human male); Vestara Khai, Sith apprentice (human female); Han Solo, captain of the *Millennium Falcon* (human male); Leia Organa Solo, Jedi Knight (human female); Jaina Solo, Jedi Knight (human female); Jagged Fel, Imperial Head of State (human male); Allana "Amelia" Solo, child (human female); Natasi Daala, Galactic Alliance Chief of State (human female); Javis Tyrr, journalist (human male); Wynn Dorvan, assistant to the Chief of State (human male)

SUMMARY · THE PAST: The Sith meditation sphere discovered by Ben Skywalker during the Second Galactic Civil War rejects an invitation by the One Sith to join their cause. Instead Ship journeys to Kesh, where it senses the presence of power. Kesh is home to the Lost Tribe of the Sith, and the long-stranded dark siders are abuzz with Ship's arrival. Vestara Khai, a teenage Sith student, makes telepathic contact with Ship. She is summoned before the Circle of Lords, who have decreed that the Sith will use Ship to voyage offworld for the first time, and that Vestara will become apprentice to Lady Rhea. Communing with Ship reveals to Vestara the shocking truth: the Sith are extinct in the galaxy. The Lost Tribe is all that remains. Seeking to rebuild a great empire, the Tribe harries the space lanes around Kesh, conquering wandering vessels to build a new armada.

THE PRESENT: Jysella Horn, younger sister to Valin, succumbs to the strange delusion that imposters have surrounded her. She flees the Jedi Temple, desperate to avoid capture, battering her way past her friends, Jedi Knights Bazel "Barv" Warv and Yaqeel Saav'etu. Sensationalist journalist Javis Tyrr broadcasts the capture of the dangerous Jysella by Galactic Alliance security forces. Thanks to the quick reaction of her personal assistant, Wynn Dorvan, Chief of State Daala is soon on the scene, capitalizing on the chaos by publicly proclaiming that Jysella, like her brother, will be frozen in carbonite while her government continues its zero-tolerance stance on Jedi transgressions.

Cilghal contacts Luke Skywalker to discuss the medical findings she garnered while studying the afflicted Jedi. Each Jedi has exhibited esoteric Force abilities seen in Jacen Solo. The other threads connecting the victims are childhoods spent at Shelter Base during the Yuuzhan Vong War. This gives Ben pause since he, too, was kept there as an infant.

SHORT STORY — "First Blood"

Star Wars Insider #125 (May 2011) features this short story by Christie Golden. After arriving on Kesh, Ship leads a Sith party into the stars to target valuable starships. The Sith shoot down a cargo vessel onto an uncharted world. The elder Sith hunt and slaughter the surviving crewmembers, but Vestara is excluded from this action due to her inexperience. She is instead assigned to inventory the cargo of the crashed freighter. Vestara discovers an escaped slave. Though the slave begs for her life, Vestara kills her in cold blood. It is Vestara's first kill, and she feels her power in the dark side grow.

With Jysella and Valin both held by the government, Cilghal continues her research on Seff Hellin. The Jedi chafe under the passive leadership of Kenth Hamner, who repeatedly defers to Daala.

On Coruscant, the scheming Moff Lecersen is keeping a close eye on the relationship between Jagged Fel and Jaina Solo, as well as the growing tensions between the Alliance and the Jedi. He seeks to exploit this into something that will benefit the Moffs of the Imperial Remnant.

On a family outing to buy young Allana a pet, Han, Leia, and Jaina travel with the child to the Coruscant Livestock Exchange and Exhibition. One of their Jedi escorts, Natua Wan, suffers a violent psychosis, threatening innocents as she drives a panicking crowd into the area holding the more dangerous animals. Making matters worse, Javis Tyrr is there, recording the incident. The Solos stop Natua and help settle the chaos. In her effort to save lives, Leia has no choice but to kill a mother nexu. Allana later pleads for the Solos to take the nexu's orphaned cub as a pet.

Following the incident, Daala demands that the Order hand over all afflicted Jedi to the Alliance. Kenth agrees and punishes Jaina for her involvement in capturing Hellin by confining her to the Temple. It's not all gloom, however; Jag surprises Jaina with a marriage proposal that she enthusiastically accepts.

Within the turbulent nebula known as the Kathol Rift, Luke and Ben Skywalker contact the mysterious Aing-Tii. One of their order, Tadar'Ro, greets them and leads them to his homeworld. The Aing-Tii look to the Skywalkers to settle a rift among the normally harmonious people, hoping that the off-worlders may find wisdom among Force-imbued relics that the Aing-Tii are forbidden to touch. In exchange, Tadar'Ro will tell them about Jacen's visit years earlier. While examining the relics, Luke comes in contact with a powerful Force artifact called the Codex. His touch is transmitted across the Force, where it is felt by Ship and Vestara. Luke senses a disturbance in the Force, based in the Maw Cluster. The Skywalkers tell the Aing-Tii that the relics do not offer any guidance in their dispute; they must settle it themselves. Knowing that Jacen, too, touched the Codex and was directed to the disturbance in the Maw, Luke and Ben follow this path.

On Kesh, the Lost Tribe's discussion of the Force disturbance is suddenly interrupted when Ship departs the planet without warning, prompting the Sith to pursue.

Meanwhile, on Coruscant, Galactic Alliance officers arrest Tahiri Veila for obstruction of justice, treason, and the murder of Gilad Pellaeon.

OMEN BRINGS the descendants of the ancient Lost Tribe of the Sith into the modern *Star Wars* time frame. Concurrent with the publication of the Fate of the Jedi series were the *Lost Tribe of the Sith* e-novellas, allowing readers to learn the history and the current state of the Lost Tribe simultaneously.

The Codex kept by the Aing-Tii first appeared in the *Star Wars Gamemaster Handbook* (1993) as a sample artifact to use in roleplaying games, and was incorporated into the epic DarkStryder saga in the adventure module *The Kathol Rift* (1996). Its appearance in *Omen* marks its sole use in a novel narrative. Also found on the Aing-Tii world is Jorj Car'das's house. His past history with the Aing-Tii was established in *Vision of the Future* (1998).

ABYSS

AUTHOR · Troy Denning

COVER ARTIST · Ian Keltie

PUBLICATION HISTORY · Novel, Del Rey Books
- Hardcover, August 2009
- Paperback, June 2010

TIME LINE PLACEMENT · 43 ABY

WORLDS VISITED · Abeloth's planet [T-10]; Coruscant [L-9]; Sinkhole Station [T-10]

MAIN CHARACTERS · Luke Skywalker, Grand Master in exile of the Jedi Order (human male); Ben Skywalker, Jedi apprentice (human male); Vestara Khai, Sith apprentice (human female); Han Solo, captain of the *Millennium Falcon* (human male); Leia Organa Solo, Jedi Knight (human female); Jaina Solo, Jedi Knight (human female); Jagged Fel, Imperial Head of State (human male); Allana "Amelia" Solo, child (human female); Natasi Daala, Galactic Alliance Chief of State (human female); Abeloth, destroyer (female entity); Javis Tyrr, journalist (human male); Wynn Dorvan, assistant to the Chief of State (human male)

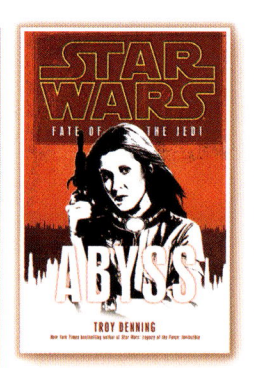

SUMMARY · Deep within a sequestered and heavily protected area called the Asylum Block of the Jedi Temple, Cilghal studies the psychosis-stricken Jedi Knights Seff Hellin and Natua Wan. They are contained in ysalamiri fields so they cannot touch the Force, but their madness prevails. The next Jedi to succumb are Yaqeel Saav'etu and Bazel Warv. Han, Leia, Jaina, and Jagged team up to incapacitate these two latest victims. Galactic Alliance security forces try to collect the fallen Jedi, but Han and Leia outsmart them. They figure out that the Alliance was so prompt in responding to the sudden outbreak of violence because they have been spying on the Temple.

The *Jade Shadow* plunges into the Maw Cluster as Luke and Ben Skywalker continue to follow a path previously blazed by Jacen Solo. Inside a gravitational oasis, they discover a miniature version of Centerpoint Station called Sinkhole Station. Landing aboard the mysterious construct, Ben feels a disturbing presence in the Force: a cold tentacle of longing that he recognizes from his childhood at Shelter Base.

The inside of the station is filled with ancient, abandoned starships and littered with Killik corpses, as well as the desiccated bodies of the Mind Walkers.

In the Asylum Block of the Jedi Temple, Leia and Han Solo check in with Jedi Master Cilghal on the status of Jedi Knight Seff Hellin.

These Force-sensitives have gathered at Sinkhole Station from across the galaxy to enter a state of catatonic meditation, wherein their consciousnesses reside in a realm they call "beyond shadows." Seeking to re-create as much as possible the circumstances of Jacen's lengthy trek, Luke agrees to enter beyond shadows.

Elsewhere in the Maw Cluster, the Lost Sith Tribe continue their pursuit of the Sith meditation sphere known as Ship. The ancient self-aware vessel leads them to an unknown jungle world that is home to a powerful presence that has beckoned to Ship. As the Tribe members debark to scour the jungles, they are attacked by carnivorous plants. The surviving Sith, including Vestara Khai and her Master, Lady Rhea, are led by Ship to a mysterious woman named Abeloth. Seemingly humanoid, the quizzical Abeloth can change her form at will. Vestara is immediately wary of this person, and she detects through the Force that it is Abeloth who has lured Ship's loyalty away from the Tribe. Vestara alone can peer beyond Abeloth's beguiling beauty to see a horrifying monster lurking beneath. Still, the Sith strike an accord with Abeloth, and she allows the Tribe to take Ship to Sinkhole Station to destroy the powerful Jedi Knight they had sensed earlier.

Jaina and Jag examine high-tech surveillance equipment secreted within a captured cleaning droid from the Jedi Temple, the instrument used to spy on the Jedi. Jag finds proof that the technology is the work of Moff Lecersen, given to reporter Javis Tyrr to spy on the Jedi. He offers this evidence to

LEGACY 451

Daala, hoping to soften her antagonistic stance against the Jedi by showing that the tension between the Alliance and the Jedi is specifically being exploited by the Imperial Remnant. Though Daala has no love for the Moffs, it doesn't change her hard-line view against the Jedi.

Knowing that the Jedi Temple has been compromised by spies and that Coruscant is increasingly unwelcoming, the Jedi secretly transport their unstable Jedi Knights from the capital to their base on Shedu Maad. The transfer, abetted by Han and Leia, is ambushed by Mandalorian commandos hired by Daala. Though the transfer succeeds, it is clear that Daala will not be pushed any further.

The realm beyond shadows can be reached only by meditating so deeply as to hover at the brink of death. There Luke and Ben encounter the ghostly forms of Anakin Solo, Mara Jade Skywalker, and even an aspect of Jacen. Luke gets a hazy glimpse into the future, of a red-haired Jedi Queen—the adult Allana Solo—sitting on the Throne of Balance, a position that seemingly rules the galaxy. He senses a dangerous female form whom he cannot identify. The ghostly Jacen confides to Luke that Jacen's path to the dark side was preceded by knowledge that a great evil threatened the galaxy, and Jacen needed to do whatever he could to prevent it from succeeding.

The Skywalkers return to the corporeal realm as the Sith survivors arrive to ambush Sinkhole Station. Defending themselves, Luke and Ben cut through all of the highly skilled Sith warriors, including Lady Rhea. Vestara Khai survives, and Luke marks her with his blood so that he can track her flight to wherever she may flee and learn more about these newly revealed dark warriors.

In an allusion to *The Odyssey*, the Mind Walkers whom Luke and Ben meet resemble the lotus-eaters encountered by Odysseus.

BACKLASH

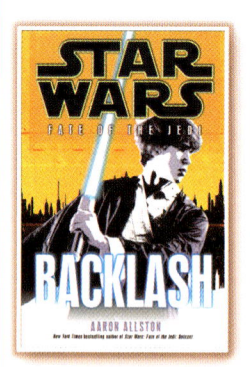

AUTHOR · Aaron Allston
COVER ARTIST · Ian Keltie
PUBLICATION HISTORY ·
Novel, Del Rey Books
· Hardcover, March 2010
· Paperback, February 2011
TIME LINE PLACEMENT ·
43 ABY

WORLDS VISITED · Coruscant [L-9]; Dathomir [O-6]; Kessel [T-10]

MAIN CHARACTERS · Luke Skywalker, Grand Master in exile of the Jedi Order (human male); Ben Skywalker, Jedi apprentice (human male); Vestara Khai, Sith apprentice (human female); Han Solo, captain of the *Millennium Falcon* (human male); Leia Organa Solo, Jedi Knight (human female); Jaina Solo, Jedi Knight (human female); Jagged Fel, Imperial Head of State (human male); Allana "Amelia" Solo, child (human female); Natasi Daala, Galactic Alliance Chief of State (human female); Dyon Stadd, former Jedi candidate (human male); Kaminne Sihn, chief of the Raining Leaves Clan (Dathomiri female); Drikl Lecersen, Imperial Moff (human male); Wynn Dorvan, assistant to the Chief of State (human male); C-3PO, protocol droid; R2-D2, astromech droid

SUMMARY · Having escaped a deadly confrontation with the Skywalkers, Vestara Khai flies an abandoned space yacht captured at Sinkhole Station to Dathomir, hoping to hide among its Force-sensitive populace and warn the Lost Tribe of the Jedi's power. Luke and Ben follow her to the planet and recruit

LEGACY

help from locals to find her. One such local is Dyon Stadd, an unsuccessful candidate from the Jedi academy who is nonetheless resourceful and gifted in the Force despite his lack of formal training. Luke and Ben also inform the Jedi Order that the Sith have returned. The Solos—Han, Leia, and Allana—journey to Dathomir aboard the *Millennium Falcon* to offer their aid in finding Vestara. Hoping to keep Allana safe, Han and Leia have her stay aboard the *Falcon* with R2-D2, C-3PO, and her pet nexu, Anji, for company.

The Skywalkers and Solos reunite and come into contact with two competing Dathomirian tribes: the Raining Leaves and the Broken Columns. Both are engaged in contests of raw physical and Force-attuned abilities in anticipation of their merger, but they are plagued by attacks from the Nightsisters. Luke and Ben help unite the tribes to better defend themselves. The Skywalkers find Vestara within the Raining Leaves Clan, where she has been adopted by Olianne Sihn, a clan member who took sympathy upon the stranded girl. Olianne is very protective of Vestara, not allowing the Skywalkers to apprehend her. Vestara works with the clans to help repulse the Nightsisters, though Luke and Ben remain suspicious of her motives.

On Coruscant, Jagged Fel is ambushed in his supposedly secure quarters by would-be kidnappers. Jagged and Jaina wonder who would have ordered so bold, yet so sloppy, an attack. The true mastermind is Senator Haydnat Treen of Kuat, who wants to depose Fel and engineer a greater union between the Alliance and the Imperial Remnant with Moff Lecersen ruling as a new emperor and herself as second in command.

Waiting aboard the *Falcon*, a restless Allana cannot stay put, especially when it appears that R2-D2 has been abducted. Allana fools C-3PO into playing an endless game of hide-and-seek and uses the opportunity to sneak away from the ship to follow clues to a garage owned by a gruff dockworker named Monarg. Allana is able to free R2-D2 from Monarg's clutches and narrowly escapes the dockworker's wrath. Returning to the *Falcon*, Allana rashly decides to pilot the ship away from the landing pad, soaring safely (albeit bumpily) into the surrounding jungle. She is met by a relieved Han and Leia, who decide to take Allana back to Coruscant.

At the capital, Jedi Knight Sothais Saar compiles a report on the rise of slavery in the galaxy. He hopes to bring it to Chief of State Daala's attention and meets with her aide, Wynn Dorvan. But during his meeting, Saar is gripped by the same psychosis that has been afflicting other Jedi and rushes about in a mad fit of paranoia before being stopped. In response, Daala has Mandalorian warriors blockade the Jedi Temple, thus preventing the Jedi from sending Luke reinforcements against the resurgent Sith.

Though convinced she is in the right, Daala weathers souring public sentiment for her controversial handling of the Jedi. Some wags hyperbolically compare her forceful measures to the draconian rule of Palpatine. Dorvan offers some advice to help Daala appear more evenhanded: her targeting of Tahiri for arrest and trial, for example, seems to be a biased pursuit, especially since Admiral Niathal, who was similarly allied to Jacen Solo during the Second Galactic Civil War, escaped consequence. In the interests of fairness, Daala begrudgingly agrees to pursue legal action against Niathal, and out of courtesy sends a warning to the admiral on Mon Calamari. Niathal, though, stands by her convictions and refuses to denounce her past actions. Recognizing the ramifications of a trial, Niathal commits suicide. Daala is both saddened and politically hurt by the death. She cannot attend the state funeral because of fears for her safety.

Upon their return to Coruscant, the Solos are met by Daala. She requests their help in serving as

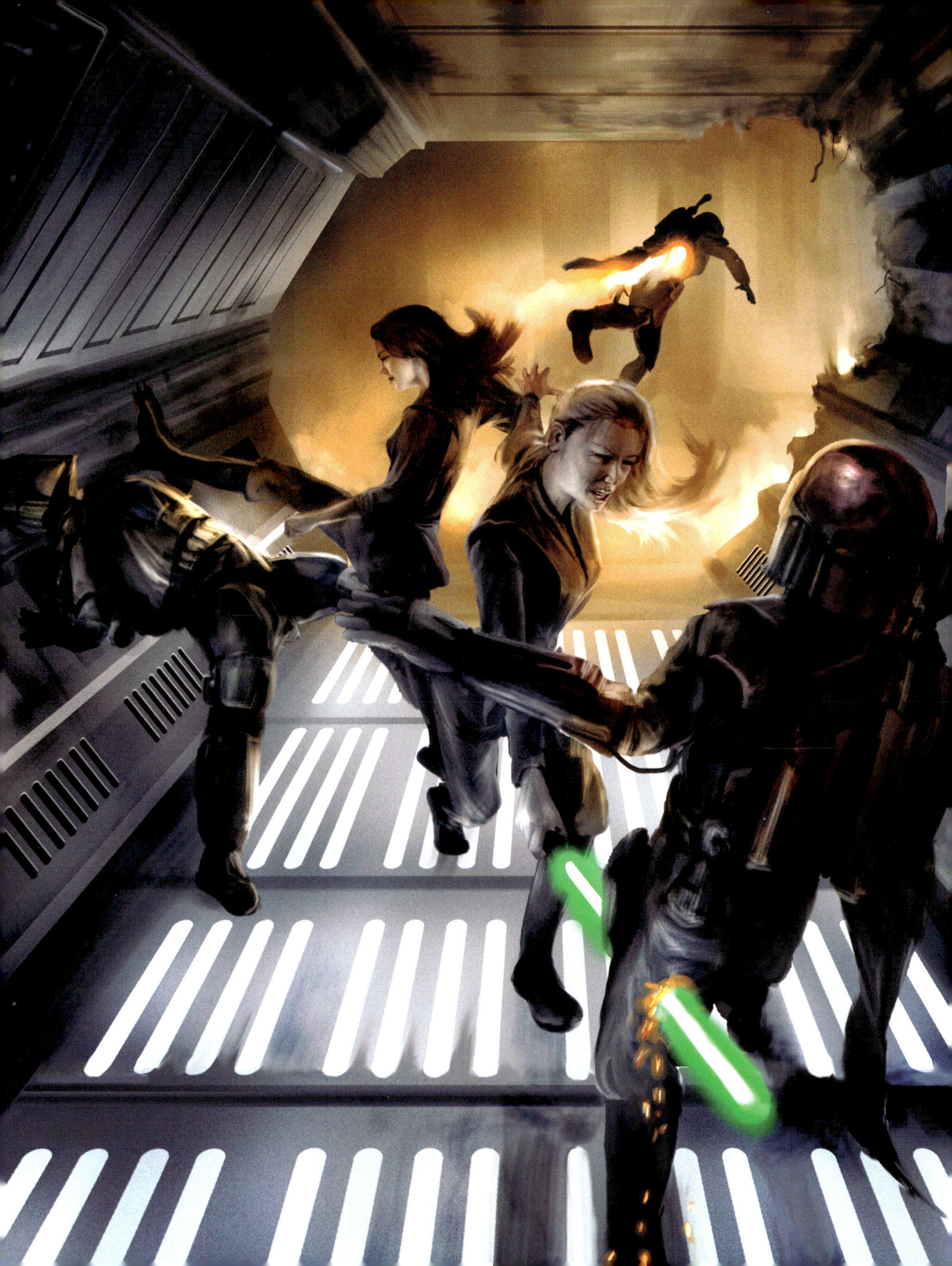

intermediaries to negotiate a truce between the Alliance and the Jedi. In exchange for their assistance, Daala agrees to overlook past transgressions of the law. Interested in a peaceful resolution to the growing conflict, Leia agrees.

Later, Jaina and Jag join Han, Leia, and Allana for a family dinner. The gathering is attacked by terrorists hired by Moff Lecersen—an ambush calculated by the Moff to appear engineered by Daala. Though Jag and the Solos are able to defeat the attackers, Lecersen does not count this as a loss. His plot against Daala is one meant to build in subtle layers over time.

On Dathomir, the conclave of the Raining Leaves and Broken Columns clans is attacked by Nightsisters. Vestara quietly allies herself with Halliava Vurse, a Nightsister spy hidden within the Raining Leaves ranks. Vestara awaits the arrival of a landing party of her fellow Sith, whom she contacted upon arrival on Dathomir. Vestara clandestinely meets the gathered Nightsister survivors as well as her newly arrived tribe-mates, under the pretense of forging an alliance. The Sith easily overpower the Witches and capture them, taking them back to their fleet. Vestara then returns to the clans to retrieve Halliava while four Sith stay behind to wait for her. Following Vestara, the Skywalkers and Dyon confront and defeat the Sith quartet. When Vestara returns with Halliava, the Skywalkers apprehend her and expose her treachery to the now merged and renamed Bright Suns clan. Luke, Ben, and Dyon take Vestara captive and leave Dathomir, only to find themselves surrounded by a flotilla of the Lost Tribe's ChaseMaster frigates.

THE OUTLINE OF THE NOVEL describes the locals who help Luke track Vestara as similar to the Argonauts who accompanied Jason in his search for the Golden Fleece, another allusion to epic Greek mythology. Similarly, Allana must defeat Monarg, a dockworker with an old injury that left him one-eyed like a Cyclops.

ALLIES

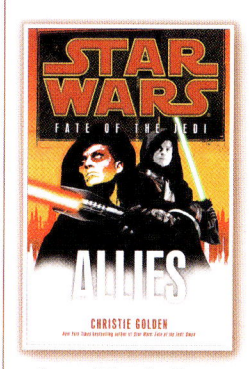

AUTHOR · Christie Golden
COVER ARTIST · Ian Keltie
PUBLICATION HISTORY ·
Novel, Del Rey Books
· Hardcover, May 2010
· Paperback, April 2011
TIME LINE PLACEMENT ·
44 ABY
WORLDS VISITED · Abeloth's planet [T-10]; Coruscant [L-9]; Klatooine [S-9]; Tatooine [R-16]; Vinsoth [N-5]
MAIN CHARACTERS · Luke Skywalker, Grand Master in exile of the Jedi Order (human male); Ben Skywalker, Jedi apprentice (human male); Vestara Khai, Sith apprentice (human female); Han Solo, captain of the *Millennium Falcon* (human male); Leia Organa Solo, Jedi Knight (human female); Jaina Solo, Jedi Knight (human female); Lando Calrissian, entrepreneur (human male); Sarasu Taalon, Sith High Lord (Keshiri male); Jagged Fel, Imperial Head of State (human male); Allana "Amelia" Solo, child (human female); Natasi Daala, Galactic Alliance Chief of State (human female); Madhi Vaandt, reporter (Devaronian female); Abeloth, destroyer (female entity); Wynn Dorvan, assistant to the Chief of State (human male)

Tyria Sarkin Tainer and Jaina Solo defend the Jedi Temple from Mandalorian mercenary invaders.

SUMMARY · Surrounded by Sith frigates, the *Jade Shadow* receives a transmission from Sith High Lord Sarasu Taalon. He proposes an alliance with the Skywalkers to counter the threat of Abeloth. Gavar Khai, Vestara's father, boards the *Jade Shadow* to speak with his daughter. Alone, Gavar reveals to Vestara that the Sith are conspiring to betray the Skywalkers once Abeloth is destroyed. Luke, unable to understand their Keshiri language, nonetheless records their conversation. Gavar intuits that Vestara has developed an attraction to Ben, emotions that the young Skywalker reciprocates. Gavar encourages his daughter to use this against Ben. Luke accepts the Sith offer to help defeat Abeloth, and the *Jade Shadow* and Sith vessels depart for nearby Klatooine to resupply. Luke calls Lando Calrissian for assistance in traversing the Maw Cluster to where Abeloth resides, and Lando agrees to deliver Luke a specialized ship. Luke also contacts C-3PO at the Solo residence with his recording of the Keshiri conversation to translate.

Fearing that Chief of State Daala will take out her frustrations against the Jedi on Tahiri Veila, Jaina Solo barges into Jagged Fel's office and demands his help in the upcoming trial against the former Jedi. Jag agrees, although he worries about getting too enmeshed in the political affairs of the Alliance and the Jedi. He discreetly arranges for Eramuth Bwua'tu, an elder Bothan lawyer, to serve as Tahiri's defense attorney.

At Klatooine, Luke sends Ben and Vestara to the surface to acquire supplies and asks Dyon Stadd to watch over the teenagers. Luke worries about Vestara's influence on his son. Dyon is suddenly stricken by the psychosis that has been plaguing the Jedi, and in his frenzied dash to escape capture, he trespasses at an ancient and sacred Klatooinian landmark: the Fountain of the Hutt Ancients. When Ben and Vestara try to stop Dyon from desecrating the site, all three of them are arrested. The Klatooinians turn over the trio to Luke and Gavar Khai, who arrive to bail out their children. Luke warns Ben away from Vestara. The young man resents his father's intrusion.

On Coruscant, the Jedi Temple is still surrounded by Daala's Mandalorian mercenaries, who await the surrender of psychotic Jedi Knights held within. Jaina cannot convince Kenth Hamner to challenge Daala's decree. She again asks Jag to help, but he cannot do so without severely destabilizing the political relationships among the Imperial Remnant, the Jedi Order, and the Galactic Alliance. Jaina realizes that Jag's political duties and her duties as a Jedi are incompatible. Jaina returns Jag's engagement ring.

After receiving C-3PO's translation of Vestara and Gavar's conversation, Luke reveals Vestara's duplicity to his sullen son. Ben realizes his father was right about Vestara, but he cannot shake his feelings for her. Luke feels compelled to proceed to the Maw before Lando's arrival, so in agreement with Lord Taalon, the *Jade Shadow* and several of the Sith vessels depart. Lord Taalon leaves some Sith vessels behind to await Lando, but gives them the secret order to collect material samples from the sacred site on Klatooine. This attempted raid on the fountain causes an uproar among the Klatooinians, prompting uprisings. Lando and Jaina Solo arrive at Klatooine separately, but both become involved in the turmoil as the Klatooinian elders ask for their help to sort through this crisis created by the Sith.

At stake is the future of the Klatooinian people. For over a thousand generations, the Klatooinians have been enslaved by the Hutts. In exchange for their servitude, the Hutts promised to protect their most sacred site. If the Hutts were derelict in their duty, the Klatooinians could be free of their overlords. Jaina and Lando decide that the Hutts did do all they could to protect the site, and blame rests with the Sith. With the prospect of freedom dangling before them, Klatooinian uprisings continue, and this unrest is echoed across the galaxy, where similarly disadvantaged cultures have begun fomenting rebellion against their rulers. An underground movement called Freedom Flight is helping this cause on other worlds, which creates political turbulence felt by Daala's administration.

The siege at the Jedi Temple turns bloody when Kenth Hamner's assistant attempts to negotiate with the Mandalorians and the mercenaries gun down the young woman in cold blood. Though urged by the other Jedi Masters to act against Daala, Kenth does not—he bides his time because he is in secret communication with Admiral Nek Bwua'tu. The admiral, who is in a relationship with Daala, promises to use his influence to change Daala's tactics.

Lando finally reunites with Luke and delivers the starship, *Rockhound*, as promised. The enormous asteroid tug can use its tractor beam array to help defend the expedition into the treacherous Maw Cluster. As the Sith and Skywalkers approach Sinkhole Station, they find only debris in its place. Vestara leads the expedition to Abeloth's planet.

On the overgrown jungle world, Vestara frees Dyon from captivity, intent on tracking the mad Jedi as he makes his way to Abeloth. The Sith and the Jedi confront the strange entity, who adopts a physical form resembling Luke's long-lost love Callista. Despite her appearance, Luke battles and eventually defeats Abeloth. The being's death ripples through the Force, and those Jedi afflicted with madness are suddenly cured.

On Coruscant, Nek Bwua'tu fails to convince Daala to call off her Mandalorian siege of the Jedi Temple. Heading home after his dinner with Daala, Nek is attacked by two crazed Jedi. He realizes they cannot be Jedi, as he is capable of defending himself against their attacks, and kills one of them. But before he can do anything with this insight, he blacks out due to injuries sustained from a lightsaber during the attack.

IN A BRIEF CUTAWAY to Tatooine to introduce the Freedom Flight story line, the novel includes an appearance by Ackmena, the cantina bartender played by Bea Arthur in "The *Star Wars* Holiday Special," the *Star Wars* variety TV special that aired in 1978.

The slave uprising subplot was not part of the original story outline for the series. As part of the process of writing multibook epics, the authors would stay in constant communication and convene in person, when possible, to have supplemental story conferences to assess where the flow of the plot and characters was going. It was during one of these secondary meetings that the slave plotline was proposed to further galvanize the Jedi into action and give them a cause with a moral clarity that stood apart from the conspiracies of Coruscant.

VORTEX

AUTHOR · Troy Denning

COVER ARTIST · Ian Keltie

PUBLICATION HISTORY · Novel, Del Rey Books
· Hardcover, November 2010
· Paperback, March 2012

TIME LINE PLACEMENT · 44 ABY

WORLDS VISITED · Abeloth's planet [T-10]; Blaudu Sextus [U-12]; Coruscant [L-9]; Pydyr (moon of Almania) [S-5]

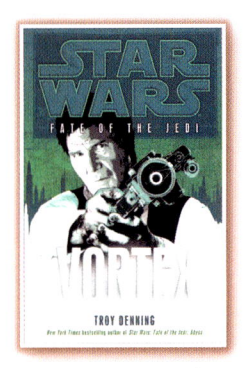

MAIN CHARACTERS · Luke Skywalker, Grand Master in exile of the Jedi Order (human male); Ben Skywalker, Jedi apprentice (human male); Vestara Khai, Sith apprentice (human female); Han Solo, captain of the *Millennium Falcon* (human male); Sarasu Taalon, Sith High Lord (Keshiri male); Abeloth, destroyer (female entity); Leia Organa Solo, Jedi Knight (human female); Jaina Solo, Jedi Knight (human female); Jagged Fel, Imperial Head of State (human male); Allana "Amelia" Solo, child (human female); Natasi Daala, Galactic Alliance Chief of State (human female); Kenth Hamner, interim Grand Jedi Master (human male); Saba Sebatyne, Jedi Master (Barabel female); Madhi Vaandt, reporter (Devaronian female); Wynn Dorvan, assistant to the Chief of State (human male)

SUMMARY · On Abeloth's planet, Luke Skywalker and the Lost Tribe Sith Lords examine the caves to learn more about their bizarre foe. Through the Force, Vestara Khai can sense that Ship, the Sith meditation sphere that fled upon Abeloth's apparent death, is returning to the planet to serve the Sith. To ensure that her father knows this information first, Vestara betrays Ben and locks him aboard the *Jade Shadow*. While she races through the jungle Vestara gets tangled in deadly plants. Still smitten, Ben comes to her rescue and cuts her free on the condition that she not betray the Skywalkers again. The Sith and Jedi examine Abeloth's body only to find that it is actually Dyon Stadd. The mysterious entity has covered her survival with a convincing illusion.

On Coruscant, when Han Solo emerges with Jedi once believed insane and a psychiatrist in Daala's employ diagnoses them as competent and cured, Daala is forced to call off her Mandalorian siege of the Jedi Temple. Though it is evident the psychosis plague has abated, Daala refuses to hand over the carbon-frozen Jysella and Valin Horn until she has more time to further investigate the matter. This causes great contention within the Jedi Council. Some Jedi want to push against Daala, but Kenth Hamner refuses to risk war with the Alliance.

On Abeloth's planet, the Sith and Jedi alliance crumbles when, in the Pool of Knowledge dark side nexus, Lord Taalon sees a Force vision of the future with a Jedi Queen (Allana) ruling the galaxy. The Lost Tribe fear this image portends the end of the Sith. Luke and Ben want to keep Allana's true identity secret, which forces a fight with the Sith Lords. Both Skywalkers narrowly escape with their lives. Taalon wishes for Vestara to serve as a spy for the Sith. To cover her true loyalties, Taalon beats Vestara to appropriately scar her for her assignment, then releases her to tag along with the Skywalkers. With Vestara accompanying them, Luke and Ben escape Abeloth's planet aboard the captured Sith vessel *Emiax* to pursue Abeloth, who has fled aboard the *Jade Shadow* with Ship following.

Meanwhile, Daala investigates the circumstances surrounding the attack on Admiral Nek Bwua'tu. She knows the Jedi were not behind it, but she doesn't know who would seek to discredit the Order in this manner, and Bwua'tu cannot provide any answers as he is in a coma.

On Blaudu Sextus, a world undergoing revolt fueled by an anti-slavery uprising, Mandalorians hired by Daala crack down on the unrest. The violent mercenaries kill a popular journalist, Madhi Vaandt, which only further fuels the Jedi desire to stop Daala's actions. When it comes to light that Kenth Hamner had been brokering secret deals

LEGACY

with Alliance admiral Nek Bwua'tu, he loses further favor with the Jedi under his command. They choose to disregard his edicts and free Valin and Jysella Horn.

Luke has tracked Abeloth to the Almanian moon of Pydyr. He calls for Jedi StealthX fighters as reinforcements while he, Ben, and Vestara venture into the Force illusions cast by the Fallanassi. Corrupted by Abeloth, the Fallanassi are harboring Vestara, protecting her from pursuit with repulsive mirages of a world suffering a deadly plague. Vestara, still loyal to her Sith masters, summons the Lost Tribe to Pydyr. This results in a confrontation between Lord Taalon and Luke. Taalon is undergoing a bizarre transformation due to his deep exposure to the Pool of Knowledge. The Sith Lord grows in power but suffers immensely. Though Taalon wants to destroy Skywalker, he needs Luke to find Abeloth so as to understand and discover his fate.

Abeloth possesses Akanah Norand Pell's body and leads the Fallanassi in illusory attacks against the interlopers. The Sith turn on the Skywalkers, and as Ben fends off attacks from Taalon and Vestara, Luke once again strikes down Abeloth, but she yet again takes on the form of Callista. The Skywalkers are outnumbered, but Vestara recognizes that the High Lord has become little more than a pawn of Abeloth. Realizing that Luke stands the best chance of destroying the monstrous entity, Vestara betrays the High Lord and kills Taalon, thus sparing Luke's life.

With the arrival of the *Errant Venture* over Coruscant, the Jedi engineer a distraction that consumes the Galactic Alliance's attention. Booster Terrik hosts a sabacc tournament aboard his Star Destroyer, drawing such notables as Moff Lecersen and Wynn Dorvan aboard. He holds them hostage while using his ship to attack satellites around Coruscant—all in a bid to keep the orbital security of Coruscant focused on him while the Jedi launch their StealthX fighters. Meanwhile Han, Leia, Jaina, and several allies raid the Alliance detention center and take Valin and Jysella, in their carbonite slabs, back to the Jedi Temple.

Kenth's attempts to regain control of the Jedi sparks a duel with fellow Master Saba Sebatyne. When he tries to seal the Temple's hangar doors to prevent the Jedi from launching the StealthX fleet, Saba slays Kenth. She becomes the interim leader of the Jedi, and the Jedi fleet arrives at Pydyr and battles with the Sith ships. Having slain a Sith High Lord, Vestara has no choice but to continue to ally with Luke and Ben. The trio is determined to stop Abeloth once and for all.

CONVICTION

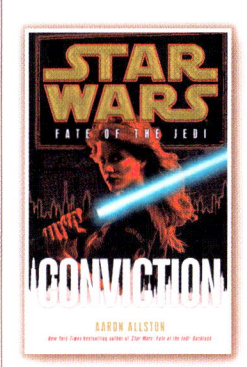

AUTHOR · Aaron Allston
COVER ARTIST · Ian Keltie
PUBLICATION HISTORY ·
Novel, Del Rey Books
· Hardcover, May 2011
· Paperback, August 2012
TIME LINE PLACEMENT ·
44 ABY
WORLDS VISITED · Almania (system) [S-5]; Borleias [K-9]; Coruscant [L-9]; Hapes [O-9]; Klatooine [S-9]; Meliflar Station, Mendenbatt (system) [R-5]; Nam Chorios [R-7]
MAIN CHARACTERS · Luke Skywalker, Grand Master of the Jedi Order (human male); Ben Skywalker, Jedi apprentice (human male); Vestara Khai, Sith apprentice (human female); Han Solo, captain of

LEGACY 459

the *Millennium Falcon* (human male); Abeloth, destroyer (female entity); Leia Organa Solo, Jedi Knight (human female); Jaina Solo, Jedi Knight (human female); Jagged Fel, Imperial Head of State (human male); Allana "Amelia" Solo, child (human female); Natasi Daala, Galactic Alliance Chief of State (human female); Wynn Dorvan, assistant to the Chief of State (human male); Tenel Ka, Hapan Queen Mother (human female); Gavar Khai, Sith Saber (human male); C-3PO, protocol droid; Boba Fett, bounty hunter (human male); Drikl Lecersen, Imperial Moff (human male)

SUMMARY · Valin and Jysella Horn are at long last freed from their carbonite imprisonment, but they are still secretly afflicted by the psychosis that causes them to believe that everyone around them is an imposter. Outwardly they pretend all is normal, but together they conspire to contact Abeloth.

Hammered by the Jedi StealthXs at the Almanian system, the Sith frigate fleet disengages and makes good its escape. Luke Skywalker, his son Ben, and Vestara Khai track the fleeing Abeloth to Nam Chorios. This poses a disturbing threat, for if Abeloth can control the Theran Listeners and the intelligent crystals of the planet, she can effectively bring an entire world under her sway. Furthermore, the Sith flotilla is already there to help Abeloth, battering away at the planetary defenses. Luke alerts the Jedi Temple; then he, Ben, and Vestara head down to the planet's surface.

The near assassination of Nek Bwua'tu has greatly unsettled Chief of State Natasi Daala. She lashes out against those who would destabilize her rule, intensifying her police actions against slave uprisings. This spurs the Jedi to move against her. The *Errant Venture*, meanwhile, releases its hostages on Borleias. The freed Moff Lecersen, Senator Haydnat Treen, and others within their conspiratorial circle move forward with their plan to overthrow Daala, only to find that the Jedi have beaten them to it. Saba Sebatyne leads the charge of Jedi Masters who capture Daala, imprisoning her in a cell across from Tahiri Veila. With no Chief of State to rule the Alliance, Saba moves into the power vacuum, sharing the title with Haydnat Treen and General Merratt Jaxton of Alliance Starfighter Command. Jagged Fel comes down in favor of the coup against Daala, a move that would put him in opposition to most in the Imperial government. As Jaina wonders if Jag is trying to sabotage his political career to be closer to her, she is reminded of her love for him, and the two continue to mend their relationship.

With the Jedi now in control of the Alliance, they overturn Skywalker's sentence of exile and recall the Mandalorians operating against the slave revolts. This opens the way to diplomatic resolutions to the growing uprisings. Leia Organa Solo goes to Klatooine to explore inviting the Klatooinians to be members of the Galactic Alliance and thus end the rule of the Hutts. Also serving as diplomatic envoys are the Hapans, led by Queen Mother Tenel Ka. The Lost Tribe, led by Gavar Khai, tracks Tenel Ka's movements, for they believe her to be connected to the dangerous Jedi Queen of Lord Taalon's visions. Soon the Sith are able to puzzle out the connection between Tenel Ka and young Amelia Solo, and they target both for assassination by covertly planting a bomb in C-3PO's body. Allana thwarts this plan, and Leia uncovers the would-be assassin, defeating the Sith in a lightsaber duel. The diplomatic mission succeeds, with Klatooine given full Alliance membership.

Tahiri Veila's trial comes to an end when she is convicted and bound over for sentencing. This creates a storm of controversy, as members of the media see flaws in the trial and in the judge's concluding remarks, which appear to be those of a Daala partisan rather than of an impartial jurist. Tahiri is sentenced to death, but she escapes into the Coruscant cityscape in the chaos caused when Boba Fett breaks Daala out of prison.

On Nam Chorios, Valin and Jysella arrive to help Abeloth, harrying Luke, Ben, and Vestara with intense Force storms. Nonetheless, Luke finds Abeloth among the tsils, the native crystalline lifeforms. Abeloth once again presents herself as an avatar of Callista to weaken Luke's resolve. Luke realizes that the Callista likeness is not just an illusion—Abeloth absorbed the real Callista in an encounter with her. Luke uses a special Force technique to draw the Callista remnant out of Abeloth and finally free her from the entity's grasp. In addition to this trauma, Vestara destroys a tsil, creating an agonizing backlash wave that ripples through the Force, crippling Abeloth. Abeloth again flees. As she departs, she encounters Gavar Khai and invites him to enter into an alliance to destroy Luke Skywalker.

THIS BOOK MAKES CLEAR Callista's fate, which had long been unresolved in the Expanded Universe. At some point after her last appearance in *Planet of Twilight* (1997), Callista encountered Abeloth and was absorbed into her being. The return of Callista had been broached in the very first story explorations for the Fate of the Jedi series.

ASCENSION

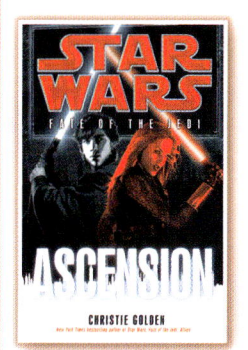

AUTHOR · Christie Golden
COVER ARTIST · Ian Keltie
PUBLICATION HISTORY ·
Novel, Del Rey Books
· Hardcover, August 2011
· Paperback, November 2012
TIME LINE PLACEMENT · 44 ABY
WORLDS VISITED · Dromund Kaas [R-5]; Exodo II [R-7]; Kesh [U-10]; Korriban [R-5]; Pedducis Chorios [R-7]; Roonadan [S-3]; Upekzar [R-5]

MAIN CHARACTERS · Luke Skywalker, Grand Master of the Jedi Order (human male); Ben Skywalker, Jedi apprentice (human male); Vestara Khai, Sith apprentice (human female); Han Solo, captain of the *Millennium Falcon* (human male); Leia Organa Solo, Jedi Knight (human female); Jaina Solo, Jedi Knight (human female); Abeloth, destroyer (female entity); Jagged Fel, Imperial Head of State (human male); Allana "Amelia" Solo, child (human female); Natasi Daala, Galactic Alliance Chief of State in exile (human female); Wynn Dorvan, acting Joint Chief of State (human male); Saba Sebatyne, Jedi Master (Barabel female); Boba Fett, bounty hunter (human male); Drikl Lecersen, Imperial Moff (human male)

SUMMARY · On Kesh, the Circle of Lords gathers to discuss Abeloth's proposal of an alliance to defeat Luke Skywalker. Though the Lost Tribe is wary of Abeloth's inscrutable motives and power, Grand Lord Darish Vol decrees that they need her to ensure victory over the Jedi. The Sith celebrate Abeloth's arrival in grand fashion, complete with parade. As he sleeps that night, Vol is visited by Abeloth in his dreams. She attacks the Grand Lord in this state, but he fights back with his keen mind. He is able to peer past Abeloth's illusions and see her as a painfully lonely being desperate to be loved. Frustrated with Vol's tenacity, Abeloth reacts by blasting a Force shock wave that devastates the city of Tahv. Millions of citizens die in the disaster—among them Vestara Khai's mother, Lahka—though Vol survives. Abeloth boards Ship and departs Kesh with loyal Sith followers, including Gavar Khai.

The Skywalkers, joined by Vestara Khai and Jaina Solo, continue their hunt for Ship and Abeloth, starting on the ancient Sith world of Korriban. In the Valley of the Dark Lords, they survive attacks by guardian beasts. Vestara helps the Skywalkers, though Luke remains skeptical of her intentions.

The Galactic Alliance continues to reform in Chief of State Daala's absence—command of the government falls to a triumvirate consisting of Jedi Master Saba Sebatyne, Senator Haydnat Treen, and Wynn Dorvan, Daala's former aide. Meanwhile, the fugitive Daala learns from her rescuer Boba Fett that the Freedom Flight movement that so complicated her days in office was engineered by Moff Lecersen in a bid to keep her distracted and off balance. In retaliation, Daala aligns with Moff Porrak Vansyn, an Imperial official opposed to the coup. Together they are able to lure Lecersen into a trap. Daala threatens the treacherous Moff into helping her.

The search for Abeloth leads the Skywalkers, Vestara, and Jaina to the ancient Sith world of Dromund Kaas, to the site of a dark side temple. There they encounter Abeloth's loyal Sith Sabers. The Skywalkers and Jaina duel and defeat the Sith, leaving Vestara to battle her father. She slays her father, Gavar, and mourns him. Ben believes that Vestara can leave her dark side past behind her and perhaps one day embark upon the path of the Jedi. Ben and Vestara admit their love for each other and share their first kiss.

Returning to Coruscant for the first time since his exile, Luke resumes command of the Jedi Order as Grand Master. He absolves Saba Sebatyne of Kenth Hamner's death, given the circumstances that surrounded it. Luke declares that the Jedi Order will separate from the galactic government and move off Coruscant. With Sebatyne no longer part of the Alliance triumvirate, the Senate holds an emergency session to elect an interim Chief of State. A cabal of anti-Jedi Senators votes Padnel Ovin into office, thinking him to be an easily manipulated politician. Recognizing this, Ovin has Wynn Dorvan serve as his adviser.

Rather than live as an escaped convict, Tahiri Veila surrenders herself to the Solos, seeking to atone for her past crimes. But the sentence handed down under Daala's administration is no longer valid, and since Tahiri's central crime was the murder of an Imperial Remnant officer, the Solos turn her over to Jagged Fel. Given the threats directed against his life by the conspiring Moffs, Jag assigns Tahiri to be his Force-sensitive bodyguard.

The anti-Jedi cabal determined to steer the Alliance government secretly includes human members of the Lost Tribe of the Sith. At their decree, Leia Organa Solo is arrested on spurious charges. Luke has anticipated this course of action—while the Sith focus on such machinations, they are too busy to interfere with his crusade to wipe out Ship and Abeloth. As scheming as the Sith are, they are rivaled by the Bothans. The so-called Club Bwua'tu surfaces to help Leia escape—it is a conspiracy that includes Nek Bwua'tu (awakened from his coma), Eramuth Bwua'tu, Wynn Dorvan, Chief of State Ovin, Lando Calrissian, and Han Solo. Club

LEGACY

Bwua'tu moves clandestinely to counter the Sith infiltration, and in the process causes Moff Lecersen and Senator Treen's bids for power to collapse.

With the help of Moff Tol Getelles, Jag Fel is able to expose Daala's alliance with Moff Lecersen. Backed by fighting forces from the Empire of the Hand as well as Imperial loyalists, Fel ambushes Daala's Maw Irregular Fleet and Lecersen's vessels. Though Fel lands a mighty blow on the conspirators, he is forced to retreat from the engagement when Lecersen's forces rally.

On Coruscant, interim Chief of State Ovin is assassinated under mysterious circumstances. Senator Rokari Kem of Qaras rides a wave of popularity, stemming from her role in fighting slavery in the galaxy, to become elected Chief of State of the Galactic Alliance. She is, in fact, possessed by Abeloth, who has used her persuasive abilities to rise to power.

The Jedi hunt for Abeloth leads to a Sith trap in the subterranean lava tunnels of Upekzar. Ben, Vestara, and Jedi Knight Natua Wan search the caverns for the dark side entity but are attacked by mutated native insectoid creatures called Rhak-skuri. To save Ben's life, Vestara sacrifices Natua to the beasts' ravenous appetites. She realizes her aspirations to be a Jedi may be misguided, for so callously tossing aside a Jedi's life still comes as second nature to her as a Sith.

APOCALYPSE

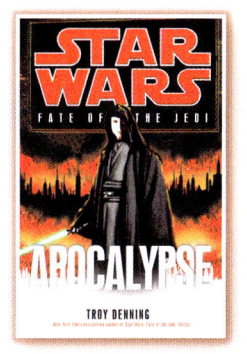

AUTHOR · Troy Denning
COVER ARTIST · Ian Keltie
PUBLICATION HISTORY · Novel, Del Rey Books
· Hardcover, March 2012
· Paperback, February 2013
TIME LINE PLACEMENT · 44 ABY
WORLDS VISITED · Bastion [K-3]; Coruscant [L-9]; Exodo II [R-7]; Hagamoor 3 [R-7]; Kesh [U-10]; Ossus [R-6]; Reo (system) [I-7]
MAIN CHARACTERS · Luke Skywalker, Grand Master of the Jedi Order (human male); Ben Skywalker, Jedi apprentice (human male); Vestara Khai, Sith apprentice (human female); Abeloth, destroyer (female entity); Han Solo, captain of the *Millennium Falcon* (human male); Leia Organa Solo, Jedi Knight (human female); Jaina Solo, Jedi Knight (human female); Jagged Fel, Imperial Head of State (human male); Allana "Amelia" Solo, child (human female); Natasi Daala, former Galactic Alliance Chief of State (human female); Wynn Dorvan, adviser (human male); Raynar Thul, Jedi Knight (human male)
SUMMARY · Luke Skywalker's Jedi Knights begin their covert operation to infiltrate Coruscant, slipping past the hidden Sith agents who have insinuated themselves into the Alliance government. Abeloth possesses the form of Chief of State Rokari Kem, and she has broken Wynn Dorvan to her will by torturing him, turning the resourceful aide into her Joint Chief of State and adviser.

Though Vestara has earned the tentative trust of Ben and Luke Skywalker, her loyalty to the Jedi Order is hardly firm. She assists the Jedi mission, but mostly out of self-preservation—to ensure that the Jedi destroy the High Lords who would mark her for death for the killing of Lord Taalon and Gavar Khai.

Helping the Jedi with the evacuation of their students on Ossus are the Hapans, led by Queen Mother Tenel Ka, along with Han Solo, Leia Organa Solo, and Allana Solo. Tenel Ka survives an assassination attempt by the Sith, who are still determined to prevent her or her descendants from sitting upon a future throne, as suggested by the vision in the Force witnessed by Lord Taalon. With the evacuation completed, the Solos return to Coruscant, where Allana is desperate to save her Barabel Jedi friends who have secretly built a nest below the Jedi Temple.

Researching Abeloth's history, Jedi Knights Raynar Thul, Tekli, and Lowbacca bring the protocol droid C-3PO to the Celestial Palace in the Reo system, site of a Killik hive nest. They ask the Killiks if Abeloth is indeed connected to the Celestials, a primordial race in the galaxy said to be behind phenomenal examples of ancient cosmic architecture such as the Maw and Centerpoint Station. The Killiks are shocked to learn that Abeloth has been unleashed as a threat to the galaxy, for they were tasked, eons earlier, with keeping her imprisoned on her overgrown world. Especially attuned to communicating with the Killiks, Raynar learns the hive's version of a legend that appears to describe Abeloth. She was once part of a group that embodied the balance of the Force, but she ultimately became the Bringer of Chaos, an apocalyptic entity that intermittently wipes out life in the galaxy to allow it to begin anew. To prevent such cataclysm, the Celestials had penned Abeloth in the Maw, holding her in place with the power of Centerpoint Station.

When Luke's Jedi infiltrators, bolstered by Nek Bwua'tu's Void Jumper commandos, enter the Jedi Temple on Coruscant, they are met by Sith entrenched in preparation for an attack. In the battle, Vestara is pulled away from the rest of the Jedi. Once again prioritizing her own survival, she bargains for her life by revealing to the Sith that the woman seen in the visions of the future is Allana Solo. The Sith force her to prove her loyalty by assassinating Allana. Vestara botches the attempt on purpose, but her strike damages the *Millennium Falcon* and results in the death of Bazel Warv, Allana's protector. This course of action brands Vestara a traitor in the eyes of the Solos.

Abeloth's next tactic is to abandon the mortal shell of Rokari Kem and transfer her disembodied spirit into the computer systems of the Jedi Temple, where she can thwart the invading Jedi. She simultaneously possesses the body of Lady Korelei, a Sith Lord. In the Imperial Remnant, Jagged Fel and his bodyguard Tahiri Veila are able to stop Abeloth's attempts to meddle with Imperial politics by destroying another of her avatars. Jag capitalizes on this event to maneuver himself out of his position, leaving Vitor Reige as the Imperial Head of State. Jag and Tahiri depart the Empire to help their Jedi allies on Coruscant.

Abeloth unleashes destruction on Coruscant using powerful quakes and volcanic eruptions. She kidnaps Vestara and Ben on Ship, bringing them back to her prison planet. Tekli and Lowbacca return to Coruscant with their discoveries about Abeloth's history and insight into her objectives. Noting similarities between the Killik legend and the ancient Jedi tale of Mortis, they postulate that Abeloth is trying to re-create a family of godlike Force-wielders, with Luke as the father and Ben and

After the defeat of Abeloth, Vestara Khai escapes Abeloth's planet and the pursuit of Jaina Solo with the help of Ship.

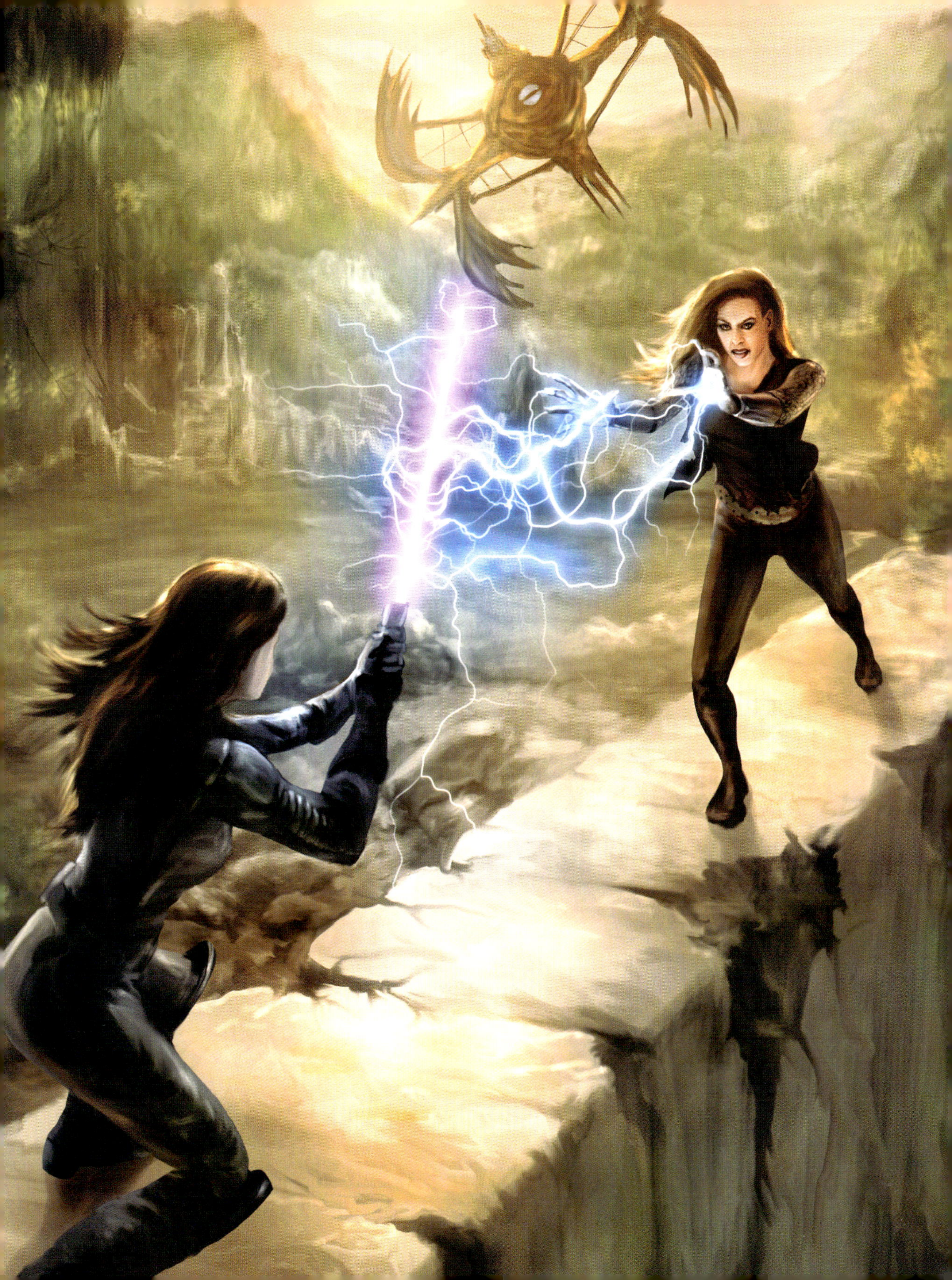

Vestara as the children embodying the light and dark sides of the Force, respectively.

As Abeloth's computer presence is destroyed, Luke departs the capital with Jaina Solo in an effort to rescue Ben and Vestara from Abeloth's clutches. Jaina battles Ship in space combat while Luke enters the twilight realm beyond shadows, where he seeks help in defeating Abeloth. He communicates with the spirit of Mara, who cannot help him; neither can the spirit of Jacen. A dark stranger emerges from the shadows, claiming to be part of the Lost Tribe. Luke doesn't believe this, but he does recognize the stranger as a powerful Sith. They band together to battle a common threat, engaging in combat with Abeloth in the astral plane beyond shadows. The strain of battling on so many fronts weakens her. Together Luke and the stranger slay Abeloth. On Coruscant, Saba Sebatyne kills an avatar of Abeloth with her powerful jaws. On Abeloth's planet, Ben and Vestara kill the Korelei avatar.

Beyond shadows, Luke confronts Jacen about his turn to the dark side. He tells Jacen his actions did not prevent the rise of Abeloth—in fact, Jacen's fall to darkness ensured her release. Jacen claims that he had seen the same dark stranger in a Force vision with Allana serving at his side, and strove to prevent that future from occurring. While both Luke and Jacen sought to prevent the stranger from sitting on the throne of power in the distant future, the stranger is confident that his time to rule has only been delayed, not destroyed.

In the aftermath of Abeloth's destruction, Vestara flees aboard Ship, who has accepted her as its Sith Master. Ben is saddened and betrayed by the loss. Vestara mourns as well, but reasons that the pain of her loss will provide fuel for her power in the dark side.

In the months that follow, the war-weary populace of Coruscant blames the Jedi for the tide of destruction that swept the world. The Jedi willingly depart the capital. Luke believes vestiges of Abeloth remain—her destructive rise to power is cyclical, according to legend, and Luke fears she will return, as evidence suggests the galaxy is slipping into darkness. In a proactive measure, Luke dispatches a special team of Jedi—the Ten Knights—to seek out the monolith of Mortis, where they might find the Dagger of Mortis, a legendary object capable of slaying a Force-wielder from beyond the mortal realm.

With Allana's identity and destiny revealed, she discards her alias of Amelia and accepts her place in the Hapan aristocracy. Wynn Dorvan serves as the interim Chief of State as the Alliance rebuilds. And after much delay, Jaina and Jag finally exchange their vows as husband and wife.

THE THREAT OF ABELOTH was part of the Fate of the Jedi story from the very first planning stages, though her true nature was left undefined. She was sketched out as a powerful Force being from beyond the mortal realm, and the ancient Celestials took pains to keep her at bay. Using Centerpoint Station, these powerful primordial aliens built the Maw Cluster to keep Abeloth trapped. During the Yuuzhan Vong War, when the Jedi hid their children at Shelter Base so close to Abeloth's prison, she reached out through the Force and connected with the unprotected infant minds. After Centerpoint was destroyed in the Legacy of the Force series, Abeloth began to pry apart the bars holding her in place, and gravitated toward the brightest point in the Force she could sense: Luke Skywalker. In pulling herself toward Luke, she used the minds she had previously made contact with as stepping-stones, creating the plague of Jedi madness that would form a growing crisis in the story line.

As the story developed, Abeloth started to become more defined. In a parallel path, the *Clone*

Wars animated series delved into godlike beings that were a part of the Force in the Mortis Trilogy (2011). Lucas Licensing suggested to author Troy Denning that he use the Mortis backstory as part of Abeloth's history that would be revealed in the final book.

Though he is never named, the stranger who helps Luke defeat Abeloth is Darth Krayt, the hidden founder of the One Sith movement that would rule the galaxy in the *Star Wars: Legacy* comics.

"GETAWAY"

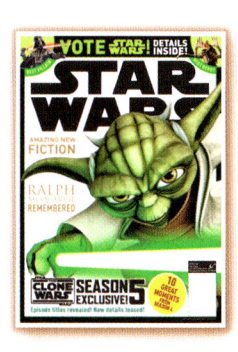

AUTHOR · Christie Golden
PUBLICATION HISTORY ·
Short story, Titan Publishing
· *Star Wars Insider* #134, June 2012
TIME LINE PLACEMENT · 44 ABY
WORLD VISITED · Sakuub [R-18]

MAIN CHARACTERS · Jaina Solo Fel, Jedi Master (human female); Jagged Fel, honeymooner (human male)

SUMMARY · Rather than have a relaxing honeymoon, Jaina brings her husband, Jag, to the remote world of Sakuub for a rugged hike. She is investigating ancient ruins to see if they point to clues about Abeloth. Their treasure-seeking guide betrays them to bandits once Jaina finds an ancient Jedi Holocron, but they are chased off by an unlikely ally: a visiting Hutt. He saves Jaina's life, hoping to square the debt with Jaina for ruling in favor of the Hutts during the Klatooinian uprising.

X-WING: MERCY KILL

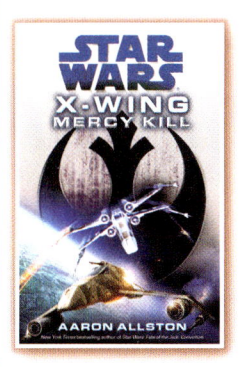

AUTHOR · Aaron Allston
COVER ARTIST · Mike Bryan
PUBLICATION HISTORY ·
Novel, Del Rey Books
 · Hardcover, August 2012
 · Paperback, June 2013
TIME LINE PLACEMENT · 13 ABY, 19 ABY, 29 ABY (flashbacks); 44 ABY (present)
WORLDS VISITED · Ayceezee [N-4]; Badfellow Station [M-10]; Chashima [S-6]; Coruscant [L-9]; Gagrew Station [S-9]; Kuratooine (and its moon, Tildin) [J-5]; Mulvar Sensor Station (flashback) [K-3]; Parabow Station [S-7]; Ryvester (flashback) [R-7]; Vandor 3 [L-9]

MAIN CHARACTERS · Voort "Piggy" saBinring, mathematics professor (Gamorrean male); Myri Antilles, gambler (human female); Garik "Face" Loran, retired intelligence officer (human male); Bhindi Drayson, retired intelligence officer (human female); Jesmin Tainer, Antarian Ranger (human female); Viull "Scut" Gorsat, biofabricator (Yuuzhan Vong male); Stavin Thaal, general (human male); Turman Darra, actor (Clawdite male); Trey Courser, mechanical engineer (human male); Sharr Latt, psychological warfare specialist (human male); Wran Narcassan, sniper (human male); Drikall Bessarah, medic (Devaronian male); Thaymes Fodrick, slicer (human male); Huhunna, warrior (Wookiee female); Wedge Antilles, retired pilot (human male)

SUMMARY · Mathematics professor Voort saBinring receives a surprise visit from Garik "Face" Loran.

LEGACY

467

His old friend needs Voort's strategic and mathematical genius for his newly reconstituted Wraith Squadron. General Maddeus wants the team to confirm whether or not a key Alliance military officer, General Stavin Thaal, is a double agent involved with Moff Lecersen and his conspiracy to gain control of the Imperial Remnant and Alliance governments. Voort agrees to help, joining fellow Wraiths Bhindi Drayson, Jesmin Tainer, the shapeshifting Clawdite Turman Darra, and the well-built engineer Trey Courser. Making Voort particularly uncomfortable are new Wraiths Myri Antilles and Viull "Scut" Gorsat—the former because he does not want to be involved in any action that may risk the life of Wedge's daughter, and the latter because Scut is Yuuzhan Vong. Throughout the assignment, a melancholy Voort thinks back to his Wraith assignments, including a horrible mission during the Yuuzhan Vong War when he had no choice but to kill his best friend, Runt, to save Runt from continued suffering at the hands of the barbaric alien invaders.

The Wraiths conceal parasite droids disguised as blaster ammunition packs into Alliance service via the military base on Vandor 3 in order to glean information regarding Thaal's "extracurricular" activities. The Wraiths also commandeer the Imperial pocket cruiser *Concusser* in an elaborate effort to fake a missive from an Imperial commander attempting to suborn an Alliance officer. General Thaal's reaction to the fake entreaty—ordering an Alliance corvette to attack the *Concusser*—leads Voort to believe Thaal is guilty of *something*. It's too clumsy a move from a seasoned officer such as Thaal, and Voort thinks it's an attempt by Thaal to purposely look incompetent in order to deflect attention from his main goal.

The Wraiths' covert surveillance uncovers secret barracks hidden beneath the surface of Vandor 3 that belong to General Thaal's private army, the Pop-Dogs. They also find leads that Thaal intends to biologically alter his identity. The Wraiths are further surprised to find *another* team of Wraiths assembled by Face—six agents including Sharr Latt, Wran Narcassan, Drikall Bessarah, Thaymes Fodrick, and Huhunna—on a parallel assignment.

The combined Wraith teams leave the barracks under fire from Thaal's Pop-Dogs and hole up at an abandoned observatory on Mount Lyss. The Pop-Dogs call in artillery reinforcements. Bhindi dies in an attack, leaving a distraught Voort to assume command. Scut confronts him, accusing Voort of a depressed fatalism that has poisoned his judgment and left him unfit to lead the team. Voort and Scut eventually settle their differences when Voort understands Scut's hostility comes from disillusionment. The young Yuuzhan Vong, raised by human parents who had past dealings with the Wraiths, was taught to idolize the pilots. Eventually, the Wraiths are saved by the sudden appearance of StealthXs piloted by Wedge Antilles and Tycho Celchu—reinforcements arranged by Myri Antilles. The fighters strafe the artillery emplacements and fly cover for the extraction shuttle.

The Wraiths move their operation to a temporary headquarters at Kuratooine. Voort has pieced together a plausible course of action for Thaal—he believes the dirty officer is setting up his own private force. Voort develops a plan to entrap Thaal. Scut uses his advanced bioengineering knowledge to create a living disguise to be worn by Turman, accessorized with elaborate gems. Turman then makes "first contact" with the Pop-Dogs, demanding to meet with their leader and promising riches in return. Thaal's scientists take the alien into custody and Thaal, intrigued, comes to Kuratooine.

Turman escapes Pop-Dog custody and sheds his alien disguise, extracted from Thaal's base by Jesmin and Huhunna. Trey, disguised as Thaal, kidnaps Thaal's mistress Ledina Chott, a young and popular

LEGACY

SHORT STORY: "Roll of the Dice"

The short story "Roll of the Dice" by author Karen Miller, written as a tie-in to X-Wing: Mercy Kill, was published in Star Wars Insider #135 (July 2012). It stars Myri Antilles, undercover as a gambler aboard the converted freighter Galactic Princess. The ship's proprietor, Captain Oobolo, has worked out a deal with a Besalisk cheater to smuggle information. Myri was to capture imagery of the thief and the handoff, but her covert surveillance equipment—organic crystals embedded into her garish makeup—has been detected and countered. Myri's operation is exposed, but her father, Wedge, helps extricate her. A disguised Wedge leads Myri away from the casinos into the ship's cargo area—filled with a shipment of pungent dwarf banthas—in order to get into the ship's escape pods. Myri and Wedge launch separately to rendezvous with a pursuing Alliance cruiser. The Galactic Princess is surprisingly aggressive, opening fire on the pods, but Myri uses her pod to steer her father's into the waiting cruiser hold, earning his gratitude.

chanteuse. Voort and Myri, disguised and piloting surplus X-wing fighters, tangle with Thaal's E-wing fighters, broadcasting the IDs of Phanan One and Phanan Two as they fly to further sow confusion among Thaal's followers. Voort and Myri land at a crowded square, hoping to draw the attention of the populace, but the crowds are completely distracted by the sudden news that Ledina Chott has been kidnapped. To command the crowd's attention, Voort bribes a band to play loudly, and he doffs his clothing to dance to their music.

Amid this chaos, Thaal is incensed by the bizarre turns of fortune that have plagued him on Kuratooine. A Wraith-commandeered droid emerges from the gawking audience to broadcast a hologram of Ton Phanan (in actuality, Turman in disguise) accusing Thaal of being an imposter. Sure enough, Thaal's current likeness is cosmetic—he has already undergone biological alteration to become his alias, Thadley Biolan. The entire operation has been engineered by Voort not only to trap Thaal, but also to neutralize his proposed disguise.

Thaal is incarcerated. Face confronts General Maddeus, who proves to be an ally of Thaal. Face has figured this out by purposely leaking false information about the resurgent Wraiths through strategic channels—and the word that the late Ton Phanan was leading the group was passed along through a source that could only have come from Maddeus. With Thaal and Maddeus caught, Face reflects on the effectiveness of the Wraiths, and wants to keep the covert and off-the-record group active for future assignments.

APPENDIX A

WORKS IN PUBLICATION ORDER

1976
- *Star Wars: From the Adventures of Luke Skywalker* 180

1978
- *Splinter of the Mind's Eye* 226

1979
- The Han Solo Adventures: *Han Solo at Stars' End* 166
- The Han Solo Adventures: *Han Solo's Revenge* 166

1980
- *The Empire Strikes Back* 234
- The Han Solo Adventures: *Han Solo and the Lost Legacy* 166

1983
- *Return of the Jedi* 248
- The Lando Calrissian Adventures: *Lando Calrissian and the Mindharp of Sharu* 162
- The Lando Calrissian Adventures: *Lando Calrissian and the Flamewind of Oseon* 162
- The Lando Calrissian Adventures: *Lando Calrissian and the Starcave of ThonBoka* 162

1991
- The Thrawn Trilogy: *Heir to the Empire* 303

1992
- The Thrawn Trilogy: *Dark Force Rising* 303

1993
- The Thrawn Trilogy: *The Last Command* 303

1994
- *The Truce at Bakura* 266
- *Star Wars Adventure Journal* #1
    "First Contact" 293
    "A Glimmer of Hope" 282
    "Escape from Balis-Baurgh" 270
    "Breaking Free: The Adventures of Dannen Lifehold" 198
    Star Wars Stories: "Chessa's Doom" 289
- The Jedi Academy Trilogy: *Jedi Search* 314
- *The Courtship of Princess Leia* 296
- *Star Wars Adventure Journal* #2
    "Whispers in the Dark" 282
    "Out of the Cradle" 157
    Star Wars Stories: "Big Quince" 289
- The Jedi Academy Trilogy: *Dark Apprentice* 314
- *Star Wars Adventure Journal* #3
    "Mission to Zila" 302
    "When the Domino Falls" 165
    "Changing the Odds: The Adventures of Dannen Lifehold" 198
    "Droid Trouble" 199
    Star Wars Stories: "Explosive Developments" 289
- The Jedi Academy Trilogy: *Champions of the Force* 314
- *Star Wars Adventure Journal* #4
    "Tinian on Trial" 169
    "Shadows of Darkness" 303
    "The Final Exit" 155
    Star Wars Stories: "Starter's Tale" 289
- *The Crystal Star* 327

1995
- *Star Wars Adventure Journal* #5
    "One of a Kind" 273
    "A Bitter Winter" 214
    "Turning Point" 154
    Star Wars Stories: "Vengeance Strike" 289
- The Corellian Trilogy: *Ambush at Corellia* 336
- *Star Wars Galaxy* #3
    "Lumiya: Dark Star of the Empire" 272
- *Star Wars Adventure Journal* #6
    "To Fight Another Day" 200
    "Finder's Fee" 223
    "Rendezvous with Destiny" 310
    "Kella Rand, Reporting . . ." 290
    "Ringers" 177
- *Children of the Jedi* 319
- Young Jedi Knights: *Heirs to the Force* 357

- The Corellian Trilogy: *Assault at Selonia* 336
- *Star Wars Adventure Journal* #7
    - "Mist Encounter" 132
    - "Missed Chance" 281
    - "Retreat from Coruscant" 312
    - "Passages" 157
- *Tales from the Mos Eisley Cantina*
    - "We Don't Do Weddings: The Band's Tale" 184
    - "A Hunter's Fate: Greedo's Tale" 186
    - "Hammertong: The Tale of the Tonnika Sisters" 186
    - "Play It Again, Figrin D'an: The Tale of Muftak and Kabe" 188
    - "The Sand Tender: The Hammerhead's Tale" 188
    - "Be Still My Heart: The Bartender's Tale" 190
    - "Nightlily: The Lovers' Tale" 190
    - "Empire Blues: The Devaronian's Tale" 190
    - "Swap Meet: The Jawa's Tale" 191
    - "Trade Wins: The Ranat's Tale" 192
    - "When the Desert Wind Turns: The Stormtrooper's Tale" 184
    - "Soup's On: The Pipe Smoker's Tale" 191
    - "At the Crossroads: The Spacer's Tale" 192
    - "Doctor Death: The Tale of Dr. Evazan and Ponda Baba" 210
    - "Drawing the Maps of Peace: The Moisture Farmer's Tale" 189
    - "One Night in the Mos Eisley Cantina: The Tale of the Wolfman and the Lamproid" 262
- *Star Wars Galaxy* #5
    - "Double-Cross on Ord Mantell" 233
- Young Jedi Knights: *Shadow Academy* 358
- The Corellian Trilogy: *Showdown at Centerpoint* 336
- Junior Jedi Knights 1: *The Golden Globe* 350
- *Star Wars Adventure Journal* #8
    - "A Certain Point of View" 199
    - "Uhl Eharl Khoehng" 222
    - "Blaze of Glory" 311
    - "Firepower" 242
- *Darksaber* 322
- Young Jedi Knights: *The Lost Ones* 358

1996
- *Tales from Jabba's Palace*
    - "A Boy and His Monster: The Rancor Keeper's Tale" 251
    - "Taster's Choice: The Tale of Jabba's Chef" 256
    - "That's Entertainment: The Tale of Salacious Crumb" 251
    - "A Time to Mourn, a Time to Dance: Oola's Tale" 252
    - "Let Us Prey: The Whiphid's Tale" 256
    - "Sleight of Hand: The Tale of Mara Jade" 252
    - "And Then There Were Some: The Gamorrean Guard's Tale" 256
    - "Old Friends: Ephant Mon's Tale" 254
    - "Goatgrass: The Tale of Ree-Yees" 257
    - "And the Band Played On: The Band's Tale" 254
    - "Of the Day's Annoyances: Bib Fortuna's Tale" 254
    - "The Great God Quay: The Tale of Barada and the Weequays" 257
    - "A Bad Feeling: The Tale of EV-9D9" 255
    - "A Free Quarren in the Palace: Tessek's Tale" 258
    - "Tongue-Tied: Bubo's Tale" 258
    - "Out of the Closet: The Assassin's Tale" 258
    - "Shaara and the Sarlacc: The Skiff Guard's Tale" 259
    - "A Barve Like That: The Tale of Boba Fett" 261
    - "Skin Deep: The Fat Dancer's Tale" 259
- Junior Jedi Knights 2: *Lyric's World* 350
- X-Wing: *Rogue Squadron* 283
- *Star Wars Galaxy* #6
    - "Hunting the Hunters" 238
- *Star Wars Adventure Journal* #9
    - "Slaying Dragons" 241
    - "Combat Moon" 228
    - "Easy Credits" 273
- Young Jedi Knights: *Lightsabers* 360
- The Black Fleet Crisis Trilogy: *Before the Storm* 329
- Junior Jedi Knights 3: *Promises* 352
- *Shadows of the Empire* 243
- *Shadows of the Empire* (junior novelization) 243
- *Star Wars Adventure Journal* #10
    - "Only Droids Serve the Maker" 214
    - "Do No Harm" 229
    - "Desperate Measures" 242
    - "The Capture of *Imperial Hazard*" 229
- X-Wing: *Wedge's Gamble* 284
- Young Jedi Knights: *Darkest Knight* 361
- *Star Wars Galaxy* #8
    - "Dark Vendetta" 152
- The Black Fleet Crisis Trilogy: *Shield of Lies* 329
- Young Jedi Knights: *Jedi Under Siege* 361
- X-Wing: *The Krytos Trap* 286
- *Star Wars Adventure Journal* #11
    - "Command Decision" 232
    - "Spare Parts" 192
    - "The Most Dangerous Foe" 209
    - "The Longest Fall" 241
- *The New Rebellion* 333
- *Tales of the Bounty Hunters*
    - "Therefore I Am: The Tale of IG-88" 262
    - "Payback: The Tale of Dengar" 260
    - "The Prize Pelt: The Tale of Bossk" 238
    - "Of Possible Futures: The Tale of Zuckuss and 4-LOM" 239
    - "The Last One Standing: The Tale of Boba Fett" 340

1997
- The Black Fleet Crisis Trilogy: *Tyrant's Test* 329
- X-Wing: *The Bacta War* 287
- Galaxy of Fear: *Eaten Alive* 211
- Young Jedi Knights: *Shards of Alderaan* 362
- Dark Forces: *Soldier for the Empire* 169

APPENDIX A · *Works in Publication Order*

- Galaxy of Fear: *City of the Dead* 212
- *Star Wars Galaxy* #10
    - "Sandbound on Tatooine" 201
- *Star Wars Adventure Journal* #12
    - "Side Trip, Part One" 231
    - "Side Trip, Part Two" 231
    - "Betrayal by Knight" 311
    - "Small Favors" 201
    - "Idol Intentions" 230
- Junior Jedi Knights 4: *Anakin's Quest* 352
- Galaxy of Fear: *Planet Plague* 212
- Young Jedi Knights: *Diversity Alliance* 363
- *Star Wars Adventure Journal* #13
    - "Side Trip, Part Three" 231
    - "Side Trip, Part Four" 231
    - "Conflict of Interest" 288
    - "The Last Hand" 230
    - "Day of the Sepulchral Night" 271
    - "The Occupation of Rhamalai" 200
- *Star Wars Galaxy* #11
    - "The Emperor's Trophy" 240
- The Han Solo Trilogy: *The Paradise Snare* 152
- Galaxy of Fear: *The Nightmare Machine* 213
- *Planet of Twilight* 325
- Young Jedi Knights: *Delusions of Grandeur* 363
- Galaxy of Fear: *Ghost of the Jedi* 215
- Junior Jedi Knights 5: *Vader's Fortress* 353
- *Star Wars Galaxy* #12
    - "Priority: X" 221
- *Star Wars Adventure Journal* #14
    - "Murder in Slushtime" 324
    - "The Breath of Gelgelar" 223
    - "No Disintegrations, Please" 312
    - "Crimson Bounty" 228
- The Han Solo Trilogy: *The Hutt Gambit* 155
- Galaxy of Fear: *Army of Terror* 215
- Junior Jedi Knights 6: *Kenobi's Blade* 353
- Young Jedi Knights: *Jedi Bounty* 364
- *Star Wars Adventure Journal* #15
    - "Firestorm" 316
    - "Laughter After Dark" 233
    - "The Great Herdship Heist" 210
    - "Two for One" 334
    - "The Draw" 233
- Galaxy of Fear: *The Brain Spiders* 216
- *Tales from the Empire* 155
- *Specter of the Past* 342

1998
- Young Jedi Knights: *The Emperor's Plague* 365
- Galaxy of Fear: *The Swarm* 216
- X-Wing: *Wraith Squadron* 290
- The Han Solo Trilogy: *Rebel Dawn* 175
- Galaxy of Fear: *Spore* 220
- Dark Forces: *Rebel Agent* 277
- Young Jedi Knights: *Return to Ord Mantell* 365
- *I, Jedi* 318
- Galaxy of Fear: *The Doomsday Ship* 221
- The Bounty Hunter Wars: *The Mandalorian Armor* 264
- *Star Wars* Journal: *The Fight for Justice* 183
- *Star Wars* Journal: *Captive to Evil* 183
- *Star Wars* Journal: *Hero for Hire* 183
- X-Wing: *Iron Fist* 291
- Galaxy of Fear: *Clones* 222
- *Vision of the Future* 342
- Young Jedi Knights: *Trouble on Cloud City* 366
- Galaxy of Fear: *The Hunger* 224
- The Bounty Hunter Wars: *Slave Ship* 264
- Dark Forces: *Jedi Knight* 278
- Young Jedi Knights: *Crisis at Crystal Reef* 366

1999
- X-Wing: *Solo Command* 292
- X-Wing: *Isard's Revenge* 309
- *Star Wars*: Episode I *The Phantom Menace* 48
- *Star Wars*: Episode I *The Phantom Menace* (junior novelization) 48
- Jedi Apprentice 1: *The Rising Force* 30
- Jedi Apprentice 2: *The Dark Rival* 30
- Episode I Journal: *Anakin Skywalker* 50
- Episode I Journal: *Queen Amidala* 50
- The Bounty Hunter Wars: *Hard Merchandise* 264
- Jedi Apprentice 3: *The Hidden Past* 32
- X-Wing: *Starfighters of Adumar* 323
- Jedi Apprentice 4: *The Mark of the Crown* 32
- *Vector Prime* 370
- Jedi Apprentice 5: *The Defenders of the Dead* 33
- *Tales from the New Republic*
    - "Interlude at Darkknell" 172
    - "Jade Solitaire" 335
    - "Gathering Shadows" 271
    - "Hutt and Seek" 298
    - "Simple Tricks" 321

2000
- Dark Tide I: *Onslaught* 374
- Jedi Apprentice 6: *The Uncertain Path* 33
- Episode I Journal: *Darth Maul* 50
- Jedi Apprentice 7: *The Captive Temple* 34
- *Rogue Planet* 56
- Jedi Apprentice 8: *The Day of Reckoning* 34
- Dark Tide II: *Ruin* 374
- Jedi Apprentice 9: *The Fight for Truth* 37
- Agents of Chaos I: *Hero's Trial* 376
- *Star Wars Gamer* #1
    - "The Starfighter Trap" 43
    - "Fair Prey" 211
- Jedi Apprentice 10: *The Shattered Peace* 37
- Agents of Chaos II: *Jedi Eclipse* 376
- *Balance Point* 380
- *Star Wars Gamer* #2
    - "A Credit for Your Thoughts" 270

"The Monster" 42
- Jedi Apprentice 11: *The Deadly Hunter* 38

2001
- *Star Wars Gamer #3*
    "Bane of the Sith" 24
- Jedi Apprentice 12: *The Evil Experiment* 38
- Darth Maul: *Shadow Hunter* 46
- Darth Maul: *Saboteur* 43
- Jedi Apprentice 13: *The Dangerous Rescue* 39
- Edge of Victory I: *Conquest* 383
- *Star Wars Gamer #4*
    "Deep Spoilers" 55
- *Cloak of Deception* 44
- *Star Wars Gamer #5*
    "The Crystal" 367
    "Darkness Shared" 27
- Jedi Apprentice Special Edition: *Deceptions* 55
- Edge of Victory II: *Rebirth* 383
- *Star Wars Gamer #6*
    "Rebel Bass" 165
- Jedi Apprentice 14: *The Ties That Bind* 39
- Jedi Quest: *Path to Truth* 59
- Jedi Apprentice 15: *The Death of Hope* 40
- *Star by Star* 388
- *Recovery* 382
- *Star Wars Gamer #7*
    "Red Sky, Blue Flame" 346
- Jedi Apprentice 16: *The Call to Vengeance* 40

2002
- *Dark Journey* 390
- *The Approaching Storm* 71
- *Star Wars Gamer #8*
    "The Apprentice" 392
    Emissary of the Void, Part 1 386
- Jedi Apprentice 17: *The Only Witness* 41
- Jedi Apprentice 18: *The Threat Within* 42
- *Star Wars Gamer #9*
    Emissary of the Void, Part 2 386
- Enemy Lines I: *Rebel Dream* 393
- Jedi Apprentice Special Edition: *The Followers* 58
- *Star Wars*: Episode II *Attack of the Clones* 76
- *Star Wars*: Episode II *Attack of the Clones* (junior novelization) 76
- *Star Wars Gamer #10*
    Emissary of the Void, Part 3 386
    "Handoff" 272
- Jedi Quest: *The Way of the Apprentice* 60
- Jedi Quest: *The Trail of the Jedi* 64
- Boba Fett 1: *The Fight to Survive* 79
- Enemy Lines II: *Rebel Stand* 393
- *Traitor* 395
- Jedi Quest: *The Dangerous Games* 64
- *Ylesia* 399
- *Star Wars Insider #62*
    Emissary of the Void, Part 4 386
- *Destiny's Way* 396
- Jedi Quest: *The Master of Disguise* 65
- Boba Fett 2: *Crossfire* 81
- *Star Wars Insider #63*
    Emissary of the Void, Part 5 386
- *Star Wars Insider #64*
    Emissary of the Void, Part 6 386

2003
- Jedi Quest: *The School of Fear* 65
- *Star Wars Insider #65*
    "The Pengalan Trade-Off" 97
- "Corphelion Interlude" 299
- *A Forest Apart: A Chewbacca Adventure* 300
- Force Heretic I: *Remnant* 399
- *Star Wars Insider #66*
    "Elusion Illusion: A Tale of the Clone Wars" 80
- *Tatooine Ghost* 300
- Boba Fett 3: *Maze of Deception* 82
- Force Heretic II: *Refugee* 399
- Jedi Quest: *The Shadow Trap* 66
- *Star Wars Insider #67*
    "The Trouble with Squibs" 302
- *Shatterpoint* 101
- Hasbro Short Story Collection
    "Scholastic Presents: Storm Fleet Warnings" 82
    "Del Rey Presents: Equipment" 103
    "*Star Wars Insider* Presents: Duel" 100
- Force Heretic III: *Reunion* 399
- *Star Wars Insider #68*
    "Hero of Cartao: Episode I Hero's Call" 115
- *Star Wars Insider #69*
    "Hero of Cartao: Episode II Hero's Rise" 115
- *Legacy of the Jedi* 82
- *Star Wars Insider #70*
    "Hero of Cartao: Episode III Hero's End" 115
- *The Final Prophecy* 404
- Jedi Quest: *The Moment of Truth* 68
- Boba Fett 4: *Hunted* 97
- *The Unifying Force* 406

2004
- *Star Wars Galaxies: The Ruins of Dantooine* 224
- *Star Wars Insider #73*
    "The League of Spies" 98
- "Judge's Call" 350
- *Survivor's Quest* 354
- *Fool's Bargain* 356
- *Star Wars Insider #74*
    "Pearls in the Sand" 225
- Jedi Quest: *The Changing of the Guard* 68
- Boba Fett 5: *A New Threat* 118
- *Star Wars Insider #75*
    "Or Die Trying" 404
- *The Hive* 87

APPENDIX A · *Works in Publication Order*

- *The Cestus Deception* 85
- *Star Wars Insider #76*
    - "Changing Seasons, Part 1" 87
- *Jedi Quest: The False Peace* 69
- *Medstar I: Battle Surgeons* 112
- *Star Wars Insider #77*
    - "Changing Seasons, Part 2" 87
- *Star Wars: Episode IV A New Hope* (junior novelization) 180
- *Star Wars: Episode V The Empire Strikes Back* (junior novelization) 234
- *Star Wars: Episode VI Return of the Jedi* (junior novelization) 248
- *Medstar II: Jedi Healer* 112
- *Jedi Trial* 89
- *Republic Commando: Hard Contact* 98
- *Jedi Quest: The Final Showdown* 70
- *Star Wars Insider #79*
    - "Death in the Catacombs" 79
- *Yoda: Dark Rendezvous* 116
- *Boba Fett 6: Pursuit* 119

2005

- *Labyrinth of Evil* 119
- *Secrets of the Jedi* 88
- *Star Wars Insider #81*
    - "Omega Squad: Targets" 100
- *Star Wars: Episode III Revenge of the Sith* 124
- *Star Wars: Episode III Revenge of the Sith* (junior novelization) 124
- *Last of the Jedi: The Desperate Mission* 136
- *Vader: The Ultimate Guide*
    - "In His Image" 136
- *The Dark Nest Trilogy I: The Joiner King* 410
- *Star Wars Insider #83*
    - "Medstar: Intermezzo" 113
- *Last of the Jedi: Dark Warning* 138
- *The Dark Nest Trilogy II: The Unseen Queen* 410
- *Dark Lord: The Rise of Darth Vader* 128
- *Last of the Jedi: Underworld* 139
- *The Dark Nest Trilogy III: The Swarm War* 410

2006

- *Star Wars Insider #85*
    - "Two-Edged Sword" 151
- *Outbound Flight* 61
- *Republic Commando: Triple Zero* 104
- *Last of the Jedi: Death on Naboo* 139
- *Star Wars Insider #87*
    - "Odds" 109
- *Legacy of the Jedi/Secrets of the Jedi* omnibus, "The Last One Standing" 133
- *Betrayal* 418
- *Star Wars Insider #88*
    - "Ghosts of the Sith" 139
- *Last of the Jedi: A Tangled Web* 143
- *Boba Fett: A Practical Man* 379
- *Bloodlines* 421
- *Darth Bane: Path of Destruction* 21
- *Last of the Jedi: Return of the Dark Side* 143
- *Tempest* 424

2007

- *Allegiance* 207
- *Exile* 426
- *Last of the Jedi: Secret Weapon* 144
- *Sacrifice* 428
- *Inferno* 431
- *Death Star* 194
- *The Rise and Fall of Darth Vader* 263
- *Last of the Jedi: Against the Empire* 145
- *Republic Commando: True Colors* 109
- *Fury* 432
- *Darth Bane: Rule of Two* 21

2008

- *Last of the Jedi: Master of Deception* 146
- *Revelation* 434
- StarWars.com, "Labor Pains" 11
- *Last of the Jedi: Reckoning* 147
- *Invincible* 435
- StarWars.com, "Precipice" 78
- StarWars.com, "Lando Calrissian: Idiot's Array" 226
- *Coruscant Nights I: Jedi Twilight* 133
- *The Clone Wars* 91
- *The Clone Wars* (junior novelization) 91
- *The Clone Wars*: "Out Foxed" 93
- *The Force Unleashed* 157
- StarWars.com, "Deader than a Triton Moon" 281
- StarWars.com, "Crossroads" 295
- *Coruscant Nights II: Street of Shadows* 141
- *The Life and Legend of Obi-Wan Kenobi* 308
- *Republic Commando: Order 66* 127
- StarWars.com, "Interference" 11
- StarWars.com, "Fists of Ion" 280
- *Millennium Falcon* 443
- *Rebel Force: Target* 203
- *Rebel Force: Hostage* 204
- *The Clone Wars: Wild Space* 95
- *Luke Skywalker and the Shadows of Mindor* 273

2009

- *Coruscant Nights III: Patterns of Force* 149
- *The Clone Wars: Grievous Attacks!* 92
- *Outcast* 445
- *Rebel Force: Renegade* 204
- *The Clone Wars: No Prisoners* 103
- *Lost Tribe of the Sith: Precipice* 5
- *Omen* 448
- *Lost Tribe of the Sith: Skyborn* 5

APPENDIX A · *Works in Publication Order*

- *Imprint* 415
- *Abyss* 450
- *Rebel Force: Firefight* 205
- *A New Hope: The Life of Luke Skywalker* 269
- *The Clone Wars: Secret Missions 1 Breakout Squad* 93
- *Death Troopers* 171
- *Imperial Commando: 501st* 130
- StarWars.com, "Shades of Gray: From the Adventures of Alex Winger" 321
- *Darth Bane: Dynasty of Evil* 21

2010
- *Rebel Force: Trapped* 206
- *Crosscurrent* 438
- *Lost Tribe of the Sith: Paragon* 5
- *Clone Wars Gambit: Stealth* 106
- *Backlash* 452
- StarWars.com, "The Old Republic: Smuggler's Vanguard" 10
- *Lost Tribe of the Sith: Savior* 5
- *The Clone Wars: Bounty Hunter: Boba Fett* 92
- *Rebel Force: Uprising* 208
- *Allies* 455
- *Clone Wars Gambit: Siege* 106
- *The Old Republic: Fatal Alliance* 16
- *The Clone Wars: Secret Missions 2 Curse of the Black Hole Pirates* 93
- *The Force Unleashed II* 157
- *Lost Tribe of the Sith: Purgatory* 5
- StarWars.com, "Knight Errant: Influx" 21
- *The Clone Wars: Defenders of the Republic* 92
- *Vortex* 457
- *Red Harvest* 14

2011
- *Knight Errant* 18
- *Lost Tribe of the Sith: Sentinel* 5
- *The Old Republic: Deceived* 11
- *The Clone Wars: Secret Missions 3 Duel at Shattered Rock* 93
- *Star Wars Insider* #124 "The Third Lesson" 12
- *Star Wars Insider* #125 "First Blood" 449
- *Lost Tribe of the Sith: Pantheon* 5
- *Star Wars Insider* #126 "Buyer's Market" 280
- *Conviction* 459
- *Choices of One* 217
- *Star Wars Insider* #128 "And Leebo Makes Three" 175
- *Ascension* 461
- *Heir to the Empire* 20th Anniversary Edition "Crisis of Faith" 295
- *The Clone Wars: Warriors of the Deep* 92
- *Riptide* 441
- *Star Wars Insider* #129 "A Fair Trade" 440
- *The Old Republic: Revan* 7
- *Shadow Games* 173
- *Star Wars Insider* #130 "The Tenebrous Way" 54
- *Star Wars Insider* Special Edition 2012 "Vader Adrift" 243

2012
- *Darth Maul: Shadow Hunter* 2012 reissue "Restraint" 46
- *Darth Plagueis* 51
- *Star Wars: Episode I The Phantom Menace* 2012 reissue "End Game" 49
- *The Wrath of Darth Maul* 111
- *Star Wars Insider* #131 "Maze Run" 177
- *Lost Tribe of the Sith: Secrets* 5
- *The Clone Wars: Secret Missions 4 Guardians of the Chiss Key* 93
- *Apocalypse* 463
- *Star Wars Insider* #132 "The Guns of Kelrodo-Ai" 151
- *Scourge* 347
- *Star Wars Insider* #133 "Hunting the Gorach" 349
- *Star Wars Insider* #134 "Getaway" 467
- *Lost Tribe of the Sith: The Collected Stories Pandemonium* 5
- *Star Wars Insider* #135 "Roll of the Dice" 469
- *X-Wing: Mercy Kill* 467
- *Star Wars Insider* #136 "Reputation" 70
- *Star Wars Insider* #137 "The Last Battle of Colonel Jace Malcom" 18
- *The Old Republic: Annihilation* 17
- *Star Wars Insider* #138 "Heist" 203
- *Scoundrels* 202

2013
- *The Clone Wars: Darth Maul: Shadow Conspiracy* 92

APPENDIX A · *Works in Publication Order*

APPENDIX B

WORKS BY AUTHOR

ALLEN, ROGER MACBRIDE
- The Corellian Trilogy: *Ambush at Corellia* 336
- The Corellian Trilogy: *Assault at Selonia* 336
- The Corellian Trilogy: *Showdown at Centerpoint* 336

ALLSTON, AARON
- X-Wing: *Wraith Squadron* 290
- X-Wing: *Iron Fist* 291
- X-Wing: *Solo Command* 292
- X-Wing: *Starfighters of Adumar* 323
- *Star Wars Insider* #65, "The Pengalan Trade-Off" 97
- *Star Wars Insider* #73, "The League of Spies" 98
- Enemy Lines I: *Rebel Dream* 393
- Enemy Lines II: *Rebel Stand* 393
- *Betrayal* 418
- *Exile* 426
- *Fury* 432
- *Outcast* 445
- *Backlash* 452
- *Conviction* 459
- X-Wing: *Mercy Kill* 467

ANDERSON, KEVIN J.
- The Jedi Academy Trilogy: *Jedi Search* 314
- The Jedi Academy Trilogy: *Dark Apprentice* 314
- The Jedi Academy Trilogy: *Champions of the Force* 314
- *Darksaber* 322
- *Tales from the Mos Eisley Cantina*, "Swap Meet: The Jawa's Tale" 191
- *Tales from Jabba's Palace*, "A Boy and His Monster: The Rancor Keeper's Tale" 251
- *Tales of the Bounty Hunters*, "Therefore I Am: The Tale of IG-88" 262
- Young Jedi Knights: *Heirs to the Force* (coauthor) 357
- Young Jedi Knights: *Shadow Academy* (coauthor) 358
- Young Jedi Knights: *The Lost Ones* (coauthor) 358
- Young Jedi Knights: *Lightsabers* (coauthor) 360
- Young Jedi Knights: *Darkest Knight* (coauthor) 361
- Young Jedi Knights: *Jedi Under Siege* (coauthor) 361
- Young Jedi Knights: *Shards of Alderaan* (coauthor) 362

- Young Jedi Knights: *Diversity Alliance* (coauthor) 363
- Young Jedi Knights: *Delusions of Grandeur* (coauthor) 363
- Young Jedi Knights: *Jedi Bounty* (coauthor) 364
- Young Jedi Knights: *The Emperor's Plague* (coauthor) 365
- Young Jedi Knights: *Return to Ord Mantell* (coauthor) 365
- Young Jedi Knights: *Trouble on Cloud City* (coauthor) 366
- Young Jedi Knights: *Crisis at Crystal Reef* (coauthor) 366
- *Star Wars Adventure Journal* #15, "Firestorm" 316
- *Star Wars Gamer* #3, "Bane of the Sith" 24

BALSAMO, PAUL
- *Star Wars Adventure Journal* #1, "Escape from Balis-Baurgh" 270

BARNES, STEVEN
- *The Hive* 87
- *The Cestus Deception* 85

BARR, MIKE W.
- *Star Wars Insider* #79, "Death in the Catacombs" 79

BEAR, GREG
- *Rogue Planet* 56

BEASON, DOUG
- *Tales from the Mos Eisley Cantina*, "When the Desert Wind Turns: The Stormtrooper's Tale" 184

BELL, M. SHAYNE
- *Tales from the Mos Eisley Cantina*, "Drawing the Maps of Peace: The Moisture Farmer's Tale" 189
- *Tales from Jabba's Palace*, "Of the Day's Annoyances: Bib Fortuna's Tale" 254
- *Tales of the Bounty Hunters*, "Of Possible Futures: The Tale of Zuckuss and 4-LOM" 239

BETANCOURT, JOHN GREGORY
- *Tales from Jabba's Palace*, "And the Band Played On: The Band's Tale" 254

BISCHOFF, DAVID
- *Tales from the Mos Eisley Cantina*, "Be Still My Heart: The Bartender's Tale" 190

BISSON, TERRY
- Boba Fett 1: *The Fight to Survive* 79
- Boba Fett 2: *Crossfire* 81

BLACKMAN, HADEN
- *Star Wars Galaxies: The Ruins of Dantooine* 224

BOHNHOFF, MAYA KAATHRYN
- *Star Wars Insider* #128, "And Leebo Makes Three" (coauthor) 175
- *Shadow Games* (coauthor) 173

BROOKS, TERRY
- *Star Wars*: Episode I *The Phantom Menace* 48

BUDZ, MARK
- *Tales from Jabba's Palace*, "Let Us Prey: The Whiphid's Tale" (coauthor) 256

BURDETTE, KATHY
- *Tales from the New Republic*, "Gathering Shadows" 271

BURNS, LAURIE
- *Star Wars Adventure Journal* #6, "Ringers" 177
- *Star Wars Adventure Journal* #6, "Kella Rand, Reporting . . ." 290
- *Star Wars Adventure Journal* #7, "Retreat from Coruscant" 312
- *Star Wars Adventure Journal* #13, "Conflict of Interest" 288

CASSIDY, CHRIS
- *Tales from the New Republic*, "Simple Tricks" (coauthor) 321
- *Tales from the New Republic*, "Hutt and Seek" (coauthor) 298
- *Star Wars Gamer* #2, "A Credit for Your Thoughts" (coauthor) 270
- StarWars.com, "Precipice" 78

CERASI, CHRISTOPHER
- StarWars.com, "Crossroads" 295

CHESTNEY, ROBERT
- StarWars.com, "The Old Republic: Smuggler's Vanguard" 10

CRAGG, DAN
- *Jedi Trial* (coauthor) 89

CRISPIN, A. C.
- *Tales from the Mos Eisley Cantina*, "Play It Again, Figrin D'an: The Tale of Muftak and Kabe" 188
- *Tales from Jabba's Palace*, "Skin Deep: The Fat Dancer's Tale" 259
- The Han Solo Trilogy: *The Paradise Snare* 152
- The Han Solo Trilogy: *The Hutt Gambit* 155
- The Han Solo Trilogy: *Rebel Dawn* 175

CUNNINGHAM, ELAINE
- *Dark Journey* 390
- *Star Wars Gamer* #5, "The Crystal" 367
- *Star Wars Gamer* #7, "Red Sky, Blue Flame" 346
- *Star Wars Gamer* #8, "The Apprentice" 392

DALEY, BRIAN
- *Han Solo at Stars' End* 166
- *Han Solo's Revenge* 166
- *Han Solo and the Lost Legacy* 166

DANEHY-OAKES, DAN'L
- *Tales from Jabba's Palace*, "Shaara and the Sarlacc: The Skiff Guard's Tale" 259

DANNER, PAUL
- *Star Wars Adventure Journal* #5, "One of a Kind" 273
- *Star Wars Adventure Journal* #9, "Easy Credits" 273
- *Star Wars Adventure Journal* #12, "Small Favors" 201
- *Star Wars Adventure Journal* #13, "The Last Hand" 230
- *Star Wars Adventure Journal* #14, "No Disintegrations, Please" 312
- *Star Wars Adventure Journal* #15, "Two for One" 334

DENNING, TROY
- *Star by Star* 388
- *Recovery* 382
- *A Forest Apart: A Chewbacca Adventure* 300
- *Tatooine Ghost* 300
- "Corphelion Interlude" 299
- *Star Wars Insider* #67, "The Trouble with Squibs" 302
- The Dark Nest Trilogy I: *The Joiner King* 410
- The Dark Nest Trilogy II: *The Unseen Queen* 410
- The Dark Nest Trilogy III: *The Swarm War* 410
- *Tempest* 424
- *Inferno* 431
- *Invincible* 435
- *Abyss* 450
- *Vortex* 457
- *Apocalypse* 463

DIETZ, WILLIAM C.
- Dark Forces: *Soldier for the Empire* 169
- Dark Forces: *Rebel Agent* 277
- Dark Forces: *Jedi Knight* 278

DIX, SHANE
- Force Heretic I: *Remnant* (coauthor) 399
- Force Heretic II: *Refugee* (coauthor) 399
- Force Heretic III: *Reunion* (coauthor) 399
- *Star Wars Insider* #75, "Or Die Trying" (coauthor) 404

EFFINGER, GEORGE ALEC
- *Tales from Jabba's Palace*, "The Great God Quay: The Tale of Barada and the Weequays" 257

ENDOM, ERIN
- *Star Wars Adventure Journal* #10, "Do No Harm" 229

ERDELAC, ED
- StarWars.com, "Fists of Ion" 280

FITCH, MARINA
- *Tales from Jabba's Palace*, "Let Us Prey: The Whiphid's Tale" (coauthor) 256

FLINT, KENNETH C.
- *Tales from the Mos Eisley Cantina*, "Doctor Death: The Tale of Dr. Evazan and Ponda Baba" 210
- *Tales from Jabba's Palace*, "Old Friends: Ephant Mon's Tale" 254

FOSTER, ALAN DEAN
- *Star Wars: From the Adventures of Luke Skywalker* (uncredited) 180
- *Splinter of the Mind's Eye* 226
- *The Approaching Storm* 71

FREED, ALEXANDER
- *Star Wars Insider* #137, "The Last Battle of Colonel Jace Malcom" 18

FRIESNER, ESTHER M.
- *Tales from Jabba's Palace*, "That's Entertainment: The Tale of Salacious Crumb" 251

FRY, JASON
- StarWars.com, "Deader than a Triton Moon" 281
- *The Clone Wars: Bounty Hunter: Boba Fett* 92
- *Star Wars Insider* #132, "The Guns of Kelrodo-Ai" 151
- *The Clone Wars: Darth Maul: Shadow Conspiracy* 92

GLUT, DONALD F.
- *The Empire Strikes Back* 234

GOLDEN, CHRISTIE
- *Imprint* 415
- *Omen* 448
- *Star Wars Insider* #125, "First Blood" 449
- *Allies* 455
- *Ascension* 461
- *Star Wars Insider* #134, "Getaway" 467

GOLDEN, CHRISTOPHER
- *Shadows of the Empire* (juvenile novel) 243

GOLLEDGE, CAROLYN
- *Star Wars Adventure Journal* #8, "Firepower" 242

GRUBB, JEFF
- *Scourge* 347
- *Star Wars Insider* #133, "Hunting the Gorach" 349

HAMBLY, BARBARA
- *Children of the Jedi* 319
- *Tales from the Mos Eisley Cantina*, "Nightlily: The Lovers' Tale" 190
- *Tales from Jabba's Palace*, "Taster's Choice: The Tale of Jabba's Chef" 256
- *Planet of Twilight* 325
- *Star Wars Adventure Journal* #14, "Murder in Slushtime" 324

HAND, ELIZABETH
- *Boba Fett 3: Maze of Deception* 82
- *Boba Fett 4: Hunted* 97
- *Boba Fett 5: A New Threat* 118
- *Boba Fett 6: Pursuit* 119

HANDLEY, RICH
- *Star Wars Adventure Journal* #14, "Crimson Bounty" (coauthor) 228
- StarWars.com, "Lando Calrissian: Idiot's Array" 226

HIDALGO, PABLO
- *Star Wars Adventure Journal* #11, "Spare Parts" 192

JACKSON, PATRICIA A.
- *Star Wars Adventure Journal* #2, "Out of the Cradle" 157
- *Star Wars Adventure Journal* #3, "When the Domino Falls" 165
- *Star Wars Adventure Journal* #4, "The Final Exit" 155
- *Star Wars Adventure Journal* #5, "A Bitter Winter" 214
- *Star Wars Adventure Journal* #8, "Uhl Eharl Khoehng" 222
- *Star Wars Adventure Journal* #11, "The Longest Fall" 241
- *Star Wars Adventure Journal* #12, "Idol Intentions" 230
- *Star Wars Adventure Journal* #12, "Betrayal by Knight" (coauthor) 311
- *Star Wars Adventure Journal* #15, "Laughter After Dark" 233

JETER, K. W.
- *The Bounty Hunter Wars: The Mandalorian Armor* 264
- *The Bounty Hunter Wars: Slave Ship* 264
- *The Bounty Hunter Wars: Hard Merchandise* 264

KAHN, JAMES
- *Return of the Jedi* 248

KARPYSHYN, DREW
- *Darth Bane: Path of Destruction* 21
- *Darth Bane: Rule of Two* 21

- Darth Bane: *Dynasty of Evil* 21
- The Old Republic: *Revan* 7
- The Old Republic: *Annihilation* 17

KEMP, PAUL S.
- The Old Republic: *Deceived* 11
- *Star Wars Insider* #124, "The Third Lesson" 12
- *Star Wars Insider* #129, "A Fair Trade" 440
- *Crosscurrent* 438
- *Riptide* 441

KEYES, GREG
- Edge of Victory I: *Conquest* 383
- Edge of Victory II: *Rebirth* 383
- *Star Wars Gamer* #8, *Emissary of the Void*, Part 1 386
- *Star Wars Gamer* #9, *Emissary of the Void*, Part 2 386
- *Star Wars Gamer* #10, *Emissary of the Void*, Part 3 386
- *Star Wars Insider* #62, *Emissary of the Void*, Part 4 386
- *Star Wars Insider* #63, *Emissary of the Void*, Part 5 386
- *Star Wars Insider* #64, *Emissary of the Void*, Part 6 386
- *The Final Prophecy* 404

KUBE-MCDOWELL, MICHAEL P.
- The Black Fleet Crisis Trilogy: *Before the Storm* 329
- The Black Fleet Crisis Trilogy: *Shield of Lies* 329
- The Black Fleet Crisis Trilogy: *Tyrant's Test* 329

LUCAS, GEORGE
- *Star Wars: From the Adventures of Luke Skywalker* (ghostwritten) 180

LUCENO, JAMES
- Agents of Chaos I: *Hero's Trial* 376
- Agents of Chaos II: *Jedi Eclipse* 376
- *Cloak of Deception* 44
- Darth Maul: *Saboteur* 43
- *The Unifying Force* 406
- *Labyrinth of Evil* 119
- *Dark Lord: The Rise of Darth Vader* 128
- *Millennium Falcon* 443
- Darth Maul: *Shadow Hunter* 2012 reissue, "Restraint" 46
- *Star Wars*: Episode I *The Phantom Menace* 2012 reissue, "End Game" 49
- *Darth Plagueis* 51

MALLETT, DARYL F.
- *Tales from Jabba's Palace*, "Tongue-Tied: Bubo's Tale" 258

MARMELL, ARI
- *Star Wars Insider* #136, "Reputation" 70

MARRON, DAVE
- *Star Wars Adventure Journal* #1, "Breaking Free: The Adventures of Dannen Lifehold" 198
- *Star Wars Adventure Journal* #3, "Changing the Odds: The Adventures of Dannen Lifehold" 198

MAYERS, NORA
- *Star Wars Adventure Journal* #10, "The Capture of *Imperial Hazard*" 229

MCINTYRE, VONDA M.
- *The Crystal Star* 327

MIKAELIAN, MICHAEL
- *Star Wars Galaxy* #3, "Lumiya: Dark Star of the Empire" 272
- *Star Wars Galaxy* #5, "Double-Cross on Ord Mantell" 233

MILLER, JOHN JACKSON
- StarWars.com, "Labor Pains" 11
- StarWars.com, "Interference" 11
- StarWars.com, "Knight Errant: Influx" 21
- *Knight Errant* 18
- Lost Tribe of the Sith: *Precipice* 5
- Lost Tribe of the Sith: *Skyborn* 5
- Lost Tribe of the Sith: *Paragon* 5
- Lost Tribe of the Sith: *Savior* 5
- Lost Tribe of the Sith: *Purgatory* 5
- Lost Tribe of the Sith: *Sentinel* 5
- Lost Tribe of the Sith: *Pantheon* 5
- Lost Tribe of the Sith: *Secrets* 5
- *Lost Tribe of the Sith: The Collected Stories, Pandemonium* 5

MILLER, KAREN
- The Clone Wars: *Wild Space* 95
- Clone Wars Gambit: *Stealth* 106
- Clone Wars Gambit: *Siege* 106
- *Star Wars Insider* #135, "Roll of the Dice" 469

MILLER, STEVE
- *Star Wars Gamer* #1, "The Starfighter Trap" 43

MOESTA, REBECCA
- *Tales from the Mos Eisley Cantina*, "Trade Wins: The Ranat's Tale" 192
- Junior Jedi Knights 4: *Anakin's Quest* 352
- Junior Jedi Knights 5: *Vader's Fortress* 353
- Junior Jedi Knights 6: *Kenobi's Blade* 353
- Young Jedi Knights: *Heirs to the Force* (coauthor) 357
- Young Jedi Knights: *Shadow Academy* (coauthor) 358
- Young Jedi Knights: *The Lost Ones* (coauthor) 358
- Young Jedi Knights: *Lightsabers* (coauthor) 360
- Young Jedi Knights: *Darkest Knight* (coauthor) 361
- Young Jedi Knights: *Jedi Under Siege* (coauthor) 361
- Young Jedi Knights: *Shards of Alderaan* (coauthor) 362
- Young Jedi Knights: *Diversity Alliance* (coauthor) 363
- Young Jedi Knights: *Delusions of Grandeur* (coauthor) 363
- Young Jedi Knights: *Jedi Bounty* (coauthor) 364
- Young Jedi Knights: *The Emperor's Plague* (coauthor) 365
- Young Jedi Knights: *Return to Ord Mantell* (coauthor) 365

- Young Jedi Knights: *Trouble on Cloud City* (coauthor) 366
- Young Jedi Knights: *Crisis at Crystal Reef* (coauthor) 366

MONTGOMERY, J. D.
- *Tales from Jabba's Palace*, "A Barve Like That: The Tale of Boba Fett" 261

MORAN, DANIEL KEYES
- *Tales from the Mos Eisley Cantina*, "Empire Blues: The Devaronian's Tale" 190
- *Tales of the Bounty Hunters*, "The Last One Standing: The Tale of Boba Fett" 340

NEWCOMB, CHARLENE
- *Star Wars Adventure Journal* #1, "A Glimmer of Hope" 282
- *Star Wars Adventure Journal* #2, "Whispers in the Dark" 282
- *Star Wars Adventure Journal* #3, "Mission to Zila" 302
- *Star Wars Adventure Journal* #4, "Shadows of Darkness" 303
- *Star Wars Adventure Journal* #5, "Turning Point" 154
- *Star Wars Adventure Journal* #6, "Rendezvous with Destiny" 310
- *Star Wars Adventure Journal* #7, "Passages" 157
- *Star Wars Adventure Journal* #8, "A Certain Point of View" 199
- *Star Wars Adventure Journal* #12, "Betrayal by Knight" (coauthor) 311
- *Star Wars Adventure Journal* #14, "Crimson Bounty" (coauthor) 228
- StarWars.com, "Shades of Gray: From the Adventures of Alex Winger" 321

OLTION, JERRY
- *Tales from the Mos Eisley Cantina*, "At the Crossroads: The Spacer's Tale" 192

PAHL, TISH
- *Tales from the New Republic*, "Hutt and Seek" (coauthor) 298
- *Tales from the New Republic*, "Simple Tricks" (coauthor) 321
- *Star Wars Gamer* #2, "A Credit for Your Thoughts" (coauthor) 270

PEEL, JON
- *Star Wars Journal: The Fight for Justice* 183

PERRY, STEVE
- *Shadows of the Empire* 243
- Medstar I: *Battle Surgeons* (coauthor) 112
- *Star Wars Insider* #83, "Medstar: Intermezzo" (coauthor) 113
- Medstar II: *Jedi Healer* (coauthor) 112
- *Death Star* (coauthor) 194

PHILLIPS, ANGELA
- *Star Wars Adventure Journal* #9, "Slaying Dragons" 241

- *Star Wars Adventure Journal* #11, "The Most Dangerous Foe" 209
- *Star Wars Adventure Journal* #15, "The Draw" 233

RABE, JEAN
- *Star Wars Adventure Journal* #13, "Day of the Sepulchral Night" 271
- *Star Wars Adventure Journal* #14, "The Breath of Gelgelar" 223

REAVES, MICHAEL
- Darth Maul: *Shadow Hunter* 46
- Medstar I: *Battle Surgeons* (coauthor) 112
- *Star Wars Insider* #83, "Medstar: Intermezzo" (coauthor) 113
- Medstar II: *Jedi Healer* (coauthor) 112
- Coruscant Nights I: *Jedi Twilight* 133
- Coruscant Nights II: *Street of Shadows* 141
- Coruscant Nights III: *Patterns of Force* 149
- *Death Star* (coauthor) 194
- *Star Wars Insider* #128, "And Leebo Makes Three" (coauthor) 175
- *Shadow Games* (coauthor) 173

REEVES-STEVENS, JUDITH and GARFIELD
- *Tales from the Mos Eisley Cantina*, "One Night in the Mos Eisley Cantina: The Tale of the Wolfman and the Lamproid" 262
- *Tales from Jabba's Palace*, "A Bad Feeling: The Tale of EV-9D9" 255

RICHARDSON, NANCY
- Junior Jedi Knights 1: *The Golden Globe* 350
- Junior Jedi Knights 2: *Lyric's World* 350
- Junior Jedi Knights 3: *Promises* 352

ROBERSON, JENNIFER
- *Tales from the Mos Eisley Cantina*, "Soup's On: The Pipe Smoker's Tale" 191
- *Tales from Jabba's Palace*, "Out of the Closet: The Assassin's Tale" 258

RUSCH, KRISTINE KATHRYN
- *The New Rebellion* 333

RUSSO, ANTHONY P.
- *Star Wars Adventure Journal* #8, "Blaze of Glory" 311

SALVATORE, R. A.
- *Vector Prime* 370
- *Star Wars*: Episode II *Attack of the Clones* 76

SCHREIBER, JOE
- *Death Troopers* 171
- *Red Harvest* 14

SCHWEIGHOFER, PETER
- *Star Wars Adventure Journal* #1, "Chessa's Doom" 289
- *Star Wars Adventure Journal* #2, "Big Quince" 289
- *Star Wars Adventure Journal* #3, "Explosive Developments" 289
- *Star Wars Adventure Journal* #4, "Starter's Tale" 289
- *Star Wars Adventure Journal* #5, "Vengeance Strike" 289
- *Star Wars Adventure Journal* #6, "Finder's Fee" 223
- *Star Wars Galaxy* #10, "Sandbound on Tatooine" 201
- *Star Wars Galaxy* #11, "The Emperor's Trophy" 240

SHERMAN, DAVE
- *Jedi Trial* (coauthor) 89

SLAVICSEK, BILL
- *Star Wars Gamer* #5, "Darkness Shared" 27

SMITH, BILL
- *Star Wars Galaxy* #6, "Hunting the Hunters" 238

SMITH, L. NEIL
- *Lando Calrissian and the Mindharp of Sharu* 162
- *Lando Calrissian and the Flamewind of Oseon* 162
- *Lando Calrissian and the Starcave of ThonBoka* 162

SPERATI, CHUCK
- *Star Wars Adventure Journal* #3, "Droid Trouble" 199

STACKPOLE, MICHAEL A.
- X-Wing: *Rogue Squadron* 283
- X-Wing: *Wedge's Gamble* 284
- X-Wing: *The Krytos Trap* 286
- X-Wing: *The Bacta War* 287
- *Star Wars Adventure Journal* #7, "Missed Chance" 281
- *Star Wars Adventure Journal* #12, "Side Trip, Part Two" 231
- *Star Wars Adventure Journal* #13, "Side Trip, Part Three" 231
- *I, Jedi* 318
- X-Wing: *Isard's Revenge* 309
- *Tales from the New Republic:* "Interlude at Darkknell, Part 2" 172
- *Tales from the New Republic:* "Interlude at Darkknell, Part 3" 172
- Dark Tide I: *Onslaught* 374
- Dark Tide II: *Ruin* 374
- *Star Wars Insider* #66, "Elusion Illusion: A Tale of the Clone Wars" 80

STEWART, SEAN
- *Yoda: Dark Rendezvous* 116

STOVER, MATTHEW
- *Traitor* 395
- *Shatterpoint* 101
- Hasbro Short Story Collection, "Del Rey Presents: Equipment" 103

- *Star Wars*: Episode III *Revenge of the Sith* 124
- *Luke Skywalker and the Shadows of Mindor* 273
- *Star Wars Insider* #130, "The Tenebrous Way" 54

STRASSER, TODD
- Episode I Journal: *Anakin Skywalker* 50

STRAYTON, GEORGE R.
- *Star Wars Galaxy* #12, "Priority: X" 221

TAUSCHER, DONNA
- *Star Wars* Journal: *Hero for Hire* 183

TRAUTMANN, ERIC
- *Star Wars Galaxy* #8, "Dark Vendetta" 152

TRAVISS, KAREN
- Republic Commando: *Hard Contact* 98
- *Star Wars Insider* #81, "Omega Squad: Targets" 100
- *Vader: The Ultimate Guide*, "In His Image" 136
- *Star Wars Insider* #85, "Two-Edged Sword" 151
- Republic Commando: *Triple Zero* 104
- *Star Wars Insider* #87, "Odds" 109
- Republic Commando: *True Colors* 109
- *Boba Fett: A Practical Man* 379
- *Bloodlines* 421
- *Sacrifice* 428
- *Revelation* 434
- *The Clone Wars* 91
- Republic Commando: *Order 66* 127
- The Clone Wars: *No Prisoners* 103
- Imperial Commando: *501st* 130

TYERS, KATHY
- *The Truce at Bakura* 266
- *Star Wars Adventure Journal* #4, "Tinian on Trial" 169
- *Tales from the Mos Eisley Cantina*, "We Don't Do Weddings: The Band's Tale" 184
- *Tales from Jabba's Palace*, "A Time to Mourn, a Time to Dance: Oola's Tale" 252
- *Star Wars Adventure Journal* #6, "To Fight Another Day" 200
- *Star Wars Adventure Journal* #10, "Only Droids Serve the Maker" 214
- *Tales of the Bounty Hunters*, "The Prize Pelt: The Tale of Bossk" 238
- *Balance Point* 380
- *Star Wars Gamer* #6, "Rebel Bass" 165

VALOIS, ROB
- The Clone Wars: *Grievous Attacks!* (coauthor) 92
- The Clone Wars: *Out Foxed* 92
- The Clone Wars: *Defenders of the Republic* 92
- The Clone Wars: *Warriors of the Deep* 93

VEITCH, MARTHA
- *Tales from the Mos Eisley Cantina*, "A Hunter's Fate: Greedo's Tale" (coauthor) 186

VEITCH, TOM
- *Tales from the Mos Eisley Cantina*, "A Hunter's Fate: Greedo's Tale" (coauthor) 186

WALLACE, DANIEL
- *Star Wars Adventure Journal* #15, "The Great Herdship Heist" 210
- *Star Wars Gamer* #1, "Fair Prey" 211
- *Star Wars Gamer* #2, "The Monster" 42

WASSERMAN, VERONICA
- The Clone Wars: *Grievous Attacks!* (coauthor) 92

WATKINS, M. H.
- *Star Wars Adventure Journal* #13, "The Occupation of Rhamalai" 200

WATSON, JUDE
- *Star Wars* Journal: *Captive to Evil* 183
- Episode I Journal: *Queen Amidala* 50
- Jedi Apprentice: *The Dark Rival* 30
- Jedi Apprentice: *The Hidden Past* 32
- Jedi Apprentice: *The Mark of the Crown* 32
- Jedi Apprentice: *The Defenders of the Dead* 33
- Jedi Apprentice: *The Uncertain Path* 33
- Episode I Journal: *Darth Maul* 50
- Jedi Apprentice: *The Captive Temple* 34
- Jedi Apprentice: *The Day of Reckoning* 34
- Jedi Apprentice: *The Fight for Truth* 37
- Jedi Apprentice: *The Shattered Peace* 37
- Jedi Apprentice: *The Deadly Hunter* 38
- Jedi Apprentice: *The Evil Experiment* 38
- Jedi Apprentice: *The Dangerous Rescue* 39
- Jedi Apprentice Special Edition: *Deceptions* 55
- Jedi Apprentice: *The Ties That Bind* 39
- Jedi Quest: *Path to Truth* 59
- Jedi Apprentice: *The Death of Hope* 40
- Jedi Apprentice: *The Call to Vengeance* 40
- Jedi Apprentice: *The Only Witness* 41
- Jedi Apprentice: *The Threat Within* 42
- Jedi Apprentice Special Edition: *The Followers* 58
- Jedi Quest: *The Way of the Apprentice* 60
- Jedi Quest: *The Trail of the Jedi* 64
- Jedi Quest: *The Dangerous Games* 64
- Jedi Quest: *The Master of Disguise* 65
- Jedi Quest: *The School of Fear* 65
- Jedi Quest: *The Shadow Trap* 66
- Hasbro Short Story Collection, "Scholastic Presents: Storm Fleet Warnings" 82
- Jedi Quest: *The Moment of Truth* 68
- *Legacy of the Jedi* 82
- Jedi Quest: *The Changing of the Guard* 68
- Jedi Quest: *The False Peace* 69
- Jedi Quest: *The Final Showdown* 70
- *Secrets of the Jedi* 88
- Last of the Jedi: *The Desperate Mission* 136
- Last of the Jedi: *Dark Warning* 138
- Last of the Jedi: *Underworld* 139
- Last of the Jedi: *Death on Naboo* 139
- *Legacy of the Jedi/Secrets of the Jedi* omnibus, "The Last One Standing" 133
- *Star Wars Insider* #88, "Ghosts of the Sith" 139
- Last of the Jedi: *A Tangled Web* 143
- Last of the Jedi: *Return of the Dark Side* 143
- Last of the Jedi: *Secret Weapon* 144
- Last of the Jedi: *Against the Empire* 145
- Last of the Jedi: *Master of Deception* 146
- Last of the Jedi: *Reckoning* 147

WEST, TRACEY
- *The Clone Wars* (junior novelization) 91
- The Clone Wars: *Grievous Attacks!* (coauthor) 92

WHEELER, ALEX
- Rebel Force: *Target* 203
- Rebel Force: *Hostage* 204
- Rebel Force: *Renegade* 204
- Rebel Force: *Firefight* 205
- Rebel Force: *Trapped* 206
- Rebel Force: *Uprising* 208

WHEELER, DEBORAH
- *Tales from Jabba's Palace*, "Goatgrass: The Tale of Ree-Yees" 257

WHITMAN, JOHN
- *Star Wars Adventure Journal* #9, "Combat Moon" 228
- Galaxy of Fear: *Eaten Alive* 211
- Galaxy of Fear: *City of the Dead* 212
- Galaxy of Fear: *Planet Plague* 212
- Galaxy of Fear: *The Nightmare Machine* 213
- Galaxy of Fear: *Ghost of the Jedi* 215
- Galaxy of Fear: *Army of Terror* 215
- Galaxy of Fear: *The Brain Spiders* 216
- Galaxy of Fear: *The Swarm* 216
- Galaxy of Fear: *Spore* 220
- Galaxy of Fear: *The Doomsday Ship* 221
- Galaxy of Fear: *Clones* 222
- Galaxy of Fear: *The Hunger* 224

WHITNEY-ROBINSON, VORONICA
- *Star Wars Galaxies: The Ruins of Dantooine* (coauthor) 224
- *Star Wars Insider* #74, "Pearls in the Sand" 225

WILLIAMS, DAVID J.
- *Star Wars Insider* #131, "Maze Run" (coauthor) 177

WILLIAMS, MARK S.
- *Star Wars Insider* #131, "Maze Run" (coauthor) 177

WILLIAMS, SEAN
- Force Heretic I: *Remnant* (coauthor) 399
- Force Heretic II: *Refugee* (coauthor) 399
- Force Heretic III: *Reunion* (coauthor) 399
- *Star Wars Insider* #75, "Or Die Trying" (coauthor) 404
- *The Force Unleashed* 157
- The Old Republic: *Fatal Alliance* 16
- *The Force Unleashed II* 157

WILLIAMS, WALTER JON
- *Ylesia* 399
- *Destiny's Way* 396

WINDHAM, RYDER
- *Star Wars Gamer* #4, "Deep Spoilers" 55
- *Star Wars*: Episode IV *A New Hope* (junior novelization) 180
- *Star Wars*: Episode V *The Empire Strikes Back* (junior novelization) 234
- *Star Wars*: Episode VI *Return of the Jedi* (junior novelization) 248
- *The Rise and Fall of Darth Vader* 263
- *The Life and Legend of Obi-Wan Kenobi* 308
- The Clone Wars: Secret Missions 1 *Breakout Squad* 93
- *A New Hope: The Life of Luke Skywalker* 269
- The Clone Wars: Secret Missions 2 *Curse of the Black Hole Pirates* 93
- The Clone Wars: Secret Missions 3 *Duel at Shattered Rock* 93
- *Star Wars Insider Special Edition 2012*, "Vader Adrift" 243
- *The Wrath of Darth Maul* 111
- The Clone Wars: Secret Missions 4 *Guardians of the Chiss Key* 93

WOLVERTON, DAVE
- *The Courtship of Princess Leia* 296
- *Tales from the Mos Eisley Cantina*, "The Sand Tender: The Hammerhead's Tale" 188
- *Tales from Jabba's Palace*, "A Free Quarren in the Palace: Tessek's Tale" 258
- *Tales of the Bounty Hunters*, "Payback: The Tale of Dengar" 260
- Jedi Apprentice: *The Rising Force* 30

WREDE, PATRICIA C.
- *Star Wars*: Episode I *The Phantom Menace* (junior novelization) 48
- *Star Wars*: Episode II *Attack of the Clones* (junior novelization) 76

- *Star Wars*: Episode III *Revenge of the Sith* (junior novelization) 124

WU, WILLIAM F.
- *Tales from Jabba's Palace*, "And Then There Were Some: The Gamorrean Guard's Tale" 256

ZAHN, TIMOTHY
- The Thrawn Trilogy: *Heir to the Empire* 303
- The Thrawn Trilogy: *Dark Force Rising* 303
- The Thrawn Trilogy: *The Last Command* 303
- *Star Wars Adventure Journal* #1, "First Contact" 293
- *Star Wars Adventure Journal* #7, "Mist Encounter" 132
- *Tales from the Mos Eisley Cantina*, "Hammertong: The Tale of the Tonnika Sisters" 186
- *Tales from Jabba's Palace*, "Sleight of Hand: The Tale of Mara Jade" 252
- *Star Wars Adventure Journal* #11, "Command Decision" 232
- *Star Wars Adventure Journal* #12, "Side Trip, Part One" 231
- *Star Wars Adventure Journal* #13, "Side Trip, Part Four" 231
- *Specter of the Past* 342
- *Vision of the Future* 342
- *Tales from the New Republic:* "Interlude at Darkknell, Part 1" 172
- *Tales from the New Republic:* "Interlude at Darkknell, Part 4" 172
- *Tales from the New Republic*, "Jade Solitaire" 335
- *Star Wars Gamer* #10, "Handoff" 272
- Hasbro Short Story Collection, "*Star Wars Insider* Presents: Duel" 100
- *Star Wars Insider* #68, "Hero of Cartao: Episode I Hero's Call" 115
- *Star Wars Insider* #69, "Hero of Cartao: Episode II Hero's Rise" 115
- *Star Wars Insider* #70, "Hero of Cartao: Episode III Hero's End" 115
- Delreybooks.com, "Judge's Call" 350
- *Survivor's Quest* 354
- *Fool's Bargain* 356
- *Star Wars Insider* #76, "Changing Seasons, Part 1" 87
- *Star Wars Insider* #77, "Changing Seasons, Part 2" 87
- *Outbound Flight* 61
- *Allegiance* 207
- *Star Wars Insider* #126, "Buyer's Market" 280
- *Choices of One* 217
- *Heir to the Empire* 20th Anniversary Edition, "Crisis of Faith" 295
- *Star Wars Insider* #138, "Heist" 203
- *Scoundrels* 202

ACKNOWLEDGMENTS

A BOOK LIKE THIS does not come together overnight—it's the result of over thirty years of devotion to a fictional universe.

Special thanks to Del Rey editor Erich Schoeneweiss for his direction, enthusiasm, and, especially, patience over a huge project that kept growing. Thanks to Shelly Shapiro, Frank Parisi, and Keith Clayton at Del Rey for always including me. Thanks to Nancy Delia and Laura Jorstad for crossing all the t's and dotting all the i's. Thanks to Tom "Darth Internous" Hoeler for his research and reference skills. Thanks to the fantastic designers Simon Sullivan and Scott Biel, and to Paul Youll for a beautiful cover painting. Thanks to everyone at LucasBooks for their support along the way—Carol Roeder, Jennifer Heddle, Joanne Chan Taylor, and J. W. Rinzler—as well as past directors and editors who were generous enough to offer me an opportunity to see their work firsthand: Lucy Autrey Wilson, Amy Gary, Allan Kausch, Jane Mason, Sarah Hines Stephens, Benjamin Harper, Chris Cerasi, Michelle Vuckovich, Jane Irene Kelly, Linda Kelly, and of course Sue Rostoni were always willing to include me in the captivating process of building the Expanded Universe.

Many fellow fans have served as inspiration in this endeavor. I've been lucky to count *Star Wars* experts like Daniel Wallace, Jason Fry, and Leland Chee as not only go-to professional colleagues but also like-minded friends who delight in taking deep dives into this galaxy. A special note of gratitude to Jason for double-checking that all of the planets and moons are where they should be. Thank you to Tricia Barr for her keen eye and thoroughness. To the many Wookieepedians, time liners, and chronologists who have undertaken their own research of this universe, my humble thanks. Special mention to Robert Mullin, Jay Shepard, Nathan Butler, James McFadden, Mike Biedler, and Joe Bongiorno, who have developed some fascinating academic resources for cataloging the history of *Star Wars*.

A round of applause for artists Chris Trevas, Darren Tan, Chris Scalf, Brian Rood, Jeff Carlisle, and Joe Corroney who have visualized what I've long seen in my mind's eye.

Thank you to Matt Martin for giving this project his attention, and to Mike Kogge for his advice and input.

As always, inestimable gratitude to my wife, Kristen, whose love keeps me focused during these galaxy-consuming projects.

I also want to thank the late Brian Daley for instilling in me a love of the written word as a portal to adventure. That dog-eared copy of *Han Solo at Stars' End* I carried everywhere as a child set me along this path. Clear skies.

ABOUT THE AUTHOR

PABLO HIDALGO started writing about fantastic subject matters professionally in 1995 as a freelance author for role-playing games. In 2000, he changed careers from working as a visual-effects concept artist and digital compositor in Canada to being a full-time *Star Wars* authority at Lucasfilm Ltd., working with their marketing and online department. Since then, he has overseen the development of websites, authored several books, and developed a number of online comic books and strips.

He lives in San Francisco.

ABOUT THE ILLUSTRATORS

JEFF CARLISLE is a freelance illustrator and concept designer who has spent a good portion of the last decade in a Galaxy Far, Far Away. He has designed or illustrated for various *Star Wars* projects such as books, magazines, web comics, role-playing and miniatures games, trading cards, posters, art prints, sketchcards, and even paper airplanes. www.jeffcarlisle.com

JOE CORRONEY has been providing Lucasfilm with official *Star Wars* artwork for books, games, trading cards, comic books, posters, and magazines since 1997. Joe has illustrated numerous comic books and is currently illustrating IDW's new *True Blood* series and new *Star Trek* ongoing comic book series. He's also developing his creator-owned comic book series, *Death Avenger,* and continuing to create new *Star Wars* artwork for Lucasfilm. www.joecorroney.com

BRIAN ROOD is an illustrator who spends most of his time creating new artwork for the *Star Wars* galaxy. His work can be found on numerous licensed *Star Wars* products, including toy packaging, Blu-ray packaging, trading cards, and a large assortment of *Star Wars* fine art reproductions with ACME Archives Direct. He lives in Southeast Michigan with his wife and two awesome children. www.brianrood.com

CHRIS SCALF grew up in Michigan, the middle child of a single mother. He didn't have much so he thrived on his imagination. He began drawing his favorite moments from the science fiction and monster shows he loved watching on TV. Eventually a high school crush led to marriage and Chris's desire to provide for his new family by making a living as an artist. In 2006 Chris was hired to paint his first *Star Wars* project, the R2-D2 mailboxes for the USPS. Today, Chris spreads his work between commercial art and advertising and the genre art he loved so much as a kid. He still lives in Michigan with his wife and daughter.

Born and raised in Malaysia, **DARREN TAN** grew up drawing spaceships, dinosaurs, and the stuff of his imagination, which was fueled by movies and computer games. Inspired by these he went on to study animation and later graduated as a computer animator from Sheridan College, Canada. After a brief stint in 3D animation, he decided to trade in polygons for a Wacom tablet. Now he works as a digital concept artist at Imaginary Friends Studios and is enjoying getting paid for his hobby. Apart from his passion for art and *Star Wars,* he is also a big fan of *The Lord of the Rings* and enjoys delving into medieval and church history. He now lives with his beautiful wife in sunny Singapore.

CHRIS TREVAS has been working professionally in the *Star Wars* universe for over fifteen years, illustrating books, magazines, games, trading cards, packaging, and limited-edition prints. His books include *Jedi vs. Sith: The Essential Guide to the Force* by Ryder Windham and *The New Essential Guide to Alien Species*. Chris works from his home studio in Beverly Hills, Michigan, where he lives with his wife and daughter. www.christrevas.com